CROSSROADS

CROSSROADS

JONATHAN FRANZEN

4th ESTATE • London

4th Estate
An imprint of HarperCollins*Publishers*
1 London Bridge Street
London SE1 9GF

www.4thEstate.co.uk

HarperCollins*Publishers*
1st Floor, Watermarque Building, Ringsend Road
Dublin 4, Ireland

First published in Great Britain in 2021 by 4th Estate
First published in the United States by Farrar, Straus and Giroux in 2021

3

A catalogue record for this book is
available from the British Library

HB ISBN 978-0-00-830889-6
TPB ISBN 978-0-00-830890-2

The author is grateful to Will "I Think This Answers Your Question" Akers,
and to John Chetkovich and Anna Paganelli, for their help
with facts and background.

Designed by Gretchen Achilles

Set in Adobe Caslon Pro
Printed and bound in the UK using 100%
renewable electricity at CPI Group (UK) Ltd

MIX
Paper from
responsible sources
FSC
www.fsc.org
FSC™ C007454

For Kathy!

ADVENT

The sky broken by the bare oaks and elms of New Prospect was full of moist promise, a pair of frontal systems grayly colluding to deliver a white Christmas, when Russ Hildebrandt made his morning rounds among the homes of bedridden and senile parishioners in his Plymouth Fury wagon. A certain person, Mrs. Frances Cottrell, a member of the church, had volunteered to help him bring toys and canned goods to the Community of God that afternoon, and though he knew that only as her pastor did he have a right to rejoice in her act of free will, he couldn't have asked for a better Christmas present than four hours alone with her.

After Russ's humiliation, three years earlier, the church's senior minister, Dwight Haefle, had upped the associate minister's share of pastoral visitations. What exactly Dwight was doing with the time Russ saved him, besides taking more frequent vacations and working on his long-awaited volume of lyric poetry, wasn't clear to Russ. But he appreciated his coquettish reception by Mrs. O'Dwyer, an amputee confined by severe edema to a hospital bed in what had been her dining room. He appreciated the routine of being of service, especially to those who, unlike him, couldn't remember one thing from three years ago. At the nursing home in Hinsdale, where the mingling smells of holiday pine wreaths and geriatric feces reminded him of Arizona high-country latrines, he handed old Jim Devereaux the new church membership face-book they'd been using as a prompt for conversation and asked if Jim remembered the Pattison family. To a pastor feeling reckless with Advent spirit, Jim was an ideal confidant, a wishing well in which a penny dropped would never hit bottom and resound.

"Pattison," Jim said.

"They had a daughter, Frances." Russ leaned over his parishioner's wheelchair and paged to the Cs. "She goes by her married name now—Frances Cottrell."

He never spoke her name at home, even when it would have been natural to, for fear of what his wife might hear in his voice. Jim bent closer to the picture of Frances and her two children. "Oh . . . Frannie? I remember Frannie Pattison. What ever happened to her?"

"She's back in New Prospect. She lost her husband a year and a half ago—terrible thing. He was a test pilot for General Dynamics."

"Where is she now?"

"She's back in New Prospect."

"Oh, huh. Frannie Pattison. Where is she now?"

"She came back home. She's Mrs. Frances Cottrell now." Russ pointed at her picture and said it again. "Frances Cottrell."

She was meeting him in the First Reformed parking lot at two thirty. Like a boy who couldn't wait for Christmas, he got there at 12:45 and ate his sack lunch in the car. On his bad days, of which there'd been many in the past three years, he resorted to an elaborate detour—into the church through its function hall, up a stairwell and down a corridor lined with stacks of banished Pilgrim Hymnals, across a storage room for off-kilter music stands and a crèche ensemble last displayed eleven Advents ago, a jumble of wooden sheep and one meek steer, graying with dust, with whom he felt a sad fraternity, then down a narrow staircase where only God could see and judge him, into the sanctuary via the "secret" door in the paneling behind the altar, and finally out through the sanctuary's side entrance—to avoid passing the office of Rick Ambrose, the director of youth programming. The teenagers who massed in the hallway outside it were too young to have personally witnessed Russ's humiliation, but they surely knew the story of it, and he couldn't look at Ambrose without betraying his failure to follow their Savior's example and forgive him.

Today, however, was a very good day, and the halls of First Reformed were still empty. He went directly to his office, rolled paper into his typewriter, and considered his unwritten sermon for the Sunday after Christmas, when Dwight Haefle would be vacationing again. He slouched in his chair and combed his eyebrows with his fingernails, pinched the bridge of his nose, touching a face whose angular contours he'd learned too late were attractive to many women, not just his wife, and imagined a sermon about his Christmas mission to the South Side. He preached too often about Vietnam, too often about the Navajos. To boldly speak, from the pulpit, the words *Frances Cottrell and I had the privilege*—to pronounce her name while she sat listening from the fourth row of pews and the congregation's eyes, perhaps enviously, connected her with him—was a pleasure, alas, foreclosed by his wife, who read his sermons in advance and would also be sitting in a pew, and who didn't know that Frances was joining him today.

On his office walls were posters of Charlie Parker and his sax, Dylan Thomas and his fag; a smaller picture of Paul Robeson framed alongside a handbill for Robeson's appearance at the Judson Church in 1952; Russ's diploma from the Biblical Seminary in New York; and a blown-up photo of him and two Navajo friends in Arizona, in 1946. Ten years ago, when he'd assumed the associate ministry in New Prospect, these artfully chosen assertions of identity had resonated with the teenagers whose development in Christ had been part of his brief. But to the kids who now thronged the church's hallways in their bell-bottoms and bib overalls, their bandannas, they signified only obsolescence. The office of Rick Ambrose, him of the stringy black hair and the glistening black Fu Manchu, had a kindergarten feel to it, the walls and shelves bedecked with the crudely painted effusions of his young disciples, the special meaningful rocks and bleached bones and wildflower necklaces they'd given him, the silk-screened posters for fundraising concerts with no discernible relation to any religion Russ recognized. After his humiliation, he'd hidden in his office and ached amid the fading totems of a youth that no one but his wife found interesting anymore. And Marion didn't count, because it was Marion who'd impelled him to New York, Marion who'd turned him on to Parker and Thomas and Robeson, Marion who'd thrilled to his stories of the Navajos and urged him to heed his calling to the ministry. Marion was inseparable from an identity that had proved to be humiliating. It had taken Frances Cottrell to redeem it.

"My God, is this you?" she'd said on her first visit to his office, the previous summer, as she studied the photo from the Navajo reservation. "You look like a young Charlton Heston."

She'd come to Russ for grief counseling, another part of his brief and not his favorite, since his own most grievous loss to date was of his boyhood dog, Skipper. He'd been relieved to hear that Frances's worst complaint, a year after her husband's fiery death in Texas, was a sense of emptiness. At his suggestion that she join one of the First Reformed women's circles, she flicked her hand. "I'm not going to coffee with the ladies," she said. "I know I've got a boy starting high school, but I'm only thirty-six." Indeed, she was sagless, pouchless, flabless, lineless, an apparition of vitality in a snug paisley sleeveless dress, her hair naturally blond and boyishly short, her hands boyishly small and square. It was obvious to Russ that she'd be remarried soon enough—that the emptiness she felt was probably little more than the absence of a husband—but he remembered his anger when his mother had asked him, too soon after Skipper's passing, whether he might like another dog.

There was, he told Frances, one particular women's circle, different from the others, guided by Russ himself, that worked with members of First Reformed's inner-city partner church, the Community of God. "The ladies don't coffee," he said. "We paint houses, clear brush, haul trash. Take the elderly to their appointments, help kids with their homework. We do it every other Tuesday, all day. And, let me tell you, I look forward to those Tuesdays. It's one of the paradoxes of our faith—the more you give to the less fortunate, the fuller you feel in Christ."

"You say his name so easily," Frances said. "I've been going to Sunday service for three months, and I'm still waiting to feel something."

"Not even my own sermons have moved you."

She colored a little, fetchingly. "That's not what I meant. You've got a beautiful voice. It's just . . ."

"Honestly, you're more likely to feel something on a Tuesday than a Sunday. I'd rather be on the South Side myself than giving sermons."

"It's a Negro church?"

"A Black church, yes. Kitty Reynolds is our ringleader."

"I like Kitty. I had her for senior English."

Russ liked Kitty, too, although he sensed that she was skeptical of him, as a male of the species; Marion had invited him to consider that Kitty, never married, was likely a lesbian. She dressed like a lumberjack for their biweekly trips to the South Side, and she'd quickly asserted possession of Frances, insisting that she ride both ways with her, rather than in Russ's station wagon. Mindful of her skepticism, he'd ceded the field to Kitty and waited for a day when she might be indisposed.

On the Tuesday after Thanksgiving, when a flu-like cold was going around, only three ladies, all widows, had shown up in the First Reformed parking lot. Frances, wearing a plaid wool hunting cap like the one Russ had worn as a boy, hopped into the front seat of his Fury and left the hat on, perhaps owing to the leak in the Fury's heating system that fogged the windshield if he didn't keep a window down. Or did she know how gut-punchingly, faith-testingly, androgynously adorable she looked to him in that hat? The two older widows might have known it, because all the way in to the city, past Midway and across on Fifty-fifth Street, they pestered Russ from the back seat with seemingly pointed questions about his wife and his four children.

The Community of God was a small, unsteepled church of yellow brick, originally built by Germans, with a tar-roofed community center attached to one side. Its congregation, mostly female, was led by a middle-aged pastor, Theo Crenshaw, who did the circle the favor of accepting its suburban charity without thanks. Every second Tuesday, Theo simply presented Russ and Kitty with a prioritized to-do list; they came not to minister but to serve. Kitty had marched with Russ for civil rights, but Russ had had to counsel other women in the circle, explaining that just because they struggled to understand "urban" English it didn't mean they had to speak loudly and slowly to make themselves understood. For the women who got it, and learned to overcome their fear of walking on the 6700 block of South Morgan Street, the circle had been a powerful experience. On the women who didn't get it—some of whom had joined the circle for competitive reasons, not wanting to be left out—he'd been obliged to inflict the same humiliation he'd suffered at the hands of Rick Ambrose and ask them not to come again.

Because Kitty had kept her glued to her side, Frances hadn't been tested yet. When they arrived on Morgan Street, she left the car reluctantly and

waited to be asked before helping Russ and the other widows carry tool-
boxes and bags of cast-off winter clothes into the community center. Her
hesitancy set off a flurry of misgivings in Russ—that he'd mistaken style
for substance, a hat for an adventurous spirit—but they were melted by a
gust of compassion when Theo Crenshaw, ignoring Frances, directed the
two older widows to catalogue a shipment of secondhand books for the
Sunday school. The two men were going to install a new water heater in
the basement.

"And Frances," Russ said.

She was hovering by the street door. Theo sized her up coolly.
"There's a whole lot of books."

"Why don't you help Theo and me," Russ said.

The eagerness of her nod confirmed his compassionate instinct, dispelling the suspicion that what he really wanted was to show off how
strong he was, how skilled with tools. In the basement, he stripped down
to his undershirt and applied a bear hug to the nasty, asbestos-clad old
heater and lifted it off its seat. At forty-seven, he was no longer a tall
sapling; he'd broadened in the chest and shoulders like an oak tree. But
there wasn't much for Frances to do but watch, and when the intake pipe
snapped off flush with the wall, necessitating work with a stone chisel
and a pipe die, he was slow to notice that she'd left the basement.

What Russ most liked about Theo was his reticence, which spared
Russ from the vanity of imagining that the two of them could be in-
terracial buddies. Theo knew the essential facts about Russ—that he
didn't shy from hard work, that he'd never lived far from poverty, that
he believed in the divinity of Jesus Christ—and he neither asked nor
welcomed more open-ended questions. About, for example, the retarded
neighborhood boy Ronnie, who wandered in and out of the church in
all seasons, sometimes stopping to do a peculiar swaying dance with
his eyes closed, or to cadge a quarter from a First Reformed lady, Theo
would only say, "Best leave that boy alone." When Russ had tried to engage with Ronnie anyway, asking him where he lived, who his mother
was, Ronnie had responded, "Can I have a quarter?" and Theo had said
to Russ, more sharply, "Best just leave him be."

It was an instruction Frances hadn't received. Upstairs, at lunchtime, they found her and Ronnie on the floor of the community room with a box of crayons. Ronnie was wearing a cast-off parka recognizably from New Prospect, swaying on his knees while Frances drew an orange sun on a sheet of newsprint. Theo stopped dead, began to say something, and shook his head. Frances offered Ronnie her crayon and looked up at Russ happily. She'd found her own way to serve and to give of herself, and he was happy for her, too.

Theo, following him into the sanctuary, was not. "You need to speak to her. Tell her Ronnie is off-limits."

"I really don't see the harm."

"Isn't a matter of harm."

Theo went home to his wife for a hot meal, and Russ, not wanting to discourage Frances's act of charity, took his sack lunch up to the Sunday-school room, where the older widows had undertaken a wholesale reorganization. When you were sick in the body, you surrendered it to the touch of strangers, and when you were sick with poverty you surrendered your environment. Without asking permission, the widows had sorted all of the children's books and created bright, enticing labels for them. When you were poor, it could be hard to see what needed doing until someone showed you by doing it. Not asking permission hadn't come naturally to Russ, but it was the counterpart of not expecting to be thanked. Venturing into a back yard of bramble and shoulder-high ragweed, he didn't ask the old lady who owned it which bushes and which pieces of rusting junk weren't worth saving, and when the job was done, more often than not, the old lady didn't thank him. She said, "Now doesn't that look better."

He was chatting with the two widows when they heard a door bang downstairs, a woman's voice rising in anger. He leaped to his feet and ran down to the community room. Frances, clutching a sheet of newsprint, was shrinking from a young woman he'd never seen before. She was emaciated, filthy-haired. Even halfway across the room, he could smell the liquor on her.

"This *my* son, you understand me? *My* son."

Ronnie was still on his knees with the crayons, swaying.

"Whoa, whoa," Russ said.

The young woman wheeled around. "You the husband?"

"No, I'm the pastor."

"Well, you tell whatever she is to stay away from my boy." She addressed herself again to Frances. "Stay away from my boy, bitch! What you got there anyway?"

Russ stepped between the women. "Miss. Please."

"*What you got there?*"

"It's a drawing," Frances said. "A nice drawing. Ronnie made it. Didn't you, Ronnie?"

The drawing in question was a random red scrawl. Ronnie's mother reached and snatched it from Frances's hand. "This ain't your property."

"No," Frances said. "I think he made it for you."

"She still talking to me? Is that what I'm hearing?"

"I think we all need to calm down here," Russ said.

"*She* need to get her white ass outta my face and not be messing with my boy."

"I'm sorry," Frances said. "He's so sweet, I was only—"

"*Why is she still talking to me?*" The mother ripped the drawing into quarters and yanked Ronnie to his feet. "I told you to keep away from these folk. Didn't I tell you that?"

"Dunno," Ronnie said.

She slapped him. "You don't *know*?"

"Miss," Russ said, "if you hit the boy again, there's going to be trouble."

"Yeah, yeah, yeah." She was heading toward the street door. "Come on, Ronnie. We done here."

After they were gone, and Frances had broken down in sobs and he'd embraced her, feeling her fear expend itself in shudders, but also noticing how neatly her narrow form fit in his arms, her delicate head in his hand, he was close to tears himself. They should have asked permission. He should have kept a more protective eye on her. He should have insisted that she help the older ladies with the books.

"I don't know if I'm cut out for this," she said.

"It was just bad luck. I've never seen her before."

"But I'm afraid of them. And she knew it. And you're not, and she respected you."

"It gets easier if you keep showing up."

She shook her head, not believing him.

When Theo Crenshaw returned from his lunch, Russ was too ashamed to mention the incident. He'd had no plan for him and Frances, no specific fantasy, nothing more than a wish to be near her, and now, in his vanity and error, he'd blown his chance to see her twice a month. He was bad enough to desire a woman who wasn't his wife, but he was also bad at being bad. How hideously passive a tactic it had been to bring her down to the basement. To imagine that watching him work could make her want him, the way watching her do anything made him want her, was to be the kind of man her kind of woman wouldn't want. Watching him had bored her, and he deserved the blame for what had followed.

In his Fury, on the slow drive back to New Prospect, she was silent until one of the older widows asked her how her son, Larry, the tenth grader, was liking Crossroads. It was news to Russ that her son had joined the church's youth group.

"Rick Ambrose must be some kind of genius," Frances said. "I don't think there were thirty kids in that group when I was growing up."

"Were you in it?" the older widow asked.

"Nope. Not enough cute boys. Not any, actually."

Coming from Frances, the word *genius* was like acid on Russ's brain. He should have borne it stoically, but on his bad days he was unable not to do things he would later regret. It was almost as if he did them *because* he would later regret them. Writhing with retrospective shame, abasing himself in solitude, was how he found his way back to God's mercy.

"Do you know," he said, "why the group is named Crossroads? It's because Rick Ambrose thought kids could relate to the name of a rock song."

This was a scabrous half-truth. Russ himself had originally proposed the name.

"And so I asked him—I had to ask—if he knew the original Robert Johnson song. And he gives me a blank look. Because to him, you know, music history started with the Beatles. Believe me, I've heard the Cream version of 'Crossroads.' I know exactly what it is. It's a bunch of guys from England ripping off an authentic Black American blues master and acting like it's *their* music."

Frances, in her hunting cap, had her eyes on the truck ahead of them. The older widows were holding their breath while their associate minister trashed the director of youth programming.

"I happen to have the original recording of Johnson singing 'Cross Road Blues,'" he bragged, repellently. "Back when I lived in Greenwich Village—you know, I used to live there, in New York City—I'd find old 78s in junk stores. During the Depression, the record companies went out in the field and made amazing authentic recordings—Lead Belly, Charley Patton, Tommy Johnson. I was working with an afterschool program in Harlem, and I'd come home every night and play those records, and it was like being carried straight into the South in the twenties. There was so much *pain* in those old voices. It helped me understand the pain I was dealing with in Harlem. Because that's what the blues are really about. That's what went missing when the white bands started aping the style. I can't hear any pain at all in the new music."

An embarrassed silence fell. The last daylight of November was dying in crayon colors beneath the clouds on the suburban horizon. Russ now had more than enough to be ashamed of later, more than enough to be sure that he deserved to suffer. The sense of rightness at the bottom of his worst days, the feeling of homecoming in his humiliations, was how he knew that God existed. Already, as he drove toward the dying light, he had a foretaste of their reunion.

In the First Reformed parking lot, Frances lingered in the car after the others had taken their leave. "Why did she hate me?" she said.

"Ronnie's mother?"

"No one's ever spoken to me like that."

"I'm very sorry that happened to you," he said. "But this is what I meant about pain. Imagine being so poor that your kids are the only thing you have, the only people who care about you and need you. What if you saw some other woman treating them better than you were able to treat them? Can you imagine how that might feel?"

"It would make me try to treat them better myself."

"Yes, but that's because you're not poor. When you're poor, things just happen to you. You feel like you can't control *anything*. You're completely at God's mercy. That's why Jesus tells us that the poor are blessed—because having nothing brings you closer to God."

"That woman didn't strike me as being especially close to God."

"Actually, Frances, you have no way of knowing. She was obviously angry and troubled—"

"And stinking drunk."

"And stinking drunk at noon. But if we learn nothing else from these Tuesdays, it should be that you and I are not in a position to judge the poor. We can only try to serve them."

"So you're saying it was my fault."

"Not at all. You were listening to something generous in your heart. That's never a fault."

He was hearing something generous in his own heart: he could still be a good pastor to her.

"I know it's hard to see when you're upset," he said gently, "but what you experienced today is what people in that neighborhood experience on a daily basis. Abusive words, racial prejudice. And I know you're no stranger to pain yourself—I can't even imagine what you've been through. If you decide you've had enough pain and you'd rather not work with us right now, I won't think less of you. But you have an opportunity, if you're up for it, to turn your pain into compassion. When Jesus tells us to turn the other cheek, what is he really saying to us? That the person who's abusing us is hopelessly evil and we just have to put up with it? Or is he reminding us that the person is a person like us, a person who feels the same kind of pain that we do? I know it can be hard to see, but that perspective is always available, and I think it's one we all should strive for."

Frances considered his words for a moment. "You're right," she said. "I do have a hard time seeing it that way."

And that had seemed to be the end of it. When he phoned her the next day, as any good pastor would have done, she said her daughter had a fever and she couldn't talk right then. He didn't see her at services the following two Sundays, and she skipped the circle's next trip to the South Side. He thought of calling her again, if only to resupply himself with shame, but the purity of the hurt of losing her was of a piece with the season's dark afternoons and long nights. He would have lost her sooner or later—at the latest when one of them died, very probably much sooner than that—and his need to reconnect with God was so pressing that he seized on the hurt almost greedily.

But then, four days ago, she'd called him. She'd had a wretched cold, she said, but she couldn't stop thinking about his words in the car. She didn't think she had the strength to be like him, but she felt like she'd turned a corner, and Kitty Reynolds had mentioned a Christmas delivery to the South Side. Could she come along with them for that?

Russ would have been content to rejoice merely as her pastor, her enabler, if Frances hadn't then asked if he might loan her some of his blues recordings.

"Our turntable plays 78s," she said. "I'm thinking, if I'm going to do this, I should try to understand their culture better."

He winced at the phrase *their culture*, but even he was not so bad at being bad as not to know what sharing music signified. He went up to the unheatable third floor of his hulking church-provided house and spent a good hour on his knees, selecting and reselecting 78s, trying to guess which ten of them together were likeliest to inspire feelings like the ones he already had for her. His connection with God had vanished, but this wasn't a worry for now. The worry was Kitty Reynolds. It was imperative that he have Frances all to himself, but Kitty was sharp and he was bad at lying. Any ruse he tried, like telling her to meet him at three and then departing with Frances at two thirty, was bound to raise Kitty's suspicions. He saw that he had no choice but to level with her, sort of, and say that Frances had suffered a small trauma in the city, and that he needed to be alone with her when she bravely revisited the scene of it.

"It sounds to me," Kitty had said when he called her, "like you fell down on the job."

"You're right. I did. And now I need to try and regain her trust. It's encouraging that she wants to go back, but it's still very delicate."

"And she's a cute one, and it's Christmastime. If it were anyone but you, Russ, I might be worried about your motives."

He'd wondered about Kitty's implication—whether she considered him uniquely good and trustworthy, or uniquely unsexed and unmanly and unthreatening. Either way, the effect had been to make his impending date with Frances feel more thrillingly illicit. In anticipation of it, he'd smuggled out of his house and into the church his final selection of blues records and a grimy old coat, a sheepskin thing from Arizona, that he hoped might lend him a bit of an edge. In Arizona, he'd had an edge, and, fairly or not, he believed that what had dulled it was his marriage. When Marion, after his humiliation, had loyally undertaken to hate Rick Ambrose, calling him *that charlatan*, Russ had snapped at her— lashed out—and declared that Rick was many things but not a charlatan, the simple fact was that he, Russ, had lost his edge and couldn't relate to young people anymore. He flagellated himself and resented Marion for interfering with the pleasure of it. His subsequent daily shame, whether of walking past Ambrose's office or taking a craven detour to avoid it, had connected him to the sufferings of Christ. It was a torment that nourished him in his faith, whereas the too-gentle touch of Marion's hand on his arm, when she tried to comfort him, was a torment without spiritual upside.

From his office, as the hour finally approached two thirty, the page in his typewriter still blank, he could hear the afterschool influx of Crossroads teenagers buzzing around the honeypot of Ambrose, the pounding of running footsteps, the shouting of swear words that Mr. Fuck-Piss-Shit encouraged by using them incessantly himself. More than a hundred and twenty kids now belonged to Crossroads, among them two of Russ's own children; and it was a measure of how focused he'd been on Frances, how mad with anticipation of their date, that only now, as he stood up from his desk and pulled on the sheepskin coat, did he consider that he and she might run into his son Perry.

Bad criminals overlook obvious things. Relations with his daughter, Becky, had been strained ever since she'd joined Crossroads, gratuitously, in October, but at least she was aware of how deeply she'd wounded him by joining, and he rarely saw her at the church after school. Perry, however, knew nothing of tact. Perry, whose IQ had been measured at 160, saw too much and smirked too much at what he saw. Perry was fully capable of chatting up Frances, his manner seemingly forthright and respectful but somehow neither, and he would definitely notice the sheepskin coat.

Russ could have used the detour to the parking lot, but the man who resorted to it wasn't the man he meant to be today. He squared his shoulders, deliberately forgot to take the blues recordings, so that he and Frances would have a reason to return to his office after dark, and stepped into a dense bank of smoke from the cigarettes of a dozen kids camped out in the hallway. There was no immediate sign of Perry. One chubby, apple-cheeked girl was splayed out happily on the laps of three boys on the saggy old divan that someone, over Russ's quiet objections to Dwight Haefle (the hallway was a fire escape route), had dragged in for kids waiting their turn to be confronted by Ambrose, with brutal but loving honesty, in the privacy of his office.

Russ moved forward with his eyes on the floor, stepping around blue-jeaned shins and sneakered feet. But as he approached his adversary's office he could see, peripherally, that its door was halfway open; and then he heard her voice.

He stopped without having wanted to.

"It's so great," he heard Frances gush. "A year ago, I practically had to put a gun to his head to get him to church."

Of Ambrose, through the doorway, only ragged denim cuffs and beat-up work boots were visible. But the chair Frances was sitting in faced the hallway. She saw Russ, waved to him, and said, "See you outside?"

God only knew what expression was on his face. He walked on, blindly overshot the main entrance, and found himself outside the function hall. He was taking on dark water through large holes in his hull. The stupidity of never once imagining that she could go to Ambrose. The clairvoyant certainty that Ambrose would take her away from him. The guilt of having hardened his heart against the wife he'd vowed to cherish. The vanity of believing that his sheepskin coat made him look like anything but a fatuous, obsolete, repellent clown. He wanted to tear off the coat and retrieve his regular wool one, but he was too much of a coward to walk back up the hallway, and he was afraid that if he took the detour and saw the dusty crèche steer, in the state he was in, he might cry.

Oh God, he prayed from within the loathsomeness of his coat. *Please help me.*

If God answered his prayer, it was by reminding him that the way to endure misery was to humble himself, think of the poor, and be of service. He went to the church secretary's office and ferried cartons of toys and canned goods to the parking lot. Each passing minute deepened the late-dawning badness of the day. Why was she with Ambrose? What could they be discussing that was taking so long? The toys all appeared to be new or indestructible enough to pass as new, but Russ was able to survive further minutes by rooting through the food cartons, culling the lazy or thoughtless donations (cocktail onions, water chestnuts) and taking comfort in the weight of jumbo cans of pork and beans, of Chef Boyardee, of pear halves in syrup: the thought of how welcome each would be to a person who was genuinely hungry and not merely, like him, starved in spirit.

It was 2:52 when Frances came bounding up to him, like a boy, full of bounce. She was wearing the hunting cap and, today, a matching wool jacket. "Where's Kitty?" she said brightly.

"Kitty was afraid she wouldn't fit, with all the boxes."

"She's not coming?"

Unable to look Frances in the eye, he couldn't tell if she was disappointed or, worse yet, suspicious. He shook his head.

"That's silly," she said. "I could have sat on her lap."

"Do you mind?"

"Mind? It's a privilege! I'm feeling *very* special today. I've turned a corner."

She made an airy little ballet move, expressive of turning a corner. He wondered if her feeling had preceded or been caused by her visit with Ambrose.

"Good, then," he said, slamming the Fury's rear door. "We should probably get going."

It was a subtle reference to her lateness, the only one he intended to permit himself, and she didn't pick up on it. "Is there anything I need to bring?"

"No. Just yourself."

"The one thing I never leave home without! Let me just make sure I locked my car."

He watched her bounce over to her own, newer car. Her spirits seemed higher than his not only at this moment but possibly in his entire life. Certainly higher than he'd ever seen Marion's.

"Ha!" Frances exulted from across the lot. "Locked!"

He gave her two thumbs up. He never gave anyone two thumbs up. It felt so strange he wasn't sure he'd done it right. He looked around to see if anyone else, Perry in particular, had witnessed it. There was no one in sight but a pair of teenagers carrying guitar cases toward the church, not looking in his direction, perhaps intentionally. One was a boy he'd known since he was a second grader in Sunday school.

What would it be like to live with a person capable of joy?

As he was getting into the Fury, a single, floppy snowflake, the first of the multitude the sky had promised all day, came to rest on his forearm and dissolved in itself. Frances, climbing in from the other side, said, "That's a great old coat. Where'd you get it?"

Resolved: that the soul is independent of the body and immutable. First affirmative speaker: Perry Hildebrandt, New Prospect Township High School.

Ahem.

Tempting though it may be, let's not make the mistake of misreading the experience, familiar to any pothead worthy of the name, of being in one place, doing one thing—say, struggling to tear open a bag of marshmallows in Ansel Roder's kitchen—and then, the very next instant, finding one's bodily self performing an entirely different task in a wholly different setting. Such spatio-temporal elisions or (in common but misleading parlance) "blackouts" need not suggest a division of soul and body; any decent mechanistic theory of mind can account for them. Let's begin, instead, by considering a question that may at first glance seem trivial or unanswerable or even nonsensical: Why am I me and not someone else? *Let's peer into the dizzying depths of this question . . .*

It was curious the way time slowed, almost stopped, when he was feeling well: wonderful (but also not, because of the sleepless night it augured) the number of laps his mind could run in the seconds it took him to climb one staircase. The pulsing nowness of it all, body and soul in sync, his skin registering each degree of falling temperature as he approached the third floor of the Crappier Parsonage, his nose the mustiness of the cold air flowing down toward the door at the bottom of the stairs, which he'd left open in case his mother came home unexpectedly; his ears the assurance that she hadn't, his retinas the slightly less gloomy December light in windows nearer to the sky, less shaded by trees, his soul the almost déjà vu familiarity of climbing these stairs alone.

He had once (only once) asked the higher powers if one of the third-floor rooms could be his, or really not so much asked as rationally pointed out the third floor's suitability for the third child he ineluctably was, and when the answer had come down from on maternal high—no, sweetie, it's too cold in the winter, too hot in the summer, and Judson likes sharing a room with you—he'd accepted it without protest or renewed entreaty, because, by his own rational assessment, he was the one child in the family with no rightful claim to a room of his own, being neither the oldest nor the youngest nor the prettiest, and he was used to operating at a level of rationality inaccessible to others.

Nevertheless, in his mind, the third floor belonged to him. Many a lungful of depleted smoke had been puffed out the storage-room window, many an ash smudged into the polleny dust on the outer sill, and the Reverend Father's home office, which he now brazenly entered, had no secrets from him. He had read, partly out of curiosity, partly to gauge just how miserable a worm he could be, the entirety of his mother's premarital correspondence with his father, except for two letters that his father himself had never opened. Searching, with little optimism, for *Playboy*s, he'd exhumed his father's stacks of *The Other Side* and *The Witness*, the fruit of minds so woody that not a drop of sweetness could be pressed from them, along with a year's worth of *Psychology Today*s, in one of which he'd dwelled on the words *clitoris* and *clitoral orgasm*, sadly not illustrated. (Ansel Roder's father stored his collection of *Playboy*s in hinged archival cardboard boxes, labeled by calendar year, which was impressive but discouraged pilferage.) The Reverend's jazz and blues recordings were so much mute plastic and moldering sleeve, and the old coats in the slope-ceilinged closet weren't covetable, cut as they were for a man much bigger than Perry, who could feel, literally in his bones, that he would end up as the physical runt of the Hildebrandt litter, his growth spurt, the year before, having resembled the bottle rocket that goes off at a faltering angle and dies with a dull pop. The closet interested him only in December, when the floor of it filled up with presents.

A noteworthy fact, possibly bearing on the question of the soul's immutability, was that a person named Perry Hildebrandt had existed on earth for nine Christmases, his consciousness alive and functioning on five of them, before it occurred to him that the presents that appeared under the tree on Christmas Eve *must have been in the house, not yet wrapped, for some days or even weeks before their appearance.* His blindness had had nothing to do with Santa Claus. Of Santa the Hildebrandts had always said, Bah, humbug. And yet somehow, long past the age of understanding that presents don't just buy and wrap themselves, he'd accepted their sudden annual appearance as, if not a miraculous provision, then a phenomenon like his bladder filling with urine, part of the normal course of things. How had he not grasped at nine a truth so obvious to him at ten? The epistemological disjunction was absolute. His nine-year-old self seemed to him a total stranger, and not in a good way. It was a figure of vague menace to the older Perry, who couldn't escape the suspicion that, although the cherubic face in photos from 1965 was identifiably his own, the two Perrys did not have the same soul. That somehow there had been a switcheroo. In which case, where had his current soul come from? And where had the other one gone?

He opened the closet door and dropped to his knees. The nakedness of the presents on the floor was a sad premonition of their naked future, after the brief, false glory of being wrapped. A shirt, a velour pullover, socks. An argyle sweater, further socks. A ribboned box from Marshall Field's—pretty tony! Gentle shaking indicated a lightweight garment within, doubtless for Becky. Reaching in deeper, he uncrimped the paper bags of books and records. Among the latter was the Yes album he'd mentioned to his mother in a sideways conversation of the sort that gave them pleasure. (Transmitting a Christmas list without referring to Christmas was a very elementary game, and yet the Reverend Father couldn't have managed it without winking, and Becky would have spoiled it altogether: "Are you trying to tell me what you want for Christmas?" Only his mother and his little brother had proper ludic faculties.) In hindsight, it was a pity he'd hinted at the Yes record before he formed his new resolution. Yes paired outstandingly with reefer, but he feared that its music might forfeit a certain luster if listened to with head unaltered.

At the back of the closet were heavier items, a small yellow Samsonite suitcase (for Becky, certainly), what appeared to be a secondhand microscope (had to be Clem), a portable cassette player/recorder (hinted at but by no means counted on!), and, oh dear, an electric NFL Football game. Poor Judson. He was still young enough that he needed to be given a game, but Perry had already played this particular game at Roder's and nearly passed out laughing at its shittiness. The sheet-metal playing field vibrated electrically, with a sound like a Norelco shaver's, beneath two teams of tiny plastic gridders with oblongs of plastic turf glued to their feet, the quarterbacks eternally frozen in he-man forward-passing posture, the halfbacks carrying a "ball" that was more like a pellet of pocket lint and frequently fumbling it, or becoming so disoriented in the buzzy scrum that they speeded toward their own end zone and scored a safety for their opponent. Nothing was more hilarious to the stupidly stoned than stupidly stoned-looking behavior; but Judson, of course, would not be playing it while stoned.

On the plus side: no sign of a camera. Perry had been fairly sure that only he knew what his little brother most wanted, because Judson was a superior human being, to whom it wouldn't occur to engage in avaricious hinting with their mother, and the paternal style was so anti-materialistic that Christmas lists were never solicited. Still, there was such a thing as bad luck, intuitive guesses, and so he had to ransack the closet—a small infraction, smaller yet in the context of a greater good.

Because this was his new resolution: to be good.

Or, failing that, at least less bad.

Although his motives for so resolving suggested that the badness was underlying and perhaps intractable.

For example: the reluctance he now felt, as he stood up and headed back down the drafty staircase, to liquidate the asset. The liquidation was a sentence he'd passed on himself, a punitive fine he'd levied at the peak of his resolution, but now he wondered if it was really necessary. He had in his billfold the twenty-dollar bill his mother had slipped him for Christmas shopping, plus eleven dollars he'd managed not to spend on poisoning his central nervous system. The camera that he and Judson had admired in the window of New Prospect Photo cost $24.99, not including sales tax and rolls of film. Even if he could find a cheap used frame for his gouache portrait of his mother and bought paperbacks for everyone else—and his irritation at having to buy *anything* for Becky or Clem or the Reverend was already an ominous violation of his resolution—he was facing a shortfall.

And there was a cheaper way. Judson would also have liked to get the game of Risk, a new one of which cost less than half the camera, and to play it with Perry in their bedroom, which Perry would gladly have done as a further gift to Judson, being fond of the game himself. But along with every other game involving war or killing, any toy that shot projectiles or could be imagined to shoot them, any representations of soldiers, warplanes, tanks, etc.—in short, every thing a normal boy like Judson most wanted—Risk was forbidden in the house, owing to the Reverend's violent pacifism. Perry did have an arsenal of rational arguments at his disposal: Wasn't the object of *all* games a kind of warlike vanquishment? How come the virtual slaughter in chess and checkers didn't run afoul of the ban? Was it truly obligatory to view the pleasing enameled lozenges of Risk as "armies," rather than as abstract markers in a game of topological strategy and dice-rolling? If only it were possible to argue with his father without flushing and choking up with tears of anger and hating himself for being smarter, but also less good, than the old man! A fine gift to Judson a fight would be on Christmas morning.

Concluding, reluctantly, that there was no saving the asset, he shut the stairway door behind him and found Judson where he'd left him, in their bedroom, reading a book beneath the homemade reading light that Perry had rigged up for him above his captain's bed. Judson's corner of their room recalled the cabin of the *Spray*, the globe-circling vessel of his hero Joshua Slocum—everything in its place, clothes folded and stowed beneath the bed, fifty-cent paperbacks ordered alphabetically by title, Dinky cars parked on a little shelf at parallel diagonals, alarm clock tightly wound—outside which raged the sea of Perry, for whom folding clothes was an irrational waste of time and ordering his possessions a superfluity, since he remembered exactly where he'd left them. The asset was under his bed, in the padlocked plywood strongbox that he'd built as his final project in eighth-grade shop class.

"Hey, kiddo, sorry to bother you," he said from the doorway. "But I need you to go somewhere else."

Judson's book was *The Incredible Journey*. He frowned elaborately. "First you tell me I have to stay here and then you tell me I have to leave."

"Just for a minute. Unusual commands must be obeyed at Christmas time."

Judson, not budging, said, "What do you feel like doing today?"

A sideways question.

"Right now," Perry said, "I feel like doing something you need to leave the room for."

"Later, though."

"I have to go downtown. Why don't you go over to Kevin's? Or Brett's."

"They're both sick. How long will you be gone?"

"Possibly until dinnertime."

"I have a new idea for how to set the game up. Can I do it while you're gone and we can play it after dinner?"

"I don't know, Jay. Maybe."

A bruise of disappointment in Judson's face returned Perry to his resolution.

"I mean, yes," he said. "But the game's not coming out before then, you understand?"

Judson nodded and hopped off the bed with his book. "Promise?"

Perry promised and locked the door behind him. Ever since he'd manufactured a copy of Stratego, rather cunningly, out of shirt cardboard, his brother had been mad to play it with him. Because it was nominally a game of bombs and killing, it carried the risk of confiscation by the higher powers, and Judson had needed no telling to keep it a secret. There were many worse little brothers in New Prospect. Not only was Judson Perry's best evidence of the reality of love, he was such an appealing and well-regulated youngster, nearly as smart as Perry and much better able to sleep at night, that Perry sometimes wished that he, Perry, *were* his little brother.

But what did that even mean? If the soul was merely a psychic artifact created by the body, it was tautologically self-evident why Perry's soul was in Perry and not in Judson. And yet it didn't feel self-evident. The reason he wondered if the soul might be independent and immutable was his persistent sense of how odd it was, how seemingly random, that his soul had landed where it had. Try as he might, altered or sober, he could never quite solve—or even properly articulate—the mystery of his happening to be Perry. It wasn't at all clear to him what Becky, for example, had done to deserve being Becky, or when exactly (in an earlier incarnation?) she'd earned that privilege. She just found herself being Becky, around whom the heavens revolved; and this, too, confounded him.

A delicious faint skunk smell wafted off the asset when he opened the strongbox. The asset consisted of three ounces of weed, in double Baggies, and twenty-one Quaaludes, the remnant of a wholesale buy that, like every previous buy, had cost him nearly unendurable anxiety and shame. He stared at it in frank disbelief that he was going to part with it for nothing in return but the putative joy of Christmas giving. So very cruel, his resolution. He thought he might love being high a little less than he loved his brother, but he wasn't sure that when his mind was racing and one night in bed felt like a month of nights he didn't love two Quaaludes better. Aye, that was the question: whether to shove the whole fucking asset in the pocket of his parka and be done with it, or to sleep tonight. The weed alone would fetch him thirty dollars, more cash than he needed. Why not hold back a few 'ludes? For that matter, why not hold back all of them?

Eleven days earlier, in an eerie correlative of the cosmic lottery in which his soul had drawn the name Perry, he'd plucked the name *Becky H* from a pile of folded slips on the linoleum floor of the function hall at First Reformed. (What were the chances? About one in fifty-five—a hundred million times greater than the chances of being Perry, but still rather low.) As soon as he'd seen his sister's name, he'd sidled back toward the pile, hoping to trade in his slip for a different one, but a Crossroads adviser was standing there to guard against this sort of cheating. Ordinarily, when it came time to choose partners for a "dyad" exercise, Rick Ambrose directed everyone to pick a person they didn't know well or hadn't shared with recently. The previous Sunday, however, one of the inner-circle twelfth graders, Ike Isner, had stood up and complained to the group that people were choosing too many "safe" partners and avoiding risky ones. In good Stalinist show-trial fashion, with a display of strong emotion, Isner confessed that he was guilty of this himself. The group immediately drenched him with approval for his courageous honesty. Someone then proposed a lottery system, against which another inner-circler argued that they ought to take personal responsibility for their choices, rather than relying on a mechanical system, but the proposal carried a group vote by a wide margin—Perry, as was his habit, waiting to see which way the wind was blowing before raising his hand in favor.

Becky had been one of the few people voting against. Seeing her name on the slip now, he wondered if she'd foreseen this very eventuality; had been, in this rare instance, sharper than he was. All across the church function hall, people were running up to their partners. Becky was looking around innocently to see who hers would be. As Perry approached her, he saw the situation dawn on her. Her expression matched his own. It said *Oh, shit*.

"All right, listen up," Ambrose barked. "In this exercise, I want each of us to tell our partner something we really admire about them. First one of us, then the other. And then I want each of us to tell our partner something they're doing that's a barrier to getting to know them better. I'm talking about *barriers*, not character assassination. Everyone got it? Are we all clear on what comes first?"

The group was big enough that Perry and Becky had easily avoided each other since the night, six weeks earlier, when she'd shocked the world by joining Crossroads. He personally had been shocked because Becky was rather too obviously the Reverend Father's favorite child and she knew very well how much their father hated Rick Ambrose; Perry's own defection to Crossroads had merely deepened an existing chill between him and the Reverend, whereas Becky's was a brutal betrayal. More universally shocking was the sheer sight of her face on a Sunday night at First Reformed. Perry had been there. He'd seen the heads turning, he'd heard the murmurs of astonishment. It was as if a Cleopatra had shown up at one of Jesus's rallies in Galilee, a diademed queen sitting down among the freaks and the lepers and trying to blend in; because Becky, too, came from a different world—the social royalty of New Prospect Township High.

Perry as a boy hadn't been a student of his sister's doings. Along with Clem, with whom she was tight, she'd constituted a generic Older Siblings unit, notable mainly for always being more advanced than Perry, better with scissors, better at hopscotch, better (much better) at control of emotion and mood. Only when he started junior high did he become aware of Becky as a distinct individual, about whom the larger world had strong opinions. She was the captain of the Lifton Central cheerleading squad and could have won any other popularity contest she cared to enter. Whichever lunch table she sat down at filled up instantly with the prettiest girls, the cocksurest boys. Strangely, she herself was held to be very pretty. To Perry, the tall and bony girl with whom he impatiently shared a bathroom, and whose face twisted into something haglike when he corrected her on a point of fact or grammar, was more like vaguely disgusting, but the group of older Lifton Central boys he'd quickly fallen in with, Ansel Roder among them, assured him that he was mistaken. He was never able to agree with them, though he did eventually concede that his sister had *something*—an aura of singularity, a force at once attractive and unapproachable (no one had ever dared claim to be her boyfriend), a kind of *expensiveness* that had nothing to do with money (it was said that she wasn't stuck up like the other cheerleaders, as if she didn't even notice the attention she effortlessly commanded)—because he himself, Perry, the negligible sibling satellite, reflected a glow of his own from her preeminence.

In New Prospect the words *Becky Hildebrandt* were magical in the strict sense, their mere utterance sufficing to ensure massive attendance at a party or to induce self-reported boners in shop class (Perry regrettably within earshot for that one). As the sharer of half of her name, he'd found *himself* immediately noticed at Lifton Central, at least by the set of eighth- and ninth-grade boys whose parents' high incomes and large homes accorded them a certain elevated status. He started as their runty mascot but soon proved himself their equal or better. No one could hold a pipe hit longer in his lungs, no one could drink more shots without slurring his speech, no one knew more words in the English language. Even his hair, being flax-colored and having natural wave and body, looked better than his friends' at shoulder length. Roder had gotten so tired of brushing his lank, dull hair from his eyes that he'd finally cut it off; he was the biggest freak of them all and looked like G.I. Joe now.

It had seemed appropriate to Perry that his friends should all be older than he was. Becky might have provided the initial entrée to them, and they might never have forgotten whose brother he was, but in his own way he was singular, too. This became especially evident in ninth grade, when the last of his friends had gone on to high school. Surrounded by contemporaries of paltrier intelligence, and having no one to get him high at lunch hour, he felt like an astronaut who'd moonwalked too long and missed the flight home. This was when his sleeping troubles started. During a period of weeks between January and March, now blessedly largely lost to memory, he experienced his first nights of being 100% awake until dawn, other dawns when he felt physically incapable of raising his eyelids, a number of mornings when he crept back into the Crappier Parsonage and up the third-floor stairs and slept under an old throw rug until dinnertime, many incidents of falling asleep in his uniformly profitless classes, an excruciating conference with his principal and his parents at which he also briefly fell asleep, intermittent intense phobia of his mother, and level-voiced lectures from his father. Was it not impressive that he'd nonetheless maintained straight As that quarter? He had his sleepless nights to thank for that. There was also the psychic respite of seeing his friends after school and on weekends, but these get-togethers were shadowed, during the dark months, by his sense of wanting—of *needing*—larger quantities of whatever was being smoked or swallowed than the others seemed to need. To a man, his friends all could have afforded to buy more drugs. Only he, whose craving for relief didn't peak until he was alone at home and facing another night on the rack, had a churchmouse for a father.

Right around the time he determined that he had no choice but to start dealing drugs, three of his best friends had joined Crossroads. For Bobby Jett it was a matter of a girl he was chasing, for Keith Stratton the allure of nine undersupervised days on the Crossroads spring trip to Arizona, and for David Goya, whose mother belonged to First Reformed, a not terribly punishing punishment for multiple curfew violations. Under Rick Ambrose, Crossroads had begun to undermine traditional social categories. Seemingly unlikely candidates for Christian fellowship drifted in, gave it a try. Among the ones who stuck with it, to Perry's surprise, were all three of his friends. They still partied of a weekend, but their center of conversational gravity had shifted. Referring warmly to the Arizona trip, or more archly to the sensitivity training they did on Sunday nights, or more lubriciously to certain choice girls on the Crossroads roster, they made Perry feel excluded from a thing that sounded fun.

After a harrowing spring, followed by a summer of inhaling lawn-mower exhaust and getting wasted and rereading Tolkien, he proposed to Ansel Roder that the two of them check out Crossroads. Roder refused emphatically ("I'm not into cults"), and so Perry, on his first Sunday night in tenth grade, walked by himself into the vault-ceilinged third-floor room that Crossroads had appropriated in his father's church. The air was blue with tobacco smoke, the walls and the ceiling vaults covered with hand-painted quotations from e. e. cummings, John Lennon, Bob Dylan, even Jesus, and with more inscrutable, unattributed lines, such as Why guess? Get the facts. DEATH KILLS. Before Perry knew it, he was being *hugged* by David Goya, physical contact with whom he'd heretofore naturally avoided. In the ensuing minutes, he was touched by—squeezed by, pulled into the exciting breasts of—twenty times more female bodies than he'd touched like that in his entire life. Very pleasant! After greetings and administrative business, the group marched downstairs, a hundred strong, to the church's function hall, where the touching, male and female, in various formats, continued for another two hours. The only uncomfortable moment came when Perry, introducing himself to the group, alluded to his dad's being the associate minister "here." He glanced at Rick Ambrose and was pierced by a pair of burning dark eyes, slightly narrowed in puzzlement or suspicion, as if to ask, *Does your dad know you're here?*

The Reverend did not know it. Since Perry seemed unable to argue with him without crying, he habitually concealed as much as he could for as long as he could. The following Sunday, to forestall any questions, he told his mother that he was having dinner at Roder's, and he did stop in there, for a while, to consume freezer pizza and apparently quite a volume of gin and grape soda in front of the color TV in the Roders' comfortably appointed cellar. Though he was noted for holding his liquor well, things started happening so fast when he arrived at Crossroads that he couldn't remember them all later. It was possible he'd stumbled or lurched. He found himself confronted by two older advisers, alumni of the group, and informed that he was drunk. Rick Ambrose came wading through the crowd and led him out into a hallway.

"I don't care if you want to be drunk," Ambrose said, "but you're not doing it here."

"Okay."

"Why are you even here? Why did you come?"

"I don't know. My friends . . ."

"Are they drunk?"

Fear of punishment was killing Perry's buzz. He shook his head.

"You're damn right they're not," Ambrose said. "I ought to just send you home."

"I'm sorry."

"Are you really? Do you want to talk about that? Do you want to be part of this group?"

Perry hadn't decided yet. But it was undeniably pleasant to have the full attention of the mustachioed leader about whom his irreverent friends spoke admiringly; to be in frank conversation, for once, with an adult. "Yes," he said. "I do."

Ambrose took him back into the smoke-filled room and interrupted regular programming for one of the plenary Confrontations that were at the heart of Crossroads praxis. The issues at hand were alcohol use, respect for one's peers, and self-respect. Kids Perry barely knew addressed him as if they knew him very well. David Goya told him that he was an amazing person but that he, David, sometimes worried that he, Perry, used drugs and liquor to avoid his real emotions. Keith Stratton and Bobby Jett piped up in the same key. The thing went on and on and on. Although in some respects Perry had never experienced anything more horrible, he was also thrilled by the quantity and intensity of attention he was getting, as a sophomore and a newcomer, just for having drunk some gin. When he broke down in tears, weeping with shame, authentically, the group responded in a kind of ecstasy of supportiveness, advisers praising him for his courage, girls crawling over to hug him and stroke his hair. It was a crash course in the fundamental economy of Crossroads: public display of emotion purchased overwhelming approval. To be affirmed and fondled by a roomful of peers, most of them older, many of them cute, was exceedingly pleasant. Perry wanted more of this drug.

When the group headed down to the function hall for activities, Rick Ambrose held him back and collared him in a headlock evidently meant to be affectionate. "Well done," Ambrose said, releasing him.

"Frankly, I'd assumed I'd be severely punished."

"You didn't think that was severe? They really let you have it."

"I do feel a bit put through the ringer."

"One thing, though." Ambrose lowered his voice. "I don't know if you're aware of it, but there were some hard feelings when your father left the group. I feel bad about it, and I really don't know what to do. But if you want to be here, I need to know your dad's okay with it. I need to know you're here for your own sake, not because of something going on with you and him."

"He doesn't even know. I wasn't even thinking of him."

"Well, you need to fix that. He needs to know. Are we clear?"

Perry's conversation with the Reverend, later that night, was thankfully short. His father made a trembling steeple of his fingers and regarded them sadly. "I'd be lying," he said, "if I told you that your mother and I aren't worried about you. I think you need some kind of purpose in your life. If this is what you want it to be, I won't stop you." Perry's analysis was that he was actually of such small concern to his father that his joining the enemy camp didn't even merit anger.

By the time Becky joined Crossroads, he'd already mastered the game of it. The object was to move closer to the center of the group, to become an inner-circler, by following the rules exemplified by Ambrose and the other advisers. The rules required counterintuitive behaviors. Instead of comforting a friend with fibs, you told him unwelcome truths. Instead of avoiding the socially awkward, the hopelessly uncool, you sought them out and engaged with them (making sure, of course, that you were noticed doing this). Instead of choosing friends as exercise partners, you (conspicuously) introduced yourself to newcomers and conveyed your belief in their *unqualified worth*. Instead of being strong, you blubbered. Where his tears on the night of drinking gin had been cathartic, his tears later on came more easily and were a more fungible currency, redeemable for progress toward the inner circle. Because it was a game, he was good at it, and although intimacies achieved by game-theoretical calculation were hard to feel great about, he sensed that other people genuinely valued his insights and were genuinely moved by his emotional displays.

The person he feared he wasn't fooling was the one whose approval really mattered to him, Rick Ambrose. He admired Ambrose for, among other things, his intellectually plausible faith in God. Perry himself had yet to hear from God; maybe the lines were down, or maybe there was simply no one at the other end. One boring summer afternoon, he'd gone through one of his father's religious magazines with a ballpoint and replaced every reference to God with "Steve," for the hilarity of it. (Who was Steve? Why were otherwise sane-seeming people going on and on about Steve?) But Ambrose had an idea so elegant that Perry wondered if there might be something to it. The idea was that God was to be found in relationships, not in liturgy and ritual, and that the way to worship Him and approach Him was to emulate Christ in his relationships with his disciples, by exercising honesty, confrontation, and unconditional love. Ambrose had a way of talking about this stuff that didn't seem insane. He'd inspired Perry to devise a theory of how all religion worked: Along comes a leader who's uninhibited enough to use everyday words in a new and strong and counterintuitive way, which emboldens the people around him to use this rhetoric themselves, and the very act of using it creates sensations unlike anything they're used to in everyday life; they find they know who Steve is. Perry was altogether fascinated by Ambrose, and he felt that his own singularity entitled him to a place near his side, and so he was disappointed that Ambrose, after the night of gin, had seemed to shun him. He was forced to conclude that Ambrose detected the fraudulence in his playing of the Crossroads game and didn't trust him. The other likely explanation—that Ambrose was sensitive about encroaching on the Reverend's family—had been demolished by the visibly close attention he'd been paying to Becky since she'd joined the group.

And now the dangerous lottery system, for which Perry had unwisely voted, had thrown him together with her. Being a furtive and curious little worm, he knew every nook in First Reformed. In the function hall, behind a door that looked locked but wasn't, was a spacious coat closet into which, as the other "dyad" partners dispersed around the first floor of the church, he led his sister. They sat down crosslegged on the linoleum beneath rows of empty wooden hangers. A bare overhead bulb lit a dusty punch bowl, packages of waxed-paper cups, two orphaned umbrellas.

"So," he said, his eyes on the floor.

"Yeah, so."

"We could use some sort of system of marking slips to avoid this."

"Agreed."

Grateful that she agreed, he looked up at her. She didn't have a Crossroads wardrobe yet, no overalls, no painter's pants, no army jacket, but she was wearing an old sweater that at least had some holes in it. He still couldn't believe she'd joined Crossroads; it upset the natural order of things.

"I really admire how smart you are," she said in a rote kind of tone, not looking at him.

"Thank you, sister. And I admire, I really do, how sincere you always are. You've got a lot of phony friends, but you're not phony. It's actually kind of amazing." Seeing her mouth harden, he added, "That came out wrong. I didn't mean to criticize your friends. I was trying to say something positive about you."

Her mouth remained set.

"Maybe we should move right along to the barriers," he said. "I suspect it's more fruitful terrain."

She nodded. "What is a thing I'm doing that's a barrier to you getting to know me better."

Perry realized that the wording of the exercise left something to be desired. It presupposed, for example, that he and Becky *wanted* to get to know each other better.

"I would say," he said, "that the fact that you don't seem to like me, and always seem vaguely pissed off with me, including right now, and haven't tried to have a personal conversation with me in the last three or four years, at least not one that I can remember, despite our living in the same house, could be considered something of a barrier."

She laughed, but in a shaky way, as if a sob had also been an option. "Guilty as charged," she said.

"You don't like me."

"I mean the part about us never having a personal conversation."

Her face, which he took this unusual opportunity to observe from up close, was faultless. One's eye sought for a blemish (he himself had several raging) or some underlying feature that detracted, a thinness of lip, a squareness of jaw, a defect of nose, and found none. Same thing with her long, straight, shining hair, which was of a richer color than the slightly false-seeming yellow of his own: she had the platonic teen-girl hair to which other girls compared their own invidiously. Perry could see why the world considered Becky attractive, but also why it was wrong to. An absence of negatives wasn't necessarily a positive. It could be a thing that merely offered no resistance to the eye, like an invisible balloon on a string. Maddened by the sight of a taut vertical string that ended in nothingness, people followed it around and concluded, from their following it, that it must be highly desirable.

He didn't like her either.

"So it's something *I'm* doing," she said. "Is that the idea?"

"In this half of the exercise, yes. I'm naming what appears to me to be a barrier."

"Well, one thing that's kind of a barrier for me is the way you speak. Are you aware of how you sound?"

"Let the character assassination begin."

"That's what I'm talking about. The way you just said that. Like you're an English aristocrat."

"I have a Midwestern accent, Becky."

The flaw of redness entered her face. "How do you think it feels to the rest of us to be around a person who's always looking down on us, like we're funny to him? Who's always smirking like he knows something we don't know."

Perry frowned. To object that he didn't look down on Judson, except in the most literal physical sense, would have conceded her larger point.

"Who acts like I'm mentally deficient because I got a B in chemistry."

"Chemistry isn't a subject for everyone."

"But you'll get an A-plus in it, won't you. Without even trying. With-out even giving a shit."

"It could happen. But you could have done it, too, if you really wanted. I don't think of you as dumb, Becky. That's just false."

He could feel himself becoming sentimental, and there were no points to be scored for it here, in the privacy of the coat closet, with his sibling.

"I'm talking about my feelings," she said. "You can't say a feeling is false."

"Yes, true. So, you're saying you feel that my being good at school is a barrier."

"No. I'm saying I don't feel like you're even *there*. Like you're a thou-sand miles away from all of us. I'm saying that doesn't make me want to get to know you better."

Despite having every conceivable social privilege at high school, Becky wasn't just day-tripping in Crossroads, wasn't just slumming—he had to grant her that. She was giving it a real go, being open about her feelings, exercising honesty and confrontation, if perhaps falling short with the unconditional love. She was in the initial phase of Crossroads fervor. He himself had advanced through this phase so rapidly that by the time of the group's first weekend retreat, in October, at a lakeside Christian conference center in Wisconsin, he'd felt a kind of nostalgic pity for the fellow sophomore, Larry Cottrell, who solemnly approached him with a broken rock. Frost by the lake had cracked the pebbles there, and some inner-circler had been inspired to give somebody one half of a pebble and keep the other, as a symbol of their being two halves of one whole, and this had quickly become a thing. Perry, who didn't know Cottrell well, was touched to receive a half pebble from him, followed by a hug, but not for the intended reason. What touched him was Cottrell's naïveté. Perry knew it was a game and Cottrell didn't yet. He might have been similarly touched by Becky's fervor if he could only figure out why she, the undisputed queen of her senior class, had deigned to join Crossroads in the first place.

He was on the verge of asking her why—confronting her—when she launched into the most extraordinary diatribe.

"The *barrier*," she said, "is that I don't actually believe you're a good person. Do you have any idea how crazy it's been for me to be in Crossroads? The first night I was here, do you know what people kept telling me? How great my younger brother is. Emotionally open, easy to relate to, incredibly supportive. And I'm thinking, are we talking about the same person? I actually wondered if I'd been a bad sister. Like, maybe I never took the time to get to know the real you. Maybe I was too self-involved to notice how emotionally open you are. But you know what? I don't think that's it. I think I've been exactly the sister you wanted me to be. Have I ever said a word to Dad or Mom about what everybody else knows about you? I could have. I could have said, Hey, Dad, are you aware that Perry's the biggest pothead at Lifton Central? Are you aware he hasn't made it through a day unstoned all year? That he goes up to the third floor after you're in bed and uses drugs? That his friends are all junior alcoholics and everybody in the high school knows it? I've protected you, Perry. And all you do is sneer at me. You sneer at all of us."

"Not true," he said. "In fact, I think each one of you is a better person than I am. I mean—'sneer'? Really? You think I sneer at Jay?"

"Judson is like your pet. That's exactly the way you treat him. You use him when you need him and you ignore him when you don't. You use your friends, you use their drugs, you use their houses. And, I swear to God, you're using Crossroads, too. You're smart enough to get away with it, but I can see what you're doing. That first Sunday, when people were telling me how great you are, I thought I was crazy. But you know who else agrees with me? Rick Ambrose."

Although the linoleum floor was cold, the closet felt overwarm to Perry, short on oxygen, bathyspheric.

"He thinks you're trouble," Becky said relentlessly. "That's what he told me."

Perry's mind started down the road of imagining the circumstances under which she'd heard this from Ambrose but stopped and turned back. It was as if he'd been born dispossessed, by his sister. No sooner had he found a game he could play well, a place where he was valued for his skill at playing it, an adult whom he could actually admire, than his sister came along and overnight turned Ambrose against him, claimed Ambrose for herself.

"So it isn't that you don't like me," he said, his voice unsteady. "That's not the barrier. The barrier is that you *hate* me."

"No. It's that—"

"I don't hate *you*."

"I don't even know you well enough to have a feeling about you. I don't think anybody really knows you. I think the people who think they do are wrong. And boy are you good at using them. Have you ever once in your life done something for another person that cost you something? All I've ever seen from you is selfishness and self-involvement and selfish pleasure."

He slumped forward and surrendered to tears, hoping they might soften her toward him, elicit a redemptive hug. But they did not. He struggled to think of a thing he'd ever done to harm her, a thing more visible than the occasionally unkind thoughts he had about her, to explain her hatred. Unable to think of one thing, he was forced to conclude that she hated him on principle, because he was an evil, selfish worm, and that she was testifying now merely to redress the abstract injustice of his being praised by other people.

"I'm sorry," she said. "I know this must be hard to hear. I mean, you are my brother. But maybe it's good you picked my name tonight, because I've lived with you my whole life. I can see you better than other people can. I . . . I do want to get to know you better. You're my brother. But first I have to see that there's a person there worth knowing."

She stood up and left him in the closet like a city leveled by a hydrogen bomb. Out of the rubble, he painfully reconstructed the gist of what she'd said. *She knew a lot more about his extracurricular activities than he might have imagined.* (The only blessing there was that she didn't seem to know that he sold drugs to seventh graders.) *Ambrose thought he was "trouble."* (The only consolation there was the certainty that Ambrose would be angry if he knew she'd betrayed this confidence.) *His seeming good works in Crossroads counted for nothing.* (But at least she'd reported that people thought well of him.) *He was a bad person. He merely used Judson.*

Too ashamed and self-pitying to leave the closet, he listened to the group reassembling in the function hall, the glad buzz of dyad partners who'd successfully worked on their relationships, the barking of Ambrose, the skillful strumming of guitars, the sing-along of "All Good Gifts" and "You've Got a Friend." He wondered if anyone noticed he was missing. Though not yet in the inner circle, he was among the sophomores most likely to get there, a fairly bright star in the Crossroads sky, and *he* certainly would have noticed if, say, one of the stars in Orion's Belt went dark. As the meeting broke up, he waited for a tap on the closet door from someone—a remorseful Becky, a worried adviser, a reassuring Ambrose, a fellow member who valued him, or even just someone who saw the strip of light under the door when the function-hall lights were turned off. That no one came to him, not one person, seemed to him a damning confirmation of Becky's judgment. He was not a person worth knowing.

It was partly to prove his sister wrong and partly to become a person whom Rick Ambrose ought to trust (and perhaps prefer to Becky) that he'd formed his new resolution that night. Not the purest-hearted of motives, surely; but one had to begin somewhere.

Leaving only two Quaaludes behind in his strongbox, as a tiny Christmas present to himself, he readmitted Judson to their bedroom and hurried forth in his parka, under snow-threatening skies, to Ansel Roder's house. A peculiarity of the Crappier Parsonage was that, although more in need of razing than of renovation, it stood in a much tonier part of town than the senior minister's house. All of Perry's old drug buddies lived close by. In his reluctance to liquidate the asset, he'd dithered past the start of Christmas vacation and now couldn't rely on finding any of his regular customers behind the Lifton Central baseball backstop, but Roder was always Mr. Liquidity. The stuccoed Roder manse had a round turret with terra-cotta shingles. Inside were beam-ceilinged rooms whose least-fine piece of furniture was finer than Perry's family's finest. Such was the heating situation that Roder came to the front door barefoot and shirtless, like G.I. Joe on a beach holiday. "Just the man I'm looking for," he said. "I'm getting this weird fuzz tone in my speakers."

Perry followed his friend up a broad staircase. "Both of them?"

"Yeah, but only with the turntable, not the tape deck."

"That's useful information. Let's have a look."

He had neither the time nor the inclination to play stereo doctor, but one of the ways he balanced accounts with his friends was by applying his manifold dexterity to petty problems of theirs, home-appliance puzzles, clogged aquarium hosing, calligraphy for signage, forgery of parental handwriting, interpretation of dreams, anything involving glue or tweezers. Upstairs, in his bedroom, Roder blasted a bit of "Whiskey Train" on his powerful stereo, and Perry readily diagnosed and fixed the looseness of the phonograph's needle cartridge. Without ceremony, he drew the asset from his parka pocket and tossed it onto Roder's bed.

Roder's eyes widened. "That is a princely Christmas present, Perry."

"I was hoping you might buy it from me."

"*Buy* it."

Between them, unspoken, the matter of Roder's perennial largesse, and the question of why Perry invariably accepted it if he had drugs of his own and didn't share them.

"I need funds," he explained. "There's something I want to get Jay for Christmas."

"*Really.* And so you're selling . . . It's like that story—Gift of the Madgie?"

"Mā-jī."

"Wouldn't it be funny if Jay sold his, I don't know, so he could buy you a water pipe? Et cetera."

"'The Gift of the Magi' is a story about irony, yes."

Roder poked at the asset, perhaps counting the pills. "How much money do you need?"

"Forty dollars would be good."

"Why don't I just loan it to you."

"Because we're friends and I don't know how I'd pay you back."

"You mowing lawns again next summer?"

"I'm supposed to be saving for college. There's some oversight of my earnings."

Roder shut his eyes, trying to make sense of it all. "Then how did you manage to buy this shit? Have you been *stealing*?"

Perry's palms began to sweat. "That's really neither here nor there."

"But don't you think it would be a little weird if you ended up burning this with me after I had to buy it off you?"

"I won't do that."

Roder made a skeptical sound. This was the moment for Perry to announce, per the terms of his resolution, that he wouldn't be burning anything with anyone anymore. But, again, the reluctance.

"Look," he said, "I know I can't be as generous as you are. But if you consider it rationally, I don't see why it matters who you bought from if the outlay is the same either way."

"Because it does, and I'm surprised you can't see why."

"I'm not stupid. I'm looking at it rationally."

"You know, for a minute, I honestly thought you'd gotten me a present."

Perry could see that he'd hurt his friend's feelings; that they'd reached a crossroads. *Are you willing to leave passive complicity behind you?* The voice of Rick Ambrose in his head. *Do you have the guts to risk the active witnessing of a real relationship?* He hadn't come to Roder's intending to end their (passive, complicit, drug-using) friendship. But it was true that all they ever did together anymore was get high.

"How about thirty dollars, then?" Perry's face, too, was sweating. "So it's partly a present, partly a, uh . . ."

Roder had turned away and opened a dresser drawer. He dropped two twenties on the bed. "You could have just asked for forty dollars. I would have given it to you." He scooped up the asset and put it in the drawer. "Since when are you a *dealer*?"

Outside again, as he made his way down Pirsig Avenue, Perry tried to reconstruct why, fifteen minutes earlier, he hadn't thought to just ask Roder for the money, perhaps as a "loan" that both of them knew would not be repaid, and then flush the asset down a toilet, achieving the same result without hurting his friend: why he hadn't imagined Roder reacting the way he had, which now made perfect sense to him. Never mind the nine-year-old Perry: the fifteen-minutes-ago Perry was a stranger to him! Did his soul change every time it achieved a new insight? The very definition of a soul was immutability. Perhaps the root of his confusion was the conflation of soul and knowledge. Perhaps the soul was one of those tools built to do exactly one specific task, *to know that I am I*, and was mutable with respect to all other forms of knowledge?

Whether it was the limitations of his intellect, vis-à-vis the mystery of the soul, or the difficulty of reconciling his new resolution with his thoughtless hurting of an old friend's feelings, he felt a little downward tug inside him, the slipping of a gear, the first shadow of the end of feeling well, as he proceeded into the central shopping district of New Prospect. Ordinarily he loved the glow of commerce on a dark winter afternoon. Almost every store contained things he wanted, and in this season every lamppost was wound with pine boughs and topped with a red bow that spoke additionally of buying, of receiving, of things brand-new and useful to him. But now, although he didn't quite have the feeling itself yet, he remembered how it would feel to be unmoved by the stores, unwanting of anything in them, and how much dimmer the lights of commerce would seem to him then, how dead the pine boughs on the lampposts.

As if the feeling could be outrun, he trotted on to New Prospect Photo. The camera he'd found for Judson was a mint-condition twin lens reflex Yashica. It had sat behind the window on a small white pedestal among twenty other used and new cameras, and Judson had agreed it was a beauty. As Perry entered the store, he almost didn't glance at the window. But the white of an empty pedestal caught his eye.

The Yashica was gone.

Gift of the Fucking Magi.

The store smelled of acid from the darkroom in the rear. Its owner, a shinily bald man, had an air of irritable oppression, understandable at a time when drugstores and shopping centers were killing his business. It was clear that when he looked up from the lens he was cleaning and saw Perry, a long-haired teenager, his first thought was shoplifter or waster of his time. Perry put his mind at ease by wishing him, with the intonation that bothered Becky, a very good afternoon. "I was hoping to purchase the twin lens reflex Yashica you've had in your window."

"Sorry," the owner said. "Sold it this morning."

"That is very distressing."

The owner tried to interest him in a shitty Instamatic, and then some ugly older cameras, while Perry tried not to show how offended he was by the suggestions. They'd arrived at an impasse when his eye fell on a beautiful thing under the glass-top counter. A compact movie camera, European-made. Burnished solid-metal body. Adjustable aperture. He recalled the old movie projector in the storage room at home, the remnant of a more optimistic era, when the Hildebrandts might still have become a family that watched home movies as a close-knit group, and before the Reverend, set upon by wasps, had lost his camera over the side of a rowboat.

"That's forty dollars," the owner said. "It sold for twice that, new, in nineteen-forties dollars. It's Regular 8, though. You have to load it in a bag."

"May I see it?"

"It's forty dollars."

"May I see it?"

When Perry wound the mainspring and took a peek through the viewfinder's luscious optics, he keenly wanted the camera for himself. Maybe Judson would share it with him?

Precisely the kind of thought that his resolution insisted that he banish.

And so he banished it. He left the store forty-eight dollars poorer but palpably richer in spirit. Imagining Judson's surprise at receiving not the camera they'd ogled but something even finer and cooler, he was certain that, for once, he was glad for another person. Snow had started falling from the Illinois sky, white crystallizations of water as pure as he felt, himself, for having parted with the asset. His thoughts had slowed to a happy medium, no slower than that, not yet. He stood for a moment on the sidewalk, amid the melting snowflakes, and wished the world could just stand still.

From the street came the rumble of a familiar engine. He turned and saw the family Fury braking for the stop sign at Maple Avenue. The rear of the car was packed with cardboard boxes. At the wheel was his father, wearing an old coat that Perry hadn't noticed missing from the third-floor closet. On the passenger side, angled to face his father, one arm draped over the backrest, was Larry Cottrell's foxy mother. She waved to Perry gaily, and now the Reverend saw him. No attempt at a smile was made. Perry had the distinct impression that he'd caught the old man doing something wrong.

Becky that morning had awakened before dawn. It was the first day of vacation, in past years a day for sleeping in, but this year everything was different. She lay in the dark and listened to the tick and wheeze of the radiator, the struggling clank of pipes below. As if for the first time, she appreciated the goodness of being snug in a house on a cold morning. Also, no less, the goodness of the cold, which made the snugness possible; the two things fit together like a pair of mouths.

Until last night, she'd put make-out sessions in the category of non-obligatory activities. For five years she'd seen people making out all around her, and she knew girls who'd allegedly gone all the way, but she hadn't felt ashamed of her inexperience. Shame of that sort was a trap girls fell into. Even the really pretty ones were afraid of losing popularity if they didn't act the way boys wanted them to. As her aunt Shirley had said, "If you sell yourself short, that's how the world will value you." Becky hadn't set out to be popular, but when popularity came to her she'd found she had a native instinct for how to manage and advance it. Being some athlete's squeeze seemed like an obvious dead end. She wouldn't have guessed how sweet it was to fall, and how much she would want to keep falling, and how altered she would feel in the aftermath, when she was by herself in bed.

Light grew in the windows half-heartedly, leaving monochrome the poster of the Eiffel Tower above her desk, the original watercolor painting of the Champs-Élyseés that Shirley had left her, the pony-themed wallpaper that she'd picked out for her father to hang for her tenth birthday, when she was too young to understand she'd have to live with it forever. In gray light, the wallpaper was more forgivable. An overcast sky was just the weather she would have wished for on the day after the night her life had become more serious. No sun to mark the hour, no change in its angle to take her out of the state of having been kissed.

When the alarm clock went off in her parents' bedroom, one door over from hers, it wasn't the usual cruel morning sound but a promise of everything the day ahead might hold. When she heard the faint buzz of her father's shaver and the footsteps of her mother in the hallway, she was amazed she'd never noticed, until today, how precious ordinary life was and how lucky she was to be a part of it. So much goodness. Other people were good. She herself was good. She felt goodwill to all mankind.

If she nevertheless waited, before getting out of bed, until the family car had whinnied to life in the driveway and her mother had come upstairs to dress, it was because she wanted to prolong her aloneness in the aftermath. She knotted herself into the Japanese silk robe that Shirley had bought her and soundlessly, in her bare feet, went down to the first-floor bathroom. The person who sat down to pee was a woman a man had kissed. Afraid of finding the change as invisible from the outside as it felt momentous from within, she avoided the eyes of this person in the mirror.

The aftersmell of toast and eggs deflected her away from the kitchen and back up to her room. It seemed as if her stomach was fluttering because she had a thousand things to begin all at once, but the only thing she could actually think of doing was to tell someone that she'd been kissed. She wanted to tell her brother first, but he wasn't home from college yet. She stood at her front window and watched a squirrel angrily send another squirrel scrambling up the trunk of an oak tree. Maybe it was a matter of a stolen acorn, or maybe her mind just went there because she herself had stolen. The nervousness in her stomach was partly a thief's adrenaline. For a moment, the aggressor squirrel seemed content to let the matter drop, but then the conflict escalated—hot pursuit up the trunk, further pursuit horizontally, a flying leap into the bushes by the driveway.

She wondered if he was awake yet, what he was thinking about her, whether he had regrets.

Outside her door, Judson was afoot and speaking to her mother about

sugar cookies. Becky didn't enjoy the domestic arts and was grateful to
have a brother who did, especially in December, when her mother had
the burden of upholding certain traditions, like the manufacture of sugar
cookies in the shape of Christmas trees and candy canes, that she'd invented for the family. As far as Becky could tell, the holidays to her
mother were just another chore, and it appeared that her own new feeling of goodwill was somewhat abstract, because it would have been a
kindness to go and sit in the kitchen, maybe help with the cookies, and
she didn't want to.

By way of compromise, she dressed in her best, faded jeans and took
her application materials down to the living room (the only person she
was *actively* avoiding, Perry, was unlikely to appear before noon) and
set up camp in the armchair by the Christmas tree, whose decoration
was another of her mother's chores. Its scent recalled the frenzy that she
and Clem as kids had whipped each other into when presents piled up
beneath it; but now she was so much older. The light in the windows
was somber, the sounds of cookie-making strangely distant. She might
have been sitting in some far-northern place that smelled of conifers. In
the kiss's aftermath, she seemed to be watching herself from a point so
elevated that she could see the earth's curvature, the world newly three-
dimensional and spreading out in all directions from her armchair.

She was applying to six colleges, five of them private and expensive.
As recently as October, college catalogues had been objects of romance,
variously flavored promises of escape from a family she'd outgrown and
a school whose social possibilities she'd exhausted. But then she'd discovered Crossroads, which had lessened her impatience to leave New
Prospect, and now, as she opened the folder of applications, she found
that the kiss had foreshortened the future more drastically. Anything
beyond the coming *day* seemed irrelevant.

Tell us about a person you admire or have learned something important from.

She removed the tooth-dented cap of a Bic pen and started writing
in a spiral notebook. Her handwriting, its upright pudginess, struck her
as childish this morning. She scratched it out and tried to make it leaner
and more slanting, more forward, more like the woman she'd felt herself
to be the night before, in the parking lot behind the Grove.

~~The person I most admire is~~

*My family lived in Southern Indiana until I was eight. My father was
the pastor of two small rural parishes. It was farm country but there were
woods and creeks to explore with my brother Clem. Unlike most brothers,
Clem never got angry if I followed him. Clem wasn't afraid of anything.
He taught me to stand still if a bee was bothering me.* ~~He liked all kinds
of critters.~~ *He called animals "critters" and was curious about all of them.
One day he scooped up a big spider and let it crawl on him and then
asked if he could put it on my arm. I learned that spiders don't bite if you
don't threaten them. There was a log over a deep creek that Clem ran
across like it was nothing. He showed me how to cross the creek by sitting
on the log and scooching along. I think most brothers would have been
happy to leave their little sister behind*~~, but not Clem. He had a baseball
glove he~~

A weariness had overcome her. Her words seemed childish, too.
She'd imagined that colleges would be charmed if she wrote about her
brother, and that it would be easy to explain why she admired Clem,
but she wasn't feeling it this morning. For one thing, Clem had come
home at Thanksgiving and told her, in strict confidence, that he had a
girlfriend in Champaign, his first ever. She ought to have been purely
happy for him, but in truth she'd felt a little bit left behind. Until then,
despite being younger, she'd considered herself the more worldly and
socially advanced one.

Clem's friends in high school had mostly been slide-rule types, guys
with dandruff-coated glasses, defiant body odor. She'd felt sorry that he
couldn't do any better than this, but he claimed to have no envy of her
social position and only a "sociological" interest in her people. Coming
home late on a Saturday night, she invariably saw light under his bedroom
door. If she knocked, he set aside the book he was reading or the science
problem he was cracking and listened, as only he in her family could, to
her little tales of life in Camelot. He pronounced clear-eyed judgments on
her friends, which she brushed aside in the moment ("Nobody's perfect")
but privately recognized the justice of. He was particularly harsh about

certain guys of her acquaintance, such as Kent Carducci, who wouldn't stop asking her out on dates and who, according to Clem, tormented Clem's friend Lester in the locker room. Still only a tenth grader, she'd walked up to Kent one day at lunch hour and spelled out, in front of his jock buddies, why she would never go out with him: "Because you're a bully and a jerk." Though Kent apparently continued to snap wet towels at Lester's butt, Becky was keenly attuned to the hierarchy and detected a subtle new shunning of Kent by the highest tier. She was tempted to report this accomplishment to Clem, but she knew it was the hierarchy itself, more than any given member of it, that he disdained. And yet, as if he recognized it as the field of her own sort of excellence, he never pushed her to drop out of it. How grateful she was for that! It was one of a hundred ways she knew he loved her. Sometimes it happened that she dozed off on his bed and awoke to find herself tenderly covered with a quilt, Clem asleep on the rug by the bed. She might have worried that there was something weird about their friendship, that she felt close to him in an almost married way that maybe wasn't healthy, that she wasn't as physically repelled by his beanstalk body, his scarred and pimpled face, as a sister ought to have been, if she hadn't been so sure that everything Clem did was good and right.

Even after he went off to college, he'd remained the star she navigated by. There were some fairly debauched, parentally unsupervised parties she found it necessary to attend because no sophomores and almost no juniors had been invited. In principle, Clem hated this kind of exclusivity even more than her parents did, but where her father gave her gentle lectures about remembering those less fortunate than her, and her mother worried aloud that she'd gotten pretty full of herself, Clem understood how important to her it was to be at the center of things. "Just be careful," he said. "Don't forget you're better than the rest of that crowd put together." She was protected at the parties, to an extent, by having been the leading vote-getter in the all-school cheerleader election, thus automatically a co-captain of the squad, despite being only a junior; if she raised her voice to wail that she hated the music, then, voilà, some unseen hand would lift up the needle and put on a Santana album. But the pressure to fuck up was still intense. She might not have

been able to wave away the burning doobies she was offered if Clem
hadn't warned her that marijuana's long-term effects on the brain were
not well studied. At the infamous New Year's party at the Bradfields',
where there was barfing in the back-yard snow and a disgusting truth-
or-dare thing happening in the basement, she might have gone upstairs
with Trip Bradfield, who was twenty and relentless, if she hadn't been
seeing him through Clem's eyes.

The Bradfield party had been her last of that sort. Her aunt Shirley
had passed away a few weeks later, and Becky had quit the cheerleading
squad and applied herself more seriously to schoolwork. It was Shirley
who'd taught her that staying home and reading a good book, letting
people wonder where you were, could get you farther than chasing after
every party. No longer exempted from family work rules by her cheerleading duties, she took an afterschool job at the florist shop on Pirsig
Avenue. She'd been secure in her popularity for long enough to know
she wasn't in danger of being forgotten. Quite the opposite. By quitting
the squad, she'd cast a diminishing light on all the girls who remained.
Shirley had given her an ankle-length navy-blue merino coat, and when
she walked in it on Pirsig after school, accompanied only by Jeannie
Cross, her best friend and her loyal lieutenant since seventh grade, she
could sense how the two of them looked to the cars full of peers driving
by. Shirley's word for it had been *mystique*.

She forced herself to take up her pen again. Her plans for the day
were predicated on finishing an essay before lunchtime.

One ~~warm hot humid summer~~ afternoon Clem and I were out exploring
near a farmhouse which had a large, vicious dog on a chain. Even Clem
was a little afraid of that dog. ~~Well, s~~Somehow the dog wasn't on its chain
that day, and it jumped over a fence and started chasing me. It bit my ankle
and I fell down. I could have been very seriously injured if Clem hadn't dove
onto the dog and started fighting with it. By the time the farmwife came to
the rescue, Clem was the one who was seriously injured. The dog bit his face
and both of his arms, and he had to have ~~thirty forty fifty~~ forty stitches. He
was lucky the dog didn't cripple his arm or bite through an artery. ~~To this
day, whenever I see the scars on his arms and his cheek, I remember how he~~

Always does the right thing without caring what other people think of him

Sticks up for kids who get picked on　　　not afraid of bullies (just like dog)

~~*He helped me realize there are more important things in life than being the*~~

Why did her writing have to make her sound like such a nitwit? She ripped the offending page out of the notebook. From the kitchen came the smell of a preheating oven, the morning slipping away. She felt unfairly stymied by the badness of what was on the page, as if she weren't, herself, the person who'd put it there.

And now came her mother, carrying a pitcher of water into the living room. "Oh," she said. "You're up."

"Yes," Becky said.

"I didn't hear you get up. Have you had breakfast?"

Her mother was already in her exercise clothes, a formless sweatshirt, saggy synthetic knit pedal pushers. It was a look that encapsulated, Becky felt, the difference between her mother and her aunt, who'd been as trim as her mother was bulky and couldn't possibly have owned such a sweatshirt. As her mother kneeled down to water the Christmas tree, Becky averted her eyes from the impending exposure of lumbar flesh. Another, more tragic difference between her mother and Shirley was that her mother was alive. Shirley had stayed trim by smoking two packs of Chesterfields a day.

Her mother asked her if she had any fun plans.

"Working on my applications," Becky said. "Christmas shopping."

"Well, just make sure you're home by six, so you have time to get ready for the Haefles' party. We'll leave as soon as your father gets home."

"I'm going to a party?"

Her mother stood up with the pitcher. "Dwight invited everyone to bring their families. Perry's staying home with Judson, and I don't know what time Clem is getting here."

"Sorry—what is this party?"

"An open house for clergy. Clem came with us last year."

"Did I say I would do this?"

"No. I'm telling you now that you will."

"Well, I'm sorry, but I have other plans. I'm going to the Crossroads concert."

She kept her eyes averted, but she could imagine her mother's expression.

"Your father won't be happy about that. But if that's your choice, we'll be home from the Haefles' by eight thirty."

"The concert starts at seven thirty."

"There's nothing wrong with being fashionably late. Missing one hour, to maintain some semblance of peace at the holidays, doesn't seem like much to ask."

Becky inclined her head mulishly. She had her reasons, but she wasn't going to explain them.

"How's it going with your essay?" her mother asked.

"Fine."

"I can help you with it, if you want to show me what you've written. Do you want to do that?"

This in a more honeyed tone, intended as a peace offering, but Becky took it as a reminder that her mother was better than her at writing, she herself better at nothing her mother valued. "I'm thinking," she said, by way of striking back, "that I might write about Aunt Shirley."

Her mother stiffened. "I thought you were writing about Clem."

"It's a personal essay. I can write whatever I want."

"True enough."

Her mother left the room. The light in the windows had brightened a little, and Becky was pleased to find her goodwill still intact. It wasn't as if her mother was a bad person. She just didn't understand how much nicer Becky's own plans were than going to the Haefles' party.

After the dog attack in Indiana, when the bite on Clem's face was iodined and stitched and his arms were in bandages, her father had come home from a church meeting and yelled at him. *How did you let this happen? What on earth were you doing at that farm? I gave you responsibility for your sister! She could have been killed! It happens all the time—a child no smaller than Becky gets killed by a dog! What were you thinking?* All this to a ten-year-old boy who'd been mauled while protecting her. And then

came the edict: Clem was henceforth forbidden to take Becky beyond
the lines of their property, except on the county road to and from their
school. When Becky thought about her and Clem's unusual friendship,
her mind went back to the word *forbidden*. Things that were forbidden
were often precisely what the heart most wanted. Things became more
attractive *because* they were forbidden by some cruel or uncomprehending authority. As a teenager, when she saw the light under Clem's door,
late on a Saturday night, it was like the beckoning glow of a forbidden
thing. She and Clem were united against the authority that wanted to
separate them.

Following the edict, her father had undertaken to replace Clem as
the person she went on walks with. For Clem, outdoors, everything was
an adventure—vines to be swung from, old wells to be sounded with
pebbles, terrible centipedes to be discovered under rocks, seed pods to be
sniffed and broken open, horses to be lured with an apple. For her father,
nature was just a glorious but unspecific thing that God had made. He
talked to Becky about Jesus, which made her uncomfortable, and about
the hard lives of local farmers, which was more interesting but maybe not
so wise of him. The stories she could tell on the playground—the Boylans
had a son in an insane asylum, Mrs. Boylan could only take nourishment
through a straw, Carl Jackson's mother was actually his grandmother—
had given her an early taste of popularity. Shocking true facts about
grownups were at a premium in grade school.

After the family moved to Chicago, her father had continued the "tradition" of taking her on walks on Sunday afternoons, usually a simple loop
around Scofield Park. Declining his invitation was seldom worth the guilt
trip her mother would have laid on her. Becky already felt guilty enough
for caring little about the church and even less about oppressed people, and
she did appreciate that her father treated her like a grownup, respected her
like that, and kept telling her things he maybe shouldn't have. She heard
a lot about his dreams of a larger life of Christian service, his frustrations
at being an associate minister in an affluent and mostly white suburb, and
she took what she heard straight to Clem. ("He's *frustrated*," Clem said,
"that he has a wife and four kids." Or, more wickedly: "Mom likes you
being the one Dad goes for walks with, because she knows he can't run off

with you.") In return, despite being prodded, she told her father nothing about her own dreams and frustrations.

She uncapped her pen again with her teeth. The first batch of sugar cookies was baking.

On January 16, it will be one year since my Aunt Shirley passed away.

This was better already. It had gravity and created immediate sympathy for the bereaved college applicant.

She was alone in the world, having lost her one true love in World War II. I had the privilege of knowing her later in life and learning the importance of culture and elegance, belief in oneself, and bravery in the face of solitude and sickness from her. ~~Whatever my mother may think, she didn't buy my affection.~~ I truly loved her. Every summer, starting when I was ten, I got to go and spend a week in her small but ~~elegantly~~ tastefully furnished apartment in ~~New York City~~ Manhattan.

It was true that Shirley had bought her a lot of stuff over the years. Also true that none of Becky's brothers ever got anything. True that the new clothes she brought home from New York had to be cleaned before she even wore them, to get the stink of Chesterfields out of them, and that on her first visit, in 1964, she cried every night on her aunt's sofa bed (Shirley called it a "convertible," as if it were a car) out of homesickness for Clem and the eye-burning oppression of the smoke in the airless apartment, and that, ironically, it was her mother who insisted that she accept Shirley's invitation again the next summer, as an act of charity. (Only later, after Becky had come to look forward to her New York trips, did her mother start using words like *vain* and *unrealistic* about her sister.)

Even early on, though, Becky had been dazzled by her aunt. On Shirley's first and last visit to the Indiana farmhouse, she'd taken Becky by her seven-year-old shoulders, looked her seriously in the eye, and informed her that she was destined to be a great beauty. That was something. Unlike her mother, who was only ever a pastor's wife, Shirley had had a career as a Broadway actress, never as a big star, apparently, but an actual career, and Becky had marveled at how imperiously she sliced through the masses of humanity at the World's Fair, in 1964, and how, when a waiter or a salesperson referred to Becky as her daughter, she merely winked at Becky, who until then had followed Clem's example and abhorred dishonesty. The difference between dishonesty and make-believe, Shirley said, was artistic imagination. Though it was obvious that Becky didn't have this kind of imagination—in New York, she preferred the mummies at the Met to the European painters, the dinosaurs across the park to the mummies, and Macy's to the dinosaurs—Shirley told her that this was just as well, because the world of art and theater was entirely controlled by cruel men, many of them literally, pardon her French, *cocksuckers*, and it was better for a woman to be the patron, the appreciator, than patronized and unappreciated. By which, though Shirley never quite spelled it out, Becky understood that she would be better off rich than talented.

How much money her aunt had and where it might have come from was long unknown to her. Shirley's apartment was small, but she had charge cards for all the department stores. Her furniture looked inexpensive, but her shoes and jewelry weren't. She took Becky out for a fancy dinner only once per visit, but she also never cooked a meal. Instead, she and Becky paged through a ring binder wonderfully populated with takeout menus, and anything else Becky needed (milk and cookies in the early years; later Fresca and tampons) was summoned for delivery by a phone call and paid for in cash at the burglar-proof front door. Shirley conveyed, through the way she shuddered at the recollection, her enduring horror at the Indiana farmhouse where she'd foretold her niece's destiny; the convulsive Maytag in the mud room, with its age-fissured rubber rollers, seemed to have made a particularly traumatic impression. Her own linens arrived clean in brown-paper packages tied up with white string.

Along with the shopping, what Becky most enjoyed about her summer visits was not having to pretend she didn't care about status and didn't want a future life in which she had it. Shirley methodically interrogated her about the professions of her friends' fathers and the size of their houses, and thereby made Becky aware that New Prospect Township wasn't a Midwestern utopia where everyone was equal, as she might have supposed, but a place where money counted socially and only good looks or athletic prowess could make up for the lack of it. In tenth grade, using funds that Shirley had provided for the purpose, and over her mother's sour disapproval, Becky had signed up for New Prospect's monthly formal dancing school, Messieurs et Mesdemoiselles, which her friends all rolled their eyes at but nevertheless attended. Still Clem's emissary, but also inspired by her aunt's insight that snobs were insecure and the true aristocracy gracious, she didn't avoid the greasier and clumsier dancers the way her friends did (although she did notice, and enjoy what it said about her status, that a clumsy boy became even clumsier when she astonished him by picking him as a partner). Inclusiveness, as she practiced it at M&M, was not only gracious but no less valuable than exclusivity was in building popularity—witness the results of the cheerleader election the following year. To be both *feared* and *liked* was its own kind of feat, and it struck, in her mind, a happy balance between the two very different people whose example mattered to her.

Between cigarettes, on Becky's last visit to New York, her aunt had sucked on nasty-smelling medicated lozenges. Despite the July humidity, there was a frog in her throat that she couldn't get rid of. In hindsight, Becky wondered if Shirley had known what it meant, because she couldn't keep it in her head that Becky still had two years of high school left, not one. The next summer, Shirley said, just as soon as Becky graduated, she wanted to take her on a grand tour of Europe: London for theater, Paris for the Louvre, Salzburg for music, Stockholm for white nights, Venice for atmosphere, Rome for antiquities. How did that sound to her? "I think," Becky said, "you mean *two* summers from now." Sad to say, she didn't share her aunt's impatience. Seeing Paris sounded good to her, but Shirley's favoritism wasn't playing well at home, and a grand tour of Europe would be an entirely different level of expense. Also, as Becky got older, the seeds of criticism planted by her mother had grown into an awareness that Shirley was somewhat loony and didn't have close friends. Becky still loved her and valued her insights. She understood, as her mother didn't seem to, how much Shirley envied her younger sister for having a husband and a family; how lonely she was. But she and her cigarettes weren't the companions Becky would have chosen, in an ideal world, for a trip to Europe.

Four days after she returned from New York, before she'd even written her thank-you letter, her mother had taken a phone call from Shirley and sobbed when it was over. Her tears were appropriate but still surprising, a lesson in the power of sisterly love to overcome sisterly dislike. Becky herself didn't cry at the news that her mother then gave her; cancer seemed to her both terrifying and unreal. Her own tears came later, when she wrote the thank-you and tried to think of how to end it (*Get well soon? I hope you feel better soon?*), and again when Shirley sent her a copy of *Fodor's Europe* filled with underlinings and annotations, along with a letter in which she went into great detail about European rail passes and spoke of beating her cancer and how important it would be, in the difficult months ahead, to have something to look forward to "next summer."

That fall, Becky's mother became real to her, as a person of independent capability, in a way she hadn't been before. She made two long trips to New York, where Shirley was getting radiation. When Becky asked if she could go there herself, her mother not only didn't discourage her but said it would be a wonderful gift to her aunt. But Shirley didn't want Becky to come, didn't want her to see her looking the way she did, didn't want her to remember her like that. Becky could come in the spring, when the treatments were behind her and she was more like herself. If everything went well, the two of them would then have the trip of a lifetime in the historic capitals of Europe.

She died alone in a room at Lenox Hill Hospital. There was no funeral. It was like Eleanor Rigby.

When I was younger I thought her elegance was effortless, but when I got to know her better I saw it was anything but. Now I think about all the things she did every day to put a brave face on. All the makeup supplies in her bathroom, her Chanel No. 19 spritzer, the hose she threw out if they got the tiniest run in them, the old white gloves she put on to read the newspaper to keep the ink off her fingers, the gold-rimmed cup she drank her tea from with her pinkie raised like a lady. And for what. Just to maintain her dignity in a world where she went by herself to the theater

*or a concert. No wonder, I thought, her little routines meant so much to
her. She gave me so many insights into my own life but, too, an insight
into the lives of people who wake up alone every morning and find the
courage to get out of bed and show their face. I was always blessed with
having many friends. I was "popular" and sometimes conceited about it.
All that changed when Shirley passed away. She gave me new admiration
for people who are lonely in the world.*

Becky's mother had gone to New York, one last time, to have Shirley's body cremated and to deal with her estate. She came home with an old wicker suitcase of Shirley's that contained a mink stole, the watercolor painting, silver earrings, a gold bracelet, and other keepsakes, all of it for Becky, who wept when her mother showed it to her.

"I understand why you're crying," her mother said coldly. "But you shouldn't romanticize your aunt. She made nothing but mistakes in life. In fact, *mistakes* may be too kind a word for it."

"I thought you were sad," Becky said.

"She was my sister. I couldn't help feeling sorry for her." Her mother seemed to soften, but only for a moment. "I should have known that people don't change."

"What do you mean?"

"Shirley was the kind of woman who has no use for other women. All she wanted was men. And she had plenty of them in her day. Funnily enough, though, none of them stuck around. The good ones figured out in a hurry what kind of person they were dealing with, the bad ones disappointed her, and she was vicious on the subject of homosexuals. I never met the man she actually married, but I gather he had some family money. He left her an annuity when he was killed in the Pacific, and it was a good thing he did, because she wasn't an actress. She was a pretty face who could memorize her lines. By the time your father and I moved to New York, she was 'between roles.' She was still between roles when we left. She lived in a fantasy world where nobody appreciated her talent and the men all either exploited her or disappointed her, but maybe the next man wouldn't. She was one of the most miserable people I've ever known."

The coldness of this speech shocked Becky. "But it's so sad," she said.

"Yes, it is," her mother said. "That's why I didn't mind you going out there in the summer. You have a good head, a good heart, and God knows she was lonely."

"If she didn't like other women, then why did she like me?"

"I wondered that myself. But people like her never change."

Eight months went by before Becky learned the reason for her mother's coldness. It happened that her birthday, her eighteenth, fell on a Saturday. Jeannie Cross had organized a blowout party that everyone who counted was coming to. Everyone wanted to see Hildebrandt get drunk, which was Jeannie's stated object and, God help her, Becky's private intention. Unlike her dissolute younger brother, she'd always been sensitive to her father's position as a man of the cloth, the unseemliness of a minister's daughter getting shit-faced, but now she was old enough to vote, and her social instincts told her it was time to mix things up a little. After working the lunch shift at the Grove—she'd quit her florist job and taken a less dorky one, waiting tables—she hurried home to shower and dress and have an early dinner with her family. The parsonage seemed curiously empty. There were October sunbeams in the living room, a fading smell of baked cake. She went up to her room and was startled to see her mother seated on her bed. "You need to come upstairs with me," she said.

"I need to shower," Becky said.

"You can do that later."

On the third floor, they found her father waiting in his home office, his windows open, cool autumn air filtering into the attic-like stuffiness. He motioned to Becky to sit down. Her mother shut the door and stayed standing. Becky was quite alarmed. It was as if she were facing punishment for the heavy drinking she hadn't done yet.

"Marion?" her father said.

Her mother cleared her throat. "As you know," she said to Becky, "my sister named me as the executrix of her will. What I have to say to you, I'm saying as the executrix. Your aunt left you a great deal of money. Now that you're eighteen, the money is yours. The will doesn't specify that it be held in trust. All it says is—Russ, will you read it?"

Her father unlocked a drawer and took out a document. "'To my

niece Rebecca Hildebrandt I will, devise, and bequeath the sum of thirteen thousand dollars for a Grand Tour of Europe, to be taken in my
memory.' That's all there is. No mention of trustees."

Becky was smiling broadly; she couldn't help it.

"I put the money in your savings account yesterday," her mother said.
"Wow."

"I was legally obligated," her mother said. "The lawyer said we could
wait until your eighteenth birthday, but no longer than that. Shirley's
intentions were clear."

"Wow. That's so nice of her."

"It's not nice," her father said. "It's a foolish bequest, and we need to
talk about it."

"Thirteen thousand dollars," her mother said, "is almost the entirety
of your aunt's estate. There were a few odd thousands left over for various
museums, but you're the main beneficiary. If you'd happened to prede-
cease her, the money would have gone to the museums."

Now Becky saw the problem. In case she hadn't, her mother laid it
out for her: not only had Shirley ignored Clem, Perry, and Judson, but
she'd stipulated that Becky use the money for something frivolous. She'd
lived in a fantasy world to the end, and beyond. "And she knew very well
how I would feel about it. That was part of the equation."

So everything is about you, Becky thought.

Her father might have had the same thought, because he suggested
that her mother leave the two of them alone. When she was gone, he
shifted into his gentle dad-to-daughter tone. "I can't believe you're eighteen already. It seems like only yesterday that we brought you home from
the hospital."

How many times had Becky heard that it seemed like only yesterday?

"But now here you are, eighteen years old, and I want you to think
hard about this money. You're not legally bound by the wording of your
aunt's will, and thirteen thousand dollars seems to me an awful lot to
spend on a trip to Europe. Unless you're staying at the Ritz, you could
travel for two years on that."

Staying at the Ritz, Becky thought, was exactly what Shirley had had
in mind.

"I can't tell you what to do, but it seems to me that you could honor Shirley's intention by using a small portion of the money to travel abroad next summer. If you wanted to do something nice for your mother, you could bring her along. Again, I'm not telling you what to do—"

Really?

"But there's also a question of fairness. I know you had a special fondness for Shirley, and she for you, but I do think she may have been trying to hurt your mother with this bequest. Your mother and I love all of you kids equally, and we think you should all be treated equally. For better or worse, we're not a well-to-do family. Your mother and I want all of you to go to college, and a quarter of the bequest would make a real difference to each of you. I can't tell you what the right thing to do is—"

Really?

"But I hope you'll think carefully about how you want to proceed. Will you do that for me?"

"Yep," Becky said.

"I know it's not easy. Thirteen thousand dollars is a lot of—"

"I get it," she said. "You don't have to say anything else."

"I just want you to know that I'm very—"

"I said I get it. Okay?"

She jumped to her feet, ran down to her room, and jerked open the top drawer of her dresser, where she kept her savings passbook. The balance had indeed been updated. It was $13,753.60. Christening money, birthday money, paychecks for the hours she'd spent in a stupid green florist's apron, and tips and paychecks from the Grove added up to $753.60. Dear Aunt Shirley! She'd known what Becky wanted, and it was all the better for being unexpected. Becky had never, *not once*, wondered if her aunt had left her any money; the little suitcase of treasures had been enough. Only now, as she imagined the figure in her passbook reduced to a sad nubbin, did her mind spring to life with greedy rationalizations. Maybe she wasn't legally bound to follow the letter of the will, but wasn't she *morally* bound to honor the spirit? Wouldn't it be an insult to Shirley's memory to submit to her father's wishes? And why should she give anything to her pothead little brother, who could probably get a full scholarship to Harvard anyway? Wouldn't there be more money for

Judson in the future, when her father got his own church and there were fewer mouths at home to feed? The only person she felt at all inclined to share with was Clem.

At the party that night, she quickly downed two Seagram's and 7UPs, after which it was possible to slow down without being noticed. The main effect of the alcohol was to create a powerful but hazy sense of importance; of being on the verge of a great, warm insight. As her buzz began to fade, the sense of importance faded with it, leaving behind a small, cold insight: she was bored. She didn't care who had a crush on who, what kind of prank was played on Lyons Township before the football game. The world was full of better places.

> *It's because of an inheritance I received from Shirley, following her tragic death, that I'm able to consider attending a private college. She herself never attended college, having been a noted actress in her youth and busy with her career, but she loved the higher things in life and knew more about art and theater and music and coteur than ~~many experts~~ anyone I've ever known. It was from her that I learned to dream big and really make something of myself. I'm blessed to have an opportunity to educate myself in a way she never could, and learn more about the world. I intend to seize this opportunity fully.*

She read what she'd written and wrinkled her nose. There seemed to be no way back to the pure feeling she'd had for Shirley before her mother clouded it with criticisms. Or maybe the morning after being kissed was simply not a good time to experience admiration. Considering her state, she felt good about having written anything at all.

She closed her notebook and went to the kitchen, where Judson was applying colored sugar to a tray of cookies. Through the open basement door came the sound of laundry chores.

"These look great, Jay," she said.

"I need a better tool. It clumps on the spoon."

"Which one is your least favorite? I bet I can make it disappear."

"This one," he said, pointing.

She ate the cookie and immediately wished she could eat another. "Is there anything special you want for Christmas? Something you haven't told anyone about?"

"Nobody asks."

"Perry didn't ask you?"

Judson hesitated and shook his head.

"I'm asking," she said.

"Colored pencils," he said, intent on the cookies. "With interesting colors."

"Got it. This tape will self-destruct in five seconds."

"If you or any of your I-enforcers are caught or killed, the Secretary will disavow any knowledge of your actions."

"I think it's 'I.M. force.' Impossible Mission."

"I wondered about that."

"You're a good kid," she said, brimming with goodwill.

"Thank you."

Her mother was trudging up the basement stairs, so she fled to her room again. Seeing her unmade bed, she was drawn to lie down on it, as a way of falling back into the kiss. The day already seemed to have lasted longer than an entire ordinary day, and it had still barely started.

It was generally assumed, and specifically assumed by her father, in his jealousy, that Rick Ambrose was the reason Crossroads had exploded in popularity. According to Clem, though, there were two reasons, and the other one was Tanner Evans. Tanner's parents belonged to First Reformed, and he'd come up with Clem through Sunday school and gone with Becky's father on the first spring work camp in Arizona. Tanner was a nice person, from a nice family, but he was also a gifted musician and *the* coolest guy at New Prospect Township, one of the first to grow his hair long, a bell-bottomed dreamboat. In Clem's telling, Crossroads had exploded when Tanner invited his music-playing friends, male and female, white and black, to come to Sunday meetings. Crossroads became as much a musical happening as a religious thing, Tanner's coolness the counterweight to Ambrose's intensity.

Tanner had postponed college to develop his skills and write songs. He had a regular Friday-night gig in the back room at the Grove, where liquor was served. He and his girlfriend, Laura Dobrinsky, who'd been his female counterpart in Crossroads, played together in a band called the Bleu Notes. Laura was short and somewhat chunky, but she had an impressive head of wavy hair and a face flattered by pink-tinted wire-frames, and her voice, when she sang solo, made walls shake and hearts break. She was one of New Prospect's original hippies, a walking yes to the question *Are You Experienced?* It was hard to imagine Tanner with anyone else, and so when Becky went to work at the Grove and started running into him, and he asked her how Clem was doing at college, and sent greetings to her parents, she assumed she was only a little sister to whom, being nice, he was being nice.

The night before she turned eighteen, after her shift ended, she stood in the doorway of the back room and listened to the last song of the Bleu Notes' first set. Tanner's voice and mustache resembled James Taylor's, and he wore a fringed suede jacket. His hands were strong and lanky from playing guitar, his mouth full-lipped and fascinating when he sang. After the song ended and Becky had turned to leave, she heard him call her name. He came weaving through the bar tables and motioned to her to sit down with him. Laura Dobrinsky had disappeared somewhere.

"There's a question I've been meaning to ask you," he said. "Why aren't you in Crossroads?"

Becky frowned. "Why would I be?"

"Um, because it's an incredible experience? Because you're a member of First Reformed?"

She was not, in fact, a member of the church. She was so obviously not a religious person that her parents hadn't bothered to pressure her to join.

"Even if I wanted to be in Crossroads, which I don't," she said, "I wouldn't do that to my father."

"What does your father have to do with it?"

"The group kicked him out?"

Tanner winced. "I know. That scene was messed up. But I'm asking about you, not him. Why don't you want to be in Crossroads?"

It was true that Clem had joined the youth group, before it was called Crossroads, and that he was even less religious than she was. But Clem enjoyed service to poor people, the Arizona trip especially, and was naturally generous (or willfully perverse) in his choice of companions. Becky was turned off by the Crossroads look, the painter's pants and flannel shirts, and by the superior air of Crossroads people at their tables in the high-school cafeteria, their ostentatious closeness, their indifference to the hierarchy. Though Clem had dismissed the hierarchy himself, he'd never seemed smug about it. The Crossroads people did.

"I just don't," she told Tanner. "It's not my kind of thing."

"How do you know it's not your kind of thing if you haven't tried it?"

"Why do you care if I try it?"

Tanner shrugged, stirring his suede fringes. "I heard Perry's been going. I thought, 'That's cool, but what about Becky?' It seemed weird that you weren't in the group."

"Perry and I are very different."

"Right. You're Becky Hildebrandt. You're the queen of the soshies. What would all your friends say?"

It was nice that he'd paid enough attention to know her social standing. But she'd always hated being teased. "I'm not going to Crossroads. I don't have to tell you why."

"It's not because you're afraid of what you might learn about yourself."

"Nope."

"Really? It sounds to me like you're afraid."

"I am what I am."

"That's what God said, too."

"You believe in God?"

"I think so." Tanner leaned back in his chair. "I think He's there in our relationships, if they're honest. And the first place I ever had honest relationships, and felt close to God, was in Crossroads."

"Then why did it kick my dad out?"

Tanner seemed genuinely pained. "Your dad is great," he said. "I love your dad. But people couldn't relate to him."

"I can relate to him. So I guess there's something wrong with me, too."

"Whoa. That is, like, textbook passive aggression. You wouldn't get away with that for five minutes in Crossroads."

"Perry's a total bullshitter, and he seems to be doing great there."

"When I look at you, I see the girl who's got everything, the girl everybody wishes they could be. But inside you're so scared you can hardly breathe."

"Maybe I'm holding my breath until I can get away from this town."

"You were chosen for bigger and better things."

She wasn't accustomed to being mocked. Everywhere at New Prospect Township, the mere threat of her disdain carried weight. "Just so you know," she said, in a frosty tone she rarely found it necessary to use outside her family, "I don't enjoy being teased."

"Sorry about that," Tanner said. "It just seems like a waste, to hold your breath for a year. You're supposed to be living. That's the way we honor God—by being present in the moment."

As Becky tried to think of a tart comeback, Laura Dobrinsky reappeared. Her cumulus of hair reeked of pot smoked in chill autumn air, which had hardened the nipples clearly visible through the crepe of her blouse, beneath her unzipped biker jacket. She sat down backward on Tanner, straddling one of his thighs.

"I've been telling Becky she needs to go to Crossroads," Tanner said.

Laura appeared only then to notice Becky. "It's not for everyone," she said.

"You loved it," Tanner said, his beautiful hands clasped low on Laura's belly.

"I liked the intensity. Not everyone does. There were people who got fucked up by it."

"Like who?"

"Like Brenda Maser. She had a nervous breakdown on the spring retreat."

"She had a freakout," Tanner said, "because Glen Kiel dumped her for Marcie Ackerman the day before the retreat."

Laura asked Becky if she could imagine someone bawling for twenty hours straight. "It started with a screaming exercise," she said. "You scream and then you stop, except that Brenda didn't. I was in Ambrose's car with her on the drive home. You could hug her, you could leave her alone, it didn't matter. We ended up just sitting there listening to her cry. Kind of wanting to strangle her to make it stop. We got to her house, and

Ambrose took her inside and handed her off to her parents. Like, here's your daughter, there seems to be a problem, uh, we don't know anything else about it."

Becky tried to imagine Clem on a retreat, screaming, and could not.

"It wasn't a nervous breakdown," Tanner said. "Brenda was in school the next morning."

"Oh, well, then." Laura gave Becky a funny overbright smile. "Only twenty hours of crying. What's not to like?"

Another thing Becky had enjoyed about her aunt was her disdain. Shirley had exercised it constantly, often with salty language. After she died and Becky's mother pronounced her judgment, Becky understood what a survival mechanism disdain had been for her aunt, who had few other defenses against an uncaring world. For Becky herself, disdain was more of an emergency measure, taken only when someone directly tried to make her feel bad. Leaving the Grove that night, rattled by an un-accustomed sense of inferiority, she tried to summon it, but there was nothing to disdain about Laura Dobrinsky except her shortness, which Becky, even in an emergency, could see wasn't fair. Laura was the Natu-ral Woman that Becky had heard her sing about being made to feel like, in her giant voice, and there was no disdaining Tanner for anything. She went to bed that night wondering if Tanner had been right about her—if she really was afraid of life. The boredom she felt at her birthday party, the following night, was another sign that she needed to start living.

If Shirley hadn't left her thirteen thousand dollars, she might not have chosen Crossroads as the place to start. She did have an instinct that showing up at Crossroads would be a delicious kind of shock to those who paid attention to such things. If she happened to like it, Tanner would be more respectful of her, and if she thought it was stupid, well, then she would have something to disdain. But she knew how her father loathed Rick Ambrose. She wasn't exactly *forbidden* to go to Crossroads, but she might as well have been.

Only after he'd lectured her about Shirley's money did she decide to defy him. It wasn't that she thought he was wrong. She got that her loony aunt had played favorites and that it was up to her to make things right, by sharing her money. And yet she felt betrayed, in a way that hurt no less for being childish. How many times had her mother told her how specially dear she was to her father? How many stupid walks had she taken on the assumption that the walks were super-important to him? If she'd known he was going to yank away her inheritance before she could even be excited about it, she would never have gone on so many walks. What was the point if all she got out of it was a sermon about fairness? He couldn't even wait for her to find her own way to a generous impulse. It was wham, bam, share the money with your brothers. Who, speaking of fairness, had never done anything for Shirley, never written her, never sacrificed valuable days of summer vacation for her, never lain awake on her convertible with eyes and nose assaulted by smoke. If her father was so fond of her, shouldn't he at least have acknowledged that?

She invited Jeannie Cross to come with her to Crossroads. Jeannie would have run through a hail of bullets for Becky, and might have preferred it to visiting a Christian youth group, but Becky explained that Tanner Evans had dared her to go. Jeannie was duly impressed. "You've been hanging out with Tanner Evans?"

"Just casually. We talk."

"Isn't he with what's her face?"

"Laura, yeah. She's cool."

"So . . ."

"I said. It's just casual."

"Would you go out with him if he asked you?"

"He's not going to ask me."

"I can actually sort of see it," Jeannie said. "You and him together."

"You haven't seen the way he is with Laura."

"You know what I mean, though. You're going to be with someone, sometime. And, Jesus—Tanner Evans? I can really almost see it."

So, now, suddenly, could Becky. She had only to picture it as it would appear to people like Jeannie, as a crowning confirmation of her status, a punishing lesson to every lesser boy who'd imagined he could date her, and the thought became lodged in her head. Why, after all, had Tanner challenged her to try Crossroads? Wasn't this evidence of interest in her? Even his teasing—maybe especially his teasing—was evidence.

From Clem's involvement with the group, she knew enough to dress down for it, but she wasn't Jeannie's keeper. When Jeannie picked her up, in the silver Mustang her parents had given her, she was wearing dress slacks, an expensive brocade vest, and a lot of makeup. Becky felt sorry for her, but she didn't mind having an overdressed friend to feel cooler than. The Crossroads meeting room was shockingly crowded with people she knew the names of, had given many a congenial smile to in classrooms and hallways, and would never have dreamed of seeing socially. In a far corner was a tangle of bodies like a collapsed game of Twister with her brother Perry at the bottom of it, fighting a battle of tickles with a fat girl in bib overalls, his face red with happiness, quite a bizarre sight. Becky and Jeannie sat down with two former friends from Lifton Central. One of them, Kim Perkins, a cheerleader who'd strayed into promiscuity and drugs, gave Becky a welcoming hug and petted her head as if it were she, not Kim, who had strayed. Kim tried to hug Jeannie as well, but Jeannie raised a hand to ward her off.

And so it went. Downstairs, in the function hall, Becky opened herself to the activities because Jeannie couldn't. When people taped a sheet of newsprint to their back and wrote messages on other backs with felt-tip pens, Becky scrawled *Looking forward to getting to know you!* ☺ *Becky* on back after back, stopping only to be scrawled upon, while Jeannie, looking miserable in her dress slacks, stood to the side and frowned at her pen as if its workings were a mystery. The group then formed a circle of crosshatched bodies, everyone's head resting on their neighbor's belly. There was no obvious point to the exercise except to start laughing as a group and feel your head bouncing on a laughing belly and another head bouncing on yours, but to Becky, positioned between two boys she'd never spoken to, it seemed strange that she'd spent her life surrounded by bellies, all of them as familiar to their owners as her own belly was to her, all of them potentially touchable, and yet they were almost never touched. Strange that a possibility constantly present was so seldom acted on. She was sorry when the exercise ended.

"We're going to break into groups of six," Rick Ambrose said. "I want each of us in the group to talk about something we've done that was wrong. Something we're ashamed of. And then I want each of us to talk about something we've done that we're proud of. The point here is to *listen*, all right? Really listen. We'll meet back here at nine."

Not wanting to be in a group where she knew nobody, Becky pounced on the one Kim Perkins was forming and left Jeannie to fend for herself. A friend of Perry's, David Goya, tried to join Kim's group, but Rick Ambrose stepped in front of him and blocked him out. Becky hadn't expected that Ambrose himself would participate in the exercise. She and the others followed him upstairs and sat down in the hallway outside her father's office. At the sight of her father's name on the door, her chest constricted with the consequence of what she was doing to him. She'd had every right to try Crossroads, but a betrayal was a betrayal.

Rick Ambrose was smaller than he loomed in her parents' demonology. He was like a little black-mustached satyr with stack-heeled hooves. Following his own instructions, he listened intently while a tough kid Becky had known only by face told the story of breaking windows at Lifton Central with a slingshot after he'd gotten a D-minus in physical science, Kim Perkins the story of having sex with a summer-camp counselor whose girlfriend was the counselor in her cabin.

"And you think that was wrong," Ambrose said.

"Definitely it was shitty of me," Kim said.

"But I'm listening to you," Ambrose said, "and what I'm hearing is more like bragging. Is anyone else hearing that?"

What Becky was hearing was more like statutory rape. Kim had long had a bad reputation, but at some level Becky hadn't quite believed the rumors about her. Becky was three years older than Kim had been at summer camp, and she hadn't even kissed anyone. What story could she tell when it was her turn? Behaving irresponsibly had never been her thing.

"I liked that I could have him," Kim said. "Like, how easy it was. Maybe I was proud of that. But when I went back to my cabin and saw his girlfriend, I felt awful. I still feel awful. I hate that I was ever the kind of person who would do that to someone, just because I could."

"That, I'm hearing," Ambrose said. "Becky?"

"I'm hearing it, too."

"Do you want to tell us something about yourself?"

She opened her mouth but nothing came out. Ambrose and the others waited.

"Actually," she said, "right now I'm feeling bad about my friend Jeannie. I made her come with me tonight, and I don't know where she went."

She looked down at her hands. The church was very quiet, the other groups dispersed, their guilty disclosures a distant murmur.

"I think she might have gone home," Kim said.

"Okay, now I'm feeling really bad," Becky said. "She's my best friend, and I . . . I think I'm a bad friend. Everywhere I go, I want everyone to like me, and this is my first time here—I want to be liked. But I should have been taking care of Jeannie."

The girl next to her, whose back she'd scrawled on without learning her name, put a soft hand on her arm. Becky shuddered and sort of sobbed. It was more emotion than the situation perhaps called for, but something about Crossroads brought emotion to the surface. *I want to be liked* might have been the most honest words she'd ever uttered. Recognizing the truth of them, she bent forward and surrendered to her emotion, and now other hands were on her, hands of comfort and acceptance.

Only Ambrose held back. "What are you waiting for?" he said.

She wiped her nose. "What do you mean?"

"Why aren't you looking for your friend?"

"Now?"

"Yes, now."

The silver Mustang was still in the parking lot. As Becky approached the driver's side, Jeannie started the engine and turned down the radio, which was tuned to WLS and playing "Save the Country." She lowered the window.

"I'm sorry," Becky said. "You don't have to wait for me."

"You're *staying*?"

"Are you sure you don't want to come back inside? I'll stick close to you."

Come on down to the glory river, the radio said. Jeannie shook her head. "I thought you were only doing this because Tanner dared you."

"He dared me to *try* it. Not just go for one hour."

"One hour was plenty for me."

"I'm sorry."

"You're forgiven," Jeannie said. "I swear to God, though, Bex. You'd better not go religious on me."

To her own surprise, she went religious. It began with being bored and wanting to be liked, but even on her first night she was forced into interactions with kids less fortunate than she was, forced to listen to them, forced in turn to account for the person she really was, undefended by status, and thereby, just as Tanner had promised, forced to learn things about herself, not all of them flattering. Crossroads didn't *look* religious— there was nary a Bible in sight, and whole evenings went by without reference to Jesus—but here again Tanner had been right: simply by trying to speak honestly, surrendering to emotion, supporting other people in their honesty and emotion, she experienced her first glimmerings of spirituality. She could feel herself vindicating Clem's long-standing faith in her, as a person of substance.

A hundred and twenty kids were in Crossroads, and only one exciting leader. In two hours on a Sunday night, every member could hope for one minute of Ambrose's attention. Becky, in the weeks that followed, averaged a lot more than that. Ambrose twice chose her as a dyad partner, praised her for her guts in joining the group, and called her out in larger discussions, praising her honesty. She would have been more self-conscious about hogging him if she hadn't felt a natural affinity with him. She, too, had been a person other people measured and compared their time with; she knew the pleasure but also the burden of that. Plus she'd come painfully late to Crossroads—she had two years of lost time with Ambrose to make up for.

Her father, meanwhile, was barely speaking to her. She was theoretically sorry to have hurt him, but she didn't miss the charade of closeness. He'd needed to be shown that she was eighteen years old and had a right to her own life. The ancient edict needed punishing as well.

The action that had truly taken guts occurred in the school cafeteria some weeks later. She'd already stopped putting on makeup in the morning and taken to wearing only jeans, never skirts, but she didn't think she'd ever felt more glaringly visible than the day she plunked her sack lunch down between Kim Perkins and David Goya. They acted like it was nothing, but every eye at Becky's usual table was on her, especially Jeannie Cross's. Though Jeannie should arguably have been grateful to her, for vacating a rung on the ladder that she herself could then ascend to, Jeannie didn't see it that way. She continued to give Becky rides to school in her Mustang, and Becky still enjoyed hearing her gossip, but a line had been crossed when she sat down at a Crossroads table. Jeannie referred to Crossroads as Kumbaya, which wasn't funny even the first time she said it, and Becky, although she couldn't prove it, sensed that Jeannie was no longer telling her every secret she learned.

Offsetting her self-imposed demotion was her rise in Tanner Evans's estimation. Not only had the thought of her with Tanner not left her; after she publicly declared herself a Crossroads person, the thought had acquired new urgency. Certain people who thought less of her for going religious might think again if they saw her with Tanner Evans. This was a calculation, but her feelings had quickly fallen in line with it. She imagined holding one of Tanner's hands in hers, touching the tips of his long fingers one by one. She imagined his hands clasped on her belly, the way she'd seen them clasped on Laura Dobrinsky's. She imagined him writing a song about her.

At the Grove, on the Friday after her first Crossroads meeting, she resisted the urge to find him and tell him what she'd done. She'd enjoyed the meeting, and she planned to go to the next one, but as soon as she saw Tanner arrive with his guitars she wondered if she'd capitulated too easily. If she'd offered more resistance, he might have kept pressing her, and teasing her.

The Bleu Notes were playing without the Natural Woman that night. By the time their first set ended, Becky was putting chairs up on tables in the empty dining room. The urge was there but she resisted it. And was rewarded when Tanner came looking for her.

"Hey," he said, "I saw Rick Ambrose. You know what he told me?"

"No."

"You actually went! I couldn't believe it. I thought I'd totally pissed you off."

"You did piss me off."

"Well, and apparently it worked."

"Yeah, once. I'm not sure I'll go back."

"You didn't like it?"

She shrugged, trying to maintain her resistance.

"You're still pissed off with me," he said.

"I still don't see why you care if I'm in Crossroads."

She hoisted a chair onto a table, feeling his eyes on her. She expected him to ask what she'd made of Crossroads. Instead he asked her if she wanted to stay for the second set.

"I'm not allowed in the back room," she said, "except to get drink orders."

"You work here. No one's going to card you."

"Where's Laura?"

"She went to Milwaukee for the weekend."

"Well, then, I don't think I'd better."

Tanner looked away, blinking. He had wonderful eyelashes.

"Okay," he said. "That's cool."

All the way home and well into the night, she revised the evening in her head. Her chance had come and gone so suddenly, she hadn't had time to think it through. Had she said no because she considered it unethical to sneak around behind Laura's back? Or was it because the idea of being a temporary replacement, a second-stringer, was insulting? If only she hadn't said no so quickly! Deflection of male advances had become a re-flex, because until now the advances had always been deflection-worthy. But what if she'd stayed for the second set? And hung out afterward with Tanner and the band, and let him drive her home, and then seen him again the next day, and the day after that, while Laura was in Milwaukee?

She didn't get a second chance. The following Friday, Laura was back at the Grove, playing with Tanner, doing harmonies with him and then a solo song at the piano, "Up on the Roof," that Becky fled into the kitchen to avoid hearing even distantly. That Sunday, she almost didn't go to Crossroads, since there seemed to be nothing further to be gained with Tanner by going. But when seven o'clock rolled around she expe-rienced a pang of actual loneliness, not a feeling she was used to. She threw on her only halfway scruffy coat, a corduroy jacket that Clem had outgrown, and ran-walked down to First Reformed, arriving just in time to be chosen by Rick Ambrose as a dyad partner.

The instruction was *Share something you're struggling with that the group might help you with*. Ambrose led her to his office, which he had the privilege of using for dyad exercises, and offered to share first. His dark eyes uncharacteristically cast down, rather than boring into hers, he spoke of being frightened by the size and intensity of the group he'd helped create, the power that so many kids had given him over their lives. It was hard for him to maintain humility, and he worried that his relationship with God was suffering, because the horizontal relationships within the group were so compelling. "It's easier to pray when you feel weak," he said. "It's easier to pray for strength than for humility, because humility is what you need to pray in the first place. Do you know what I mean?"

"I haven't really tried to pray yet," Becky said.

"That's the next step," Ambrose said. "I don't just mean for you. This group started as a Christian fellowship, but it's taken on a life of its own. I'm a little worried about what we've unleashed. What *I've* unleashed. I'm worried that, if it doesn't end up leading us back to God, it's just an intense kind of psychological experiment. Which could just as easily end up hurting people as liberating them."

Even by Crossroads standards, his disclosure seemed extreme to Becky. She was flattered by his openness with her, which she took as another token of their affinity. But she was only a high-school kid, not his spiritual adviser.

"I know it's a sore subject," she found herself saying, "but one thing my dad is good at is keeping religion front and center. It's always made me uncomfortable. But maybe it was a good contribution he made to the group?"

Ambrose winced. "I hear what you're saying."

"I mean, it's great, what you're doing. I'm not a pray-er. I like that I don't have to do that. But . . ."

But what? Suggest that her father be reinstated in Crossroads? She cringed at the thought of him and his Christ talk at a Sunday-night meeting. She would quit the group in a minute if he came back.

"And what about you?" Ambrose said. "What are you struggling with?"

To reciprocate his openness, she told him that she had feelings for Tanner Evans. That Tanner was the reason she'd joined Crossroads. That, if she was not mistaken, Tanner was interested in her, too. That she wanted to pursue a relationship with him, but she didn't think it was right to get between him and Laura. What should she do?

If Ambrose was surprised, he didn't show it. "I love Tanner," he said. "I'm not sure anyone's ever had a better experience in this group. If everyone were like him, I wouldn't be worried about where we're going. He really did find his way back to God, and he had a beautiful way of keeping it light."

"But Laura," Becky suggested.

"Laura gave me constant shit. And I respected that. If Laura's got a problem with a person, the person's going to hear about it."

"Okay."

"But Tanner is mellow, and that cuts both ways. I can't tell you what the right thing to do is. But I can tell you my impression, which is that Laura was always the one driving that relationship. For Tanner it was more like the path of least resistance."

Helpful information.

"But maybe," Becky said, "I should just keep away?"

"If you want to be safe, yes. Do you want to be safe?"

She already knew that *safety*, like *passive aggression*, was a dirty word in Crossroads. Safety was the opposite of risk-taking, without which personal growth could not occur.

"It's not your job to hide your feelings," Ambrose said. "It's Tanner's job to deal with them, and with his own feelings."

Like her father, Ambrose had told her what to do while claiming not to, but it didn't bother her when Ambrose did it. The problem was how to show her feelings. She loved safety! Her entire life to date had been organized around it! But since she'd blown her chance with Tanner, it was now up to her to take some kind of initiative, and she didn't like the image of herself coming on to him. It would be extremely unsafe, not to mention difficult to manage if Laura was in the vicinity, and she wasn't sure she'd be good at it anyway. She decided instead, as a semi-unsafe measure, to write him a letter.

> *Dear Tanner,*
>
> *I was lying when I said I was still mad at you. In fact, I owe you a big debt of gratitude for introducing me to Crossroads. After just three weeks I can feel myself expanding as a person and taking new risks. You were right that I was just holding my breath. Well, I'm not holding it anymore. I'm trying to be more forthright about my feelings, and one of those feelings is that I'd like to get to know you better. If you feel the same way, maybe we can meet up sometime and take a walk or something? I would like that very much.*
>
> *Your friend (I hope),*
> *Becky*

The letter, which she rewrote and copied three times to get the tone right, terrified her. She sealed it in an envelope, tore open the envelope to read it again, and sealed it in a new envelope that she then hid in her dresser. It was waiting to be delivered to Tanner, in person, forthrightly, the next time she saw him, when Clem returned from college for Thanksgiving.

She was glad that her father was the one to bring her brother home from the train station, so that she could pointedly exclude him when she invited Clem to take a walk with her. Since the summer, Clem had grown a sort of beard, and let his hair go long, and somewhere acquired a black peacoat. He looked a lot more than just three months older. As they walked in the low afterschool sunlight, he in the peacoat, she in his corduroy jacket, she had an elated sense of her own imminent adulthood; of their new formidableness as the pair of older siblings. They were the next generation. They had to be reckoned with.

From their mother's letters to him, Clem had learned that Becky had joined Crossroads. He approved, but he wondered why she'd done it.

"I was mad at Dad," she said.

"About what?"

"I'm more interested in why *you* were in it. I mean, now that I'm there and I see what it's like. Some of those exercises . . ."

"The exercises weren't that big a thing until Dad left. I stayed in for the work and the music. The sensitivity training was just a price you had to pay. There were enough other guys like me that we could pick each other as partners and talk about books or politics."

"Did you ever do a screaming exercise?"

"I didn't mind that one. It was better than the hugging. You were supposed to go around the room and give people hugs. Which, A, there were kids that nobody wanted to hug, and B, how did you know if a person wanted a hug? You were supposed to ask if it was okay, and the answer was supposed to be yes. I remember walking up to Laura Dobrinsky and asking her, and her saying no. She told me she wasn't into doing things unless she really felt them. And I'm thinking, thanks, Laura. Glad we got that straight. I'd really been worrying about whether you felt like hugging me."

"What do you think of Laura?"

"She's got a real gift for humiliating people. You wouldn't believe the way she spoke to Dad. She was at the center of that whole mess."

"I didn't realize that."

"It wasn't just her, but she was definitely the ringleader."

Though Clem had explained it to her at the time, Becky had only a sketchy sense of why their father had left Crossroads. Her understanding was that he'd preached too much, and that Rick Ambrose had asked him to leave. She wasn't feeling very loyal to him, but she was offended to think of Laura hurting him. "What did she do?"

"The whole scene was horrible. I can't even tell you."

"I've been talking to Tanner Evans, at the Grove. He and Laura play there every Friday."

"Good old Tanner."

"I know. It's kind of strange that he's with Laura."

"How so?"

"Well, I mean, they're both musicians. But he's so nice, and tall, and she's so—midgety. You know what I mean?"

Clem spoke sharply. "Laura can't help how tall she is, Becky."

"No, of course not."

"You shouldn't be hung up on superficial appearances."

Becky felt stung. She had made, she thought, an innocuous point—that Tanner's superficial appearance was extremely pleasing, Laura's less so. All she wanted was that Clem agree that they looked strange together.

Instead, he launched into a telling of how Tanner and his musician friends had doubled the size of Crossroads. She appreciated the confirmation of Tanner's social status, but Clem seemed to have changed more than just physically. It wasn't just the beard, the hair, the peacoat. It was that he seemed more interested in talking than in listening to her. As they sat on a picnic table in Scofield Park, watching tree shadows lengthen on the yellowed grass, she learned the reason.

The reason's name was Sharon. She was a junior at U of I, and he'd met her in a philosophy class. As he related to Becky how he'd boldly asked Sharon on a date, and how, on that date, they'd had a heated argument about Vietnam, and how amazing it was to find a woman who could more than hold her own in an argument with him, Becky had the unprecedented sensation of not wanting the details. Of being, herself, less interested in listening. The antipathy she felt toward Sharon, the discomfort it caused her to hear about Clem's happiness, was inappropriate. It seemed to confirm, retrospectively, the inappropriateness of other things about her and Clem's friendship. When he went on to effuse about what a revelation it was to experience a powerful animal attraction for the first time, and intense animal pleasure, by which he apparently meant full-on sex, and what a revelation it would be for Becky, someday, when she was ready for it, to connect with her own animal nature, her ears started roaring and she had to walk away from the picnic table.

Clem hopped off the table and followed her. "I'm such an idiot," he said. "You didn't want to hear about any of that."

"It's okay. I'm glad you're happy."

"I just wanted to tell somebody, and you're the person I always want to tell. You'll always be that person, Becky. You know that, right?"

She nodded.

"Is it okay if I give you a hug?"

It took her a second to get the joke. She laughed, and things were right with them again, and so she told him about the money from Shirley and what their father had said. Clem's response was "Fuck him. Fuck that guy."

Things were right with them again.

"Seriously, Becky, that is so fucked up. That money is yours. You totally earned it, Shirley loved you. You can do whatever the hell you want with it."

"What if I want to give you half of it?"

"Me? Don't give it to me. Go to Europe, go to a great college."

"But what if I *want* you to have it? You could transfer to a better school next year."

"There's nothing wrong with U of I."

"But you're smarter than I am."

"Not true. I just never had a social life."

"But if U of I is okay for you, why isn't it okay for me?"

"Because—I don't mind farm kids. I don't care what kind of room I'm in. You should be at Lawrence, or Beloit. That's the kind of place I picture you."

That was the kind of place she pictured herself, too.

"But with sixty-five hundred dollars," she said, "I could still go there. And you could save your half for graduate school."

Only now did Clem get that she was offering him thousands of dollars. In a calmer voice, he explained that she had two choices, either to keep all of the money or to share it equally. Singling him out was hurtful to Perry and Judson; it looked bad. And since three thousand dollars wasn't enough money to make a difference to anyone, whatever the old man might think, she should keep the entire sum.

His analysis made perfect sense—he was, in fact, smarter than she was, also more considerate of other people's feelings, also less greedy— and she was undeniably happy to think of keeping all the money. But her gratitude made her even more inclined to share it with him.

"I can't do it," he said. "Don't you see how bad it would look?"

"But Dad's going to kill me if I keep all of it."

"Let me talk to him."

"You don't have to do that."

"No, I want to. I'm sick of this pious shit."

Night had fallen when they returned to the parsonage. Clem marched straight up to the third floor, and it was strange to be Becky then, sitting on her bed one floor below, hearing him and her father fighting over her. She didn't know Sharon and didn't want to, but it seemed to her unlikely that Sharon fully understood how good a person Clem was. He came back downstairs and appeared in her doorway.

"I set him straight," he said. "Let me know if he bothers you again."

Her passbook, which had been radiating unease in its drawer, settled down as soon as its five figures were secure. She had the money, and this seemed right to her, since she was the sibling who most wanted money and had the clearest idea of what to do with it, and now Clem, the only judge who mattered, had certified that it was right. Her father couldn't be any colder to her than he already was, and when her mother expressed her own unhappiness Becky threw her off balance by inviting her to join her in Europe the following summer, and by promising to spend the remaining money on education. Though not originally her idea, the invitation was a brilliant stroke. Her mother had no great selfish interest in seeing Europe, but family life was like a microcosm of high school. Her mother wasn't popular, and Becky's invitation was gracious.

The night after Thanksgiving, she took her frightening letter to the Grove and put it in the pocket of her apron. All nerves, she proceeded to mix up orders, twice bring the wrong salad dressing to the same diner, and get stiffed on her tip by a red-faced father who'd had to track her down to get his check. Why was she even still working at the Grove? She had thirteen thousand dollars. If she could just deliver the letter, she thought, she might quit. But the back room was jammed with friends and fans of Tanner's home from college, and when the first set ended, a mob of well-wishers blocked her way to him.

From her blind side, as she hesitated on the margins, came the voice of Laura Dobrinsky. "I hear you're in Crossroads."

Becky looked down and flashed hot. The pink-spectacled shorty she meant to steal from was putting a match to a cigarette.

"Tanner convinced you, I gather?"

"Well, it is my church."

Laura shook the match and frowned. "You go to church?"

"You mean, on Sunday?"

"I wasn't aware that you're a churchgoer."

"I guess you don't know me."

"Is that a yes?"

Becky didn't see why it mattered. "I'm saying you don't know me."

"Yeah, and maybe I don't know Crossroads, either. Kind of makes me glad I got out when I did."

Again Becky flashed hot. "I'm sorry—do you have a problem with me?"

"Only in a general way. I hope it's a good experience for you."

Leaving Becky trembling, Laura plunged into the oily ponytails and embroidered denim surrounding Tanner and dispensed some of the hugs she hadn't felt like giving Clem. *Only in a general way?* So far, at least, Becky had done nothing more threatening than join Crossroads. It was almost as if the Natural Woman had smelled the letter she was carrying.

Seeing no chance of catching Tanner alone, she went home with the letter. It now had a spot of salad oil on it, but she couldn't bear to open it again. She also couldn't bear to keep it for another week. She thought of mailing it, but she didn't know if Tanner still lived with his parents; she had only the dimmest sense of his life outside the Grove. She was at the point of looking for his name in the phonebook when she recalled the word *churchgoer.*

In the morning, she asked her mother if she ever saw Tanner Evans at Sunday services. Her mother conveyed, with a look and a pause, that her curiosity about Tanner had been noted. "Not the nine o'clock," she said. "I think I have seen him on Sunday, though. You can ask your father."

It was none of her father's business. On Sunday morning, when Clem and Perry were sleeping and her parents and Judson had left for the early service, she put on a demure full-skirted dress and walked down to First Reformed with the letter in her purse. Except for "midnight" Christmas services (which, like all things Midwestern, happened an hour early), she hadn't gone to a service since she finished Sunday school. The faces of older parishioners brightened with pleasure and surprise when she crossed the sanctuary's carpeted parlor. Her mother, in a church dress, and her father, in his vestments, were chatting with some nine o'clockers who'd lingered at the inter-service coffee hour. Judson sat in a corner reading a book, waiting to be taken home. When her mother saw Becky, it was clear from the slyness of her smile that she knew why she was there.

Taking a program from the greeters, she sat down in the last row of pews and waited to see if she'd guessed right about Laura's peculiar question. Might Laura come here, too? From the way she'd said *church-goer*, Becky doubted it. The organist started up, playing something that her aunt could have named the composer of, and the late crowd began to fill the pews. With each new arrival, she turned to see if it was Tanner, until she became self-conscious about turning too often. She smoothed her skirt, folded her program into a small triangle, and fixed her eyes on the huge wood-and-brass cross hanging behind the altar. The longer she stared at it, the odder it seemed. The fact of its being manufactured somewhere, with the same kind of tools that made useful cabinets and furniture. Cross maker: what a weird nine-to-five to have. And paid how? With the money that people unaccountably, in exchange for nothing, dropped into wood-and-brass collection plates, possibly made by the same worker.

The Tanner who entered the sanctuary, by himself, just after eleven, was hardly the Tanner she knew. He was wearing a dopey plaid sport coat and an actual necktie, albeit loose-knit and lumpily knotted. He slipped into the pew across the aisle from her, and she returned her eyes to the altar, where her father and Reverend Haefle were entering through a side door, but her skin knew precisely when Tanner turned and saw her; she felt it go hot. The music stopped, and Tanner, half standing, crossed the aisle and sat down by her.

"What are you doing here?" he whispered.

She shook her head to shush him.

"Heavenly Father," her father prayerfully intoned from the pulpit; and that was all she heard before her ears went deaf. He was a tall and handsome man, but to Becky the black robe he was wearing and the devout sincerity of his delivery more than negated any standing he had as a man in the world. She sat frozen but squirmed inside, counting the seconds until he shut up. It came to her now, with a clarity brought by her return after long absence, how much she must have always hated being a minister's daughter. The fathers of her friends designed buildings, cured illness, prosecuted criminals. Her father was like a cross maker, only worse. His earnest faith and sanctity were an odor that had forever threatened to adhere to her, like the smell of Chesterfields, only worse, because it couldn't be washed off.

But then, when the congregation rose to sing the Gloria Patri and Tanner, at her side, in his ridiculous sport coat, sang forth in a clear, strong voice, unlike her own self-conscious murmur, and when she tried raising her own voice accordingly, *As it was in the Beginning, is now and ever shall be*, she caught a strange flashing glimpse of a desire, buried somewhere inside her, to belong and to believe in something. She wondered if the desire might always have been there; if it had only been her father, the shame of him, that repelled her from pursuing it. If maybe the fact of the brass cross, its manufacture, wasn't so dumb. Maybe it was more like amazing that two thousand years after Jesus's crucifixion people were still filling collection plates to make crosses in his honor.

In a further flash, she saw that Laura did not like Tanner's churchgoing; that it might be a fault line between them; that she, Becky, if she opened herself to the possibility of belief, might gain an unforeseen advantage; and that it therefore might be wiser, after all, not to put her letter in Tanner's hand now, since this would suggest that delivering it was the only reason she'd come to church, but instead to keep coming on Sunday mornings.

They shared a hymnal for the singing of "For the Beauty of the Earth," Becky's hair touching Tanner's shoulder as she leaned in, and then Reverend Haefle gave the sermon. During the one year she'd been obliged to attend entire services, Becky had sat still for her father's sermons, for fear of making other congregants restless with her restlessness, which would have embarrassed her as a Hildebrandt, but Dwight Haefle's interminable slabs of lyrical abstraction had defeated her. Listening to him now, hoping greater age might bring greater understanding, she followed him only as far as Reinhold Niebuhr before losing herself in admiration of Tanner's hands. She had to will herself not to touch them. In his jacket and necktie, he looked like a boy dressed up for church by his mother. Haefle had moved on to the importance of humility, not Becky's favorite subject, though one she would need to work on if she got more serious about religion, and it occurred to her that, for Tanner, leaving his fringed jacket and his Frye boots at home was exactly what Haefle was talking about. All but one hour a week, Tanner's coolness was beyond question, but he humbled himself for church, and this struck her as extremely dear.

Rising with him to recite the Lord's Prayer, she might already have been his girlfriend, not to say his wife of many years, and the trespass for which she asked their Father's forgiveness her theft of him from Laura.

"You're here," he said, when the service was over.

"Yeah, everything's changing. I'm trying new things."

He was looking at her as if he couldn't figure her out. This was good.

"I owe you a big debt of gratitude," she said. "For making me try Crossroads. I'm learning to be more open with my feelings. And—" She faltered, her face hot. He kept looking at her. "Will you be here next Sunday?"

"It's what I do."

She nodded, too vigorously, and stood up. "Okay, I'll see you then."

On her way out through the parlor, she paused to be noticed by her father, hoping to take some free credit for having come to a service, but he was engaged with Kitty Reynolds and a petite blond woman whom Becky didn't recognize. Her father was smiling, and the blond woman was apparently a magnet for his eyes. When they flicked up to Becky, his smile faded. When he returned them to the woman, it came back to life.

The message was unmistakable. He'd written her off and moved on. As she left the church, the word *asshole* popped into her head. Clem had uttered it, blasphemously, but it was new to her. Her growing interest in First Reformed, which ought to have pleased her father, was clearly of less consequence to him than his grudge against Rick Ambrose. And he a Christian minister.

"Yes Tanner was there," she announced to her mother when she got home, before her mother could annoy her by asking.

"That's nice," her mother said. "He's spoiling Rick Ambrose's other-wise perfect record of turning young people off church services."

Becky declined the bait. "I'm sure Tanner would be thrilled to know he has your approval."

"I imagine he'd rather have yours," her mother said. "As I'm gathering he does."

"Not talking about it," Becky said, leaving the room.

A few days later, she was felled by a cold so bad that she had to call in sick at the Grove and couldn't go to church on Sunday. As soon as she recovered, she took the new step of hanging out at First Reformed after school, joining the girls outside Ambrose's office, who kindly explained the stories behind their Crossroads gossip, helping her understand what was funny and what was appalling. When she tired of being the newcomer, she wandered down to the function hall and found a team of three boys, led by her own brother, silk-screening posters for the Christmas concert. In theory, she should have lent a hand, because she needed to start accumulating "hours" toward the Arizona trip—to be eligible for Arizona, you had to perform at least forty hours of service or paid work for the group—but Perry was the one thing about Crossroads she didn't like. Perry was the brother who was brilliant at everything, including art (the poster design bore the mark of his hand), but lately the mere sight of him had made her scalp tighten and prickle, as if she were a dog in the presence of the occult; as if she shared a house with a psychopath whose brilliance was undergirded by all manner of dark doings. She knew about some of those doings but not, she suspected, all of them. He looked up from the silk screen, red-handed with Christmas ink, and smirked at her. She turned and fled.

When she finally gained admittance to Ambrose's office and he asked her how things were at home, she found herself saying that she was worried about her mother. Even two weeks ago, she would have considered it treasonous to pass family information to her father's enemy. Now she positively relished it.

"My mom keeps up a good front," she said. "But underneath I get the sense she's falling apart, and meanwhile Clem is convinced that my dad is going to leave her. It could just be an idea in Clem's head, but he really harps on it."

"Clem is smart," Ambrose said.

"I know. I love him so much. But I'm worried about my mom. She's so dependent on my dad, and the only time she *ever* stands up to him is when he criticizes Perry. She thinks Perry is a genius. Which, I mean, he is sort of a genius. But he does all this bad shit that she doesn't have a clue about."

"Are you sure about that?"

"She doesn't know anything from me, that's for sure."

"You protect him."

"It's not him I'm protecting. I feel bad for her—she's having a hard enough time already. But I also don't want Perry to hurt her."

"Do you think we can help him?"

"Crossroads? I think he only joined because his friends were in it, and then suddenly he's like Mr. Gung Ho. I don't know—maybe that's good?"

Ambrose waited, his dark eyes on her.

"It's just," she said, "some part of me doesn't believe it."

"Me neither," Ambrose said. "The minute he walked in the door, I said to myself, 'That kid is trouble.'"

Becky felt breathless. She couldn't believe Ambrose trusted her enough to say that. For a disorienting moment, her heart confused him with Tanner. His honesty with her was like an eighty-proof version of Tanner's gentler brew. There was no wedding ring on his dark-haired hand, but she'd heard he had a girlfriend at the seminary where he was nominally still a student. It was a little like hearing that Jesus had a girlfriend.

A burst of female laughter outside his door reminded her that she was one of many. As if to preempt a rejection, to save her dignity, she excused herself hastily and ran from the church, reorienting her heart.

The following Sunday, after the service ended, she and Tanner sat in the rearmost pew and talked for more than an hour. When someone turned off the sanctuary lights, and the last distant voices died away, they stayed on in the more solemn light of the stained-glass windows. Becky was relieved that she did not, after all, need to do the Crossroads thing of telling Tanner she wanted to get to know him better.

An exchange of past impressions yielded the interesting fact that Becky, even as a sophomore in high school, had seemed to Tanner impossibly unapproachable. When she countered that, no, *he* had been that person, he laughed and denied it, as befit his unconceited nature, but she could tell that he was pleased. While they skated around on the subject of Crossroads and the friends of Tanner's who now served as advisers in the group, her mind worked furiously below the surface. It ought to have followed logically, even irresistibly, that two such singularly unapproachable-seeming people were meant to be together. But what if being together only meant being friends?

She saw that she had no choice but to take a risk. In a studiously off-hand tone, she asked Tanner why Laura didn't come to church with him.

"She was raised Catholic," he said, with a shrug. "She hates institutional religion."

Becky waited.

"Laura's way more radical than me. She was ready to split for San Francisco as soon as we finished high school. Sleep in the van, be part of the scene."

"Why didn't you?" Becky said, barely breathing.

"I don't know. I guess I'm not that into the scene—going back to someone's house and staying up all night. That's okay once a week, or if you're into drugs, but I'd rather be sleeping and getting up early to practice. I've still got so far to go as a musician."

"You already sound amazing."

He looked at her gratefully. "You're not just saying that?"

"No! I love listening to you."

She watched him take this in. It seemed to go down well. He squared his shoulders and said, "I want to cut a demo album. That's my whole focus right now. Twelve songs good enough to record before I'm twenty-one. I was afraid, if we hit the road, I'd lose sight of that."

"I understand that."

"Really? I'm not sure Laura does. She's so gifted, but she doesn't care about being a professional. If it were up to me, we'd be doing three or four gigs a week. Blues, jazz, Top Forty, whatever. Putting in the hours, developing an audience. The only thing bar owners care about is making money, and Laura hates that. If somebody asked her to do Peggy Lee, she'd just laugh in their face. But me . . ."

"You're more ambitious," Becky suggested.

"Maybe. Laura's got a lot going on, she's working the crisis hotline, she's got her women's group. For me, it's enough to work on my music and try to feel closer to God. You know, I really like going to church. I like seeing you here."

"I like seeing you, too."

"Truly? I was starting to worry that you didn't."

She looked into his eyes, wordlessly telling him he had nothing to fear. God only knew what might have happened if they hadn't heard footsteps in the vestry, the reverberant bang of metal. Dwight Haefle, no longer in his robe, had popped the release on one of the sanctuary doors. "You don't have to leave," he told them. "The doors open from the inside."

But Tanner was already on his feet, and Becky stood up, too. Their moment had been too fragile to be reassembled now. As they left the sanctuary, he told her how Danny Dickman and Toby Isner and Topper Morgan had smoked grass and drunk whiskey in the sanctuary on the night before the third Arizona trip, and how Ambrose, in the church parking lot, beside the idling and fully loaded trip buses, had led the group in reaming out the miscreants and debating whether they should be barred from the trip. The confrontation had lasted two hours. Topper Morgan had cried so violently he burst a blood vessel in his eye. And the church had started locking the sanctuary doors.

Becky went home frustrated by her failure to get a clear statement on Tanner and Laura. She needed to be more than just his experiment. She was, admittedly, inexperienced in love, but her pride and her ethics and her basic sense of tidiness insisted that, before she consented to be added, Laura be explicitly subtracted. The only useful nugget she'd gleaned in this regard was that Tanner still lived with his parents. Since he wasn't shacked up with Laura, there was no decisive action he could take. But this made a formal renunciation all the more necessary. She considered this requirement absolute, and so it was with a confusing sense of self-betrayal, of observing a person she morally disapproved of and didn't understand but nevertheless *was*, that she let Tanner kiss her before he'd satisfied it.

At the Grove, five nights after their seemingly crucial conversation in the sanctuary, she'd seen Laura Dobrinsky standing on tiptoes to press her face to Tanner's, and him letting himself be nuzzled, a contented smile on his face. Becky had felt stabbed in the gut. She'd fled to a bathroom stall and shed her first tears on account of a man. In her ensuing misery, she'd skipped both Sunday service and Crossroads, which she felt had failed to warn her that the risk in risk-taking was stabbing pain, and dragged herself through the last days of school before vacation.

And then, last night, she'd subbed at the Grove. It wasn't her usual night. When Tanner walked into the restaurant, alone, it shouldn't have been with the expectation of finding her there. Assuming it was just wretched luck, she asked a veteran waitress, Maria, to take his table. She could feel him looking at her, but she didn't look at him, not once, until the last of the other diners were leaving. He was slouched low, the picture of composure, an emptied dessert plate on his table. He waved her over.

"What," she said.

"Are you okay? I looked for you in church on Sunday."

"I didn't go. I'm not sure I'm into it anymore."

A taste from childhood was in her throat, a horrible self-spiting taste that she couldn't help wanting more of.

"Becky," he said. "Did I do something? You seem pissed off with me."

"Nope. Just tired."

"I called your house. Your mom said you were here."

There was no law against just walking away. She walked away.

"Hey, come on," Tanner said, jumping up to pursue her. "I came here to see you. I thought we were friends. If you're pissed off with me, you could at least tell me why."

Maria was watching them from the table she was wiping down. Becky continued on into the kitchen, but Tanner wasn't afraid of the kitchen. She turned on her heel.

"Figure it out," she said bitterly.

She knew her worth. He was required to say that he was done with the Natural Woman. Nothing less would do.

"Whatever it is," he said, "I'm sorry."

"Thank you for being sorry."

"Becky—"

"What."

"I really like you."

It wasn't enough. She picked up a rag and returned to the dining room to wipe down tables. It wasn't enough, and then she heard how hard he slammed the front door behind him. She heard the hurt of his having called her house and come looking for her, only to be treated so meanly, and suddenly the person she was but didn't understand was running out into the night. Tanner was slumped against the side of his Volkswagen bus, his head bowed. At the sound of her feet, as they out-ran her better judgment, he looked up. She ran straight into his arms. A breeze from the south had risen, more springlike than autumnal. The hands she'd dreamed of were on her head, in her hair. And then, just like that, in the most unplanned and unconsidered way, it had happened.

She was awakened by the telephone. She'd fallen asleep on her back, crossways on her bed, and opened her eyes to a gray sky framed by her window and broken by black branches. Her mother was tapping on her door.

"Becky? It's Jeannie Cross."

She went to the phone in her parents' bedroom and waited for her mother to hang up downstairs. Jeannie was calling about a party that night at the Carduccis'. Becky appreciated that Jeannie was still includ-ing her, and she might have liked to accept the invitation for friendship's sake. But she was going to the concert.

"There's a concert?"

"Crossroads," Becky said.

A silence.

"I see," Jeannie said.

"You know what, though? I'm going with Tanner."

"Tanner Evans?"

"Yeah, he's the headliner, and he's taking me."

"Well, well, *well*."

Becky was tempted to say more, but she might already have said too much. Tanner didn't quite know yet that he was taking her to the concert. In her mind, their very long kiss had been definitive, but much had been left unspoken, and she wouldn't feel secure until the world had seen her walk into First Reformed on his arm. She asked Jeannie if she wanted to go shopping with her. It was almost funny how eagerly Jeannie said yes, after all these weeks of distance. But Jeannie wasn't free until three thirty.

"Shoot," Becky said. "I'm meeting Tanner at four."

"Wow, Bex. Too busy with a *guy*."

"I know," she said happily. "It's weird."

"Tomorrow, though? I'm not doing anything all day."

Becky took a long shower and performed delicate work at the bathroom mirror, applying makeup that was enhancing without, she hoped, being noticeable. Perry banged rudely on the locked door, offered some commentary which she ignored, and went away. Dressing, too, she labored to strike a balance between elegance and Crossroads. She had to look good for at least the next ten hours, beginning especially at four o'clock. By the time she went down to the kitchen, her mother was bundling herself into a frightful old coat.

"I'm late to my class," her mother said. "Can you make sure you're home by six?"

Becky filled her mouth with a sugar cookie. "I'm not going to the Haefles' party."

"I'm afraid that's not negotiable."

"I'm not negotiating."

"You can discuss it with your father, then."

"There's nothing to discuss."

Her mother sighed. "You know, honey, it's not the worst thing in the world to make a young man wait. I know it doesn't feel that way to you, but there is always tomorrow."

"Thank you for your input."

"I take it he managed to find you last night?"

"I thought you were late for your exercise class."

Her mother sighed more heavily and turned away. Becky was sorry to have to freeze her out. Her goodwill was boundless, but her mother was wrong. Tomorrow was too late for the work she had to do. Tanner wasn't headlining the concert, he was co-headlining it with Laura Dobrinsky. Becky needed every minute she could get with him before it started.

The time had come to take action. A dull red gash had opened and closed below the clouds on the eastern horizon, over the fields of broken cornstalks distantly visible from the window of Clem's room, while he typed the last sentences of his Roman history term paper. His desk, in the uneasy light, was stubbled over with red eraser morsels and cloud-colored ash. His clean-living roommate, Gus, had already decamped to Moline for the holidays, and Clem had seized on his absence to smoke heavily all night, powering himself forward with nicotine and with rage at his primary sources, Livy and Polybius, for contradicting each other, rage also at the dwindling of his hoped-for hours of sleep from six to three to zero, and rage, most of all, at himself for having spent Monday seeking pleasure in his girlfriend's bed, allowing himself to believe that he could research and write a fifteen-page paper in two twelve-hour workdays. The pleasure he'd experienced on Monday now amounted to nothing. His eyes and his throat were on fire, his stomach on the verge of digesting itself. The paper he'd produced, on Scipio Africanus, was an ill-argued tangle of repetitive phrases for which he'd be lucky to get a B-minus. Its badness was the final confirmation of a thing he'd known for weeks.

Without giving himself time to think, without even standing up to stretch, he rolled a clean sheet of erasable onionskin into his typewriter.

December 23, 1971
Selective Service Local Board
U.S. Post Office Building
Berwyn, Illinois

Dear Sirs,

I write to inform you that as of today I will no longer be enrolled as a student at the University of Illinois, thus no longer eligible for the student deferment that I was granted on March 10, 1971. I am prepared to serve in the U.S. Armed Forces if I am called upon. My date of birth is December 12, 1951. My draft number is 29 4 13 88 403. Please advise if/when you would like me to report for induction.

Sincerely,

Clement R. Hildebrandt

215 Highland Street

New Prospect, Illinois

Unlike his paper, the letter had the clarity of extensive forethought. But did typing it constitute an action? The words were barely more substantial on paper than they'd been in his head. Not until they'd been received and replied to would they attain power over him. At which point, exactly, could he be said to have taken an action?

He gazed for a while at the ceiling of cloud above the distant cornfields, the ground-level haze that industrial agriculture seemed to generate in winter, a smog part dampness and part nitrates. Then he signed the letter, addressed an envelope, and applied one of the postage stamps he'd bought for writing to his parents.

"This is what your son is doing," he said. "This is how it had to be."

Feeling less alone for having heard a voice, if only his own, he ventured out to the bathroom. Its eternally burning lights seemed all the brighter now that everyone else had gone home. Some departed hall mate's whiskers adhered to the sides of the sink at which he splashed water on his face. He considered taking a shower, but his core body temperature was at a low ebb and he thought he might convulse with shivers if he undressed.

As he left the bathroom, the hall telephone rang. Its loudness was extraordinary and jolted him with dread, because he knew that only Sharon could be calling; she'd already called at midnight for a progress report and a pep talk. With regard to Sharon, his typing of the letter most definitely constituted an action. He stood outside the bathroom, immobilized by the ringing, and waited for it to stop. After the debacle of his wasted Monday, he no longer had a shred of faith in his power to resist the pleasure he took from her. The only safe plan now was to pack up his things, catch the first available bus to Chicago, and inform her of his action from New Prospect, by letter.

To his surprise, a door at the end of the hall flew open. A hall mate in gym shorts stomped out and answered the phone. He saw Clem and shook the receiver at him.

"Sorry," Clem said, hurrying to take it. "I didn't think anyone else was here."

The hall mate slammed his door behind him.

"Did you finish?" Sharon said eagerly.

"Yeah. Ten minutes ago."

"Hurrah! I bet you could use some breakfast."

"What I really need is sleep."

"Come have breakfast. I want to take care of you."

A wave of light-headedness washed over him. The mere sound of her voice was rushing blood to his groin. Change of plan.

"All right," he said. "But there's something I need to tell you."

"What is it?"

"I'll tell you when I come over."

His room, when he returned to it, was like a lidded charcoal fire. He opened the window and put on the peacoat that Sharon had chosen for him. The tissue-swelling elevation of his blood pressure was surely related to sex, but also perhaps to what he had to tell her. The letter he'd written had elements of aggression, and aggression was known to induce erections in men. The letter could lead to his going to Vietnam, where, although there was nothing arousing about being killed, he might be called upon to defend himself with a weapon. In his rational mind, he knew that killing was morally wrong and psychologically devastating, but he suspected that his animal self took a different view.

Letter and term paper in hand, he left his building through the rear stairwell, which had never lost its smell of fresh concrete. The damp morning air penetrated straight through his coat to his core, but it was a relief to be free of the smoke-filled tunnel that sex and all-nighters had made of his existence since regular classes ended. In the hush of the emptied campus, he could faintly hear the mightiness of Illinois, the rumble of a freight train, the moan of eighteen-wheelers, coal transported from the south, car parts from the north, fattened livestock and staggering corn yields from the middle, all roads leading to the broad-shouldered city on the lake. It did him good to find the larger world still extant; it made him feel less crazy.

Down the lane from the Foreign Languages Building, after he'd slipped his paper under the door of the classics department office, he came upon a mailbox. The next collection time was eleven a.m., and today was not a holiday. He faced the mailbox and considered his existential freedom to act or not to act. The strong thing to do was to drop his letter in the box. He might curse himself in the future—however wretched he felt now, army life was bound to bring worse—but if an action was morally right, a strong man was obliged to take it in the present. If he didn't mail the letter now, he would arrive at Sharon's with only the intention of mailing it, and he'd been down the intention-paved road before.

He closed his eyes and fell asleep in a heartbeat, reawakening in time to catch himself from falling over. In his hand he found a letter to his draft board. The throat of the mailbox made a rusty-jointed gulp as the letter went down it. He turned away and broke into a sprint, as if he might outrun what he'd done.

In the philosophy course he'd taken the previous spring, there was a curly-haired little mouse who sat in the same row he did, often wearing a pleated velvet French-style cap, and kept looking at him. One afternoon, when the bearded and beaded professor was holding forth on Sartre's *Nausea*, extolling the idea that what we make of existence has nothing to do with what existence rawly is, Clem raised his hand to disagree. Reality, he said, operated according to laws discoverable and testable by scientific method. The professor seemed to think this proved his larger point—we *impose* our laws of science on a stubbornly unknowable reality. "But what about math?" Clem said. "One plus one will always equal two. We didn't invent the truth of that equation. We discovered a truth that was always there." The professor joked that they had a Platonist in their midst, and the hippies in the lecture hall turned to look at the square who'd challenged him, and the little mouse moved over to sit by Clem. After class, she praised his independence of mind. She adored Camus but couldn't forgive Sartre for his communism.

Sharon was an Honors student, the first person in her immediate family to attend college. She'd grown up on a farm outside the downstate town of Eltonville, where communists were held in very low esteem. For the rest of the semester, she and Clem had sat together in class, and when she asked him for his home address he was happy to provide it. He'd never had a female friend besides Becky. In the letter Sharon then sent him, while he was at home in New Prospect, doing shovel work for the local nursery, she wrote about the heat and desolation of her family's farmhouse in the summer. Her mother had died when she was twelve, her brother Mike was in Vietnam, her father and her younger brother made the farm run, and a hired Croatian woman did the cooking and housework. Her father had always excused Sharon from chores, and in her boredom as a child and her sorrow as a teenager she'd found refuge in reading. Her ambition was to be a writer or, as a fallback, to teach English in Europe. She'd already vowed never to spend another summer in Eltonville.

Clem wrote back to her and received a second letter so long she'd put three stamps on the envelope. It began with questions, devolved into stream of consciousness, short on punctuation, devoid of capital letters, and ended with a passage from Camus she'd copied out in French. He kept intending to take an evening and reply, but he never found the evening. He hung out with his friend Lester or watched TV with Becky, who'd cut back on her social life. Only when he returned to school and saw Sharon, walking by herself on the Main Quad, did the wrongness of his inaction come home to him. She threw him a hurt look, and this wasn't right, he wasn't a hurter, and so he pursued her. She greeted his apology with a shrug. She said, "I think I had a wrong idea about you." Whether it was the challenge implicit in this, or the thing that people called guilt but was actually just a self-interested wish not to be thought ill of, he was moved to ask her out for pizza.

What had started their fight was the olive-drab jacket he wore to the pizzeria. For an antiwar protest the previous spring, he'd fashioned an electrical-tape peace sign for the back of it, and Sharon didn't like it. She couldn't stand the college peaceniks. Every morning, she said, she woke up afraid of hearing that her brother had been killed or maimed in Vietnam. Mike wasn't a reader, he enjoyed hunting and fishing and had no ambition beyond inheriting the farm, but he was the kindest and most honorable person she'd ever known, and the peaceniks had only contempt for him. Who were they to spit on a person like her brother? They all had their student deferments, they got to smoke pot and have sex while people like her brother were dying, and they weren't even grateful. They thought they were morally *superior.* Lucky white kids from the suburbs flashing their peace signs while other kids fought a war for them: it made her sick.

Clem's first response to her tirade had been condescension. Being female, and sentimental, Sharon didn't seem to realize how grotesquely immoral the war was, or that her brother had been free to refuse to serve in it. He, Clem, in her brother's place, would have refused to serve. But Sharon wouldn't budge. Her brother loved his country and was a real man; when duty called, he reported. And what about all the boys from Black slums and Indian reservations her brother was serving with? They didn't even know that not serving was an option. The result was that people like Clem got to be both safe *and* self-righteous.

"What was your lottery number?" she asked him.

"Terrible. Nineteen."

"So somebody right now is in the jungle because your parents sent you to college."

"But I wouldn't have gone anyway."

"*It's the same thing.* Somebody is there because you're not. Somebody like Mike. You're all about the 'grotesque immorality' of the war. What about the grotesque immorality of making poor people and uneducated people and Black people be the ones to fight it? Why isn't that equally grotesque? Why aren't you protesting *that*?"

"It's kind of implied, don't you think?"

"No. I never hear anyone here talk about it. All I hear is contempt for the military."

She was little, and female, but her thoughts were original. In Arizona, on his church group's spring trip, he'd worked for a Navajo man, Keith Durochie, who'd lost a son in Vietnam. Only seventeen, uncomfortable in the presence of a parent's loss, Clem had tried to sympathize with Durochie by lamenting how unjust it was to die in such a war, and Durochie had gone morose and silent. Clem had said the wrong thing, but he hadn't known why. Listening to Sharon, he understood that, far from consoling Durochie, he'd dishonored his son's death. What an ass he'd been.

"I'm really sorry I didn't write back to you," he said.

Her dark brown eyes were on him. "Walk me home?"

Already, that first night, he'd had the heart-fluttering sense that he would have to take action; that he'd glimpsed a moral truth which there was no going back and unglimpsing. He might have been spared if he'd had a higher draft number, but lottery ball 19 had followed an incalculable ("random") trajectory to pairing with his birthday, and his heart went out to the uneducated kid who was serving in his rightful place. He didn't want to be like his father, who merely professed to have sympathy for the underprivileged. Giving up his student deferment was an insanely steep price to pay for being more consistent than his father, but by the time he and Sharon reached her house, on one of the shabbier side streets of Urbana, his moral intuition was telling him to pay it.

At the top of the stairs to her front porch, she turned around and kissed him. He was one step below her, the stairs compensating for their rather extreme height difference. The kiss was the beginning of a long reprieve from the judgment he'd passed on himself. When he finally tore himself away from her, with a promise to call her the next day, the thought of Vietnam had been banished by the sweetness of her mouth, the welcoming scent of her skin, the parting of his lips by her bold little tongue, the great surprise of it all.

Her house was a clapboard wreck with a hippie-run bicycle store on the ground floor, hippie common rooms on the second floor, hippie bedrooms on the third, and Sharon, who detested hippies, in the only habitable room on the fourth. She looked to the world like a harmless small creature, but she had a way of getting what she wanted. The year before, after her sorority had expelled her for violating its rules, the hippies had given her the best room in their house. Among other things, it was the perfect room for uninterrupted sex. Clem would later come to see the wisdom of parietal regulations, which, outmoded norms of behavior aside, served to keep undergraduates from falling into a pit of pleasure and neglecting their studies, but on his second visit he'd gone up to her room in all innocence. After some hours of necking on her bed, in their clothes, Sharon went to the bathroom and returned wearing only a terry-cloth robe. It transpired that she'd got impatient with the necking, also sore of chin and nose. She pushed Clem onto his back and undid his belt buckle. He said, "Wait, though." She said it was okay, she was on the Pill. She'd lost her own virginity when she was seventeen, an exchange student in Lyon, France. The family she'd boarded with had an older son who went to the university but lived at home and was her lover for two and a half months, until they were detected. The ensuing shitstorm had resulted in her being sent home to Eltonville. A monumental embarrassment, she said, but worth it. After exchanging letters for a year, her lover had found someone else and she'd had further adventures on which she didn't care to elaborate. Clem, supine, his belt unbuckled, was still trying to slow things down, to extend a discussion that seemed mandatory, when she took off the robe and lay down on him. "It's easy," she said. "I'll show you." In short order, he found himself looking up at the naked entirety of a girl he might have expected to uncover part by part, with much asking of permission, over a span of weeks or months. Seeing her altogether was such a visual overload he had to shut his eyes against it. She moved up and down on his erection until there was a cracking rip in the fabric of the universe. She fell forward and kissed him with her indeed very abraded mouth. He needed to know if she'd liked what had just happened. She said she had, very much. But, he persisted, had she . . . ? "All in good time," she said. "I'll show you."

For a twenty-year-old farm girl from southern Illinois, Sharon knew a lot about sex. Some of it she'd learned in France, the rest she knew from reading books. To Clem the most shocking thing she knew was that she really, really liked to have her vulva licked. Licking a vulva hadn't been on his most distant radar; the Latin word for it, although he'd seen it in a dictionary, had only been a word. If pressed, he might have guessed that it was a technique for seasoned lovers, a sort of hard drug to which ordinary intercourse was a gateway. He certainly couldn't have imagined doing it with a girl who was still confusing the names of his two brothers. Still less could he have imagined loving it. The only thing better than seeing and smelling and tasting her vulva was the moment when he got to put his penis in it; and therein lay the problem.

He now saw that his supposed self-discipline, the outstanding study habits his parents and his teachers had always praised, had not been discipline at all. He'd excelled at school because he'd *enjoyed* learning things, not because he had superior willpower. As soon as Sharon introduced him to more intense forms of pleasure, he discovered how hopelessly undeveloped the muscles of his will really were. He found himself skipping organic chem lab for hardly any reason, just to take a long walk with her, not even to have sex, just to be near her. He had his first experience of fellatio on a morning when he should have been in Roman history. He failed to prepare for his cellular biology midterm because putting his penis in Sharon's vulva had offered more pleasure, in the moment, than studying did. What this said about his self-control was bad enough. Worse yet was how it undermined his best moral argument for keeping his deferment—the idea that he could better serve humanity by working diligently at school, becoming a leader in the field of science, than by serving as a grunt in Vietnam. If he couldn't keep his grade point average above 3.5, he truly had no right to a deferment.

Sharon, for her part, was wonderfully untroubled. She couldn't be drafted, and she only took the kind of courses where a gifted writer got an automatic A. She could outline a paper just by talking it through with Clem, whereas he needed to study hard, by himself, to memorize organic radicals. She was a true reader, accustomed to solitude, and preferred having no friends to having friends less remarkable than she was. Clem didn't have good friends at U of I yet himself, but one of his science study mates, Gus, had asked him to room with him, clearly hoping to deepen their friendship, and now Gus was barely speaking to him, because Clem had hurt his feelings by spending all his time with Sharon. She was every bit as hungry for pleasure as he was, but it didn't seem to derail her life the way it did his. She was never in a hurry to be somewhere, and he'd come to crave what she did to his sense of time, her serene indifference to the clock, nearly as much as he craved her body. As long as he could stay curled up inside her neatly ordered life, as if it were his own life, and never leave her room, he felt all right. Only when he left her room was he engulfed by anxiety, and only by returning could he relieve it.

Though he would have denied it, vehemently, if she'd asked him, another reason he preferred to be in her room was that he felt awkward with her in public. The difficulty, such as it was, lay not in what she was in herself. He was proud of her intelligence, proud of her pretty face and prettier figure, proud of her limpidly unaffected manner. The difficulty lay in what she was in relation to *him*, namely, fourteen inches shorter. She had never, not once, made reference to their height difference, and he hated himself for even being aware of it. The way the world judged people by their physical appearance, which they had no control over, and which had nothing to do with their mind or their personality, was totally unjust. In theory, he was happy to be so much taller than Sharon, because it demonstrated his commitment to equality and to the marriage of true minds, irrespective of physical impediment. In practice, too, when they were alone in bed, the almost illicit littleness of her naked body was an added turn-on. But in public, try as he might, he couldn't help feeling that people were staring at them and drawing conclusions about him.

At Thanksgiving, when he went home to New Prospect and saw Becky, who was now a fully grown woman, his discomfort had become acute. Becky and her friends, especially Jeannie Cross, were so resplendent that they might have been a different species, and Becky had made an uncharacteristically cutting remark about the height difference of Tanner Evans and Laura Dobrinsky. Although Clem had looked forward to telling his sister that he had a girlfriend, he sensed right away that Becky had no interest in Sharon—didn't want to meet her, didn't want to hear about her, wouldn't approve of her. When he proceeded to gush about the beauty of Sharon's mind, and to describe the extremity of her allure, the depth of the sensual pit he'd fallen into, his words sounded hollow and abstract. The whole conversation was deeply embarrassing.

He came away from it ashamed of his sexuality, ashamed by extension of Sharon herself, and more painfully aware of their dimensional incongruity. Their relationship, which until then had seemed open-ended, now felt temporary, as if Sharon were merely his "first girlfriend," the sweet but dimensionally unsuitable person with whom he'd lost his virginity. Intentionally or not, Becky had caused him to scrutinize his feelings for Sharon, and he found them lacking. They weren't rugged enough for him to declare to his sister, "I don't care about your superficial judgment, she's the person I love," and they weren't powerful enough—didn't strongly enough suggest an enduring future of togetherness—to serve as an argument against giving up his student deferment. They were more like an escape, a reprieve, from his moral duty.

He'd returned to school with a strict plan for himself. He would see Sharon only two evenings a week, and not stay over at her house at all, and he would study ten hours every day and try to ace every one of his finals and term papers. If he ran the table with A-pluses, he could still keep his GPA above 3.5—the figure which, though basically arbitrary, was his last plausible defense against the action he would otherwise be called upon to take.

His plan was sensible but not, it turned out, achievable. When he stopped by Sharon's house, it was as if they'd been apart for five months, not five days. He had a thousand things to tell her, and as soon as he took down her corduroys it seemed mean and silly to have worried about their height difference. Not until he returned to his room, the following afternoon, did he lament his lack of willpower. He recalibrated his plan, assigning himself eleven hours of daily study, and stuck to this schedule until Friday, when he treated himself to another evening with Sharon. By the time he left her, on Sunday afternoon, he would have had to study fifteen hours a day to make the numbers work. He told himself that he was living in the moment, like an existentialist, and savoring their togetherness while it lasted, but he sensed something darker going on. Something almost spiteful—as if, by surrendering to Sharon's elastic sense of time, and thereby ensuring that his grades would suffer, which would leave him no moral choice but to drop out of school, he were secretly preparing to punish her. She had no inkling of what the figure 3.5 signified to him, but she would understand it soon enough, and rue that she hadn't insisted that he study.

What had made the coming punishment crueler was that Sharon was giving signs of loving him in an old-fashioned, romantic, totalizing way. Despite having presented herself as a free spirit, a Colette-reading sexual adventurer, and despite being too sophisticated to use mushy language, she seemed to have a longer-range vision for the two of them. No sooner had he told her about his conversation with his sister at Thanksgiving, the bequest from their aunt, than she'd become fixated on going to Europe with him. She respected him for refusing the money Becky had offered, but why not at least accept a free vacation? Wouldn't it be amazing to be together in France? The two of them visiting the same places as his sister and his mother, but doing their own thing? Whenever she returned to the idea, to add or subtract some stop on their mythical itinerary, Clem simply closed his eyes and smiled. In his secret heart, he already knew that he would write to the draft board. The overriding reason to do it was that it was morally correct. He had further important reasons relating to his father and to Sharon, to whom he wanted to prove how seriously he'd taken her ideas, and who he hoped would admire the rightness of his action and compare him favorably with her brother Mike. And yet, ridiculously, in the waning days of the semester, as the reality of his academic failures had sunk in, the most salient attraction of forfeiting his deferment had been *to avoid going to France with his girlfriend and his sister.*

The morning sky was growing darker, not lighter, when he reached her house. He had a key he never used—despite a recent bicycle theft, the hippies refused to lock their back door. He let himself into the murk of their kitchen and hurried past the cheese-crusted crockery piled in and around the sink, which existed in a kind of hippie equilibrium, a steady state in which new dirty dishes were added at exactly the same rate that someone bothered to wash the older ones. Most of the hippies were too placidly self-absorbed to even know his name, but he'd received many a knowing smile in passing, and he was glad not to encounter anyone as he made his way upstairs. He sensed that the sum of his identity, in that house, consisted of being the dude who was boning the little chick on the fourth floor, which was uncomfortably close to a fair summation.

Sharon, in flannel pajamas, was mixing something at the plywood counter of the makeshift kitchenette outside her room. Clem stooped to kiss her curls and put his arms around her from behind. In his disordered mind, he was already halfway a soldier, arriving to do what soldiers did with a woman, but she shrugged him off playfully. "I'm making toast with sugar and cinnamon."

"I'm not sure I can face food right now."

"When was the last time you ate?"

"Sometime yesterday. I had a tuna-salad sub."

"You definitely need food. But first—" She crouched to open her little refrigerator. "I bought champagne."

"Champagne."

"To celebrate." She handed him the cold bottle. "You didn't believe me, but I knew you could do it."

Typing out fifteen pages of C-level work in sixty hours didn't seem like such a feat to Clem. "Champagne, Urbana," he said.

"Exactly."

Drinking anything alcoholic, at nine in the morning, in his condition, was ill-advised, but Sharon had definite ideas about how things should be done, and he didn't want to disappoint her. He peeled the foil off the bottle and popped the cork.

"To us," she said when he'd filled two jelly glasses. "To Scipio Africanus!"

"Don't even say that name. I spent all night typing *Scipoi* and having to erase it."

"Just to us, then."

She stood on tiptoe for a kiss that he bent down to give her. He caught an exciting, catfoody whiff of degraded semen from his several deposits of it in her on Monday. She took her glass and the bottle into her bedroom, and he followed her like a dog. She sat propped against the pillows on her bed while he pawed her feet, massaging her bare soles with his thumbs. The champagne was making her exceedingly lovely. Far from easing his announcement to her, it was inviting him to calculate when he would have to leave her house to intercept the postal worker emptying the mailbox and get his letter back. On the theory that his brain cells needed readily absorbable glucose to regain higher function, he drained his glass.

She immediately refilled it. "You said you had something to tell me?"

He fell back onto the bed and looked up at the canted ceiling, his vision spinning. The light coming in through her dormer seemed detached from any specific hour, by its grayness and by his body clock's confusion, the feeling that today was still yesterday and morning had followed afternoon without an intervening night.

"I have something to tell you, too," she said.

It occurred to him that he'd never kissed her feet. They were tiny and high-arched, their soles soft and cool, a balm to his fevered cheeks. She laughed and pulled them away.

"Sorry," she said. "That tickles."

He had no basis for comparison, but it was possible to worry that not all girls—perhaps very few girls—were as sweetly direct as Sharon about what they liked and didn't like. Possible to worry that few girls could have been more generous, more forgiving of his blunders, more tolerant of his incessant wish for intercourse, more interested in having it herself, less given to tears or pouting, less emotionally demanding, than Sharon had been. Possible, indeed, to worry that the three months now ending had amounted to a little Eden, an earthly paradise that he'd been stupid-lucky to land in and was a fool to be destroying. He thought of the November morning when he'd watched her hobble to the bathroom, like an old woman, and had understood how miserably sore he'd made her in his pursuit of one last, negligible orgasm. He remembered how she'd hobbled back to bed, how he'd castigated himself and begged her forgiveness, and how she'd simply laughed it off, *C'est l'amour*. He'd been living in an inverse Eden, whose Eve had eaten the apple and shared her delicious knowledge with him. Why, oh why, did he have to destroy it?

He reckoned that he could leave her room as late as 10:45 and still be back at the mailbox before a postal worker got there. For that matter, he could spend the whole morning with her and write a second letter to say he'd changed his mind and was keeping his deferment.

"Are you falling asleep?" she said.

"Not at all."

"Let me make you some toast."

"No, I'm okay. Champagne is like a glucose bomb."

He pressed his palm between her legs, testing the spring of the curls beneath the flannel. He moved up for a closer view while he pulled down her pajama bottoms. Oh, the beauty of what he uncovered! The inexhaustibleness of its invitation! It was true that, if he'd been as forthright in his preferences as she was in hers, he might have asked her to leave her pajama top on. He was on friendly enough terms with her breasts, but he'd gained access to them so early on that he hadn't had time to become properly fascinated with them, as a treasure to dream of uncovering, and they'd seemed a bit irrelevant ever since. He liked them better in a bra. Best of all would be to have her top-clad and bottomless, like a collegiate female faun, Honors student above the waist, creature of his wettest dreams below. But he'd never found a way to express this preference uninsultingly, and she seemed to prefer being fully naked.

She shed her pajama top and tugged on the shoulders of his shirt. She liked him naked, too—considered it especially bad form to leave one's socks on—but this morning he didn't feel like undressing. He'd had a taste of aggression and felt like doing what he wanted, even if he couldn't tell her what to do. He had an image of a soldier fucking in his boots, defended by his clothes. When she tugged again on his shirt, he resisted.

"Are you cold?"

"No."

He set about the only work for which he'd lately had ambition. Spread out before the horizon of her rib cage, sloping into the valley of her navel and up to a grove of wiry curls too close to be in focus, were the mobile white plains of her belly. Her hands, to either side, gripped the bed as she regulated contact with his tongue. He was amazed by his body's reserves of energy; it spoke to the primacy of reproductive function to an organism. No matter how he'd lashed his brain cells with cigarettes, they'd been too spent to pull weight in his final pages on Scipio Africanus, and yet here were the muscles of his neck and tongue, indefatigable, soldiering forward on the promise of a reward accruing not even to them but to his penis. His neck postponed its aching, his temples their pounding with champagne, his eyes the resumption of their burning, until he could obey the deeper animal imperative and release its boiling madness.

She gave a sharp cry. For a moment, rocked by its own galvanism, her body seemed to dismember itself. He lingered to push his tongue as far into her as it would reach, to taste what his penis couldn't, and then moved up to look into her eyes. They were beady, the darkest of browns; her smile was lopsided, as if he'd broken it. He put a pillow under her butt, the way she liked it, and pulled his pants halfway down. It bordered on miraculous how completely her little person accommodated him. He lowered his full weight onto her and lay still, trying to etch into his memory the feel of total penetration. He wondered how many months or years it would be before he next felt it with someone.

"Are you all right?" she said.

"Yeah. Just pausing."

"You know what I was imagining? That we were together in Paris. That we got caught in a thunderstorm and went back to our hotel room soaking wet. I was imagining you making me come while the rain came down harder and harder on the boulevards."

Even the word *come* could not overcome the turnoff of picturing them in Paris. The four of them standing in line to get inside the Louvre. Becky tall and clean and radiantly good-natured, his mother studying a guidebook and making some wry comment about it—he hated to imagine Sharon in that picture. He hated to imagine himself, condemned every morning to lie in a heavily fucked-upon French bed where everything was hot and red and sleep-depriving, with crusted semen on the sheets, condemned to wishing he could be wherever Becky was instead, maybe downstairs in a breakfast room with fresh napkins and baguettes, she and their mother having some lively conversation that he would have liked to be a part of. Becky he never regretted being near, because nearness was all he wanted from his sister. When he pictured himself and Sharon entering that Parisian breakfast room, stinking of après-sex cigarettes, their eyes red and puffy-lidded, the glowing image of Becky receded and faded like an angel's. Even in the real world, he was losing her—had been losing her ever since the night in September when Sharon had taken off her bathrobe. The more Sharon was in the picture, the less Becky could be. His penis was deflating.

"Oh, baby," Sharon said. "You must be so tired."

He nodded, glad to let her think that.

"I have an idea, though," she said. "I was thinking we could both come back here right after Christmas. Do you want to do that? We could spend all day reading ahead for classes and be together every night. I don't want you to feel like you're falling behind with your work because of me."

He'd burned through all his glucose. The imperative had dwindled to nothing.

"But that's not the thing I wanted to tell you." She repositioned herself to look into his eyes. "Can I tell you something important? I've been wanting to say it for weeks now."

He waited with dull dread.

"I'm in love with you," she said. "Am I allowed to say that?"

It was exactly as he'd feared.

"I am so in love with you, baby."

It was exactly as he'd feared, but somehow the effect was the opposite of what he might have expected. A wave of masculine well-being was sweeping through his body. The knowledge that he fully possessed this person, the thrill of that conquest, and something more savage, the sudden enhancement of his capacity to inflict pain on her: it was hitting him like a full-bore shot of testosterone. The imperative stormed back to life, and he unthinkingly obeyed it, with a thrust. It was astonishing how different it felt to be inside a woman he'd caused to fall in love with him, how comprehensively his genital nerves now felt connected to her. It was almost as if, until this moment, he'd never had sex. He gave another thrust. The pleasure was outrageous.

"So, what do you think?" she said.

"I think you're amazing," he said, humping away.

"Okay." She faintly nodded, as if to herself.

He paused and lowered his face to kiss the mouth that had spoken the magic words. She turned her face away from his.

"Why didn't you want to take your clothes off today?"

"I don't know. It seemed like it might be exciting, somehow."

Again the dubious little nod.

"Sharon," he pleaded. He knew that a conversation needed to be had, and that it would not be a good conversation, but his *very strong preference* was to have it just a little bit later. By way of expressing this preference, he shut his eyes and moved his hips again. The pleasure was undiminished, but she immediately spoke again.

"I want you to say you're in love with me, too."

He opened his eyes. As far back as September, when the needle of his mind had stuck in a groove playing Sharon, he'd had the impulse to say he was in love with her. He'd suppressed it because he was following her lead in everything and had gathered that romantic declarations weren't comme il faut. It was true that, after his crisis at Thanksgiving, he'd been glad he'd kept his mouth shut earlier. But now he could feel, in his own nerves, how transformative it might be for Sharon to hear the magic words from him. It was so transformative, in fact, that he felt he could speak them with some honesty.

"You don't even have to mean it," she said. "I'm just curious how it feels to hear it."

He nodded and said, "I'm not in love with you."

It took him a moment to realize that his tongue had slipped. He truly hadn't meant to say that. He was aghast.

"Say you are, though," she said.

"I was trying to. It just came out wrong."

"To put it mildly!"

He extended his arms, looked down at their furry point of contact, and shook his head against a bitter truth in him. "I . . . I don't know what I am. I don't think I can say it."

Her face twisted up as if the truth had scalded it.

"I'm sorry," he said.

"It's okay." She managed a wry smile. "I tried."

"God, Sharon, I am so sorry."

"It's really okay. You can go ahead and finish."

She was generous to the last, but even in his supremely inflamed state he understood the wrongness of taking more pleasure from her now. He started to withdraw.

"No, do it," she said, trying to pull him back in. "Just forget I said that thing."

"I can't."

She was weeping. "Please do it. I want you to."

He couldn't. He remembered the sex talk, or what had passed for a sex talk, that his mother had given him before he left for college. Whatever else he might hear on campus, she'd said, sex without commitment was empty and ruinous. This was the ancient wisdom. As with the parietal rules, he was realizing too late that old people weren't entirely stupid. Beneath him was a weeping girl to prove it.

Getting out of bed made him conscious of the obscenity of his erection. While Sharon lay and wept, he yanked up his jeans and put on his peacoat. In the hippie bedroom below them, a familiar bass line started up, the same Who album they'd been hearing for weeks. He shook Sharon's pack of cigarettes, pulled one out with his lips, and struck a match. Back in September, he'd tried one of her Parliaments and liked it. By the time he'd realized that smoking, like sex, did not in itself confer manhood, he was wretchedly addicted.

"Can I make you some toast?" he said.

No answer. Sharon had pulled the bedspread onto herself and was facing the wall, her crying detectable only as a faint shaking of her curls. Her bed was a double mattress on a box spring, her desk a hollow-core door on sawhorses, her bookshelves pine one-by-tens with cinder-block supports. He remembered his first sight of her books, the great quantity of French-language paperbacks, the austere whiteness and uniformity of their spines. Back then, three months ago, he couldn't have imagined anything sexier in a woman than high intelligence. Even now, if he and she had been all mind and genitals and nothing else, he might have imagined a future for them.

He wondered if he should simply leave now—whether this would be the kind thing to do or the cowardly thing. He'd planned to break up with her by letter because he wanted to speak to her mind-to-mind, rationally, well clear of the inviting pit. But now he'd hurt her, and she was crying. Maybe the situation spoke for itself? Maybe further talk would only be hurtful? He sat down on the edge of her bed, drew smoke into his abused lungs, and waited to see what he would do. Again the existential freedom, to speak or not to speak. Beneath the floor, the Who continued their thumping.

"I'm not coming back next semester," he heard himself say. "I'm dropping out."

Sharon rolled over immediately and stared at him, her cheeks wet.

"I'm giving up my deferment," he said. "I'm going to do whatever they want me to do, which probably means Vietnam."

"That's insane!"

"Really? You were the one who said it was the right thing to do."

"No, no, no." She sat up and hugged the bedspread to her chest. "It's already unbearable that Mike is there. You can't do that to me."

"I'm not doing it to you. I'm doing it because it's right. My lottery number is nineteen. It's just like you said—I should have gone already."

"God, Clem, no. That is insane."

In the year of his childhood when his genius brother had been old enough to play chess and young enough to be beaten, Clem had always, before moving to checkmate, asked Perry if he was sure about the last move he'd made. He'd considered this a gracious question for an older brother to ask, until one day Perry had choked up with tears—as a little kid, Perry had always been crying about one thing or another—and told Clem to *stop rubbing it in.* It was unclear to him now why he'd imagined that Sharon's response would be any different.

"Vietnam won't kill me," he said. "We're out of ground combat."

"When did you start thinking this? Why didn't you tell me?"

"I'm telling you now."

"Is it because I said I was in love with you?"

"No."

"It was a mistake to say that. I don't even know if it's true. It's like there are these words, they're out there in the world, and you start wondering what it would be like to say them. Words have their own power— they *create* the feeling, just by the fact of your saying them. I'm so sorry

I tried to make you say them. I love that you were honest with me. I love—oh, shit." She slumped, crying again. "I *am* in love with you."

He took a last puff on his cigarette and carefully mashed it out in her ashtray. "It wasn't anything you said. I already sent the letter."

She looked at him uncomprehendingly.

"I mailed it on the way over here."

"No! No!" She began to beat on him with her little fists, not painfully. The sex scent rising off her and the aggression of his speech act inflamed him afresh. He thought of the time he'd staggered around her room with her impaled on him, how her smallness had made this excellent thing practicable. Fearful of falling back into the pit after so nearly breaking free of it, he grabbed her wrists and made her look at him.

"You're a wonderful person," he said. "You've totally changed my life."

"That's a good-bye!" she wailed. "I don't want a good-bye!"

"I'll write to you. I'll tell you everything."

"No, no, no."

"Can't you see this isn't equal? I love who you are, but I'm not in love with you."

"Now I wish I'd never met you!"

She threw herself onto the foot of the bed. The pity he felt was infinitely realer than the idea of being a soldier. He pitied her for being so small and loving him, and for the logical bind in which he'd put her, and for the irony of her having made him the person who would leave her, by introducing him to more existential forms of knowledge. He wanted to stay and explain, to talk about Camus, to remind her of the necessity of exercising moral choice, to make her understand how indebted he was to her. But he didn't trust his animal self.

He leaned over and pressed his face into her hair. "I do love you," he said.

"If you loved me, you wouldn't leave," she replied in a clear, angry voice.

He shut his eyes and was instantly half asleep. He forced them open. "I've got to go pack up my room."

"You're breaking my heart. I hope you know that."

The only way out of the pit was to stand up, be strong, and walk away. When he opened her door and heard her cry out—"*Wait!*"—it nearly broke his own heart. Shutting the door behind him, he was seized by a spasming that he was surprised to recognize as sobbing. It was wholly autonomic, as uncontrollable as vomiting but less familiar—he hadn't cried since the day Martin Luther King was assassinated. In a salty blur, he ran down a damply carpeted flight of stairs, past a thudding mass of Who sound in which the treble now was audible, down through a sharp smell of morning pot ignited in the common rooms, and out into cold, gray Urbana.

Five hours later, at the bus station, where snow had begun to fall, he handed over his duffel bag and his mammoth suitcase, the lugging of which across campus he'd taken as a foretaste of basic training, and claimed one of the last free seats on the Chicago bus. It was an aisle seat deep in the smoking section, with a baby shrieking in the seat directly behind it. Clem was missing Sharon so much, was aching so steadily at the lost hope of any future meeting, was feeling so persistently close to further tears, that he might as well have been in love with her. Though greater concentrations of smoke than were already in the bus could hardly be achieved, he took a cigarette from his peacoat, flipped up the lid of his seat's ashtray, and tried to suppress his emotions with nicotine. The monstrous job of breaking Sharon's heart was behind him, but there was still more work ahead of him today.

Camus was wholly admirable, and his thinking made sense when Clem and Sharon discussed it. When Clem was alone, though, he could see a problem with Camus. Perhaps because he was French, Camus was a closet Cartesian—he assumed the existence of a unitary consciousness that rationally deliberated moral choices, when in fact a person's real motives were complex and uncontrollable. Clem, borrowing from Sharon, had a good moral argument for giving up his student deferment. But if the moral argument were all he'd had, he might not have written to the draft board. Other strong choices were available. For example, he could have worked to raise public awareness of the immorality of deferments; he could have broken up with Sharon simply because their relationship made it hard for him to study. The *particular* choice he'd made was aimed squarely at his father.

For the longest time, for more than sixteen years, Clem had admired his father precisely for his strength. In the beginning, in Indiana, where the parish house had been decaying faster than his father could keep up with its maintenance, Clem had been awed, even frightened, by the roping and contraction of his father's large muscles when he swung a pickax or drove a nail; by the torrents of sweat that ran off him when he scythed weeds on a hot August day. The sweat had a unique, indefinable scent—not stinky, more like the smell of a young toadstool or fresh rain, but still upsetting to Clem in its intensity. (It was a revelation, much later, when he worked for the nursery in New Prospect, to catch the exact same smell from his own soaking T-shirts. As far as he knew, no one in the world except him and his father produced that smell. He wondered, indeed, if anyone else could smell it.) One push from his father at a swing set had sent him so high that he clutched the chains in fear of falling off. One mild flick of his father's wrist, and a baseball came at Clem so hard it stung his palm through his glove. And the yelling. His father's voice, raised in anger (always at Clem, never at Becky), was a sound so blasting that a spanking, which his father did not believe in giving children, might almost have been preferable.

In Chicago, he'd come to appreciate his father's moral strength as well. When he read *To Kill a Mockingbird*, in junior high, he recognized Atticus Finch and felt proud. His political views were a perfect replica of his father's, and they must have been authentic, because they survived his mother's praise of them. He shared his father's abhorrence of the Vietnam War and his belief that the struggle for civil rights was the defining issue of the day. During his father's campaign to desegregate New Prospect's public swimming pool, he went ringing doorbells by himself, handing out literature and repeating verbatim his father's words about racial prejudice. Although he didn't have his father's scope of action, didn't have a pulpit to preach from, didn't ride a bus to Alabama, he followed his example in smaller ways. The jocks at Lifton Central who persecuted the *faggots*, the *wussies*, soon learned to keep away from him. When he saw someone weak being picked on, he became so hot with anger and so numbed to pain that he could hold his own in a fight. He mostly wasn't friends with the kids he defended—they were social pariahs for a reason. He was just doing what his father had taught him was right.

The only sore points between them were religion and Becky. Nothing metaphysical made any sense to Clem, neither God the Father nor, still less, the absurd Holy Spirit, and something had gone wrong from the start regarding Becky, some jealousy or overprotectiveness on his father's part. Being alone with Becky made Clem aware of a peculiar duality in himself. He would have had a fistfight with anyone who said a word against his father, but he couldn't stop trying to undermine his sister's respect for his father's Christianity. What made this even stranger was that his own ethics were basically Christian. He admired Jesus greatly, as a moral teacher and a champion of the poor and the marginalized. But there was an imp of perversity in him, a sarcastically dissenting alter ego, and being alone with Becky brought it out. He walked her through the absence of evidence for immaterial forces, the lack of hard corroboration for the stories in the Bible, the unprovability of the proposition that God existed, the imperviousness of "miracles" to scientific experiment; and it worked. He made a junior atheist of Becky, and this became another thing that united them, another thing to love about his sister—the way her lip curled whenever God came up at the dinner table.

If he was more circumspect with his own atheism, it was partly out of respect for Jesus and partly because he and his father worked so well together. His father was patient in teaching him to use tools, and Clem, no matter how tired he got, refused to be the first to quit when the two of them were moving earth or raking leaves or painting walls. He wanted his father's approval, for his work ethic no less than for his politics, and he appreciated how frequently and warmly his father expressed it—he couldn't have asked for a better dad in this regard. When he started tenth grade, and his father had the inspiration of reorienting his church's youth fellowship toward a work camp in Arizona, Clem saw no reason to let metaphysics stand in the way of joining it.

Rick Ambrose had come aboard at the same time. During the first year, when he was a full-time seminarian and only a part-time fellowship adviser, Ambrose had worn his hair short, shaved his face, and deferred to the associate minister. But after the political tumult of the following summer—Clem had campaigned for Eugene McCarthy, working along-side his father, who in August had his lip split open while trying to intervene between cops and protesters in Grant Park—Ambrose returned to the fellowship with long hair and a Fu Manchu. Some of the boys from the church, notably Tanner Evans, had adopted the same look. There was a new rowdiness on Sunday nights, a new impatience with authority, as long-haired kids from other churches, or from no church at all, started showing up at meetings, but it never occurred to Clem to worry about his father. Who cared if an ordained minister still carried a Bible and started every meeting with a metaphysical prayer? MLK had been devout, and no one had admired him any less for it. Clem didn't know a man who worked more passionately for social justice than his father, and when you really loved someone, the whole person, you simply accepted the little things you might have wished were different. He could see eyes being rolled when his father waxed religious at a fellowship meeting, but Becky herself rolled her eyes like that. It didn't mean she didn't love him.

By the spring of 1969, the group was so large that two chartered buses were waiting in the church parking lot on the first afternoon of Easter vacation. Two separate work camps were planned for Arizona, and it would have made sense to divide the group by destination. Instead, as quickly became clear, there was a cool bus—identified as such when Ambrose dropped his luggage next to it; promptly mobbed by the Tanner Evans crowd—and an uncool bus, with Clem and his father and the squarer kids from First Reformed. For Clem, a bus was only a means of transport to the thin air of the mesa, the smells of pinyon pine and frybread, the chance to haul rocks and pound nails for a people his country had robbed and oppressed. The whole notion of coolness was puerile. Nobody in New Prospect was more socially desirable than his sister, and he knew for a fact, from the stories Becky had told him, that popular kids had no more substance than unpopular ones. Because he had Becky, he'd never gone out of his way to make friends at school, and the few good friends he did have were not in the fellowship, but he was on friendly enough terms with many of the square kids. Even the sour fat girl, even the compulsive punster, even the immature blurter had interesting things to say if you put them at ease and took the time to listen. This was what Jesus would have done, and Clem felt good about doing it.

His father, however, seemed restless and distracted on the square bus.

Their driver was a little slower than the other driver, and his father sat directly behind him, ducking his head to peer down the road, as if he were anxious about falling behind. Clem went to sleep early. When he woke up in the night and saw that his father was still peering through the windshield, he put it down to excitement, anticipation. The real situation didn't become clear until morning, when their bus caught up with the Ambrose bus, at a Texas Panhandle truck stop, and his father made Ambrose trade places with him.

Theoretically, there was nothing wrong with this. His father was the leader of the group, and it was arguably correct to share his ministerial presence with the other bus. But when Clem saw how *eagerly* his father bounded onto it, without a backward glance, something shifted inside him. He sensed, in his gut, that his father hadn't switched buses because it was right. It was because he selfishly wanted to be on the other bus.

That evening, when they rolled into the town of Rough Rock, Arizona, Clem's instinct was confirmed in the awfulest of ways. In the dark, in a dust cloud lit by headlights, there was a melee of baggage handling as the group sorted itself into the half that would stay in Rough Rock, with his father, and the half going on to the settlement at Kitsillie, up on the mesa, with Ambrose. Weeks earlier, when everyone signed up for one location or the other, Clem had chosen Kitsillie because its primitive conditions suited him, but most of the kids boarding the Kitsillie bus had chosen it because of Ambrose. Among them were Tanner Evans and Laura Dobrinsky, their musician friends, and the group's cutest girls. The bus was fully loaded and ready to go, missing only Ambrose, when Clem's father climbed aboard with his duffel bag.

There had been, he said, a change of plan. It would be better, he'd decided, if he led the Kitsillie contingent and let Rick stay in Rough Rock, where there was dormitory housing. After a moment of stunned silence, the bus erupted with cries of protest from Laura Dobrinsky and her friends, but it was too late. The driver had already closed the door. His father took the aisle seat by Clem and clapped him on the knee. "This is great," he said. "You and I get to spend a whole week together. It's better, don't you think?"

Clem said nothing. From farther back in the bus came urgent, angry female whispering. His father had trapped him in the window seat and he thought he might die if he didn't get away. The shame of being the son of this man was new to him and searingly painful. It wasn't that he cared how he personally looked to the cool kids. It was how weak his father had made himself look to them, by abusing his petty authority to commandeer their bus. And now his father was *using* him, being all fatherly, so as to pretend that he'd done nothing wrong.

The pretending continued on the mesa. The old man seemed willfully blind to how much the Kitsillie group resented him for taking Ambrose's place. He didn't seem to realize that he was nearly fifty, twice as old as Ambrose, not interchangeable. Yes, he was stronger and more skilled than Ambrose, and, yes, he was full of energy—returning to the mesa, reconnecting with the Navajos, walking the land he loved, always fired him up. But every morning, when he organized the work crews, no one volunteered to be in his. When he went ahead and selected a crew, and busied himself with tools and supplies for the day, a funny thing happened: every girl in his crew who was friends with Laura Dobrinsky traded places with someone from a different crew. He had to have noticed this, and yet he never said a word about it. Maybe he was too cowardly to make an issue of it. Or maybe he didn't care what the girls thought of him. Maybe all he'd wanted was to prevent them from spending the week with their beloved Ambrose.

Clem was a crew leader himself, the only non-adult to whom his father gave responsibility. A year earlier, this expression of trust would have thrilled him, but now he was merely grateful that he never had to be in his father's crew. During the day, hard physical labor dulled his fear of returning to the schoolhouse where the group was camping out, but the shame was always waiting there at dinnertime. He felt obliged, by his principles, to eat with his father, who was otherwise shunned, and to submit to his fraudulently hearty talk about the trench he was digging for a septic line. Seeing his peers all laughing and eating together, Clem felt uniquely cursed and isolated. He wished he were the son of someone—anyone—else.

It was a fellowship tradition to gather as a group around a single candle after dinner and share thoughts and feelings about the day. Every night at Kitsillie, there was a wall of stony silence from the cool girls. Late in the week, his father went so far as to ask the prettiest of them, Sally Perkins, if she had anything to tell the group. Sally just stared at the candle and shook her head. Her refusal to speak was so pointed, the tension around the candle so high, that it ought to have triggered a full-on confrontation, but Tanner Evans knew exactly when to strike a chord on his twelve-string and lead the group in song.

If Clem's father was relieved to avoid a confrontation, he shouldn't have been. The explosion that followed ten days later, at the first Sunday meeting after the Arizona trip, was more violent for having been suppressed. The evening was unusually hot for April, the fellowship meeting room as airless and rafter-smelling as an attic. Everyone was in a hurry to get downstairs for activities, and most of the room quieted when Clem's father stepped forward to deliver his opening prayer. He glanced at Sally Perkins and her friends, who were continuing to talk, and raised his voice. "Heavenly Father," he said.

"This room could sure use an air conditioner," Sally remarked, loudly, to Laura Dobrinsky.

"Sally," Rick Ambrose growled from a corner of the room.

"What."

"Be quiet."

After a pause, Clem's father tried again. "Heavenly Father—"

"No!" Sally said. "I'm sorry, but no. I'm sick of his stupid prayers." She jumped to her feet and looked around the room. "Is anyone else here as sick of them as I am? He already ruined my spring trip. I'm literally going to throw up if he keeps doing this."

The contempt in her voice was shocking. Whatever might be happening in the country at large, however angrily authority was being questioned, nobody could speak like this at church.

"I'm sick of it, too," Laura Dobrinsky said, standing up. "So that makes two of us. Anyone else?"

En masse, the rest of the cool girls stood up. The heat in the room was suffocating Clem. Laura Dobrinsky addressed his father directly.

"The younger Navajos don't like you, either," she said. "They're sick of being ministered to. They don't want a white guy condescending to them and telling them what his white God wants them to do. Are you even aware of how you sound to other people? Maybe you had a good thing going with the elders, way back when. And maybe they're still cool with that. But they're *elders*. The missionary bullshit won't cut it anymore."

Rick Ambrose was glowering at his boots, his arms tightly crossed. Clem's father's face had gone white. "May I say something?" he said.

"How about trying to listen for a change?" Laura said.

"If I can do nothing else, Laura, I believe I do know how to listen. It is my job to listen."

"How about listening to yourself, then? I don't see much evidence of that."

"Laura," Ambrose said.

Laura turned on him. "You're defending him? Because he's, what, the ordained minister? That's a strike *against* him as far as I'm concerned."

"If you have an issue with Russ," Ambrose said, "you should take it up with him directly."

"That's exactly what I'm doing."

"One on one."

"Fuck that. I have no interest in that." Laura addressed Clem's father again. "I have no interest in a relationship with you."

"I'm very sorry to hear you say that, Laura."

"Yeah? I seriously don't think I'm the only one here who feels that way."

"I don't either," Sally Perkins said. "I don't want to have a relationship with you. In fact, I don't even want to be in this group if you're in it."

More than half the group was on its feet now. Over the tumult of voices came Ambrose's bellowing. "Sit DOWN. Everyone SIT DOWN NOW and SHUT THE FUCK UP."

The mob obeyed him. Though Ambrose was technically subordinate to Clem's father, everyone knew who the group's real leader was: who was strong and who was weak.

"We're going to skip the prayer tonight," Ambrose said. "Is that okay with you, Russ?"

The older man nodded meekly. He was weak! weak!

"You're not listening to us," Laura Dobrinsky said. "You don't get it. We're telling you either *he* goes or *we* go."

There were shouts of agreement, and Clem couldn't stand it. However ashamed he'd been of his father in Arizona, he couldn't stand to see a weak person beaten up. He raised his hand and waved it. "Can I say something?"

Immediately all eyes were on him. Ambrose nodded with approval, and Clem stood up unsteadily, his face burning.

"I can't believe how mean you guys are being," he said. "You're going to walk away because you don't like a two-minute prayer? I'm not into it, either, but I'm not here for prayers. I'm here because we're a community committed to service to the poor and the downtrodden. And you know what? My dad has been committed to that for longer than anyone here has been alive. He's more committed than anyone in this room. I think that ought to count for something."

He sat down again. A girl next to him touched his arm supportively.

"Clem is right," Ambrose said. "We need to respect each other. If we don't have the guts to work through this as a group, we don't deserve to call ourselves a community."

Sally Perkins was staring at Clem's father. She seemed to take cruel satisfaction in his inability to look at her. "No," she said.

"Sally," Ambrose said.

"Let's put it to a vote," she said. "How many people want to stay in this group if *he's* in it?"

"We're absolutely not doing that," Ambrose said.

"Then I'm leaving."

She stood up again. More than half the group stood up. Clem's father's eyes were wide with pain. "I'd like to say something," he said. "Hear me out, all right? I'm not sure where all this is coming from—"

Laura Dobrinsky laughed and walked out of the room.

"I'm sorry if I'm not the person you want me to be," the old man said. "I guess I still have a lot to learn from you guys. I care about this group, deeply. We've been doing great work, and I'd like to help us continue to do that. If you want Rick to lead the prayers, or Rick to lead the group, I'm okay with that. But if you care about personal growth, I'd like the chance to experience it myself. I'm asking you to give me that chance."

Clem experienced a petrification so literal it seemed as if his body might shatter if tapped with a hammer. His father was *begging*. And not even to any avail. Sally Perkins had walked out, and half the group was following her, crowding the doorway in their eagerness to side with her. The old man watched them with dumb animal bewilderment.

Ambrose, whose position was unenviable, suggested that Russ lead a breathing exercise while he went and reasoned with the defectors. Again the old man nodded submissively. Among the church kids who remained when Ambrose was gone, Clem was surprised to see Tanner Evans.

"I want us all to breathe," the old man said, a tremor in his voice. "I'm going to lie down—we're all going to lie down and shut our eyes. All right?"

He was supposed to keep speaking, to lead the group in a visualization, but the only sound was the buzz of the defectors downstairs. As Clem lay in the heat and tried to breathe, his mind went back to Becky: how his father had always wanted her to be his special friend, and had seemed to resent that Clem was also her special friend, had tried to separate her and Clem and have a private relationship with each of them, and how peculiar it was that he'd singled them out, since Becky was popular and Clem could take care of himself. Neither she nor he needed extra attention the way, for example, their younger brother did. Perry was rich in gifts but poor in spirit, and their father, who in public made such a big deal of attending to the poor, found nothing but fault in Perry. And now the same thing had happened in the fellowship. Instead of ministering to the socially needy, his father had tried to separate the popular kids from Ambrose and take them for himself. He wasn't just weak. He was disgusting—a moral fraud.

Hearing footsteps, Clem sat up and saw his father following Ambrose out of the room. No one was even pretending to do the breathing exercise now. Tanner Evans looked at Clem and shook his head.

"You know what?" Clem said. "I don't want to talk about it. Can we just not talk about it?"

There were murmurs of relief. His peers understood.

"I'm not quitting the group," he added. "But I think I might go home now."

He tottered from the room and down the stairs as if he'd been excused for medical reasons. Back at the parsonage, he went straight to his room and locked the door, picked up an Arthur C. Clarke novel he'd borrowed from the library, and absorbed himself in someone else's world. Two hours disappeared before he heard a tap on his door.

"Clem?" his father said.

"Go away."

"May I come in?"

"No. I'm reading."

"I just want to thank you. Clem. I want to thank you for what you said tonight. Can you open your door?"

"No. Go away."

The pain his father's weakness caused him was like an illness, and it persisted in the weeks that followed. At the next Sunday meeting, he reminded himself of Tim Schaeffer, a boy from the group who'd had surgery for brain cancer and returned to meetings for two months before he died. Everyone wanted to be Clem's partner in trust-building exercises, no one gave him shit if he didn't feel like opening up with his feelings. Rick Ambrose told him, privately, that he'd witnessed few acts of greater strength and courage than Clem's standing up to defend his father. Ambrose proceeded to confide in him, ask for his help with logistical decisions, and make an affectionate running joke of his atheism. Never referred to, but obvious to Clem, was Ambrose's recognition of his need for a new father figure.

He no longer respected the old man. Having glimpsed his fundamental weakness, he now saw it at every turn. Saw him exploiting Becky's politeness to drag her on their Sunday walks, saw him distancing himself from their mother at church functions and chatting with other men's wives, heard him blackening Rick Ambrose's name because young people liked him, heard him reminding people who didn't need reminding that he'd marched with Stokely Carmichael and integrated the swimming pool, saw him gazing at himself in the bathroom mirror, touching his shaggy eyebrows with his fingertips. The man whose strength Clem had admired now seemed to him a raw blot of egregiousness. Clem couldn't stand to be in the same room with him. He was giving up his student deferment to show his father what a strong man did.

The smoke in the Chicago-bound bus and the weather outside it were enforcing an early twilight. Snow falling on the cornfields dimmed and smudged the furrows and stubble, the distant cribs. The baby in the seat behind Clem had invented a word, *buh*, and fallen in love with it. Each time she said it—*Buh!*—she squealed with fresh delight, at intervals timed perfectly to keep him wide awake. Without his taking any action, the bus was carrying him forward, toward the task of telling his parents that he'd written to the draft board, away from the violence of what he'd done to Sharon. The depth of the violence was becoming ever more apparent, his aching more grievous. The only relief he could imagine was Becky's blessing.

Disgusted with herself, the overweight person who was Marion fled the parsonage. For breakfast she'd eaten one hard-boiled egg and one piece of toast very slowly, in tiny bites, per the advice of a writer for *Redbook* who claimed to have shed forty pounds in ten months, and whom *Redbook* had photographed in a Barbarella sort of jumpsuit, showing off her futuristically insectile waistline, and who had also advised pouring oneself a can of a nationally advertised weight-loss drink in lieu of lunch, engaging in three hours of vigorous exercise each week, repeating mantras such as *A moment on the lips, a lifetime on the hips*, and buying and wrapping a small present for oneself to open whenever one succeeded in losing x number of pounds. Excepting a decade's supply of sleeping pills, there was no present that Marion wanted enough to serve as a reward, but she'd duly been going to Tuesday and Thursday morning exercise classes at the Presbyterian church and would have gone there today if Judson hadn't been home. Deprived of the proper half sandwich, with mayonnaise, to which an hour of Presbyterian calorie-burning would have entitled her, she'd lunched on two stalks of celery with cream cheese in their grooves. These had almost got her out the door, into the chute of an afternoon without temptations, but one of the cookies she'd baked with Judson had broken in half. Seeing it broken on a cooling rack, among its whole fellows, she'd felt sorry for it. She was its Creator, and to eat it was a kind of mercy. But its sweetness had unleashed her appetite. By the time her disgust caught up with her, she'd eaten five more cookies.

In her tennis shoes and her oft-mended gabardine overcoat, she proceeded past trees whose bark was darkened by the moisture their frozenness had condensed, past residential façades no longer promising the marital stability they had in the forties, when they were built. Her gait felt more waddling than striding, but at least she didn't have to worry about being noticed. Unless it was to pity her for not owning a car, no one gave a thought to a pastor's wife out walking by herself. As soon as people had met her and identified her position in the community, situated her at the Very Nice end of the all-important niceness spectrum, she became invisible to them. Sexually, there was no angle from which a man on the street might catch a glimpse of her and be curious to see her from a different angle, no point of relief from what she and time had done to her. She'd become invisible especially to her husband in this respect. Invisible to her kids as well—rendered featureless by the dense, warm cloud of momminess through which they apprehended her. Although she considered it possible that not one person in New Prospect actively disliked her, there was no one she could call a close friend. However short on money she was, perennially, she was even poorer in the currency of friendship, the little secrets that friends shared to build trust. She had plenty of secrets, but they were all too large for a pastor's wife to safely betray.

What she had instead of friends, on the sly, was a psychiatrist, and she was late for her appointment with her. She detested jogging, the thudding downward flesh-tug of her heavy parts, but when she turned onto Maple Avenue she started running with short and shallow steps, which conceivably burned more calories, per unit of distance, than walking did. The houses along Maple were a free-for-all of competitive decoration, their shrubbery and railings and rooflines infested with green plastic vines bearing fruits in dull colors. It wasn't clear to Marion that the charm of Christmas lights at night was enough to offset how ugly the hardware looked in daylight hours, of which there were many. Nor was it clear that the excitement of Christmas for children was enough to make up for the disenchanted drudgery of it in their adult years, of which there were likewise many.

At Pirsig Avenue, she slowed to a marching pace. The only person in New Prospect who knew she was seeing a psychiatrist was the receptionist at the thriving dentistry practice of Costa Serafimides, in a low brick building near the train station. Dr. Serafimides's wife, Sophie, saw her psychiatric patients in a small, unmarked room between identical rooms in which plaque was scraped and cavities filled. Anyone who noticed Marion in the waiting room would assume that she was there for such work. Once she was in Sophie's office, she could hear the squeak of rubber-soled comfort shoes, the whine of motive cords on pulleys, and smell the pleasant antiseptic peculiar to dentistry. The office contained two leather chairs, shelves of reference works, framed certificates (Sofia Serafimides, MD), and a deep-drawered credenza full of drugs. It was like a modernized confessional box, a not greatly secluded place to have the inside of one's head scraped, with payment exacted not in future Hail Marys but in cash on the spot.

Marion in her early twenties had been a seriously practicing Catholic. She'd believed, at the time, that the Church had saved her life, or at least her sanity, but later on, after she'd met Russ and made herself a level-headed Protestant, she'd come to see her youthful Catholicism as another form of craziness, more sustainable than the form that had landed her in a hospital at the age of twenty, but morbid nonetheless. It was as if, in her Catholic phase, she'd lived under a vault that made the sunniest day dark. She'd been obsessed with sin and redemption, prone to being overwhelmed by the significance of insignificant things—a leaf that fell and landed at her feet, a song she heard playing in two different places on the same day—and paranoid with the sense that God was watching everything she did. When she'd fallen in love with Russ, and had received the wonderfully concrete blessings of her marriage to him, one healthy child after another, each one of them precious enough to have sufficed, she'd closed a mental door on the years when the sun had been dark and her only friend, if one could call an infinite Being a friend, had been God. The incessantly praying girl she'd been at twenty-two signified mainly as the person she was blessed not to be anymore.

Not until the previous spring, when Perry had had his sleep troubles, his problems at school, had she opened the mental door again, to compare his symptoms with what she remembered of her own, and not until her first visit to Sophie Serafimides, in the clinically scented little room, did she experience real nostalgia for her Catholic years. She remembered how soothing the transactions of the confessional had been and how she'd loved the immensity of the Church's edifice, the majesty of its history, which had made her sins, grievous though they were, feel like tiny drops in a very large bucket—richly precedented, more manageably antique. Christianity as Russ preached and practiced it laid very little stress on sin. Marion had long been inspired, intellectually, by Russ's conviction that a gospel of love and community was truer to Christ's teachings than a gospel of guilt and damnation. But lately she'd begun to wonder. She loved her children more than she loved Jesus, whose divinity remained something of a question mark, and whose resurrection from the dead she basically didn't believe in, but she absolutely believed in God. She could feel His presence inside her and around her all the time. God was *there*—no less now, when she was fifty, than when she'd been twenty-two. And to love God even a little bit, even only when she happened to ask herself if she did, was to love Him more than she could love any person, even her children, because God was infinite. She wondered if good Protestant churches like First Reformed, in placing so much emphasis on Jesus's ethical teachings, and thereby straying so far from the concept of mortal sin, were making a mistake. Guilt at First Reformed wasn't all that different from guilt at the Ethical Culture Society. It was a version of liberal guilt, an emotion that inspired people to help the less fortunate. For a Catholic, guilt was more than just a feeling. It was the inescapable consequence of sin. It was an objective thing, plainly visible to God. He'd seen her eat six sugar cookies, and the name of her sin was gluttony.

As she marched through the Pirsig Avenue business district, she tried not to look at the store windows, whose displays of merchandise reproached her for the gifts she was giving her kids. It was true that Russ opposed the commercialization of Christmas and had set a meager budget for it, but this was hard on the kids, especially Judson, who was growing up in such a prosperous suburb. She'd bought him a football game that a toy-store salesman had assured her every boy wanted but Judson was probably too bright to enjoy for long. For Becky she'd bought a cute suitcase that had been marked down in price, probably because it was the wrong size to be useful. For Clem, as a token of his scientific ambitions, she'd bought a secondhand microscope that was probably obsolete in comparison with the ones at his school. And for Perry—oh, Perry wanted so many things, and would have made creative use of all of them, and was so considerate of her, so much on her wavelength, that he'd hinted only at presents he knew she could afford. She'd bought him the cheapest of cassette recorders, the kind of thing that an appliance store displayed to assure the buyers of other cassette recorders that they weren't getting the worst one. And all the while, at the back of her hosiery drawer, *all the while* she'd had an envelope containing the eight hundred dollars in cash she hadn't yet spent on her sessions with Sophie Serafimides, whom she was paying to be her friend.

Beneath this selfishness lay deeper circles of guilt. She lied and she stole, and once upon a time she'd done far worse than that. She'd lied to her husband from the moment she met him, and she'd lied to her daughter not fifteen minutes ago, on her way out the back door—"I'm late for my exercise class." She was late, all right. Two hours late for a one-hour class! The dollars in the pocket of her gabardine coat were twenty of the fourteen hundred she'd received from the Wabash Avenue jeweler to whom she'd taken the pearls and the diamond rings she'd set aside when she emptied her sister's apartment in Manhattan. At the time, as the executrix, she'd told herself that she was redressing an injustice perpetrated by her sister; that Becky already had too much money coming to her and didn't need costly jewelry. The theft might still have been forgivable if Marion had followed through on her intention to spend the money on Perry and Clem and Judson, to whom Shirley had left nothing. But after her first "hour" with Sophie, in June, when Sophie had suggested that weekly counseling would be more valuable than a sleeping-pill prescription, and had explained her sliding fee scale and asked Marion if she could afford, say, twenty dollars a week, and Marion had replied that she did, in fact, have a small personal fund at her disposal, there was no more denying the evil of her theft.

Thanks to her running on Maple Avenue, she arrived at the dental office just five minutes late. The parking lot was emptier than usual, the waiting room occupied only by a mother and a boy reading *Highlights for Children*, apparently unconcerned about the oral discomforts awaiting him. That the mother and her son were Black spoke to the liberalism of the Serafimideses, whose educations had taken them not only to the suburbs but also, as Marion knew, because she'd asked, out of the Greek Orthodoxy of their childhoods; they belonged to the Ethical Culture Society. The receptionist, a paragon of discretion, sixtyish and Greek herself, gave Marion a silent nod of permission to go straight to the sanctum.

Sophie Serafimides was a chair-filling dumpling of a woman with beautiful olive skin and a great volume of crinkly white hair. Although Marion had been struck by her angelic surname when she found it in the Yellow Pages, she'd chosen Sophie for her given name. The attending psychiatrists who'd treated her in Los Angeles had been men of such insufferable male condescension that it was surprising she'd recovered her sanity at all. To have found a female clinician in New Prospect was something of a miracle, and if she'd "transferred" onto Sophie any of her issues with her unloving, reality-avoidant mother, who'd died of liver disease in 1961, fully estranged from Marion, she had yet to become aware of it. Sophie Serafimides was all about reality. She radiated— exemplified—Mediterranean warmth and good sense, which itself could be insufferable, but not in a way for which Marion could blame her.

Nothing pleased the dumpling more than to be brought a fresh dream, but Marion didn't have any dreams for her today and preferred confession anyway. After hanging up her coat, she sat down and confessed that she was wearing her exercise clothes because she'd had to lie to Becky about where she was going. She confessed that she'd gobbled up—crammed into her mouth, stuffed herself with—six sugar cookies. Sophie smiled pleasantly at these confessions. "Christmas comes but once a year," she suggested.

"I know you think I'm too obsessed with this," Marion said. "I know you think it's beside the point. But do you know what I weighed this morning? A hundred and forty-three pounds! I've been starving myself since September, doing my knee bends and my sit-ups, avoiding sweets, and I've lost six pounds in three months."

"We've talked about counting things. The way we use numbers to punish ourselves."

"I'm sorry, but, for a person my height, a hundred and forty-three pounds is objectively a lot."

Sophie smiled pleasantly, her hands folded on her belly, the ampleness of which didn't seem to embarrass her. "Eating cookies is an interesting response to feeling overweight."

"Well, Becky was being a pill—she's suddenly unbearable. I could handle it if it was just a matter of being irritable and secretive, but Tanner Evans called the house last night, trying to find her, and I didn't hear her come home until after midnight, and this morning she was up bright and early, which is unusual. She isn't telling me anything, but it's obvious how happy she is. And I was thinking about the sweetness of being in love for the first time—how nothing in the world is sweeter."

"Yes."

"Tanner is a great kid. He's talented, he goes to church, he's really quite beautiful. When I think about my own adolescence, what a disaster it was . . . Becky is the total opposite. She's a good person who makes good choices. I'm proud of her—I'm happy for her."

Sophie smiled pleasantly. "So proud and happy, you had to eat six cookies."

"Why not? I could starve myself for a year, it still wouldn't make me eighteen again."

"You really want to be eighteen again?"

"If I could go back and be like Becky? Unlive my life and do it over again? Absolutely."

The dumpling seemed to resist an impulse to argue the point. "Okay," she said. "And what else?"

She already knew the answer. The what-else was always Russ. Marion, in the waiting room, had seen patients emerging from the clinic with expressions more distraught than dental work could account for, and every one of them had been a middle-aged woman. From this she'd gathered that Sophie's clientele consisted mainly of wives, depressed wives, wives whose husbands had left them or were about to, as the epidemic of divorce ravaged New Prospect. Given a clientele like this, it was understandable that Sophie would view all husbands as a priori suspect. To a hammer, everything looked like a nail. During their first "hour" together, Marion had sensed that Sophie disliked Russ sight unseen. In subsequent "hours," she'd tried to explain that her marriage wasn't the problem, that Russ wasn't like other husbands, that he'd merely been shaken by a humiliating career crisis, while Sophie, in her pleasantly smiling way, had asked Marion why, if she wasn't worried about her marriage, she kept showing up on Thursdays to talk about it. Finally, in August, Marion admitted that something had come over Russ—he was standing up straighter, taking better care of himself, while seeming acutely repelled by her and snapping at every little thing she said—and that she was no longer so sure what he might do. To Sophie, this represented a "breakthrough" on Marion's part, and she'd graciously allowed that her marriage might be worth fighting to keep. She suggested that Marion put herself out into the world more, develop more of an independent life, give Russ a new context in which to see her. Maybe, since money was an issue anyway, she could take a half-time job? Or a university-extension course? Marion's own plan of action for her marriage was to lose twenty pounds by Christmas. Sophie, who was far heavier than Marion, and yet apparently still attractive to her wiry little dentist husband, had approved her plan reluctantly. If she wanted to lose weight, she should do it for her own sake, as a way of taking control of her life.

"I think Russ lied to me at breakfast," Marion said now, to please her paid friend, who took each fresh complaint about Russ as a sign of progress toward—what? A realistic recognition that her marriage was dead? "The minute he came downstairs, I could tell he was excited. His legs kind of waggle when he's happy, he's like a little boy. Or like Elvis—he can't keep his hips still. He was wearing the shirt I got him for his birthday, which I knew would look nice on him, the blue in it picks up the blue in his eyes, and *that* seemed strange, because all he's doing today is pastoral visits and a delivery run to the church in Chicago and an open house tonight, which he would have changed his clothes for anyway. So I asked him if he had any other plans, and he said no, and I started wondering about the delivery, because Frances Cottrell is in that circle. Frances—"

"The young widow," Sophie said.

"Exactly. She's going to wreck *someone's* marriage, and now she's in the service circle Russ leads in the inner city, and so I asked him who else was making the delivery with him. And it was like he was expecting the question. He practically interrupted me to answer. He said, 'Just Kitty Reynolds.' Kitty's in the circle, too. She's retired now—she used to teach at the high school. The thing was how quickly Russ answered. And then the shirt, and his legs waggling, so."

"So."

"Well, he never mentions her. Frances. I happened to see her in the parking lot one day when they were leaving for the city. The only time he's *ever* referred to her was when I asked him about her that night."

"She's young."

"Young*er*. She has a boy in high school."

"Young is young," Sophie said. "Costa likes to talk about the first warm day of spring, when the young women all come out in their summer dresses. It lifts a man's spirits to be around attractive younger women. There's nothing necessarily wrong with that. I like seeing those summer dresses myself."

It was interesting how Sophie, who played the prosecutor when Marion defended Russ, turned around and argued for tolerance when Marion impugned him. She wondered if this was a subtle therapeutic strategy or just a way to keep her coming back every week with twenty dollars.

"I guess I haven't reached that higher plane," she said irritably. "You know what I think made me eat the cookies? I think Becky was one too many happy people to handle in one morning."

"You preferred it when Russ was suffering."

"Maybe. Yes. Did we somehow determine that I'm not a bad person? If we did, I must have missed it."

"You feel you're a bad person."

"I *know* I'm a bad person. You don't have any idea how bad."

Sophie's smile gave way to a more censorious expression. The timing of her therapeutic frowns was comically predictable. Marion felt infantilized by it.

"I could have eaten the whole batch of cookies," she said. "The only reason I didn't was there wouldn't have been any left for Judson. But I definitely could have eaten all of them. Six pounds in three months of starving myself, and it's not as if anyone has noticed. It's not as if I deserve to be thin. The disgusting thing I see in the mirror every morning is what I deserve."

Sophie glanced at the spiral-bound notepad on her little side table. She hadn't written on the notepad since the summer. There was a hint of threat in the glance.

"It's not just me, by the way," Marion said. "I think everyone is bad. I think badness is the fundamental condition of humanity. If I really loved Russ, shouldn't I be rejoicing to see him happy again? Even if it meant him being with the fair young widow and lying to me about it? I don't really want him to be happy. I only want him not to leave me. When I saw him in that shirt this morning, I wished I'd never given it to him. If suffering is what it takes for him to stay married to me, I'd rather that he suffer."

"You say that," Sophie said, "but I'm not sure you believe it."

"Also, for your information," Marion said, her voice rising, "I'm paying you money I can't afford to be here, so I don't really care to hear about how well adjusted you and your husband are."

"You may have misunderstood what I was saying."

"No, I understood you very well."

Sophie glanced again at her notepad. "What did you hear me to be saying?"

"That you're not depressed. That you have a happy marriage. That you have no idea what it's like to look at a girl in a summer dress and wish a terrible life on her, a life as terrible as your own. That you're lucky enough not to know how lucky you are. That you've never had to find out how selfish *all* human love is, how bad *all* people are, and how the only love you can be sure isn't selfish is loving God, which isn't much of a consolation prize, but it's all we've really got."

Sophie drew a slow breath. "You're giving me a lot today," she said. "I'd like to understand better where it's coming from."

"I hate Christmas. I can't lose weight."

"Yes. I'm sure that's a disappointment. But I'm sensing something else here."

Marion turned her face toward the door. She thought of the money in her hosiery drawer and the ugly cheap cassette recorder she'd bought for Perry. It wasn't too late to go out and get him a set of good stereo components, or a really nice camera, something he would truly enjoy having, something to atone in some tiny way for the blackness she'd put in his head by being his mother. The other kids would be all right, but she was very much afraid that Perry wouldn't, and it was unbearable to know that the instability she could sense in him had come from her. If she kept seeing Sophie, the money would be gone by summer, and all she'd have to show for it would be the biweekly moments when Sophie, with an odd backhanded motion, without looking, reached behind her and opened a credenza drawer to fish out another handful of free physician samples of Sopor™, methaqualone, 300 mg. The samples were the one indisputably useful thing Marion got for her twenty dollars a week. A prescription would have been cheaper, but she hadn't wanted to be a woman with a prescription. She'd preferred to pretend that her anxious depression was temporary and the drug samples were an ad hoc way of managing it. Perry's most worrisome symptoms had abated, and in the fall he'd joined the church's youth fellowship, and she'd allowed herself to believe that Sophie was right—that the problem was her marriage. She'd believed that Sophie could help her *get better*. But she wasn't getting better. The Sopors did help her sleep more soundly than being confessed once had, but at least in the confessional she'd been able to speak the worst truths about herself. She could be as crazy and unhappy as she wanted without being expected to *fight to save her marriage*, which she now believed there was no saving, because she'd never deserved it in the first place, because she'd obtained it by fraud. What she deserved was punishment.

"Marion?" Sophie said.

"It's not working."

"What isn't working?"

"You. This. Me. None of it."

"The holidays are very hard. The end of the year is hard. But the feelings that get stirred up can be useful to work with."

"A breakthrough," Marion said bitterly. "Are we having another *breakthrough*?"

"You feel you're a bad person," Sophie prompted. Twenty dollars was the bottom of her fee scale, but it evidently still bought Marion the right to be hateful, as she never allowed herself to be with anyone else, and to receive pleasant smiles in return.

"It's a fact, not a feeling," she said.

"What exactly do you mean by that?"

Marion closed her eyes and didn't answer. After a while, she began to wonder what would happen if she continued to say nothing, stayed silent for the rest of their "hour," and then left the office without another word. She had enough Sopors to last another week, and she was very tempted to refuse to give Sophie anything more to *work with*, to make the dumpling just sit there and look at a patient whose eyes were closed, to punish her for not having helped her get better, to drive home how little she was better; to be the person who was withholding, not the wife and mother being withheld from. Each potentially therapeutic minute she stayed silent was another forty cents wasted, and the deliberate waste of minutes was tempting in the same self-spiting way that eating cookies had been. The only waste more evilly satisfying than to say nothing for the rest of the "hour" would have been to be silent from the moment she sat down. She wished she'd done that.

After several minutes of silence, marked only by the whir of dental equipment down the hall, she gave Sophie a half-lidded peek and saw that her eyes, too, were closed, her expression neutral, her hands loosely clasped on her lap, as if to demonstrate her powers of professional patience. Well, two could play at that game.

In the summer, in the early rush of their paid friendship, Marion had told Sophie the truth about certain things she'd outright lied to Russ about, or had omitted to mention and now could never tell him. The principal facts were that she'd spent fourteen weeks in a mental hospital in Los Angeles in 1941, following a severe psychotic episode, and that, contrary to what she'd told Russ in Arizona, soon after she'd met him, she had not had a brief, failed marriage to an unsuitable man in Los Angeles. There really had been a man, who really had been married, albeit not to her, and she'd felt obliged to warn Russ that she was previously used goods. She'd made her "confession" in a legitimate storm of tears, fearing that her having been "married" and "divorced" would cause her beautiful good Mennonite boy to recoil in horror and refuse to see her again. Thankfully, Russ's forgiving heart and his sexual attraction to her had carried the day. (It was his more sternly Mennonite parents who later recoiled.) She'd believed that she'd become a new person in Arizona, firmly grounded in reality by her conversion to Catholicism, and that the ghastly events in Los Angeles no longer mattered. By the time she gave Russ half the truth of half her story, she'd stopped going to confession.

It wasn't until she found her way into Sophie's box, more than twenty years later, that she realized how much she'd needed to unburden herself. Because patient confidentiality was as strict as the confessional's, she could have safely gone ahead and told the dumpling *everything*, but some things were only for her and God (and, once upon a time, in Arizona, God's priestly intercessor) to know. The absolution Sophie had given her was not of her sins but of her fear that she was manic-depressive. Apparently, she was merely chronically depressed, with obsessional and mildly schizoid tendencies. Compared to manic depression, these terms were a comfort.

Up to a point, the story she'd told Sophie in the summer, while Sophie jotted on her notepad, was the same story she'd told the young Russ. It began with her father, Ruben, the capable son of a German Jewish widower in the San Francisco shoe-repair trade, who'd attended Berkeley around the time of the great earthquake. Rooting for Berkeley's football team, the Golden Bears, Ruben had gotten the idea of starting his own business to manufacture athletic uniforms. The nation had gone crazy for high-school and collegiate sports, and after he finished college he had some success selling uniforms to high schools. The universities, however, were controlled by men from old California families who conducted all their business in the same Jew-excluding milieu. Marion reckoned it was partly cold business calculation, partly social ambition, and presumably some modicum of sexual attraction that led Ruben to pursue an "artistic" young woman from that milieu. Marion's mother, Isabel, was a fourth-generation Californian from a family whose once-extensive property holdings, in the city and Sonoma County, had largely been squandered—poorly husbanded, inopportunely liquidated, charitably donated to garner status points, inadvisably divided among shiftless offspring—by the time she met Ruben. One of Isabel's brothers ruthlessly managed what was left of the family's land in Sonoma, the other was a landscape painter of scant means and little note. Isabel herself had vague musical aspirations, but all she actually seemed to have done with herself was appreciate culture in San Francisco, ride around in the cars of richer friends, and spend long weekends at their country houses. How exactly Ruben found his way into one of those houses, Marion never learned, but within two years he'd parlayed an advantageous marriage into contracts with the Stanford and Cal athletic departments. By the time Marion was born, he was the largest manufacturer of athletic gear west of the Rocky Mountains. He built Isabel a three-story house in Pacific Heights, and it was there, as a rich girl (for a while), that Marion had grown up.

In her memory, the house was darker than a Catholic sky. Thick curtains further dimmed the fog-enfeebled daylight falling on the heavy, stained-oak furniture then in style. Her mother seemed to view both her and Shirley as aberrations that her body had unaccountably twice housed for nine months, their births a regrettable interruption of her social life but otherwise a relief on the order of passing a kidney stone. Her father's heart might have had room for two daughters if the first one, Shirley, hadn't filled it inordinately. His obsessionality (the dumpling's word) served him well in his business, Western All-Sport, to which he devoted sixty and seventy hours a week, but at home it served to make Marion feel invisible. Ruben's darling was Shirley. When he happened to look at Marion directly, it was often to ask, "Where's your sister?" Shirley was the really pretty one, even as an infant, and took his adoration as her due. On Christmas morning, she didn't tear through her immense haul of presents with a normal child's greed. She unwrapped them like a wary retailer, carefully inspecting each of them for flaws of manufacture, and sorted them by category, as if checking them against a mental invoice. The repeated chiming of her voice—"Thank you Daddy"—was like the chinging of a cash register. Marion took refuge from the excess by absorbing herself in a single doll, a single toy, while her mother yawned with open boredom.

Christmas for her mother was an enforced separation from the four friends with whom she did everything. The friends were from old families with less depleted fortunes, and, although three of them had husbands and children of their own, all five were in love with themselves as a unit. They'd been the marvelous fivesome of the Class of 1912 at Lowell, where they'd jointly decided that, if the world had a problem with their marvelousness, it was the world's problem, not theirs, and for the rest of their lives they never tired of lunching together, shopping together, attending lectures and theater together, reading books together, advancing worthy civic causes together. Marion came to see that her mother's place in the fivesome had always been the most precarious—she'd begun with the least money and then married a Jew—and therefore the most fanatically defended. Isabel lived in fear of being the fifth wheel, and at Christmas she fretted about the three friends whose husbands were also good friends, the non-fivesome gatherings that might be happening without her.

Spoiling Shirley wasn't the only thing her father couldn't stop doing. Beginning when Marion was six or seven, he never seemed to sleep at all. Awakening at a small hour, she could hear him playing ragtime, self-taught, on the piano two floors below. He was also a self-taught architect and spent other nights alone with his drafting tools, forever redesigning an even bigger house. At work, he bought businesses above and below him—his obsessive goal was to open a nationwide chain of sporting-goods stores—and he made more speculative investments as well, employing his special insight as a stock picker, his special gift for well-timed margin purchases. He smoked enormous cigars and wore a coonskin coat to Cal football games, sometimes taking Marion to sit with him in his fifty-yard-line seats, since Shirley and her mother had no interest. He talked nonstop throughout the game, in a technical language mostly beyond a seven-year-old's comprehension. He knew the name of every Golden Bear player and carried a little notebook in which he drew Xs and Os to show Marion how a play had worked, or to design new plays that he intended to show Cal's head coach, Nibs Price, whose job, he confided to her, he could have done better. He never behaved rudely, but his voice was loud and excited, and Marion was uncomfortably aware that other fans kept looking at him.

How like a mental illness a nation's economy was! She later wondered how much longer, if the stock market hadn't crashed when it did,
her father's manic period might have lasted, and whether, if his illness
had set in later, he could have managed to be manic in the midst of a
depression. These hypotheticals were hard to entertain, because the coin-
cidence of the market's crash and her father's crash seemed so inevitable
in hindsight. In the weeks following Black Tuesday, he duly scrambled to
salvage what he could of his highly leveraged holdings, but his voice, on
the phone in his study, from which he communicated with New York before going to the office, sounded the way it had when he'd made funeral
arrangements for his father. Marion came home from school and found
him in the parlor in his shirtsleeves and suspenders, staring at the cold
grate of the fireplace. Sometimes he spoke to her about the singular misfortune that had befallen him, and the little she understood of margin
purchases and mining futures, as an eight-year-old, was still more than
her mother and her older sister cared to know. Her mother was scarcer
than ever, and Shirley was coldly disappointed by the diminished flow of
goods to her, the meagerness of Christmas in 1929, the vaporization
of the Larkspur weekend house in whose pool she'd been assured she
would be swimming the following summer.

It was a testament to her father's abilities that, even when the light
in his eyes had gone out, he not only saved the house but put meat on
the table and continued to pay for Shirley's dancing and voice lessons.
He now worked as the sales manager for Western All-Sport, which he'd
sold, for less than its book value, to cover his other losses. In a mental
state like the one for which Marion was later hospitalized, if not worse,
he dragged himself out of bed every weekday morning, dragged a ra-
zor across his cheeks, dragged himself to the streetcar, dragged himself
through meetings for a company he had no hope of making his again,
and then dragged himself home to an unforgiving wife, a favored daughter whose disappointment tortured him, and Marion, who felt responsible for what had happened. Because she was invisible, she'd noticed
things the other three of them hadn't. She'd known that something
wasn't right.

As her father, too, became invisible—a gray-skinned ghost who slept in his study, spoke in a murmur, shook his head when asked to repeat himself—she did her best to be his caretaker. She met him at the street-car in the evening and asked him how his Golden Bears were doing. She tapped on the terrible closed door of his study and braved the bad smell in it to bring him a piece of fruit she'd cut up. He'd always loved fruit above all other foods, the Californian freshness and variety of it, and even now a light flickered in his eyes when she urged a cut-up pear on him. He didn't smile when he ate it, but he nodded as if it had to be admitted: the pear was good. And Marion, at ten and eleven and twelve, was already aware of how inextricably mixed up good and evil were. When she got her father to enjoy a piece of fruit, there was no telling if the glow she felt was purely love or also the satisfaction of being a better daughter than her sister.

Like the Great Depression, the dark years seemed to have no end. In the fall of 1935, Shirley boarded an eastbound Pullman sleeper, as happy to be escaping San Francisco as Marion was glad to see her go. With something of his old financial magic, her father had come up with a semester's tuition money for Vassar College, thereby fulfilling a long-standing promise to Shirley. But the effort seemed to have finished him. Within weeks of his darling's departure, nothing could induce him to dress and go to work. Isabel, who for six years had occupied herself with such threats to her way of life as the rage for contract bridge, a game which, horribly, *only four women at a time could play*, now finally was forced to reacquaint herself with reality. She obtained a small loan from her Jew-hating brother in Sonoma and persuaded the owners of West-ern All-Sport to grant her husband a short furlough. Although Marion always felt that she and Shirley had drawn very poorly in the mother lottery, she had a grudging admiration for Isabel's resourcefulness in a pinch. Isabel's self-preservative instincts, her ultimately successful battles to maintain her standing in her fivesome, were both laudable and pitiable in their way. And so, as ever, Marion blamed herself for what her father did.

The problem was that she'd discovered theater. Shirley had been the family's presumptive talent, Marion the invisible one, but as soon as her sister left for Vassar, Marion and her best friend had tried out for their school's fall production of *The Five Little Peppers*. Aided, perhaps, by the fact that she was short, she'd landed the part of the smallest and most adored Pepper, Phronsie, and discovered that she, too, had talent. With a familiar sense of ambiguity, uncertain if she was doing something good or something bad, she became a different person in rehearsals, became visible to the other players, entered a kind of trance of not-herselfness. Because the school theater was where this happened, she was smitten with the wobbly paint-smelling flats, the great thunking toggle switches of the light board, the backstage hanging sheet of tin that was endlessly fun to make thunder. After school, instead of going home to look after her father, she stayed to rehearse and paint flats.

In early December, during the play's first dress rehearsal, she was being Phronsie, preparing to charm a real audience, when a gray-braided school administrator entered the theater and called her down from the stage. It was a rainy afternoon, already dark at four thirty. The administrator silently walked her to her house, where all four of her mother's friends had already gathered. Her mother was sitting by the cold grate, her expression blank, a folded sheet of stationery in her lap. There had been, she said, an accident. Perhaps embarrassed to be mincing words in front of her friends, she shook her head and corrected herself. Her expression still blank, she told Marion that her father had taken his own life. She spread her arms, beckoning Marion to come and be embraced, but Marion turned and ran from the room. To get to her father's study, to find him there and show them they were wrong, she had to run up two flights of stairs, but it seemed to her that she was going down, hurtling down a tunnel of guilt toward her punishment. She could hear, strangely distant, the screaming of the girl being punished.

A boat captain that morning had seen a man pulling a child's red wagon on a pier below Fort Mason. When the captain looked again, too soon for the man to have gone back up the pier, the wagon was standing at the end of it. Two hours later, when a body was raised from the water, the police deduced that the wagon had contained the heavy chain the man had locked around his neck and shoulders before jumping. The wagon, a well-made toy of solid steel, its red enamel still bright, had once been a Christmas gift to Shirley, later a stand for potted geraniums behind the house. Marion never read the note that her father had left behind while her mother was out breakfasting with her friends, but it was apparently not an apology or a farewell but simply a confession of the financial situation he'd hidden from her. The family's debts were hopeless, there were liens on everything, multiple liens, a tissue of fraud and bankruptcy. The last conceivably leverageable dollars had been spent on Shirley's first semester at Vassar.

In the story Marion told Sophie about herself, a story she'd worked out in the hospital and in her years of Catholic introspection, her guilt was inextricable from her ability to dissociate. Two nights after her father's death, with the definitive thunk of a light-board switch, she turned herself into Phronsie Pepper, telling herself that the show must go on, and proceeded to be adorable onstage for two hours. After each of the show's three performances, she returned to her grief and her guilt. But now she knew that a switch inside her could be flipped at will. She could turn off her self-awareness and do bad things for the momentary gratification of them. The trick of dissociation was the beginning of her own illness, although she didn't know it yet.

She and Shirley were allowed to finish the semester at their respective schools, but the house was about to be repossessed, its furnishings sold at auction. Her mother crisply informed her that she, Isabel, was going to stay for a while as a houseguest of the richest of her friends. Shirley, who hadn't bothered to come home for the funeral, which some previously unseen cousins of her father had materialized to pay for, intended to find work and lodging in New York City. But what to do about Marion? Her maternal grandmother was senile, and Marion would be one houseguest too many at her mother's friend's. The only people who might take her in were her mother's brothers. If her mother had sent her to her uncle in Arizona, James, the landscape painter, Marion still might have been saved from herself. But Isabel believed that Jimmy was a homosexual, unsuitable as a guardian, and so her younger brother, Roy, in Sonoma, had agreed to house Marion until she finished high school.

Roy Collins was a man of many hatreds. He hated his forebears for pissing away money that should have been his. He hated Roosevelt, labor unions, Mexicans, artists, fairies, and socialite phonies. He especially hated Jews and the socialite phony sister who'd married one. But he wasn't one of those weak men, like his fairy brother or his suicide brother-in-law, who shirked a man's family duties. He had four kids of his own whom he supported by working hard at the farm-machinery distributorship he'd started with the pittance his grandparents had left him. Although his wife and his children were too cowed to disagree with him, he liked to remind them, at nearly every meal, how hard he worked. Marion didn't find Roy especially suitable as a guardian, but he did have money. He was the opposite of her father, a lot richer than one might have guessed from the plainness of his house in Santa Rosa. He'd kept his business solvent through the heart of the Depression, and, as the sole trustee of the family orchards and vineyards, he'd borrowed from himself so heavily, on the trust's behalf, that his own name ended up on the titles to the land. Marion didn't learn about this until she went to Arizona, but it went some way toward explaining why Roy had fed and clothed her for three and a half years, and why he so hated his sister and his brother. It would have been harder to rob them if he hadn't.

Until she was fifteen, Marion had been the mild daughter, the easy daughter, but to live with Roy Collins was to flip the switch in her. The two of them fought about the cigarettes she'd started smoking. They fought about the way she wore her socks, the friends she brought home from Santa Rosa High, the lipstick he couldn't prove she'd stolen from the drugstore. Once she flipped the switch, she hardly knew what she was shouting. At her new school, she gravitated toward the theatrical girls, the fast girls, and the boys who chased them. Her own fast credentials were in order because she came from the city and her father had killed himself. She smoked fiendishly and used the suicide to upset people. She thought that if she was bad enough, hateful enough, Roy might give up and send her somewhere else. But he knew what she wanted, and he sadistically refused to give it to her. Much later, she had the thought that he'd been sexually attracted to her; that people were cruel to what they were afraid of loving.

Her best friend, Isabelle Washburn, was prettier and taller than Marion, a shining blonde with a sharp little nose that drove the boys wild, but Marion was smarter and more daring and made Isabelle laugh. Isabelle fancied herself an actress, but she couldn't be bothered to join the Thespian Society. She preferred going to the movie house, where the ushers, in deference to her nose, would often let in her and Marion for free. Marion's former self was now mostly a memory, but to her the theater was still the place that had distracted her from her father, a place of guilt, and so, although she might have ruled the thespians, she never tried out for another play. She threw herself instead into the real-life drama of discussing boys, provoking boys, and, finally, falling in love with a boy, Dick Stabler, who lived down the street from the Collinses.

Dick was beetle-browed and husky-voiced, with a mild congenital lisp that made her weak in the knees; he looked and sounded the way she imagined Heathcliff. His parents rightly distrusted her, and her senior year was a serial drama of subterfuge and secret outdoor locations where she could be alone with Dick and kiss him and let him touch her breasts. She'd determined that she was "oversexed"—at times, she was literally cross-eyed with her urges, ill with them, dying of them. She was ready to do whatever Dick wanted, including marrying him, but he was bound for college and a higher grade of wife. In the spring, there came a night when his parents heard a noise in their parlor, well after midnight, and his father crept downstairs to investigate, switched on the most glaring light in all of Santa Rosa, and discovered her and Dick on the parlor sofa, clothed but fully horizontal. After this embarrassment, and under the steady pressure of his parents' disapproval, Dick's passion for her faltered. She was left feeling dirty and bad. Her uncle, in one of his rages, went so far as to use the word *slut*, and instead of shouting back at him, as she'd done so many times, she collapsed in tears of self-reproach.

Her mother, in San Francisco, was still a houseguest. In her infrequent letters to Marion, she claimed to miss her *baby*, but she couldn't impose on her hosts by inviting her baby to stay with her, and she wouldn't subject herself to Roy's hostility by coming to Santa Rosa. When Marion took a bus to the city to meet her for lunch at Tadich's, a month before she finished high school, it was eight months since she'd last seen her. She was there to discuss her future, but her mother, whose hair had turned white, and whose cheeks offered red evidence of morning drinking, had exciting news of Shirley in New York. After some difficult years at a Gimbels perfume counter, Shirley was now *on Broadway*—in a small role, to be sure, but launched as an actress, with prospects for larger roles. Isabel's maternal pride, a quality hitherto absent in her, might have seemed poignant to Marion, suggesting as it did a woman desperate to keep up with friends whose sons were Ivy Leaguers, if Marion hadn't felt so enragingly effaced by the news. She felt that someone, probably she herself, ought to murder both Shirley and her mother, to avenge what they'd done to her father. Her "talented" sister in particular needed murdering. When a waiter brought her a plate of fried sand dabs, a Tadich specialty, she ashed her cigarette on them.

At home, in Santa Rosa, Roy Collins had been wearing her down, preying on her shame and self-reproach, and had just about convinced her that she would, indeed, be *very lucky* to start work as a clerk in his distributorship after she graduated. An earlier dream, which was to head to Los Angeles with Isabelle Washburn and try to break into the movies, had gone dormant in the months of her obsession with Dick Stabler. She'd seen less of Isabelle and become more realistic. Although she'd smoked her way to weighing one hundred and three pounds at the doctor's office, careful attention to the calves and ankles flashed onscreen at the California Theatre had led her to suspect that her legs were too peasanty for Hollywood. Isabelle, however, whose legs were better, still intended to go to Los Angeles, and she'd never retracted her invitation to Marion. Sitting in Tadich's, her cigarette ends soaking up melted parsley butter while her mother nattered about the doings of the Francisca Club musical committee, evidently too repelled by the scowling of her baby to broach the subject of her future, Marion experienced a rage so murderous that her decision made itself. She was going to go to Los Angeles and flip the switch and see what happened. She would make herself visible, and she was definitely going to murder someone. She just didn't know who.

Isabelle had a plan for being discovered by Hollywood, involving a cousin who was William Powell's physician, and although she gamely allowed that Marion could be a part of it, she seemed unthrilled that Marion was going with her. In Los Angeles, at the Jericho Hotel, to which they'd retreated after learning that the homes for aspiring actresses all had waiting lists, Isabelle no longer laughed at the things Marion said. When her doctor cousin asked her out to lunch, she decided it was better, after all, if she met him alone. Getting the picture, and adding Isabelle to her list of people in need of murdering, Marion moved into a ladies' rooming house on Figueroa Street. She went to some of the agencies that advertised in the newspaper, but there were a million other girls like her. When she'd exhausted the three hundred dollars that Roy Collins had given her, with an angry vow never to give her anything else, she took a job in the back office of Lerner Motors, which was the largest General Motors dealership in Los Angeles. With her first paycheck, she bought a stack of old plays for a nickel apiece and read them aloud in her room, trying to recapture the feeling of not-herselfness, but she needed a theater and had no idea how to get into one. How had Shirley done it? Had someone discovered her at the perfume counter?

Her first Christmas alone wasn't so bad that it didn't later seem good. A girl in the Lerner back office had invited her to dinner with her family, but she'd had enough of other families' Christmases. In the afternoon, she rode the streetcar to the end of the line in Santa Monica and sat by herself on a bench by the water, parceling out her cigarettes, writing in her diary. She read the entry from exactly one year earlier, when Dick Stabler had given her a silverplate chain and she'd given him a leather-bound volume of Khalil Gibran and her longing for his touch had colored every minute. The weather in Santa Monica was fine, the far snow-capped peaks floating bodyless above the winter haze. Everything seemed more or less in balance. A breeze from the east kept the marine layer offshore, and the sun's downward progress was made tolerable, less alarmingly a reminder of life escaping from her, by the timeless repetition of the waves, their breathlike breaking on the wide, flat beach. The pressure that was lately always in her head, the loneliness and something less definable, a low-grade dread, was balanced by her outward composure. She was a girl interesting enough to herself to sit alone, pretty enough to draw glances from men walking by with their families, tough enough that no one bothered her for long, and smart enough to know that being discovered while sitting on a bench was just a daydream. When the sun finally sank into fog, she walked to the first diner she found open and ate pressed turkey with canned gravy, potato puree, a slice of cranberry jelly.

"Marion?" Sophie Serafimides said.

One of Marion's hips had gone dead and prickly. She was used to an arm or a foot going to sleep, but not a hip muscle, not since the last time she was pregnant. She suspected she had her heaviness to blame for it.

"I'm afraid our time is almost up," Sophie said.

Marion shifted her weight, allowing blood back into her hip, and opened her eyes. Snow was falling on the rail tracks outside the window. The white flakes seemed speeded up by the half-closed slats of the venetian blinds.

"I'd like to know what you mean with your silence," Sophie said. "If you think you might tell me, we could do a double session. I had some cancellations—you're my last patient today."

"I only brought twenty dollars."

"Well." Sophie smiled pleasantly. "You can think of it as a Christmas present, if you want."

Marion shuddered.

"The holiday seems to have a particular association for you," Sophie said. "Will you tell me what it is?"

Marion shut her eyes again. The Christmas she'd spent alone in Santa Monica later seemed like the last day that she and the outside world had been in balance. In the first weeks of 1940, storm after chaotic storm dumped rain on Southern California. The streets were black and oily with it on the evening she stayed late at Lerner Motors to type up papers on the preposterous sale that Bradley Grant had made. Sideways rain was slapping the window of her boardinghouse room long after midnight, when she wrote in her diary, *Something awful has happened and I don't know what to do. It must never, ever happen again.*

Bradley Grant was the star salesman at Lerner. Although Marion was lonely, she'd taken to eating her lunchtime sandwich in an unused room in the parts department. There, she at least had the undivided companionship of a book, until Bradley Grant began intruding on her. Bradley was fifteen years older than she was, but he had the fatless body of a teenager and a face whose handsomeness was hard to judge; there was something cartoonlike about the stretchiness of his features, especially his wide mouth. When he saw Marion with a volume of Maupassant stories, he invaded her lunch-hour sanctuary to hold forth on Maupassant. He was an avid reader, a literary man by training. He struck her as being most interested in himself, so overflowing with words that he had to troll the parts department to find an outlet for them, but one day he brought her his own copy of *Homage to Catalonia*, by the English writer George Orwell. He was distressed about the rise of Fascism in Europe, about which she knew essentially nothing. She duly read the Orwell and began to pay attention to the front page of the newspaper, in order to seem less ignorant to Bradley. One day, he remarked that a girl as intelligent and pretty as Marion ought to be in the front office, and the very next day she was transferred to the front office. At Lerner, the lesser salesmen were rank perspirers, changing their undershirts at midday, afraid of the pink slip every Friday, but Bradley Grant was so valuable to the dealership that only the owner, Harry Lerner, could overrule him. After her transfer, Marion continued to eat her lunchtime sandwich in the back. Becoming a front-office typist and file fetcher was hardly her idea of being discovered.

On the day a person was born, only one date on the calendar, her birthday, was significant, but as she proceeded through life other dates became permanently exalted or befouled, the date her father killed himself, the date she married, the dates her children were born, until the calendar was densely checkered with significance. On the evening of January 24, a young man in a dripping fedora walked into the Lerner showroom shortly before closing time. A lesser salesman sidled up to him and got the brush-off. At Lerner, they called any man who came inside to flaunt his automotive knowledge, or to be fawned over for a couple of minutes, or just to get out of the weather, with no intention of buying, a Jake Barnes. Bradley Grant, who'd coined the name, and who'd already closed three sales that day, strolled up to Marion's desk with an apple and ate it carefully while he studied the young Jake Barnes. "I like his shoes," he said, dropping the apple core in her wastebasket. "Is there somewhere you need to be?" There was never anyplace Marion needed to be. Within a minute, on the floor, Bradley had a hand on the Jake Barnes's shoulder and was helping him into a brand-new Buick Century. She watched Bradley's features stretch into cartoons of astonishment, indifference, compassion, stern admonition. With a gliding tread that let him hurry without seeming to hurry, he returned to her and told her to keep the showroom open and a manager on duty. "Jake and I are making a little cash run," he said, gliding away again. An hour later, he and the young buyer were back on the floor and Marion was typing up the paperwork.

"How easy was that?" Bradley exulted when the buyer was gone. He was bumping one fist on the other like a dice roller. "What do you want to bet I can't move another car today?" His energy reminded Marion of her father's in the pre-crash years. They were the only ones left in the office, and he couldn't sell a car without authorization from a manager. "There's a T-bone steak in it for you," he said to Marion. "What do you want to bet?" Before she could answer, he grabbed an umbrella and ran out of the showroom. From the front door, smoking a cigarette, she saw him working the cars braking at the corner of Hope and Pico, saw drivers rolling down their windows, saw him gesturing at their vehicles and then at the dealership. It was insane, and she didn't know who he was doing it for, himself or her, but watching him brought her latent dread to the surface. Later, in Arizona, she came to think that the sight of Bradley in the rain, with his umbrella, had been a premonition of pure evil. People who weren't seriously Catholic didn't understand that Satan wasn't a charmingly literate tempter, or a funny red-faced devil with a pitchfork. Satan was pain without limit, annihilation of the mind.

"This gentleman has come to the sensible realization that he no longer wishes to drive a Pontiac," Bradley said, ushering into the showroom a heavyset bald man who smelled of drink. It had taken him less than half an hour to find a customer, but he was soaked with sideways rain and street spray. He asked Marion to get the gentleman a cup of coffee while—he winked at her—he had a word with his manager, and then he asked her to pull the keys for the cherry-red '35 Oldsmobile coupe for which the gentleman wished to trade in his Pontiac. The gentleman, he added, would be paying by personal check. The two men returned to the back lot, where the red car was parked. Marion might have walked out and let Bradley close the sale by himself if Roy Collins hadn't made her such a rule-breaker. When the sucker drove away in his Oldsmobile, Bradley produced a flat pint bottle of whiskey and two clean coffee cups.

Perched on a seat warmed by the sucker's fat butt, at Bradley's desk, she could see a small studio photograph of Bradley and his wife and their two little boys. She wondered if the T-bone steak was still coming or if he'd forgotten. She lit another cigarette and sipped the whiskey. "I sure hope that check doesn't bounce."

"It won't," Bradley said, "but I'll cover it if it does. Even without it, we did better than break even."

"His car was worth more?"

"It's one year old! I could have offered him a straight swap, but then he would have started thinking, 'Hey, wait a minute . . .' So I made up a number and let him take me down to half of it."

"That was mean," she said.

"Not at all. Half the fun of owning a superior brand of car is knowing you could pay for it."

"You were doing him a favor."

"It's psychology. This job is all psychology. My problem is I'm so damned good at it. Did you see me in the street? Have you ever seen anything like it?"

She shook her head and took another sip of whiskey.

"It's like a compulsion," Bradley said. "I'm in it and I can't get out of it, because I'm so damned good. People know they're being suckered and they let me do it anyway. They come in here, they've made a solemn vow to themselves, they're going to be strong, they're going to drive a hard bargain. But they only buy a car once a year, or once a decade, or maybe they've never bought a car, and here's *me* who sells cars day in and day out. They have no chance! I'm going to make them weak, and they're going to go home and lie to their wife. They're going to tell her they got a great deal. There's only one red car on the lot, and the guy's got to have it because it's red and, goddamn it, there's only one of them, and what are we going to do tomorrow morning? Get another red car out there. I swear this job is killing my soul."

Marion set her cup on his desk, intending to drink no more. She wondered if she should mention food, or simply go home to bed hungry, but the words kept pouring out of Bradley. In college, in Michigan, he said, he'd written plays and published poems in the college magazine, and then he'd come to Los Angeles to break into the movies as a writer. His soul was still alive then, but he'd met a girl who had dreams of her own, and one thing led to another, and now he was just another member of the goddamned middle class, suckering people for a living. Ideas came to him in the night, original script ideas—like, during the Spanish Civil War, the daughter of Hitler's ambassador to Spain is secretly in love with a Republican intelligence officer, the Fascists are holding the officer's wife and children hostage, he asks the daughter to help them escape from Spain, and she can't be sure if he really loves her or if he's only using her to save his family—he had a million ideas, but when was he supposed to work on them? At the end of a day, his soul was too deadened. The only shred of human decency still left in him, the only way he knew he wasn't the worst person in the world, was how much he loved his boys. They were a weight on him, yeah, a drain on his creative energy, but the responsibility was the only thing standing between him and perdition. Did Marion understand what he was saying? The boys weren't negotiable. His marriage wasn't negotiable. He was never leaving Isabelle.

There was an upsurge in Marion's dread. "Your wife is named Isabel?"

The woman in the studio portrait actually looked a little like Isabelle Washburn. She was older and thicker but similarly blond and small-nosed. Marion stared at the picture, and Bradley stood up and came around his desk and crouched at her feet.

"There's so much soul in your eyes," he said. "Your soul is so alive, I see you and I feel like I'm dying. I'm—God! Do you have any idea how much soul there is in you? I look at you and I think I can't live if I don't have you, but I know I can't have you . . . because . . . Or unless. Because. Unless. Do you understand what I'm saying?"

No amount of whiskey could have overcome her dread, but she drank what was left in her cup. The view from the street was obstructed by shiny floor models, but there were angles from which a person walking by could see Bradley at her feet in the showroom lights.

"Say something," he whispered. "Say anything."

"I think I should go home."

"Okay."

"And maybe find someplace else to work."

"God, no. Marion. I'd die if I couldn't see your face anymore. Please don't do that. I swear I won't pester you."

It was strange to think that the man crouched at her feet had been having such thoughts about her. He was a fascinating person, but in the end, even if one discounted that he was married, he was just a car sales-man. She'd weathered the upwelling of dread with her good sense intact. She made a move to stand up, but Bradley caught one of her hands and held her in place. "I wrote something about you," he said. "Can I tell you what I wrote?"

Taking her silence as consent, he recited a poem.

A woman walks, her name is Marion
Her hair is dark but smells of bright
Sun piercing clouds with clarion splendor
Her eyes downcast but full of light
And darkness both, her mind a wide sky
Both serene and threatening: untouchable

"Who wrote that?" she said.
"I did."
"You wrote that."
"It's the first thing I've written since I don't know when."
"You wrote that about me?"
"Yes."
"Say it again."

He recited it again, with a bashful sincerity that made him definitely handsome. She was having a delayed reaction to the whiskey, an opening of certain floodgates. The apparent tilting of the showroom floor seemed to prove that the cars had their parking brakes set. Despite having seen Bradley persuade a stranger, twice in three hours, that the stranger wanted something he shouldn't have wanted, she wondered if he really might have talent as a writer. The subject of his poem was specific, not interchangeable. She herself had felt herself to be dark and light, sky-wide, and he'd made a rhyme with her name.

"One more time," she said.

She thought a third hearing might tell her, for sure, if he had real talent. In fact, it told her nothing, because all she could hear was that he'd written a poem about her. She leaned back in the chair and let the whiskey shut her eyes. "Hoo-eee," she admitted. The switch in her was in the Off position, which was another way of saying she didn't care. Her father with a chain around his neck, dead on the bottom of the bay. Her sister uncatchable no matter how Marion might run. She didn't care.

When Bradley drew her to her feet and kissed her, it was as if her body were picking up at exactly the oversexed point it had left off with Dick Stabler. It was horrifying how much a man wanting her was what it wanted. She felt she couldn't press herself against Bradley hard enough, she needed harder pressing, and Bradley gave it to her. He backed her against the immovable weight of a gleaming Cadillac 75 and pressed her where Dick Stabler hadn't dared to. There was a thing that her hips were capable of doing but hadn't ever done. To let them do it, to fully relax them, even upright, even in a dress, with Bradley between her knees in his still-damp trousers, felt momentous. Roy Collins, on the eve of her departure from Santa Rosa, had predicted what would happen if she wasn't careful in Los Angeles. Roy hadn't used the word *slut* again, but he'd made it very clear that if Marion got in trouble she could expect no further help from him. And now here she was, opening her legs for a married man. Over Bradley's head, when he happened to lower it to her neck, she saw the uneven steps the office wall clock was taking toward eleven o'clock, the hour at which she'd be locked out of her rooming house. She was feeling ill with hunger as the whiskey wore off.

As if putting a bookmark in a novel, she pushed him away and wordlessly moved to get a cigarette. He, too, said nothing while he turned off the bright lights, locked the front door, and led her to his '37 LaSalle. By the time they reached her house, they had only ten minutes to talk before the night manageress threw the deadbolt.

She put out the third of the cigarettes she'd chain-smoked. "I don't see how I'm going to go to work in the morning."

"Same as you always do," he said.

There was a problem that needed solving before it worsened, but she suspected that the problem had no solution—that she was no stronger than the man who came to Lerner and saw the only red car. Rather than waste her last minutes on pointless talk, she slid over and put her arms around Bradley. The car shook in the gusts of wind and she with it. Inside the house, as soon as she'd shut her door behind her, she touched herself the way she'd learned to in the frustrated aftermath of making out with Dick Stabler. But those had been more innocent days. Now she felt too lonely to concentrate on dispelling her sexual urge, too scared of her badness to surrender to it. She needed to cry instead; and this was the first time the slippage occurred.

It was one in the morning and she couldn't account for two hours. Her sad little room, with its nicked and peeling furniture and its smoke-saturated fabrics, its lamp overbright but wrongly positioned for reading in bed, presented itself as a collection of random places that she thought she might have stared at, pushed her face into, banged her forehead against. Her bedspread lay in a heap in a corner. There was no fresh smoke, but her ashtray was upended on her bed, a dirty avalanche of old butts and ashes at the base of the pillow. Her impression was of a person who'd frantically defended herself against evil spirits beating on the window in the form of sideways rain. Now she was painfully hungry, but she appeared to be uninjured. *No one in the world is more alone than I,* she wrote in her diary.

The next morning brought a break between storms. She ate a big plate of eggs before she went to work, and the sky above the city, the startling blue gaps between the rushing clouds, was an encouraging reminder of more innocent San Francisco winters. She thought she might be all right if she changed her routine, ate her lunch with the other office girls, and made sure never to be alone again with Bradley Grant. But when she arrived at Lerner and tried to say good morning to her manager, she discovered that the slippage hadn't left her uninjured.

Her condition was that she could barely speak. The impulse that should have led to speaking was diverted into swallowing and blushing, a clotted sensation in her chest, an involuntary recollection of opening her legs. All morning, on and off the floor, her mind was so scrambled with self-consciousness that when she opened her mouth her mind lagged behind and then dashed forward, propelled by the anxiety that what she was saying was unintelligible. Each time, she found that she'd spoken halfway appropriately, and each time this seemed like amazing luck.

At lunchtime, in the lounge with some other girls, she sat in a posture of friendly attentiveness and tried to listen to their conversation, but her eyes refused to look at whoever was speaking.

". . . on sale at Woolworth's, you wouldn't think they'd . . ."

". . . an inch too wide to fit, how on earth do you measure it three times and get . . ."

". . . me to the premiere last Thursday, he knows the guy who . . ."

". . . but then your hands smell like orange all day, even if you wash them . . ."

". . . Marion?"

Without raising her eyes, she turned toward the girl, Anne, who'd said her name. Anne was the one who'd invited her to Christmas with her family. Anne was kind.

"I'm sorry." Despite great effort to breathe, Marion's voice was choked. "What did you say?"

"What happened last night?" Anne repeated with a kind smile.

"Oh." Marion's face burned. "Oh."

"Mr. Peters said Bradley was still selling at nine o'clock."

She thought her head might explode. "I'm so tired," she found that she had said.

"I bet you are," Anne said.

"What . . . do you mean?"

"I don't know where that man gets his energy. He's like a selling *fiend.*"

The lounge was a minefield of female eyes on her. She tried to say more but quickly realized it was hopeless. All she could do was stand up and go back to her desk. Behind her, in her imagination, there ensued an appalled discussion of her sluttiness.

Although she'd spent an inordinate amount of time alone in Los Angeles, she didn't consider herself shy. The way her new condition felt to her was that every person who spoke to her was somehow Bradley Grant; every exchange of words, no matter how trivial, a rehearsal of the dire conversation she feared she would be having with him. A year later, in the hospital, one of the psychiatrists asked her if she wouldn't rather be like other girls, not always so deathly serious—there was nothing wrong with small talk—gaiety was attractive in a girl—wouldn't it be nice to escape from her thoughts in the flow of a light conversation? Marion wanted to file a criminal complaint about the psychiatrist. She happened to know that not all men required gaiety. She wondered how many other women on the ward had encountered the kind of man excited by morbid taciturnity: the literary kind of man, for whom craziness was romantic, or the sensualist kind, to whom still waters betokened sexually churning depths, or the chivalrous kind, who dreamed of saving someone broken.

Bradley was all of those kinds of man. At least two other unmarried girls at Lerner were prettier than Marion, and Anne was as much a book reader as she was, so something else must have attracted Bradley. He'd detected craziness in her before she'd sensed it herself. Without her knowing it, her new condition made her more interesting to him, not less. On January 31, another fateful date, she returned from a protracted afternoon bathroom break and found, on her desk, an envelope with her name typed on it. Bradley was outside on the lot with a customer while the lesser salesmen stood at the windows, watching their lives go down the drain. It seemed likely to her that she'd been pink-slipped, and she opened the envelope to make sure. Seeing a typewritten poem, she ought to have thrown it in her wastebasket or at least waited until evening to read it. Instead, she took it back to the bathroom and locked herself in a stall.

SONNET FOR MARION

I dream I'm at the wheel and I've forgotten how
To drive or never learned. I'm dreaming I'm
Nineteen again. The car is young and powerful,
It seems to drive itself, and by the time
I find the brakes I've gone into a spin,
A blur of storm-tossed palms and traffic lights.
And you are at the wheel, not I. Within

You a calm capability, as on that night—
Oh, that night, when I was spinning and you
Were speed and safety both. Did I only dream
That, too? In your sustaining arms I knew
What I had doubted: I'm younger than I seem.
To dream of happiness, wake up, and walk on air
Is to know the chance of happiness awake is there.

Sitting in the stall, she tried to read past the sheer fact of the poem and understand what he was saying. The word that made no sense to her was *capability*. She was hardly even capable of speaking! It didn't occur to her that Bradley might simply have used a faulty noun. She wondered if he'd meant that she was capable of saving him: if somehow, in the showroom of a car dealership, she'd been discovered after all, by a man of sufficient talent to fulfill his dream of writing for Hollywood, a dream his marriage had smothered but Marion might be capable of reviving and might yet join her own dream with. Wasn't that what the poem was saying? That some dreams were so vivid that they became reality?

She returned to the floor feeling elated, incipiently capable, and was disappointed when she could barely decipher her manager's words to her. Now it was elation, not shame, that scrambled her mind, while the more general and important fact—that there was something diseased about a mind so easily scrambled—continued to elude her. When Bradley came back into the showroom with his customer, he was like a powerful magnetic field and she a charged needle. The field repelled her when she turned in his direction and attracted her when she turned away.

In the evening, as closing time approached, the field approached her desk. "I'm such an ass," he said.

The manager, Mr. Peters, was standing within earshot. Bradley sat down sideways on a desk. "I promised you a T-bone steak last week," he said. "You've probably been thinking, yeah, another salesman's promise."

"I don't need a steak," Marion managed to say.

"Sorry, doll, I'm a man of my word. Unless there's somewhere else you need to be?" It was clever of him to approach her in the presence of Mr. Peters, who was older and sexually blind to her. It made the invitation seem innocent. "I thought we'd go to Dino's, if that's okay with you." Bradley turned to Mr. Peters. "What do you think, George? Dino's for a steak?"

"If you don't mind the noise," Mr. Peters said.

The rain outside was hurling itself down vertically, the car lot a shallow lake with currents rippling in the showroom lights and cresting at the storm drains. Marion sat in Bradley's dark LaSalle with him, facing a fence in an unlighted corner of the lot, while the rain made a warlike sound on the roof. In her head, she rehearsed a short sentence, *I'm actually not hungry.* Even in her head, she stumbled over the words.

Bradley asked her if she'd read his poem. She nodded.

"It's a tricky form, the sonnet," he said, "if you're strict about the rhyme and meter. In the old days, the word order was more flexible, you know, *In me thou seest, where late the sweet birds sang,* but who talks like that anymore? I wonder if anyone ever really said *In me thou seest.*"

"Your poem is good," she said.

"You liked it?"

She nodded again.

"Will you let me buy you dinner?"

"I'm not actually . . . actually not I'm—not hungry."

"Hmm."

"Maybe just take me home?"

The rain came down harder and then abruptly let up, as if the car had gone under a bridge. When Bradley leaned toward Marion, she shied from the magnetism.

"This is wrong," she said, finding the voice she used to have. "This isn't fair."

"You don't like me."

She didn't know if she liked him. The question somehow wasn't pertinent.

"I think you have talent as a writer," she said.

"On the basis of two little poems?"

"You do. I could never write a sonnet."

"Sure you could. You could make one up right now. Da-*duh*, da-*duh*, da-*duh*, da-*duh*, rhyme *A.* Da-*duh*, da-*duh*, da-*duh*, da-*duh*, rhyme *B.*"

"Don't ruin it," she said.

"What?"

"Don't ruin what you wrote for me. It's so beautiful."

He tried again to kiss her, and this time she had to push him away.

"Marion," he said.

"I don't want to be that kind of girl."

"Which kind is that?"

"You know which kind." Her face cramped up with tears. "I don't want to be a slut."

"You could never in a million years be that kind of girl."

She pressed on her face to stop the cramp. "You hardly know anything about me."

"I can see into your soul. You're the opposite of that kind of girl."

"But you said your marriage is not negotiable."

"I did say that."

"Do you write poems for your wife?"

"Not since a very long time ago."

"I don't mind if you write poems for me. I like it. In fact, I love it. I wish—" She shook her head.

"Wish what?"

"I wish you'd write a play, or a movie, and I could star in it."

Bradley seemed astonished. "That's what you want?"

"It's just a dream," she hastened to say. "It isn't real."

He put his hands on the wheel and bowed his head. He could so easily have opened the door a crack and said he wasn't sure about his marriage. He must have sensed that she wasn't well. Perhaps he felt that lying to a nutty girl wasn't sporting.

"What if I did," he said. "What if I wrote a part for you. Maybe the daughter of the German ambassador—I almost think I could do it, as long as I could picture you in the role. That's what I'm missing, something beautiful to picture instead of all the ugliness I bring home. I don't get any support at all from Isabelle. She doesn't even like it when I read a book. She's jealous of a book! And boy does she get angry when I try to tell her about a new idea. It's like she's Dr. Freud and I'm the patient, just because I have ideas for a screenplay. 'Oh dear, the patient is displaying symptoms again. We thought we'd cured him of ambition, and now he's had a relapse.' She's so bitter about her own dreams, she can't stand the fact that I still have my own."

"Do you love her?" Marion said. Hearing herself ask this question made her feel older and wiser: capable.

"She's good with the boys," Bradley said. "She's a good mother. Maybe a little too anxious—every little sniffle is a sure sign of whooping cough. But you wouldn't believe how quickly the most interesting person in the world can turn into the most boring person you'll ever meet."

"She used to be interesting."

"I don't know. I don't know. She sure as hell isn't now."

Marion could simply have offered him friendship and inspiration. She wasn't yet nutty enough to believe she could star in a movie he'd written. His stroke of genius salesmanship was to describe a person she felt like murdering. He didn't know that his wife had the same name as Marion's mother and her faithless school friend, but as soon as he gave her a more detailed Isabelle to hate, the door was open for nuttier thoughts to rush in. The thought that she, Marion, really was more capable than he. The thought that he was too kindhearted to face the obvious truth. The thought that only she could save him from unhappiness, only she could rescue him as a writer, by believing in him and helping him face the truth about his love-less marriage. What kind of vengeful witch got jealous of a *book*? Isabelle needed murdering for that, and the way for Marion to do it was to move over on the seat. She was short enough to kneel on it, slender enough to fit between him and the steering wheel, and once she was in his arms the dimension of moral significance disappeared.

Bradley Grant took her virginity on the seat of a 1937 LaSalle Series 50 with fogged-up windows, on the lot of Lerner Motors. The act hurt less than certain girls in Santa Rosa had led her to suppose it would, but later, in the bathroom at her rooming house, she discovered more blood than she expected. The white porcelain ran red as she rinsed her under-linens. Only in the morning did she realize that her monthly period had started.

There wasn't much room for her condition to worsen, but in February it worsened. She felt trapped in a metal cube that was filling up with water, leaving only a tiny pocket of air at the top to breathe. The air was sanity. At every turn, she encountered constriction, most cruelly in how little time she had alone with Bradley. All day, she worked within a hundred paces of him, but he said they had to be very careful. At lunchtime she pressed him into a corner of her old sanctuary in the parts department, but the room had a window through which their corner was obliquely visible. Harry Lerner had forbidden further selling of cars after closing time, and Bradley kept finding reasons he had to go home in the evening. They finally resorted, again, to the seat of his LaSalle. Although it seemed a lot riskier on a moonlit night, without fog on the windows, she kept him there until 10:45. The following week, on his day off, he took her to a motel in Culver City, but even there she felt constricted, because it wasn't enough to make love. They needed to discuss the future, because surely Bradley now understood that he couldn't stay married to Isabelle, and their lovemaking left no time for talk. Not until they were back in his car did she ask him if he'd started writing again.

"Not yet," he said.

It was a reasonable and honest answer, but it greatly upset her. The distance to her house was diminishing as he drove, their time for talking dwindling, the cube filling up with water.

"I don't know if I can do it," he said.

"Have you tried?"

"All I can think about is you."

"That's all I can think about, too. I mean—you."

"I just don't know if I can do it."

"I know you can."

"Not writing," he said. "This. I don't know if I'm cut out for loving two women at the same time."

Less than a mouthful of air was left in the cube. All Marion was able to say with it was "Oh."

"It's tearing me in two," he said. "I've never met anyone I've wanted like you. Everything about you is exactly right. It's like I was born with your face imprinted on my brain."

She didn't have the same feeling about him. If she'd passed him on the street a year ago, she wouldn't have looked twice. For a moment, as if from outside herself, she could glimpse the outlines of the thing inside her, the obsession that was growing in her, and recognize it as an object foreign to a normal person's desires. But then, in a blink, she was inside it again.

"Let's go back to the motel," she said.

"We can't."

"It wasn't enough. I need more time with you."

"I want more, too, but we can't. I'm already late."

Late meant Isabelle. The prospect of relinquishing Bradley felt so life-threatening to Marion that if she murdered Isabelle it would be an act of self-defense. She began to hyperventilate.

"Marion," he said. "I know it's hard for you, but it's even harder for me. It's tearing me in two."

He said more, but her breathing drowned it out. Black cars and white buildings, winos with paper bags and women in sheer stockings, *loving two people* and *tearing me in two*. Either she breathed so hard she passed out or another slippage was occurring. The hand that Bradley put on hers, in front of her rooming house, was burning cold. She still couldn't hear what he was saying, she only knew she had to get away.

The second slippage was worse, the number of hours unaccounted for greater, and afterward she found scrapes on her knuckles, a red bump on her forehead. She was an hour late for work the next morning and wept disproportionately when Mr. Peters mildly chided her. At lunchtime, fearing suffocation if she stayed inside, fearing death if Bradley tried to speak to her, she fled the dealership and walked randomly on named and numbered streets. Snowfall from the storms extended down the spectral mountains, but the March sun was strong, spring already in the air. She was beginning to breathe more freely when she caught sight of a familiar face. Coming toward her, in the crosswalk at Grand Avenue and Ninth Street, was Isabelle Washburn. Marion lowered her head, but Isabelle stopped her by the arm.

"Hey, kid. Aren't you even gonna say hi?"

Underneath a light coat with a sheen both lavender and green, Isabelle wore a green-on-white polka-dot dress, not cheap. She'd side-curled her hair and adopted a slack-jawed way of speaking that sounded copied from the movies. It transpired that she blamed her nincompoop cousin, rather than her utter lack of acting talent, for the failure of her plan for being discovered, but she was making okay money as a photography model and living with some other gals in a bungalow behind the Egyptian Theatre. It could have been Marion's imagination, diseased by her own wantonness, but Isabelle's repeated references to her landlord gave her the impression that he was more than just a landlord. Her artificial new way of speaking suggested a heart hardened by rough experience. "So anyways, that's me," she said. "Whatcha been up to yourself?"

"I'm well," Marion said, which was so funny to her she almost laughed.

"Landed on your feet and all that?"

"Fine, fine. Yes. I have a steady job. Which I should probably get back to."

Isabelle frowned. "Whadja do to your head?"

"I couldn't tell you."

Isabelle dug in her purse. "Lemme put some powder on that."

Right there on the street corner, Marion let her erstwhile friend apply makeup to the bump on her forehead. The casual sisterliness of the ministration choked her up. Isabelle raised her chin with her finger and inspected her with a professional eye. "That's a little better," she said, closing her compact. "You know, we really ought to get together sometime. You used to crack me up so much. Remember Hal Chalmers and Pokie Turner? Dick Thtabler? You ought to just drop in if you're ever out my way. I'm literally right behind the Egyptian, on Selma, it's a bright-red house, you can't miss it."

Isabelle seemed to have forgotten that she'd dumped Marion nine months ago. Her life in the meantime had been so crowded with event that high school was already historical to her, and indeed it did now seem remarkable that Marion had ever imagined their remaining friends after graduation. But she no longer felt like murdering Isabelle. Instead, she felt sad about what life was doing to her. Nine months later, when life had done even worse to Marion and she had no one to turn to, she not only remembered Isabelle's sloppy kindness at the corner of Ninth and Grand. She remembered that Isabelle lived in a bright-red bungalow behind the Egyptian Theatre.

She'd become—had made herself—a problem Bradley had to man-age. A few days after her second slippage, a blond customer in her thirties had come to the showroom. Nearly all the customers at Lerner were men, and Marion hadn't seen Bradley work his magic on a woman since she'd become obsessed with him. Suddenly the cartoonish plasticity of his fea-tures seemed grotesque. After the woman left, without buying, Marion's hatred of his wife came to a screaming boil and blew a gasket in her head. When he went to the men's room, she followed him into it and threw her arms around his neck, tried to climb him. Her question was when they could make love again. She desperately needed to make love with him again, and in his fear of being caught in the men's room he agreed. They went back to Culver City that very evening. The pleasure sex gave her was increasing exponentially with each encounter. Bradley avowed that, until that night, he'd never understood what passion was. He avowed that he was absolutely mad for her. When he drove her home, he told her she had to quit working at Lerner and find a better place to live.

She went to work in the steno pool at a property-management com-pany where a former Lerner salesman, a friend of Bradley's, worked. The friend found her an efficiency apartment in Westlake, and Bradley paid three months' rent in advance, peeling bills off the stack he kept folded in his front pocket. Technically, this made her a kind of prosti-tute, but to her the bills represented so many dollars that wouldn't go to his wife and his boys, dollars rightfully hers, redeemable against a future in which she'd be his wife. Her surety was their rightness for each other. Through April and May and June, she experienced the rightness on the apartment's Murphy bed, among the cigarette burns on the carpet, on the checkered oilcloth that covered the little dining table. After sex, the words she struggled to speak elsewhere came easily. Bradley brought her new books to read, and she now followed the war in Europe avidly, be-cause it interested him. Most thrilling to her was his Spanish screenplay, for which she was acting out the character of the German ambassador's daughter. As their joint idea for the story emerged in detail, she made shorthand notes on it in bed, a nude stenographer. Working on the story excited her extremely and excited Bradley, too. When he took the pad and pencil from her and set them aside, she lay back for him in a state of not-herselfness, imagining herself as the ambassador's daughter, as if she were the actress playing her. At work, it wasn't hard to find an idle hour for typing out the story notes, sometimes adding new ideas of her own. The unattached young men in the office might have known about her situation with Bradley—she seemed to be invisible to them. She was the taciturn girl who was proficient in Gregg and didn't misspell words.

In July, Bradley took Isabelle and his boys on a car trip to Sequoia and Yosemite. Marion had begged him to use his vacation to get started on the screenplay, which she'd now completely outlined for him, but he said he owed the vacation to his boys, and off they went. As long as she hadn't had to go more than four days without seeing him, as long as their rightness for each other was regularly confirmed, she'd avoided further episodes of slippage. But a weekend alone, after a week with no hope of seeing Bradley, was endless. The very sun seemed evil to her in the way it dawdled in her windows, took its insolent time in going down. She couldn't read a book or go to the pictures. The passage of time needed vigilant monitoring. She sat perfectly still, trying not to even blink, until the fear of relaxing her vigilance became apocalyptic, as though the world might end if she so much as flexed a muscle in her foot. She was very, very low. For some reason, she was especially averse to bathing, the sensation of water on her skin.

Bradley was due back on the night of Saturday the 27th and had promised to come and see her on Sunday. She spent Saturday night on her back with her eyes open, because to close them was to picture him in bed with his Isabelle, to consider the countless hours that Isabelle had had to undermine his confidence as a writer, and to entertain the suspicion that Isabelle was right: to see him as he really was and see herself as she really was, a lonely girl trading her body for a fantasy. Time was the enemy when she was alone, because the fantasy required effort to sustain and her strength was finite. In the morning, unslept, unbathed, she boiled and ate two eggs and lay down again. The sun had an evil new trick of changing its position suddenly, jumping forward, as if to mock her for Bradley's non-arrival. It was setting by the time she heard a tapping on her door, the turning of a key. How she must have looked when he saw her on the bed! Flat-haired, puffy-eyed, parched-lipped, mad. He kneeled on the floor and kissed her cheek. She didn't feel a thing.

"I'm sorry I didn't come sooner," he said. "We had a mouse problem. Mouse poop all over the kitchen. I finally found a nest of them in the space behind the phonebook drawer. Four little baby mice in chewed-up phonebook paper. I tried to ladle them out with a metal spoon, so I could let them go outside, but they started crawling away—it was horrible. I had to crush them with the spoon, which turns out to be pretty hard when you're reaching inside a cabinet and you can't see what you're doing and your wife is screaming in your ear."

How many times did you fuck her? someone said loudly. The atrocious word argued against its having been her, but who else could it have been?

"I wanted to be here earlier," Bradley said, as if he hadn't heard the question, "but everything was such a mess. The boys were fighting, they had too much time together in the car, and, Jesus, the mice. The parents are still in the cabinets somewhere. I can't stay long."

"Why stay at all?" she definitely said.

"I'm sorry. I know it was hard for you, but it was hard for me, too."

"You don't know what hard is."

"Marion. Honey. I do know." With a mouse-butchering hand, he brushed hair from her eyes and stroked her head. "I've done a bad thing—a bad thing to you. You're so beautiful, so fragile, so serious. Oh God, you're serious. And I'm just a goddamned car salesman."

She began to cry, hysterically. It ate into the little time they had, but it was a release from the desiccated paralysis she'd suffered for two weeks. It restored her to sensation again, and by and by it had the added cruel benefit of making Bradley stay far longer than he'd intended to—of complicating the lies he'd have to tell when he got home—because he couldn't resist her fragility. Her tear-wet face compelled a rough undressing of her, and she was serious, all right. As he had his way with her, she focused intensely on his face, alert to any subtle sign that his pleasure in her had diminished. Her own pleasure had become incidental. The only thing that mattered was Bradley.

Three nights later, he surprised her by showing up at her office and asking her out for a hamburger. As he drove to a Carpenter's, her feral intelligence, which was warning her that no good could come of surprise changes to their routine, was at war with the hope that he'd finally found the courage to leave Isabelle. Her feral intelligence was correct. In his car, at the drive-in, after eating his burger in nervously wolfing bites, while hers sat untouched on her lap, he licked a bit of bloody ketchup from his finger and said he'd done some hard thinking on his vacation. He said—oh, what was it he was saying?—*find my way to putting them through the pain of made my bed and now I've got to lie deserve a man who's worthy of your one-hundred percent not fifty percent because fifty percent is not be alone with you again because you'll never stop being the person not fair to you isn't fair to I'm never going to be a realistically realistic it's just not fair to I should have known worst thing terrible realistically so terrible get over it never get over it . . .* While Bradley's rubbery features stretched expressively, she could feel the varieties of redness surging in her own face, tomato, scarlet, crimson, garnet, beet, as if she were a chameleon. Imagining how comical she looked, she started laughing.

He stared at her, and the worry in his face was even funnier to her. She waved a limp hand, as helplessly laughing people did by way of apology, and tried to control herself. "I'm sorry," she said. Another mirthful snort escaped her. "I was thinking about the baby mice."

"Jesus. Why are you laughing at that?"

"Because—poor you. Having to mash them with a spoon." She giggled and then laughed harder, caving forward with it. Perhaps she was aware that Bradley couldn't very well abandon her while she was acting crazy, but she was legitimately in the grip of her hilarity. He would certainly think twice before he took her out in public again. This thought, too, was hilarious to her.

"Should I be worried about you?" he said when she'd finally regained control.

"You should worry about yourself," she said. "I'm a lot bigger than a mouse."

"What does that mean?"

"What does it sound like it means?"

He glanced at the Ford coupe parked to his left, the uniformed backside of a female carhop leaning in the passenger-side window.

"I need you to believe that I will never get over this," he said, his expression very serious. Marion adjusted her own expression correspondingly, but her attempted severe frown felt so ridiculous that she giggled at it.

"Please, please, please," he said.

"I'm trying to be serious, but maybe you had me wrong."

"We have to stop," he said.

"Oh. Why?"

"I told you. It was the very first thing I told you. I'm not going to destroy my family. I'm not going to leave the mother of my children."

"You also said you'd die if you couldn't be with me. Does that mean you're going to die now?"

He covered his face with his hands. If she'd ever really liked him, she definitely didn't now, but the matter of liking was more irrelevant than ever. She could clearly perceive the contours of her obsession with him. It would have been sensible to tear it from her skull, but the object had grown too large to be removed without splitting her head open. Despite its sick enormity, it was also too beautiful to her.

"I'll probably die if I can't be with you," she said, in a factual tone.

"No, you won't. You're going to find somebody who's better for you."

"Do you see what I'm saying, though?"

"Honestly, I'm not following all of it."

"You're wrong," she said, opening her door. "That's all. I know you're wrong."

As she made her way home, past Westlake Park, she didn't feel low. She felt nervously elated, like a general on the eve of a decisive battle. She and Bradley were in a crisis that she needed all her wits to navigate. To have walked away from the drive-in voluntarily, to not have made a screeching scene and begged him to reconsider, seemed in hindsight an inspired tactic. Now she just needed to be patient. Between his job and his family duties and his attentiveness to her, Bradley had been too overstretched to exercise his talent as a writer. The fantasy of him returning to her apartment, unannounced, in the middle of the night, after a month of separation, fired up by the screenplay he'd written and desperate to get her

opinion of it, the fantasy of their reading the pages together and her finding them magnificent, was so compelling to her, so enjoyably repeatable
and refinable, that she hardly slept that night. In the morning, she felt like
skipping on her way to work. Instead of burying her head in a newspaper,
she chatted with the other typists and smiled at the unmarried men.

For a number of weeks, she was sustainedly elated—uplifted by her
certainty that her strategy of not pestering Bradley, of letting him wonder about her and feel remorseful, of leaving him alone to write, would
bring him back. Imagining that he could somehow see her and be jealous, she let one of the young men from the office take her to dinner and
a movie. Afterward, she couldn't remember the man saying anything
at all, which led her to wonder if she'd talked nonstop about Hitler and
Ribbentrop and Churchill. Perhaps she had. The man didn't ask her on
another date, and this was fine with her, because he barely existed. The
edges of existence more generally had begun to fray, her lack of sleep
taking its toll. Finally, one evening in September, she decided to leave
work early and go and see Bradley at Lerner Motors. The date, 9/9, was
irresistibly auspicious.

Bradley was drinking coffee with Mr. Peters and blanched at the
sight of her. Nervous but residually elated, she greeted the other girls
as if they'd been great friends of hers. One of them had an engagement
ring, another was expecting and about to quit, a lesser salesman had been
fired. To reconcile her urgent need to speak with her utter lack of personal things to speak about, Marion expressed strong opinions, derived
from the newspaper, about the situation in Europe and the necessity of
American intervention. One by one, the girls excused themselves, until
only Anne remained. Anne remarked, kindly, that Marion didn't seem
well, and Marion allowed that she'd been having trouble sleeping. Anne
asked if she'd like to come home with her and have some soup.

"No, I'm here to see Bradley," Marion said. "He still owes me a T-bone
steak."

Anne's expression became grave.

"He's a man of his word."

"Why don't you come home with me instead," Anne said.

"Another time," Marion said, walking away. Her head was pounding and her body felt made entirely of chalk. She might have preferred to be asleep if sleep had been a possibility. Bradley was standing by the still-unsold Cadillac 75 with a red-haired man, an obvious Jake Barnes, and listening with cartoonish raptness. He had a way of making every customer feel astonishingly interesting. Marion walked up to the Jake Barnes and said, "I'm very sorry, but I believe I was here before you."

Bradley's gaze looped all around her without alighting on her. "Marion," he said.

The Jake looked at his watch. "It's all right."

"No, no." Bradley placed a hand on her back and turned her away. "You need to wait," he told her, as if speaking to a child.

"Is that not what I've been doing?"

"Just—wait. All right?"

She waited, prominently, smoking a cigarette, on one of the leather couches for customers. The inside of her mouth was chalky, too. Her lack of sleep had broken the formerly continuous world into sharp fragments. The worried looks of Anne and Mr. Peters, at their desks, glanced off her like arrows off a thing of chalk.

Without knowing how she got there, she found herself outside with Bradley, on the sidewalk around the corner from Lerner. The tops of the street-shadowing buildings blazed in the setting sun. The air was acrid with motor exhaust.

"Oh, honey," he was saying. "You look so tired."

"I'm sorry."

"I didn't mean it in a bad way. Just—have you been eating enough?"

"I eat eggs. I like eggs. I'm sorry."

"You keep saying you're sorry when it's me who should be sorry."

"I'm sorry."

Bradley squeezed his eyes shut. "Oh, God."

"What?" she said eagerly.

"It's killing me to see you again."

"Will you come home with me?"

"It's better if I don't."

"You don't have to stay long."

He sighed. "There's a PTA meeting I promised Isabelle I'd go to."

"Is it an important meeting?" she said, genuinely curious.

The long wait was over. She stood patiently outside a phone booth while he lied to his wife. She was patient in his car with him, too. It was he who was impatient—as soon as they were inside her building, he pushed her against the wall by the mailboxes and kissed her savagely. She still felt chalky, but apparently to him her flesh was pliable, and that was enough.

Except that it wasn't. The goal of her waiting had been achieved, but the waiting had stretched the connection between her obsession and its object past the breaking point. Their lovemaking, repeated several times before he left her apartment, delighted her only in what it signified. The actual person on top of her, the panting car salesman with coffee breath, was a stranger to the world she lived in now. Although she clearly signified something to him, too, she was beyond trying to imagine what it was.

Later, in Arizona, she couldn't remember why she'd told him he didn't need to be careful. Maybe, being confused about so many things, she'd been confused about her time of month. Maybe, knowing that Bradley didn't love the alternative to being careful, and not daring to diminish his pleasure in their reunion, she'd simply hoped for the best. Or maybe, although she definitely didn't remember *wanting* to be pregnant, her feral intelligence had disastrously miscalculated without her being aware of it. But there was also the fact that, despite her obvious unwellness in the head, Bradley had believed her when she said he didn't have to be careful. Was it possible that he, too, without being aware of it, had wanted to make a baby? In Arizona, in the absence of any clear memory, she concluded that her pregnancy had been God's plan for her, His way of testing her: that His will manifested itself in the actions of His children, regardless of their reasons. This settled the question.

When she told the story of her crack-up to Sophie Serafimides, it wasn't hard to omit the pregnancy, because more than enough other things had happened to explain her landing in a locked ward. There was the late night, a week after the first reunion, when Bradley showed up at her door with a half-emptied whiskey bottle. There was the second night of that sort. There were the two weeks in which she didn't see him, and then the dreadful letter he sent her. There was her second visit to Lerner Motors, which didn't go well, and her third visit, when she tried to make Bradley smell her hand, with which she'd touched herself privately, and was hustled out the door by Mr. Peters. There was her ensuing catatonia at the property-management company, which resulted in her being fired. There was the stretch of days that she mostly couldn't account for, interminable days in an apartment on which rent would soon be due. Finally, there was the warm November afternoon when she went to Bradley's house, whose address she'd found in the phonebook, to have a word with his wife.

The neat, nearly identical houses on Keniston Avenue looked to her like toy houses or a movie set. She was very frightened when she rang Bradley's doorbell, but she couldn't think of any other way to show him he was wrong. Paradoxically, she needed to enlist his wife's help. When Isabelle learned that Bradley was in love with someone else, namely Marion, whose face had been imprinted on his brain at birth, she'd understand the folly of her marriage. Imagining Bradley divorced was more pleasurable and less strenuous to Marion than wondering why she hadn't had her monthly period. She hoped it was only because she was malnourished and emotionally stressed—she'd heard of such things—because her chances with Bradley depended on her being his liberation. A baby would make him feel trapped and disgusted, and she could never play the German ambassador's daughter if she was fat with one.

To her great surprise, a blond boy of seven or eight opened the front door. In her thousand imaginings of the scene, no one but Isabelle had ever come to the door.

The boy stared at her. She stared at him. The moment seemed to last about an hour.

"Mom," the boy shouted over his shoulder. "There's a lady here."

He went away, and Isabelle Grant appeared with a dish towel in her hands. She was thick in the middle, not as tall as Marion had pictured her.

Like Isabelle Washburn, she seemed more pitiable than murderable. This, too, was unexpected. "Can I help you?" she said.

In Marion's face the chameleoning reds, not the least bit funny to her now.

"Miss?" Isabelle said. "Are you all right?"

"Your, uh, your husband," Marion said.

"Yes?"

"Your husband doesn't love you anymore."

Now alarm, suspicion, anger. "Who are you?"

"It's very unfortunate. But you bore him."

"Who are you?"

"I . . . well. Do you see what I'm saying?"

"No. You must have the wrong house."

"You're not Isabelle Grant?"

"Yes, but I don't know you."

"Bradley knows me. You can ask him. I'm the person he's in love with."

The door slammed shut. Feeling that she hadn't made herself sufficiently clear, Marion rang the doorbell again. From inside she heard children's pounding footsteps. The door sprang open. "Whoever you are," Isabelle said, "please go away."

"I'm sorry," Marion said, with real remorse. "I shouldn't have tried to hurt you. But what's done is done. You just don't satisfy him. Maybe, in the long run, it'll be better for you, too."

This time, the door didn't slam, it just clicked shut. She heard the deadbolt turning. After some unaccounted-for minutes, she found herself still standing on the welcome mat. It was all so disappointing. For days, she'd imagined that speaking to Bradley's wife would entirely remake the world; that her mental pain, which had been growing steadily since he sent his dreadful letter to her, would cease in an instant and she would be in a world where decisions were easy. But the pain was still there. It now took the form of not knowing what to do next. She would have liked to simply stay standing on the welcome mat, but she was sane enough to recognize the badness of going to Bradley's house—all she'd accomplished was to cause Isabelle pain without relieving her own. She turned and walked back to the sidewalk. Coming to a small park, she saw a box hedge behind which she could discreetly lie down. She rested her cheek on a tussock of grass between bare clods of earth. Although there was dog poop close enough to be smelled, she lay there until darkness fell.

When she got back to her building, Bradley's LaSalle was parked in front of it. He could have let himself into her apartment, but he was sitting at the wheel. He jerked his head to indicate that she should get in with him. She was frightened, but she did it. She cowered against the passenger door, trying to make herself smaller.

"What do you want?" he said angrily.

"I'm sorry."

"No, seriously. What do you want? Tell me what the hell you think you want."

"I'm sorry."

"It's too late for sorry. I've got an unholy mess on my hands now. I swear to God, Marion, if you go anywhere near my wife again, I'm calling the police."

"I'm sorry."

"The same goes for Lerner. We'll call the police, and you know what they'll do? They'll put you in a hospital. You're not right in the head. It kills me to say it, but you're not."

"I'm throwing up a lot," she agreed. "It's hard to keep food down."

He sighed in frustration. "For the last time: We can't see each other again. Never, ever. Do you understand?"

"Yes. No."

"No contact of any kind. Do you understand?"

She knew that it was important to say yes, but she couldn't say it honestly.

"What you need to do now," he said, "is get yourself home. Can you do that for me? I want you to go back to San Francisco and let your family take care of you. You are the sweetest thing. It's killing me to see what's happened to you. But what you did today was just beyond the pale."

Her chest clotted up with a new worry: that she'd finally liberated Bradley but was now too wrong in the head for him to want her. The irony surged up and strangled her like stomach acid. She retched out five words. "Will she divorce you now?"

"Honey—Marion. How many ways do I have to find to say it? We can't be together."

"You and I."

"You and I."

The hyperventilating set in, and he reached into his jacket. The stack of money he put between them on the seat was thick. "I want you to take this," he said. "Buy yourself a first-class ticket north. And then, as soon as you get to San Francisco, I want you to see the best psychiatrist you can find. Somebody who can help you."

She stared at the money.

"I am so sorry," he said. "But there's nothing else I can give you. Please take it."

"I'm not a whore."

"No, you're an angel. A sweet angel who's in very bad trouble. I mean it—if there were anything else I could give you, I would do it. But this is all I've got."

She finally understood that she was nothing to him but his paid slut. The money on the seat seemed to her a dangerous, loathsome reptile. She found the door latch and half fell, backward, from his car. With a loathsome hand, he extended the money toward her. "Please, Marion. For God's sake."

When she came out of her slippage, some morning or another, probably the very next one, she felt inexplicably better. It was as if her hatred of the man trying to pay her had made a crack in her obsession with Bradley Grant. The obsession was still in her, but it was weakened now, more readily observable for what it was. Inside her front door, wrapped in an advertising flyer and slipped under the door, she found the stack of money. She methodically cut each bill into tiny pieces and flushed them all down the toilet. This was a terrible mistake she had to make to ease her mental pain.

In the first days of December, less distracted by pain, she was capable of reading the newspaper again, taking an interest in Mussolini's attack on Greece, and venturing forth to seek work. Her employer references weren't in order, but she still had her looks. She found a job as a greeter at a big Safeway supermarket, offering customers bite-size samples of featured food products, and was surprised by how little she minded it. She liked having only one thing to say and saying it over and over. Repetition calmed her fear of the thing she was now able to admit was inside her. But the smell of certain foods, meat products especially, was revoltingly intense to her, and her fear was growing with the thing inside her. One day, when she was sticking toothpicks in miniature canned franks, her fear impelled her to walk out of the store, run home, and obey the commands of her feral intelligence. She hit herself in the stomach and jumped up and down violently. She swallowed a mouthful of ammonia and couldn't keep it down. When she tried again and blew the ammonia out her nose, the explosion in her head was so extreme she thought she was dying.

In her narrative to Sophie, a straight line led from Bradley's offer of money to the night she wandered the streets of downtown Los Angeles in the rain, raving on themes of sluttiness and murder, barefoot, her blouse soaking and unbuttoned, until she was picked up by the police. But the line hadn't been straight. It had led through an eviction notice; a tearful scene with her property manager; telegrams to her mother and to Roy Collins, asking both of them for emergency money; and a phone call to Bradley at Lerner Motors. The property manager gave her until the end of December to pay her overdue rent. Her mother, it later turned out, was on a ski vacation with her friends. Roy Collins wired her twenty dollars of travel money, along with a terse offer to employ her. Bradley hung up the phone as soon as he heard her voice.

Definitely pregnant and definitely not interested in carrying his baby, she took a streetcar out to Hollywood. The streets were dry and dusk was falling, the holiday tinsel and ribbons in store windows emerging from the cheapening glare of daylight to glow and beckon. She was able to entertain rational thoughts and ordinary feelings—resentment of her mother, the thought of the darkness that had fallen on Europe, hatred of Bradley and his wife, appreciation of the fender lines of a custom-body Cadillac passing the streetcar, curiosity about her sister in New York, the question of Shirley's own sexual experience or lack thereof—for no more than a few seconds before the terror of her situation welled up in her afresh and scattered them. When she saw the Egyptian Theatre, she stepped off the streetcar and asked a newspaper seller where Selma Avenue was. Her main hope now was Isabelle Washburn. Even if Isabelle couldn't give her money, she could provide sisterly advice and sympathy, which Marion was very much in need of. In the dark, it was hard to tell the colors of houses, but eventually she found a distinctly red one. Dim, warm light was in the curtained front windows. She walked right up to the door and knocked. Almost immediately, the door opened; and there stood Satan.

She didn't know it was Satan. The man was short, almost elfin, with a full white beard and suntanned cheeks, a large shiny tanned bald spot on his head, and kindly wrinkles around his eyes. "Come in, come in," he said, as if he'd been expecting her. Marion said she was looking for Isabelle Washburn. "Isabelle no longer lives here," the man said, "but come in. Please."

"Are you the landlord?"

"Why, yes, I am. Please come in."

In the living room were comfortably weary chairs, framed soft-focus head shots of young actresses or models, also a framed poster for *King Kong*. A bottle of red wine and a stemmed glass of it stood on a coffee table. "Let me get you a glass," the man said, disappearing.

Farther back in the house, water was splashing in a bathtub, skin squeaking resonantly on porcelain. The white-bearded man returned with a glass, sat down, and filled it. He seemed very happy to see Marion.

"I just need to find Isabelle," she said.

"I understand. But you're shaking like a leaf."

This was undeniable, and the wine looked good to her. She sat down and drank some. It was much weaker than the whiskey she'd drunk with Bradley. By the time she'd explained how she knew Isabelle and had come to the red house, her glass was empty. When the man moved to refill it, she didn't stop him. The wine helped her rise with the upwellings of her fear, like a buoy on deep ocean.

"I'm afraid I don't actually know where Isabelle is at present," the man said, "with respect to her street address and so forth. But I know one girl who might."

"That would be good," Marion said, drinking.

"You're a very comely young woman," he added for no obvious reason.

Marion reddened. The wine was both weak and not so weak. She heard a door open, water draining from a tub, the soft stepping of bare feet, a door closing.

"So the girl," she said. "The person who knows where she lives."

"Oh, dear, you look *terrified*," the man said. "Are you frightened? Marion? Why are you so frightened?"

"I just want to find Isabelle."

"Of course," he said. "I can help you with that."

There was a kindly light in his eyes, a sort of gentle mirth.

"I'm a helpful person," he said. "You wouldn't be the first girl to come here in trouble. Is that what it is? Are you looking for Isabelle because you're in some kind of trouble?"

She couldn't answer.

"Marion? You can tell me. Are you in trouble?"

Her trouble was too large to be spoken. To emerge from her in words, it needed to be broken into smaller pieces and arranged in a coherent sequence, and even if she'd been capable of the breaking and the arranging she would have been telling a total stranger that she was carrying a married man's child. As the stranger waited for her to answer, she noticed a different, less kindly sort of light in his eyes. She noticed that his shirt was untucked and that he had quite a potbelly. She must have been mistaken about Isabelle's romantic interest in her landlord.

"It's man trouble, isn't it," he said.

She couldn't breathe, and she had no intention of answering, not even with a nod.

"I see," he said. "And is your man still in the picture?"

Had she nodded? Apparently she had. She went ahead and shook her head.

"I'm very sorry," the man said.

"But the girl you mentioned. The one who knows where Isabelle is."

"Would you like me to telephone her?"

"Yes. Please."

He left the room. Marion's glass was empty, as was the bottle. While she waited, a series of small noises culminated in a clicking of heels, a woman entering the room. She stopped when she saw Marion. She was dressed in a narrow skirt and a matching jacket with padded shoulders. Her mouth, crimson-lipsticked, had a hard set to it. "You here about the room?"

"No," Marion said.

"Good for you."

The woman turned and left the house. The man returned with a cork-screw and a second bottle of wine. Marion waited in suspense while he opened it.

"No luck," he said, pouring. "Jane hasn't seen her since before Thanks-giving. She thinks she might have gone back to Santa Rosa. Apparently she'd talked about doing that."

Isabelle's returning to Santa Rosa seemed strange to Marion, but ev-erything seemed strange to her. She wished she hadn't already spent the travel money Roy Collins had wired her. Imagining Isabelle in Santa Rosa made her homesick for the place.

"We'll have to think of something else for you," the man said.

"I think I'll go to Santa Rosa."

"Yes, that would be one plan. Although, of course, we're not sure that Isabelle is actually there. She could have gone anywhere. She could still be right here. All Jane said was that she hadn't seen her in a while."

"But it sounds like . . . I'll bet she went home to Santa Rosa."

"Mm."

He took a sip of wine, possibly to hide a smile. Why would he be smiling? Marion stood up and thanked him for making the call.

"Sit down, dear," he said. "You don't want to go back to Santa Rosa. It's a Podunk town—people talk. You're much better off in the big city. We can arrange things here that would be difficult, if not impossible, in Santa Rosa. Do you understand what I'm saying?"

She did understand. Bradley had once asked her exactly the same question, and she was fast. Sitting down again, accelerated by the wine in her, she landed unexpectedly and tilted sideways.

"You don't have to be embarrassed," the man said. "I've had this house for fifteen years, and there's nothing I haven't seen. So why don't we speak frankly, you and I."

The thing was growing in her, and it was Bradley's. This was the fact she couldn't get around. She didn't want to have the thing inside her. It reminded her of the boy who'd answered the door at his house, the horror of Bradley having children, the horror of his marriage, the horror of what she'd done to herself.

"Perhaps you've missed a monthly," the man said. "Perhaps more than one?"

She affirmed it with a whimper.

"How many?" he said. "Surely not more than two—you're skinnier than a post."

She shook her head.

"I like a skinny pretty little girl," he commented in a throatier way. "And you are definitely that."

She could sooner have recited the Koran than raise her eyes to Isabelle's former landlord. Except for the ticking of a clock on the mantel, the house was silent. She was certain that no one but the two of them was in it.

"Luckily for you, I can help you," he said. "I happen to know just the man—he's very good. Tip-top hygiene. Nice office. Complete discretion."

She was breathing either far too fast or not at all. The man's words came from a distance and receded further as he spoke them. "Do you have a hundred fifty dollars? That would include the twenty-five for me. And, let's see, today is Thursday, isn't it. We could have you good as gold again by Saturday night."

She heard wine being poured.

"Do you have a hundred fifty dollars?" he said.

The question came through clearly. She indicated that she didn't.

"How much money do you have?" He waited for a response and got none. "Marion, do you have any money at all?"

The answer must have been obvious. She heard him leave the room and return, felt the heat of him as he crouched by her. "I know how frightened you are," he said. "You're terribly frightened. Understandably frightened. You'll feel better if you take these."

He opened one of her clenched hands and pressed two tablets into it.

"It's only Seconal. It'll help you sleep."

She felt the heat of his hand on her knee.

"I imagine you're wondering if I can really solve your problem. I suppose I could give you references, but the other girls I've helped may be reluctant to talk about it. The way I see it, you'll just have to trust me. I've run an honest business here for fifteen years. I never take anything I haven't paid for, and I never give a girl anything she hasn't paid for. That's the rule in this house. Everything here is quid pro quo."

By bodily reflex, she removed the hand that was creeping up her leg. As soon as she let it go, he put it back.

"I'm going to Palm Springs for the holidays," he said. "If you'll stay with me until then, we'll have you good as gold by Christmas. That is a solemn promise. A mere eleven days. If I may say so, the terms are rather advantageous to you. Luckily for you, you're just my kind of girlie. Very, very much my kind of girlie."

Her feral intelligence understood perfectly well what he was proposing. To agree to it, all she had to do was not stand up and leave. She raised her hand and put the two pills in her mouth. Her arms felt too short to reach for her glass, so she chewed them.

Her mental illness, compounded by a Seconal fog, spared her from remembering much from her eleven days in the red house. She did remember listening for footsteps outside her door, the landlord's and the other tenant's, the latter even more dreadful than the former. She thought she would die if the other woman's gaze so much as brushed her, she cowered at the clatter of high heels in the hallway, she let the landlord bring food to her room. Disgusting things were visited on her, but they rarely seemed to last long. As long as she stayed in the house, she remained entirely a victim and would have had nothing to confess to her priest in Arizona—in fact, she might have had grounds for going to the police. The Satanic thing about the landlord was that he'd struck a deal with her. Satan was a stickler when it came to contracts, and by following through with his side of the

bargain, punctiliously delivering her to the doctor and paying for the abortion, he deprived her of her victimhood. By keeping his word, he made
her submission to his lechery one half of a transaction, a quid pro quo,
in which she was complicit. She couldn't claim ignorance or innocence.
She'd knowingly committed adultery with Bradley Grant, and then she'd
knowingly sold herself to pay for the murder of her baby.

Satan was gone, vanished seemingly for good, when she emerged from
the scene of the crime, a few blocks from Lerner Motors. It was late in
the afternoon of December 24. The leading edge of a storm system had
crept across the city sky, scalloping it with cloud. The last Seconal she'd
swallowed, in the morning, was wearing off. She was light-headed, and
the pain in her belly, though not severe yet, felt evil in its novelty. In place
of her specific dread, now put to rest, a more general dread was creeping
across her sky-wide mind. She still had six dollars and change in her
purse, but she couldn't bring herself to board a streetcar. Weaving a little,
pausing to rest against the sides of buildings, she made her way toward
her apartment.

It wasn't more than twenty blocks away, but traversing that distance
finished her off, because she couldn't get away from him. His elfin face
loomed up in window after window. Twinkling-eyed. White-bearded.
Dressed in a bright red suit with ermine trim. Posters and greeting
cards and cookie tins and life-size manikins all advertised his pawing,
wine-breathed malice. She needed more Seconals to get away from
him. He was watching her from every direction. His penis was short
and fat and tan, like a miniature him. He stood potbellied on a corner,
in a red suit, and rang a bell beside a red can into which passersby
dropped money. Everywhere, red. She couldn't get away from red. It
was the color of his house. It was how he signaled that wherever she
turned he was already there. Red bows, red ribbons. Red-striped candy
canes. Shiny stars and crescent moons of metallic red cardboard. The
red house. The red car. The red in the sink at her old rooming house.
The red wagon. The red wagon. The red wagon. The red wagon. Evil
had pursued her all her life, and now the world was exploding with the
color of it, and nowhere was there refuge. It found her in her bathroom,

the bathroom of her apartment. Red was inside her, too, and it was coming out. She was nothing but a thin-skinned bladder bursting-full of red. Her hands were red, her things were red, there was red on the floor, red on the walls she wiped her hands on. Red annihilated her mind. Merry Christmas.

"So here's a memory," she said. "It's the best memory I have of Christmas. Do you want to hear it?"

"I would," Sophie Serafimides said. "If you're sure you're done punishing me."

Marion opened her eyes. Out on the rail tracks, snow was falling heavily. The tracks already had a thick coconut frosting.

"You needed punishing," she said.

Sophie didn't smile. "Tell me your memory."

"It was 1946, in Arizona. Russ and I had been together for the better part of a year—we were already a couple in every way except marriage. He still had his alternative service to finish, even though the war was over, but things had gotten very lax at the camp. He could get some days off almost whenever he wanted, and that was nice for me. I'd invited him to Christmas at my uncle Jimmy's, but he said he had a better idea. There was an old Willys truck that the camp director was willing to let him borrow, and Russ wanted to see more of the Southwest. Jimmy gave us some money as a Christmas present, and off we went. It was a huge deal for Russ, because his parents didn't know about me, and everywhere we went we had to pretend that we were married. It was a huge act of defiance for him, and I was in love with him. It was heaven to have him all to myself, driving wherever we felt like going. We spent a day in Santa Fe, and then we were in Las Vegas—Las Vegas, New Mexico—when the snow came. Do you know Las Vegas?"

"I don't."

"It's an old, old Spanish colonial town up by the Sangre de Cristos. The Willys had bad tires and we got stuck there by the snow. There was only one hotel where people like us could have stayed, and that's where we had our Christmas. Our room was probably terrible, but we had each other, so I thought it was wonderful. The hotel was on the old town square, with a dining room on the ground floor, and that's where we ate on Christmas Eve. To be there with Russ felt like a reward beyond anything I deserved. There was frost around the edges of the windows, and actual cowboys—real cowboys in long coats were coming in to have their dinner. There was also a little family, maybe stuck by the snow like us, an Anglo family with two little girls. And it was like those little girls were the family we were going to have. Like we were looking at *ourselves* in the future, and then the most amazing thing happened. Outside on the square, there was a big truck that somebody had rigged up to look like Santa's sleigh. There were two reindeer sticking out in front of it, above the hood, and they'd rigged up lights to make it look like they were flying. They'd also lit up the sleigh on the roof of the cab. From a distance, you couldn't see the truck. All you could see was the reindeer and the sleigh and a cowboy in a Santa suit waving his hand while the truck went around and around in the snow. And—I, uh."

Marion faltered, avoiding Sophie's eyes.

"I never liked Santa Claus. I thought he was scary and creepy. I had a problem with him. But the look on those two little girls' faces, when they caught sight of the reindeer and the sleigh—I don't think I'll ever see more pure wonder and joy. The girls' eyes were just huge. One of them said, 'Oh! Oh!' And they ran to the window and looked out, and they were saying, 'Oh! Oh! Oh!' It was just pure joy and credulity. Their utter belief in what they were seeing was just the most beautiful thing. And all the . . . all the . . . I'm sorry, but all the *shit* I'd been through in California, it just got washed away. It was like I was being reborn, just by watching those girls and their reaction."

"That does sound beautiful."

"But what does this have to do with anything?"

The dumpling inclined her head suggestively.

"Russ didn't see it the way I did," Marion said. "He didn't get it at all. And I couldn't tell him what it meant to me, because I couldn't tell him what I'd been through."

"It's never too late to tell him."

"No, it's definitely too late. That Christmas Eve would have been the time to do it. 'I had an affair with a married man, I tried to break up his marriage by telling his wife, and I got so crazy they had to lock me up on Christmas morning.' There was no way that story was going to fly, not with Russ."

"You were institutionalized on Christmas?"

"Had I not mentioned that?"

"You hadn't."

"Well, there you go. That's how the leopard got his spots."

"Meaning?"

"Now you know why I hate Christmas. We can call it a breakthrough, and I can go home and eat some more sugar cookies. Tra-la-la, tra-la-la. I can live happily ever after."

Sophie frowned.

"We had a horrible fight that night," Marion said. "Russ and I, in New Mexico. It was our first real fight, and I promised myself we'd never have another one. No matter what it took, I wasn't going to raise my voice with him again. I would love him and support him and keep my mouth shut. Because he saw something very different when he looked at those two girls. He said he was disgusted by the parents—that they were encouraging their children to worship a false idol. That they were lying to their kids and neglecting the true meaning of Christmas, which had nothing to do with Santa Claus. And I went out of my mind again. I felt like I'd experienced a kind of magical rebirth—something *truly Christian*, by the way, which was to forgive, oh, not forgive, but to get over . . . well."

She felt herself going red. The dumpling's eyes were on her.

"It was . . . I'm not explaining it right. Santa was . . . Santa wasn't . . . I could see that it was only an *illusion*. It was just some cowboy in a Santa suit, not . . . And somehow that, plus the girls—I was sharing in someone else's joy and wonder. I knew it was only an illusion, but *because* it was only an illusion I could be an innocent little girl again myself. And that mattered so much to me, and Russ didn't get it. I was screaming at him, just out of control. I hated him, and I could see I was scaring the daylights out of him, and I said to myself, nope, never going to do that again, ever. And you know what? I never did. Tomorrow will be exactly twenty-five years that I've been keeping my mouth shut."

The dumpling seemed preoccupied. She glanced over her shoulder at the falling snow. "I'm sorry if this is a difficult question," she said. "But I feel I have to ask again. Is there something important you're not telling me?"

A coldness surged in Marion. "What kind of thing."

"I'm not quite sure. There was just—something in your tone of voice. I've thought I might have heard it once or twice before, and just now I heard it again, very clearly. I'm not saying I'm a world-class practitioner. And, by the way, in case you didn't know, I don't believe in Just So stories. I don't believe there's a single key that unlocks everything. But when I've heard that particular tone of voice in the past, it often turns out that the patient has experienced a particular kind of trauma."

The dumpling was relentless.

"My father killed himself," Marion said. "My mother didn't love me. I lost my mind. Is that not enough?"

"No, that's a lot," Sophie said. "And I definitely hear that in your voice, too. But that's the funny you. That's the you who survived a rotten childhood and the aftermath of that and made adjustments, made a good life for yourself, found a way to cope with the turmoil in your head. That's the survivor in you. What I was hearing was something else, and I'm not saying I'm right. I'm just asking."

Marion looked at her watch. She was two minutes past the end of their second "hour." As if the little office were the living room of a certain red bungalow, she stood up hastily and took her coat off the hook. She jammed one arm and then the other into its sleeves. She still had time to run home, raid her hosiery drawer, and buy something nicer for Perry. For twenty-five years, she'd believed that her life with Russ was the blessing she'd received from a forgiving God, a blessing she'd earned by her years of Catholic prayer and penance, a life she continued to earn daily by suppressing the badness in her and keeping her mouth shut. It was true that she'd lately hated Russ at least as much as she still loved him; there was little reason to keep pretending for his sake. But she loved Perry more than ever. His suffering, for which her side of the family was responsible, was the punishment that God had waited three decades to inflict on her.

"You don't have to leave on my account," the dumpling said from behind her. "Costa and I are here until five."

Marion faced the door, her hand on the knob. The office was godless, and she knew what God expected of her. She needed to devote herself to Perry and begin atoning for her sins. And yet to leave the office was to relinquish all hope of getting better.

"Maybe you should tell me about Santa," Sophie said.

"Oh, there's Perry," Frances Cottrell said, waving. "Speak of the devil."

Seeing the pale yellow locks of his son at the corner of Maple Avenue, not twenty seconds after he and Frances had made a clean getaway from First Reformed, Russ was tempted to drive through the stop sign, but the township police station was right across the street. He braked and made himself turn and look where Frances was waving, so as not to seem guilty. Perry was standing on the sidewalk, all-seeing, a plastic bag in his hand. Russ held his gaze for a moment and stepped hard on the gas.

Speak of the devil?

"He's an impressive kid," Frances said. "I think Larry's got a little crush on him."

Beyond Maple, the speed limit on Pirsig Avenue could safely be broken. Luckier snowflakes were blindly evading the Fury while others met their end on the windshield. If Perry had been standing anywhere but at the stop sign, he might not have seen that Russ's only passenger was Frances. Now Russ could only hope that Perry would forget; and there was little chance of that.

"So here's an awkward question," Frances said.

Russ eased up on the gas. "Mm?"

"Since I have you all to myself today, this is kind of like private counseling, right? Even though we're not in your office? It's still confidential?"

"Absolutely," Russ said.

Frances had been bouncing and repositioning her limbs ever since she got in the car. Her left foot, on the bench seat, was currently no more than an inch from his leg. "I'm wondering," she said, "how old you think your kids should be before they try marijuana."

"My kids?"

"Yes, or any kids. How young is too young?"

"Well, marijuana is illegal. I don't think any parent wants to see his children breaking laws."

Frances laughed. "Are you really that square?"

The coat he was wearing, the coat she'd admired, wasn't the coat of a square. The blues 78s he'd brought for her and left in his office weren't the records of a square. The thoughts he had about her weren't a square's thoughts.

"I'm not against breaking the law," he said. "Gandhi broke the law, Daniel Ellsberg broke the law. I don't think rules are sacred. I just don't see that breaking drug laws serves any meaningful purpose."

"Wow. Okay."

He could hear that she was smiling, but the dichotomy of square and hip, the unfairness of it, was offensive to him.

"There's nothing wrong with being a square," she said. "I think it's cute. But I gather you've never tried pot yourself?"

"Ah, no. Have you?"

"Not—yet."

There was a twinkle in her voice. He took his eyes off the road and saw that she was watching him for a reaction. She seemed very activated, very happy with herself; seemed ready to play. He, too, had come to play, but his game wasn't flirting. He had no faith in his skills there.

"Your question," he said. "Were you asking about your son?"

"Yes, partly. But also partly about yours."

"*My* son? You mean Perry?"

"Yes."

His son? Using drugs? Well, of course. It made such perfect sense, Russ couldn't believe he hadn't suspected it before. God damn Marion.

"Can I tell you some things?" Frances said. "Since we're having a confidential session?"

The white flurry on the road ahead of them was thick and disorienting.

He kept his eyes on it, but he could feel her leaning toward him in her hunting cap.

"Do you remember," she said, "when I came to see you last summer?"

"I do. I remember it very well."

"So, I was in a bad place, but I wasn't very honest with you. Actually, I wasn't even a little bit honest. You were so nice about Bobby, about losing a husband, but that wasn't really why I was there. I was upset because I'd just found out that the man I'd been seeing was also seeing someone else."

The brittle rubber of the Fury's wipers shuddered on the windshield. Russ wanted to ask a clarifying question, to confirm that *seeing* meant what it seemed to, but he didn't trust his voice. A day that had begun well was now conclusively terrible. As stupid as he'd been about Perry, he'd been even stupider about Frances. It had never occurred to him that another man might already have swooped in on her. Last summer, she'd been widowed for barely a year.

She leaned back into her corner of the front seat. "It was one of those things that seemed too good to be true because it was. One of my old girlfriends set us up on a date, and it just immediately felt right—we clicked right away. Philip's a surgeon, and he'd been in the service. He'd served on one of the same bases Bobby had, so we had that in common, and heart surgery is like the medical equivalent of being a fighter pilot—not for the faint of heart. Philip's got a gorgeous apartment in one of the high-rises on the lake, just north of the Loop, with an incredible view. As soon as I saw it, I thought, 'Okay, sign me up!' In hindsight, it was way too early for me to be thinking that way, but I just wanted everything to be right again. I wanted there to be four of us, not three."

Russ tried to imagine the scenario in which Frances had been in the heart surgeon's apartment and not had intimate relations with him.

"I wanted Larry and Amy to meet him," she said. "I thought we could all have lunch and go to the Field Museum. I kept pushing until finally one night he tells me, *in the spirit of full disclosure*, that there's something I should know. Apparently, the entire time I've known him, he's been seeing someone else. A nurse, of course. Younger than me, of course. So that's where my head was when I came to see you. I really was missing Bobby, but not for the right reasons. I'd kind of had my heart broken."

The black exhaust of a dump truck in front of Russ was soiling the snow before it even reached the ground. "I see," he said.

"But here's something else I didn't tell you. Things hadn't actually been so wonderful with me and Bobby. I was only twenty-one when we got married. He was my brother's best friend, he was piloting planes that broke the sound barrier, he was awesomely good-looking, and I was the girl who got to marry him. He was gone a lot, but I didn't mind that—I was an officer's wife, which had its privileges. He was stationed at Edwards when the kids were born, and I would have followed him anywhere—it wasn't me who made him quit the air force. But he wanted the kids to grow up in one place, in one school district, and the pay was a lot better with General Dynamics. And then as soon as we were there in Texas he decided he'd made a mistake. He missed the military, and I could tell he blamed me, even though it wasn't my fault. Year after year, I watched him get more angry. Everyone knew he was a stud, and it wasn't like I was giving him an argument, but he kept making me pass these loyalty tests. If I laughed too hard at something a neighbor said, it meant I was flirting with him, and Bobby wouldn't let it go until I admitted that the neighbor was less of a man than he was. If I watched the news and made some comment about the war not going well, he'd start interrogating me. Didn't I agree that America was the most powerful country on earth? With the best economic system? Weren't we morally obliged to keep the Communists from expanding their blah-blah-blah? He honestly believed the reason so many troops were getting killed was that the protesters at home were undermining their morale. *I* was getting boys killed, by having doubts about the war. And Larry, he wanted to be an astronaut, but he wasn't exceptional at sports, wasn't a straight-A student, and Bobby was constantly yelling at him. 'Do you think you get to be an astronaut by not sliding hard into second base? Do you think John Glenn ever got a B on an algebra test?' Larry was just a dreamy kid who was interested in space, and he was so proud of Bobby, so desperate to please him, his disapproval was a torture. Have you ever seen the cockpit of an F-111?"

Russ should have been glad that she was opening up to him, but all he could hear was that she commanded the attention of test pilots and heart surgeons. He was an associate minister with a wife, four kids, and no money. What had he been thinking?

"It's incredible," she said. "The amount of instruments they have. They give you the sense that you're utterly in control, and that's the way Bobby was with us. We needed his approval, and he controlled us by making it conditional. Larry had to be a star athlete, and I couldn't have a little fun talking to a neighbor. For me, the most terrible thing about the crash was imagining him losing control of the aircraft. He must have felt so *furious*."

The sky was darkening, the traffic slow. How many millions of dollars did an F-111 cost? How could a nation that called itself Christian spend billions of dollars on weapons of death? The instrument panel of Russ's Fury consisted of a speedometer and three gauges, one of them broken. The car urgently needed new brakes and new snow tires, but Marion had asked for two hundred dollars for Christmas shopping. The sum had struck him as excessive, but he'd been mindful of how little else he'd given her lately, mindful of the four hours alone with Frances that he'd contrived to give himself for Christmas. He'd imagined that the four hours would fly by all too quickly. Now he wondered how he could survive another minute of hearing about the kind of man she loved. There was a hard, sour knot in his throat.

"I've been talking a lot to Kitty about this," Frances said. "I'm never going to be a bra-burner, but she's given me some books that make a lot of sense to me. It's not that Bobby was physically abusive. He was just cold, cold, cold. In a way, though, that was almost worse. I was the little wife, and the only thing that mattered was that I do everything exactly right. It was the opposite of a marriage of equals. When I look back now, I realize that our neighbors all thought I was married to a jerk. The only people who didn't think so were his pilot buddies, and they were jerks, too. I mean, obviously, it's terrible, the way he died—I feel so sorry for him. But sometimes I almost wonder if I'm better off without him. Is that bad of me?"

"Marriage is difficult," Russ said.

"But does it have to be difficult? Is yours difficult? Or—sorry, maybe I can't ask that."

If Russ had had the nerves of a test pilot or a heart surgeon, now would have been the time to open his heart and declare that his marriage was a miserable thing, held together by habit and vow and duty. Now would have been the time to make his pitch. But his complaint with Marion was that she was heavy and joyless, unexciting to him, dulling of his edge. He didn't see how he could voice this complaint without sounding like a jerk.

"Anyway," Frances said, "you did me a huge favor, putting me in touch with Kitty and getting me into the Tuesday circle. It's exactly what I needed. I've been taking a class at Triton College, and that's been good, too. All in all, I was having a pretty good fall. But then—"

"I know," Russ said. "I want to apologize again for what happened with Ronnie. That was my mistake."

"Oh, yeah. Thanks. You don't have to apologize. What happened was that Philip got in touch with me again. He called me out of the blue and said his mind was clearer now. He'd broken things off with the nurse, and could I find it in my heart to forgive him? I didn't think I could, but he sent me roses and called me up again. He really turned on the charm, and things just kind of clicked. The weekend after Thanksgiving, after the thing with Ronnie, I went in to the city and had a whole afternoon and evening with him."

The snow was still melting when it hit the pavement, but the forecast called for as much as eight inches. If Russ and Frances got stuck somewhere, it would mean additional hours with a heart surgeon's girlfriend.

"Everything felt different, though," she said. "It was partly the books I've been reading, but it was partly—it was partly what you've given me. I mean, the Tuesday circle, and, I don't know, just the example of a different kind of man. Philip took me to Binyon's, and when the waiter came he took the menu out of my hand and ordered for me. The old me would have liked that—it would have made me feel safe. But—and then we were in his apartment, with the amazing view, and I was looking at the family pictures on his piano. I picked one up, and I must have set it down wrong, because he came over and moved it, like, one inch further back. He came all the way across the room to move the picture one inch.

Which probably makes him a great surgeon, but I thought to myself: Uh-oh. Here we go again. You know what I mean?"

Russ was feeling whipsawed, despairing one moment, daring to hope the next.

"It was like I'd wanted to replace Bobby with someone like Bobby. I guess that's the kind of man I'm attracted to, or one kind of man. Bobby could be charming, too, when he'd been a jerk to me and I was mad at him. I realized that if I stayed with Philip I'd probably have another kid or two—I think he wants his own kids—and that would be the end of me. He'd be controlling everything. But so, anyway, I didn't get home till nearly midnight—"

After having intimate relations with the surgeon? Russ had no grasp of contemporary dating protocol.

"And I found Larry in the family room by himself, watching TV. He's old enough to babysit for Amy, but he seemed a little weird. I bent over to give him a kiss, and I couldn't believe it. He smelled like pot and mouthwash. He'd gotten high after Amy went to bed! I couldn't believe it. I knew he'd had a hard time after Bobby died, and starting a new school in ninth grade wasn't any picnic, but he's a good kid, and he's doing a lot better this year, thanks to Crossroads. He still has bad posture, he still hides his face with his hair, but he seems to be maturing. When I realized he was high, my impulse was to feel guilty about leaving him and Amy alone for so many hours. I told him I was disappointed that he'd taken a stupid risk while he had responsibility for his sister, but I wasn't going to punish him. I just needed to know some things, such as where he got the marijuana. But his hair is hanging in his face, he won't look at me, won't answer. I ask him if there's marijuana in the house. He still won't answer, and that's when I kind of lose it. I demand that he show me where his pot is, I march him up to his room, and you know what? He's got a whole bag of it! I take it away from him, I ask him again where he got it, and you know what he says? He says, 'I'm not a nark.' It made me so angry, I took away his TV privileges for a month."

Russ had an uneasy sense of where her story was heading. The coin had dropped when she mentioned Perry.

"So, like I said, this is awkward," she said. "But I thought you should know."

"You think Larry got the marijuana from my son."

"I don't know for sure. But the two of them are together a lot, and Larry—it's sweet—he's obviously smitten with Perry. They come home from school and go straight to his room. Larry builds models, and I can smell the glue and the paint when they're up there. I don't care if they spend their time building models. I'm not sure I even care if they smoke pot. Larry says half the kids at school have tried it, which is probably an exaggeration, but I gather it's pretty common. But to have a whole bag of it, a good-size bag—that didn't seem like Larry."

God damn Marion.

The previous spring, when the gross extent of Perry's misbehavior had come to light, Marion had thrown religion in Russ's face—had accused him of an Old Testament fixation on commandments, accused him of forgetting the New Testament forgiveness he preached on Sundays. According to Marion, Perry needed love and support, not punishment. He'd skipped a total of eleven days of school and had forged Russ's handwriting on notes explaining his absence, but Marion insisted that his problems were psychological, not moral. The boy was hypersensitive and moody and couldn't sleep at night. Marion, pleading for compassion, had proposed psychiatric counseling for him (as if they had the money for that). In Russ's view, Marion herself was the problem. From the very beginning, she'd indulged Perry in his moods and his whims, his incessant whining and crying as a toddler, his pompous superiority as he got older. Although Russ was aware that all four of his kids, to varying degrees, preferred Marion to him, because she was always near them, always at home while he was away serving others, Perry's preference for his mother was the most glaring and exclusive. Russ might have felt jealous of their closeness if he'd liked Perry better and Marion still excited him. He'd chosen to leave them to each other, and now, as a consequence of her coddling and his indifference to it, Perry had embarrassed them in front of the junior high school authorities.

He'd clearly sensed moral fault in Perry, and he should have suspected drug use, but he'd been led astray by Marion's story of a gifted, sensitive child who only wanted to get some sleep. Summoning Perry to his office in the parsonage, where he had a stack of handwritten notes addressed to the junior-high principal and penned in a hand that he had to admit was uncannily like his own—Perry was undeniably a boy of many talents—Russ had undertaken to impose, on his girly-haired son, the discipline that Marion had failed to.

"You can't be sleeping in the daytime," he'd said. "You need to sleep at night like the rest of us."

"Dad, I would love to," Perry said. "But I can't."

"There are plenty of mornings when I don't feel like getting up and going to work. But you know what? I get up and do it. If you just make yourself do it, one day, you'll be so tired at night you'll go to sleep. And then you're on a normal schedule again."

"With all due respect, that's easier said than done."

"You're very bright, and I'm sorry if you're not challenged enough at school. But part of growing up is learning to be disciplined. All I ever see is you reading a book or messing around with your art supplies. You should be outside, tiring yourself out. I wonder if you should join an intramural softball team."

Perry stared at him with insolent incredulity. Russ tried to contain his irritation.

"You need to do *something*," he said. "Starting this summer, I want to see you working. That's the rule in this family: we work. I want you to set a goal of earning fifty dollars a week."

"Becky didn't have to work in tenth grade."

"Becky was involved in cheerleading, and she's working now."

"She hates that job."

"Well, that's what self-discipline is. You may not like it, but you work anyway. I'm not trying to punish you, Perry. I'm doing this for your own good. I want you to start looking for work tomorrow. That way, you'll have it lined up when summer comes."

To Russ's disgust, Perry began to weep.

"Frankly," Russ said, "I'm letting you off very lightly. I should be taking away all your privileges for what you did."

"This *is* punishment."

"Stop crying. You're too old to be crying. This is not punishment. You can always mow lawns if you can't find anything else. If mowing lawns was good enough for Clem, it's good enough for you. I guarantee you'll sleep at night if you've been mowing grass all day."

Marion had complained to Russ, in her mild but stubborn way, that mowing lawns was a senseless waste of Perry's talents, a painful assault on his sensitivities, but Russ had been vindicated by the ensuing improvement in Perry's habits. In the summer, Perry had slept from midnight to late morning, normal for a teenager, and in September, on his own initiative, he'd joined Crossroads. Aligning himself with Rick Ambrose was probably his idea of revenge for having been forced to mow lawns, and Russ had refused him the satisfaction of disapproving. The truth was that he'd felt increasingly repelled by Perry, vaguely nauseated by his adolescent body. The afterschool hours that Perry spent in Crossroads, the entire weekend he was away on a Crossroads retreat, had been a relief from the corporeal affront of him.

But now Russ wondered if what had repelled him was simply Perry's bad character, his smug enjoyment of the secret of his drug use. It was all the goddamned fault of Marion. She wouldn't hear a word against her precious son, and Perry had exploited her trust in him, and now, in the eyes of Frances, who'd become the source of delight in Russ's life, Perry had reduced him to an unsuspecting square whose son had lured her Larry into drugs. God damn Marion. He could already taste the cruel pleasure of informing her that Perry was a drug user, of rubbing her nose in what her coddling had wrought: of making her pay for the humiliation of his learning it from Frances. He would make Perry pay, too.

But if Perry turned around and made insinuations? If he asked Russ, in Marion's presence, where he'd been going with Mrs. Cottrell and a car full of boxes? Russ, God help him, had felt compelled to lie to Marion at breakfast—to tell her that he was delivering the food and toys with Kitty Reynolds.

"Don't you want to take the turn here?" Frances said.

Skidding a little, rattling toys in the rear cargo area, he veered across two slushy lanes to make the turn onto Ogden Avenue. Horns blared behind him.

"You shouldn't feel bad," she said. "Rick Ambrose says a lot of other parents are dealing with the same thing."

Street-credible Rick Ambrose, his finger on the pulse of contemporary youth.

"You were talking to Rick about Larry?" Russ managed to say.

"Yeah, but don't worry—I didn't nark out Perry. I mean, I just did, to you. But not to Rick. I only wanted a little guidance on how to think about fifteen-year-olds smoking pot. Rick said the one thing I don't have to worry about is Crossroads. Apparently they have very strict rules against drugs and drinking on Crossroads time. Against sex, too. Although, poor Larry, I don't think I have to worry about that one yet. I've never even seen him *look* at a girl. The person he has a crush on is Perry."

Russ struggled to think of something wise to say, something to compete with Ambrose's special insight into young people.

"Coming home and finding Larry high," she said, "was a real eye-opener. I came down with a wretched cold, and when I finally got over it I felt like I'd turned a corner. Like I needed to get my life on a different kind of track—be more involved with my kids, stop chasing the fantasy second husband. I want to roll up my sleeves and get my hands dirty. I want to get more involved with you and Kitty and your work, and I asked Rick if there's a way for me to get involved in Crossroads, too. Part of it is feeling I have to be a kind of father for Larry and Amy, not just a mother. But part of it is just—do you ever feel like you were born too early?"

"You mean, do I wish I were younger?"

"Yeah, I guess we all end up wishing that. But I'm talking about what's happening now. I mean, the simple fact that girls can wear the same clothes as boys now—I missed all that. I missed the Beatles. I missed living with a guy before I decided if I should marry him, which wouldn't have been a bad idea in my case. I feel like I was born fifteen years too early."

"But what you're describing," Russ said, "was already happening in the early fifties. The spirit in New York, in Greenwich Village, when I was there, was everything you're describing, except, in a way, it was purer."

"In New York, maybe. It sure wasn't happening in New Prospect."

"Well, personally, I'm not sure I wish I'd been born any later." He warned himself not to oversell Greenwich Village, since he and Marion had lived there for only two months, following two years in seminary housing on East Forty-ninth Street. "What galls me about so-called youth culture now is that people seem to think it came out of nowhere. The kids today think they invented radical politics, invented premarital sex, invented civil rights and women's rights. Most of them have never even heard of Eugene Debs, John Dewey. Margaret Sanger, Richard Wright. When I was in Birmingham in 1963, a lot of the protesters were my age or older. The only real difference now is the fashions—different music, different hair. And that's just superficial."

"You really think that's the only difference? If there'd been a group like Crossroads when I was in high school, I would have joined it in a heartbeat. If I'd read Betty Friedan and Gloria Steinem when I was twenty, my whole life might have gone differently."

Russ frowned. He'd known that Ambrose was a menace, but the gravity of the threat from Kitty Reynolds was unanticipated.

"I'm only saying," he said, "that civil rights and the antiwar movement and, yes, feminism are the fruit of seeds that were planted a long time ago."

"Okay, noted. But can I tell you one other terrible thing?"

She repositioned herself again, putting her back against the passenger door and one of her feet against his seat belt. He felt a tug in the belt, across his groin.

"I still have Larry's bag of pot," she said. "Can you believe it? I went to flush it down the toilet, so he could hear me doing it, but somehow I didn't do it. I hid it in my bedroom."

Everything Russ had just said about his youth was hogwash. The age he wanted to be was exactly the age of Frances.

"I'm waiting, Reverend Hildebrandt. Are you going to tell me I did a bad thing?"

"Legally, I suppose there is some hazard."

"Oh, come on. No one's going to kick my door down."

"Still. What are you planning to do with it?"

"Well, um—what do you think I'm going to do with it?"

He nodded. He felt some pastoral responsibility to steer her from the path of iniquity, but he didn't want to seem like a square. "In that case," he said, "I suppose my concern would be that it complicates your message to Larry. If you're telling him that drugs are bad for him—"

"That's why I asked you how young is too young. Because I'm not too young. I'm trying to start my life all over at thirty-seven. I'm curious to try new things, and I had this image . . . I was thinking, you know, maybe I could invite Kitty, and you could invite your wife. The four of us could do a little experiment together, to see what all the fuss is about. If we're forbidding our kids to do something, shouldn't we know what we're forbidding?"

"I don't need to jump off a cliff to know that children shouldn't be jumping off a cliff."

"But what if it turns out to be great? What if it helps us understand our kids better? Or, I don't know, just generally expands our minds. I was thinking, if you were there with me, it would be okay to try it. You're a man of God, and you're not a fearful person. You're the opposite of the usual kind of minister."

She could hardly have said anything more warming to his heart and loins. An early dusk was gathering, snow whitening the metal surfaces along the road, slush mottling the sidewalks. It was the best of days again.

"I don't think my wife would be interested," he said.

"Okay. Just you and me and Kitty, then."

While he groped for a plausible reason to exclude Kitty as well, Frances gave him a playful little kick on the hip.

"Unless you don't think we need a chaperone," she said.

Among the revelations of the night before, in the front seat of Tanner's VW bus, had been the excellence of lips. In the past, Becky's lips had mostly just annoyed her, by being chapped or by wearing off her lipstick unevenly, their sensitivity in spin-the-bottle situations a matter of ticklishness and grossness. Only when they found their way to Tanner's lips, which mirrored hers but had their own unpredictable volition, did she discover their connection to every nerve in her body. His mustache was at once plushy and sharp-bristled, his tongue shy at first but then less so, his teeth unexpectedly close to the action. Every sensation was a novelty, every angle of contact subtly different. The reality of kissing Tanner Evans was shockingly much better than the idea of it. She could have done it for hours, insensible of the discomfort of twisting sideways on the passenger seat, if they hadn't been interrupted by noises in the parking lot.

"Hey, that's Tanner's van," they heard a girl say.

In the imperfect darkness, he pulled away from Becky and cocked an ear. The voices of the girl and a second girl receded, presumably heading into the back room of the Grove.

"We should get out of here," he said.

Having thrown herself at him, Becky understood his not wanting to be caught with her, but to her the hazard of being caught was thrilling. She drew him close and kissed him again. Moments later, the voices were back.

"Tanner?" the girl called, approaching the bus. "Laura?"

Tanner jerked away and peered out the window. Catching his panic, Becky bent over double and tried to hide her face in her hair, but it was obviously insufficient cover. She groped behind her, felt the Navajo blanket that was draped over the passenger seat, and pulled it over her head. From under its dusty woolenness she heard Tanner rolling down the window.

"Sally, yeah, hey," he said.

"Are you guys coming in?"

It was Sally Perkins, Laura Dobrinsky's good friend.

"Yeah," Tanner said. "Yeah, I'm just helping a friend here for a second."

Through the wool, Becky could feel Sally Perkins's eyes on her ridiculous blanketed form.

"Laura's not here?" Sally said.

"Uh, no."

"Marcie and I are celebrating, if you felt like joining us. She just turned legal."

"Yeah, um. That sounds—yeah."

"See you inside?"

When Sally was gone, Becky sat up giggling and shrugged off the blanket. "Oops," she said. This would have been a natural moment to ask about the status of Tanner and Laura as a couple, but he was giggling, too. For now, Becky thought, it was enough to share a secret with him, to be his partner in crime. She already had a sleepless night's worth of new sensations to process and relive, and it seemed unwise to overstay her welcome. "You should go inside," she told him.

"I don't even like Marcie Ackerman."

"It's okay." She leaned over and kissed his cheek. "You do like *me*?"

"Yes! Why do you think I came down here?"

"So maybe I'll see you tomorrow."

"Definitely. We could—" He slumped. "Actually, tomorrow's not so great."

"I don't have anything all day until the concert."

"Yeah, that's the thing. I have to work until four, and then we'll be setting up."

By *we* he meant his band. He meant the Natural Woman. Becky's nerves, hypersensitized by kissing, were defenseless against her disappointment.

"I'm really sorry," he said. "What about Friday?"

"Friday's Christmas Eve. Clem's coming home. I'll be busy with my family."

"Right."

"So I guess I'll just see you when I see you." She reached for the door latch. "Maybe in church, if I decide to go again."

"Becky—"

"It's okay. I understand. You're really busy tomorrow."

As she opened the door, he grabbed her shoulder. "I don't have to be at the church until five thirty. I could meet you somewhere before then."

"You don't have to."

"No, I want to." His expression was pleading. "I want to."

Satisfied that she had power over him, unsure only about the extent of it, she declined his offer of a ride and left him to Sally and Marcie. As she walked home, alone, the image of herself cowering beneath the Navajo blanket became less funny, more troubling. She was now officially the kind of girl who stole another girl's boyfriend. She couldn't tell if she sincerely felt guilty or was just scared of being confronted by the Natural Woman.

They'd agreed to meet at Treble Clef, the music store where he worked. As the appointed hour approached, Becky forced herself to linger at New Prospect Books, leafing through European travel guides, until she was a few minutes late. It was Tanner's job to be eager now, not hers. In her shoulder bag she had the colored pencils that Judson had requested, a velveteen-boxed pen and mechanical pencil for Clem, and a Laura Nyro album so desirable to her she didn't care if Perry wanted it himself. She'd stuck to her usual Christmas budget, despite the thirteen thousand dollars in her savings account, and had postponed the last of her buying until she could ride to the shopping mall in Jeannie Cross's Mustang in the morning. The cellophane-wrapped newness of the items in her bag, which was the thing about Christmas presents—that they passed unused through the hands of the giver, were wonderfully new-feeling and new-smelling when the recipient unwrapped them—was of a piece with the freshness of the snow beneath her feet, the world's rebirth in whiteness, when she finally walked around the corner to the music store. Being kissed had made her feel like a brand-new person, a just-opened present whose life was imminent but unbegun. When she saw Tanner standing in the snow by his bus, outside the store, he seemed equally new to her, because she had an actual date with him. She recognized his fringed jacket, the dark fall of his hair on his shoulders, but what a difference there was between wishing for a thing and finding it yours on Christmas morning.

Instead of embracing her, he helped her—not to say hustled her—into the bus and ran around to the driver's side. Wet snow on the windows had made an ice cave of the interior, private but dreary. The rear of the bus was piled with amps and instrument cases that seemed impatient to be unloaded. After Tanner had started the engine and turned up the heater, Becky waited for him to lean over. She'd made the first move the night before, so now it was his turn. Her entire self was poised to open itself up to him as soon as he kissed her. But he was nodding to himself, drumming his fingers on the steering wheel.

"I just got some news," he said. "It's pretty far-out."

She turned to him and presented her face, to suggest that his news could wait.

"Do you remember that time we were talking in the sanctuary?"

"Do I *remember* it?"

"Well, it got me thinking," he said. "You got me thinking. I realized it was time for me to take the next step."

In Becky's mind, his next step was to make a definitive break with Laura Dobrinsky. If the news was that he'd done it without her having insisted on it, she was happy to hear it.

"So, you know Quincy, right?"

Quincy Travers was one of Tanner's black friends, the drummer for the Bleu Notes.

"So Quincy's been playing with this guy from Cicero whose cousin is an agent. A really good agent—he gets his acts into clubs all over Chicago. And you know what? He's going to be there tonight. I just got a call back from him."

Becky shivered in the long coat her aunt had given her. The seat of the bus was much colder than it had been the night before. "That's great," she said.

"I know. This is our biggest crowd of the year by far. It's the perfect showcase."

The VW's little vents were blowing nothing but freezing air.

"Congratulations," Becky said.

"I only made the call because of you." Tanner took her gloved hands in his bare hands and squeezed them, as if to infuse her with enthusiasm. "Just knowing you understood what I'm trying to do—that made a huge difference."

Only abstractly did she appreciate being thanked. She didn't like sitting in an ice cave, talking about his music career and not about the night before. She didn't like imagining him and Laura and the Bleu Notes playing more gigs around Chicago.

"What's wrong?" he said.

"Nothing. That's great news."

He tenderly put two fingers on her cheek, but she averted her face. The lumpy, shadowy snow coating her window was like the cellulite pictured in her mother's *Redbook*s. Tanner rested his chin on her shoulder, his mouth near her ear. "When I see you, I feel like I can do anything."

She tried to speak, shivered, tried again. "And Laura?"

"What do you mean?"

"I thought she was your girlfriend."

He sat up straight. Outside the bus, teenaged boys were bellowing in the snow.

"I'm just wondering where I stand," Becky said. "I mean, after last night."

"Yeah."

"I mean, shouldn't we talk about it? Or is that too Crossroads?"

"It's pretty Crossroads."

"I only joined because of you. I thought you loved it."

"Yeah. I know. I have to have a conversation with her. It's just—here's the thing."

A snowball hit the frosted windshield. It stuck there, a darker blurry mass, and now a red-fingered hand was swiping snow off Becky's window. Through the cleared glass, she saw a junior-high kid packing a snowball. He fired it across the street, and another one slammed into the side of the bus. Tanner popped open his door, shouted at the kids, and shut the door again. "Stupid juvies."

Becky waited.

"So, it's hard," he said. "Everybody sees Laura as this intense, scary person, but there's a side of her that's really insecure. Really vulnerable. And—well, here's the thing."

"Who you want to be with," Becky said firmly.

"I know. I know what I need to do. It's just—tonight is not the night to have that conversation. Laura doesn't even care if we get an agent, but the rest of us do, and she's so radical, I can see her just walking out. Which—there go our keyboards, there go my harmonies. Even if she plays, and she's up there pissed off with me, it's going to be a mess."

Realistically, Becky knew there wasn't any rush. The fact of their having kissed, the fact of her sitting in his bus with him now, the fact of their having this conversation, was evidence of the inroads she'd made on his heart. If only she hadn't set her own heart on going to the concert with him! It was too late to undo how fervidly she'd imagined walking into the church on his arm, showing the world that he was hers, and telling Jeannie Cross about it in the morning.

"Aren't there other agents?"

"There are tons of agents," Tanner said. "But this guy, Benedetti, he's supposed to be really good, and this isn't like playing the Grove. Darryl Bruce is home from college, he's sitting in on lead guitar, and Biff Allard is bringing his congas. We've got a really full sound tonight, and the perfect audience."

"I thought the main thing was your record. Your demo, with your songs."

"Yeah. It still is. But you were right—I need to think bigger. I need to be playing four times as many gigs, building up an audience, making contacts."

Becky hoped he couldn't see, in the dreary cave light, that she was clenching her face muscles to keep from crying. "But so . . . if Laura's in the band . . . and you're playing gigs . . . how does that work?"

"I can find someone to replace her. I just can't do it in the next three hours."

An embarrassing squeak escaped from Becky's throat. She cleared it loudly. "So," she said. "You're breaking up with her?"

When Tanner didn't answer, she looked and saw that his eyes were closed, his hands pressed together between his knees.

"It's kind of important for me to know," she said. "After what happened last night."

"I know. I know. It's just hard. When you've been with a person for so long, and she's still so into you. It's hard."

"Or maybe you just don't really want to."

"That's not it. I swear to God, Becky. This is just a bad night to do it."

The need to cry could be as urgent as the need to pee. She picked up her shoulder bag. "I should probably go."

"You just got here."

"It's all right. There's a reception I told my mom I couldn't go to because I was going to the concert. I can at least make her happy."

"I'm not saying you can't go to the concert."

"You want me to go there and act like nothing happened? Or, what, I'm supposed to put a blanket over my head again?"

He filled his fists with his hair and pulled on it.

"It's almost like you're ashamed of me," she said.

"No, no, no. This is just—"

"I know, a bad night. I was really looking forward to it, but now— I'm not."

Before he could stop her, she jumped out of the bus. Leaving the door hanging open, she narrowed her eyes against the stinging snow and ran up the alley behind the bookstore, where the bus couldn't follow her. She could only hope that she was disappointing him as much as he'd disappointed her. She'd felt so *certain* of how their date was going to go: a delicious resumption of their kissing, followed by testimonials of amazement that they'd found their way to each other, followed by lengthier kissing, followed by her triumphal entry into the church with him. Now even the snow was unromantic, a painful hindrance. Everything had gone to shit.

She could feel wetness creeping into her only decent boots, which she was probably damaging irreparably, as she trudged the long blocks home in slanting snow. It was getting too dark to see well, and the physical effort of not slipping and falling kept her tears at bay until she reached the parsonage. She'd held out hope that Tanner might be waiting in his bus there, waiting to apologize and beg her to come to the concert with him, the consequences be damned. But except for a forlorn distant scraping of a shovel and a pair of unrecent tire tracks, nearly refilled with snow, her block of Highland Street was desolate. The only light in the parsonage was in Perry and Judson's room.

Inside, there was no sign of her mother. Was she still not back from her exercise class? Becky now felt ashamed of having been so unforthcoming with her, so certain she knew better how to handle Tanner. Her mother seemed to her the one person with whom she might safely share her disappointment. She brushed snow out of her hair and hurried upstairs, past the closed door of her brothers' room. At the sight of her bed, where just a few hours earlier she'd innocently dreamed of going to the concert, her disappointment came bursting out.

As she lay on the bed and wallowed in her conviction that Tanner was still in love with Laura, that he cared more about Laura's feelings than he did about hers, she thought she was crying not too loudly. But after some minutes there came a gentle knocking on her door. She went rigid.

"Becky?" Perry said.

"Go away."

"Are you all right?"

"Yes. Leave me alone."

"You sure?"

She wasn't all right. An anguished sound came out of her, the disappointment erupting again. It must have been audible to Perry, because he entered her room and shut the door behind him. Her irritation stopped her tears.

"Go away," she said. "I didn't say you could come in."

Increasing her irritation, he sat down beside her. Skin-crawling repugnance was probably a normal response to a pubescent brother's proximity, the abnormal thing her lack of a similar response to Clem, but the badness she sensed in Perry made the repugnance especially intense. She scooched away from him and wiped her face on her pillowcase.

"What's going on?" he said.

"Nothing you would understand."

"I see. You think I lack empathy."

She did suspect that he lacked empathy, but this wasn't the point. "I'm upset," she said, "about something that has nothing to do with you."

"I'm sensing a barrier to our getting to know each other better."

"Get out of my room!"

"Joke, sister. That was a joke."

"I got the joke. Okay? Now please get out of my room."

"There's something I need to say to you. But I have the distinct impression that you've been trying to stay away from me."

It was true that she'd been avoiding him, even more than usual, since the night he'd drawn her as his partner in a Crossroads dyad exercise. During the exercise, she'd felt proud of confronting him with his selfishness and self-involvement; excited to think that Crossroads was empowering her to become the family truth-teller. She'd guessed that she was hurting him, to the extent that an amoral brainiac was capable of being hurt, but she'd hoped that her honest witnessing might foster his own personal growth. Ever since that night, though, the sight of him had troubled her. No matter how on-target her assessment of his faults had been, no matter how much the truth had needed airing, she felt that somehow she, not he, had done a wrong thing.

"Here's what I've been wanting to say," he said. "To put it very simply, you were right. In our coat-closet conversation, which you'll no doubt remember. I've come to the conclusion that you were right."

His highbrow intonations were repellent. She reared away from him and stood up. "Where's Judson?"

"Judson is mulling the Stratego board. He luxuriates in the planning aspect."

"And Mom? Did she come home?"

"I've seen neither hide nor hair all day."

"That's weird," Becky said, heading to the door.

"Excuse me?" Perry jumped up and blocked her escape. "Did you not hear what I just said to you?"

"Please get out of my way."

"I think I'm entitled to two minutes of your attention, Becky. You said you wanted a relationship with me. You said, 'You're my brother.' That is a direct quote."

"That was Crossroads. You're supposed to say you want a relationship with everybody."

"Ah, so, in fact, you don't want a relationship with me."

"Will you give me a break? I'm having a really shitty day."

"And that's your response? Just walk away?"

Walking away was a well-known Crossroads no-no. Becky rolled her eyes and said, "Fine. Thank you for saying I was right. I'm not sure I was, but thank you for saying it. Now can I please go blow my nose?"

Perry stepped aside but followed her into the bathroom. For no fathomable reason, its Depression-era tub and sink had been installed in one cramped corner, leaving a needlessly large expanse of floor tiles, now cracked and discolored. Perry shut the door and sat down on the laundry hamper while Becky blew her nose.

"When I say you were right," he said, "I mean that you were right that I've never taken you seriously enough. We can skip over my reasons for that—they do me no honor. Suffice it to say I've never given you the credit you deserve. You were right to call me on that."

"Perry, come on. You don't have to do this."

"I need to say it. I've been unjust to you. And you were honest with me."

She threw up her arms in frustration. Wrong time, wrong place for a Crossroads dyad.

"I need you to believe," he went on, "that I'm trying to become a better person. That I've taken everything you said to me to heart. I won't bore you with every detail, but I've made some changes. I've sworn off intoxicants, for one thing."

She narrowed her eyes. "Is that what this is about? Were you afraid I was going to nark on you?"

"Not at all."

"You sure about that?"

"Yes!"

"Well, good. I'm glad to hear you've done some thinking. I'm glad my criticism was constructive."

"I need your help, though. I need—"

He broke off, his face reddening. She prayed that he wouldn't start crying on her. The one time she'd seen him cry at Crossroads, a hundred other people had been there to perform the task of touching him. It was strange that a person so visibly emotional, so ready to cry, both in public and in private, should persistently give her the impression that his emotings were detached from any real thing inside him. It made her feel as if something were wrong with *her* head.

"It's hard enough," he said, "to be in the same house with you and feel like I'm your enemy. But if we're going to be together in Crossroads, too, we need to find a way to have a better relationship." He took a deep breath. "I want to be your friend, Becky. Will you be my friend?"

Too late, she saw that she'd been cornered. She well knew, as did he, that the biggest of all Crossroad no-nos was to reject a person's offer of friendship. You had to accept the offer even if you didn't really mean to spend time with the person. If she spurned Perry's offer, and then went to Crossroads and practiced unconditional love, accepted the unqualified worth of everyone else in the group, became "friends" with whoever asked her, he would know she was a hypocrite. She would *be* a hypocrite. Craftily or not, he'd cornered her.

Overcoming her natural repugnance, the way Jesus had done with lepers, she went and crouched at his feet by the hamper. "I have a lot of trust issues with you," she said.

"For good reason. I am so sorry."

"You're right, though. We should try to get to know each other better. If you're willing to try, so am I."

Now he did let out a sob, but only one, a kind of gulp. He slid off the hamper and put his arms around her. "Thank you," he said into her shoulder.

Returning his hug wasn't so bad. Whatever precociously illicit things he might have done in secret, he was still a human being, still basically just a boy. He was small for a Hildebrandt, truly her little brother. At the feel of his narrow shoulders in her arms, something maternal stirred in her. He tried to cling to her when she stood up.

"I wonder where Mom is," she said. "Are you sure she didn't come home?"

"Jay said he hadn't seen her. It's conceivable she went straight to the Haefles'."

"Not in her exercise clothes."

"Good point."

She had to admit that in the wake of their embrace she felt slightly more at ease with him.

"It's weird," she said. "She made such a big deal about me being home by six."

"What for?"

"So I can go to the reception."

"What are you doing that for? You'll miss half the concert."

Disappointment welled up in her again. She turned away to hide it from him. "I'm not going."

"*What?*"

"I don't want to talk about it."

"Is that what you were crying about?" He jumped up and put a hot little hand on her shoulder. "Do you want to tell me what happened?"

She almost laughed. "You mean, now that we're friends? That's pretty slick, Perry."

"I guess I deserve that, but you have me all wrong."

"Part of being a friend is respecting a person's boundaries."

"Fair enough. I just wish you'd give me a chance. I know I haven't earned your trust. I haven't earned anybody's trust. But when I heard you crying, I thought, 'She's my sister.'"

"Judson's probably wondering when you're coming back."

"I'm going right now. Unless you want to tell me—"

"I don't."

"Okay, but listen. If you change your mind about the concert, I'll be here with Jay. You and I can walk over together when you're back."

Returning to her room, lying down on her bed, she tried to make sense of Perry's sudden kindness to her. Ordinarily, she would have assumed he had some hidden selfish motive. But in hugging him she'd caught a glimmer of the unqualified worth of every human being. Perry had no choice but to be his hot-handed, overly articulate little self, and the vulnerability he'd revealed to her hadn't seemed like just an act. Walking to the church with her pothead little brother, being together in the snow with him, was the bizarrest of scenarios, but the chance of their becoming friends was exciting in its very slenderness. She'd always had, in Clem, the only brother she needed, but now Clem was far away, preoccupied with his evidently fascinating girlfriend. The biggest barrier to Becky's relationship with Perry had been her feeling that he disdained her for her lesser intelligence. Maybe all she'd needed was some sign that he respected her and was interested in her as a person. Now that he'd given her such a sign, maybe they really could be friends. Maybe her whole family could be happier, beginning with the unlikely duo of her and Perry.

The feeling of goodwill with which she'd awakened in the morning, before losing it in the ice cave of Tanner's bus, was coming back. She felt a particular glow of gratitude for Crossroads, which had taught her to take risks. The risk she'd taken with Tanner had brought her pain, but in the glow of her goodwill she could see that she might have overreacted, might have pushed him too hard on the wrong night, might have set too much store on the outward appearance of going to the concert with him. Meanwhile, the risk of confronting Perry, in the coat closet at church, had encouraged him to take his own risk, by offering her his friendship. For better and for worse, but mostly for better, Crossroads was making her more alive.

At six o'clock, though there was still no sign of either of her parents, she got up to make herself presentable. The spectacle of blotch reflected in the bathroom mirror discouraged her, but she brushed her hair, reapplied her makeup, and went and knocked on Perry and Judson's door.

"Who is it?" Perry answered sharply.

"The war-game police. I'm coming in."

Opening the door, she saw Perry reclining on one elbow and Judson kneeling over their homemade board game, his ankles crossed beneath him in a position that would have excruciated anyone older than ten. With a subtle movement of her head, she beckoned Perry into the hall-way. He hopped right up.

"Do you have any eye drops?" she asked him in a low voice.

"Yes, as it happens, I do."

She waited while he ran upstairs to the third floor, thereby betraying where he'd been hiding his paraphernalia. The complicity in their trans-action, like the complicity of being in on the secret of his and Judson's war game, was giving her a sense of what life might be like in a happier family, with her at the center of it.

"You can keep this," Perry said, returning with a bottle. "My eye-drop-using days are over."

"Are you worried about Mom? The fact that she hasn't even called?"

"You think she's lying frozen in a snowdrift."

"It's just weird."

Perry frowned. "What time does the reception start?"

"Six thirty."

"So here's an idea. Why don't you go to the concert and let Jay and me go to the Haefles'? Admittedly, I'm judging only by appearances, but I have the sense you don't actually want to miss the concert."

"I don't think the Haefles want little kids there."

"Assuming you don't put me in that category, I think you're underes-timating Jay. He has an old soul."

Becky considered her long-haired brother. To feel allied with his brainpower, rather than mocked and threatened by it, was a strange sen-sation. "You would do that for me?"

It was painful to recall, but Russ had loved Rick Ambrose.

Once upon a time, in New York, at the seminary on East Forty-ninth Street, Russ and Marion had been the It couple, into whose married-student apartment other young seminarians crowded three or four nights a week to smoke their cigarettes, listen to jazz, and inspire one another with visions of modern Christianity's renaissance in social action. Twiggy, pretty Marion, more deeply and eclectically read than anyone else, wearing snug pedal pushers and bulky sweaters that evoked the Welsh countryside of Dylan Thomas, was the envy of Russ's fellow seminarians. Whatever she and Russ did was ipso facto the hip thing. Even pulling up stakes and relocating to rural Indiana, which he'd felt obliged to do when Marion became pregnant and his applications for more exotic postings were rejected, had seemed like an edgy move. Only when Marion withdrew into motherhood, grew heavier and wearier, and Russ needed to come up with fifty sermons a year, rewritten by Marion and delivered in two churches with a combined flock of fewer than three hundred, at eight thirty and ten o'clock every Sunday, did the life she'd once made large for him begin to feel inescapably small. Whenever he contrived a respite from the Indiana farmhouse, by begging favors of pastors from nearby churches, and attended conferences in Columbus or Chicago or protested for civil rights, he was bittersweetly reminded of the edge that he and Marion had lost.

In prosperous New Prospect, although he continued to agitate for social justice, the political sleepiness of First Reformed had just about defeated him when Rick Ambrose arrived to wake it up. Where Russ came by his alienation from the suburbs honestly, by virtue of his Mennonite childhood, Ambrose's was adopted. He'd been the causeless young rebel in the otherwise happy family of an endocrinologist in Shaker Heights, Ohio. On the night of his high-school graduation, he and his girlfriend had ridden his motorcycle down the main drag of Shaker Heights and straight out of town. A month later, on a highway in Idaho, he and the girl had been passed by four teenagers doing a hundred miles an hour in a Chevy that broadsided a rancher crossing in front of them in his pickup. Beside the road, staring at teenaged death, Ambrose had heard a bell-clear calling from God. Seven years later, as a minister in training, he felt called to work with troubled young people. When he came to Russ's office to accept, in person, the job of director of youth programming, he flattered Russ. A congregation in Oak Park had offered him a position with better pay, but he'd chosen First Reformed because, he said, he admired Russ's vocal commitment to peace and justice. He said, "I think we'll make a great team."

Warmed by the sense of being recognized, and taken with the simmering charisma of his young associate, imagining they might become friends, Russ repeatedly invited him to dinner at the parsonage. When Ambrose finally accepted, and lingered at the table after the kids had been excused, he paid so much attention to Marion that Russ felt uneasy about the scant attention he'd lately given her himself. Marion had never been a flirt, but she seemed enjoyably energized by Ambrose's intensity. After he left, Russ was surprised to hear she hadn't liked him. "That glower of his," she said. "It's like a mind-control trick he picked up somewhere and fell in love with. It's a car salesman's trick—making people afraid they don't have your approval. They'll do anything to get it, and they never stop to wonder why they even want it."

It was true that, for all his foul-mouthed forthrightness, there was something unknowable about Ambrose, and Russ never quite shook the awareness of his affluent background, in contrast to his own. But Russ had an eager and generous heart, which suited him well to the ministry, and Ambrose had been right: they made a good team. Their mentoring styles were complementary, Ambrose's psychological and streetwise, Russ's more political and Bible-oriented, and he was grateful that Ambrose took charge of the stormier kids in the youth fellowship, leaving him to lead the others by example.

After hearing Russ's stories of his time among the Navajos, Ambrose had proposed that the fellowship refocus itself on a spring work camp in Arizona. Russ loved the idea so much that he soon forgot it hadn't been his. Arizona was *his* place, after all. Arriving on the arid reservation, landing in waste and privation beyond what anyone else on the bus had experienced, he felt forty pairs of suburban teenage eyes looking to him for courage and guidance. It transpired that Ambrose, though he had the swagger of a tough who didn't shy from manual labor, couldn't so much as drive a clean nail without first bending two of them. Time and again, he came to Russ, or even to Clem, for help with seemingly elementary tasks. Although his ineptitude later became a real issue—was arguably, indeed, the catalyst of Russ's humiliation—on the first spring trip it served to highlight Russ's capability.

By the following October, so many teenagers were thronging to the fellowship that Russ worried about a surprise inspection by the fire marshal. Beyond the sheer numbers, what excited him was the kind of kids who were joining. There were long-haired musicians, there was a raft of blond girls from the Episcopal church, there were even some Black kids, and they weren't just seeking spiritual renewal. They wanted to invite guest speakers from the inner city and the peace movement, they wanted to examine their suburban affluence. For six years, in his sermons, Russ had tried to awaken the adult congregation of First Reformed to the implications of its privilege. Now, suddenly, for the first time since New York, he was at the center of the It place. He knew he had Ambrose to thank for this, but he also knew that reports of the Arizona trip had set the high school afire, and that the promise of a second trip was driving the rise in membership numbers. In November, after a rollicking Sunday-night meeting, Ambrose, who so rarely smiled, turned to Russ with a cockeyed grin.

"Pretty wild, isn't it."

"Incredible," Russ said.

"I counted fourteen kids who weren't here last week."

"Absolutely incredible."

"It was Arizona," Ambrose said, more seriously. "That trip completely changed the dynamic. That's what made this whole thing real."

Russ, already giddy, felt even giddier. Arizona was *his* place. He, no less than Ambrose, had changed the dynamic. In his giddiness, through the winter and into the early spring, he plunged into the spirit of the times. He took the risk of rapping about his feelings, he opened himself to new styles of music. He found that shutting his eyes and raising a clenched fist, while speaking of Dr. King or Stokely Carmichael, whose hand he'd once shaken, had a powerful effect on the young people. Though it never sounded quite convincing, he took to using curse words such as *bullshit*. He let his hair grow over his collar and started a beard, the latter lasting until Marion remarked on his resemblance to John the Baptist. He was stung enough to shave the beard, but he felt that Marion was becoming a drag. He preferred the excitement of the attention he was getting from the new breed of girls in the fellowship. They swore as bluely as the boys did, they were loud and gross in the sexual innuendoes they traded with the boys, and yet, being suburban, their naïveté was even greater than his had been at their age. None of them had decapitated a chicken or seen a bank seize a man's ancestral farm. Russ believed he could offer them a depth of authentic experience lacking in young Ambrose. He put more thought into his Sunday-night prayers than he put into his Sunday-morning sermons (Marion did much of that thinking for him anyway), because the dream he'd once had in New York, the vision of a nation transformed by vigorously Christian ethics, was alive in the blue-jeaned throng in the First Reformed function hall, not in the sleepy gray heads in the sanctuary.

Among the new converts to the fellowship was a young woman, Laura Dobrinsky, who was tight with Tanner Evans and thus instantly popular. At her first meeting, Russ had greeted her with a hug that she did not return, and at subsequent meetings he'd been unsettled by the openly hostile way she stared at him. It seemed strangely personal, unlike anything he could remember being the object of. Per the discussions of adolescent psychology he'd had with Ambrose, Russ hypothesized that Laura had a problem with her father and was seeing him in Russ. But one afternoon in March, ten days before the Arizona trip, he emerged from the church library, where he'd been consulting references for a sermon, and heard Laura Dobrinsky uttering the words *That dude is such an unbelievable fucking dork*. From the silence that fell as he rounded a corner and saw half a dozen girls seated in the corridor, and from the glances the girls then exchanged, the smirks they imperfectly suppressed, he conceived the hurtful suspicion that Laura had been referring to *him*. Especially hurtful was that one of the girls smirking was the popular, blond Sally Perkins, who a few weeks earlier, after school, had come to his office and opened up to him about her unhappiness at home. Most of the popular kids preferred to go to Ambrose with their troubles, and Russ had been surprised and gratified that Sally had come to him.

Returning to his office, he tried to cheer himself with the thought that Sally Perkins wouldn't have come to him if she thought he was a dork, and that, even if Laura Dobrinsky did think so, it was silly to let himself be hurt by a girl with wildly unresolved anger issues, and also that maybe she *hadn't* been referring to him, maybe the dork in question was Clem, which would explain the girls' embarrassment when they saw Clem's father; but he was still in distress when Rick Ambrose came knocking on his door.

Taking a seat, his expression pained, Ambrose told Russ that he'd been hearing some complaints—or not complaints, concerns—about Russ's style of ministry. Some of the kids seemed uncomfortable, in particular, with Russ's weekly prayers. Ambrose himself was fine with them, but he suggested that Russ consider "toning it down a bit" with the scriptural language. "Do you know what I mean?"

He could hardly have found a worse moment to criticize Russ. "I put a lot of thought into those prayers," Russ said. "When I cite Scripture, it's always in direct relation to the theme that you and I have chosen for the week."

Ambrose nodded judiciously. "Like I said, I don't have a problem with it myself. It's just something you should be aware of. Some of the kids we're drawing don't have any religious background. Obviously, the hope is that everyone will find their way to an authentic faith, but people need to find their own way, and that takes time."

Because of Laura's remark, Russ felt angrier than Ambrose's tactful words merited. "I don't care," he said. "This is a church for believers, not a social club. I'd rather lose a few members than lose sight of our mission."

Ambrose pursed his lips and blew a silent whistle.

"Who are the people complaining?" Russ said. "Is there anyone besides Laura Dobrinsky?"

"Laura is definitely the most outspoken of them."

"Well, and I would not be sorry to see her leave."

"She's a handful, I agree. But the energy she brings is really valuable."

"I'm not going to change my style because one angry girl is complaining to you about me."

"It's not just her, Russ. This is something we need to deal with before we leave on Spring Trip. I wonder if you'd be willing . . ." Ambrose glowered at the floor. "I wonder if we should open up part of the meeting on Sunday and talk about where we stand, as a group, with expressions of Christian doctrine. You could hear Laura, she could hear you. I think it could be a really valuable conversation for the group to have before we all get on the bus."

"I'm not interested in a public shouting match with Laura Dobrinsky."

"I'll be there to make sure it doesn't get out of hand. I promise, I will back you up. I just—"

"No." Russ stood up angrily. "I'm sorry, but no. That does not sound right to me. I'm happy to let you do your thing, but I would ask that you let me do mine."

Ambrose sighed, as if to suggest a withholding of approval, but he said nothing more. Russ was left with the impression that much whispering was being done behind his back, and that he would do well to strengthen his relationships with the group's rowdier element. At the next Sunday meeting, the last before Arizona, he made friendly forays into that element. Whether the negative vibe he got from it was real or just the product of his paranoia, it gave his movements a marionette-like clumsiness; a dorkiness. Sitting in the huge group circle at the end of the meeting, he sought the eyes of Sally Perkins, hoping to exchange a warm smile, but she seemed determined not to look at him.

On the Friday afternoon before Palm Sunday, aware of the emotional bonding that occurred on long bus rides, he stationed himself between the two interstate buses in the First Reformed parking lot and waited to see which of them would be preferred by the kids with whom he needed to bond, so that he could board it. But the normally visible forces of teenaged social physics were scrambled in the parking lot. Parents stood chattering among haphazard piles of luggage, preteen siblings ran on and off the buses, latecomers arrived with tooting car horns, and everyone kept pestering Russ with logistical questions. He was loading five-gallon drums of paint into a bus's luggage bay when, behind his back, the hidden social forces resolved into a mob of long-haired kids outside the other bus, which Ambrose had chosen.

Too late, he saw that he and Ambrose should have discussed their bus assignments—that he should have insisted on having a chance to repair his rapport with Laura Dobrinsky's clique. Riding west into the night, in the unpreferred bus, he felt exiled. Even when he succeeded, the next morning, in trading places with Ambrose, the scene on the other bus was unsatisfactory. The kids had been awake all night, laughing and singing, and now they only wanted to sleep. Tanner Evans kindly sat down with him, but soon Tanner, too, was sleeping. By the time they reached the reservation, Russ had become afraid to look over his shoulder at the kids behind him. It was a relief to know that most of them were going on with Ambrose to the demonstration school at Kitsillie, up high on the mesa.

Waiting in the settlement of Rough Rock was Russ's Navajo friend Keith Durochie. The back of Keith's Ford pickup was heaped with new and scavenged plumbing supplies. He informed Russ that he and the other elders were expecting him to install a septic line and put a sink and toilet in the school. When Russ replied that Ambrose, not he, was leading the Kitsillie contingent, Keith didn't hide his displeasure. He'd seen, the year before, the kind of skills Ambrose had.

Russ waved Ambrose over and explained the situation. "How would you feel about doing some plumbing work up there?"

"I would need help," Ambrose said.

"This is the job at Kitsillie," Keith said to Russ. "This is what we have for you this year."

"Shoot," Russ said.

"I kept the equipment safe all winter."

"I'm willing to give it a try," Ambrose said. "Between Keith and Clem, we'll probably be okay."

Keith threw Russ a look—Clem was seventeen—and turned to Ambrose. "You stay here," he said firmly. "Let Russ go to Kitsillie."

"That's fine."

"Rick," Russ said. He didn't want to be the white guy arguing with a Navajo, but the kids going to Kitsillie had counted on being with Ambrose. "I think we should talk about this."

"I'm no kind of plumber," Ambrose said. "If that's the job, I'd be more comfortable trading places with you."

Keith walked away, satisfied that the matter was settled, and Ambrose hurried off to the kids with whom he was unexpectedly spending a week in Rough Rock. Russ could have pursued him and made him speak to the Kitsillie group, made him explain why he'd chosen not to join it, but instead he placed his trust in God. He thought that God's will might be at work in Keith, guiding the course of events, offering Russ a providential chance to forge better relationships with the popular kids. Submitting to His will, he shouldered his duffel bag and boarded the Kitsillie bus; and there it was instantly clear that God had harsher plans for him.

The week on the mesa was torture. Everyone, even his own son, thought he was lying about why he'd replaced Ambrose, and to tell them the full truth—that Keith Durochie had a low opinion of Ambrose—would have been unfair to Keith and unkind to Ambrose. Russ was still stupid about Ambrose, still considered him a friend worth protecting. But he wasn't stupid otherwise. He saw how acidly the group resented him for being there. He saw the lengths to which Laura Dobrinsky and her friends went to avoid working with him, he felt their hatred at every nightly candle talk, and he knew he had a pastoral responsibility to raise the issue. He tried repeatedly to have a private word with Sally Perkins, who not long ago had trusted him enough to confide in him, but she kept eluding him. Afraid that terrible things might be said to his face in a group confrontation, he chose to endure his misery in silence until Ambrose could confirm the reason he'd stayed behind in Rough Rock.

By the time the two groups reunited, Russ was too low to beg Ambrose to make a clarifying statement. He waited for Ambrose to do it voluntarily, but Ambrose had had an amazing week in Rough Rock—had wowed the half of the group that still related to Russ; had gained ground on Russ's own turf—and he seemed oblivious to Russ's misery. Witnessing the pointedly joyous hugs with which the Kitsillie group greeted Ambrose, Russ lamented his heart's generosity. He rued that he hadn't heeded Marion's warnings. Only now could he see that he and his young associate had been engaged, from the beginning, in a competition of which only one of them had been aware.

And even then, even knowing that Ambrose was not his friend, had never been his friend, he was shocked by the audacity of Ambrose's betrayal of him. At the first Sunday meeting after Arizona, when Laura and Sally stood up to lacerate Russ's heart and hurl their teenaged acid in his face, Ambrose did nothing to stop it—just stood in a corner and glowered with disapproval, presumably of Russ himself—and when the majority of the group walked out of the fellowship room, which was baking in an April heat wave, Ambrose sided not with his colleague, not with the well-mannered kids from the church that employed him, but with the rabble from outside the church, the hip kids, the popular girls, and left Russ to ask God what he'd done to deserve such punishment.

He got the answer, or at least an answer, some endless minutes later. Ambrose returned to Russ and asked him to come downstairs. "I tried to warn you," he said as they descended the stairs. "I really think this could have been avoided."

"You said you would back me up," Russ said. "You said, quote, you wouldn't let it get out of hand."

"And you refused to have the conversation."

"I'd say this qualifies as out of hand!"

"This is serious, Russ. You need to hear what Sally just told me."

The air was scarcely cooler on the second floor. Ambrose led Russ into his unventilated office, where Laura and Sally were seated on his sofa, and shut the door. Laura gave Russ a cruel smile of victory. Sally stared sullenly at her hands.

"Sally?" Ambrose said.

"I don't really see the point," Sally said. "I'm done with this church."

"I think Russ has a right to hear from you directly."

Sally closed her eyes. "It's just that I'm totally creeped out. It's just what a nightmare Spring Trip turned out to be. It was like my worst nightmare when he walked onto that bus. I couldn't believe it."

"There was a reason Russ and I traded places," Ambrose said. "He was better at the work that needed to be done up there."

"Yeah, I'm sure. I'm sure he found some reason. But the way it felt to me was that I couldn't get away from him."

The office was unbearably hot. Russ was appalled and frightened and perplexed. "Sally, look at me," he said. "Please open your eyes and look at me."

"She doesn't feel like opening her eyes," Laura said in a righteous tone.

"I just wanted him to leave me alone," Sally said. "I got a really creepy feeling, that time in his office. And then, I couldn't believe it, he followed me to Kitsillie."

Worse even than her refusal to look at Russ were the words *he, his, him*. They reduced him to the It in an I–It relationship.

"I don't understand," he said to Sally. "You and I had a good conversation in my office, and it would have been wrong of me not to follow up. That's what I do as a minister. I don't know why you think I'm somehow singling you out."

"Because that's how it feels to me," she said. "How many ways do I have to find to tell you to leave me alone?"

"I truly wasn't aware of trying to push you. I just wanted you to know that I'm available. That I'm a person you can trust and open up with."

"That's the thing," Laura said. "She doesn't trust you."

"Laura," Ambrose said. "Let Sally speak for herself."

"No, I'm done," Sally said, jumping to her feet. "He ruined Spring Trip for me. He gives me a bad feeling about this whole group. I'm done."

She fled the office. With a withering glance at the It that was Russ, Laura stood up and followed her. It seemed to Russ, in the silence that ensued, that only he was sweating. When Ambrose leaned back in his desk chair and clasped his hands behind his head, the underarms of his denim shirt were enviably dry.

"I don't know what to do here, Russ."

"I was only trying to help her."

"Really? She says you complained to her about your sex life with Marion."

Sweat flowed from so many of Russ's pores, it felt like a skin he was shedding. "Are you out of your mind? That is simply a lie."

"I'm just reporting what she said."

Blindsided by the accusation, Russ tried to shake his head clear, tried to remember his exact words in his conversation with Sally.

"That's not correct," he said. "What I said to her was—I said that marriage is a blessing but can also be a struggle. That the enemy in a long relationship is boredom. That sometimes there's not enough love in a marriage to overcome that boredom. And then—you have to understand, there was a context to it."

Ambrose waited, glowering.

"We'd been talking about her parents' divorce, how angry she is at them, and I thought we were close to a breakthrough. When she asked me if I was ever bored in *my* marriage, I felt I had to share something honest with her. I thought it was important for her to know that even a man of the cloth, even a pastor she respects—"

"Russ, Russ, Russ."

"What was I supposed to do? Not answer honestly?"

"Within reason. There's a certain art to it."

"*She* asked *me*, 'Are you bored in your marriage?'"

"I'm sorry to say that's not how she remembers it. As she understood it, you were coming on to her."

"Are you out of your mind? I have a fifteen-year-old daughter!"

"I'm not saying that's what you were doing. But can you see why she might have perceived it that way?"

"*She* came to see *me*. If anyone was doing the coming-on, it was—do you know what I think happened? It was Laura. As soon as she saw Sally getting closer to me, putting her trust in me, Laura turned her against me. The person with the dirty mind here is Laura. Sally was perfectly comfortable with me until Laura got ahold of her."

Ambrose seemed unexcited by Russ's theory. "I know you don't like Laura," he said.

"Laura does not like me."

"But take a step back and look at yourself. What were you thinking, talking about your sexual boredom to a vulnerable seventeen-year-old? Even if she was coming on to you, which I don't believe, you had a clear responsibility to shut that down. Hard. Right away. Unambiguously."

It didn't matter if Ambrose's glowering was just a trick. Under the pressure of it, Russ stepped back and was mortified by what he saw: not the sexual creepiness he stood accused of (the girls of the fellowship were taboo to him in umpteen ways) but the fatuousness of thinking he could ever be as hip as Ambrose. More than once, he'd heard Ambrose confess to the group that he'd been an arrogant, heartless prick as a teenager, and Russ had seen how thrilled the group was, not only by Ambrose's honesty but by the image of him breaking female hearts. Made giddy by attention from a popular girl, Russ had imagined that he'd mastered the skill of honesty himself and could somehow erase his own timidity as a teenager, retroactively become a boy at ease with the likes of Sally Perkins. In his giddiness, he'd confessed, at least by implication, that Marion no longer turned him on. He'd felt the need to shed Marion, break free of her, in order to be more like Ambrose; and now his vanity stood shamefully revealed. His only thought was to get away, find fresher air, and seek comfort in God's mercy.

"I guess I need to apologize," he said.

"It's too late for that," Ambrose said. "Those kids aren't coming back."

"Maybe you should tell them why you weren't in Kitsillie. If they heard it from you—"

"Kitsillie's not the issue. Didn't you hear what they were saying? The issue is your style of ministry. It's simply not compatible with the kids I'm trying to reach."

"The groovy kids."

"The troubled kids. The ones who need an adult they can relate to. There are plenty of other kids who appreciate a more traditional style, and you'll be fine with them. The numbers should be small enough for you to handle by yourself."

"What are you saying?"

"I'm saying I can't keep working here."

Ambrose's eyes were on him, but Russ felt too loathsomely sweaty to raise his own. The trip he'd been on since October had been the fantasy of a dork freeloading on another man's charisma. Picturing the sorry little rump group that would remain after tonight, he could see only shame. Even the kids who stayed would never respect him after what they'd witnessed.

"You can't leave," he said. "You're still under contract."

"I will finish out the school year."

"No," Russ said. "It's your group now. I'm not going to fight you for it."

"I'm not saying you should quit. I'm saying I will find another church."

"And I'm saying take it. I don't want it." Fearing he would cry, Russ stood up and went to the door. "You didn't say one goddamned word in my defense up there."

"You're right," Ambrose said. "I'm sorry about that."

"The hell you are."

"It's unfortunate that the whole group got pulled into this. I know that was brutal for you."

"I don't want your compassion. In fact, you can shove it up your ass."

Those were the last words he ever spoke to Ambrose. He left the church that night with a shame so crippling that he didn't see how he could set foot in it again. His impulse was to resign from First Reformed and never again have anything to do with teenagers. But he couldn't put his family through another move—Becky especially was having a splendid time at school—and so, the next morning, he went to Dwight Haefle and asked that Ambrose be given full charge of the youth group. Haefle, alarmed, asked why. Embracing his shame, not going into detail, Russ said he couldn't relate to high-school kids. He said he would still run Sunday school and confirmation classes, would happily do more pastoral visitation, and might like to start an outreach program in the inner city.

"Hmm," Haefle said. "Perhaps a few more sermons, too?"

"Absolutely."

"More committee work."

"Definitely."

Haefle, who was sixty-three, seemed to weigh Russ's failure against the agreeable prospect of working less. "Rick does seem to be doing a bang-up job," he said.

From the senior minister's office, Russ went to the church secretary and asked her to instruct Ambrose to direct any future communications to him in written form. Later that day, after getting the message, Ambrose came and tapped on Russ's door, which Russ had locked. "Hey Russ," he said. "You in there?"

Russ said nothing.

"Written communication? What the fuck?"

Russ knew he was being childish, but his hurt and hatred had a horizonless totality, unrelieved by adult perspective, and beneath them was the sweetness of being thrown upon God's mercy: of making himself so alone and so wretched that only God could love him. He refused to speak to Ambrose, either on the day following his humiliation or ever after. While he performed his other duties vigorously, starting a women's circle in the inner city, reaching new heights of political eloquence in his sermons, earning his paychecks and proving that everyone else still valued him, he avoided Ambrose and lowered his eyes when they accidentally met. By and by—Russ could sense it—Ambrose began to hate him for hating him. This, too, was sweet, because it gave Russ company and helped sustain his own hatred. Though he had some hope that the congregation was unaware of their feud, there was no hiding it in the church offices. Dwight Haefle kept trying to broker a peace, calling meetings, and the shamefulness of Russ's refusals, the knowledge of how childish he appeared to Haefle and the secretarial staff, even to the janitor, compounded his wretchedness. His grievance with Ambrose was like a hair shirt, like a strand of barbed wire he wore wrapped around his chest. He suffered and in his suffering felt close to God.

The torment for which there was no reward came from Marion. Never having trusted Ambrose, she blamed him entirely for Russ's humiliation. Russ ought to have been grateful for her loyalty, but instead it made him feel all the more alone. The difficulty was that he could never tell her the real story of the shaming that Ambrose and Sally had inflicted on him, because the story hinged on his having admitted to Sally, in a fit of admittedly poor judgment, that he and his wife very rarely made love anymore.

This had obviously been a terrible betrayal of Marion. And yet, by a curious alchemy, as the months went by, he came to feel that Marion herself
had been the cause of his humiliation, by having become unattractive to
him. In the illogic of the alchemy, the more Marion was to blame, the
less Sally was. Finally there came a night when Sally appeared to him in
a dream, wearing an innocent but breast-accentuating argyle sweater, and
meltingly gave him to understand that she preferred him to Ambrose and
was ready to be his. Some unsleeping shred of superego steered the dream
away from consummation, but he woke up in a state of maximum arousal.
Creeping from the bed, his self-awareness attenuated by the darkness of
the parsonage, he paid an onanistic visit to the bathroom. Into the sink
came concrete substantiation of Sally's complaint with him. He saw that it
had been inside him all along.

Every man seeking salvation had a signature weakness to remind him
of his nullity before the Lord and complicate communion with Him.
Russ's own weakness had been revealed to him in 1946, in Arizona,
where his susceptibility to female beauty had aggravated a crisis of faith
in the religion of his brethren. The image of Marion's dewy dark eyes, her
kiss-inviting mouth, her narrow waist and slender neck and fine-boned
wrists, had come buzzing, like a huge and never resting hornet, into the
formerly chaste chamber of his soul. Neither the imagined fires of Hell
nor the very real prospect of breaking with his brethren could still the
buzzing of that hornet. Although the result had been a permanent estrangement from his parents, he'd resolved his spiritual crisis by adopting
a less stringent but still legitimate form of Christian faith, and he'd solved
the problem of his weakness by lawfully wedding Marion.

Or so it had seemed. In the wake of his taboo-upending dream, he saw
that he hadn't actually overcome his weakness—that he'd merely repressed
it from his consciousness. Now the dream had opened his eyes. Now, at
forty-five, he saw beauty at every turn—in the forty-year-old women who
turned to him with startling friendliness on Pirsig Avenue, the thirty-
year-olds he glimpsed in passing cars, the twenty-year-old candy stripers
at the hospital. Now he was beset not by a single hornet but by a chaotically
swirling swarm of them. Try as he might, he couldn't shut the windows of
his soul against them. And then along came Frances Cottrell.

The afterfeel of her teasing little kick was persisting in his hip as he piloted the Fury through heavy snow on Archer Avenue. Three cars ahead of him, an orange truck was flashing yellow lights and strewing salt, but he had yet to see a snowplow. Frances had fallen silent, and he felt obliged to say something, if only to defuse the charge of her having foot-prodded her pastor in the vicinity of his genitals, but the Fury's tractionless tires were palpably shimmying. If he got stuck in the snow, significantly delayed, the outing would become a misadventure that Marion, the next time she saw Kitty at church, might naturally remark on and thereby learn that Frances, not Kitty, had come along with him. As if he were one with the Fury, he willed himself to keep a grip. It was vital to avoid hard braking, but the momentum of events was frightening—Perry's giving drugs to Frances's son, the painful conversation that Russ was now obliged to have with him, Frances's invitation to smoke marijuana with her, and the risk that if Russ declined her invitation she would look elsewhere for company on her youth quest; the upsetting fact that she'd *already* been looking elsewhere, not more than an hour ago. She'd sat chatting away with Rick Ambrose, against whose hipness Russ had abundantly demonstrated he could not contend.

"So, ah," he said, when he'd safely braked for a stoplight. "You had a good talk with Rick?"

"I did."

"I don't suppose he mentioned that he and I are not on speaking terms."

"No, I already knew that. Everybody knows that."

So much for his hope that their feud wasn't universal knowledge.

"Why do you ask?" she said. "Am I not allowed to talk to him if I want to be friends with you?"

"Of course not. You can talk to whoever you like. Just be aware that everything with Rick Ambrose is always about Rick Ambrose. He can be very seductive, and you might think he's your friend. But you'd better watch your back."

"Why, Reverend Hildebrandt," she said with a lilt. "I do believe you're jealous."

The traffic light turned green, and he nudged the gas pedal. The rear wheels squealed and fishtailed a little.

"I mean jealous of Crossroads," she said. "Rick's got a hundred and fifty kids adoring him every Sunday. You get eight old ladies twice a month. I'd be jealous, too, if I were you."

"I'm not jealous. There's nowhere I'd rather be right now than here."

"That's nice of you to say."

"I mean it."

"Okay. But then why the hard feelings about Rick? I guess it's none of my business. But if he's great at what he does and you're great at what you do—I don't see the problem."

Even on a straight stretch of road, the car was subtly bucking, wanting to spin.

"It's a long story," Russ said.

"In other words, none of my business."

Russ's refusal to forgive Ambrose, which for nearly three years had organized his interior life and received daily support from Marion, seemed silly when he imagined explaining it to Frances. Worse than silly: unattractive. He saw that, to have a chance with her, he might need to let go of his hatred. But his heart didn't want to. The loss would be huge, would waste a thousand days of nursing his grudge, would render them meaningless in retrospect. There was also the danger that, if he made peace with Ambrose, Frances would feel even freer to admire Ambrose, and that he, Russ, would end up with nothing—neither his righteous pain nor Frances as his private reward for bearing it. He and Ambrose would still be competing, and he would lose the competition.

"Not to be all Mrs. Fix-It," she said, "but Crossroads has been so good for Larry, and you've been so good for me. It seems like there ought to be some solution."

"Rick doesn't like me, and I don't like Rick. It's just a natural antipathy."

"But why? Why? It goes against everything you say in your sermons. It goes against what you said to me about turning the other cheek. I can't stop thinking about that. It's the reason I wanted to come along with you today."

The spot on his hip where she'd kicked him was still buzzing. He understood her to be saying that she was attracted to his goodness, and that, in order to do a very bad thing, to break his vows of marriage, he was now required to practice goodness.

"It means a lot to me," he said. "That you came along today."

"Oh, pooh. It's an honor."

"You mentioned getting involved in Crossroads yourself." A tremor in his voice betrayed his anxiety. "Were you serious about that?"

"God, you really are jealous."

Again—*again*—she prodded his upper leg with her toe.

"My only job," she said, "is being a mother. I only get to work with you and Kitty twice a month, so, yes, I asked Rick if I could work in Crossroads as an adviser. He didn't seem too enthusiastic, but they always take a couple of parents on the Arizona trip, and he put me on the list for that."

"For the spring trip," Russ said, aghast.

"Yes!"

Arizona was *his* place. The thought of her being there with Ambrose was atrocious.

"I'm sorry," she said, "I know I shouldn't try to save the day. But you should be going on those trips yourself. You obviously love the Navajos, you lived there for however many years. If you and Rick could patch things up, we could all be there together. Wouldn't that be fun? I would love that."

She bounced on the seat, so lovely in her energy that Russ became confused. *Lo, I bring you tidings of great joy—peace on earth among all men.* The opposing headlights on Archer Avenue were tightly bunched, in every car a stewing driver. There was nothing of Christmas in the mess the weather was making. The joy of the season was in Frances, in her childlike questioning of the strife between Russ and Ambrose, and a tendril of her joy was reaching into Russ's hardened heart. Was it possible? Might he finally forgive Rick Ambrose? If his reward on earth were Frances? A week in Arizona in her hopeful, playful, eye-delighting presence? Or maybe more than just a week—maybe half a lifetime? Was she the second chance that God was giving him? The chance to entirely transform his life? To joyfully make love with a joyful woman? He'd been hating himself and Ambrose for a thousand Marion-darkened days, imagining that he was close to God, while all along, every second of every day, a simple turn of his heart toward forgiveness, which was the essence of Christ's message to the world, the true meaning of Christmas, had been there to be freely chosen.

"I'm going to think about that," he said.

"Please do," she said. "There's no earthly reason you and Rick can't get along."

In medieval romances, a lady set her suitor an impossible task to perform, the retrieval of the Grail, the slaying of a dragon. It seemed to Russ that his fair lady, in her hunting cap, was requiring him to slay a dragon in his heart.

Mayor Daley didn't plow Englewood until the streets of white neighborhoods were cleared to bare pavement. Russ zigzagged through side streets, where the snow was more powdery and gave better traction, and maintained his momentum by rolling through stop signs. By the time the Community of God came into view, the hour was approaching five o'clock. To get home by seven, so that the trip didn't become a thing that Marion might comment on to Kitty Reynolds, he needed to unload the Fury quickly.

The door to the community center was locked, the light above it off. Russ rang the bell, and they waited in the invisibly falling snow, Frances stamping her feet against the chill, until the light came on and Theo Crenshaw opened the door.

"I'd almost given up on you," he said to Russ.

"Yeah, pretty serious snow."

An impression that Russ had had before—that Theo was reluctant to acknowledge Frances's presence—deepened when Theo turned away and kicked a wooden wedge under the door.

"I'm Frances," she said brightly. "Remember me?"

Theo nodded without looking at her. He was dressed in a saggy velour pullover and ill-fitting stretch trousers. He seemed immune to the vanity that had led Russ to wear his favorite shirt and his sheepskin coat for Frances. The poignancy of an urban preacher, beloved on Sundays to the women of his congregation but otherwise so very alone in his church, with no support staff, no associate, his annual salary paltry, his primary sustenance spiritual, was especially keen on a raw December evening. Russ thought there might be no one he admired more than Theo, no one he knew more authentically Christian. Theo made him feel as privileged as Rick Ambrose made him feel disadvantaged, and he could imagine how Frances, showing up in her suburban blond loveliness, might be an unwelcome apparition to Theo.

He was pleased to see her pitch right in and hustle boxes into the community center. He hoped that Theo, seeing her cheerful industry, might better acknowledge her in the future. As always, the delivery of food and toys was a straightforward transaction. Russ expected no thanks for the donations, and Theo expected no lingering for sociability. When all the boxes were inside, Theo put his hands on his hips and said, "Good. Some ladies will be here in the morning for anybody who wants to stop by."

"And we will see you here again on Tuesday," Russ said. He clapped his hands and turned to Frances. "Shall we?"

He saw that she was holding a small, flat package. It was wrapped in Santa Claus paper and red ribbon.

"Will you do something for me?" she asked Theo. "Will you give this to Ronnie tomorrow? Tell him it's from the lady he made the drawings with?"

Russ hadn't seen the package in any of the boxes. She must have had it in her coat pocket. He wished she'd mentioned it to him earlier, because Theo was frowning.

"I don't think that's a good idea."

"It's just a set of Flair pens. They're great for coloring-books."

"That's nice," Theo said. "Some little boy or girl be happy to get that."

"No, it's for Ronnie. I got it specially for him."

"All well and good. But I think you should put that with the other toys."

"Why? He's such a sweet boy—why can't I give him a little present?"

She seemed innocently surprised, innocently hurt. An instinct to protect her welled up in Russ so strongly, he thought he might really be in love with her.

Theo wasn't similarly moved. "I was given to understand," he said, "that you and Ronnie's mother had some words."

"It's a *gift*," Frances said.

"I already asked you once to leave that boy be. Now I'm asking you again, politely."

Frances's hurt was turning to anger. It was an emotion Russ had never seen in her, and the sight of it turned him on. He imagined her angry at *him*, the full womanly range of her emotions bared to him, in the kind of spat that lovers sometimes had.

"Why?" she said. "I don't understand."

Theo rolled his eyes toward Russ, as if she were his woman to control.

"Frances," Russ said, moving toward her. "Maybe we should trust Theo on this. We don't know the situation."

"What is the situation?"

"The situation," Theo said, "is that Clarice, the boy's mother, doesn't want you talking to him. She came and complained to me about that."

Frances laughed. "Because why? Because she's such a perfect mother?"

Her derision, too, was sexually exciting to Russ, but morally it was unattractive. He placed a hand on her shoulder and tried to turn her away. "You and I can talk about this later," he said.

She shrugged off his hand. "I'm sorry, but how is it right for a boy who should be in a special school, getting special attention—how is it okay for him to be wandering around the neighborhood during school hours, cadging quarters?"

"Frances," Russ said.

"I appreciate your concern," Theo said evenly. "But I suggest you head home. It's a long drive in the snow."

"We really should be going," Russ agreed.

Frances now did direct her anger at him. "Does this seem right to *you*? Why isn't someone calling social services? Isn't this something the state should know about?"

"The state?" Theo smiled at Russ as if they were in on a joke. "You think the State of Illinois has a functioning child-protection system?"

"What are you smiling at?" Frances said to Russ. "Did I say something funny?"

He erased his smile. "Not at all. Theo is just saying it's not a perfect system. It's understaffed and overwhelmed. We can talk about it in the car."

Again he tried to steer her toward the door, and again she shed his hand. "I want to know," she said, "why I can't give a needy boy one tiny little Christmas present."

The time on the community center's wall clock was 5:18. Each passing minute deepened the trouble Russ would be in with Marion, and he knew he should insist that they leave. But again his lady was asking him to perform a difficult task—to side with her against an urban minister with whom he'd painstakingly cultivated a relationship.

"I take your point about the gift," he said to Theo. "But I'm kind of with Frances here. It doesn't seem right that Ronnie's on the street by himself."

Theo threw him a disappointed look and turned to Frances. "You want to take charge of that boy? You want to take that on? Retarded South Side nine-year-old? You ready for that?"

"No," she said. "That would be a lot for me to take on. But I can't help—"

"He's already been in foster care once. Are you familiar with that system?"

"Not—no. Not really."

"We're here to learn," Russ said—managing, in one breath, to patronize Frances and sound idiotic to Theo.

"You got to go pretty far down the list," Theo said, "to find the family that will take a boy like Ronnie. That's going to be a family collecting checks for half a dozen kids—to see any profit, you need volume. And how do you handle half a dozen kids?"

"You lock them in a room," Russ said, to sound less stupid.

"You lock them all up in a room. You don't spare the rod."

"That's a bad system, I agree," Frances said.

"Then work on changing it, if you want to try to help. Clarice isn't all bad, she was just too young when she had Ronnie. When she gets herself together, she takes him to the school in Washington Park. That's on a good day. On bad days he falls through the cracks. He knows to come here when she's strung out, and sooner or later she always comes to find him. The problem is the men who give her drugs. She gets lost in that, and the only thing that gets her out of it is mother's pride. If she didn't have Ronnie, I reckon she'd be dead by now."

"I can understand that," Frances said. "I just want to give him something he might like."

"That's right. That's what you want. What *I* want is for Clarice not to up and tell Ronnie to keep away from a church where he's safe."

"Well, so, let me write her a note. Is there a piece of paper I can write on?"

"Frances," Russ said.

"She needs to know I'm not trying to take Ronnie away from her. Theo can give her the note with the present."

Theo made his eyes very wide, suggesting a limit to his patience.

"Look," Russ said. "This is silly. If you want Ronnie to have colored pens, Theo can take off the wrapping paper and give them to him. I don't think writing a note is a good idea."

"I wanted him to have a present to unwrap on Christmas."

Theo, his limit reached, shook his head and walked away. Russ snatched the gift from Frances and hurried after him, into the sanctuary.

"Do me a favor and take this," he said, pressing the gift on Theo. "She means well. She really does care about Ronnie. She's just . . ."

"I was surprised to see her," Theo said. "I assumed you were coming with Kitty."

"Yeah, ah. Change of plan."

The single fluorescent light burning above the altar, behind an old upright piano and a freestanding organ, seemed to intensify the sanctuary's chill.

"Your private affairs are none of my business," Theo said. "But I'd appreciate it if you'd take the log out of your eye and tell her to keep clear of that boy. If she won't do it, she needs to find someplace else to go with her good intentions. I don't need that kind of thing here."

Two years of bridge-building with Theo were in jeopardy. Russ knew exactly why Theo was impatient with Frances. He himself had been impatient with other First Reformed ladies who'd joined the circle,

Juanita Fuller, Wilma St. John, June Goya. They'd spoken to people in the neighborhood, including Theo, with a treacly sort of maternal condescension, partly a product of fear, partly racism repackaged in self-flattering form. He'd had to ask each of them to leave the circle, and if Theo had now been complaining about anyone but Frances, Russ would have deferred to him and kicked her out. He did believe that the flavor of Frances's offense was different, more a matter of high spirits and irreverence. But it was possible that he only believed this because he was falling in love with her.

"I'll speak to her," he said.

"All righty," Theo said. "You get yourself home safe."

An inch of fresh snow had fallen on the Fury's windshield. The lightening of its rear load made its handling even more floaty as Russ steered it homeward. Frances was now sitting in normal passenger posture, her feet on the floor, and seemed coldly aggrieved with him.

"I don't suppose I can ask," she said, "what the two men had to say about me behind my back."

"Yeah, I'm sorry," Russ said. "Theo can be stubborn. Sometimes you just have to defer to how he wants things done."

"I'm sure the two of you think I'm a dunce, but it wouldn't have killed him to give Ronnie my present."

"Your gesture was lovely. I'm all for it."

"But apparently there's just something about me that makes black people hate me."

"Not at all."

"I don't hate *them*."

"Of course not. It's just . . ." He took a deep breath, for courage. "It might not be a bad idea," he said, "to step back and think about how you're coming across. It's one thing to be in New Prospect, in your own milieu, with people like yourself. You can be as outspoken as you want. You can openly disagree with people, and they'll take it as a sign of respect. But that kind of spirit comes across differently when you're a visitor in a Black community."

"I'm not allowed to disagree with them?"

"No, that's—"

"Because it's not like every black person is so perfect. I'm sure they do plenty of disagreeing among themselves."

"I'm not saying you can't disagree with Theo Crenshaw. I disagreed with him myself today."

"I didn't see much sign of that."

"I'm talking about an inner attitude. The first thing I do, when I feel myself disagreeing, is acknowledge my own ignorance. Maybe there's something in Theo's experience that leads him to think the way he does, something I can't immediately see. Instead of just shooting from the hip, I stop and ask myself, 'Why does he feel differently about this than I do?' And then I listen to his answer. He and I may still disagree, but at least I've acknowledged that a Black man's experience in this country is profoundly different than mine."

Frances offered no rejoinder, and Russ dared to hope that he was getting through to her. He had selfish reasons to keep her in the Tuesday circle, but they didn't make his message less sincere.

"You have a good heart, Frances. A wonderful heart. But you can't really blame Theo for not immediately seeing that. If you want him to trust you, you need to try to cultivate a different attitude. Begin with the assumption that you don't know anything about being Black. If you make that adjustment, I guarantee he'll notice the difference."

She sighed so heavily that the windshield fogged. "I embarrassed you, didn't I."

"Not at all."

"No, I did. I can see that now. I was trying to be Mrs. Fix-It."

Russ glowed with pride. He, not Theo, had been right about her true nature.

"You didn't do anything so wrong," he said. "But the next time you see Theo, it wouldn't hurt to tell him you're sorry. A simple heartfelt apology goes a long way. Theo's a good man, a good Christian. If you change your inner attitude, he'll know it. It is so important to me, Frances, so very important, that you keep coming on our Tuesdays."

This was the mildest of allusions to his pride in her, his hopes for a deepening of their intimacy, but he worried that it was still too much; and, indeed, the allusion wasn't lost on her.

"Why, Reverend Hildebrandt," she said. "The things you do say."

Desire surged in him so powerfully, it felt like a premonition of its fulfillment. He thought of the blues recordings he'd left in his office, the excuse they would give him to bring Frances inside the church, the course that events might take in the dark of his office, if he kept up his nerve and didn't get them back too late. Feeling one with the Fury, he urged it across Fifty-ninth Street, where the snow was heavily furrowed.

The furrows were deeper than he'd judged. They absorbed his momentum and deflected him into a sideways skid. For a very bad moment, neither steering nor braking had any effect. He clutched the wheel helplessly while Frances cried out and the Fury slid backward through the intersection. There was a bump and a bang and a crunch of metal on metal.

Resolved: that goodness is an inverse function of intelligence. First affirmative speaker: Perry Hildebrandt, New Prospect Township High School.

Let's begin by positing that the essence of goodness is unselfishness: loving others as one loves oneself, performing costly acts of charity, denying oneself pleasures that harm others, and so forth. And then let's imagine an act of spontaneous kindness to a previously hostile party—to one's sister, for example—that accords with our posited definition of goodness. If the actor lacks intelligence, we need inquire no further: this person is good. But suppose that the actor is helpless not to calculate the ancillary selfish advantages accruing from his charitable act. Suppose that his mind works so quickly that, even as he's performing the act, he's fully aware of these advantages. Is his goodness not thereby fully compromised? Can we designate as "good" an act that he might also have performed through the sheerly selfish calculations of his intellect?

Returning to his room, where Judson was kneeling over the home-made Stratego board, Perry weighed the benefits and costs of taking his sister's place at the Haefles' reception. On the credit side were the goodness of this action, the satisfaction of adhering to his new resolution, the unprecedented look of gratitude with which Becky had accepted his offer, and the advancement of his self-interested campaign to secure her silence regarding his earlier bad actions. On the debit side, he now had to attend a reception for clergymen, with Judson.

"Listen, kiddo," Perry said, sitting down across the board from him. "I need to ask you a favor. How would you feel about going to a party where there aren't any kids your age?"

"When."

"As soon as Mom and Dad get home. We'll go with them."

Judson's brow creased. "I thought we were playing the game."

"We can slide it under my bed. It'll be there tomorrow."

"Why do I have to go?"

"Because I have to go. You don't want to be home alone, do you?"

A brief silence.

"I don't mind," Judson said.

"Really? You kind of freaked out, that time in the fall. It wasn't even at night."

Judson stared at the game board with an odd little smile, as if the boy who'd freaked out about some noises in the basement, though undeniably him, were an object of faint amusement; as if the shame of that time in the fall, when he'd been left home alone for too long, might pass over him and land somewhere else.

"The snacks will be good," Perry said. "You can bring your book and find a place to read."

"Why do you have to go?"

"It's something I'm doing for Becky."

Perry waited for the obvious question: Why do a good thing for Becky and not for his little brother? But this wasn't the way a superior human being's mind worked.

"Can we finish the game first?"

"Probably not."

"You promised we'd play tonight."

"We *started* it tonight. We'll *finish* it tomorrow."

Absorbing this sophistry, Judson stared at the board. "It's your move," he said.

Each player had forty pieces whose identities were concealed to his opponent. The object was to capture your opponent's flag, via the slaughter of lesser pieces by pieces of greater rank, while avoiding deadly collisions with your opponent's bombs, which were immotile and removable only by your very low-ranking miners. In classical strategy, you planted your flag at the rear of your forces and surrounded it with bombs, but Judson had apparently now grasped the weakness of this strategy: as soon as your opponent could advance a miner, unscathed, to the protecting bombs, your flag was helpless and the game was over. Observing Judson's guileless excitement about his *new idea*, Perry could have pretended to be surprised by it and let him win the game. Instead, anticipating Judson's more freewheeling placement of bombs, he'd deployed his own miners in more forward positions. It was plausibly good to beat Judson again and again, teaching him to not betray his strategy, forcing him to develop his skills, until he was able to win fair and square. Wouldn't Judson's happiness then be all the greater for being hard earned? Or was this merely the rationalization of an intelligent person who selfishly hated losing, even to his little brother?

Becky in her boots had clattered down the stairs, bound for the Crossroads concert, and Perry had defused the third of Judson's bombs, at the nugatory sacrifice of a miner to a captain, when the telephone rang. He went and picked up on the extension in the parental bedroom.

"Yeah, ah—Perry?" his father said. His voice sounded strained and metallically distorted. There was street noise in the background. "Can I speak to your mother?"

"She's not here."

"She already went to the Haefles'?"

"No. I haven't seen her all day."

"Ah, okay, so. When you see her, can you tell her not to wait for me? There's a problem with the car—I'm still in the city. Can you tell her she should just go on without me? It's important that one of us be there."

"Sure. But what if she—"

"Thanks, Perry. Thank you so much. Thank you. Thank you."

With notable haste, his father ended the call. Likewise notable had been the guilty look he'd given Perry some hours earlier, when Perry spotted him and Mrs. Cottrell in the family car.

Perry placed the receiver in its cradle and pondered what to do. Mrs. Cottrell was, without question, a fox—not only in the salacious sense of the word but in her slyness. In his encounters with her since Larry Cottrell had made the dumb mistake of getting high while babysitting, Perry had detected a sharpening of her interest in him, a glint of mischief in her eyes. Larry had sworn to Perry that he hadn't narked him out, but his mother obviously suspected who'd sold him the dime bag. And now

Perry had discovered, by accident, at the corner of Pirsig and Maple, a dangerous liaison between Mrs. Cottrell and the Reverend Father. To be busted by the Reverend now, after forming his resolution and liquidating the asset, would be the height of irony.

Impelled by worry, after watching his father speed away on Pirsig, he'd postponed the rest of his Christmas shopping and walked to the Cottrell residence for a word with Larry. If all Larry's mother had was a suspicion, and if she happened to voice it to the Reverend, Perry could simply deny everything. The worry was that Larry was weak. If he'd fingered Perry by name, despite swearing that he hadn't, denials would not avail.

Larry could have been Exhibit A in Becky's contention that Perry merely used people. For a while, Perry had dodged him at Crossroads meetings and inventively deflected his invitations to hang out. Larry was immature, a squeaker, a newcomer, and thus of scant utility to Perry in his quest to reach the center of Crossroads. But Perry couldn't baldly reject him without running afoul of Crossroads precepts. One day, after school, Larry attached himself to Perry and Ansel Roder as they made their way to Roder's house. Roder was in a magnanimous mood that day. Learning that Larry had never tried pot and very much wanted to, he included him in the passing of the bong, whereupon Larry embarrassed Perry. With ear-grating giggles, he offered a running play-by-play of his mind's reaction to chemical insult, and when Roder finally told him to shut the fuck up he gigglingly explicated his insulted mind's reaction to it. He giggled, too, when he bumped into Roder's turntable and harmed the LP that was playing. Roder took Perry aside and said, "I don't want that kid here again." Perry was of similar opinion, but Larry, serenely unaware of how uncoolly he'd behaved, proceeded to pester him to be included in future festivities. He was a poignant figure, messed up by the recent death of his father. To sell him drugs would have been a pure kindness if it hadn't also made rationally self-interested sense: here was a loyal customer, a known quantity, whose mother gave him a handsome allowance. To then smoke with him the pot he bought might likewise have been construable as charity, an act of friendship, if it hadn't accorded with Perry's strategic desire to be less dependent on Roder's generosity, and with certain other benefits. It was proving pleasant to Perry to have an adoring acolyte in Crossroads, pleasant to see his foxy mother up close, in her den, pleasant to exercise his dexterity on the model airplanes that Larry could afford with his allowance, pleasant to dip brushes into the nifty square bottles of paint he'd long coveted at the hobby shop. Not until Larry got himself busted by his mother—semi-deliberately, as a self-destructive way of defying her, Perry suspected—did the costs of their friendship outweigh the benefits. Larry had promised his mother he wouldn't buy more pot, and Perry, despite having lost him as a customer, was obliged to remain friends with him, lest he be hurt and nark him out.

The Cottrell house was a white brick Colonial, impressively large for a widow and two children. Larry was at home with his kid sister and invited Perry in from the snow.

"We have a problem," Perry said when they were in Larry's bedroom. "I just saw your mother with my father."

"Yeah, they're doing some church thing in the city."

"Well, so, I have to ask again. Is our secret safe with you?"

Among Larry's insecure tics was rubbing the sebaceous nodes around his nose and sniffing his fingertips. Perry, too, enjoyed the smell of his own sebum, but such sniffing was better done privately.

"You understand why I'm asking."

"You don't have to be paranoid," Larry said. "The whole thing's over, except that I can't watch TV for another nine days. I'm going to miss the Orange Bowl."

"No mention of my name, then."

"I already swore to you. Do you want me to get a Bible?"

"No need. I just hadn't imagined your mom going into the city with my dad. It was only the two of them. I have a bad feeling that we haven't heard the last of this."

"What did you expect? You're the one who sells dope."

"Exactly my point. My exposure is potentially far more serious than yours."

"I'm already the one who got punished."

"You're the one who made the mistake, my friend."

Larry nodded, touching his face again. "What's in the bag?"

"A present for my brother. Do you want to see it?"

He was glad of the chance to let Larry admire the movie camera, to wind it up and shoot imaginary footage with him, before it became irrevocably Judson's. After an hour, which was the minimum duration for his visit to pass as a friendly social call, rather than the targeted instrumentality it actually had been, he headed home through snow swirling down from a dark sky. He didn't think Larry would break, even under renewed pressure, but the irony of getting busted now, when he'd resolved to be a better person, was persuasively vivid to him. He still feared mischief from Mrs. Cottrell, and there was another worrisome loose end. In the days since Becky had annihilated him as a person, in the coat closet at First Reformed, she'd seemed more pissed off with him than ever. He imagined a full-scale family Confrontation in which he insisted on his innocence—with a kind of retroactive honesty, since he'd now forsworn the use and sale of mind-altering substances—only to be undercut by his sister's denunciation.

What providence it therefore was when, ensconced in his room with Judson, he'd heard Becky crying. His ensuing exchange with her had ended in a warm embrace, a sense of being rewarded for his resolution. This would have been entirely satisfactory if he hadn't then felt so deliciously relieved of his worry about her. The relief, its selfishness, negated all the goodness he'd displayed, and it cast an unfortunate light on his feeling of being rewarded. Shouldn't true goodness be its own reward? He wondered if an action, to qualify as authentically good, needed not only to be untainted by self-interest but also to bring no pleasure of any kind.

The parental alarm clock, which he knew to be two minutes slow, showed 6:45. His mother was now so bizarrely late that all bets on her arrival time were off. He considered a good action that would almost certainly bring him no pleasure: going to the Haefles' without waiting for his mother. The action had only the faintest taint of self-interest, in the form of the credit he might get for ensuring that the Hildebrandt family was represented at the party. This credit would be too feeble to be fungible if he was accused of selling drugs, and so could be discounted.

He wrote a short note to his mother, on the scratch pad by the phone, and went to collect Judson. "Time for a walk in the snow."

"I thought we were waiting for Mom and Dad."

"Nope, just you and me, kiddo. We are the Hildebrandts tonight."

A minor mystery of adulthood was that his parents referred to latex overshoes as *rubbers*. Even Becky, that vessel of purity, had been seen to suppress a snigger at the word. The parents surely knew its other meaning, and yet they persisted in using it, with a confounding absence of embarrassment: *Make sure you wear your rubbers.* Though Judson's rubbers were innocent, Perry was ashamed of his. Ansel Roder and his moneyed friends wore alpine hiking boots in the snow.

It was still coming down heavily when he and Judson ventured out in their rubbers. Judson ran ahead, kicking up sheets and clumps of it, the interruption of Stratego forgotten in the excitement of a winter storm. Watching him fall down and pick himself back up, Perry mourned no longer being small enough that falling didn't hurt. He no longer even remembered how it felt to have the ground so unthreateningly proximate. Why had he been in such a hurry to grow up? It was as if he'd never experienced the grace of childhood. As he watched his little brother frolic, he felt another downward tug in his mood, stronger than the tug he'd felt while shopping but also less painful, because it was occasioned by a feeling of metempsychosis. More surely than before, he sensed that he was going down, was irredeemably bad in the head, but this time it seemed to matter less, because his soul was connected to Judson's by love and fraternity, at some mystical level interchangeable, and Judson was a blessed child, literally born on a Sunday, and would always be okay, even if he, Perry, wasn't.

On the front stoop of the Superior Parsonage, between rows of bushes with Christmas lights dimmed by snow, he crouched to brush off Judson's parka and help him with the buckles of his rubbers, which were encrusted with ice and difficult to undo.

"I still don't see why we're here."

"Because Dad is stuck in the city and Mom is AWOL."

"What is AWOL."

Perry rang the doorbell. "It means absent without leave. Dad said it's important that the family be here. By process of elimination, that leaves you and me."

The door was opened by a very large white bunny, Mrs. Haefle, in a red apron embroidered with holly leaves. Perry quickly and cogently explained why he and Judson were there, but Mrs. Haefle seemed slow on the uptake. "Do your parents know you're here?"

"They were unavoidably detained. I left them a note."

She looked over her shoulder. "Dwight?"

Reverend Haefle appeared in the doorway. "Perry! Judson! What a nice surprise."

He ushered them inside and took their coats. Functioning home insulation being a perk of senior ministry, the house was hot and steamy. Clergymen and their spouses filled the living room, obeying the obscure social imperatives of adult life, apparently enjoying themselves. Reverend Haefle led the Hildebrandts into the dining room, which was acridly scented with the combustion of Sterno cans beneath a copper-clad pan of Swedish meatballs, a tray of potatoes in a sauce of cream and onions, and a cauldron of something fumingly alcoholic, with blanched almonds and bloated raisins floating in it. Through the open kitchen door, Perry saw wine jugs and a vodka bottle on a counter.

"Take a plate and load up," Reverend Haefle said. "Doris's heritage is Swedish, and she makes a mean meatball—don't forget the gravy. The potatoes are a dish called Jannson's Temptation. It wouldn't be a Swedish Christmas without a lot of heavy cream."

Judson, though he must have been starving, politely hesitated.

"Don't hold back, lad. We can use a young appetite. If you'd like some company your own age, our granddaughters are in the basement."

Thinking of the Crappier Parsonage's appalling basement, Perry pictured the granddaughters clad in rags and chained to a filthy stone wall. *Yes, we keep them in the basement . . .*

"And what is this?" he said, indicating the cauldron.

"That is a Scandinavian Christmas drink for grownups. We call it gløgg."

Left alone with Judson, who evinced his native moderation by taking three meatballs, a spoon of potatoes, a quantity of raw carrots and broccoli florets, and, from a triple-decker stand laden with homemade cookies, two dry-looking balls dusted with powdered sugar, Perry considered the incredible intensity of the alcohol fumes wafting off the cauldron. It was like sticking his nose in a bottle of rubbing alcohol. There was, he realized only now, some ambiguity in his resolution, some scenarios not explicitly addressed by its terms. To wit: Was he required to abjure alcohol? Perhaps one cup of gløgg, taken on an empty stomach to maximize its clout, might be permissible on a night when he had no other antidote to the sinking of his mood? With an unsteady hand, splashing a little, he ladled the wine-dark substance into a ceramic cup and glanced behind him. No one was watching.

Escaping to the hallway, he took a slurp of the most delicious drink he'd ever tasted. It was clovey and cinnamony, full of vodka. The ordinarily nauseating gastric sourness of wine was overwhelmed by sugar. His face went warm immediately.

"Where am I supposed to go?" Judson said, holding his plate and a fork.

At the end of the hallway, they found stairs leading down to a proper recreation room, shag-carpeted, paneled with knotty pine, and dominated by a pool table. Sprawled on the carpeting, near an empty but usable fireplace, was a pair of girls younger than Perry and older than Judson, playing Yahtzee. Perry as a boy, when asked to play with female strangers, had routinely been paralyzed by self-consciousness. He was impressed by how naturally Judson sat down with the girls and introduced himself. Judson truly was a blessed child, rightly sure that strangers would like him. Or maybe the lure of Yahtzee was so powerful that it simply swept away all shyness.

Somehow, though Perry hadn't been conscious of drinking, his cup was already empty. He ate two sodden raisins from the bottom, extracting precious liquid. A thin line of spice scum marked the level of his tragically modest initial serving, and as he went back up the stairs he reasoned that, not having taken the entire "one cup" permitted by the loophole in his resolution, he was entitled to a refill. His face was flaming, but he hadn't achieved a proper buzz yet.

Now standing by the food and drink were two men in lumpy sweaters and priestly black slacks, selecting cookies. Perry sidled up to them and waited. Before he could refill his cup, Mrs. Haefle came swooping toward him.

"Have you had any meatballs?"

Palming the cup against his hip, out of sight, he borrowed a concept from her husband. "Still working up an *appetite*," he said.

Unilaterally, as if he were a toddler, or a dog, Mrs. Haefle loaded a plate for him. She was stout and rabbity and meddling, a poor advertisement for Swedish heritage. She handed him enough meatballs and Temptation to thwart formation of a buzz, and he had no choice but to take the plate. With a meddling hand, she turned him away from the fuming cauldron. "The other teenagers are in the sunroom," she said.

As he walked away, he felt her following him, making sure he conformed to her patronizing wishes. Uninterested in teenagers in the sunroom, he weaved through the living room to a bookcase, set his plate on an end table, selected a volume at random, and pretended to absorb himself in it. Mrs. Haefle had been buttonholed, but she was still monitoring him. Her vigilance reminded him of certain teachers at Lifton Central whose lives were evidently devoid of every pleasure but the sadism of denying younger people pleasure.

Finally the doorbell rang. Mrs. Haefle went to answer it, and Perry darted back to the dining room with his cup. Two white-haired ladies were at the cookie station, but he didn't know them, had no relationship with them, and brazenly filled his cup with steaming gløgg. Hearing Mrs. Haefle's voice, as she returned from the coat closet, he escaped through the kitchen and from there to the basement stairs, where he sat down. From below came the rattle of dice in the Yahtzee shaker, the brooklike patter of Judson's voice.

In no time, again, Perry emptied the cup. As with every illicit substance he'd ever sampled, his thirst for gløgg seemed inordinate, abnormal. It occurred to him that standing on the kitchen counter was a bottle of pure vodka. Since the accounting of what constituted "one cup" was already fubar, he went ahead and crept back into the kitchen, poured several ounces of vodka, and quickly downed it. He left the cup in the sink.

Now in possession of a satisfactory buzz, his spirits rising a little, his resolution affronted but arguably unviolated, he went to test his liquor-holding powers on the clergy in the living room. Beside the neglected fire in the fireplace, two men, one tall and one short, stood side by side as if they'd run out of things to say but hadn't yet moved on to greener conversational pastures. Perry introduced himself.

The taller man was wearing a red turtleneck beneath a camel-hair blazer. "I'm Adam Walsh, from Trinity Lutheran. This is Rabbi Meyer from Temple Beth-El."

The rabbi, who had hair only behind his ears, shook Perry's hand. "Happy Hanukkah."

In case this was a quip, Perry produced a laugh, perhaps overloud. From the corner of his eye, he could see Mrs. Haefle sourly watching him.

"Is your father here?" Reverend Walsh said.

"No, he's on a pastoral mission in the city. He got stuck in the snow."

There ensued talk of snow. Perry had not yet developed the fascination with weather that every adult seemed to have. After voicing his meaningless opinion that the snow was already eight inches deep, he broached the subject of goodness and its relation to intelligence. He'd come to the reception for selfless reasons, but he now saw that he might get not only a free buzz but free advice from, as it were, two professionals.

"I suppose what I'm asking," he said, "is whether goodness can ever truly be its own reward, or whether, consciously or not, it always serves some personal instrumentality."

Reverend Walsh and the rabbi exchanged glances in which Perry detected pleasant surprise. It gratified him to upset their expectations of a fifteen-year-old.

"Adam may have a different answer," the rabbi said, "but in the Jewish faith there is really only one measure of righteousness: Do you celebrate God and obey His commandments?"

"That would suggest," Perry said, "that goodness and God are essentially synonymous."

"That is the idea," the rabbi said. "In biblical times, when God manifested Himself more directly, He could seem like quite the hard-ass—striking people blind for trivial offenses, telling Abraham to kill his son. But the essence of Jewish faith is that God does what He does, and we obey Him."

"So, in other words, it doesn't matter what a righteous person's private thoughts are, so long as he obeys the letter of God's commandments?"

"And worships Him, yes. Of course, at the level of folk wisdom, a man can be righteous without being a *mensch*. I'm sure you see this, too, Adam—the pious man who makes everyone around him miserable. That might be more what Perry is asking about."

"My question," Perry said, "is whether we can ever escape our selfishness. Even if you bring in God, and make Him the measure of goodness, the person who worships and obeys Him still wants something for himself. He enjoys the feeling of being righteous, or he wants eternal life, or what have you. If you're smart enough to think about it, there's always some selfish angle."

The rabbi smiled. "There may be no way around it, when you put it like that. But we 'bring in God,' as you say—for the believer, of course, it's God who brought *us* in—to establish a moral order in which your question becomes irrelevant. When obedience is the defining principle, we don't need to police every little private thought we might have."

"I think there's more to Perry's question, though," Reverend Walsh said. "I think he's pointing to sinfulness, which is our fundamental condition. In Christian faith, only one man has ever exemplified perfect goodness, and he was the Son of God. The rest of us can only hope for glimmers of what it's like to be truly good. When we perform an act of charity, or forgive an enemy, we feel the goodness of Christ in our hearts. We all have an innate capacity to recognize true goodness, but we're also full of sin, and those two parts of us are constantly at war."

"Exactly," Perry said. "How do I know if I'm really being good or if I'm just pursuing a sinful advantage?"

"The answer, I would say, is by listening to your heart. Only your heart can tell you what your true motive is—whether it partakes of Christ. I think my position is similar to Rabbi Meyer's. The reason we need faith—in our case, faith in the Lord Jesus Christ—is that it gives us a rock-solid basis for evaluating our actions. Only through faith in the perfection of our Savior, only by comparing our actions to his example, only by experiencing his living presence in our hearts, can we hope to be forgiven for the more selfish thoughts we might have. Only faith in Christ redeems us. Without him, we're lost in a sea of second-guessing our motives."

Perry was enjoying his ability to converse on the level of men three times his age, enjoying how well he'd calibrated his alcohol intake, enjoying the easy but unslurred flow of his words. But now Mrs. Haefle, as if she'd smelled a pleasure in need of immediate stamping out, was approaching them. He repositioned himself, squaring his back to her.

"I understand what you're saying," he said to Reverend Walsh. "But what if a person isn't able to have faith?"

"Not everyone finds faith overnight. Faith is rarely easy. But if you've ever done a good thing, and felt a glow in your heart, then that's a little message from God. He's telling you that Christ is in you, and that you have the freedom and capacity to pursue a closer relationship with him. 'Seek, and ye shall find.'"

"It's approximately the same if you're a Jew," the rabbi said, "although we tend to emphasize that you're a Jew whether you like it or not. It's more a matter of God tracking you down than of you finding God."

"I don't think our positions are so dissimilar in that respect," Reverend Walsh said stiffly.

Perry tried to ignore the hovering of Mrs. Haefle at his shoulder.

"But so," he said, "what if I feel the kind of glow you're talking about, but it doesn't lead me to God? What if it's just one of the feelings that any sentient animal might have? If I never find God, or He never finds me, it sounds like you're saying that, basically, I'm damned."

"In principle, I suppose that is the doctrine," Reverend Walsh said. "But you're very young, and life is long. There's a near infinity of moments when you might receive God's grace. All it takes is one moment."

"In the meantime," the rabbi said, "I think it's enough to be a mensch."

"Perry?" Mrs. Haefle said, pushing her way in. "I want you to come meet Reverend Walsh's son Ricky. He's a junior at Lyons Township."

Her voice was syrupy. Perry's irritation was more intense than any feeling of goodness he'd yet experienced. "Excuse me?"

"The young people are in the sunroom."

"I'm aware of that. We're in the middle of a conversation here. Is that so hard to grasp?"

Evidently, though it hadn't slurred his speech, gløgg was very disinhibiting.

"I think we've touched on the main points," Reverend Walsh said. "Is anyone else ready for cookies?"

Perry appealed to the rabbi. "Was I boring you? Did my questions seem childish? Should I be consigned to the sunroom?"

"Not at all," the rabbi said. "These are important questions."

With a vindicated gesture, Perry turned to Mrs. Haefle. Open animosity had now replaced her phony sweetness. "Gløgg is not for children," she said.

"What?"

"I said gløgg is not for children."

"I don't know what you're talking about."

"I think you do."

"Well, I think you should mind your own business." The disinhibitions of gløgg were an unfolding surprise. "Seriously, do you not have anything better to do than follow me around?"

In proportion to the rising of his voice, the living room was quieting.

"What's going on?" Reverend Haefle said, looming up.

"Nothing at all," Perry said. "I was in the midst of an interesting conversation with Rabbi Meyer and Reverend Adams when your wife interrupted us."

Mrs. Haefle whispered something in her husband's ear. He nodded gravely.

"So, Perry," he said. "It was good of you to come. But—"

"But what? It's time for me to leave? I am not the one at social fault here."

Reverend Haefle placed a gentle hand on Perry's shoulder. More roughly than necessary, Perry shook it off. He knew he needed to calm down, but the heat in his head was extraordinary.

"This is what I'm talking about," he said very loudly. "No matter what I do, it's always me who's in the wrong. You're all saved, but apparently I'm damned. Do you think I enjoy being damned?" A sob of self-pity escaped him. "I'm doing the best I can!"

The living room was now completely quiet. Through tears, he saw twenty pairs of clerical and spousal eyes on him. Among them, near the front door, to his shame and dismay, were his mother's.

Along streets so muffled she could hear the faint collective hiss of snowflakes landing, and then Pirsig Avenue, where cars with snow-blurred headlights proceeded at a funereal crawl, Becky moved as fast as she could in her long blue coat. She felt late for a date that half an hour ago she hadn't even meant to keep. She had an urgent need to see Tanner again, to give him a chance to redeem himself. Failing that, she needed to make a show of not caring—to plunge into the concert, let Tanner see that other people valued her, and let him wonder where he stood with her.

Outside First Reformed, three Crossroads sophomores were shoveling snow with a zeal that suggested their work was voluntary. Becky was pleased to be able to greet each of them by name; to be developing the same inclusive popularity in Crossroads that she enjoyed at school. She also knew the names of the girls manning the cash box in the function-hall foyer. The concert wouldn't start for another half hour, but the hall was filling with alumni and other paying guests, the air already smoky. Amp lights glowed in the shadows of the elevated stage. Current Crossroads members, earning "hours" toward Spring Trip, were lugging crates of pop bottles and arranging tables of desserts and festive breads, whose bakers had likewise earned hours.

Becky was uneasily reminded that she had to start earning some hours herself. Forty were required, she currently had zero, and Spring Trip was only three months away. It wasn't an attractive thought, but she wished that an exception could be made for her.

Crossing the hall to meet her were Kim Perkins and David Goya, who'd recently become an item. Horsey of face, weirdly thin of hair,

David was no one Becky would have liked to kiss, but she could imagine him seeming like a safe harbor to Kim. Previous heavy pot smoking had erased all traces of harm in him.

"The lunatics have taken over the asylum," he said gravely.

"Yeah," Becky said. "Is there anybody over twenty-one here?"

"Ambrose is hiding in his office. Otherwise, we appear to be unmonitored."

"Speaking of which," Kim said, with a pointed clearing of her throat. Kim had lately gained some pounds, as if to reduce the looks differential between herself and David. Her face was barren of cosmetics and she was wearing bib overalls.

"Yes, maybe you can help us," David said to Becky. "We're having a little disagreement. Kim seems to feel that the concert is a public event, not a Crossroads activity. I would argue that it's clearly a Crossroads activity—just look at the posters. I'm guessing you don't have a dog in this fight, so I wonder which one of us you agree with."

"Sorry," Becky said. "What dog? Which fight?"

"Rule Number Two. No drinking or drugs at a Crossroads activity."

"Oh."

"I probably shouldn't have told you that. It could bias your answer."

"I don't know if you smelled it, coming in," Kim said, "but the alumni are all totally lighting up in the parking lot. Like they'd do for any public concert. Which is what this is."

"It's a gathering at the church," David said. "To raise funds for the group. I rest my case."

"Gosh, guys." Becky was happy to be trusted as their arbiter. "I guess I'm kind of with David here."

"Oh, come on," Kim said. "It's Friday night."

"Thursday night," David corrected.

"I'm just giving you my opinion," Becky said.

"Okay, but here's another question. What if we did some partaking earlier, in the afternoon, not on church property, and we're still the tiniest bit high when we show up here. Is *that* against the rules?"

"You're on a slippery slope," David said.

"Let Becky answer."

"I guess it depends," Becky said, "on what the purpose of the rule is."

"The purpose of the rule," David said, "is to not have parents pissed off with Crossroads."

"I disagree," Kim said. "I think it's that you can't have an authentic witnessing relationship if one of the people is high."

"But then why forbid sex? Rule Number One. This is clearly about the group's reputation."

"No, it's the same as with drugs. Sex messes with the kind of relationship we're supposed to be developing at meetings. It's the wrong kind of intensity."

"Hmm."

"It could be for both reasons," Becky said.

"My point," Kim said, "is that we're not doing any activities tonight. We're not trying to relate to each other. We're just listening to music. If we happen to smoke a little pot on our way here, *when we're not on church property*, what difference does it make?"

David gestured to Becky. "Agree? Disagree?"

Becky smiled.

"I personally am beginning to think Kim's point has merit," David said.

Still smiling, Becky looked out across the hall. Through a clearing in the crowd, in a cluster of alumni, she glimpsed the back of a suede jacket. She knew it was Tanner's because the stumpy one, the Natural Woman, had her arm around him, her wild-haired head against his ribs. It was a posture of secure possession. The smile dropped from Becky's face.

"I think you should do whatever you want," she said.

"Permission from Hildebrandt!" Kim exulted.

"Reassuringly untainted by self-interest," David said. "Or so I presume?"

Tanner's suede-fringed arm was now around the Natural Woman. Becky saw that coming to the concert had been a bad mistake. She liked Kim and David well enough, but they weren't core friends of hers. Nobody in Crossroads was. The best she could hope to demonstrate to Tanner was a skin-deep popularity. Fearing a return of tears, she wondered if she should turn around and leave. But Kim and David were looking at her expectantly.

"What?" she said.

"Just wondering," David said casually, "if you'd care to join us."

It occurred to her that they were worried about Rule Number Three: Any failure to report a rules violation was itself a rules violation.

"Are you saying you don't trust me?"

"Not an issue," Kim said. "You said it yourself—we're not doing anything wrong."

"Just extending a friendly offer," David agreed.

Long ago, Clem had scared Becky off marijuana, telling her that the human brain was an instrument too delicate to mess with chemically, and she'd never been much tempted. But now, although she could see other friendly faces in the function hall, she felt she had only two choices—either leave and go home, or go along with her new friends. Wasn't safety the enemy? Hadn't she joined Crossroads to become less fearful? To take new risks? It could hardly be worse than standing and watching Tanner be clutched by Laura Dobrinsky. At least her friends were offering to include her.

"No, sure," she said to David. "I mean, yes, thank you. I'd like to."

Her assent was a bigger deal to her than to David. He simply turned to follow Kim, who was already moving toward the fire exit by the stage. Reacting to some invisible signal, two other senior girls, Darra Jernigan and Carol Pinella, peeled away from the crowd and joined her. By the time Becky and David caught up with them, her brain was already feeling altered, by the rush of blood in it.

Beyond the exit door, off a hallway leading to the church's attic stairs, was a second door, dangerously difficult (from a fire-hazard perspective) to push open against the snow. Outside was a narrow alley, lit only by Chicagoland sky, against a retaining wall that marked the boundary of church property. In a nod to the rules, everyone climbed up onto the snow-covered grass above the wall. Becky stuck close to David, feeling safest with him; he was one of Perry's best friends.

"For the record," Kim said to the others, "Hildebrandt gave her okay for this."

Becky chuckled in a voice she didn't recognize. "Put it all on me, why don't you."

"I think her presence here speaks for itself," David said. From a neat metal case, he produced a doobie smaller than the ones Becky had seen at parties, and Kim reached over to light it with a Bic. The smell of pot smoke was autumnal. Holding it in, David offered the doobie first to Becky.

"Sorry," she said, taking it. "How do I do this?"

"Long, slow breath and keep it in," Kim said kindly.

Becky took a puff, coughed, and tried a deeper breath. It was as if she'd swallowed a burning sword. Smoke was deadly—people died from inhaling it—she wondered if this thought was the first sign of being high or just an ordinary thought, and then if wondering this was itself a sign of being high—but she managed, with watering eyes, to hold it longer than David had held his. After Kim and Darra and Carol had taken their turns, the doobie came back to David, who offered it again to Becky.

"Um," she said. Her throat was full of scorch. "Is it okay?"

"There's more where this came from."

She nodded and filled her lungs again. She was smoking marijuana! Either the drug itself or the excitement of smoking it was flooding the same nerves that kissing Tanner had lit up the night before. Suddenly her life was changing fast. She was being initiated into sensations she'd barely been aware were possible.

When David grabbed her arm, she understood that she was fainting from too conscientiously holding her breath. She let out smoke and took in winter air. What had been a dark alley seemed almost daylit in the whiteness of the sky and snow, as if the darkness had only been her starting to pass out. The taste in her mouth was Octobery. The heat surging in her face and behind her eyes was like molten fudge. She felt walled off by the heavy hot sensation, not at all connected to the other miscreants, who were expertly snapping drags off the dwindling doobie. Which now came back.

Again a foreign-sounding chuckle, hers.

"Okay," she said. "Why not."

Her third hit hurt her throat less, not more, than the first two. This had to mean that she was getting high. The molten-fudge sensation seemed to be receding, boiling off through the top of her head, fizzing away through her skin. For a moment, she felt entirely poised, entirely present in a winter wonderland, safe with friends. She wondered what would happen next.

From inside the fire door, right below her, came a shout and a thud. The door swung open and stuck in the snow; and there stood Sally Perkins.

"Aha!" she cried.

A hairy mass in the dimness behind her resolved into the shape of Laura Dobrinsky. Becky violently coughed.

"Jesus Christ, Kim," Sally said, clambering up onto the retaining wall. "What ever happened to sisters sharing?" She extended a hand to Laura and yanked her up.

"I didn't see you," Kim said.

"Ho-ho-ho, right."

Becky was definitely high. She seemed to be standing next to herself, wondering where to place herself. She took a step backward, away from Laura. Her foot came down in a hole of some sort, which sent her falling back into a snow-laden shrub. The shrub embraced her and held her unsteadily upright.

David had taken out his little case again. "You and Sally have such keen noses," he observed to Laura, "you could be of service to law enforcement."

"Not true," Laura said. "I can only smell the high-grade stuff."

"Well, isn't this your lucky day."

He lit up a second joint and handed it to her.

"Jesus," Sally said. "Is that Becky Hildebrandt?"

"The very one," David said.

"My, how the mighty have fallen."

Laura exhaled smoke, turned toward Becky, and pierced her with a terrifying look.

"Becky's like her father," she said. "She doesn't know when she's not wanted."

Becky extricated herself from the shrub and brushed snow off her coat. It seemed important to keep on brushing, down to the last flake, to make herself presentable. Then she found that she'd lost interest in it.

"Hey, Sally," she said. "Hey, Laura."

Laura tossed her head and turned away. Now no one was actually looking at Becky, but it seemed as if the entire world were examining her. It seemed as if she'd said the wrong thing and had been somewhere else, not present, in the moments since she'd said it. There was no telling where she'd been or what she'd done there. She only knew that she'd broken the law, poisoned her brain, destroyed her mystique. She wanted to run away and be alone, but if she ran away the others would know she was having a less cool experience than they were, which would be even worse than staying. She needed to be cool, but there wasn't a particle of coolness in her. She didn't like being high. In fact, getting high was the most horrible thing she'd ever done to herself. She wished she could undo it, but she could feel that, if anything, she was getting higher. In her mind's eye, her thoughts were laid out like snacks on a lazy Susan. They weren't evaporating the way thoughts were supposed to. They just sat there, going round and round, available for second helpings. Why had she had to take a third puff on the doobie? Why even the first? Some evil thing in her, whose presence it now seemed she'd always sensed in herself but done her best to ignore, some vain and greedy and sexual thing rooted in a deeper self-loathing, had seized control of her and made the worst decisions.

But then, unaccountably, came another moment of clarity, another brightening. She saw herself as one of seven young people standing just over the property line of First Reformed. Carol Pinella and Darra Jernigan and Kim Perkins were giggling uncontrollably. David Goya and Laura Dobrinsky were discussing different grades of pot. Sally Perkins, indisputably the prettiest girl in her graduating class, three years ahead of Becky, was staring at Becky with narrowed eyes.

"It was *you*," Sally said.

"What?"

"Last night, in Tanner's van. That was you. Wasn't it."

Becky tried to answer, but all she produced was a fatuously guilty grin. It seemed to spread through her entire body. Kim and Carol and Darra were still engaged in their gigglefest, but Tanner's name had attracted Laura's attention.

"I saw Tanner last night at the Grove," Sally explained. "There was somebody in his van with a blanket over her head. She looked totally busted. And you know who it was?"

"The Grove is Becky's workplace," David affably remarked.

"It was *you*," Sally said.

"I don't think so," Becky croaked, aflame with guilt.

"No, I'm sure of it. You were sitting there trying to hide from me."

There followed a wordless moment. The giggling had stopped.

"You think I'm surprised?" Laura said, her voice flat.

Becky's gaze had become glued to the stone flank of the church. Everything she was hearing, including *I don't think so*, was staying in her head, but in a jumble. She tried to latch on to the words and arrange them in a sequence, but they just spiraled around a central pit of horribleness.

"Hey, you," Laura said. "Prom Queen. I asked you a question. Do you think I'm surprised?"

The sound of landing snowflakes was oceanic. Every eye was on Becky, even the eyes in the house behind the shrub, the eyes in the trees above it, the eyes in the sky. Anything she could say would be catastrophically revealing.

"What a fucking family," Laura muttered, jumping down from the ledge.

"Hey, now," David said. "That's not cool."

Some interval of time later, there were still six of them in the snow. Becky found herself consumed by a feeling of intolerable exposure and impending punishment, but each direction she considered turning was the wrong one. Her mind was damaged, she'd messed with its chemistry, and, oh, how she regretted it. She bent forward as if to vomit but instead put her hands on the edge of the ledge and awkwardly, sort of sideways, whoopsie, rolled off it and righted herself. She hurried through the fire door, which Laura Dobrinsky had left wide open.

To her right lurked a hall full of eyes, so she ran up the stairs to the church attic. For a while, in the dark, after the door had fallen shut behind her, she groped along a wall for a light switch, but then she forgot about doing this, only to remember and be struck by having forgotten—*it's because I am horribly stoned.* She groped forward sideways, whimpering, an arm stretched out ahead of her. She collided with something sharp and metallic, a music stand, but nothing crashed. In the distance was a glimmer of bluish light. She tried to navigate by it but lost sight of it and questioned its reality. The next thing she encountered was cool and edge-less, extensive, hollow-sounding. It ended in a curving tapered tube. Apparently a hollow horned cow. It proved to be quite an impediment to her progress. An incalculably huge amount of time had passed since she entered the attic, and she had the sudden, clear insight that time couldn't be measured without light. This seemed to her a crucial realization. She made a mental note to remember it, although she'd already lost her grip on what it meant. If she could just remember the words *time can't be mea-sured without light*, she might recapture their meaning later. But into her mind's eye came an image of quicksand, a hideously vivid image of sand crumbling and sucking itself downward, the instability and insolidity of thinking. Terrified again, she shoved past the hollow cow and thought she was free until it caught her from behind, one of its horns snagging on the pocket of her beautiful merino coat and audibly ripping a seam. Fuck oh fuck oh *fuck*. She stumbled over a smaller hollow animal, got a lungful of dust, and dropped to her hands and knees. The bluish glimmer had reappeared. It was coming from beneath a door, and she crawled toward it.

Beyond the door, lighted by a round stained-glass window, was a staircase narrowed by stacks of hymnals. She followed it down to a wood-paneled space behind the sanctuary altar. As she pushed open the "secret" door behind the pulpit, she experienced another insight: the sanctuary was a *sanctuary*. A single warm light illuminated the hanging brass cross, and all the other doors were locked—she knew this.

With a shudder of deliverance, she traversed the altar and sat down in the first row of pews. Safe for the moment, she shut her eyes and surrendered to the waves of awfulness welling up in the blackness of her head. Between each of them was a space for regretting what she'd done and wishing it could be undone. But the waves kept coming. They wore her down until her only recourse was crying.

Please make it stop, please make it stop . . .

She was praying, but nobody was listening. After the next wave of stonedness, she addressed her plea more specifically.

Please, God. Please make it stop.

There was no answer. When she returned to herself again, she thought she saw the reason why.

I'm sorry, she prayed. *God? Please? I'm sorry I did what I did. It was an evil thing and I shouldn't have done it. If you make it stop, I promise I'll never do it again. Please, God. Can you help me?*

Still no answer.

God? I love you. I love you. Please have mercy on me.

When the next evil wave welled up in her head, she peered down and saw, beneath it, not a bottomless blackness but a kind of golden light. The wave was transparent, the evil insubstantial. The golden light was the real, substantial thing. The more deeply she peered into it, the brighter it got. She saw that she'd been looking outside herself for God, not understanding that God was *in* her. God was pure goodness, and the goodness had been there all along. She'd glimpsed it in the early morning, in her feeling of goodwill, and then more intensely in Perry's kindness to her, the glow of forgiveness she'd felt. Goodness was the best thing in the universe, and she was capable of moving toward it— and yet how utterly awful she'd been! Mean to her mother, uncharitable to Perry, competitive with Laura, greedy with her inheritance, sneering with Clem at other people's faith, conceited, selfish, God-denying, *awful.* With a sob more like a paroxysm, an ecstasy, she opened her eyes to the cross above the altar.

Christ had died for her sins.

And could she do it? Could she cast aside the evil in her, cast aside her vanity and her fear of other people's opinions, and humble herself before the Lord? This had always seemed impossible to her, an onerous expectation with no upside. Only now did she understand that it could bring her deeper into the golden light.

She ran up to the cross, dropped to her knees on the altar carpeting, closed her eyes again, and put her hands together prayerfully.

Please, God. Please, Jesus. I've been a bad person. I've always thought so highly of myself, I've wanted popularity, and money, and social standing, and I've had so many cruel thoughts about other people. All my life, I've been selfish and inconsiderate. I've been the most disgusting sinner, and I am so, so sorry.

Can you forgive me? If I promise to be a better and more humble person? If I promise to serve you cheerfully? I'll take the worst kind of jobs to earn hours. I'll be more loving to my enemies and more open with my family, I'll share everything I have, I'll live a clean life and not care what other people think of me, if only you'll forgive me . . .

She hoped for a clear answer, Jesus speaking to her in her heart, but there was nothing; the golden light had faded. But she also felt delivered from her stonedness, at peace again. She'd glimpsed the light of God, if only for a moment, and her prayers had been answered.

The public library was a tall-windowed brick building, built in the twenties and seated on a lawn enclosed by dog-proof hedges. It stayed open until nine on weeknights, but it was desolate at the dinner hour, a single librarian holding down the circulation desk amid the silence of books waiting to be wanted.

Into it, through its little-used front door—most patrons arrived by car and parked in the rear—walked a disturbed person stinking of wet gabardine and cigarettes. Her face was shiny, her hair matted with melting snow. She shook herself and stamped her feet on an industrial rug that had been rolled out for the storm. From numberless hours of waiting for her kids to choose their books, she knew exactly where to go. In the reference room, behind the circulation desk, was a cabinet that housed the White Pages of major American cities and minor Illinoisan ones. Tax dollars at work, the phonebooks were all more or less current.

She crouched down in front of them, pulled out the thickest of them, and opened it on the floor. After the Gordons and Gowans, before the many Greens, was a short column of Grants. She was prepared to be disappointed, called back to reason, but her state of mind was so intense that the world seemed likely to fall in line with it. Sure enough, beside a drop of snowmelt that had hit the page and puckered it, was one of the most erotic things she'd ever laid eyes on.

Grant B. 2607 Via Rivera............... **962–3504**

She produced a kind of humming sigh, like the first note of a cello that had sat for decades in an attic. How much a phonebook entry could

suggest! The hours and days and years of being B. Grant, alive in a specific house on a specific street, reachable by anyone who knew his dear
number. She couldn't be sure it was Bradley, but there was no reason it
couldn't be. All the weekly visits to the library, all the idle browsing of its
shelves, and she'd never once thought to look for him. A key to her heart
had been hidden in plain sight.

She took a pencil and a card from a wooden tray, copied the address
and the number, and put the card in her coat pocket with her cigarettes.
In her rush to escape the dental office, after three-plus hours with Sophie
Serafimides, she'd neglected to hand over her twenty-dollar bill. The
money, ill-gotten in any case, had come in handy when she passed the
town drugstore and recalled a more effective means of losing weight and
managing anxiety. She'd procured the means, and now she had a motive,
too. In her mind, she'd already lost thirty pounds and was writing a chatty,
warm letter to Bradley, letting him know that she was very well, telling
him something specific and vivid about each of her four children, tacitly
assuring him that she'd made the fullest of recoveries, had built an ordinary good life for herself, was no longer a person he had to be afraid of
hearing from. And you? Do you still write poetry? How is Isabelle? How
are your boys? They must have families of their own now . . .

Outside the library's rear entrance, on a patch of snow made mangy
by unevenly scattered salt, she lit another cigarette. It turned out that
she'd been wanting one for thirty years. Making her confession to Sophie had rolled the stone from a tomb of emotion, inside which, miracu-
lously intact, she'd found her obsession with Bradley Grant. Describing
it to Sophie in proper detail, reliving the sins she'd committed in its
grip, had brought her back into contact with its contours, and she'd remembered how perfectly they fit the shape of who she was. If anything,
her desire for Bradley felt stronger for the thirty-year rest she'd given it,
stronger than any over-flogged sentiment she had for Russ. Bradley had
excited her at levels deeper than Russ ever could or ever would, because
only with Bradley had she been her entire, crazy, sinning self. Standing
in the snow behind the library, inhaling smoke on a cold Midwestern
night, she was carried back to rainy Los Angeles. She was a mother of
four with a twenty-year-old's heart.

As she'd recounted to Sophie the events leading up to her destruction of the unborn life in her, the filthy bargain she'd struck with Isabelle Washburn's former landlord, she'd had a growing sense of dumpling–patient disconnect. She might have imagined her story emerging with much guilty gasping, much reaching for Kleenexes, but confessing her worst sins to a psychiatrist was nothing like her Catholic confessions. There was no terror of God's judgment on her puny self, no pity for her sweet Lord's suffering on the cross for what she'd done. With Sophie, a female layperson, a maternal Greek American, she felt more like very naughty. The mental switch she'd flipped as a teenager was still there to be flipped Off. She told her story crisply, her spirits rising with the resurrection of the reckless girl who'd loved Bradley. Sophie's expression, meanwhile, grew ever sadder, to the point of amusing her. The satisfaction of showing the dumpling how bad she really was recalled the pleasure of taunting her guardian uncle, Roy Collins, with her misbehavior. By the end, as she related how a Los Angeles police officer had been obliged to tackle a raving girl in pouring rain, she went so far as to snicker at the memory.

Perhaps it was the snicker that brought out the dumpling's frown.

"I'm very sorry for what you went through," Sophie said. "It explains so much, and it makes me even more impressed with your resilience. But there's still something I'm not understanding."

"We both know what that means, don't we."

"What does it mean?"

Marion caricatured the therapeutic frown. "You disapprove."

"By your own account," Sophie said, unamused, "you were seduced by a married man when you were very young. Then you married a man you weren't allowed to be yourself with. And now you tell me that you were atrociously abused by a sexual predator. Doesn't it seem—"

"I knew what I was doing," Marion said proudly. "In every case. I knew it was wrong, and I did it anyway."

"I'm sorry—what did you do to Russ?"

"I lied to him. And now he's lying to me. So what?"

"You offered him your life and he took it. Now he's tired of it and wants something new."

"I admit I'm not very happy with Russ at the moment. But you're way out of line if you're comparing him to that landlord. Russ is like a little boy."

"I'm not comparing them. That landlord—"

"And you're even more out of line if you're comparing Bradley. Bradley was honorable—he wanted the same thing I did. We fell in love, and he never lied to me. It wasn't his fault I went crazy."

"Really?"

"Yes, really. I hated him when I was falling apart, but as soon as I was sane again I wasn't angry at him. I was only sorry for what I'd put him through."

"You felt guilty."

"Definitely."

"Why is it that, every time a man injures you, you respond by feeling guilty?"

Marion, flying, was impatient with Sophie's slowness. "Didn't I just explain this to you? I'm not a good person. I wanted to kill my baby, and I did it the only way I could. I didn't even hate that landlord, I was just insanely afraid of him. I mean, yes, he was evil. But I was seeing my own evil nature reflected in him. That's what made him so frightening."

Sophie briefly shut her eyes. Evidently the impatience was mutual.

"Try to see what I'm seeing," she said. "Try to picture a sweet, vulnerable girl not much older than your daughter is now. Think about how frightened and helpless she is. And then imagine a man whose first thought, when he sees a girl like that, is to take out his penis and abuse her. *That's* the person you think that girl resembles?"

"Well, I don't have a penis, so."

"But your first thought would be to exploit someone vulnerable?"

"You're forgetting what I did to Bradley's wife. I went to her house and deliberately hurt her. She was vulnerable, wasn't she?"

"My understanding is that Bradley was the person you were actually angry with."

"Only because I was out of my mind."

"Anger strikes me as quite a reasonable response to how he'd treated you."

Marion shook her head. No sooner had she refound a treasure than the dumpling was trying to take it away from her.

"You've told me a horrific story," Sophie said. "In your own words, you met Satan himself. I wouldn't expect a self-described believer to be so forgiving of Satan."

"That's because you're not a believer. I might as well be angry at the rain for falling on me. I knew perfectly well who he was. I let him into me anyway, and I got the punishment I deserved."

"You blame yourself, not him."

"What's wrong with that? There's a reason why anger is a deadly sin. I was full of anger when I was young—I felt like murdering people. If I hadn't been so angry, I might have made better decisions. I know you think it's sick to blame myself, but spiritually I think it's healthier."

"Maybe," Sophie said. "As long as you're happy with where it's gotten you."

"Meaning?"

"Meaning anxious and depressed. Unable to sleep. Hating your body. I have a hard time believing that any religion would condemn an emotion as natural as anger. Think about the civil rights movement. Do you think Dr. King wasn't angry when his people were murdered by Klansmen? He may have preached nonviolence, but sometimes, when a problem is intractable, only anger can change things."

"I would never compare my situation to a Black person's in Alabama. That's really almost offensive."

Sophie smiled pleasantly. "I didn't mean to be offensive."

"I was lucky to find someone to marry me at all, after what I'd been through. And even then I married him under false pretenses. I can hardly go complaining that I'm oppressed by him now. Even the business with his widow friend—I didn't blame Bradley for losing interest in his wife. Why should I blame Russ for losing interest in me? I'm a lot older and fatter than Bradley's wife was."

"Anger is an emotion," Sophie said. "It doesn't have to be logical. Right now, for example, I'm feeling very angry at your abuser. I'm also a little bit angry with you."

"What for?"

"Listen to your assumptions. You were *lucky* to find someone to marry you? Why? What was so wrong with you? You were sexually experienced? You'd had a nervous breakdown? Would that have been a problem if you were male? Would you have been *lucky* to find a wife? And why was it so important to be married in the first place? Because a woman isn't really a woman if she can't find a husband and procreate? Because she—"

Sophie stopped herself and shook her head, as if she'd said too much. And Marion indeed was disappointed in her. The dumpling was so soft and slippery in her manner that her underlying conceptual program, whether Freudian or medical or political or what, had been hard to pinpoint. Now the program stood revealed. Marion guessed that it applied to every one of the neglected or discarded wives who came here—One Size Fits All. Was she supposed to be delighted that it fit her, too?

"You must get tired of it," she said, not kindly. "All the ladies coming to you and complaining about their men. Week after week, men men men. It must be frustrating for you—that we can't talk about something else. That we can't see how oppressed we are."

Sophie, who'd regained her composure, smiled pleasantly. "It's interesting that you assume my other female patients only talk about men."

"Are you telling me they don't?"

"It doesn't matter if they do or don't. What matters is how you imagine them. Do you think I think *you* talk too much about men?"

"I think you do," Marion said. "You keep telling me I need to develop more of an independent life. I think what you're really saying is 'Enough about men already—go liberate yourself.'"

"You don't care for the idea of women's liberation."

"If that's your program, I don't object to it. If it works for your other patients, more power to them."

"But it's not for you."

"That landlord was a sicko. I never saw my friend again, I never saw Isabelle, but I'll bet you he'd found a way to have sex with her. She got behind with her rent, or she needed a professional favor, and he used his power to take advantage of her. He was fat and repulsive, and he only ran that house as a way to have sex with lots of girls. I was one of them, and what he did to me was sick. Even the part that was normal sex wasn't normal. It was all happening in his head—I was just a thing."

"Exactly."

"But let's say he went to a psychiatrist: *Sir, you're making me a little bit angry. Isn't it time you developed a more independent life? All you ever talk about is girls!*"

Sophie drew a slow breath and slowly let it out. "A good psychiatrist might have helped him identify the trauma he felt compelled to reenact."

"Ah, there we go. What am *I* reenacting?"

"What's your guess?"

"I don't know. Guilt about my father's suicide. Is that the idea?"

"If that's what you say."

"I've stopped feeling guilty about Russ. I certainly don't feel guilty about the landlord. I *was* guilty, but that's different from a feeling. That's an objective fact. The people I feel guilty about are Perry and the child of Bradley's I killed without telling him. They were innocent, and I'm responsible for them."

The dumpling looked down at her pudgy hands. Darkness had fallen outside the window. Elsewhere in the dental office, late units of pain were being manufactured with a drill.

"Your mother," Sophie said. "You said she was skiing with her friends when you needed help with your pregnancy. Did you feel angry about that?"

"My mother was a self-centered alcoholic nightmare."

"I'll take that as a yes. You've also told me about your anger at your sister. But it was your father who bankrupted your family—"

"Shirley and my mother made him do it."

"He committed fraud and lied to you. Then your car salesman takes advantage of you, despite knowing how sensitive you are. A sexual deviant does unspeakable things to you. You support your husband for twenty-five years, and now he's chasing someone else. And yet the only people you seem to be angry with are your mother and your sister. Do you see what I'm not understanding?"

"I guess I'm not a women's libber."

"I'm not asking you to be one. I'm asking you to try to see yourself."

"The person I see isn't good."

"Marion, listen to me." The dumpling leaned forward. "Do you want to know a thing I really am getting tired of hearing? That particular refrain of yours."

"But it's true."

"Really? You've raised four great kids. You've given your husband as much as any man could deserve. You did everything you could for your father. You even took care of your sister when she was dying."

"That wasn't me, though. It was me playing a role. The real me . . ." She shook her head.

"Tell me about the real you," Sophie said. "Besides being a 'bad' person, how would you describe her? What is she like?"

"She's thin," Marion said emphatically.

"She's thin."

"She feels everything intensely. She's a sinner, and she's honest with God about that. She hopes He understands that sinning is inseparable from feeling alive, but she doesn't care if He forgives her, because she's not really capable of regret. She's probably an actress—she wants attention. She's fairly crazy, but not in a way that hurts anyone. She was never suicidal."

The dumpling seemed unimpressed.

"Your sister was an actress," she remarked. "You've also described her as nutty and thin."

"Oh, thanks for that."

Sophie gestured suggestively, not retracting her remark.

"Shirley was spoiled and bitter," Marion said. "She wasn't a real actress."

"Okay."

"The person I'm describing is the opposite of bitter."

"Okay. Let's say that's the real you. What do you think is stopping you from being that person?"

"Isn't it obvious? I'm fifty years old. Being divorced would be a disaster. Even if I found a way to make it work, I'd still be responsible for my kids, especially Perry. There's no escaping the consequences of the life I've made."

"Not to nitpick," Sophie said, smiling pleasantly, "but if the real you is incapable of regret, why does she care about the consequences?"

"You asked me for my fantasy."

"No, I asked you for the opposite. It's interesting that you interpreted me to mean a fantasy."

The dumpling's endurance was extraordinary. Marion could talk to her forever, going around and around, and never get anywhere. It was nothing but a waste of money.

"I wonder if it has to be an either-or," Sophie said. "Maybe there's a way to feel truer to yourself and still be a good mother. What if you started with the local theater? Tried getting involved and seeing where it leads."

This was the kind of suggestion—moderate, sensible, incremental— that Marion might have made to one of her kids, but waddling around on a stage with other middle-aged suburbanites held no appeal. She needed to be the intense, skinny woman smoking a cigarette at the back of the theater, watching the actors fail and finally losing her patience, striding up to the stage to show them how to do a scene. A fantasy? Maybe, but maybe not. Once upon a time, on a Murphy bed in Los Angeles, her acting had mesmerized Bradley Grant.

"What are you thinking?" Sophie asked.

"I'm thinking I'm going to let you go home."

"Yes, in a few minutes. I feel we're—"

"No." Marion stood up. "Russ and I have to go to the open house for clergy. Doesn't that sound fun?"

She went to the door and took her gabardine coat off its hook.

"I guarantee you," she said, "it won't be fun for Russ unless one of the wives is good-looking. Otherwise it's just another occasion for his insecurity, and I'm no help with that. I'm the fat little humiliation he's married to. His only consolation is how good I am at playing nice, re-membering the name of every wife, making sure they all get greeted by a Hildebrandt. Later on, he'll tell me how bad it felt to be the oldest junior minister at the party, how frustrated he is, and I'll tell him he deserves his own church. I'll tell him how much better his sermons are than Dwight's, how much harder he works than Dwight, how much I admire him. That's another role I'm insanely good at. Except then, if the party was hard enough for him, he'll complain that his sermons are only good because I write them for him. Ha!"

Batting her eyelashes, exaggerating her role, she turned back to Sophie.

"Oh that's not true at all, honey. The ideas are all yours, I just do a little tidying up to help you express your ideas more clearly. I couldn't do anything without you. I'm just an empty vessel who knows how to write a clean English sentence—Ha!"

Her audience of one was watching her with somber compassion.

"You wanted mad?" Marion said to her. "I can do mad."

She meant *mad* as in *angry*, but the way she exited the office, jerking open the door and closing it too hard, was mad in both senses. She was mad at herself for using the word *fantasy*, mad at Sophie for pouncing on the slip. The self she'd unearthed was only a fantasy? They'd see about that. The important thing, she told herself, as she sailed past the Greek receptionist and out into the weather, was to not eat one more goddamned cookie, ever again. To properly starve herself; to see food as the enemy it was; to glow white-hot with the burning of her fat, false self. If it was mad to be obsessed with her weight, then let her be mad. Her fat-loss program in the fall had been a feeble thing, born of a dumpling-sanctioned hope of rekindling Russ's interest in her, of avoiding a split from which she stood to lose far more than he did. Her heart hadn't been in it, and now she knew why: she'd never gotten over Bradley. The man in whom she'd invested herself had been a second choice—as insecure as Bradley was confident, as clumsy at writing and tentative at sex as Bradley was magnificent. Maybe, at the time, in Arizona, she'd needed a man she could manage and be more brilliant than, but the marriage had long since dwindled to a mere arrangement: in return for her services, Russ didn't throw her to the wolves. She still had Christian compassion for him, but when she thought about his *penis*, vis-à-vis Frances Cottrell and the other pretty women of New Prospect, it wasn't quite true that there was no comparing him to her long-ago abuser. That much the dumpling had been right about.

The old corner drugstore had been Rockwellian when the Hildebrandts moved to town, but the owner had since remodeled it with ugly

laminates, covered the wooden floor with linoleum, and installed fluorescent lighting. In the same improving spirit, the Christmas tree inside
the door was artificial, its needles silver, not even fake green. Behind
the front counter, doing the *Sun-Times* crossword with a pencil, was a
large-eared man in his late twenties, too old to be working as a clerk if
it wasn't a career path he'd somehow, heartbreakingly, chosen. Marion
stepped up to the counter and surveyed the candy-bar display with mili-

"I need cigarettes," she said.

"Strangely," she said, "the only brand that comes to mind is Benson &
Hedges. It's because of that TV commercial, the one with the elevator

"'They take some getting used to.'"

"Are Benson & Hedges any good?"

"What's a popular brand these days?"

"Marlboro, Winston. Lucky Strike."

"Lucky Strike! Of course! I used to smoke them. One of those,

"Good Lord. I have no idea. How about one of each?"

Handing over her money, she was tempted to explain that she hadn't
had a cigarette in thirty years; that she'd quit smoking after being released from a locked ward and moving in with her uncle Jimmy in Arizona; that cigarette smoke had aggravated Jimmy's asthma and tasted
wrong to her at high altitude; that she'd filled the hole of her missing
habit with rosary beads and daily visits to the Church of the Nativity,
a walk of two thousand four hundred and forty-two steps (habitually
counted) from Jimmy's front door; that she'd discovered Nativity when,
eager to be helpful, she'd accompanied Rosalia, the mother of Jimmy's
man, Antonio, to a Sunday mass, because the men were late sleepers and
Rosalia kept forgetting where she was going; that Marion, whose state
of mind was like the high country in spring weather, strong sunlight
snuffed by clouds and breaking out again, over and over, all day long

the alternation, brightsummerwarm, darkwinterchilly, had thrown her soul open to every single thing she encountered, because none of these things was a locked ward, and that the presence and majesty of God, revealed in a womblike little Catholic church where her uncle's lover's senile mother received Communion, had happened to be one of them; that God had become a better friend to her than cigarettes. It saddened her to think that the big-eared young man had no larger ambition than working in retail, and she would have liked to enlarge his evening by sharing some of the high-country vividness with which, all of a sudden, she was recalling her life pre-Russ. But the clerk had already picked up his crossword again.

Heedless of the slush in her shoes, she ran across the street and took shelter beneath the awning of a travel agency. She wasted two matches before she got a filterless Lucky lit. Her first drag was reminiscent of losing her virginity—painful and awful and excellent. She knew very well that cigarettes had killed her sister. She also knew, from reports in the paper, that the risk of cancer was proportional to total lifetime exposure. Shirley had erred in not taking a thirty-year break from her exposure. Marion didn't intend to smoke forever, just long enough to regain the figure of the girl who'd given her virginity to Bradley Grant.

A measure of her disturbance was that, although she felt light-headed, the Lucky didn't make her sick. It made her want another one. She walked only two blocks, jumping at the sound of every passing car, jangled and buffeted by the snowy mayhem of it all, before she sat down on a bench outside the town hall and lit up again. Had cigarettes always been so delicious? She gladly noted her lack of hunger. The thought of Doris Haefle's Swedish meatballs—how many of which Marion had eaten, exactly a year earlier, she'd enjoined herself to keep count of, before losing count—turned her stomach. Snowmelt was seeping through her coat beneath her butt. The boughs of the town hall's ornamental hemlocks sagged under heavy loads of white. She was smoking the second Lucky faster than the first one; an elation long lost to her was building in her chest. To do something with it, she spoke aloud a word she didn't think she'd used since the morning the police picked her up in Los Angeles. She said, "Fuck!"

Oh, it felt good.

"Fuck Doris Haefle. Fuck her meatballs."

A hatted commuter, briefcase in hand, head lowered against the driving snow, paused on the sidewalk to look at her. She raised the hand with the Lucky in it and waved to him.

"Everything okay?" the man said.

"Never better, thank you."

He continued down the sidewalk. Something about his gait, the determined slant of his body, reminded her of Bradley. Bringing her Lucky to her lips, she saw that its coal was about to burn her fingers. She frantically shook it into the snow.

Bradley would be sixty-five now. Old, but not so very old, not in a preservative clime like Southern California's. Did he still think about her? Or had he, like her, entombed his memories and tried to make himself a different person? It would be terrible if he'd forgotten her. But even worse if he remembered her only as the girl who'd behaved unforgivably: if their months of bliss had all been blotted out by the day she'd gone to his house and spoken to his wife. Why had she had to do that? Why had she had to hurt an innocent third party? Everything might be perfect if she hadn't.

The matches were damp now—she scorched a fingertip lighting one. To make an informed guess about which version of her had stayed with Bradley, whether the good might outweigh the very bad, she tried to summon her memories of his passion for her. The memories wouldn't sit still, one bled into another, but she had the impression of a great many instances of passion. Even when she'd lost her mind and frightened him, he'd had to struggle to keep away from her. Later, yes, surely, he'd hated her for going to his wife. But so what? She'd hated him, too, for rejecting her. The hatred had quickly faded. What remained in her memory was the thrilling rightness of being with him. Maybe, with the passage of time, he'd come to feel the same way?

She imagined abandoning Russ before he could get around to abandoning her. Wouldn't *that* be a surprise. The fantasy of losing thirty pounds and ditching Russ was so satisfying that she might have been content to keep indulging in it, sitting on her bench, if it hadn't occurred to her that the library had a collection of phonebooks . . .

In the mangy snow behind the library, she flicked the end of her fourth cigarette into the parking lot. The facts of the world had submitted to her state of mind. She now had good reason to hope that Bradley was alive in Los Angeles; she had an address and a phone number. Electrified by nicotine, she wondered what to do next with her disturbance. Low on the list of options was smelling the meatballs of Dwight Haefle's nasty wife. For a moment, she worried that Becky might be waiting at home to go to the open house; that her sense of duty had prevailed over her need to be with Tanner Evans. But this seemed unlikely, and Becky, if it came to that, could go by herself to the open house with Russ, who'd be happier with that arrangement anyway. He was proud of Becky's beauty and preferred parading it in public, every Sunday afternoon, to being seen with his wife.

"Fuck you, Russ."

Remembering how it felt to want to murder someone, she thought she might yet become a women's libber. But she was done with the psychiatric dumpling. No imaginable breakthrough could leave her more broken through than she was now. She felt like going home and emptying her hosiery drawer of its remaining cash, to forestall any temptation to crawl back to Sophie, and spending it on an extravagant present for Perry, but the stores were all closing.

She saw what she had to do next. She had to confess to Perry, too. Confiding in Sophie had only been practice, a warm-up. Someone in her family needed to know what she'd done, and it sure as fucking hell wasn't Russ. Perry was the person most like her, the person in danger of disturbance like her own, the person she had to warn. Wherever her disturbance might lead her, whether back into Bradley's arms or merely to a divorcée's career in local theater, she would have to bring Perry along with her. Her responsibility for him would keep her from flying too dangerously high. This would be the deal she made with God.

Insulated by her fatness, she went around the side of the library, pushed through a weak spot in its hedge, and made tracks across its front lawn, which she'd never seen one person set foot on. New Prospect was lovely in the snow but not as beautiful as Arizona, because it was already shadowed by a tomorrow of gray slush-puddles, of salt-corroded snowbanks blackened by the exhaust pipes of cars gunning their engines, spinning their wheels. In Arizona, the white purity had persisted for weeks.

Fighting uphill against the wind on Maple Avenue made her aware of nicotine's poisoning of the heart. At the corner of Highland, she stopped to catch her breath and check her watch. It was nearly seven o'clock. With all the snow, Russ might only now be getting home himself. She could always say to him, "Fuck the reception—I'm not going." But a sweeter way to punish him would be to let him wonder why she hadn't come home. She was pretty sure he'd lied to her at breakfast, pretty sure he was with his widow friend. And there was, she realized, an easy way to be certain. Kitty Reynolds, his putative companion for the outing in the city, lived in one of the little houses farther up on Maple, near the high school.

Decisions being simple for a person unafraid of consequences, Marion crossed Highland and proceeded up Maple, into the wind. Her feet were frozen, her fingers getting there. She couldn't quite picture Kitty's house, but she recognized it when she came to it. There was light in every down-stairs window, a sports car with a Michigan license in the driveway, no wreath on the door, no lights on the bushes. Marion marched up the front walk, noting that it had been shoveled perhaps an hour earlier, and rang the doorbell. For a heart-clutching moment, she confused what she was doing with the thing she'd done to Bradley's wife, as if she were reenact-ing it. Then clarity returned. Her situation now was exactly the reverse.

An elderly man in a thick cardigan opened the door. She was afraid she had the wrong house, but he identified himself as Kitty's brother. "She's just draining the spaghetti," he said.

"Oh, I'm so sorry to bother you at dinnertime."

"Who can I tell her is here?"

"I—it's not important. I should have stopped by earlier. Was she here in the afternoon?"

"Yep. Trouncing me at Scrabble. It was the perfect day for sitting by the fire. Would you like to come in?"

"No, I, no," Marion said, turning away. "Thank you. I'll see her in church on Sunday."

"And you are . . . ?"

She raised a hand and waved it as she walked away. As soon as she heard the door close, she took out her Luckies. One of her match packs was sodden, the other still usable. Suspicious though she'd been that Russ had lied to her, it had taken conclusive proof to make her furious about it. His lie had been stupid, easily found out, the lie of a little boy, and this made her even angrier. Did he think *she* was stupid? Probably not even. She'd barely registered as a person at all. She'd been little more than an inconvenient object at the breakfast table, an annoying vase in the way of his sugar bowl, not even worth telling a decent lie to. Soon enough, when she'd lost her fat, she would have more ways to make him pay. For now, the sweetest punishment would be to say nothing, let him think she knew nothing, let him damn himself by telling further lies.

It was nearly seven thirty when she got back to the parsonage. There was no sign of the car, no car tracks in the driveway. Inside the back door, she took off her shoes and coat and ran her fingers through her slushy hair. On the kitchen counter were sugar cookies whose allure she could no longer fathom. Everything in the kitchen seemed lusterless and alien. She might have been entering the house of someone recently deceased.

"Perry?" she called. "Becky?"

Climbing the stairs, she called their names again. Maybe the boys had gone out sledding? Their bedroom was dark, the door ajar. She turned on a light in her and Russ's room. On the foot of the bed was a note in Perry's artistic hand.

> *Dear Mom,*
>   *Dad is stuck in the city, so I'm taking Jay to the Haefles. Becky waited for you. I told her to go to the concert.*
>   *Perry*

Now came, without warning, the tears she hadn't shed in her confession. Whatever Russ might mean or not mean to her, however poorly he and Perry got along, he would always be the person Perry called *Dad*— would forever be his father. And how unjust she'd been to Becky, imagining that she wouldn't come to the open house. How poignant Perry's striving to behave like an adult, how generous his mentioning that his sister had waited; how dear and real her children were, how lucky she was to have them; what a difference there was between proclaiming her badness to the dumpling, the abstract fact of it, and experiencing it in relation to her children. She'd let them down. Becky had obediently waited for her, and Perry had made the best decision he could.

Clumsy, her eyesight teary, she tore off her exercise clothes and rubbed her hair with a towel. She truly was a bad person, because along with love and remorse, no less strongly, she was feeling self-pity for having been wrenched from the vividness of memory and fantasy; resentment for the interruption of her disturbance. Also hatred of the sack of a dress in which she was now obliged to encase the sausage of her body. In the bathroom, after brushing her hair, she forced herself to step onto the corroded old scale by the toilet, to establish a new baseline. Counting clothes, she weighed one hundred and forty-four pounds. It was almost enough to make a person cry again. When she went back to the kitchen for her cigarettes, wearing her good winter coat and her good fur-trimmed boots, the sugar cookies had regained their allure.

Eating cookies is an interesting response to feeling overweight.

"Really?" she said aloud, to the dumpling in her head. "Is that really so goddamned fucking hard to understand? Have you never in your life felt sorry for yourself?"

After a fortifying smoke on the front porch, she set out for the Haefles'. The snow was still coming down heavily, but the air's flavor had turned Canadian as the cold front gained the upper hand. Her only consolation for having let her children down was that Russ was letting them down even worse. Whom she felt more like murdering, him or the slender widow with whom he was stuck in the city, was a toss-up.

Leaving the Haefles' house as she approached it were two priests in identical sable-collared overcoats. Her fear of priests outside a church, which dated from her Catholic years, was related to an atavistic fear of all things monstrous, even the ostensibly laudable monstrosity of being half human and half divinely anointed: of being celibate. She lurked on the sidewalk until the priests had climbed into a Country Squire station wagon. That it looked brand-new was itself vaguely monstrous.

She knew the Haefles well enough to let herself inside without knocking. Smelling meatballs, blessedly also cigarette smoke, she took her Luckies from her coat before she hung it in the closet by the basement stairs. From the basement came the sound of Hollywood violins and then a familiar little voice, Judson's.

Downstairs, in the rec room, she found him on a sofa between two girls in whose faces the unfortunate lineaments of Doris Haefle were discernible. They were watching *Miracle on 34th Street* on a portable Zenith. On the screen, Kris Kringle was seated on the bed of a little-girl character whose mother, as Marion recalled, saw nothing wrong with leaving her alone with strange men and their penises. As the camera framed Santa's face, her chest tightened. Not her favorite movie. She went behind the TV to avoid it.

"Hi, Mom," Judson said.

"Hello, dear. I'm sorry I'm so late. Did you have some dinner?"

"Yes, but now we're watching this movie."

"I'm Judson's mother," Marion explained to the girls.

They mumbled hellos. Judson was slouched low on the sofa, the girls inclining toward each other, their bodies touching his. Although he was a happy child in general, Marion was struck by the heavy-lidded dreaminess of his expression. He seemed to be enjoying more than just the movie. He looked like a cat transported by petting. She had the uneasy sense that she was interrupting something.

"Well, I'll leave you to your movie," she said. "Perry is upstairs?"

Judson's gaze stayed on the screen. "Pre*sum*ably," he said.

There was an edge of sarcasm in his voice, as if he were performing for the girls. Marion went upstairs feeling like no better a mother than the one in the movie. Judson was nine years old. She knew it was time for Becky to have a boyfriend, past time for Clem to have a girl in his life, but she was not remotely ready for Judson to lose his innocence.

In the hallway, standing with her back to the party and popping a whole cookie into her mouth, was the Lutheran pastor's wife—Jane. Definitely *Jane* Walsh, not Janet. On her dessert plate were four more cookies, and she was even heavier than Marion.

"Hello, Jane. Marion Hildebrandt—Russ's wife."

One greeting down, a million to go.

"This party is a lovely tradition," Jane said, "but Doris's cookies are *not* what I need at this time of year. I always seem to overdo."

Marion herself preferred the meatballs. The cookies here, though impeccably Swedish, were dry and flavorless. She was on the verge of expressing this judgment, on the theory that she was done with censoring herself, when the sociable din in the living room died down suddenly. She wondered if Dwight Haefle might be making a little speech. Instead, she heard another familiar voice rising. It was Perry, shouting something about . . . being damned?

She hurried past Jane Walsh and pushed through the party's margins. Perry was standing by the fireplace, his face extremely red, a Haefle to either side of him. Everyone else in the room was watching them.

"What's going on?" Marion said.

Perry swallowed a sob. "Mom, I'm sorry."

"What is it? What's happening?"

"Son," Dwight Haefle said, putting an arm around Perry. "Let's, ah. Let's take a little walk."

Perry bowed his head and let himself be led away. Marion tried to follow, but Doris Haefle arrested her. Her expression blazed with triumph. "Your son is intoxicated."

"I'm very sorry to hear it."

"Hm, yes, this is what happens when children aren't supervised. Did you only get here now?"

"A few minutes ago."

"It's quite unusual that your children came without you."

"I know. The weather is just . . . Perry was trying to do a good thing."

"You didn't tell him to come?"

"God, no."

"That's good, then, dear." Doris patted Marion on the shoulder. "You didn't do anything wrong. You just need to take him home now."

Doris Haefle had a grossly inflated sense of the importance of a pastor's wife, was sensitive to every slight to it, and therefore, because the world didn't share her regard for the role, existed in a state of perpetual grievance. Among the crosses she bore was being married to a pastor who ironically deprecated his own role. For Marion, the miserable thing was that she, too, was a pastor's wife and thus, in Doris's view, worthy of the highest respect. She had to endure not only Doris's unsolicited suggestions on how to comport herself, in her exalted role, but the unfailingly tender manner in which she offered them. It was awkward to be called *dear* by a person you felt like calling *insufferable bitch*.

Perry was slumped forward on a chair in the dining room, his hair draping his face. Dwight came over to Marion and spoke in a low voice. "He does seem to have been drinking gløgg."

"I'll take care of it," she said. "I apologize for this."

"Should we be worried about Russ?"

"No, he's on a date with Frances Cottrell."

The widening of Dwight's eyes amused her.

"They're delivering toys and canned goods in the city."

"Ah."

"But listen," she said. "Judson's in the basement watching *Miracle on 34th Street*. Would you mind if I left him here and came back later?"

"Not at all," Dwight said. "If you don't want to come back, I can run him home."

How often a marriage consisted of nasty paired with nice. If her own marriage didn't strike people this way, it was only because they'd never met the real her. She needed to go down and tell Judson that she was taking Perry home, but the scene in the basement had left an unsettling aftertaste, and so she asked nice Dwight to do it. When he was gone, she went to Perry and crouched at his feet.

"Sweetie," she said. "How drunk are you? A lot, or not very?"

"Relatively not very," he said, his face still hidden. "Mrs. Haefle overreacted."

The word *relatively* didn't surprise Marion. She herself had done her first drinking when she was his age. Then again, look how she'd turned out.

"What were you thinking?" she said. "You brought Judson here. You were responsible for him—did you not think of that?"

"Mother. Please. I am very sorry, all right?"

"Sweetie, look at me. Will you look at me? I'm not angry with you. I'm just surprised—you're always so considerate of Judson."

"I'm sorry!"

The poor boy. She took his hands and kissed his head.

"Jay was fine," he said. "He was playing Yahtzee, and I wasn't that buzzed. Everything was fine until . . ."

"You picked the wrong woman's house to get drunk in."

He gave a little snort. Her opinion of Doris Haefle was known to him. She'd told him all sorts of things she didn't tell the other kids. And now she had new things to tell him. The hotness of his hands, the reality of the boy she so especially loved, was burning a hole in the tissue of her fantasies of Bradley. "Let's get you home," she said.

When she returned from the closet with their coats, Perry was eating from a plate of meatballs. They were tempting, but so were cigarettes. The old cycles of nicotine, of hunger and its suppression, of anxiety and relief, were coming back to her. Leaving Perry to get some food in him, she stepped out onto the front stoop.

She was only halfway through the Lucky when he opened the door. She had a red-handed impulse to drop the cigarette, but it was important that he see her as she really was.

He goggled in cartoonish astonishment. "What, may I ask, are you doing?"

"I have my own contraband tonight."

"You *smoke*?"

"I used to, a long time ago. But it's a terrible habit and you must never try it."

"Do as I say, not as I do."

"Exactly."

He shut the door and stepped into his rubbers. "Can I try one anyway?"

Too late, she realized her mistake. At some point, she was sure of it, he'd take her smoking as permission to smoke himself, and it would be yet another thing to feel guilty about having done to him. To quell this new anxiety, she sucked hard on the cigarette.

"Perry, listen to me. There's one thing you can do that I will not forgive. I will never forgive you if you become a smoker. Do you understand?"

"Honestly, no," he said, buckling his rubbers. "I don't think of you as being a hypocrite."

"I started smoking before anyone knew how dangerous it is. You're too intelligent to make the same mistake."

"And yet here you are, smoking."

"Well, there's a reason for that. Would you like me to tell you what it is?"

"I want you not to *die*."

"I don't intend to die, sweetie. But there are some things you need to know about me. How are you feeling now?"

"The buzz no longer buzzeth. *Buzzeth buzzeth buzzeth*—see?"

In the story she began to tell him, as they made their way home, there was nothing of Bradley Grant, nothing of any man except her father. The snow, deep on the ground and still falling, gave her voice a curious distinctness while dampening its carry, as if the world were an enlargement of her skull. Perry listened in silence, wordlessly offering her a hand where the snow had formed drifts. Until now, she'd kept the suicide a secret from her kids. Even to Russ she hadn't spoken of it in many years; she had the sense that it frightened him, or embarrassed him; as did, for that matter, everything else related to her innermost self. Perry's face was hidden by the hood of his parka, and as she proceeded to describe her own mental disturbance, following the suicide—the dissociation, the episodes of slippage, the months of insomnia, the weeks of catatonic lowness—she had no idea what he was making of it.

They reached the parsonage before she'd finished. In the driveway were two sets of recent footprints, one coming, one going. Guessing that they were Clem's, she called his name as soon as she and Perry were in the kitchen, but the house was obviously empty.

"I wonder if he went to the concert," she said. "You probably want to get down there, too. We can talk more in the morning."

Perry was eating a cookie. "If you have more to say, let's hear it."

She retrieved the Luckies from her coat and opened the back door for ventilation.

"I'm sorry, sweetie. This is hard for me to do without smoking."

Her hands were too shaky to get a match lit. Perry took the matches and flared one for her. She was feeling somehow younger than he was; more daughter than mother. She gratefully inhaled the smoke and tried to blow it out the door, but the wind pushed it in.

"Put that out," he said. "I have a better idea."

"The front porch."

"No. Third floor."

In the gloom of the front hall, she was surprised to see two massive pieces of luggage. For a moment, as in a dream, she thought that they were hers—that she was leaving tonight, perhaps for Los Angeles. Then she understood that they were Clem's. Why had he brought so much luggage?

Perry had run up the stairs. Huffing, with poisoned heart, she followed him to the third-floor storage room. No guilty secrets were buried here. She'd arrived at her uncle Jimmy's with only one suitcase, and before she married Russ she'd burned her diaries in Jimmy's fireplace, destroying the last evidence of the person she'd been. The oldest relics now were from Indiana—a crib and a high chair last used by Judson, an old movie projector, a cedar chest of blankets and linens not worth keeping, a wardrobe of fashions unlikely to return, a mildewed army-surplus tent that Russ had wrongly imagined the family might camp in. It was all just sadness.

Without turning on a light, Perry opened the mullioned dormer window. "The house has some kind of chimney effect," he said. "Even with the door closed, there's always a draft going out."

"You seem to really know your way around up here."

"You can use the outer sill as an ashtray."

"Wait a minute. Are you telling me you smoke?"

"Finish your story. I thought you had more to say."

There was indeed an outflowing draft. She could put her head out the window and still be in relative warmth—*in* the snow, feeling the flakes on her face, without being *of* it. Smoking but not in smoke.

"So, well, so," she said. "I ended up losing my mind. I got picked up by the police when I was wandering around on Christmas morning. Thirty years ago tomorrow. They took me to the county hospital, and then I was committed to the women's ward at Rancho Los Amigos, which is not the kind of place you ever want to be. Obviously, they couldn't let me back out on the street, but to be locked up in a place with bars on the windows, surrounded by women even crazier than me—I still don't really understand how I got better. The psychiatrists told me that my brain was still adolescent. The word they used was *plastic*. They said it was possible my hormones would settle down—that I'd stressed them by spending too much time alone, and by . . . other things. I didn't really believe them, but there was a list of behaviors I had to exhibit before they'd let me leave, and I was so desperate to get out that I eventually exhibited every one of them. So. That's another important fact about me. I was institutionalized for mental illness when I was twenty."

She crushed her cigarette on the outer sill.

"Do you see why I was so worried about you in the spring? We're so much alike—we're not like the others. Your trouble sleeping, your mood swings, I think that's something you get from me. From my side of the family. I feel terrible about it, but it's something you need to know. I don't want you to ever have to go through what I did."

It was hard to turn away from the window, but she did it. The room seemed brighter now that her eyes had adjusted. Perry was sitting on the cedar chest, his own eyes on the floor. When she sat down in his line of vision, he lowered his chin to his chest.

"Your father doesn't know about any of this," she said. "I never told him I'd been in a hospital—because I got better. I'd been better for a number of years when I met him, and I want you to remember that. The psychiatrists were right. It was something I outgrew."

This was to some extent a lie, so she repeated it.

"You don't have to worry about me, sweetie. But I am worried about you. You're still a teenager, and you're so precious to me. You need to tell me what's happening in your head. If there's a problem, we can work on it, but you need to be honest with me. Will you do that? Will you tell me what you're thinking?"

His breath was hot and she could smell the liquor on it. To have named, aloud, to him, the thing for which she felt guiltiest made it larger; realer; inescapable-seeming. She thought of her earlier hesitation at the door of the dumpling's office—her sense that she had only two choices, either submit to God's will and devote herself to Perry, or godlessly devote herself to herself. It was cruel how mutually exclusive the choices seemed to be. In the heat of her son's breath, she could feel her elation evaporating, her longing for Bradley escaping her grasp.

"Sweetie? Please say something."

With a breathy sound, almost a laugh, he sat up straight and looked around the room as if he didn't see her at his feet. "What's there to say? It's not like this is any great surprise."

"How so?"

He was smiling. "I already knew I was damned. Right?"

"No, no, no."

"I'm not saying it's your fault. It's just a fact. There's something bad in my head."

"No, sweetie. You're just intelligent and sensitive. That doesn't have to be a bad thing. It can be a very good thing, too."

"Not true. Here, you want to see?"

He stood up with surprising energy and stepped onto the cedar chest. From the top of the wardrobe, he took down a shoe box. He wasn't reacting at all the way she'd expected. There was no distress on her behalf, no fear on his own. It was as if a switch had been flipped and he wasn't reacting at all. And she knew that switch. It was the worst sort of punishment to see her son flipping it.

He removed the lid of the shoe box and held up a clear plastic bag that appeared to be filled with plant matter. "These," he said, "are the seeds and stems from what I've smoked up here. They correspond to maybe ten percent of my total intake, counting other locations." He rooted in the box. "Here we have my papers. Here's the pipe I thought would be great but didn't quite work for me. Trusty Bic lighter, of course. Roach clip. Miniature mouthwash bottle. And this—" He held up a gleaming apparatus. "You might as well know about this, too. This is a more or less serviceable hand scale. Useful if you're in the business of selling pot."

"Holy Mary."

"You asked me to be honest with you."

He put the lid back on the box. All business, no emotion. It occurred to her that the Perry in her head had been nothing but a sentimental projection, extrapolated from the little boy he'd been. She didn't know the real Perry any more than Russ knew the real her.

"How did this all happen so quickly?" she said, meaning his becoming a stranger.

"Three years isn't quick."

"Oh my. Three years? I must be very stupid and very blind."

"Not necessarily. It isn't hard to hide a drug habit if you're sedulous about the protocols."

"I thought we had a close relationship."

"We do, in a way. It's not like I thought I knew everything about *you*. As, indeed, I'm now learning, I didn't."

"If you're selling drugs, though. That is not at all the same kind of thing."

"I'm not proud of it."

"You mustn't sell drugs."

"For the record, I no longer do. I've been trying to turn over a new leaf. You can thank Becky for that."

"*Becky?* Becky knows about this?"

"Not the selling part, I don't think. But otherwise, yes, she's pretty well apprised."

At the vista that was opening, the image of her children conspiring to exclude her, Marion felt a dizzying resurgence of her disturbance. Evidently, she was anything but the indispensable, confided-in mother she'd imagined herself to be. She'd fooled Russ, but she hadn't fooled her kids, and her feral intelligence was quick to recognize a kind of permission in this: if she ever managed to walk away, she might not be so missed.

"I'm going to have one more cigarette," she said.

"Permission granted."

She went back to the window and lit up. There was still some juice in her; the old organs of longing still functioned. Either-or, either-or. It was almost comical to watch her mind flip back and forth between irreconcilable contraries, God-fearing mother, unregretting sinner. She leaned as far as she dared out the window, trying to escape the house's leaking warmth and feel the winter air on her skin. She leaned out even farther and caught a little gust of wind. Snowflakes were melting on her cheeks. Everything was a mess, and it was wonderful.

"Whoa, Mom, careful," Perry said.

The amplified harmonies of "Leaving on a Jet Plane," stripped of reverb by the density of the crowd inside the function hall, came through the open doors. Two girls in mittens and pom-pommed stocking caps were at a table in the vestibule. They wanted three dollars.

"I'm not here for the concert," Clem said. "I'm looking for Becky Hildebrandt."

"She's here. But we're not supposed to—"

"I'm not giving you three dollars."

Inside, the heads of taller concertgoers were silhouetted by stage lights. Seated in a half circle, with dreadnought guitars, behind cantilevered mics, were the Isner brothers and a statuesque girl, Amy Jenner, whose hair was longer than her torso. Clem remembered Amy well. Two years ago, in a Crossroads exercise, she'd given him a note that said *You're sexy*. The assertion was so absurd that he'd taken it to be a joke, but seeing Amy now, having learned from Sharon what the world was made of, he understood it differently. The prettiness of Amy's voice, as she sang of hating to see her lover go, salted the wound he'd inflicted on himself in Sharon's bedroom.

On the bus to Chicago, he and the baby behind him had finally slept, but it hadn't been worth the cost of waking up. Returning to his consciousness of the actions he'd taken, to his aloneness with the knowledge of them, was like the reverse of awakening from a bad dream. After a brutal portage to the train station, he'd caught the 7:25 to New Prospect, where a good Samaritan had offered him a ride. He'd dropped his bags at the parsonage and charged back out into the snow, lashing himself forward. He was determined not to sleep until he could wake up know-ing he wasn't alone.

He moved into the crowd, looking for Becky, but the concert was also a reunion. He was immediately pounced upon by a mature edition of Kelly Woehlke, a girl he'd grown up with at First Reformed. They'd never been friends, and on any other night the hug she gave him might have seemed unwarranted. Tonight the touch of a warm body nearly made him cry. His few real Crossroads friends were too anti-sentimental to bother with a reunion, but other alumni were crowding around him, and despite how peripheral he'd felt in the fellowship, how unwowed by the trust-building exercises and the rhetoric of personal growth, he re-ceived their hugs gratefully, as if they were the condolences of family. He wondered what Sharon would make of all the hugging. Then he wished he hadn't wondered, because every specific thought of Sharon, no matter how innocuous, triggered another wave of guilt and hurt.

By the time he'd circled through the crowd, not finding Becky, the Isner brothers and Amy Jenner were rousingly singing of what they would do with a hammer at various times of day. Clem's energy was spent, and the loudness of the scene had become somewhat hellish. He'd run aground by the stage, stalled out in front of a stack of speakers, when his friend John Goya's little brother Davy approached him. Not only was Davy no longer little, he looked strangely middle-aged. "Are you looking for Becky?" he shouted.

"Yeah, is she here?"

"I'm worried about her. Did she go home?"

"No," Clem shouted. "I just came from home."

Davy frowned.

"Did something happen?" Clem shouted.

The singing mercifully stopped, leaving only a low hum in the speakers.

"I don't know," Davy said. "She's probably just lying down somewhere."

Into Clem's ear came the amplified mellifluence of Toby Isner, the elder of the two musical brothers. "Thank you, all. Thank you. I'm afraid we only have time for one more song."

Toby paused for expressions of disappointment, and someone in the audience politely moaned. Toby had an unctuous sensitive-guy sincerity, a self-pleasuring way of smiling when he sang, that never failed to make Clem's skin crawl. Now he'd grown a dark beard of biblical dimensions.

"You know," Toby said, "I love that we're all gathered here tonight, so many amazing people, so many wonderful friends, so much love, so much laughter. But I want to get serious for a minute. Can we do that? I want us all to remember there's still a war going on. Right now, right this minute, it's morning in Vietnam. People are still getting slaughtered, and, man, we gotta put a stop to that. Stop that war. We need America out of Vietnam *right now*. You dig me?"

Toby was such a preening asshole that Clem almost pitied him. And yet quite a few people were clapping and whooping. Toby, encouraged, shouted, "I want to hear it from you, people! All together now! What do we want?"

He cupped his ear with his hand, and a smattering of voices, mostly female, obliged him. "We want peace!"

"Louder, man! What do we want?"

"We want peace!"

"What do we want?"

"WE WANT PEACE!"

"When do we want it?"

"RIGHT NOW!"

"We want peace!"

"RIGHT NOW!"

Although Davy Goya, God bless him, was coolly inspecting his fingernails, it seemed to Clem that every other person in the hall had taken up the chant. He'd done his share of chanting at various protests, before he met Sharon, but the sound of it now was so alienating that he felt ashamed of himself, ashamed of his weakness, for having hugged the other alumni. Not only were they safe and self-righteous, they weren't appalled by Toby Isner. If they'd ever been Clem's people, they definitely weren't now.

Toby lowered his fist, which he'd been pumping to the rhythm of the chanting, and hit the opening notes to "Blowin' in the Wind." A shout went up from the audience, and Clem couldn't take it anymore. He pushed through the crowd and escaped into the church's central hallway, where the bathrooms were. He opened the ladies'-room door a crack. "Becky?"

No answer. He checked the other rooms along the hallway—also empty. He could still hear Toby Isner's voice, could picture him simpering through his beard, when he reached the main church entrance. Sitting on the floor inside the door, smoking a cigarette, was a girl in a biker jacket. It was Laura Dobrinsky.

"Hey Laura, good to see you. I wonder—have you seen my sister?"

Laura took a sideways puff as if she hadn't heard him. She looked like she'd been crying.

"Sorry to bother you," he said. "I'm just looking for Becky."

Between him and Laura was the social ease of having long ago established that they didn't like each other. She took another sideways puff. "Last I saw her, she was stoned off her ass."

"She was—what?"

"Stoned off her ass."

His vision swam as if he'd been punched. Now he understood why Davy Goya was worried. Leaving Laura to her private woe, he ran up two flights of stairs to the Crossroads meeting room. In the dimness of it, from the doorway, he saw a girl supine on a sofa, beneath a skinny boy. Both of them were clothed, and thankfully the girl wasn't Becky.

"Sorry. Have either of you seen Becky Hildebrandt?"

"No," the girl said. "Go away."

As he descended the stairs, he was hammered by his lack of sleep. He would have sat down for a smoke if he'd believed it would make him feel anything but worse. His eyes were fried, his head full of rottenness, his shoulders aching from carrying his luggage, his mouth sour from the cookies he'd grabbed on his way out of the parsonage, and the complication of Becky made it almost unbearable. He knew Perry smoked pot, but Becky? He needed her to be her shining, clearheaded self. He needed her on his side before he told his parents what he'd done.

The second-floor hallway was dark, but the door of Rick Ambrose's office was ajar. Clem had always appreciated Ambrose for understanding his ambivalent relationship with Crossroads, and he appreciated him now for wanting nothing to do with the concert. On the chance that his sister might be in the office, safe, Clem peeked inside. Ambrose was slouched in his desk chair, reading a book, and appeared to be alone.

Farther up the hallway to the sanctuary, Clem noticed a strip of light beneath the associate minister's office door. Evidently his father, who would now be at the Haefles' annual party, had forgotten to turn out the lights. As he walked past the door, he heard a laugh that sounded like Becky's.

He stopped. Did she somehow have an office key? He tapped on the door. "Becky?"

"Who's there?"

His blood pressure jumped. The voice was his father's. Clem hadn't expected to see him—had counted on *not* seeing him—before he'd talked to Becky and gotten her blessing.

"It's me," he said. "It's Clem. Is Becky in there?"

There was a silence, long enough to be unnatural. Then the door was opened by his father. He was wearing his old Arizona coat, and his face was strangely pale. "Clem, hi."

He seemed not at all happy to see his son. Behind him, in a hunting jacket and a matching cap, stood a clear-skinned boy who was, in fact, Clem realized, a short-haired woman.

"Is Becky here?"

"Becky? No. No, ah, this is one of our parishioners, Mrs. Cottrell."

The woman gave Clem a little wave. Her face was very pretty.

"This is my son Clem," his father said. "Mrs. Cottrell and I were just, uh—actually, maybe you can help us. Whoever shoveled the parking lot blocked her car in. We need to dig her out. Would you mind?"

Mrs. Cottrell came over and offered Clem a hand. It was cool and firm.

"Frances, don't forget your records. I think—oh, Clem, I think I saw a couple of shovels by the front door. Mrs. Cottrell and I were late getting—we were down at Theo's church and. So, and, yes, we had a, uh. Little accident."

Whatever it was that Clem had interrupted, his father couldn't have been more nervous.

"I don't think I'm up for shoveling snow."

"You—? It won't take any time at all with two of us. Shall we?" The old man turned off the overhead light and said, again, "Don't forget the records."

"If it takes no time at all with two people," Clem said, "how much time can it take with one person?"

"Clem, she really needs to get home."

"But if I hadn't happened to knock on your door."

"I'm asking you a favor. Since when do you mind a little work?"

His father held the door for Mrs. Cottrell, who emerged with a stack of old records. Everything about her was delicate, desirable, and it gave Clem an ill feeling. Even though he'd warned Becky that men like their father, weak men whose vanity needed stroking, were liable to cheat on their wives, it was hideous to think that it might actually be happening—that his father, having failed to be as groovy as Rick Ambrose, had gotten his hands on someone closer to his age. Couldn't she see how weak he was?

In the parking lot, in less densely falling snow, clusters of alumni were enjoying intermission cigarettes. While Mrs. Cottrell cleared the windows of her sedan, he and his father hacked at the mountain of snow in front of it. To get the car over the layer of hardened slush they uncovered, they had to push it from behind—just like the old days, dad and son working side by side—while Mrs. Cottrell rocked it with the accelerator. When it finally broke free, she drove a short distance and lowered her window.

Out of the window came a delicate hand. It beckoned with one finger. Not the typical gesture of a parishioner to a pastor.

The finger beckoned again.

"Ah—one second," the old man said. He trotted over to the car and bent down to the open window. Clem couldn't hear what Mrs. Cottrell was saying, but it must have been fascinating, because his father seemed to forget that Clem was there.

He waited for at least a minute, sickened by the spectacle of their tête-à-tête. Then he walked back toward the church with the shovels. He'd already noticed the family station wagon parked outside the main entrance, but only now did he see that the back end of it was maimed, the bumper missing, a taillight smashed. The bumper was inside the car.

There was a squeal of tires, and his father came hurrying up behind him. "This is something else you can help me with tomorrow," he said. "If we hammer out the dent, I think we can reattach the bumper."

Clem stared at the damage. His chest was so full of anger that speaking was an effort. "Why aren't you at the Haefles' party?"

"Oh, well," his father said, "you're looking at the reason. Frances and—Mrs. Cottrell and I were badly delayed in the city. I also had to change a tire."

Clem nodded. His neck, too, was stiff with anger. "I wonder," he said, "what she was doing in your office. If she was in such a hurry to get home."

"Aha. Yes. She was just picking up some records I'd . . . borrowed." His father jingled his car keys. "I'd offer you a ride, but I'm guessing you want to stay for the concert."

Bumperless, the Fury's rear end resembled a face without a mouth.

"She didn't strike me," Clem said, "as being in any hurry to get home."

"She—just now? She was—it was just some business about the Tuesday circle."

"Really."

"Yes, really."

"Bullshit."

"Excuse me?"

A cheer went up inside the function hall.

"You're lying," Clem said.

"Now, wait a minute—"

"Because I know what you're like. I've been watching it my whole life and I'm sick of it."

"That's—whatever you're imputing, you're—that's not right."

Clem turned to his father. The fear in his face made him laugh. "Liar."

"I don't know what you're thinking, but—"

"I'm thinking Mom is at the Haefles' and you're falling all over a woman who isn't her."

"That's—there is nothing wrong with a pastor attending to one of his parishioners."

"Jesus Christ. The fact that you even have to say that."

A drum intro, congas, drifted from the function hall, followed by another cheer. The last of the alumni smokers were heading inside. As if music ever solved anything. No more war, man. Gotta put a stop to that war. Clem's disgust with the hippie-dippie Crossroads people intensified his disgust with his father. He'd always hated bullies, but now he understood how enraging another person's fear could be. How the sight of it incited taunting. Incited violence.

His father spoke again, in a low unsteady voice. "Mrs. Cottrell and I were making a delivery to Theo's church. We got a bit of a late start, and then there was—"

"Yeah, you know what? Fuck that. I don't care what your story is. If you feel like going and boning some other woman, it's a free country. If it makes you feel better about yourself, I don't fucking care."

His father looked at him in horror.

"I'm out of here anyway," Clem said. "I wasn't going to tell you this tonight, but you might as well know it. I quit school. I already sent a letter to the draft board. I'm going to Vietnam."

He dropped the snow shovels and stalked away.

"Clem," his father shouted. "Come back here."

Clem raised his arm and gave him the middle finger as he went into the church. The entry hall was empty. Laura Dobrinsky had left two butts and a mess of ashes on the floor. He paused to consider where else to look for Becky, and the door behind him burst open.

"Don't you walk away from me."

He ran up a flight of stairs. He still hadn't checked the parlor or the sanctuary. He was halfway down the hallway when his father caught up with him and grabbed his shoulder. "Why are you walking away from me?"

"Take your hands off me. I'm looking for Becky."

"She's at the Haefles' with your mother."

"No, she's not. Becky is sick of you, too."

His father glanced at Ambrose's open door, unlocked his own office, and lowered his voice. "If you have something to say to me, you could pay me the courtesy of not walking away before I can answer."

"Courtesy?" Clem followed him into the office. "You mean, like the courtesy of leaving Mom at the Haefles' while you entertain your little lady friend?"

His father turned on the light and closed the door. "If you would calm down, I would be happy to explain what happened tonight."

"Yeah, but look me in the eye, Dad. Look me in the eye and see if I believe a word of it."

"That's enough." The old man was angry now, too. "You were out of line at Thanksgiving, and you're very much out of line now."

"Because I'm so fucking sick of you."

"And I am sick of your disrespect."

"Do you have any idea how embarrassing it is to be your son?"

"I said that's enough!"

Clem would have welcomed a fight. He hadn't thrown a punch since junior high. "You want to hit me? You want to try me?"

"No, Clem."

"Mister Nonviolence?"

There was Christian forbearance in the way his father shook his head. Clem would have loved to at least shove him against the wall, but this would merely have fed his Christian victimhood. The only thing Clem could hit him with was words.

"Did you even hear what I said in the parking lot? I quit school."

"I heard that you were very angry and trying to provoke me."

"I wasn't being provoking. I was conveying a fact."

His father sank into his swivel chair. A blank sheet of paper was in his typewriter. He rolled it out and smoothed it. "I'm sorry we got off on such a wrong foot. Tomorrow I hope we can be more civil to each other."

"I wrote to the draft board, Dad. I mailed the letter this morning."

The old man nodded to himself, as if he knew better. "You can threaten me all you want, but you're not going to Vietnam."

"The hell I'm not."

"We have our differences, but I know who you are. You can't seriously expect me to believe you intend to be a soldier. It makes no sense."

The complacency of his father's certainty—that no son of his could be anything but a replica of himself—inflamed the bully in Clem.

"I know it's hard for you to imagine," he said, "but some people actually pay a price for what they believe in. You and your little *parishioner* can go and be the nice white people at Theo Crenshaw's church. You can pull some weeds in Englewood and feel good about yourself. You can march in your marches and brag about it to your all-white congregation. But when it's time to put your money where your mouth is, you don't see any problem with me being in college and letting some Black kid fight for me in Vietnam. Or some poor white kid from Appalachia. Or some poor Navajo, like Keith Durochie's son. Do you think you're better than Keith? Do you think my life is worth more than Tommy Durochie's? Do you think it's right that I get to be in college while Navajo boys are dying? Is that what you're saying makes sense to you?"

It satisfied the bully to see his father's confusion, as it dawned on him that Clem was serious.

"No American boy should be in Vietnam," he said quietly. "I thought you and I agreed on that."

"I do agree. It's a shitty war. But that doesn't—"

"It's an *immoral* war. All war is immoral, but this one especially. Whoever fights in it partakes of the immorality. I'm surprised I have to explain that to you."

"Yeah, well, I'm not the same as you. Dad. In case you hadn't noticed. I don't have the luxury of being born a Mennonite. I don't believe in a metaphysical deity whose commandments I have to obey. I have to follow my own personal ethics, and I don't know if you remember, but my lottery number was nineteen."

"Of course I remember. And you're right—it was an immense relief, for your mother and me, that you had a student deferment. I seem to recall you feeling the same way."

"Only because I hadn't given it any thought."

"And now you've thought about it. Fine. I understand why student deferments seem unfair to you—you raise a legitimate point. I also understand feeling obliged to serve your country, because of your lottery number. But to go and serve in that war, it makes no sense."

"Maybe not to you. To me there's no alternative."

"You already waited a year—why not wait one more semester? Most of our troops are already home. Six months from now, I doubt they'll even be taking new recruits."

"That's exactly why I'm doing it now."

"Why? To make a point? You could do that by giving up your deferment and conscientiously objecting. The son of a CO, from a family of pastors—you'd have a very strong case."

"Right. That's what *you* did. But you know what? The man who took your place in 1944 was probably white and middle-class. That's a moral luxury I don't have."

"Luxury?" His father banged the arm of his chair. "It wasn't a moral luxury. It was a moral *choice*, and the fact that most Americans supported the war made it harder, not easier. They called us traitors. They called us cowards, they tried to run our parents out of town—some of us even went to prison. Every one of us paid a price."

Recalling the pride he'd once taken in his father's principles, Clem felt the reins of his argument going slack in his hands. He gave them a savage tug. "Yeah, luckily for you, plenty of other people were willing to fight the Fascists."

"That was their own moral choice. I grant that, under the circumstances, their choice was defensible. But Vietnam? There's no defense whatsoever for our involvement there. It's senseless slaughter. The boys we're killing are even younger than you are."

"They're killing other Vietnamese, Dad. You can sentimentalize it all you want, but the North Vietnamese are the aggressors. They signed up to kill, and they're killing."

His father made a sour face. "Since when do you parrot Lyndon Johnson?"

"LBJ was a fraud. He signed the Civil Rights Act with one hand and sent ghetto boys to Vietnam with the other. This is what I'm talking about—moral hypocrisy."

His father sighed as if it were pointless to keep arguing. "And you don't care how I might feel as your father. You don't care how your mother might feel about it."

"Since when do you care about Mom's feelings?"

"I care about them very much."

"Bullshit. She's loyal to you, and you treat her like garbage. Do you think I can't see it? Do you think Becky can't see it? How cold you are to Mom? It's like you wish she didn't exist."

His father winced. The punch had landed. Clem waited for him to say something else, so that he could knock it down, but his father just sat there. He was defenseless against Clem's superior reasoning, his intimate knowledge of his failings. Into the silence, through the door, through the floor, came the pulse of a distant bass guitar.

"Anyway," Clem said. "There's nothing you can do to stop me. I've sent the letter."

"That's right," his father said. "Legally, you're free to do as you please. But emotionally you're still very young. Very young and, if I may say so, very self-involved. The only thing that seems to matter to you is moral consistency."

"It's hard work, but somebody's got to do it."

"You seem to think you're thinking clearly, but what I'm hearing is a person who's forgotten how to listen to his heart. You think I don't understand you, but I know how devastated you would be, how utterly shattered, if you had to see a child burned up with napalm, a village bombed for no reason. You can do all the rationalizing you want, you can try to reason your way out of having a heart, but I know it's there in you. I've been watching it grow, my God, for twenty years. You've made me so proud that you're my son. Your kindness—your generosity—your loyalty—your sense of justice—your *goodness*—"

His father broke off, overcome with emotion. Until this moment, it hadn't occurred to Clem that he could be anything but an adversary to his father; that his animosity might not be reciprocated. It seemed unfair to him—intolerable—that his father still loved him. Unable to think of a rejoinder, he jerked open the door and ran out into the hallway. For relief from the remorse that was rising in him, his mind went reflexively to the person who validated his reasoning, who shared his convictions, who freely and wholly gave herself to him. But the thought of Sharon only deepened his remorse, because he'd broken her heart that very day. Broken it violently, with merciless rationality. He'd shot her down with her own moral arguments, and she'd said it in so many words: "You're breaking my heart." He could hear the words so clearly, she might have been standing next to him.

There was no telling how long Becky might have stayed in the sanctuary, exploring what it meant to have found religion, if she'd eaten anything but sugar cookies since the night before. As God's goodness routed the evil of marijuana, leaving only a fluish hotness in her eyes and chest, stray wisps of strange thought, she was beset by images of the baked goods in the function hall. She recalled a moist-looking chocolate layer cake, a loaf of cheese-and-chive bread, practically a balanced meal in itself, and a tray of lemon bars—she'd noticed lemon bars. She was so famished that she finally gave up on praying. By way of apology, she stood up and kissed the brass of the hanging cross.

"I'm your girl now," she told it. "I promise."

Hearing her own words, she felt a quake in her nether parts, as if her promise were romantic. It was akin to the shudder of ecstasy with which she'd beheld the golden light inside her. She wondered if the satisfaction of accepting Christ, becoming his girl, might enable her to renounce more worldly pleasures, such as kissing Tanner. The wrongness of kissing him before he'd broken up with Laura was clear to her now. So was the wrongness of her behavior in the ice cave of his van. Instead of celebrating the news that an agent was coming to hear the Bleu Notes, instead of sharing in his joy, she'd selfishly pressured him to dump Laura, and now God had shown her what to do. She needed to apologize for pressuring him. She needed to tell him that if he just wanted to be friends with her, see her in church on Sunday, explore Christianity with her, forget they'd ever kissed, she would cherish his friendship and be glad of heart.

First, however, she needed to see if any chocolate cake was left. It was nearly nine thirty and the concertgoers would be hungry. Letting the sanctuary door lock itself behind her, she paused in the front hall to collect herself. There was a scraping rumble from a snowplow in the street, a nasty rip in her beloved coat. She pulled on the loose threads, wondering if it could be repaired. She'd reentered a mundane world in which it wouldn't be so easy to stay connected with God. For the first time, she understood how a person might actually look forward to Sunday worship in the sanctuary.

She must still have been lingeringly stoned, because her torn coat pocket had absorbed her for quite a while, without her reaching any conclusions, when she heard footsteps in the church parlor. Into the front hall came an older man with permed-looking hair and thick sideburns. He wore a wide-lapelled jacket of apricot-colored leather. His face brightened as if he knew her. "Oh, hey," he said. "Hey."

"Can I help you?"

"Nah, just looking around."

She waited for the man to leave, so she could proceed to the baked goods, but he approached her and extended a hand. "Gig Benedetti."

It would have been rude not to shake his hand.

"Sorry, didn't catch your name," he said.

"Becky."

"Nice to meet you, Becky."

He smiled at her expectantly, as if he had nowhere else to be. He was an inch or two shorter than she was.

"Are you . . . here for the concert?" she asked.

"That was the plan. Although, a night like this, it really makes me question. They already canceled the other show I wanted to catch out here."

She was definitely still a bit stoned. There was a delay in her processing. Then sudden clarity: "Are you a music agent?"

"In my own little way."

"Tell me your name again?"

"It's Gig—Guglielmo, for the adventurous. Gig Benedetti."

"You're here to see the Bleu Notes."

He seemed delighted with her. His eyes darted down to her body and back up to her face. "Either you're a very good guesser, or you're the person I'm hoping you might be."

"Which person is that?"

"The one with the voice. I'm told it's gotta be heard to be believed."

There was another delay in her comprehension and then a clutching fear. The voice could only be Laura's. Until this moment, Becky hadn't given one thought to her encounter with Laura behind the church. It was like a drunk-driving accident she'd fled the scene of and forgotten.

"You must mean Laura," she said.

"Laura, yeah, that sounds right. Obviously, if you're Becky, you're not Laura."

"Definitely not Laura."

"You had my hopes up for a minute. There's ten freaking inches of snow out there. The only reason I'm waiting around is to hear that girl sing."

Now there was no delay in Becky's comprehension—she was immediately offended. Gig ought to have been waiting to hear Tanner, who was at least as talented as Laura and was the one with the ambition. Laura didn't even care about getting an agent.

"It's really more Tanner's band," she said.

"Tanner, right. Talked to him this afternoon. Nice guy. Friend of yours?"

"Very good friend, yes."

Again his eyes went up and down her body, lingering at her breasts. It was a thing older men had been doing more and more often, especially at the Grove. It was gross.

"So, his girlfriend?" Gig said casually.

"Not exactly."

"Oh, well then. How would you feel about grabbing a drink with me?"

"No, thank you."

"I thought, they're playing a church, how late can this thing go? I thought I'd be outta here by nine, nine thirty at the latest. But, no, we gotta hear from Peter Paul and Betty Lou. We gotta hear from Donny Osmond Santana and the Lilywhites. I'm not hitting on you, Becky. Or, like you say, not exactly. I just happened to notice a little tavern down the street. It could be an another freaking hour before we see your headliners."

"I don't drink," she said, as if this were the issue.

"Pfff."

"Also, I'm pretty much with Tanner, so."

"Good, good. We're up to pretty much. But that's all the more reason you should get to know me. I'm praying to God these guys are—wait. Are *you* in the band?"

"No."

"More's the pity. My point is, if I can't sign them, I suffered through Peter Paul and Betty Lou and drove eight miles in a blizzard for no reason. I'm already favorably predisposed, if you take my meaning, and if they end up signing I'll be seeing you around. Why not start things off with a little drink?"

"I can't. In fact, I should be—"

"Follow-up question: Why aren't you in the band?"

"Me? I'm not musical."

"Everybody's musical. Have you tried the tambourine?"

She stared at him. There was a gold chain around his neck.

"The reason I ask," he said, "is your presentation is extremely classy. I could really dig seeing you on a stage."

She tried to unfog her brain and calculate whether being nice to Gig would further incline him to sign the Bleu Notes, or whether she should even want him to be Tanner's agent, given his apparently icky character. Deeper in the fog was the upsetting news that he was there to hear Laura.

"Ugh, listen to me," he said. "I totally sound like I'm hitting on you, although I bet you get that all the time. You're a seriously good-looking girl. If I may say so, it's good to see you dressing like you know it. I don't think I ever saw a dowdier crowd than what's downstairs. Clodhoppers and overalls and thermal underwear—is it a religious thing?"

"It's just the style of the youth group."

"Which you don't want any part of. I get it. I presume that's why you're up here hiding?"

In the sanctuary, Becky had promised Jesus that she would live in accordance with his teachings and not shy from proclaiming it. Now she could see how much courage it would take to be a Christian in the mundane world. "No," she said. "I came up here to pray."

"Oh boy." Gig laughed. "I guess it shouldn't surprise me, being as we're in a church. But—pardon my forwardness. I didn't realize."

"It's okay. It's actually the first time I've ever really prayed."

"My timing perfect as always."

It was wrong to apologize for praying, but she didn't want to hurt the Bleu Notes' chances. "It's just me," she said. "The band isn't, you know, religious or anything."

"I don't care if they're Hare Krishnas, as long as they show up on time and play some Billboard hits. Which, by the way, I'm serious about the tambourine. You can be as Christian as you want on the inside—it's all about keeping people buying drinks. That is the sad little secret of the business I'm in. Something for the ears, something for the eyes." His own eyes went up and down her yet again. "'Why, yes, we'll have another round.'"

"I'm sorry," Becky said, "but I'm so hungry. I need to go eat something."

Gig peeled back an apricot leather sleeve and exposed an enormous watch. "Not sure we quite have time for dinner, but there's bound to be something salty at the tavern."

"The band is really excited that you're here, I—I'll see you later, okay?"

She ran away, actually ran, for fear of being pursued. At New Prospect Township, one little flick of her disdain was enough to drive away aggressive boys, and at the Grove, whenever an older man tried to flirt with her, she frostily asked him for his order. If she ended up with Tanner, despite her new willingness to renounce him, she would be entering a world of older men, men like Gig. If only to help Tanner professionally, she would need to learn to play the game. It was disturbing to think that her looks might be of use to him. When she saw people flirting, she saw people who wanted to have sex, and sex still seemed more than gross to her; it seemed—wrong. In the light of her religious experience, it seemed even wronger. Sweet though Tanner was, there was little doubt that he had sex with Laura. Maybe it really would be better to leave them to it and simply be his friend.

Halfway down the church's central staircase was a landing that led to the rear parking lot. Outside the glass door, someone in a peacoat was smoking a cigarette in the snow. With a lurch in her heart, she saw that it was Clem.

She hesitated on the landing. Catching sight of Clem usually brought a rush of happiness, but the feeling she had now was the opposite of happy. His new peacoat reminded her of the walk they'd taken at Thanksgiving, his boasting about sex with his college girlfriend, but it was more than that. She was afraid of his judgment. She'd smoked marijuana, and, worse yet, she'd been praying. He was so contemptuous of religion, he would make her ashamed of finding God.

Worried that he'd come to the church specifically to see her, she continued down the stairs. She thought she was in the clear, but the door behind her clanked open, and Clem called her name. She looked back guiltily. "Oh, hey."

"Hi, hi, hi," he said, running down to her.

His peacoat, when he hugged her, smelled of winter air and cigarettes, and he wouldn't let go. She had to squirm to extricate herself.

"Where have you been?" he accused. "I've been looking for you everywhere."

"I was just . . . I'm getting something to eat."

She started down the corridor to the function hall.

"Wait," Clem said, grabbing her arm. "We need to talk. There's stuff I have to tell you."

She yanked her arm away. "I'm really hungry."

"Becky—"

"I'm sorry, okay? I need food."

The function hall was much hotter than the corridor. Raising her arms to make herself narrower, she entered a humid thicket of dark bodies. Hands were clapping to the beat of Biff Allard and his congas, and Gig was right: he looked like Donny Osmond. The crowd was so large that it pressed against the food tables in the back. Becky went around behind them, pursued by Clem. The first table was nearly depleted, but there was still a respectable wedge of Bundt cake, spangled with red and green cherries. She took out her pocketbook, paid for a slice, and retreated to the back wall to eat it.

"Where have you been?" Clem shouted.

Her mouth full, she waved a limp hand. Clem was practically thrashing with impatience. She was relieved to see Kim Perkins and David Goya coming their way.

"*There* you are," Kim shouted. "You had us worried."

"I'm fine."

Kim reached for a fragment of Bundt cake, and Becky raised the paper plate above her head. Kim made a jumping pass at it.

"Down, girl," David shouted.

From the stage came a thunderous coda, every instrument at full volume. The hall erupted in applause.

"Thank you," Biff Allard shouted. "We've still got one act coming, our own Tanner Evans and Laura Dobrinsky, with the one and only Bleu Notes, so stick around! Good night!"

The hall lights came up. Becky ate the last bite of cake feeling more famished, not less.

"I should have warned you," David said to her. "That shit is pretty killer. They grow it indoors in Montreal." He patted her arm, as if to make sure she really was intact, and nodded to Clem. "Thanks for finding her."

Clem was watching them with a demented kind of fixity, his face haggard.

"I need more food," she said.

"Somebody has the munchies," Kim said.

A woman on a mission, Becky marched over to the other food table. In the middle of it, as in a holy vision, sat two-thirds of a loaf of cheese-and-chive bread.

"Can I have, like, all of that?" she asked the sophomore boy taking money.

"Sure. Buck-fifty?"

This was too little, but she didn't offer more. When she turned away from the table, clutching the bread like a squirrel, Kim was there to grab at it.

"Fine, fine," Becky said, tearing off a hunk.

David, in his harmless way, had engaged Clem in some topic of interest to himself, and she took the opportunity to slip through the crowd and back out to the corridor, where there was a drinking fountain. The bread was delicious but her throat was parched. While she was bent over the fountain, someone came up behind her. Afraid that it was Clem, she kept drinking.

"Becky."

The voice was Tanner's. Turning around, she experienced the rush of joy that seeing Clem hadn't given her. Somehow her intention to renounce Tanner had made him even more gorgeous. He was like a young Jesus in a fringed suede jacket. Without saying a word, he took her head in his hands and kissed her hard on the mouth.

She was too surprised to kiss him back. Her arms hung at her sides, the ridiculous bread in one hand. By the time she got over her surprise, he was pulling her away from the fountain and leading her up the hallway.

"We're so fucked," he said. "Laura's gone. She went home."

"She went home?"

"An hour ago. She quit the band."

Becky was horrified. It was like learning that the accident she'd fled the scene of had been fatal. So much for Gig hearing the voice he'd come to hear.

"Just play," she bravely said. "You'll be great. I saw the agent upstairs—he's been waiting to hear you."

Tanner stopped in the front hall and looked around it, very agitated. When his eyes alighted on Becky, it was as if she was the very thing he'd been looking for. He took her head in his hands again. "I did what you asked me to."

"Oh."

"But now—I had to redo the whole playlist. I'm not sure Biff and Darryl know half of it."

"It'll be fine. Gig told me he wants to sign you."

"You talked to him? What's he like?"

"I don't know. Just—a guy."

"Shit. Shit shit shit." Tanner let go of her and gazed down the corridor, toward the function hall, where failure awaited him. "Tonight of all nights. I really didn't—and now—shit. It's going to be a mess."

"I'm sorry."

"Don't be sorry. You were right. It had to be done."

"Okay, but . . ." She took a breath. "Something amazing just happened to me. Upstairs, in the sanctuary. Tanner, it was so amazing. I think I saw God."

This got his attention.

"I want to be a Christian," she said. "I want you to help me be a real Christian. Even if it means—I don't know what it means. For us, I mean. Will you help me?"

"You saw *God*?"

"I think so. I was praying for the longest time. I could feel God in me—I could feel Jesus. He was there."

"Wow."

"Have you ever felt that?"

He didn't answer. He seemed a little frightened of her.

"You can go back to Laura," she said. "I shouldn't have tried to pressure you. It was selfish of me, and I wanted to tell you that. I want to be a better person. If you just want to be friends with me, or whatever, it's really all right. I'm sorry I pressured you."

He stared at her. "Do you not want this?"

"I don't know. I did, but—I'm saying there's no hurry. I bet if you went back to her now—maybe you should go back to her. Tell her you're sorry and see if she'll play with you."

"We're going on in ten minutes!"

"You can be a little late, no one's going to leave. You should go. Just go. Go get Laura."

Tanner seemed confounded. "But you made such a big deal out of this."

"I'm sorry! It was wrong! I'm sorry!" Becky threw up her hands and found a loaf of bread in one of them. She set it down on a table arrayed with church-related literature. Tanner enveloped her again.

"You're the person I want to be with," he said. "I should have been clear about that. I'm crazy about you. This is going to be a really hard show, but I'm not sorry about Laura."

Over Tanner's shoulder, Becky saw Clem standing halfway down the corridor. He looked—demented. A few hours ago, she'd wanted nothing more than to be seen in Tanner's arms, and now the impediment of Laura had been removed, now her wish was coming true; but the person seeing her was Clem.

She wriggled free of Tanner. "You need to go and get her."

"No way."

"Well, someone needs to get her. You need your full sound tonight."

"I don't even care. The only thing that matters is that you believe in me."

"Yes, but you still need to get her. Just say—whatever it takes, just say it."

"Are you saying you don't believe in me?"

"No, I do, but . . ." Becky imagined Gig Benedetti's disappointment, his anger, when the Bleu Notes took the stage without the singer he'd come to hear. It was all her fault, and she had to make it right. "Where does she live?"

"At this point, I doubt she'd even let me in the door."

"I'm saying let *me* go. I owe her a huge apology anyway."

"Are you kidding me? The only person she's madder at than me is you."

"Where does she live?"

"In the apartment above the drugstore. With Kay and Louise. But, Becky, there's no way."

She buttoned her coat. She was reluctant to part with the cheese-and-chive bread, but it wasn't a convenient thing to carry around. While she considered where to hide it, Clem walked up.

"Clem," Tanner said nervously. "Welcome back."

"I need to talk to my sister."

Becky unfolded a church bulletin and draped it over the bread, concealing it no better than she'd been concealed by Tanner's blanket the night before. Tanner collared her from behind and kissed her cheek. "Don't go anywhere," he said. "I need to know you're in the audience."

He hurried off toward the function hall. The pleasure of his kiss had been killed by the discomfort of Clem's seeing it. Without looking at her brother, she ran outside. There was a new layer of snow on the shoveled pavement, and Clem was right behind her.

"Stop following me," she said.

"Why won't you talk to me? Are you high on drugs? I've never seen you like this."

"Leave me alone!"

She slipped on underlying ice, and he caught her by the wrist. "Tell me what is going on."

"Nothing. I have to talk to Laura."

"Dobrinsky? Why?"

She wrenched her wrist free and pressed onward. "Because Tanner needs her to play and she won't do it."

"So, wait. Are you and he—"

"Yes! Okay? I'm with Tanner! Okay?"

"But when did this happen?"

"Stop *following* me."

"I'm just trying to—you're with Tanner?"

"How many times do I have to say it?"

"You only said it once."

"I'm with Tanner and he's with me. Is there something wrong with that?"

"No. I'm just surprised. Davy Goya said—are you smoking pot now, too? Is that because of Tanner?"

She strode alongside a ridge of plowed snow on Pirsig Avenue. "It had nothing to do with Tanner. It was just a mistake."

"I always wondered if he smoked pot."

"I can make my own decisions, Clem. I don't need you to tell me what's right and what's wrong. What I need right now is for you to stay out of my business."

She could see the drugstore ahead of her. Lights were on upstairs.

"Fine," Clem said huskily. "I'll stay out of your business. Although I must say . . ."

"What must you say."

"I don't know. I'm just surprised. I mean—Tanner Evans? He's a good guy. He's super nice, but . . . not exactly a live wire. He's kind of the definition of passive."

The sensation of hating Clem was new and overwhelming. It was like love ripped brutally inside out.

"Go to hell," she said.

"Becky, come on. I'm not trying to tell you what to do. It's just that you've got so much going on. You're about to start college, you've got your whole life ahead of you. And Tanner—I wouldn't be surprised if he never leaves New Prospect."

She stopped and wheeled around. "Go to hell! I'm sick of you! I'm sick of you judging me and my friends! You've been doing it my whole life and I'm sick of it! I'm not six years old anymore! You've got your amazing life-changing sex-loving girlfriend—why don't you stop bossing me around and tell *her* what to do? Or is she not *passive*?"

She hardly knew what she was saying. An evil spirit had possessed her, and Clem's shock was apparent in the streetlight. She struggled to regain her Christian bearings, but her hatred was too intense. She turned and ran full-tilt toward the drugstore.

Russ was happy with his Christmas present. He'd had more than six hours with Frances, enough to feel like an entire day, and every seeming setback had turned into an advance. She'd no sooner disclosed her affair with the heart surgeon than she contrasted him unfavorably with Russ, no sooner threatened to go to Arizona than pushed Russ to join her there, no sooner antagonized Theo Crenshaw than commended herself to Russ's guidance. Even the accident on Fifty-ninth Street had been a boon. He'd wrestled with the Fury's mangled bumper and its frozen lug nuts, displaying strength of body and coolness of head, and when a group of teenagers loomed up in the snow, causing her to clutch his arm in suburban terror, she'd learned an important lesson about racial prejudice: the young men were only offering to help. The accident had made Russ so late that he now had no choice but to tell Marion he'd been with Frances, thus sparing him from fretting that Perry would tell her. Frances still claimed to be in a hurry to get home, but when he proposed a quick stop at McDonald's she'd admitted she was starving, and when they finally returned to First Reformed her reluctance to go inside with him had yielded, piquantly, to his insistence.

In his office, he'd handed her his blues records one by one, relating what little was known of Robert Johnson, what a tragic alcoholic Tommy Johnson had been, what a miracle that Victor and Paramount and Vocalion had made recordings of the early greats. The 78s were among his most valuable possessions, and she accepted them with appropriate reverence. She was sitting on his desk with her legs uncrossed, snowmelt dripping from her dangling feet. He was a short step away from standing between her legs, if he'd had the nerve of a heart surgeon.

"I'm going to go straight home and listen to these," she said. "I'd ask you to join me, but I've already kept you way too long."

"Not at all," he said. "It's been a rare pleasure."

"The other ladies will be jealous. But you know what? Tough luck. Fortune favors the bold."

He found it necessary to clear his throat. "I'm not sure I'd have time to listen to all ten of the records, but I could certainly—"

"No, I don't want to be greedy. You should get home."

"I'm not in any rush."

"Plus, what if I decide to get high with Larry's pot? They say it's great for appreciating music, but I don't imagine you'd consider that a *meaningful reason* to break the law."

"Now you're teasing me."

"You're such a square, it's irresistible."

"I already told you I'm open to experimenting with you."

"Yeah, I don't know what to do with that." She laughed. "Has the church ever had to excommunicate someone? I could see me being the first, if it came out I'd lured you into reefer madness. You'd see me down at the A&P, wearing a scarlet letter."

"*R* for reefer," he said, trying to keep up with her.

"*R* for Russ. It could also stand for Russ."

He couldn't remember her having spoken his first name. It was somehow astonishing that she even knew it, so breathtaking was the intimacy it seemed to promise.

"I'm willing to take the chance if you are."

"Okay, noted," she said, hopping off his desk. "But not tonight. I'm sure your wife is wondering where you are."

"She's not. I left a message with Perry."

What he wanted must have been plain to her. She looked him in the eye and scrunched up her face, as if she smelled something off and wondered if he did, too. "This has been enough, don't you think?"

"If you say so."

"I—you don't think so?"

"I am in no hurry at all for this evening to end."

He could hardly have been plainer, and he saw her blanch. Then she laughed and touched him on the nose. "I like you, Reverend Hilde-brandt. But I think it's time for me to go."

That Clem had found that very moment to knock on his door, be-fore the cataclysm of being beeped on the nose had fully registered, was simply an embarrassment, not a setback, but it had been followed, in the church parking lot, after he and Clem had dug out her Buick, by yet an-other advance. Frances beckoned him over and said, "It's probably good he came when he did. Things were getting a little tensy-tense."

"I'm sorry I tried to keep you. I should be grateful you donated as much time as you did."

"Mission accomplished. Deliverables delivered."

"I truly am grateful," he said with feeling.

"Oh, pooh. I'm grateful, too. But if you really want to show your gratitude . . ."

"Yes."

"You could go and talk to Rick. It looked like he was still in his office."

"Talk to him now?"

"No time like the present."

It seemed to Russ that any other time would be better than the present.

"I'm serious about going to Arizona," she said, "and it won't be half as rewarding if you aren't there. I know that sounds selfish, but I'm not just being selfish. I hate to see you holding on to a grudge."

"I'll—see what I can do."

"Good. I'll be waiting. I want you to call me and tell me how it goes."

"Call you on the telephone."

"Is there some other kind of calling? I suppose I could ask you to drop by, but who knows what kind of reefer madness you'd be walking into."

"Seriously, Frances. You should not be doing that experiment by yourself."

"Okay, I'll make sure to have a pastor present. I was going to say a pastor *and* a physician, but maybe we can do without the physician. I suspect he wouldn't approve of—you."

Russ didn't know what to say. Was the heart surgeon still a threat?

"Anyway," she said, "I hope you'll make peace with Rick. Until you do, you're not allowed to call me." She shifted her car into forward gear. "Ha, listen to *her*. Giving ultimatums to a pastor. Who does she think she is?"

And away she went.

Russ had once devoted a Sunday sermon to Jesus's disturbing prophesy to Peter at the Last Supper—his prediction that his most faithful disciple would thrice, before the cock crowed, deny that he knew him. The conclusion Russ had drawn from Peter's fulfillment of the prophesy, and from the tears he then shed for his betrayal of his Lord, was that the prophesy had in fact been a profound parting gift. Jesus had told Peter, in effect, that he knew that Peter was only human; was fearful of worldly censure and punishment. The prophesy was his assurance that he would still be there in Peter at the moment when Peter most bitterly failed him—would always be there, would always understand him, always love him, in spite of his human weakness. In Russ's interpretation, Peter had wept not simply with remorse but with gratitude for the assurance.

Though the comparison was profane, Russ had been reminded of Peter's denials when he denied to Clem, at least three times, that he lusted after Mrs. Cottrell. Frances was his joy of the season—she'd beeped him on the nose!—and he ought to have been shouting the good news from every rooftop, but Clem's accusations had caught him off guard. The accusations, and even more the crazy talk of Vietnam, had reeked of adolescent moral absolutism. Clem was too young to understand that, although commandments were important, the callings of the heart amounted to a higher law. This had been Christ's revision of the Covenant, his message of love, and Russ regretted having lacked the courage to level with his son and make an example of his own heart's calling for Frances. Clem needed to be cured of his absolutism. By denying his feelings, Russ had done a disservice not only to them but arguably to his son as well.

Left alone in his office, he sat at his desk and tried to clear his head, telling himself that Clem might yet change his mind or fail to be drafted, and that, in any case, with American infantry no longer in combat, his risk of physical injury was low, so that he could devote his thoughts again to

Frances. His outing with her hadn't exceeded his wildest dreams, because it hadn't ended with her sliding her hands inside his sheepskin coat and gazing up into his eyes, but it had come pretty close. She'd given him a dozen reasons to hope, and the tensy-tension she'd alluded to, in the parking lot, was unmistakably sexual.

The tension was still in him, palpable in the rapid beating of his heart. He'd never profaned the church by abusing himself in his office, but he was so deeply in the thrall of Frances that he was tempted to do it now. Turn out the light, lower his zipper, and declare his allegiance. Beneath his feet was a bass rhythm from the function hall, so blurred and diffracted that it was more of a random hum. Slipping in beneath his door was the attenuated smoke of countless concert cigarettes. The church was already profaned; there was license in the air. But the thought of Rick Ambrose stayed his hand.

Heart beating in a less agreeable way, he stood and opened his door. He couldn't help hoping that Ambrose had gone home—had spared him from taking any action until after the holidays. But Ambrose's door was still ajar. The very light spilling out of it was hateful to Russ. The last time he'd set foot in that office, three years ago, he'd been accused of coming on to Sally Perkins, and Ambrose had stabbed him in the back.

He closed his own door again and sat down to pray.

Heavenly Father, I come to you seeking the spirit of forgiveness. Already, as you know, I've broken your commandments by following my heart, and I pray you'll forgive me for wanting to experience more joy in your Creation—to more fully rejoice in the life you've given me. What I need now is to find forgiveness in myself. Earlier tonight, when I felt moved to make peace with my enemy, I heard your Son speaking in my heart, and I allowed myself to hope that you were working your will through Frances. But now I've lost hold of the impulse. Now I worry that what I heard speaking wasn't love of your Son but simply lust for Frances—a selfish wish to be with her in Arizona. Now I worry that "making peace" without love in my heart will only compound my offenses against you. I'm alone with my doubts and my weakness, and I beg you, humbly, to instill me again with the spirit of Christmas. Please help me sincerely want to forgive Rick.

He knew better than to expect a direct response. Prayer was an inflection of the soul in God's direction, an inner movement. God's answer, if it came at all, would seem to him his own idea. The thing to do was wait quietly and make himself receptive to it.

The first words that came to him were lacerating. *Do you have any idea how embarrassing it is to be your son?* In hindsight, of all the abuses Clem had rained on him, this was the hardest to dismiss, because it seemed to refer to more than just Russ's weakness for Frances. It was an explicit eruption of a disrespect that had been building in Clem for several years. Russ had attributed the disrespect to adolescence, but it came to him now, all at once, that his humiliation at the hands of Rick Ambrose had been painful not only to him. The humiliation must have been painful to his son as well. He'd been too preoccupied with his own pain to see it.

At the humiliating fellowship meeting, the Clem who'd stood up to defend him against Sally Perkins and Laura Dobrinsky was still the Clem he knew and loved. But Clem had become less and less recognizable since then. He'd grossly overstepped at Thanksgiving, styling himself as Becky's defender, ordering Russ to let her make her own decision about her inheritance. And now he wanted to go to Vietnam. What had happened to the boy who'd marched against the war's immorality? Even allowing for his absolutism, even granting the validity of his point about student deferments, it made little sense to join the army when the war was winding down and he wasn't saving some other boy's life, just derailing his own. As an act of principle, it didn't add up. He was clearly doing it to hurt his father.

How terribly Russ must have embarrassed him. It was all very well to be privately deplorable, cowering in his office, nursing his grudge, creeping through the attic for fear of running into Ambrose. He could bear the private shame; he could square his own accounts with God. But to be so deplorable in his son's eyes? He saw that if he only thought of Frances he would never sincerely forgive Ambrose, because the impulse was impure. It was hopelessly tangled up with his desire to (in Clem's outrageous word) *bone* her. But if he performed the act of forgiveness as a gift to Clem? To make himself a father more worthy of respect?

Keeping his eyes half shut, to protect his fragile idea, he left his office and went up the hallway to the hateful door. With someone's volition, his own or God's, he knocked.

The response was immediate and sharp. "Yep."

Russ pushed the door farther open. Ambrose, seated at his desk, looked over his shoulder. To judge from his expression, Russ might have been a blood-soaked apparition.

"We need to talk," he said.

"Um—sure," Ambrose said. "Come in."

Russ shut the door and sat down on the sofa where the young crowd received its counseling. Its springs were so shot that his knees ended up higher than his head. He shifted to the edge of a cushion, trying to gain height, but the sofa insisted on his being lower than Ambrose. And just like that, in no time at all, despite his loving intentions, he was engulfed in hatred. Engulfed in the misery of being made to feel smaller than a man half his age. There was a reason he'd shunned Ambrose for three years. It was only in the madness of Frances that he'd forgotten. She had no concept of the enormity of what she'd asked of him.

"I suppose," he said stiffly, "I should begin with an apology."

Ambrose was now glowering. "You can skip it."

"No, I have to say it. It's long overdue. I've been—childish—and I apologize for that. I don't expect you to forgive me, but I apologize."

The words rang completely hollow. Not only did he not expect to be forgiven, he didn't even want to be. He struggled to find a way around his hatred, but it had grown so large in three years, and thinking of Clem helped him not at all.

"So," Ambrose said. "What can I do for you?"

Russ leaned back on the sofa and looked at the ceiling. He wanted to be gone, but to run away now, it seemed to him, would be to admit that he would never have Frances, never regain Clem's respect. He opened his mouth to see what he might say. "What do you make of all this?"

"All this what."

"You, me, the situation. What do you make of it?"

Ambrose sighed. "I think it's a misfortune. I won't pretend I don't blame you for it, but I understand that your pride was badly wounded.

To the extent I made it worse, I regret it. I apologized to you at the time. I can apologize again if you'd like."

"No. Skip it."

"Then tell me what I can do for you."

The tokens of love and adulation in Ambrose's office had proliferated since Russ was last in it. Above the desk were poems and messages in female handwriting, on pages ripped from spiral notebooks. Hundreds of snapshots were thumbtacked on top of one another, teen faces peeking out from the lower strata. Silk-screened posters now entirely covered one wall, right up to the ceiling. Feathers and rocks and carved sticks and scraps of watercolor painting crowded two long shelves. The cup of Ambrose ranneth over.

"I don't even know how it happened," Russ said. "How I came to hate you so much. It goes way beyond pride—it's basically consumed my life, and I don't understand it. How I can be a servant of God and feel this way. Just being in this office is a torture. The only thing I can say in my defense is that I can't control it. I can't think of you for five seconds without feeling sick. I can't even look at you now—your face makes me sick."

He sounded like a little girl running to her parents with hurt feelings. Mean Rick made me feel bad.

"If it's any comfort," Ambrose said, "I don't like you, either. I used to have a lot of respect for you, but that's long gone."

Beneath them, the bass vibrations crescendoed and stopped. That Russ could hear the crowd's cheering at all, at this distance, suggested that it was very large. It really should have been a comfort to know that his hatred was reciprocated, but now it only reminded him of Clem's disrespect.

"Be that as it may," he said, "we can't keep doing this to the church. It's just too obscene. I don't know how to get out of it, but we have to find a way to be more—civil."

"It was brave of you to knock on my door. To take that step."

"Oh my God." Russ clutched at the air and made his hands into fists. "Talk about things that make me sick. That little tremor in your voice when you tell someone they're brave. As if you're the world's leading authority on courage. As if your opinion is of the utmost importance."

Ambrose laughed. "That was a brave thing to say."

"I used to love you, Rick. I thought we were friends." Again the hurt little girl.

"It was good while it lasted," Ambrose said.

"No. I don't think so. I think I was always basically a fraud. I had no business trying to be a youth minister—I was never any good at it. And then you came into my church, and you're right, it was a blow to my pride. How good at it you were. It was stupid of me to envy that, because I'm good at other things—things you're not good at. But none of them seemed to matter."

"I'll have you know I've gotten better at carpentry and plumbing."

"You'll never be as good as me. I've got any number of skills to feel good about. But all I have to do is think of you, and—none of them matters."

Russ glanced at Ambrose, caught the gaze of his dark eyes, and quickly looked away again.

"I feel for you, Russ. But you probably don't want to hear that."

"You're damn right I don't. It's easier for me if you're an asshole. Which, by the way, I think you are. I think you're a raging egomaniac. I think Crossroads for you is one big power trip. I think you get off on having all the pretty girls lined up outside your office. You're an even bigger fraud than I was, but it doesn't matter, because the kids still love you. You really do help them, because they're too stupid to see through you. And then I don't just hate you—I hate the kids for loving you."

"What if I told you that I worry about the same thing? That I wrestle with these questions all the time?"

"That would be interesting. It's interesting to imagine you as a person more or less like me, trying to be good, trying to serve God, but constantly doubting yourself. Rationally, I ought to be able to build on that and find a way to forgive you. But as soon as I put *your* face to the person I'm imagining, I'm sick with hatred. All I can see is you having it both ways. Getting off on your power and feeling good about the fact that it worries you. Being an asshole and congratulating yourself on your 'honesty' about it. And maybe everyone does that. Maybe everyone finds a way to feel good about their fundamental sinfulness, but it doesn't make me hate you any less. It's the other way around. I hate you so much that

I start hating all of humanity, including myself. The idea that you and I are in any way alike—it's disgusting."

"Wow." Ambrose shook his head, as if in wonder. "I knew things were bad, but I had no idea."

"Do you see what I've been dealing with?"

"I guess I should be honored that I loom so large in your imagination."

"Really? I thought you were the Second Coming. I'd have thought you'd be used to looming large."

"But what you're saying now, the way you're speaking to me—there's a level to this that I never saw when you were in the group. A level of honesty, vulnerability. If you could have opened yourself up like this even once . . . It's kind of amazing to see it now."

"Yeah, screw that. Screw you. I mean, Jesus Christ, Rick—you approve of my honesty? *Who the hell are you to approve of me?* I'm an ordained minister—I'm twice your age! I'm supposed to sit here and be grateful that some posturing upper-middle-class asshole from Shaker Heights approves of me? When he couldn't care less if I approve of *him*?"

"You misunderstood me."

"I've been thinking about Joseph and his brothers. I know how you feel about citing Scripture, but you'll remember that the Bible is very clear on who the bad guys were. The older brothers sold Joseph into slavery, because why? Because they were envious. Because the Lord was with Joseph. That's the refrain in Genesis: *The Lord was with Joseph.* He was the wunderkind, the favorite son, the person everyone went to with their dreams, because he had the gift from God. Everywhere he went, people put him in charge, they raised him up and praised him. And boy, did his approval matter to them. When I used to read Genesis as a young person, it seemed crystal clear who was good and who was bad. But you know what? When I read that book now, Joseph makes me sick. My sympathies are completely with the brothers, because God didn't choose them. It was all preordained, and they were the unlucky ones, and it's incredible: I hate you so much, I've started hating God!"

"Yikes."

"I ask myself what I did to offend Him, what kind of abominations

I committed, that I deserved the curse of you coming to this church. Or whether it was just His plan when He created me. That I be the bad guy. How am I supposed to love a God like that?"

Ambrose leaned forward, bringing his head closer to the height of Russ's.

"Try to think," he said. "Let's both try to think. Is there anything I could say to you that wouldn't set you off? I can't express sympathy, I can't say I admire you, I can't apologize. It seems like literally any human response I could give you, you'll turn it against me."

"That's exactly right."

"Then what did you come here for? What do you want?"

"I want you to be a person you could never be."

"What kind of person is that?"

Russ considered the question. It was a relief to finally air his feelings, but he was following a familiar pattern. Later on—soon—he would be mortified by everything he'd said. For better or worse, this was who he was. When he saw the answer to Ambrose's question, he went ahead and spoke it.

"I want you to be a person who needs something. Who cares about *my* approval. You ask me what you could say that wouldn't set me off, well, there is one thing. You could say you loved me, the way I used to love you."

Ambrose sat up straight again.

"Don't worry," Russ said. "Even if you could say it, I wouldn't believe you. You never loved me, and both of us know it."

Afraid that he might cry, like a little girl, he closed his eyes. It seemed unfair that he'd been punished for loving Ambrose. Punished for loving Clem, too. Punished even for loving Marion, because she was the one person who loved him in return, and she was the very person he seemed fated to injure. Shouldn't his capacity for love, which was the essence of Christ's gospel, have earned him a modicum of credit with God?

"Wait here," Ambrose said.

Russ heard him get up and leave the office. Even on his worst days, especially on his worst days, his unhappiness had been a portal to God's mercy. Now he could find no reward in it at all. He couldn't even count on the reward of being allowed to call Frances, because he'd failed at the task she'd set him.

Ambrose returned holding a collection plate from the sanctuary. When he crouched and set it on the floor, Russ saw that it was filled with water. Ambrose loosened the laces of the work shoes Russ was wearing. He'd bought them at Sears. "Lift your foot," Ambrose said.

"Don't."

Ambrose lifted the foot himself and took off the shoe. Russ squirmed, but Ambrose held his leg and pulled off his sock. The ritual was too sacred, had too many biblical associations, for Russ to resist it by kicking him away.

"Rick. Really."

Intent on his work, Ambrose pulled off the other shoe and sock.

"Seriously," Russ said. "You want to play Jesus?"

"By that logic, anything we ever do to emulate him is grandiose."

"I don't want you washing my feet."

"The gesture wasn't original to him. It had a more general meaning, as an act of humility."

The water in the plate was very cold—it must have come from a drinking fountain. Russ watched powerlessly while Ambrose, on his knees, his black hair hanging in his eyes, washed one foot and then the other. He took a flannel shirt from the back of his desk chair and gently dried Russ's feet with it. Then, leaning forward, head bowed, he grasped Russ's hand.

"What are you doing now?"

"I'm praying for you."

"I don't want your prayers."

"Then I'm praying for myself. Shut the fuck up."

Russ knew better than to try to pray his way out of his hatred—he'd tried it a hundred times to no avail. What moved him now was the hand grasping his. It was slender, black-haired, still youthful. It was just a human hand, a young man's hand, and it reminded him of Clem. His chest began to shake. Ambrose tightened his grip; and Russ surrendered to his weakness.

He must have wept for ten minutes, with Ambrose kneeling at his feet. The goodness of Christ, the meaning of Christmas, was in him again. He'd forgotten its sweetness, but now he remembered. Remembered that when he was bathed in God's goodness it was enough to simply remain in it, experience the joy of it, not think of anything, just be there. When Ambrose finally released his hand, Russ clutched at it. He didn't want the moment to end.

Ambrose went away with the collection plate, and Russ put on his socks and shoes. His previous experiences of grace, most of them in his adolescence and his early twenties, had left his mind in a state of calm clarity, a kind of early-morning stillness that daily life would soon dispel. With the same clarity, now, he accepted that the Lord was with Ambrose.

"I feel better," he announced when Ambrose returned.

"Then I'm not going to say another word. Let's not mess it up."

Standing up, Russ was reminded of how short his nemesis was. He looked like a long-haired boy with a bandito costume mustache. Russ suspected that his hatred was merely subdued, not vanquished, but his clarity was holding. He felt no envy of the shelves of gifts the teenagers had given Ambrose. On the lower shelf was a long feather, doubtless from Arizona, the tail feather of a hawk. He picked it up and twirled the quill between his fingers. It was *better* to have nothing. Better to be like the Navajos, the Diné, as they called themselves, in Diné Bikéyah, among the four sacred mountains. The Diné had nothing. In their hogans, they lived with almost nothing. Even in better times, before the Europeans came, they had never had much. But spiritually they were the richest people he'd ever known.

"I want to go to Arizona," he said.

Becky was literally following in Laura Dobrinsky's steps. Behind the drugstore, she found a single set of deep footprints leading up a flight of wooden stairs. At the top of them, outside a weather-beaten door, she looked down to make sure Clem hadn't followed her. She was very afraid of Laura, but she had no time to waste. She knocked on the door and waited. Hearing nothing from within, she knocked again and tried the doorknob. It wasn't locked.

Stepping inside, into a kitchenette, she saw Laura kneeling on a floor carpeted in tangerine shag. She was wearing her biker jacket and stuffing a fiberfill sleeping bag into a nylon sack. Beside it was a jumble of toiletries, a stack of books, and a military-style backpack, a sweater sleeve dangling from its mouth. An electrical space heater was scenting the air with burned dust.

"Laura?"

Laura stiffened, not turning her head.

"I know you don't want to see me," Becky said, "but this isn't about me. This is about Tanner's career. He really needs you to play tonight. Will you please do that?"

"Get the fuck out of my house."

"I talked to the agent. I talked to Gig, and you know why he's here? Because of *you*. I mean, you're such an amazing singer. I know you must be hurt, but—Gig's dying to hear you."

"*I know you must be hurt*," Laura echoed in a babyish voice. She punched the last of the sleeping bag into the nylon sack and tightened the drawstring.

"I'm sorry," Becky said, moving toward her. "I wish I could take everything back. I wish I'd known yesterday—that there's a right path. A right way to live. I was on the wrong path."

"And praise be to Jesus for showing you the way."

Becky struggled to forbear. "My point is, you shouldn't take it out on Tanner. It's my fault, not his. Can't you take one hour to help him when he truly needs you?"

"Nope."

"Why not?"

"Because I'm splitting. Going to San Francisco."

"I'm saying right now, though."

"Right now is when I'm doing it."

"Now? There's like a foot of snow out there."

"No better time to thumb a ride. Everybody wants to help a stranger."

Laura loosened straps on the backpack and pushed the sleeping bag under them. Tanner had said it himself—she was radical.

"I just think," Becky said, "if you cared enough about Tanner to be with him for however long—"

"Four years, sister."

"Don't you still want the best for him?"

Laura looked up through her pink lenses. "Are you out of your mind?"

"No, I get that you're angry. I get that I did a bad thing. But we both love Tanner—"

"Oh really. You *love* him."

"I—think so."

"Well, isn't that the sweetest thing."

Laura rooted in the pile of toiletries, and something came flying at Becky's face. She caught it defensively. It was a toothpaste tube, halfway rolled up from the bottom. Seeing the word *Gynol*, she dropped it. Not toothpaste.

"A little present for you," Laura said. "Unless—Jesus. You're probably on the Pill."

Becky's hand felt dirtied. She rubbed it on her coat.

"Not that a cheerleader would care, but you do realize you're just buying into the male-industrial complex? Messing with your hormones for their pleasure? There's nothing a dick loves better than trouble-free access. Even Tanner tried to get me on the Pill. You're going to make him sorry he ever bothered with me."

The room was underheated, but Becky was sweating. The gagging sensation in her chest was like the carsickness of her childhood, the prospect of sex unfolding like a mountain road ahead of her, a hundred curves coming to make her even sicker. She'd gotten into the car of being Tanner's. Now she wished it would slow down.

"My point is," she said unsteadily, "he really needs you to play tonight."

"Or wait. Wait." The eyes behind the pink lenses narrowed. "Have you even *had* sex?"

"Have I—?"

"Oh my God. Of course you haven't. *No, please, no, the Bible says you shouldn't touch me there.*" Laura laughed. "Not that being a churchgoer ever stopped our boy. He's quite the frisky Christian. You'd better be ready for that."

The cold sweat of carsickness.

"Or, no, I hope you're not ready. I hope the only thing you let him do with you is sing hymns. Serve him right."

"Please," Becky said. "We need to go right now. The agent is there, he came to hear you, and I just think—we should go."

"I told you to get the fuck out of here."

"Please, Laura."

Laura sprang to her feet and came at Becky. Why Becky dropped to her knees, she couldn't have said. Maybe she didn't want to be so much taller, maybe it was a gesture of supplication. But, finding herself kneeling again, she bowed her head and pressed her palms together. *Please help Laura,* she prayed. *Please forgive me.*

Laura shrieked. "What the *fuck*? Are you fucking kidding me?"

Becky kept her head bowed. From above her came a sputtering, and then a cold hand was in her hair, grabbing a fistful of it, violating her physical sanctity, trying to yank her to her feet. She could feel hairs tearing from their roots, but she refused to stand up. The hand let go. An instant later, she was walloped in the ear. The blow was vicious, there was wristbone in it, and sparks in her vision—stars. She saw stars. The blow that followed was neck-wrenching, brain-shaking. Worse than the pain was the sheer fact of violence. No one had ever hit her. She squeezed her eyes shut and tried to keep praying.

Now Laura was kneeling, too. Her fingertips brushed Becky's ear, which felt skinless and hot. "Becky, I'm sorry. Are you all right?"

Please, God. Please, God.

"I'm—shit. I'm no better than my old man."

At the change in Laura's voice, which might have been an answer to her prayer, something stirred in Becky's core—the same opening-up that she'd experienced in the sanctuary. God was still there. She concentrated, not wanting to lose her connection to Him. But Laura spoke again.

"You know about that, right? Tanner told you?"

Becky shook her head.

"He didn't tell you why I moved in with him? With his family?"

It was news to Becky that Laura had lived with the Evanses. Never mind the why of it.

"I know what it's like to be hit," Laura said. "I'm sorry I did that to you."

"It's all right. I did a bad thing to you, too."

"That's exactly how my old man made me feel. Like I deserved it." Laura touched Becky's shoulder. "Are you really all right?"

"Yes."

"An open hand can do a lot of damage. Like, I'm partially deaf in one ear. It was Tanner's mom who noticed. She was my piano teacher, and now she's basically my mother. The other one—I can't even be in the same room with her. He still hits her, and she still thinks she deserves it."

Becky felt grateful—to God—that Laura was speaking more kindly, but beneath the gratitude were the beginnings of a grievance with Tanner. He hadn't told her that Laura's father had beaten her; that Laura had lived with his family; that she was practically his sister. If Becky had understood the depths of what she was stepping into, she would have been more careful. The harm she'd proceeded to cause was partly her fault, but it seemed to her that it was partly also Tanner's.

"I'm so sorry," she said.

"It's just the left ear."

"No, I mean, about everything. I'm sorry about everything. I'm thinking—maybe I should step aside. Leave the two of you alone."

"Too late for that, sister. He's in love with you."

Again the carsick vista.

"I asked him point-blank," Laura said. "That was his answer."

"But it's only because I threw myself at him. If I just went away . . ."

"That's not how it works."

"But I know he still has feelings for you. If I just—"

"Mess with his emotions and walk away? That truly would be a cunt move. Not that I can't see you doing it."

Loudly, or angrily, it seemed, a telephone rang. The phone was on the wall in the kitchenette. Laura gave it an uninterested glance.

"I'm the one who's going to split," she said. "I should have done it years ago." She stood up and added, "I'm sorry I hit you."

She returned to her backpack, and the phone continued its angry ringing. Becky, who came from a family where ignoring a phone was unthinkable, jumped up and answered. She heard the sound of a crowd and Tanner shouting over it.

"Becky? What are you doing? I've been—Gig's here—we have to play. What are you doing?"

"Just one second, okay?" She pressed the receiver to her chest and walked it toward Laura. "It's Tanner," she said. "They need to start. Will you come with me? Please?"

The fact that Laura, after a moment, made a petulant, hand-flinging gesture of assent—the fact that she would never have done this if she hadn't hit Becky, which wouldn't have happened if Becky hadn't fallen to her knees to pray, which wouldn't have happened if the spirit of Christ hadn't brought her to Laura's apartment, which wouldn't have happened if she hadn't found God in the sanctuary, which wouldn't have happened if she hadn't smoked marijuana—seemed to Becky, as she followed Laura down the snowy stairs behind the drugstore, the most beautiful proof of God's mysterious workings. She'd done bad things, she'd accepted her punishment, and now she had her reward. She could feel a whole new life, a life in faith, beginning.

"This is so stupid," Laura said as they strode along the sidewalk. "I hope you understand what this is costing me."

The cold air stung Becky's battered ear. She didn't dare speak, lest Laura change her mind.

The crowd in the function hall was restive, the stage dimly bathed in purple light. Laura went straight to the door that led backstage while Becky hung back near the vestibule. Seeing the food tables, which were now fully denuded, she understood how considerably stoned she'd still been when she thought she was over being stoned. She was also reminded unpleasantly of Clem.

Gig Benedetti came ambling over to her, smiling. "We meet again."

"Yeah, hi."

"I can't say I'm loving the level of organization here. By which I mean it's rather low."

"Laura wasn't feeling well."

Was there a commandment in the Bible against lying? Maybe not, but the truth would come out anyway. She wondered if, having performed one amazing deed, she might perform another.

"So, actually, though," she said. "Actually, here's the thing. Laura's quitting the band."

Gig laughed. "Seriously?"

"Um, yeah."

"The act I came to hear included a female vocalist."

"I know. But I've heard them play without her, and it's actually better. Tanner really takes over when he doesn't have to share the stage. It's his band, not hers."

"Is it possible you're not the most objective critic?"

By instinct, her hand went to her hair and lifted it out from her coat collar. She gave it a luxuriant shake, nothing God could disapprove of. It wasn't her fault if Gig thought she was a good-looking girl.

"If you really want to know," she said, "I'm the reason Laura's quitting. I'm going to feel very shitty if you don't sign them because of me." Likewise instinctual was the note of hurt in her voice. She shook her hair again. "I know it sounds like I'm asking you a favor, but Tanner's the one with ambition. Laura's just an amateur."

Gig narrowed his eyes. "What's your deal?"

"What do you mean?"

"Why am I talking to you and not him?"

"I don't know. Just—if you sign the band, you'll be seeing a whole lot of me."

To really flirt, she should have looked him in the eye, but she couldn't do it.

"That's a consideration," he said.

After the blizzard came a starry-skied chill. The parsonage was dark, but the snow on the driveway was furrowed with new tracks. As Clem followed them toward the back door, he caught a whiff of tobacco smoke. He stopped and sniffed the air. He was out of cigarettes, having emptied his pack after his fight with his father. He'd intended to quit smoking in New Prospect, but that was before Becky told him to go to hell.

The smoke was coming from the parsonage itself. Sitting on the front porch, on the firewood box, in a bulky coat, was—his mother? He was tempted to continue up the driveway, slip inside, go straight to bed. But he saw that his father had been right: he hadn't considered his mother's feelings when he wrote to the draft board. Worse yet, he saw that he needed to tell her, right now, what he'd done. Better that she hear it from him than from the old man.

He retraced his steps down the driveway. By the time he reached the porch, her cigarette had vanished and she was on her feet.

"Sweetie," she said. "There you are."

He leaned down and received a smoky kiss. He knew she'd smoked as a teenager, but that was thirty years ago.

"Yes," she said, "I was having a cigarette. You caught me."

"Actually—can I bum one?"

She laughed. "This is getting ridiculous."

He didn't know what she meant, but a laugh was better than a lecture. "I'm going to quit," he said. "Tomorrow. But—just one?"

"The things I didn't know." She shook her head and reached into her pocket. "Filter? Nonfilter?"

The quicker to light up, he took a cigarette from the pack that was already open. Filterless Lucky Strikes. In the Arctic air, the smoke was abstract and nearly flavorless. He fastened his eyes on the white street, to make himself an abstraction, and told his mother about the letter and the reason he'd sent it.

Only when he'd finished did he turn to see how she was taking the news. In her hands was a coffee cup with cigarette ends in it. As if awakened by his silence, she looked down at the cup. It seemed to surprise her. She handed it to him and said, "I'm going inside."

He didn't know what exactly he'd expected, but he'd expected more than no response at all. He extinguished his Lucky and followed her into the house. His bags were at the bottom of the stairs, where he'd dropped them. The Christmas tree was dark.

In the kitchen, his mother had crouched by a seldom-opened cabinet.

"Mom, are you all right?"

She stood up with a bottle of J&B scotch. "Why do you ask? Is there a bottle of liquor in my hand? Oh, why, yes, there is." She laughed and upended the bottle over a glass. Barely a finger of scotch came out. She drank it off. "What do you want me to say? That I'm happy my son wants to fight in that war?"

"I'm not going to be morally half-assed about it."

She lowered her chin and fixed him with a dubious look, inviting him to amend what he'd said. When he didn't, she crouched again by the cabinet.

"I can't deal with this," she said. "Not tonight. If you want me to worry about you every hour of the next two years, it's your decision. It would have been nice to have a little warning, but—it's your decision."

Bottles clanked as she examined their discolored labels.

"This will devastate your father," she added. "I imagine you know that."

"Yeah, I saw him at church. He's pretty mad."

"He's at the church?"

Mrs. Cottrell and her beckoning finger were still fresh in Clem's mind, and he didn't owe the old man anything. The question was whether to spare his mother's feelings.

"He was with a parishioner," he said carefully. "We had to dig her car out."

"Let me guess. Frances Cottrell."

It was dizzying to hear the name from his mother. He wondered if she was smoking and drinking because she knew all about Mrs. Cottrell. Knew more, perhaps, than he did.

"Do you want something?" she said. "Food? A drink? There's still some bourbon here. Some ancient vermouth."

"I might have a sandwich."

She stood up with a bottle and squinted at the dram remaining in it. "Why does this happen? Why is it that, when a person finally really needs a drink, every damn bottle is empty? It can't be random. If it were random, some of the bottles would be full."

Something was definitely not right with her.

"Actually, no," she said. "I suspect it's your brother." She poured the dram into her glass. "It's sort of heartbreaking when you think about it. He keeps going back and taking a little more, but he can't leave an empty bottle. How much can he take without making it officially empty? I don't know whether to laugh or cry."

The state she was in was too much for Clem to process. In the relative warmth of the house, now that he'd told his parents what he'd done, his exhaustion was overwhelming. He sat down at the kitchen table and rested his head on his arms. He thought he might fall asleep instantly, but he'd passed that point. The exhaustion was so painful that it kept him awake. He heard his mother pouring herself a third drink, opening the refrigerator, handling utensils. He heard her setting a plate on the table.

"You should eat something," she said.

With extreme exertion, he sat up. The sandwich on the plate was ham and Swiss on rye. He was grateful that she'd made it, too sick with exhaustion to want it. He thought of the cinnamon toast that Sharon had offered him that morning, the eggs she'd scrambled him on other mornings. He thought of how happy she'd been to see him, how full of plans for their future. The pain behind his eyes became unbearable.

"Oh, honey, Clem, sweetie, what is it? Why are you crying?"

He had so much misery to express and only one way to do it. When his mother put her arms around him, he struggled to maintain some shred of strength and dignity. But, really, he had none.

It was interesting to note that, when his tears subsided, the sandwich looked more appealing. He also wanted a cigarette. These were the same appetites that returned after sexual release.

"Will you tell me what's wrong?" his mother said. "Do you not really want to be in the army?"

Someone had left a paper napkin on the table. He blew his nose with it, and his mother sat down across from him. In her glass was some brownish vermouth.

"We can call the draft board in the morning," she said. "You can say you changed your mind. No one will think any less of you."

"No. I'm just worn out."

"But that can affect your judgment. Maybe if you got some rest—this is such a crazy thing."

"It's not crazy. It's the one thing I'm sure about."

From his mother's silence, he could tell that she was disappointed. Her way as a parent had always been to offer suggestions, hoping he would see that they were sensible, rather than telling him what to do.

"Do you remember what you told me?" he said. "That sex without commitment is a bad idea?"

"Something like that, yes."

"Well, so, I've been with a girl. A woman. It's been the most amazing thing."

His mother's eyes widened as if he'd stuck her with a needle.

"But you were right," he said. "If there's no commitment, people get hurt. And that's exactly what happened. She's horribly hurt."

The misery rose in him, and his mother reached across the table for his hand. Not wanting to cry again, he pulled it away.

"We broke up," he said. "This morning. Or I broke up with her. She didn't want to."

"Oh, honey."

"I had to—I'm leaving school."

"You don't have to leave school."

"I did a horribly cruel thing to her."

The misery overcame him. While he struggled to master it, his mother stood up and went to the stove. He heard a whoosh and smelled smoke. The weirdness of her smoking brought him back out of himself.

"Don't you want to go outside?"

"No," she said. "This is my house, too."

"Why are you smoking?"

"I'm sorry. It's been one thing after another today. I'm sorry you're hurt. I'm sorry about—what's her name?"

"Sharon."

His mother drew hard on the cigarette. "It's just hard for me to understand. If you were happy with her, why are you leaving school?"

"Because my lottery number is nineteen."

"But why now? Why not wait another semester?"

"Because I'm too crazy about her to keep my grades up. As long as I'm there, I only want to be with her."

"But that's—" His mother frowned. "Are you quitting school to get away from her?"

"I'm pulling a B average. I don't deserve a deferment."

"No, no, no. You're not thinking straight. Do you love her?"

"It doesn't matter."

"Do you love her?"

"Yes. I mean—yes. But it doesn't matter. It's too late."

His mother went to the sink and ran water on her cigarette.

"It's never too late," she said. "If you love her, and she loves you, then don't leave her. It's as simple as that. Do not run away from the person you love."

"I know, but . . ."

His mother wheeled around from the sink. A strange light was in her eyes. "It's not right! There's nothing more terrible you can do!"

He'd never felt afraid of her before. She'd always only been his mother, small and soft, ever-present but diffuse. His fear deepened when she went to the wall phone by the dining-room door and took the receiver off its hook. She thrust it in his face.

"Call her."

"Mom?"

"Honey, just do it. You'll feel better. I want you to call her and tell her you're sorry. Please. She'll take you back."

The receiver was emitting a dial tone. His mother's hand was shaking.

"Is Sharon with her family? Did she go home, too?"

"Tomorrow, I think."

"Then tell her you want to come and see her. It's fine with me."

"Mom, it's Christmas."

"So what? You have my permission. I mean, honestly—is this where you want to be? Here?" She made a sweeping gesture with the receiver. "In *this?*"

The disgust in her voice was shocking. And yet she had a point. He really didn't want to be in the parsonage, not after what Becky had said to him.

"It's too late to go back," he said. "She's leaving in the morning."

The receiver burst into an off-the-hook yammering.

"Then go there now," his mother said.

Why Perry, late in the evening, was on the far side of the tracks, in the prospectless part of New Prospect where streets of sorry little houses dead-ended at the rail embankment, was a question answerable only in the narrowest pragmatic sense. To address the greater why of it required a framework of ratiocination whose pointlessness was now evident. As he trotted along Terminal Street, the snow squeaking beneath his feet, he felt pursued by an expanding black crater. Before it caught up and swallowed him, he needed to reach the house whose threshold he hadn't expected to cross again. Under the circumstances, this seemed excusable.

The crater had appeared after he confessed to his mother that he'd sold contraband. Although the confession had been strategic, a matter of securing her complicity against the raging of his father, should his misconduct ever come to general light, he'd been prepared to shed some tears, as he'd done with impressive success at Crossroads, in order to be forgiven. But his mother hadn't seemed to care. She hadn't scolded him; hadn't even asked questions. The effect, when he left her to her cigarette and went downstairs, had been to render him defenseless against the mental crater that had opened.

He'd set out in the snow for Ansel Roder's house. Surely, if only tonight, he was permitted to get very high. The anticipation of toke after toke in the trusty seclusion of the Roder swimming-pool shed, the foretaste of deliberately massive excess, the imminence of futurity-banishing befuddlement, was giving him a boner that grew harder as he imagined the pleasure of servicing it, while extremely high, in the bathroom Roder shared with his skinny, non-bra-wearing sister, Annette, when she was home from college. Annette was dry of wit, a junior at Grinnell, and had an oily, rough complexion that only added to her allure. She was close to Perry's ideal, female-wise, and seemed approximately as attainable to him as the Andromeda Galaxy.

Embarrassingly, Annette herself answered his ringing of the Roder doorbell. He couldn't look at her face; could barely find the voice to ask for Ansel. In his cheap parka, his dorkoid rubbers, his arrant craving, he was every inch the repulsive little worm. All he could do was wait for her to turn away. His desperation to be high and by himself, in a locked bathroom, was approaching intolerable. Through the open front door, he saw scintillant orange in the Roder fireplace. The fireplace was outsized, manorial, and burned longer split logs than he'd seen anywhere else.

Roder, when he came to the door, barefoot, seemed pre-annoyed. "What do you want?"

"I'd like to come in," Perry said. "If I may."

"Not a good time. We're playing canasta."

"Canasta."

"It's a holiday tradition. It's actually pretty fun."

"You and your family are playing a card game."

"Troll the ancient yuletide carol and the like. Yes."

The Roders were even less a family unit than the Hildebrandts. Their doing a fun thing together was unusual to the point of seeming cosmically unjust. Without looking behind him, Perry could sense the dark crater widening toward him.

"Well, then," he said, his throat thick with disappointment, "I wonder, if you have a second—I made a small error in judgment today. A miscalculation."

"Seriously, man." Roder began to close the door. "Not a good time."

"If you could just quickly run and get me one of the bags. Help a friend."

"We're playing a game here."

"You mentioned that. If you'd like, I can give you some cash."

Roder made a face, as if repulsed by a worm.

"Ansel, come on. When have I ever come to you like this?"

"What is wrong with you?"

"I shouldn't have mentioned money. That was a mistake—I'm sorry."

Roder shut the door in his face. Out of reach, not fifty feet from where he stood, in a drawer in Roder's bedroom, were three ounces of weed, schoolyard in quality but adequate to the task at hand, and he couldn't even blame the cosmos. It was he who'd offended Roder. By proposing a deal today, he'd rendered glaring a fact heretofore overlookable in the bonhomie of being high, of Roder's generosity and his own capacity to amuse. The fact was that he didn't love Roder. He loved drugs.

Pursued by the crater's edge, he made his way to First Reformed. Of the friends of his who might be holding, only Roder wasn't in Crossroads, and so the concert was his only recourse. His mother had lost her mind. She'd been committed to a loony bin, her father had drowned himself, *and she'd named these facts to Perry*—named two outcomes that had lurked behind doors in his head which he'd never permitted himself to open, not even on the most sleepless of nights. And yet, as if with X-ray vision, telekinetic intelligence, he must have seen through the shut doors, because nothing she'd told him had surprised him. He'd had only a dull sense of recognition. The outcomes were ugly but not shocking; he knew their faces.

He would tell her nothing more. Not now, not ever. In a sense, the crater he was fleeing was his mother.

He'd hoped to find a party in the church parking lot, but he'd arrived too late—the lot was empty. Inside the function hall, at the rear margin of the crowd, a couple of Crossroads alumnae were dancing with a blissy sloppiness to the instrumental jam in "Wooden Ships," performed by a band Perry recognized by general repute, and also from having silk-screened its name on the concert posters, as the Bleu Notes. Through shifting lanes in the crowd, he caught glimpses of the fabled Laura Dobrinsky frowning over an electric keyboard, studious in her syncopations, and a tall Afro'd guitarist vaguely moving his lips to his riffing, and Tanner Evans behaving more like a rock star, tossing his hair and making little lunges as he whaled away on rhythm. They sounded note for note like Crosby, Stills and Nash on their first record, and the crowd, unfortunately, was totally into it. Except for the dancing girls, all he could see was the backs of nodding heads. Disappointment was rising in his throat when someone touched him on the shoulder.

Of all the useless people, it was Larry Cottrell. Larry had done something dumb to his hair, overcombed it, and the result was to make everything else about him—jean jacket, straight-legged corduroys, hiking boots—seem similarly overconsidered. He spread his arms as if, Jesus Christ, he expected a hug. Perry turned toward the stage and craned his neck, pretending to be greatly interested in the band. Having admitted to his mother that he'd been a dealer, and thereby inoculated himself against paternal discovery, he no longer had anything to fear from Larry.

We are lea-ea-ving, came the refrain onstage. *You don't nee-ee-eed us.*

Larry, undiscouraged, shouted into Perry's ear. "Where were you?"

As in a game of chess, Perry saw that, unless he took bold action, his little pawn would be dogging him at every turn, complicating the task of finding drugs. Again the sense of cosmic unfairness. Again the recognition that he had no one but himself to blame.

What to do? A bold move came to him as it did on a chessboard, with a frisson of do-I-dare. He beckoned Larry to follow him, which Larry eagerly did, out into the deserted vestibule.

"I had a thought," he said.

"What, what," Larry said.

"We need to get drunk."

Larry's fingers went straight to the sebaceous sides of his nose. "Okay."

"I assume your mother has a liquor shelf?"

The fingers rubbed. The nose sniffed sebum. The eyes were wide.

"I want you to go there now," Perry said. "Take something she won't notice, triple sec or crème de menthe. Any bottle that's more or less full."

"Yeah, um. What about the rules, though?"

"You can hide the bottle in a snowdrift—it won't freeze. Will you do that for me?"

Larry was obviously scared. "You have to come with me."

"No. Too suspicious. You can take however long it takes—I'll wait."

"I don't know about this."

Perry grasped the arms of his pawn and looked into his eyes. "Just do it. You'll thank me for it later."

To observe his power over Larry was to push back the edge of the crater. There was a kind of liberation in jettisoning all thought of being a good person. From the outer doorway, he watched Larry hustle across the parking lot.

While Laura Dobrinsky, now seated at the church's baby grand piano, belted out a Carole King song, he returned to the crowd and maneuvered through it, stopping for a hug from a Crossroads girl who'd confessed to being awed by his vocabulary, and a hug from a girl who'd challenged him to be more emotionally open, and a hug from a girl with whom he'd improvised a skit about the hazards of dishonesty, to much approbation, and a hug from a girl who'd vouchsafed to him, in a dyad, that she'd gotten her first period before she turned eleven, and then a thumbs-up from the boy who'd helped him with the concert posters, and a friendly nod from no less an eminence than Ike Isner, whose face he'd once palpated, while blindfolded, in a trust exercise, and whose blind fingers had then palpated his own face. None of these people could see inside his cranium, all had been fooled into applauding his emotional candor and collectively propelling him, with a kind of gently pulsing group action, like macroscopic cilia, in the direction of belonging to the Crossroads inner circle. The hugs in particular were still pleasant, but the edge of the crater was creeping up on him again, now taking the form of a classic depressive question: What was the point? The inner circle had no actual power. It was merely the goal of an abstract game.

Near the corner of the stage, by an American flag, which the church for unknowable reasons felt obliged to display on a pole, he found all his old friends in one tight group. Bobby Jett and Keith Stratton were there with David Goya and his ill-complected girlfriend, Kim, and also Becky, by whose side stood an older man, unfamiliar to Perry, lavishly sideburned and wearing a belted orange leather coat, who might have stepped off the set of *The Mod Squad*. Kim promptly hugged Perry, and he was pleased to detect a whiff of skunk in her hair. Where there was dope, there was hope. Becky only waved to him, but not unkindly. She looked taller to him somehow, radiantly okay, as if to accentuate his own runtiness, his galloping not-okayness.

Onstage, Tanner Evans had taken up an acoustic guitar, his Afro'd friend a banjo, and the Bleu Notes had rolled into a theologically tendentious ballad whose lyrics were known to Perry, because it was the semiofficial theme song of Crossroads, purportedly written by Tanner Evans himself, and was often sung at the end of Sunday-night meetings.

> *The song is in the changes not the notes*
> *I was looking for a thing*
> *Couldn't find it in myself*
> *Until I met somebody else*
> *And I found it in between*
> *Yeah, the song is in the changes not the notes*

Becky seemed enthralled by the performance, the sideburned modster possibly a bit enthralled with Becky, but David Goya, who enjoyed amending the line *I found it in between* to *I found it between her legs*, was gazing at the crowd like a deaf old man puzzled by visual evidence of sound. Perry tugged on his sleeve and led him out into the hallway.

"Are you holding?" he said.

In the hallway light, Goya's eyes were bloodshot, his expression wistful. "Sadly, I am not."

"Then who is? If I may ask."

"At this late hour, I couldn't tell you. Demand was early and brisk."

"David. Did you think I wasn't coming?"

"What can I say? Events have taken their course. And now, yes, all pockets are empty. You should have been here with your sister."

"My *sister?*"

"Is there a problem? Do we not like Becky?"

Something evil, the edge of the crater, was nipping the undersides of Perry's heels. Evidently, despite the recent forward stride in relations with his sister, the cessation of hostilities, her larger project of dispossessing him was ongoing.

"Apropos of which," Goya said. "Were you aware that she's with Tanner Evans? Did you know this and not tell us?"

Perry stared at the brass handles of the doors to the function hall, behind which the Bleu Notes were doing better justice to "The Song Is in the Changes" than was done on Sunday nights.

"We have eyewitness reports of smooching," Goya said. "Kim is—what's the word. Kim is agog."

Down down down. Perry was going down.

"Can we go to your house?" he said. "I was—that is . . . Can we do a resupply run?"

"There's talk of pancakes," Goya said. "Becky wants midnight pancakes, and who could blame her? Kim's going. And whither Kim goest . . ."

"We could catch up with them later."

The desperate edge in Perry's voice seemed to cut through Goya's mellowness. His eyes, though red, became alert. "Is something up with you?"

The cosmos was unjust. By dallying in conversation with his mother, Perry had made himself too late to procure relief from the disturbance the conversation had caused him, whereas, if he'd skipped the conversation and come to the concert earlier, when drugs were still available, he wouldn't have been disturbed and could have stuck to his resolution.

"I just," he said. "I, uh. Is—who's going?"

"Kim, Becky, me. Tanner, too, I think. Maybe others."

Perry saw an idea and pounced on it. "The band has to pack up. If we go right now, we'll be back in plenty of time."

The idea was rational and easily realized, but Goya was too stoned or too stubborn to see it. "Is something wrong?"

"No. No."

"Then let's not do this."

A tremendous closing cheer went up in the function hall. Goya turned and went back in, and Perry, after a hesitation, followed. One might have expected an encore, but Laura Dobrinsky was hopping down from the stage. She lowered her head and charged into the crowd, jostling Perry as she hurried out the door. Over his shoulder, he saw her sprinting down the hallway.

The house lights had come up, and Tanner Evans, too, was in the crowd, his hair damp with musical exertion. He shook the modster's hand

and draped his arm around Becky. Perry couldn't see her face, but he could see the few people who'd hugged him, the many who hadn't. Every one of them was looking at his sister, who had both arms around Tanner Evans. She'd been in Crossroads for less than two months, and already, it was clear, she'd leaped past Perry and advanced to the center of it.

How happy her soul must have been with the person in whom it had chanced to land.

From the ensuing blackness in his head, he'd returned to himself on Pirsig Avenue, walking with apparent intention toward the Shell station. In his wallet were twenty-three dollars, currently earmarked for Christmas presents for Becky, Clem, and the Reverend, but the world wouldn't end if he spent only a few dollars on each of them. He also had coins in the flat, clear-plastic coin purse that Judson had given him for his birthday. Reaching the gas station, he took a dime from the purse and put it in the frigid pay phone by the restrooms. Behind him, in the snow, a tow truck idled with its roof lights flashing, no driver at the wheel. The phone number, 241–7642, was a cinch to remember, the fourth digit being the sum of the first three, which also recurred in the decimal inverse of the fourth, and the concluding two-digit number being the product of the two foregoing integers.

The guy answered on the sixth ring. Perry got no further than pronouncing his first and last names when the guy interrupted him. "Sorry, man. Closed for the holidays."

"It's something of an emergency."

The guy hung up on him.

At this point, Perry might wisely have conceded defeat and gone back to First Reformed to content himself with whatever bottle Larry Cottrell had managed to poach, but Larry's success was by no means assured, perhaps more like the opposite, and Perry had money, the guy had drugs—what could be simpler?

He'd been to the guy's house only once, not to cop but simply to be introduced to him by a disagreeable upperclassman, Randy Toft, who'd been Keith Stratton's dealer. Subsequent guy–Perry meetings had occurred among potholes in the parking lot behind the old A&P, which was boarded up but not yet demolished or repurposed, and had invariably involved lengthy waiting for the guy's anonymous white Dodge to nose into view, Perry stewing about his lack of punctuality but never brave enough, when the guy finally arrived, to raise the issue. Both of them knew who had the power and who didn't.

The house was easy to find again, because it was on a dead-end street by the cheerful name of Felix and its street-side mailbox bore a weathered NIXON AGNEW bumper sticker, possibly humor, possibly a red herring for the township police, or possibly, who could say, a heartfelt statement. As Perry came up the street named Felix toward the rail embankment, he saw the white Dodge in the driveway, buried in whiter snow. Light showed around the edges of sagging shades in the house's living-room windows. The front walk was unshoveled, altogether untrodden.

Resolved: that embracing badness accords power.

Because what else, the first affirmative speaker asked rhetorically, *distinguishes the person who needs to score from the person who needs to sell? The buyer, after all, is as free to withhold money as the seller is free to withhold his goods. Doesn't it follow that the difference in power must relate to the gravity of the offense? A high-school dealer is nothing worse than a dispersing nozzle on a hose, dispensing good times to his peers and to himself, whereas the man who makes a career of being the hose has chosen to flout stern federal statutes. He's morally far worse than the young dealer, and this is why the latter silently endures the former's lack of punctuality. The deeper you go into badness, the more formidable you become.*

Empowered by the shittiness of what he'd done to Larry Cottrell, Perry opened the guy's chain-link gate and waded through the snow to the door, behind which he heard music. Before he could knock, there came a kind of strangled howl from a dog he'd forgotten about until this moment, followed by a cascade of savage basso barks, as the dog found the breath it had lacked for its initial howl. On Perry's only other visit to the house, the dog had stood in the open doorway, large and short-haired, slit-eyed with suspicion, its jaw muscles grotesquely bulging, while the guy met him and Randy Toft outside the gate and put his arms on their shoulders, demonstrating amity, which the dog had grudgingly conceded. Now the barking caused the porch light to come on. Through the door, he heard the guy shouting.

"What are you doing, man, it's out of control! The dog is out of control! You better just get the fuck away from here! It's nobody's business!"

The door had a fish-eye peephole through which Perry felt sure he was being observed. Even discounting for a distributor's understandable paranoia, the situation didn't seem promising, but he thought it was worth trying to signal his harmlessness before he gave up. He fished out his wallet, removed his twenty-dollar bill, and dangled it at the peephole.

"What are you doing to me?" the guy shouted, over the barking. "Wrong house, man! Go away!"

To make his intention clear, Perry mimed taking a toke.

"Yeah, I get it! Go away!"

Perry made a beseeching gesture, and the porch light went out. This seemed to be the end of it, but the door suddenly opened. The guy was wearing only blue jeans, neither buttoned nor zipped, and had his fingers under the collar of the outraged dog, which was scratching at the air with raised forelegs. "What are you doing?" he said. "What are you standing there for? You can't be standing there. What do you think I am?"

He dragged the lunging dog back from the door. Extremely warm air was flowing out.

"Shut the fucking door already!"

Taking this as an invitation, Perry entered and closed the door. The guy was straddling the dog as if it were a canine pony, hauling it farther back into the house while Perry waited on the entry rug, the snow on his rubbers immediately liquefying. The house temperature was a good ninety degrees. The music, which came from a wooden stereo console, was Vanilla Fudge. Perry remembered neither the console nor anything else about the living room, partly because the walls were bare and the furniture nondescript, but mainly because he'd been too agitated, too full of anxiety and shame, to pay attention. The guy, that afternoon, the previous April, had introduced himself as "Bill," but his smirking intonation had led Perry to assume that Bill wasn't his real name. He had a reddish mustache too large for his face, and one of his legs was an inch or two shorter than the other. According to Randy Toft, the leg had kept him out of Vietnam, but the guy didn't seem to have much going for him otherwise. Namelessness suited his station in life.

A door slammed, and the dog howled more forlornly. The guy returned with his jeans still open, the zipper skewed by the differential in his leg lengths. His chest was nearly as hairless as Perry's, but he was much furrier below the navel. He looked around the room, at everything but Perry, with jerky motions of his head, as though seeking the source of a threat. Seeming to find it in the stereo, he lifted the needle from the record with a shaking hand. There was a sickening sound of needle droppage, scratched vinyl. He raised the needle again and moved it safely aside. His head nodding rapidly, he stood and considered what he'd done.

"So," Perry said carefully, for it was obvious that the guy was seriously amped on something, "I apologize for disturbing you—"

"Can't do, can't do, can't do," the guy said, staring at the turntable. "Nothing in the house, man, they fucked me over, why are you here?"

"I was hoping you might set me up."

"You definitely shouldn't be here—I don't like it."

"I'm aware of that, and I apologize."

"You're not listening. I'm saying I don't like it. You know what I'm saying? I'm not talking about the thing, I'm talking about the thing *behind* the thing, the thing *behind* the thing *behind* the thing. You know what I'm saying?"

"You don't have to worry about me," Perry said. "If you could just set me up, I'd be happy to pay full retail price, and I'll be on my way again."

The guy continued to nod. He'd been edgy and distracted the last time Perry saw him, six weeks ago, behind the A&P, but nothing like this. It came to Perry that he was looking at a speed freak. He'd heard about them but had never seen one. He didn't want to leave, because the crater was waiting for him, right outside the house, but a self-preservative instinct was asserting itself. He turned toward the door.

"Whoa, whoa, whoa, where you going?" The guy bounded over and put his hand on the door. There were ugly sores on the inside of his arm, a very rank odor coming off him. "What are you doing to me? I can't deal with the dimensions of this."

"If you can't help me—"

"You're fucking me over. Every one of you is fucking me over. I don't have any weed, all right? Merry Christmas, Happy New Year—where's your money?"

"I think I'd better go."

"No no no no no no. You like the pills, you like the 'ludes, I've still got Ludydudies."

"Unfortunately, I'm not in the market."

The guy nodded vigorously. "That's okay, man, we're still good. Just don't go anywhere, right? Stay here, don't move, I've got something else for you."

In his bare feet, with his hitching gait, he lumbered into the rear of the house, where the dog howled again. His eagerness, the shift in power it represented, was somewhat alleviating Perry's fear, and he wondered what the something else might be.

The guy returned shaking a glass jar like a maraca, a Planters Peanuts jar with several hundred pills in it, a quantity that told Perry they couldn't be valuable. Amphetamines, presumably. Not a substance he'd ever had reason to try.

"Take a handful," the guy said, "there's no such thing as too many."

The lid of the jar hit the entry rug with a dull clank and rolled away. The open jar was offered with a trembling hand.

"What have we here?" Perry said.

"Take like four of 'em and chew 'em—you'll see, there's no such thing as too many, you'll forget about your weed. Chew 'em up and wait a minute, it'll hit you. The first four are on me, because, shit, man, it's Christmas, I'll give you another forty for your twenty dollars, you'll forget about your weed, this shit's like a bomb, take take take. If you like it, which you will, I can set you up with the big bomb. Take take take."

The dark crater had appeared in front of Perry; it was both behind him and in front of him, which could only mean that he was falling into it. He held out his hand.

Having performed the task that Frances had set him, having secured a place on the Crossroads spring trip to Arizona, Russ returned to his office in a state of exultation. On the desk where his lady had sat in her hunting cap, her legs parted, he saw an Arizona landscape unfolding. In his mind, he was already driving deep into this landscape. He was tempted to call her immediately and report his accomplishment, but all afternoon, all evening, she'd been running the show, provoking his ardor, withholding rewards, and this needed to stop. It was he who'd slain the dragon! He who'd had the guts to knock on Ambrose's door! Better, he thought, to leave her in suspense. Better to let her wonder until she finally had to ask. And then, casually, let drop that he'd forgiven Ambrose and was going to Arizona.

He locked his office and went down to the parking lot. In the snow on his Fury's rear window, some teenaged hand had inscribed the word OOPS. Hearing the music from the function hall, he recalled that he and Frances wouldn't be alone in Arizona; there would also be busloads of potentially hostile young people. It occurred to him that he was still wearing his sheepskin coat.

He had a guilty impulse to go back for his other one, but he was done with being gutless. He could wear whatever goddamned coat he pleased. He no longer cared if Marion knew he'd spent the day with Frances. In the future, yes, if he commenced an affair and it grew into something larger, a new life, a second chance, the repercussions would be daunting, but for now his only detectable crime was the little lie he'd told at breakfast. If Marion remarked on the sheepskin coat, made the mildest insinuation, he would blast her with the news that Perry was a pot smoker. Even better, he would tell her about Ambrose. For three years, she'd been maligning Rick, reinforcing Russ's grudge against him, and when she learned that Russ had forgiven him, unilaterally, without consulting her, she was bound to feel betrayed. No doubt she'd imagined she was being a loyal wife. But she, in a sense, had betrayed him first. If she hadn't been so supportive of his failings, he might have made peace long ago. Frances had restored him to his courage, his edge, by believing he was capable of more.

Not trusting his tires on the unplowed hill on Maple, and being in no hurry to lay eyes on Marion, he drove the long way home to Highland Street. Again and again today, for six hours, he'd glanced at the face of his female companion and liked what he saw. It was such a simple thing, a lightness that so many other men took for granted, to walk into a McDonald's with Frances and not be embarrassed to be seen with her, but to him the relief of it, the contrast with the daily disappointment of seeing Marion, had felt almost miraculous. Where Frances's hair, even flattened by the hunting cap, had flattered her, each of the hairstyles that Marion had tried in recent years had been wrong in a different way, too short or too long, each serving to accentuate the redness of her skin, the thickening of her neck, the pinching of her eyes by adipose and insomnia. He knew it was unfair of him to care. It was unfair that his eye should be more painfully affronted by his wife than by the many objectively worse-looking women in New Prospect. It was unfair to have enjoyed her body when she was young and then burdened her with children and a thousand duties, only to now feel miserable whenever he had to venture into public with her and her sorry hair, her unavailing makeup, her seemingly self-spiting choice of dress. He pitied her for the unfairness; he felt guilty. But he couldn't help blaming her, too, because her unattractiveness advertised unhappiness. Sometimes, when she looked especially dumpy at a church dinner, he sensed a satisfaction in being unsightly to him, a wish to make him suffer along with her for what he and their marriage had done to her, but most of the time her unhappiness excluded him. Hating her looks was yet another of the jobs she quietly and capably took on for him. Was it any wonder he was lonely in his marriage?

When he finally reached the parsonage, a large Oldsmobile, Dwight Haefle's, was backing out of the driveway. He tried to go around it, but Dwight stopped at an angle and lowered his window. Russ could only lower his.

"We missed you at the party," Dwight said.

"Yes, I'm sorry about that."

"Marion mentioned that you and Mrs. Cottrell had some trouble in the city?"

Dwight's expression was unreadable in the incidental light. What was he doing at the parsonage? How had Marion known that Russ was with Frances and not Kitty Reynolds?

"No, ah, no injuries," he said.

"I brought you some leftovers, in case you're hungry."

"That's very thoughtful of you."

"Don't thank me, thank Doris."

Dwight's window went up again, quickly and smoothly. The Oldsmobile, its power windows, its capabilities and newness, seemed emblematic of the senior minister's invulnerability to temptations of the flesh. The Lord was with him; but so was Doris. Russ was a wreck at the wheel of a wreck, but he had Mrs. Cottrell.

Only when he'd pulled into the driveway and cut the engine did he recall that Clem might be at home. He wanted to see Clem as little as he wanted to see Marion, but he knew he needed to speak to him again. He needed to revise what he'd said earlier—take the same risk he'd taken with Ambrose and be honest, confess to the complications of his heart and forgive, as he had with Ambrose, the hurtful things his son had said. Nothing less was demanded of the man he was becoming.

Inside, in the kitchen, he found Marion and Judson at the table with a carton of eggnog. Judson was leaning back with a nog-smeared glass in his hand, coaxing the last viscous drops into his mouth. A faint scent of bacon was in the air.

"Good Lord," Marion said. "There you are."

"Hi, Dad," Judson said.

"Hello, lad. You're up pretty late."

"Perry took me to the Haefles'. I got to watch a movie, and it was excellent, it was in New York City, and there was a gigantic department store, the one that does the Macy's parade—"

"Judson, honey," Marion said, "why don't you run upstairs and get your teeth brushed. I'll come up and tuck you in."

"I'd like to hear more about that movie," Russ said heartily.

Without seeming to hear him, Judson got up and left the kitchen. Only for Marion did his children have ears. He pried off the work shoes that Ambrose had earlier unlaced.

"I'm sorry I missed the party."

"I'm sure you are," she said. "It was a laugh a minute."

From the chill in her voice, without looking at her, he gathered that his lie at breakfast hadn't gone unnoticed. He was tempted to explain it away—to volunteer that Mrs. Cottrell had unexpectedly taken Kitty's place. But this would have been the old Russ.

"Is Clem here?"

"No," she said.

"He's—have you seen him?"

"I sent him back to Champaign."

Now he looked at her. Her face was as red as ever, her hair no better, but there was something steely in her eyes.

"One of us needed to do something," she said. "I gather you did less than nothing."

"He's going back to Champaign? Now?"

"There's a midnight bus and apparently a girl he's involved with. I don't know if he'll change his mind, but it's a start."

Russ looked away from her. "That's unfortunate. I was hoping to talk to him again."

"If only you hadn't been detained . . ."

"I already apologized for being late. I didn't realize—"

"That he was having a major crisis?"

"I tried to reason with him."

"And how did that go?"

"I—not well."

She laughed at him. Laughed and stood up and went to the coat hooks by the door, removed something from a coat pocket, and shook it. Though small, the white object she extracted with her lips was so alien, had such a powerful charge, that it was like a third presence in the room. The bacony smell, he realized, was coming from his wife.

"What in God's name are you doing?"

"Smoking," she said.

"Not in my house."

"This isn't your house, Russ. That's a silly idea you need to let go of. The house is the church's, and I'm the one who's always in it. In what sense is it yours?"

The question took him aback. "It is part of my compensation as a minister."

"Oh dear." She laughed again. "You want to *argue* with me? I wouldn't recommend it."

He saw that she was angry, perhaps inordinately so, about his little lie. She lit a burner on the stove and leaned over it, holding her hair away from the flame.

"Put that out," he said. "I don't know what you think you're doing, but put that out."

With mirth in her eyes, she blew smoke in his direction.

"Marion. What is wrong with you?"

"Nothing!"

"If you're angry with me about missing the party—"

"Truth be told, I was hardly even thinking of you."

"I had an accident in the city. I ended up going with Mrs. Cottrell, by the way. Kitty couldn't, ah. Kitty couldn't make it. She, ah . . ."

He could feel himself being dragged down, by the inertia of marriage, into a well-established pattern of evasion. As long as he stayed with Marion, he would never change.

"You and I have a lot to discuss," he said threateningly. "It's not just Clem. There's also a problem with Perry you need to know about. And— I went to see Ambrose. I thought it was—"

"Russ, really. I'm just having a cigarette."

The sight of her smoking, in the middle of the kitchen, was uncanny. If she'd stripped out of her clothes and shaken her breasts at him, it wouldn't have been any stranger. There was something of sex in the gasp of her drag on the cigarette.

"Although I do wonder," she said, exhaling, "how you think it would work. Even at the level of fantasy, how do you picture it working?"

"How what would work?"

"You'd still have four kids to support. You'd still be making seven thousand dollars a year. Is the idea that you'd go and live on her charity? Forgive me for wondering how well you've thought it through."

"I have no idea what you're talking about."

Again Marion laughed. "I hope she's good at writing sermons," she said. "I hope she likes cooking your meals and washing your underwear. I hope she's ready to have the relationship with your kids that you're too busy saving the world for. I hope she's up for dealing with your insecurity every night of the week. And you know what else? I hope she keeps a close eye on you."

For the second time in two hours, he was being taunted. Although, in strict point of morality, he deserved it, he had a physical urge, stronger even than he'd had with Clem, to strike his wife. He felt like batting the cigarette from her hand, slapping her in the face, knocking the smile off it, so angering was the contrast between his family's disrespect and Frances's ingratiations.

"I didn't realize," he said stiffly, "that you resented helping me with my sermons."

"I don't, Russ. The help is freely given."

"In the future, I will write them all myself."

She took another puff on the cigarette. "Whatever you like, dear."

"As for the rest of it," he said, "I won't dignify it with an answer. I've had a very long day, and I'm going to bed. I would only thank you not to smoke in a house where the rest of us need to sleep."

In response, she made an O with her lips and blew a smoke ring. Her mouth stayed open.

"God damn it, Marion."

"Yes, dear?"

"I don't know what you're trying to prove—"

"I'm sure you don't. You have some fine qualities, but imagination was never one of them."

The insult was naked and it shocked him. Time and again, in the early years of their marriage, he'd sensed that she was angry about something small or large he'd done or failed to do. Each time, he'd expected an explosion of the sort he knew occurred in other marriages, and each time her anger had faded into soft-spoken reproach, at worst a sulking that she maintained for a day or two and then let go of, until finally he'd understood that they weren't a couple who had fights. He remembered feeling proud of this. Now it seemed like another instance of her deadness to him as a wife.

"I shouldn't have to imagine," he said. "If something is bothering you, the responsible thing is to tell me what it is, instead of making insinuations."

"Be careful what you ask for."

"Do you think I can't handle it? There's nothing I can't handle."

"Tall words."

"I mean it. If you have something to say to me, say it."

"All right." She brought the cigarette to her lips, her eyes crossing to focus on the coal. "It annoys me that you want to fuck her."

The kitchen seemed to spin beneath his feet. He'd never heard that word from her.

"It's really quite annoying, and if you think it's because I'm jealous, that's even more annoying. I mean, really—me? Jealous of that thing? Who do you think I am? Who do you think you married? I've seen the face of God."

Russ stared at her. A schizophrenic parishioner had once said the same thing to him.

"You've got your liberal religion," she said, "you've got your second-floor office, you've got your ladies on Tuesdays, but you have no idea what it means to know God. No idea what true belief is like. You think you're God's gift, you think you deserve better than what you've got, and, well, yes, I find that more than a little annoying. I don't know if you've noticed, but your children are amazing—at least one of them is a flat-out genius.

Where do you think that came from? Where do you think the brilliance in this family came from? Do you think it came from *you*? Ah—fuck!"

She shook her hand and dropped the cigarette, which had burned her. She picked it up and took it to the sink. She appeared to be having some kind of nervous breakdown, and it ought to have worried him, ought to have repelled him, but it didn't. He remembered an intensity so deeply buried in the past it might have been a dream, the intensity she'd possessed at twenty-five, the intensity with which he'd wanted her. And she was still his wife. Still lawfully his. Provoked by her abandon, he approached her from behind and put his hands on her breasts. Beneath the wool of her dress and the folds of middle-aged flesh was the off-kilter girl who'd maddened him in Arizona. The smoke in her hair and something equally foreign, a smell of liquor, were further provocations. It was exciting to touch the breasts of a drunk stranger.

He tried to turn her around, but she ducked under his elbow and broke free. When he took a step toward her, she skittered away.

"Don't you dare."

"Marion—"

"You think I'm sloppy seconds?"

She never rejected him. In matters of the bedroom, he was the rejecter.

"Fine," he said angrily. "I was simply trying to—"

"You and she deserve each other. Go ahead and see if I care. You have my permission."

The contempt in her voice robbed him of any joy he might have taken in her permission. She really was smarter than he was. As crazy as she was acting, she was right about that, and it didn't matter if she was squat and red-faced, it didn't matter if he slew dragons. As long as they stayed married—even if they didn't—she would always have that on him.

"You seem to think it's just me," he said, shaking, "but it's not just me. You're as much to blame as I am. You've got it set up so I'm the only one who needs support. You've got your whole litany—support, support, support. No joy, no nothing, just support. Is it any wonder I'm sick of it?"

"You can't be half as sick of it as I am."

"But you're the one who wanted this."

"This?"

"You wanted the kids. You wanted this life."

"You didn't?"

"If it had been up to me, we'd be devoted to service. You wouldn't be a housewife, and I damn sure wouldn't be giving sermons to bankers and the bridge club."

"You're saying that *I'm* the one who dragged you down? That *you're* the one who sacrificed? That you're doing *me* a favor with this marriage?"

"At this point? Yes. That is what I think. If you want to know why, take a look at yourself in the goddamned mirror."

It was the cruelest thing he'd ever said.

"That hurts me," she said quietly, "but not as much as you wish it did."

"I—apologize."

"You don't have the faintest idea who you married."

"Since I'm so stupid, maybe you should go ahead and tell me."

"No. You'll just have to wait and see."

"What does that mean?"

She came over to him, stood on her toes, and tilted her face toward his. For a moment, he thought she might kiss him after all. But she merely blew a puff of air at him. It stank of tar and alcohol.

"Wait and see."

"Do not crowd the gate area. If you insist on standing up, I'm going to need to see an orderly line. There is no reason to crowd the gate. Everyone holding a ticket will get a seat. If a second bus is needed, there will be a second bus. That bus will be making all the same stops. Due to inclement weather, we have system-wide delays, but there is equipment on the way. All you do by jostling is make yourself unhappy. The bus will not be boarding as long as I see jostling. No, ma'am, we do not have an estimated departure time as of yet. As soon as the equipment arrives and I see an orderly line, the boarding process will commence . . ."

On and on the voice went. It belonged to a heavy, dark-skinned woman whose exhaustion could not have exceeded Clem's. On the lap of the very young mother seated next to him, a baby was sleeping with its arms outflung, its head dangling off the side of her thigh. Sixty or seventy people were at the gate, most of them Black, all traveling south to St. Louis, to Cairo, to Jackson, to New Orleans, in the cruel first hour of Christmas Eve. The station was reasonably warm, but Clem was still chilled in his core. He sat hugging himself tightly, his ticket clenched in his fist. A kiosk in the station was selling coffee, and he objectively observed the thing he rawly was, wondering if the thing might stand up and go to the kiosk. His exhaustion made his condition existential, beyond motive, like Meursault's in *The Stranger*.

If, when he'd called the hippie house from the parsonage, the line hadn't been busy, and if his mother, before sending him away with his duffel bag, hadn't gone upstairs and returned with ten twenty-dollar bills and pressed them on him, and if he hadn't then had time, on the inbound commuter train, to revisit the question of freedom, he might have done his mother's bidding. Coming home to New Prospect and feeling loved by his father, hated by his favorite person in the world, and confused by his mother, he'd lost his bearings. His family had pulled him back into the conditioned lineaments of the self he'd taken action to escape. But the inbound train was slowed by heavy snow. By the time it dragged into Union Station, he'd recognized that he wasn't obliged to step off the bus in Urbana; that he wasn't a needle following the grooves of a familiar record; that radical freedom was still available. He'd had a month of mornings to wake up and reconsider his decision to quit school. Shouldn't a decision so long and well considered outweigh a few hours with his family, on a night when he was wrecked by lack of sleep? He'd already seen his way clear of Sharon. If he went back to her now, his earlier reasoning would still be valid. He didn't have the strength to meet the challenge of a woman, he wasn't yet man enough. All that would come of going back to her was the pain of leaving her again. And so, when he reached the Trailways station, he'd bought a ticket for New Orleans. He'd never been to New Orleans. He had two hundred dollars, and he was glad to think of being alone.

EASTER

Russ awoke in a strange house. Wind was banging on the windows, repulverizing the snow on the branches outside them, and Marion's side of their bed had not been slept in. Frightened that she hadn't softened toward him, frightened by the permission she'd given him, frightened also by the problem of Perry's drug use, he could feel how very reliant he'd become on her support. Turning instead to God, he prayed in bed until he was able to put on a robe and venture into the hallway. Behind closed doors, his three younger children were still asleep. The door and the curtains of Clem's room were open wide, his absence stark in the morning light. Downstairs, in the kitchen, a pot of coffee was on the stove. He took a mug of it up to his office, and there he found Marion. She was kneeling amid gifts and ribbons and didn't even glance at him. The sight of her, in the same dress she'd worn the night before, recalled the shock of desiring her, the shame of being rejected. From the doorway, without preamble, he told her that Perry had sold or given marijuana to Larry Cottrell.

"It's interesting," she said, "that that's the first thing you have to say to me today."

"I meant to bring it up last night. We need to deal with this immediately."

"I've already dealt with it. He told me he'd sold pot."

"He what? When?"

She calmly ran scissors through a sheet of wrapping paper. Whatever Russ might do or say, she seemed to be a step ahead of him.

"Last night," she said. "He's been struggling, and I think the fact that he was open with me—he's doing better now. As far as I'm concerned, it's ancient history."

"He broke the law. He needs to understand that there are consequences."

"You want to punish him."

"Yes."

"I think that's a mistake."

"I don't care what you think. We will present a united front."

"A united front? Is that a joke?"

Her coolness was worse than coldness. He had an urge to break into it, grab hold of her, impose his will. Their fight the night before had tapped into an unguessed reservoir of rage.

She folded the wrapping paper around a shirt box. "Was there anything else, dear?"

Hatred silenced him. Returning to the second floor, he heard Perry's and Judson's voices behind their door. It was only seven thirty, strangely early for Perry to be awake. Russ was disturbed to think that his nine-year-old son, with whom he had semiformal but cordial relations, as if they were longtime next-door neighbors, had been sharing a room with a trafficker in drugs. It didn't reflect well on the nine-year-old's father. But when, an hour later, while channeling his rage into shoveling the driveway, he saw Perry and Judson heading out with their sleds, Perry was in such boyishly eager spirits that Russ didn't have the heart to confront him. It was Christmas Eve, after all.

That night, at dinner—by tradition, spaghetti and meatballs—Perry was in charming form, and his manner with Becky had changed. Gone was his condescension, gone her defensiveness. Marion wouldn't look at Russ, and all she ate was salad and a few strands of spaghetti. When she teased Becky about Tanner Evans, it fell to Judson to explain to Russ that Becky had a *boyfriend*, and Russ didn't know which was more incriminating, that he was the last to learn this news or that he didn't much care. He'd been living in a world consisting of Frances, God, Rick Ambrose, and the negative blot of Marion. Of his children, the only one he felt at all connected to was Clem, and it grieved him that Clem was with his girlfriend for the holiday; it deprived him of a chance to atone for embarrassing him. For relief from his isolation, he let his thoughts turn to Frances. He imagined smoking marijuana with her, imagined its lowering of their inhibitions. Then he wondered what it said about God's intentions that the marijuana in question had passed through Perry's hands.

Rising abruptly from the table, he said he'd forgotten an important call to a parishioner. As he left the room, Marion's amused voice followed him. "Tell her I said Merry Christmas."

The third floor smelled of her disturbance. On the sill of the storage-room window, an ashtray brimmed with cigarette ends, and this was fine with him. It somehow ratified the permission she'd given him. Using the permission, he picked up the phone in his office.

Frances, answering, brushed aside his apology for calling on a holiday—he was her pastor! He'd intended to let her wonder if he'd made peace with Ambrose and was going to Arizona, but he couldn't help telling her immediately.

"Hooray, hooray," she said. "I knew I was right."

"You were right about Perry, too. He did sell marijuana."

"Of course I was right. Aren't I always?"

"Well, so, I could use your advice there. Are you, ah, private?"

"Sort of. My folks are here for dinner."

"Oh, I'm sorry to interrupt."

"I was just clearing the table. Tell me how I can help."

From two floors below came a burst of family laughter in which Perry's arpeggio of hilarity was uppermost. Russ wondered if, a year from now, he wouldn't have to call Frances; if he might be sitting down to dinner with her and her folks.

"Well, apparently," he said, "Perry's cleaned up his act. At this point, I could just let it drop, but I feel some sort of punishment is in order."

"You're asking the wrong gal. You may remember what's in my sock drawer."

"I do. And the fact—well, the experiment we talked about. It complicates things for me. I can't punish Perry and then—you know. It would be hypocritical."

"That's an easy one. Just don't do the second thing."

"But I want to. I want to do it with you."

"Okay, wow. I should probably get off the phone."

"Just quickly tell me if you're still interested in doing this."

"Definitely getting off the phone."

"Frances—"

"I'm not saying no. I'm saying I need to think about it."

"You were the one who suggested it!"

"Mm, not quite. The just-you-and-me part was your idea."

He couldn't have asked for a clearer indication that his desires were known to her. To be engaged in sexual implication, in his church-provided house, on a family holiday, was shameful and thrilling.

"Anyway," she said, "Merry Christmas. I'll see you in church on Sunday."

"You're not coming to the midnight service?"

"No. But your eagerness is noted, Reverend Hildebrandt."

In the manner of the early Christians, who'd believed that the Messiah who'd walked the earth within living memory would soon return—that the Day of Judgment was just around the corner—Russ imagined that his situation with Frances, already so fraught with implication, so poised to blossom into rapture, would resolve itself in a matter of days. While he awaited her judgment, which seemed imminent, he postponed a confrontation with his son, and by the time he understood how long he might have to wait, Perry's transgressions had become, as Marion had said, ancient history. Perry really did seem to be doing better. No longer an evasive, late-sleeping boy, he seemed slimmer and perhaps a little taller, and he was always in good spirits. Because Marion had taken to sleeping on the third floor and keeping odd hours, it sometimes happened that Perry, who now rose even earlier than Russ, made breakfast for him and Judson.

Beginning with old Mrs. O'Dwyer, who'd succumbed to pneumonia, the new year brought a string of funerals for which Russ did all the counseling and officiating, while the Haefles vacationed in Florida. He still had the extra duties Dwight had given him when he left Crossroads, and now that he'd been reinstated in the group he felt obliged to attend Sunday-night meetings. To show Ambrose the sincerity of his repentance, while avoiding the hazard of counseling troubled teenagers, he volunteered to handle all the logistics for the Arizona trip—hiring the buses, reviewing the church's liability policy, procuring project supplies, coordinating with the Navajos.

Mired in work, he watched Marion race ahead of him. She was visibly losing weight, abetted by smoking and a regimen of punishing walks. He was included in the dinners she continued to put on the table, but she now sorted through the laundry hamper and set aside his clothes while she washed everyone else's. He attended church functions without her, poured hours he couldn't spare into sermons that refused to come into focus without her help, while she went out to the library, to lectures at the Ethical Culture Society, and to the decaying clapboard theater that was home to the New Prospect Players. Her new independence smacked of women's liberation, which he approved of at the societal level, and he might have approved of it in his wife if he'd been getting anywhere with Frances.

But the day of judgment kept receding. On the Tuesday circle's first outing to the inner city after Christmas, Frances attached herself so tightly to Kitty Reynolds that he couldn't get a single private word with her. When he called her house, a few days later, in the guise of routine pastoral concern, she said she was late to class and would stop by his office later in the week. He waited, in vain, for eight days. Feeling unfairly at her mercy, casting about for leverage, he was inspired to invite an unmarried seminarian, Carolyn Polley, to come along on the next Tuesday outing. Carolyn was a friend of Ambrose and an adviser in Crossroads, and Russ hoped that by insisting that she ride with him, by making a fuss of introducing her to Theo Crenshaw, and by keeping her at his side throughout the day, he might provoke some jealousy in Frances. Instead he provoked a statement from Carolyn, in the awkwardly explicit style of Crossroads, that she had a boyfriend in Minneapolis. Frances herself was so chummy with Kitty Reynolds, so intimately murmuring, that Russ, in his jealousy, wondered if her hunger for new experiences might extend as far as lesbianism. Not once did she look at him directly. It was as if none of the tensy-tension between them, none of the innuendo on Christmas Eve, had ever happened.

When the Tuesday circle returned to First Reformed, in the last light of day, he caught up with her before she could escape in her car. He chided her, gently, for not having stopped by his office. "I hope you're not," he said, "avoiding me for some reason?"

She edged away from him. She was wearing a puffy parka and a stocking cap, not her fetching hunter's ensemble. "Actually I am, a little bit."

"Will you—tell me why?"

"It's terrible. You're going to hate me."

The twilight in January, the way it lingered in the western sky, partook of early spring, but the air was still bitterly dry and tasted of road salt.

"I was feeling bad," she said, "that I hadn't listened to your records. I didn't want to talk to you until I did, and so finally, last week, I had them all spread out in the living room, and then the phone rang, and I had to make dinner, and I forgot about them. When I went to turn a light on, I didn't see them on the floor."

She sounded vaguely annoyed, as if it were the records' fault.

"I already talked to the record store," she said. "They're going to try to find replacements. I only stepped on two of them, but apparently one of them is very hard to find."

Russ's heart felt stepped on.

"You don't have to replace them," he managed to say. "They're just worldly things."

"No, I'm absolutely going to."

"As you wish."

"See? You do hate me."

"No, I—just think I might have misread something. I thought that you and I were going to—I thought I could help you on your journey."

"I know. I was supposed to give you an answer about that."

"It's all right. Perry's doing much better—I'm not going to punish him."

"But I stepped on your records. The least I can do is give you an answer."

"As you wish."

"Except here's another confession. I already sort of did the experiment, by myself. I can't say it was life-altering. It was more like an hour-long head cold."

Russ turned away, to hide his disappointment.

"I want to try again, though," she said, touching his arm. "I've—there's been a lot going on with me. But let's you and me find a time. Okay?"

"It sounds like you're doing fine without me."

"No, let's do it. Just the two of us. Unless you want to ask Kitty."

"I don't want to ask Kitty."

"This'll be fun," Frances said.

Her enthusiasm sounded effortful, and when he called her that night, calendar in hand, their search for a mutually workable date had a flavor of dreary obligation. The experiment could only be done on a weekday, while her kids were at school, and his regular church duties fell precisely on the days that Frances had open. With some foreboding, he agreed to meet her on Ash Wednesday.

There was a foretaste of ash in his days of waiting for their date. The hope that Clem would reconsider his decision to quit school had already been dashed on Christmas Day, when he called to report that he hadn't gone to his girlfriend in Urbana. He was alone in New Orleans—would rather spend Christmas in a squalid hotel room than with his family. Russ knew that the fault was his, and he wanted to write to Clem, to apologize and try to set things right, but he didn't have a mailing address. In January, Clem called home periodically to ask Marion if a letter from the draft board had arrived. In February came the news that he'd spoken to the board and learned that it didn't intend to call him up. The news ought to have been a pure relief for Russ, as it was for Marion, but he was hurt that he had to hear the news from Becky, hurt that Clem still hadn't given them his address, hurt that he had no plans to come home. According to Becky, he was working at a Kentucky Fried Chicken.

One of the few bright spots in Russ's life—that Becky, against all expectations, had found her way to Christian faith and shared her inheritance with her brothers—was dimmed when she stopped attending services at First Reformed. She'd already spurned his invitation to join his confirmation class, and it now transpired that she and Tanner Evans were exploring other churches in New Prospect. When Russ asked why, she said she was looking for something more inspiring than Dwight Haefle's sermons. "Does he even *believe* in God?" she said. "It's like listening to Rod McKuen." Russ, who had his own doubts about Dwight's faith, replied that he, Russ, did believe in God. "Then maybe," Becky said, "you should talk more about your relationship with Him and less about the evening news." Her point was debatable, but he sensed that theology was just a pretext anyway; that her rejection of him was deeper and more personal; that Clem had done a thorough job of turning her against him. And perhaps rightly so. The bathroom sink into which he now regularly spent his seed, picturing Frances Cottrell and blocking from his mind all thought of God, was three steps from his daughter's bedroom door.

Even Arizona had become a clouded prospect. Enough kids had signed up for the spring trip to fill three buses, and his plan was to leave two of them at the base of the Black Mesa while he led a third group up to the school at Kitsillie. The Black Mesa was in the heart of Diné Bikéyah. Nowhere more than up in its thin air, in the mind- and landscape-bending midday sun, beneath night skies pressing down with the weight of a million stars, had he felt more connected to the Navajo spirit world. Kitsillie's primitive conditions would also be an opportunity to show Frances how capable he was of handling them, and they would test her appetite for new experiences. If, unlike Marion, she turned out to have a taste for roughing it, the possibilities for further joint adventures would be limitless. But when, after much trying, he reached Keith Durochie on the telephone, Keith bluntly told him, "Don't go there."

"To Kitsillie?"

"Don't go there. The energy is bad. You won't be welcome."

"That's nothing new," Russ said lightly. "I wasn't so welcome in the forties, either. You remember how you wouldn't even shake my hand?"

He expected Keith to laugh at the memory, as he had in the past, but Keith didn't.

"You'll be safer in Many Farms," he said. "We have plenty of work here. The people on the mesa are unhappy with the *bilagáana*."

"Well, and I know a thing or two about building bridges. Why don't we see how things look when I get there."

Keith, after a silence, said, "You and I are old, Russ. Things aren't the same."

"I'm not so old, and neither are you."

"No, I'm old. I saw my death the other day. It was on the ridge behind my house—not far."

"I don't know about that," Russ said, "but I'm happy to think I'll be seeing you again."

On the morning of Ash Wednesday, he left his car in the First Reformed parking lot, so as not to let it be seen too suspiciously long at Frances's, and walked uphill on sidewalks wet with the melting of dismal, clumpy snowflakes. The hour, nine o'clock, felt more suitable for a doctor's appointment. Frances's house was freshly painted and rather stately, a reminder of how much money she'd received from General Dynamics, and he rang her doorbell with a foreboding which he could only pray that marijuana would dispel.

"So much for my idea," she said, leading him into her kitchen, "that you wouldn't show up."

"Do you not want me here?"

"I just hope we're not making a big mistake."

She was wearing a wide-necked brown sweaterdress and thick gray socks. Seeing her as she was at home, not in one of her smart Sunday outfits, not in her Tuesday-circle tomboy attire, he had an unsettling strong hit of her *reality*—her independence as a woman, her thinking of thoughts and making of choices wholly unrelated to him. To glimpse how it must feel to be her, inhabiting her own life, round the clock, was exciting but also daunting. On the counter by the kitchen stove, she'd already set out an ashtray and a crudely fashioned marijuana cigarette.

"Shall we get right to it," she said, "or do we need to discuss it to death first?"

"No. Just assure me you're really okay with doing this."

"I've already done it—sort of. I don't think I had enough."

She reached and turned on the stove fan, and he wondered if there was underwear beneath her sweaterdress. The dress had slipped down her shoulder without exposing a bra strap. The skin of her upper back, which he'd never seen before, was smooth and lightly freckled. It, too, was real, and it gave him a pang of nostalgia for the safety of his fantasies. He'd been managing all right with fantasies; he could probably keep managing indefinitely. And yet to shy from the reality of Frances would confirm Marion's belittling assessment of him. She'd given him permission because she didn't believe he was man enough to use it.

"Let's see what happens," he said.

They hunched forward, side by side, under the exhaust fan. The marijuana smoke was scalding, and he might have stopped at one lungful if Frances hadn't insisted that one wasn't enough. She took sip after sip of smoke, holding the little cigarette like a dart, and he followed her lead. They didn't stop until the remainder was too small to be handed back and forth. She went to the sink, dropped the "roach" in the garbage disposal, and opened a window. The snowflakes outside struck Russ as peculiar, artificial, as though strewn by someone standing on the roof. Frances stretched her arms above her head, raising the hem of her dress and with it, again, the question of underwear.

"Wow," she said, splaying her raised hands. "This is *much* better. I wonder if you have to do it twice before you get the full effect."

Though this was Russ's first time, he was definitely getting an effect. The realization had hit him, like an anvil, that February was flu season—one of her kids could easily come home sick and discover him with their mother. The possibility seemed far from minimal, indeed quite strong, and he was appalled that he hadn't considered it until now. The hour also suddenly felt not at all like morning. It felt closer to the hour when school let out—he could almost hear the final bell, the tumult of liberated kids, Frances's among them. In the glare of the kitchen lights, he further realized, he was highly visible to her next-door neighbors. Looking around for a switch, he noticed that she'd left the room.

From the front of the house, at a sickeningly high volume, easily loud enough to attract the attention of neighbors, if not the police, came the sound of Robert Johnson singing "Cross Road Blues." Russ discovered that he'd turned out most of the kitchen lights, but the one overhead was still burning. In the midst of searching for the switch, he understood that he could simply leave the kitchen.

The living room was blessedly dusky. Frances had thrown herself onto a sofa and bunched up her dress in the process. Russ glimpsed a sliver of white panty and searingly wished he hadn't. His interest in the question of underwear was obscene. The loudness of Robert Johnson was an emergency.

"What do you think?" she called to him happily. "Are you feeling anything?"

"I'm thinking," he said, but this wasn't true, because, whatever he'd been thinking, he'd now forgotten it. Then, surprisingly, he remembered. "I'm thinking we should turn the music down."

Even as he said it, he knew it was hideously square. He braced himself for shaming.

"You have to tell me everything you're feeling," she said. "That was the agreement. Actually, there was no agreement, but what's the point of an experiment if we don't compare results?"

He went to the stereo console and turned down the volume—too far. He therefore raised it again—too far. He lowered it again—too far.

"Come sit with me," Frances called from the sofa. "I'm so aware of my skin—you know what I mean? It's like the Beatles, I want to hold your hand. I'm just so—it's like I'm here but my thoughts are in every corner of the room. Like I'm blowing up a gigantic balloon and the air is my thoughts. You know what I mean?"

I went down to the cross road, babe, I looked both east and west
Lord, I didn't have no sweet woman, babe, in my distress

Standing at the console, Russ was plunged into the hissing, low-fidelity world from which Robert Johnson was singing. He'd never felt more pierced by the beauty of the blues, the painful sublimity of Johnson's voice, but also never more damned by it. Wherever Johnson was singing from, Russ could never hope to get there. He was an outsider, a latter-day parasite—a fraud. It came to him that *all* white people were frauds, a race of parasitic wraith-people, and none more so than he. To have loaned Frances his records, imagining that some particle of authenticity might adhere to him and redeem him, was the pinnacle of fraudulence.

"Oh Reverend Hildebrandt," she called in a singsong voice. "A penny for your thoughts."

The record label rotating below him was not Vocalion. The record was an LP, not a 78. Dimly, through his confusion, came the fear that she'd replaced his valuable antique with a cheap modern compilation, but instead of being angered he experienced a kind of menace. The revolving vinyl was like a vortex, a dark drain down which he was being sucked

toward darker death. There had to be a special place in hell for him. If
indeed hell, its sulfurous fires, existed. If hell weren't exactly where he
was standing, in his detestable fraudulence, right this minute. He felt his
back go warm with a body's proximity.

"You seem," Frances said from close behind him, "more interested in
the music than in me."

"I'm sorry."

"Don't be. You can feel anything you want. I just want to hear about it."

"I'm sorry," he repeated, lacerated by her reproach, convinced of its
justice.

"But maybe we don't need the music."

The haste with which he took her suggestion and raised the tone
arm screamed of a too-eager accession to another person's wishes, a lack
of authentic wishes of his own. As the record slowed to a halt, Frances
put her arms around him from behind. She rested her head between his
shoulder blades.

"This is okay, right?" she said. "A friendly hug?"

Her warmth entered his body and funneled straight into his loins.

"It's so much better this time. I wonder if it's a social thing, like you need
to be with someone else to get the full experience. What do you think?"

He thought his head might burst with terror. He heard himself issue
a chuckle, prefatory to some kind of speech act. The chuckle was reek-
ingly phony, a creaking contraption of sinew and muscle, involuntarily
activated by a craven wish to please and to fit in—to pass as an authentic
person. It seemed to him that every word he'd ever uttered had been
loathsome, slimy with self-interested calculation, his fatuousness audible
to everyone and universally deplored. All his life, people had concealed
their true opinion of him—only Clem had been honest. Into his chest,
like a giant air bubble, unreleasable through lungs or stomach, came the
agony of having hurt his son. He leaned forward and opened his mouth,
trying somehow to release the bubble. He perceived his resemblance to
the parishioners whose final moment he'd witnessed, his jaw lowered
with agonal breathing, his facial skin stretched over an emerging death's-
head. It wasn't clear how he could survive another moment of the agony.

When Frances withdrew from him, he felt no relief, only reproach. She was having a joyful experience and he an abominable one. This fact, the humiliation of it, seemed to brighten the living room in a disagreeable way.

"There's something weird about the light," she said. "It seems different from one moment to the next—I wonder if it's always doing that. Maybe the pot makes my eyes more sensitive?"

Her friendly tone compounded his torture. That she wasn't recoiling from his ugliness and failure seemed impossibly merciful. He alone, of all the people in the world, was phony, he alone a wraith-person.

"It does seem brighter," he found himself saying, only to be stricken by the revolting wetness of his mouth's creation of the words.

"Are you all right?" Frances said. "I read that pot makes some people paranoid."

Before he could stop himself, he admitted that he was feeling paranoid. Instantly ashamed, he added, with croaking falsity, "Just a little—not a lot."

"Come sit with me—I'll hold your hand. Maybe you just need to feel safe."

Going anywhere near her was unthinkable. His dread of discovery by her children had struck him with renewed force, and the kitchen! Even with the fan on, the kitchen surely stank of marijuana. It was imperative to get away before he was discovered. In his mind, he formed the words *I'm sorry*, trying to gauge what more they might reveal about his native excrescence. Whether he actually uttered them, as he left the room and snatched his coat from the newel post, he never knew.

Walking back to the church, unable to find a facial expression that didn't broadcast culpability, he might have been a spider crawling across a white wall. It was a miracle that no one stared at him. When he reached his car, he locked himself inside it and lay down on the front seat, out of sight. Eventually he noticed that he was no longer psychotic, but the emotional truth of his paranoia persisted. When he returned to the parsonage, intending to hide in his office and pray, he was moved to stop first in the storage room and empty Marion's ashtray into his hands. He smeared the ashes into his face, opened his mouth to them.

The season of Lent had begun, and it wasn't all bad. Shame and self-abasement were still his portals to God's mercy. The old paradox—that weakness, honestly owned, made a man stronger in his faith—still obtained. Accepting his failure with Frances, he asked Kitty Reynolds to lead the next Tuesday circle without him. At home, he humbled himself with Marion, told her she looked nice, took an interest. When she said, with cool amusement, "I gather you've had a setback with your little friend," he turned the other cheek. He said, "Go ahead and mock me. I deserve it." The days were getting longer, and when he sat in his twilit study and labored to express a sermon-worthy thought, he could hear her clearing her throat in the adjacent room, applying her language skills to the at-home proofreading work she was doing to pay for new clothes, a better hairdresser. Now that she was looking trimmer, more like the intense young woman he'd fallen for, he wondered if there might be hope for their marriage after all—if they might yet find their way to a new arrangement.

But she still slept on the third floor and made him do his own laundry, and despite his renewed engagement with God he couldn't rid his mind of Frances. As he wore out the shame of his behavior in her living room, through incessant revisiting of it, he remembered more clearly her own behavior: that she'd asked him, more than once, to hold her hand; that she'd put her arms around him from behind, in a supposedly friendly hug (weren't friendly hugs *frontal?*); and that, moreover, she'd dressed for their date in a garment begging to be raised above her hips. With terrible hindsight, he saw that she'd offered him the very chance he'd dreamed of. And even if he'd had her only once, even if he was only a passing itch she'd felt like scratching, while high on drugs, it would have meant the world to him.

He was mourning his lost chance when God's providence intervened. Although he sensed its awkwardness for Becky and Perry, he'd attended every Crossroads meeting in the new year. He was technically an adviser, but he'd embraced his inferiority to Rick Ambrose and comported himself like a newcomer, there to participate in exercises and explore his emotions, not to enable young people's growth in Christ. On the last Sunday night in February, after Ambrose had parted the crowd in the function hall, as if it were the Red Sea, and instructed one half of it to write their names on slips of paper from which the other half would draw partners,

Russ unfolded the slip he'd drawn and saw whom God had given him. The name on the slip was *Larry Cottrell.*

"The instruction here is simple," Ambrose told the group. "Each of us tells our partner a thing that's really troubling us—at school, at home, in a relationship. The idea is to be honest, and for our partner to think honestly about how to be helpful. Remember that sometimes the most helpful thing is just to be present and listen without judging."

Russ had thus far avoided Larry Cottrell, to the point of never looking at him, and Larry seemed neither pleased nor displeased to be his partner—it was just another exercise. As the other dyads dispersed around the church, Russ led him upstairs to his office and asked what was troubling him.

Larry touched his nostrils. "So you know," he said, "my dad was killed two years ago. We had a picture of him, in his air-force uniform, it was in our upstairs hallway, and then last week it wasn't there anymore. I asked my mom why she took it down, and she told me . . . She told me she was tired of looking at it."

The pimpled half-maturity of Larry's face, the coarsening of his mother's features by male hormones, corrected Russ's notion that her looks were boyish. No boy looked like Frances.

"And then," he said, "this guy she's been dating, I mean, she's probably lonely, but she gets all fluttery when she's going out with him, and it's like my dad never existed. He was one of the youngest colonels in the history of the air force . . . he was my *dad*—and now she doesn't even want to see a picture of him?"

Russ was alarmed by the ambiguity of *has been dating*—whether the verb tense encompassed the present or referred to a period now past.

"So," he said, "your mother has been, or was, at some point . . ."

"Yeah, I finally met the guy. She made me and Amy go to lunch with him."

Russ cleared a sudden dryness from his throat. "When was this?"

"Saturday."

Ten days after the marijuana experiment.

"It was horrible," Larry said. "I mean, obviously I'm not going to like him, because he's not my dad, but he's so full of himself, he's bragging about doing surgery for sixteen hours, he's showing off to the waiter, and he talked to Amy like she was three years old. He's so full of shit, and my mom's all fluttery and fake with him."

Russ cleared his throat again. "And you think this might—be a serious relationship? Your mother and the—surgeon? Is that what's troubling you?"

"I thought he was out of the picture, and now suddenly everything is 'Philip' this and 'Philip' that."

"Since—how long?"

"I don't know. The last few weeks."

"And—does your mother know how you feel about him?"

"I said I thought he was a pompous jerk."

"And—how did she react?"

"She got mad. She said I was being selfish and hadn't given 'Philip' a chance. Which, like—*I'm* selfish? She was supposed to be an adviser on Spring Trip. She acted all hurt that I didn't want to be in the same group with her, and now she tells me she isn't sure she even wants to go. 'Philip' wants to take her to some bogus medical conference in Acapulco, that same week."

Russ's face was ashen; he could feel it.

"Sometimes I'm almost, like, why did it have to be my dad who died? He was always yelling, but at least he paid attention. My mom doesn't even care. She only cares about herself."

There was recognizably a truth in this, but it didn't bother Russ. He'd had enough of being married to a self-hating caretaker.

"Maybe you should tell her," he said, "that you want her to come on Spring Trip. Tell her how much it would mean to you."

"I don't know which would be worse, having to be around her, or her being with that creep. It's like I hate *everyone*."

"Well, it's good that you're honest about your feelings. That's what Crossroads is about. I hope you'll consider me someone you can open up to."

For the first time, Larry looked at Russ as if he were more than just a generic dyad partner. "Can I say something weird?"

"Ah?"

"She's always talking about you. She keeps asking me what I think of you."

"Yes—well. She and I have the circle together. We've gotten to be—friendly."

"I'm going, Mom, he's the minister. He's married."

"Yes."

"Sorry—was that weird of me?"

For a moment, Russ considered leveling with Larry, perhaps trying to enlist his aid, but the memory of leveling with Sally Perkins scared him off. The terms of the exercise now obliged him to offer a story of his own, but everything that troubled him pertained somehow to Larry. He obviously couldn't talk about his marriage, or about Perry's drug use. Clem's crazy attempt to join the army was also off-limits, because Larry was proud of his father's service. On Russ's desk was a copy of an engineering report on the church sanctuary's south wall, which was in danger of collapsing. It could be argued that this troubled him.

When their allotted time expired, he sent Larry downstairs and stayed in his office to call Frances; he no longer had anything to lose. As soon as she heard his voice, the line went silent. Sensing that he'd overstepped, he rushed to apologize, but she cut him off. "I'm the one who should apologize."

"Not at all," he said. "For whatever reason, I had a bad reaction to the, ah—"

"I know. It was funny how paranoid you got. But it's not like you could help it, and I totally understand why you ran away. You did the right thing—I was very, very out of line. That's why I didn't go to Tuesday circle last week. I was too ashamed of myself."

"But that's—why were you ashamed?"

"Um, because I basically tried to jump you? I can blame it on the you-know-what, but it was still completely inappropriate. I'm sorry I put you in that position. I'm in a much clearer place now. I did an honest reckoning, and, well, you don't have to worry about me. If you can manage to forgive me, I promise it will never happen again."

Whether the good news here outweighed the bad was hard to judge. His chance with her had been even better than he'd surmised, his blowing of it even more conclusive than he'd feared.

"I hope we can still be friends," Frances said.

A week later, she called to invite him to an evening with Buckminster Fuller at the Illinois Institute of Technology. No sooner had he accepted, in his capacity as a friend, than she added that this was the kind of evening that Philip *hated*. "Did I mention I'm seeing him again? I'm trying to be a good girl, but it's no fun being in an audience with him. He gets all fidgety, like he can't stand it that people are paying attention to someone else." Russ was discouraged that she imagined he cared to hear about Philip, encouraged that she complained about him. Reminding himself that she'd been attracted to him enough to try to "jump" him, despite his being married, he dressed for their date in his most flattering shirt and applied, for the first time, some of the cologne that Becky had given him for Christmas, only to find, when Frances picked him up at the parsonage, that Kitty Reynolds was in her car. Frances hadn't mentioned that Kitty was coming, and Russ, being merely her friend, had no basis for objecting. Nor did he have any great interest in Buckminster Fuller, though he was careful not to fidget in his seat.

A consolation for losing Frances to the surgeon was that she didn't avoid Russ on their next Tuesday in the city. She now evidently felt safe to ride in his Fury again, to prefer his company to Kitty's and volunteer to work with him in an old woman's Morgan Street kitchen, rolling onto its walls a paint color known as Ballerina Pink (wildly overproduced by its maker, now available for pennies) while he painted the edges. It was sad to be considered safe, but he was happy that she still wanted to be with him, happy to see her huddling companionably with Theo Crenshaw, happy to have helped her mend that fence.

The shock was therefore brutal when, on a gray March morning, she came to his church office and announced that she was quitting the Tuesday circle. It might have been the gray light, but she seemed older, more brittle. He invited her to sit down.

"No," she said. "I wanted to tell you in person, but I can't stay."

"Frances. You can't just drop a bomb like that. Did something happen?"

She looked close to tears. He stood up, closed the door, and managed to seat her in his visitor chair. Her hair, too, seemed older—darker, less silky.

"I'm just not a good enough person," she said.

"That's ridiculous. You're a wonderful person."

"No. My children don't respect me, and you—I know you like me, but you shouldn't. I don't believe in God—I don't believe in anything."

He crouched at her feet. "Will you tell me what happened?"

"There's no point in explaining—you won't understand."

"Try me."

She shut her eyes. "Philip says I can't go with you anymore. I know that sounds stupid, and if that's all it was I wouldn't—I might still go. But with everything else it's just easier not to."

The thought that the surgeon might be jealous of him—had reason to be jealous—only deepened Russ's sense of defeat.

"He knew," Frances said, "that I did volunteer work in the city. But when he found out where the church is, he said it was too dangerous. I tried to explain that it's not so bad, but he wouldn't listen, and—I hate being submissive. It's not who I want to be, but in this case it's just easier, because that really *is* who I am: I'm the person who does whatever's easiest."

"That's not true at all. Have you talked to Kitty about this?"

"I can't. Kitty won't respect me, either. I mean—I know, I know, I know. I'm with another jerk—I know. Larry's already barely speaking to me. I made him go to lunch with Philip, and Larry could see it—everyone can see it. I'm with a jerk again. A worse jerk, actually. Bobby at least wasn't a racist."

"No one should be allowed to tell you what you can and can't do."

"I know, and, like I said, if it was just Philip I might stand up to him. But the thing is, inside, I'm just like him. I still think I'm going to get raped or murdered every time I go down there."

"These are deep patterns," Russ said. "It takes time to develop new patterns."

"I know, and I've been trying. I apologized to Theo, the way you told me to, and you were right—it made a difference. But I couldn't stop thinking about Ronnie, how to help him, and so I talked to Theo again. According to him, the problem is that Ronnie's mother is a heroin addict. I asked if he could get her into a treatment program—I offered to pay for it myself and let him say the money came from his congregation."

"That is not the action of a person who isn't good."

"But he basically said it was impossible. He thinks Clarice would start using drugs again as soon as she gets out. I told Theo there has to be *some* okay foster family that would take a sweet little boy. I offered to talk to a social worker myself and make sure everything checked out. But Theo said, if I did that, the social worker would never let Clarice near Ronnie again. I said I thought that might be for the best. But Theo said Ronnie's the only thing keeping Clarice alive, and that a social worker wouldn't see that, because the state only cares about the boy's welfare, not the mother's. I tried to remember what you told me and not argue with him, but I pointed out that he's okay with a situation *no social worker would be okay with.* I said that sooner or later something terrible is going to happen. And Theo just shrugs. He says, 'That's in God's hands.' And that shut me up. I didn't argue with him."

"None of this," Russ said, "makes me think less of you. Quite the opposite."

Frances didn't seem to hear him. "I'm not like you," she said. "I can't accept that God creates a situation so terrible there's no getting out of it. To me, it's like there's a door, and behind the door is the inner city, and everywhere you turn there's a situation so terrible that no one can fix it, and I've reached the point where I just can't open the door again. I just want to shut it and forget what's behind it. When Philip said I couldn't go with you again, I had this horrid sense of relief."

"I wish you'd told me sooner," Russ said. "No situation is so hopeless that nothing can be done. Maybe, next time we're down there, you and Theo and I can do some brainstorming."

"No. I'm not going there again—it's just not for me. I wanted it to be for me. I looked at you and I said to myself, that's the person I want to be like. It was exciting to be with you, but I think I mistook being *with* you for being *like* you. The reality is I'm a crap human being."

"No, no, no."

"Apparently I'm turned on by jerks. I'm turned on by money, by trips to Acapulco, nobody judging me, nobody forcing me to open doors I don't feel like opening. The idea that I could be a different kind of person was just a fantasy."

"There's a difference between fantasy and aspiration."

"You don't know my fantasies. Actually, you did see one of them—I'm still ashamed of that."

Russ sensed that she'd come to him wanting to be saved but not knowing how; was edging toward a breakthrough and needed a push. But saved from what? From loss of faith, or from the surgeon?

"What exactly—was it?" he said. "The fantasy."

She blushed. "I imagined you were somebody who didn't let being married get in the way of—I imagined you could be a jerk." She shuddered at herself. "Do you see the kind of person I am? It's like I needed to drag you down to *my* level. If you were at my level, I wouldn't have to keep looking up to you and feeling like I was falling short."

His dilemma had never been plainer. She liked him for his goodness, it was the best thing he had going for him, and by definition goodness meant not having her.

"I'm not so good," he said. "I'm like you—I did the easy thing. I married, I had kids, I took a job in the suburbs, and it's made me nothing but unhappy. My marriage is a disaster. Marion sleeps in a different room—we barely speak—and my children don't respect me. I'm a failure as a father, worse than a failure as a husband. I'm more of a jerk than you may think."

Frances shook her head. "That only makes me feel worse."

"How so?"

She stood up and stepped around him. "I never should have flirted with you."

"Just give me a chance," he said, jumping to his feet. "At least come to Arizona. There's a spirituality in the air, in the people. It changed my life—it could change yours, too."

"Yeah, that was another mistake. Trying to make you go there with me."

"Not at all. If it weren't for you, I might never have patched things up with Rick. You did a great thing for me. You've been such a bright star in my life—I don't know what's happened to you."

"Nothing's happened. It was only dreading this conversation—having to disappoint you. I'll be fine as soon as I can close the door again."

By way of illustration, she moved toward the door, and Russ couldn't stop her. He was utterly impotent. All at once, he was seized by a hatred so intense he could have strangled her. She was insensitive and self-adoring, a careless trampler of records, a casual crusher of hearts.

"That's bullshit," he said. "Everything you say is bullshit. You're only running away because you're too chicken to face the goodness in your heart, too chicken to take responsibility. I don't believe that disengaging from the world is going to make you happy. But if that's the miserable life you want, we don't need you in the circle. We don't need you in Arizona. If you don't have the guts to honor your commitments, I say good riddance."

His emotion was authentic, but to express it so directly was a Crossroads thing. He sounded like Rick Ambrose in confrontation mode.

"I mean it," he said. "Get the hell out of here. I don't want to see you again."

"I guess I deserve that."

"Fuck deserving. You're a mess of phony self-reproach. It makes me sick."

"Wow. Ouch."

"Just leave. You really are a disappointment."

He hardly knew what he was saying, but in sounding like Ambrose he felt some of the power that Ambrose must have felt all the time. As if, however momentarily, the Lord was with him. Frances looked at him with a new kind of interest.

"I like your honesty," she said.

"I don't give a damn what you like. Just, on your way out, tell Rick you're not going to Arizona."

"Unless I decide to go. Wouldn't that be a surprise?"

"This isn't a game. Either you're going or you're not."

"Well, in that case . . ." She made a little slide-step dance move. "Maybe I will. How about that?"

In his anger, he didn't care. Her maybes were like needles to his brain. He dropped into his desk chair and turned away from her. "Suit yourself."

Only after she was gone did he reconnect with his desire. All in all, he thought, their meeting could hardly have gone better. The revelation was how positively she'd responded to his anger, how negatively to his begging. He'd stumbled upon the key to her. If he kept away from her, let her think he'd lost his patience with her, she might yet defy the surgeon and go to Arizona.

But it was a torment not to know what she was thinking. The following Sunday, at the last Crossroads meeting before Spring Trip, he searched the teenaged throng for Larry, intending to ask him what his mother's plans were. When he discovered that Larry, unaccountably, had skipped the meeting, his torment became acute. The next morning, first thing, he went to Ambrose's office and asked if he'd heard anything from Mrs. Cottrell.

Ambrose was reading the sports section of the *Trib*. "No," he said. "Why?"

"When I saw her last week, I had the sense she might bail out."

Ambrose shrugged. "No great loss. We already have Jim and Linda Stratton for Many Farms. Two parents there is plenty."

Russ was bewildered. A month earlier, when he and Ambrose had worked out the adviser assignments, he'd made sure that Frances was in his group.

"I thought—" he said. "That's not right. We had Mrs. Cottrell down for Kitsillie."

"Yeah, I switched her out and gave you Ted Jernigan. If she wants to wear blue jeans and hang out with the kids, she can do that in Many Farms. I'm not even sure why she's coming—she kind of pulled a fast one on me."

"You underestimate her. She's in my Tuesday women's circle. She really gets it."

"Then we'll see how she does in Many Farms."

"No. She needs to be in Kitsillie."

The eyes that flicked up from the sports pages were unpleasantly shrewd. "Why?"

"Because I've worked with her. I want her in my group."

Ambrose nodded as if something made sense to him. "You know, I did wonder. Back in December, I wondered what moved you to come and see me. It was only because she'd been in my office the same day. She was hell-bent on going to Arizona, and then there you were, wanting to go to Arizona. I'm not taking anything away from the courage of what you did—I just had a little glimmer of wondering. I wouldn't have thought of it if it weren't for the business with you and Sally Perkins."

"Mrs. Cottrell is thirty-seven years old."

"I'm not judging you, Russ. Only saying I know you."

"Then tell me this. Why did you swap her and Ted Jernigan? To spite me?"

"Cool your jets. I don't care what you do on your own time. Just keep it out of Crossroads."

"You need to put her back in Kitsillie."

"Nope."

"Please, Rick. I'm not demanding—I'm asking. Please do me this favor."

Ambrose shook his head. "I'm not running a dating service."

It seemed to Russ, as it had all winter, that every piece of good news—in this case, that Frances was evidently still on for Arizona—came paired with news more than bad enough to negate it. Ambrose had seen through him, and there was nothing he could do. He had no grounds for appeal beyond his having imagined a long walk alone with Frances, a hike up into the pinyon forest, a first kiss on a wind-scoured hilltop; and this was no argument at all. The Lord was with Ambrose.

When Russ went home that night, Becky informed him that she wasn't coming on Spring Trip. A day earlier, he would have been relieved to hear it—she and her friends had signed up for Kitsillie, where she would have observed his attentions to Frances—but now it only seemed like another sign of their estrangement. Under the influence of Tanner Evans, Becky was becoming ever more hippieish and defiant, and she'd been staying out to all hours, even during the week. When Russ had tried to impose a weeknight curfew, she'd run to Marion, which had led to an impasse, resolved in Becky's favor.

"I thought you were looking forward to the trip," he said.

She was sprawled on the living-room sofa with her Bible. In her hands, in the militancy of her rejection of him, the Bible was oddly distasteful.

"Yeah," she said, "I'm not into it."

The hippieish locution *into it* was also distasteful. "Into the trip? Or Crossroads generally?"

"Both. It's like Ambrose said—it's more of a psychological experiment than Christianity. It's teenybopper relationship dramas."

"I seem to recall that you're still a teenager yourself."

"Ha ha good point."

"I'd looked forward to some time with you in Arizona. Is the idea that you'll be alone here?"

"That is the idea, yes."

"I hope you won't burn the house down with some party."

She gave him an insulted look and reopened her Bible. He no longer understood her at all, but it was true that her social life now seemed to consist of Tanner Evans. Because she and Russ and Perry had planned to go to Arizona, Marion was taking Judson to Los Angeles for spring vacation, treating him to Disneyland and visiting her uncle Jimmy, who was in a nursing home there. The trip was an extravagance, but Russ had known better than to argue, and Marion's absence was a problem only now that Becky had decided to stay home. Very probably, Becky intended to use the empty parsonage to sleep with Tanner, which was another distasteful thought, mitigated only by Russ's fondness for Tanner. Despite her new religiosity, Becky dressed and carried herself like someone sexually active—he really didn't understand her. He only knew she'd never be his little girl again.

Early the next morning, he awakened with an idea so obvious he was amazed he hadn't seen it sooner: *Keith Durochie had told him not to go to Kitsillie.* Keith had said that there was plenty of work in Many Farms, and who was Russ to argue with a Navajo elder? More to the point: *Who was Ambrose?*

A path to a week with Frances clear ahead of him, he went to his church office and waited until the hour was late enough to call Keith's house. The woman who answered, on the fifteenth or twentieth ring, was not Keith's wife.

"He's at the hospital," she said. "He's sick."

Russ asked what had happened, but apparently the woman had said all she could. Distressed, he called the offices of the tribal council, which Keith was a longtime member of, and learned from a secretary that Keith had suffered a stroke. How bad a stroke Russ couldn't ascertain—the Navajos had taboos regarding illness. Setting aside his distress about Keith, he said he was arriving with three busloads of teenagers on Saturday night and needed to know where to go. The secretary connected him, through a loudly buzzing internal line, to a council administrator whose first name was Wanda and whose family name he didn't catch. Perhaps because of the buzzing, she spoke with plangent enunciation.

"Russ," she said, "you do not have to worry. We know that you are coming. You do not have to worry that we are not expecting you."

Over the buzzing, Russ explained that Keith had suggested he avoid the mesa and go to Many Farms instead. To this, there was no response from Wanda, only buzzing.

"Wanda? Can you hear me?"

"Let me be completely honest and straightforward with you," she said plangently. "Keith has had trouble on the mesa, but we have a federal mandate. There is work to be done at Kitsillie to conform with the mandate. We have delivered cement and lumber to the school, and we will be very grateful for your help."

"Ah—mandate?"

"It is a federal mandate and we have supplies for you. One of the women from the chapter has agreed to cook for you, as you requested in your letter. Her name is Daisy Benally."

"Yes, I know Daisy. But Keith seemed to feel we'd be better off in Many Farms."

"We know that a group is coming to Many Farms. All of the arrangements are in place."

"Well, then, maybe, if you could accommodate two groups there, instead of one—"

"Russ, I am speaking to you in all respect. We are not expecting two groups in Many Farms. I will personally meet you here on Saturday and explain the work that we are hoping you will do at Kitsillie to conform with the mandate. I will look forward to meeting you."

Russ felt powerless against Wanda's plangency, all the more so as a *bilagáana*. He hoped she might be easier to talk to in person, or that Keith would be well enough recovered to overrule her.

On Thursday night, after a long effort to fall asleep, he dreamed he was alone and lost on the Black Mesa, trying to get down from a trackless mountain. Far below him, he saw sheep and horses in a rock-strewn paddock, but to reach the trail leading down he had to climb higher, on ever stonier and steeper slopes. The terrain was unexpectedly vast, and the direction he was climbing seemed wrong, but he had to keep going to make sure. Finally he reached a cliff impossible to scale. Looking back, he saw that he was on a slope too nearly vertical to be descended. He saw sheer rock and yawning space and understood that he was going to die. Coming awake, in the barrenness of his marital bed, he recognized his situation. No path with joy at the end of it could be as arduous and convoluted as attaining Frances had become.

But this was a wee-hour recognition. By the time the buses rolled into the First Reformed parking lot, twelve hours later, his path seemed clear again. If Frances would only show up, he could sort things out in Many Farms. A cold March breeze was blowing, daffodils blooming along the church's limestone flanks, the sun bright, the air chilly. In his old sheepskin coat, a clipboard in hand, Russ directed seminarians and alumni advisers in their toting of Crossroads tool chests, cans of Ballerina Pink and Sunshine Yellow, crates of rollers and brushes, Coleman lanterns. A parent adviser, Ted Jernigan, pulled up beside Russ in a late-model Lincoln and suggested that he load the buses closer to the church doors. Ted nodded at the seminarian Carolyn Polley, who was struggling with a tool chest. "That little girl is going to get hurt."

Russ held up his clipboard, to indicate his supervisory role. "Feel free to pitch in."

Ted seemed disinclined. He was a real-estate lawyer, a soloist in the church choir, a beefy former U.S. Marine, and thought very well of himself.

"I'm concerned about drinking water," he said. "Do we have drinking water?"

"No."

"Why don't I run down to Bev-Mart and buy us a bunch of five-gallon bottles. Darra said some of the kids last year had diarrhea."

"I doubt it was from the water."

"Simple enough to bring some."

"A hundred and twenty kids, eight days—that's a lot of bottles."

"Better safe than sorry."

"The water on the reservation comes from wells. It's not a problem."

Ted made the face of a man unused to deferring. It was a mistake, Russ thought, to bring a male parishioner on a trip where he would be subordinate to a junior minister. Russ could well imagine Ted's opinion of him and his pastoral impracticality, his feeble salary, his indetectable contribution to the general good. The opinion was subtly implicit in Ted's offer to *buy* water—to open his fee-fattened wallet, to effortlessly exercise his spending power. Putting him in Russ's group had been selfish of Ambrose, if not deliberately cruel.

As the family cars streamed in, releasing kids in their paint-smeared jeans and their dirtiest coats, with their Frisbees and their sleeping bags, Russ had eyes for only one car. From within the misery of his suspense he glimpsed the relief of being free of Frances, of receiving a definitive no and moving on, of being anywhere else but where he was. When he finally spied her car on Pirsig Avenue, his misery made the moment of reckoning—whether she was joining him or simply dropping off Larry—feel curiously weightless. *Thy will be done.* As if for the first time, he appreciated the peace these words afforded.

The peace lasted until she stepped out of her car, wearing her hunting cap. When he saw Larry open the trunk and remove not only a fancy backpack, suitable for alpine trekking, but a large and feminine fabric suitcase, he was flooded with voluptuous presentiment. It swept away his equanimity, exposed its falseness, stopped his breath. He was going to have her.

Secure in his presentiment, he busied himself with his clipboard, checking off the names of Crossroads members in the Kitsillie group. Unlike three years ago, bus assignments were now determined by destination, not by clique. Someone, presumably Ambrose, had drawn a heavy line through Becky's name. Russ still half hoped and half feared that Becky would change her mind, but when he saw her and Perry pull up in the family Fury, without Marion along to drive it home, he knew she wasn't coming. She didn't even get out of the car while Perry retrieved his duffel bag.

As the Fury left the parking lot, Frances marched up to Russ. He pretended to consult his clipboard. "Oh hey," he said.

Her eyes were glittering with drama. "You didn't think I'd do it, did you. You didn't think I had the guts. It looks like you're stuck with me and my phony self-reproach after all."

He struggled not to smile. "That remains to be seen."

"What do you mean?"

"You're not going to Kitsillie. Rick wants you in the Many Farms group."

She drew her head back. "In Larry's group? Are you kidding me?"

"Nope."

"Larry doesn't want me anywhere near him. Why did Rick do that?"

"You'd have to ask him."

"Does he think I can't hack it on the mesa?"

"You'd have to ask him."

"That is extremely annoying. I hope *you* didn't make him do that."

Russ had won the fight against smiling. "No. Why would I?"

"Because you're mad at me."

"It was Rick's decision, not mine. Take it up with him if you're not happy."

"The only reason I came was to be with you on the mesa. Well, not the only reason. But I am very, very annoyed."

In her face was the disappointment of a spoiled child, a slighted VIP. Maybe she was thinking of the Acapulco trip that she'd forgone.

"Who took my place?" she said. "Who's going with you?"

"Ted Jernigan, Judy Pinella. Craig Dilkes, Biff Allard. Carolyn Polley."

"Oh great." She rolled her eyes. Russ wondered if his jealousy-provoking gambit might actually have worked. As he watched her stalk away, the arduousness of the long path behind him felt like nothing. She wanted to be with him, and he'd managed to conceal his delight.

Echoes of Biff Allard's bongo drums were bouncing off the bank across the street, cigarette smoke and Frisbees in the air, a black dog in a bandanna hurdling guitar cases and hand luggage, kids dashing in and out of the church on missions of adolescent urgency, mothers lingering to embarrass long-haired sons with loving injunctions, the three bus drivers and the swing driver conferring over a road atlas, Rick Ambrose standing in his army jacket beside Dwight Haefle, who'd come outside to behold the glory of it all. As Frances walked up to the two men, Russ averted his eyes (*Thy will be done*) and went looking for the Kitsillie kids whose names were still unchecked. They were due to leave in ten minutes, at five o'clock, and the buses were still empty. There were last-minute runs to the drugstore, tragic partings of friends on different buses, the suitcase in need of late excavation from a luggage bay, the forgotten sack dinner, and, as always, in Russ's experience, the one or two kids who were late.

"David Goya?" he shouted. "Kim Perkins? Anybody seen them?"

"I think they're upstairs," someone said.

Inside the church, as he climbed the upper stairs, he heard voices go silent at his approach. Sitting in the Crossroads meeting room, on a pair of legless couches, were David Goya, Kim Perkins, Keith Stratton, and Bobby Jett. Cool kids all; friends of Becky and Perry. Russ sensed that he'd caught them doing something wrong, but he didn't see or smell anything forbidden.

"Guys, come on," he said from the doorway. "We need you downstairs."

Glances were exchanged. Kim, in stiffly new blue overalls, jumped up and gestured to the others. "We're going, okay? Let's just go."

Keith and Bobby looked to David as if the decision was his.

"You guys go," he said.

"What's going on?" Russ said. "Do you have something to tell me?"

"No, no, no," Kim said.

She pushed past him, out the door. Keith and Bobby followed, and Russ waited for David to explain. The agedness of David's face and hair was so peculiar, it might have been endocrine.

"Seen Perry?" he said.

"Yes. Why?"

"Let me put it differently. Does Perry seem okay to you?"

Before the question was even out of David's mouth, Russ intuited its pertinence. The scenario that came to him was complete and convincing: Perry would contrive to mess things up at the last minute, and all would be lost with Frances.

"Let's go downstairs," he said to David. "You and I can talk on the bus."

"You haven't noticed anything. He hasn't seemed at all strange to you."

It was true that Perry had been notably scarce in recent weeks, more like his former furtive self, no longer rising so early, but Russ said nothing. He needed to keep the bad scenario at bay.

"I saw him last night," David said, "and he wasn't making any sense. He can be that way sometimes—his brain works too fast to keep up with. But this seemed different. More like a problem with the entire circuit board. The reason I mention it is I'm concerned he might be violating the rules."

Time was passing. Things of interest to Russ were happening in the parking lot. He forced himself to focus on the matter at hand. "So, you think—has he been smoking pot again?"

"Not to my knowledge. Laudably or regrettably, that appears to be a thing of the past—I gather he made some kind of promise to you. My concern here is that I violate the rules myself if I fail to report a rules violation. My concern is that even now, as we speak, he isn't unimpaired."

God damn Perry. The scenario now included a call to Marion, explaining that she couldn't go to Los Angeles because *her* son was messing up again, to which she might object that she'd already bought her plane tickets, to which Russ would reply that his job obliged him to lead a group in Arizona, whereas she and Judson were going to Los Angeles purely for pleasure, and that, moreover, she was the one who'd insisted that Perry was doing better.

David looked down at his long, bony hands. "I'm not just covering my ass, by the way. Something is definitely not right with him."

"I appreciate your honesty."

"Although, having taken the step of mentioning it, I'd be grateful if Kim and Keith and Bobby could be included under the umbrella of immunity."

"I'll speak to him," Russ said. "You get yourself on the bus."

His fear, as he went downstairs, was both new and familiar. His primary feeling about Perry had always been fear. At first it was fear of his operatic tantrums, later fear of his intellectual acuity, its application to mockeries too subtle to be called out and punished, its implicit piercing of Russ's every fault and weakness. Now the fear was more existentially parental. He and Marion had brought into the world a being of uncontrollable volition, for whom he was nonetheless responsible.

In the parking lot, kids were mobbing the buses, rushing to claim seats. Looking around for Perry, Russ saw the most wonderful thing. The woman he wanted was standing by the Kitsillie bus. The driver was stowing her suitcase below. With a more delicious kind of fear, Russ hurried over to her.

"Here I am," she said aggressively. "Like it or not."

"What happened?"

She shrugged. "Dwight saved the day. I asked Rick why I wasn't going to the mesa, and you know what he said? That you could use another *man* up there. I told him that was incredibly demeaning to me. I told him Larry's at an age where the last thing he wants is his mother in his hair. I said maybe *Rick* should tell Larry he'd ruined his whole trip. And you know Dwight, always the diplomat. He asks Rick if there's anyone I can trade places with. Which it turns out Judy Pinella is perfectly happy to do. I don't know what Rick was thinking, but if he thinks I don't care if I get the full experience, up on the mesa, he doesn't know me."

She was full of self-regard, full of entitlement, and Russ was smitten with every bit of it.

"Plus," he suggested, "you and I get to be together."

She made a coy face. "Is that a good thing, or a bad thing?"

"It's a good thing."

"Maybe you don't hate me so much after all?"

This time, there was no suppressing a smile, but it didn't matter—she obviously knew very well how he felt. It was inconceivable to her that anyone could resist her. And this, more than anything else, had set the hook in him. He couldn't get enough of her self-love.

Flush with the likelihood of possessing it, of carnally penetrating it, commingling with it, he went to look for Perry. As he passed the Rough Rock bus, he saw Ambrose staring at him. His lip was curled with impotent disgust. There was no more pretending that the two of them weren't enemies. It was frightening but also thrilling, because this time Russ had won.

Inside the Many Farms bus, kids were piling onto seats already taken, clambering over backrests. At the door stood Kevin Anderson, a second-year seminarian with a deep-pile mustache and the soft brown eyes of a seal pup. Before Russ could ask him if he'd seen Perry, Kevin asked him the same question. Apparently Perry had not been seen since he checked in.

Russ's intuition of warning signs ignored, of necessary actions not taken, returned in force. The sun had sunk behind the church's roofline but was still shining on the bank clock, which showed eight minutes past five. Except for Perry, the buses appeared to be fully loaded. Car engines were starting up, a few determined parents lingering to wave good-bye. It occurred to Russ that they could simply leave without Perry—let Marion deal with the fallout. But Kevin, whose heart was as soft as his eyes, insisted that they look inside the church.

Spring-smelling air followed them in through doors still propped open. Kevin ran upstairs, calling Perry's name, while Russ checked the ground floor. Not just the air but the emptiness of the hallway, which minutes ago had teemed with activity, had a flavor of Easter. In the middle chapters of the Gospels, crowds of people followed Jesus everywhere, gathering around him on the Mount, receiving fishes and loaves by the five thousand and the four thousand, welcoming him with palm fronds on the road into Jerusalem, but in the late chapters the focus narrowed to scenes of individual departure, private pain. The Last Supper: clandestine and death-haunted. Peter alone with his betrayals. Judas going away to hang himself. Jesus feeling forsaken on the cross. Mary Magdalene weeping at the sepulcher. The crowds had dispersed and everything was over. The worst thing in human history had happened sickeningly fast, and now it was another Sunday morning in Judea, the first day of the Jewish week, a particular spring morning with a particular spring smell to the air. Even the truth revealed that morning—the truth of Christ's divinity and resurrection—was austere in its transcendence of human particularity, in its own way no less melancholy. Spring to Russ was a season more of loss than of joy.

In the first-floor men's room, even before he saw Perry's feet in the farther stall, he sensed an airless stickiness, a male adolescent anxious to be left alone.

"Perry?"

The voice in the stall was muffled. "Yeah, Dad. One second."

"Are you not feeling well?"

"Coming coming coming."

"A hundred and forty people are waiting for you."

On the rim of the sink were Perry's wire-framed eyeglasses, newly prescribed for astigmatism. The frames weren't the least expensive or most rugged that Marion could have let him choose, and indeed he'd already broken them. Finer wire was tightly wound around the damaged bridge.

The toilet roared, and Perry banged out of the stall, went to the sink, and splashed water on his face. His corduroys, though belted, were halfway down his hips. He no longer had any bottom to speak of; had altogether lost a lot of weight.

"What's going on?" Russ said.

Perry violently pumped the paper-towel dispenser and tore off a yard-long sheet. "Sorry to keep you waiting. Everything is A-OK."

"You don't seem right to me."

"Just pre-road nerves. A little episode of you-know-what."

But there was no smell of diarrhea in the air.

"Are you on drugs?"

"Nope." Perry put on his glasses and snagged his knapsack from the stall. "All set."

Russ gripped him by his scrawny shoulder. "If you're on drugs, I can't let you on the bus."

"Drugs, drugs, what kind of drugs."

"I don't know."

"Well, there you go. I'm not on drugs."

"Look me in the eye."

Perry did so. His face was blotched with crimson, clear mucus seeping from his nose. "I swear to God, Dad. I'm clean as a whistle."

"You don't seem clean to me."

"Clean as a whistle and frankly wondering why you're asking."

"David Goya is worried about you."

"David should worry about his own pot dependency. As a matter of fact, I wonder what a search of his luggage might turn up." Perry held up his knapsack. "You're free to search mine. Go ahead and pat me down. I'll even drop my pants, if you can stand the embarrassment."

He was giving off a very sour mildew smell. Russ had never felt more repelled by him, but he didn't have hard enough evidence to send him home to Marion. Time was passing, and the responsibility was his. He made himself take it.

"I want you in Kitsillie with me. You can have Becky's place."

A laugh burst from Perry like a sneeze.

"What?" Russ said.

"Could there *be* anything that either of us wants less than that?"

"I'm concerned that you don't seem well."

"I'm trying to help you, Dad. Don't you want me to help you?"

"What do you mean?"

"I'll stay out of your business if you'll stay out of mine."

"My business is your welfare."

"Then you must be—" Perry snickered. "Very busy." He shouldered his knapsack and wiped his nose.

"Perry, listen to me."

"I'm not going to Kitsillie. You've got your business, I've got mine."

"You're not making any sense."

"Really? You think I don't know why you're going on this trip? It would be too hilarious if I knew it and you didn't. Do you need me to spell it out for you? She's a total F-O-X. And I don't mean some esoteric oxyfluoride salt of xenon, although, interestingly, they've synthesized some salts like that, in spite of the supposed completeness of xenon's outermost electron shell, which you'd think couldn't happen, and, yes, I realize I digress. My point in mentioning chemistry was that it's not the point, but you must admit it's pretty incredible. Everyone assumed that xenon was inert, I mean it's such a credit to the fluorine atom—its oxidizing powers. Wouldn't you agree that it's incredible?"

Perry smiled at Russ as if he believed he was following his nonsense and enjoying it.

"You need to calm down," Russ said. "I'm not at all sure you should be coming with us."

"I'm talking about a valence of zero, Dad. If we're comparing your qualifications with mine, do you even know what a chemical valence is?"

Russ made a helpless gesture.

"I didn't think so."

Outside the bathroom, in the hallway, Kevin Anderson was calling Perry's name.

"Coming," Perry shouted cheerfully.

Before Russ could stop him, he was out the door.

Glancing at the mirror above the sink, he was dismayed to see a father with responsibilities. What he wanted more than anything was to have nothing to do with his son. At the thought of letting Perry's disturbance and his mildew stink be Kevin's problem, he felt a melting warmth in his loins. The warmth, which also related to Frances, plainly told him that the thought was evil. But every other scenario—getting Ambrose involved, locating Marion and making her deal with Perry, forcibly removing Perry from the bus, forgoing the trip himself or dragging Perry to Kitsillie—seemed worse than the next. Each of them would grossly delay the group's departure, and Frances was waiting on the bus. To have her even once seemed worth whatever price God might later make him pay.

◆

After Jesus had returned to his friends, eaten breakfast with them, let them touch him, he ascended to heaven and was never on earth again in body. What followed, as recounted in Acts, was a radical insurgency. The earliest Christians *had all things in common*—sold their possessions, shared whatever they had—and were militant in their counterculture. They never passed up a chance to remind the Pharisees of their hand in nailing the Christ to a tree. Their leaders were persecuted and forever on the run, but their ranks kept growing. It no doubt helped that Peter and Paul could perform miracles, but more crucial was Peter's inspiration to extend his ministry to the Gentiles. From a fire that had started within the Jewish community and might have been safely contained there, sparks flew into the greater Roman Empire. Paul, who'd begun his career as the most zealous of persecutors, holding the cloaks of the mob that stoned Stephen to death, was the most tireless of the fire spreaders. When last seen, in Acts, he'd made it all the way to Rome and was living, unmolested, in a rented house. Unmolested but still an outsider, still an insurgent.

What gave the new religion its edge was its paradoxical inversion of human nature, its exalting of poverty and rejection of worldly power, but a religion founded on paradox was inherently unstable. Once the old religions had been routed, the insurgents became the Pharisees. They became the Holy Roman Church and did their own persecuting, fell into their own complacency and corruption, and betrayed the spirit of Christ. Antithetical to power, the spirit took refuge and expressed itself in opposition—in the gentle renunciations of Saint Francis, the violent rebellion of the Reformation. True Christian faith always burned from the edge.

And no one understood this better than the Anabaptists. They began as a rebuke to the Reformation in northern Europe, which had retained the practice of universal infant baptism. For the Anabaptists, the voluntary choice of baptism, as an adult, was decisive. The book of Acts, an account of Christians so original that some of them had known Jesus personally, abounded with stories of adults seeing the light and requesting baptism. The Anabaptists were radical in the strict sense, returning to the earliest roots of their faith. They were correspondingly feared by Reformation authorities, such as Zwingli, and cruelly persecuted—banished, tortured, burned at the stake—in the first half of the sixteenth century. The effect was to confirm the radicalism of the Anabaptists who survived. In the Bible, after all, to be Christian was to suffer persecution.

Four centuries later, when Russ was a boy, memories of Anabaptist martyrdom were still vivid. The stories of Felix Manz and Michael Sattler, and of others killed for their beliefs, were part of the group identity of his parents' Mennonite community, part of its apartness, in the farm country around Lesser Hebron, Indiana. The kingdom of heaven would never encircle the earth, but it could be approached on a small scale in rural communities that practiced self-sufficiency, lived in strict accordance with the Word, and pointedly removed themselves from the present age. The Mennonites chose to be "the quiet in the land." To aspire to more was to risk losing all.

The Anabaptists of Lesser Hebron weren't Old Order—they used machines; the men wore ordinary clothes—and they weren't as communist as the Hutterites, but Russ as a boy heard little of the wider world and saw little of money. When he was twelve, he worked a long unpaid summer for a couple who'd lost their son to influenza, Fritz and Susanna Niedermayer, milking their cows and shoveling their manure in the assurance that they'd have done the same for the Hildebrandts had their situations been reversed. His older sisters disappeared for months at a time, helping families with new babies and leaving Russ with extra duties on the small farm his mother owned. They had a few cows, a large garden and a larger orchard, and ten acres for row crops that must have earned a bit of cash.

Like his own father before him, Russ's father was the pastor of the church in Lesser Hebron. Unlike other men in the community, he wore a long, collarless coat that buttoned at the neck. In the parlor of the family's house in town was a cabinet containing birth and marriage records, minutes of Anabaptist councils from more disputatious eras, and genealogies stretching back to Europe. Small groups of men could be found in the parlor at all hours of the day, conferring with his father and courteously accepting slices of his mother's pies. There seemed to be no limit to their patience in maintaining their apartness, their nonconforming obedience to the Word. A dispute between neighbors or a fine point of worship could occupy them for weeks before his father effected a reconciliation.

Blessed are the peacemakers: Russ was proud of his father but afraid of his seriousness, his forbidding coat, the sober male voices in the parlor. He preferred the kitchen and felt closer to God there. His mother worked fourteen and sixteen hours a day, placid in her plain dress and her hair covering. According to Scripture, earthly life was but a moment, but the moment seemed spacious when he was with her. In the time it took her to listen, actively, with clear-hearted questions, to one story he had to tell from school or the farm, she could make dough for a pie crust and roll it out, core and slice apples, and assemble a pie. And then, neither pausing nor rushing, she was on to the next chore. She made emulating Christ seem effortlessly rewarding. It horrified Russ to think that, four hundred years earlier, a person so quietly devout might have been put to death; it filled him with pity for the martyrs.

His other favorite place was the blacksmith shop of his mother's father, his Opa Clement, whose work included the repair of automobiles and tractors. Clement showed Russ how to hold a glowing horseshoe with tongs, how to use tin snips to fashion cookie cutters (a Christmas present for Russ's mother in 1936), how to rebuild a carburetor, how to hammer out a dented wheel and check its roundness with calipers. Clement's wife had died before Russ was born, and although he had his daughter's meditative way of working, her limpid rightness with the things around him, he'd become eccentric in his solitude. He subscribed to the *Saturday Evening Post*, neglected his shaving and bathing, and sometimes omitted to worship with his brethren. At the end of an afternoon when Russ had helped him, he reached into the pocket of his pinstripe overalls, removed a fistful of money, and invited Russ to choose, from his blackened hand, any coin that had silver in it. Even as a teenager, Russ was too innocently devout to spend the money only on himself. It was unthinkable not to get his mother something, a package of gingersnaps, a bottle of peppermint extract.

Except for rendering taxes unto the government, as Jesus had sensibly advised, the community was quietly but firmly anti-state. They schooled their children separately, avoided polling places and courts of law, and declined to swear on the Bible if called as witnesses. Most central to their identity was their pacifism. On few points was the Gospel clearer than on the incompatibility of violence with love. As the community's pastor, in 1917, Russ's paternal grandfather had contended, on the one hand, with the anger and prejudice of non-Mennonite farmers—rocks thrown through windows of the Kaiser-lovers, a barn defaced with ugly words—and, on the other, with families in his congregation who'd permitted their sons to go to war. Two of the families eventually quit the community.

Russ was seventeen when the country entered the Second World War. He would have been obliged to lodge an objection of conscience sooner if the president of the local draft board hadn't grown up on a farm adjoining the Niedermayers'. Cal Sanborn liked and admired the Mennonites and did everything he could to protect their sons. Russ was among the last to be called up, in 1944, and by then he'd completed five semesters at Goshen College. He'd also had his first crisis of faith, not in Jesus Christ but in his parents.

He'd enjoyed his classes at Goshen, but his only close friend was likewise the son of a pastor. In his ungainly tallness, as in the seriousness he'd inherited from his father, he felt uncomfortable with the earthier and more athletic boys, especially when their talk turned to girls. His father had told him that there would be girls at the college, and that he shouldn't shy from fellowship with them, but Russ couldn't look at a girl without thinking of his mother. Even to return a girl's friendly smile was somehow to offend against the person he most loved and revered; it made him queasy. The cure was to take a walk of five or ten miles, in the country around the college, until his body was exhausted and his soul open to grace.

In his third semester he studied European history, and he was keen to hear what Clement, who paid attention to the world, had to say about the war. The blacksmith shop, with its bellows and its potbellied stove, was especially congenial at Christmastime. Each tool in it was known to Russ, each evoked memories of afternoons slowed and deepened by unspoken love. Each year at Christmas there was also a new tool, for Russ to keep as a gift, a hammer or a coping saw, an auger drill, a set of chisels. He felt bad about how little he'd used the gifts, but Clement assured him that someday they would come in handy. Russ's experiences of grace seemed to presage a future as a pastor, like his father, and the only tool his father had any skill with was his letter opener, but he imagined that when he was settled, with a wife and family, he might take up woodworking as a hobby, a little eccentricity of his own.

Lesser Hebron was buried in snow when he got home. His father took him into the parlor, shut the door, and told him that Opa Clement wasn't coming for Christmas and that Russ was not to visit him. "Clement is a drunkard and an adulterer," his father explained. "We're resolved to avoid him in the hope that he'll repent."

Greatly upset, Russ went to his mother for a fuller explanation and permission to see her father. He got the explanation—Opa Clement had taken up with an unmarried schoolteacher, a woman scarcely older than thirty, and had been drinking whiskey when his brethren went to reason with him—but not the permission. Although their community didn't practice strict shunning, his mother said, a higher standard applied to a pastor's family, and this included Russ.

"But it's Opa. I can't be home for Christmas and not see Opa."

"We're praying that he'll repent," his mother said placidly. "Then we can all be together again."

Her equanimity was consonant with the primacy of Christ in her life, the secondary nature of everything else. The commandment to honor one's parents came from the Old Testament. In the New Testament, although the rejoicing at a sinner's reclamation was hundredfold, the sinner was first required to repent. Never mind an offending parent— you were supposed to pluck your own offending eye out. His mother was only as radical as the Gospel itself.

On Christmas morning, on the snow-dusted porch of their house, Russ found a small chest of white oak, the size of a child's coffin. The wood was smoothly planed and fragrant, the brass fittings stippled with hand manufacture. Inside it was a note. *For Russell on Christmas, I reckon you have enough tools to fill this, Love from your Opa.*

Russ, weeping, carried the chest inside. He wept again later in the morning, when his father instructed him to get an ax and chop it up for kindling.

"No," he said, "that's a waste. Someone else can use it."

"You will do as I say," his father said. "I want you to look into the fire and watch it burn."

"I don't think that's necessary," his mother said mildly. "Let's just put it away for now. My father may yet repent."

"He won't," his father said. "Nothing in this world is certain, but I know his mind better than you do. Russell will do as I say."

"No," Russ said.

"You will obey me. Go and get an ax."

Russ put on his overcoat, took the chest outside, as if he intended to obey, and carried it through the streets of Lesser Hebron. Because he loved his grandfather and love was the essence of the Gospel, he didn't even feel defiant. He felt, instead, that his parents were somehow mistaken.

The blacksmith shop was shuttered, chimney smoke rising from the low rooms in back. Russ was less afraid of his father's wrath than of finding his grandfather with a harlot, but Clement was alone in his little kitchen, boiling coffee on the woodstove. He looked like a new man—closely shaved and freshly barbered, his fingernails clean. Russ explained what had happened.

"I've made my peace with it," Clement said. "I already lost your mother when she married, and that's as it should be. No more than what the Scripture asks."

"She's praying for you. She wants you to—repent."

"I don't hold it against her. Your father, yes, but not her. She's godlier than any of us. If Estelle were baptized again and married me, I don't doubt that your mother would accept her. But I'll be a sick old man soon enough. I don't want Estelle feeling she has to take care of me. It's blessing enough to have her now."

The verb *to have*, the very name Estelle, the carnality they evoked, made Russ queasy.

"If God can't forgive me," Clement said, "so be it. But who's to say if your father knows what God forgives? I've been to the Lutheran church, over to Dobbsville, with Estelle. Good people, plenty Christian—there are many ways to skin a cat. I can't say as I've tried any of them, but I've skinned a raccoon, and the adage has it right. There are different ways of doing it."

Leaving the beautiful chest safe with Clement, Russ went home and confessed to his mother what he'd done. She kissed him and forgave him, but his father never really did, because Russ had made his choice. When he went to Arizona and discovered for himself the different ways a cat could be skinned, the only disclosive letters he wrote were to his grandfather.

The alternative service camp was in the national forest outside Flagstaff, on the site of a former CCC camp. It was administered by the American Friends Service Committee, but a good third of the workers shared Russ's faith. After he'd shoveled dirt for some months, painted picnic tables, planted trees, the camp director asked him if he could use a typewriter. Though still only twenty, Russ was among the older workers, and he'd had five semesters of college. The director, George Ginchy, set him up with a foot-tall Remington, its keys yellowed to the color of custard, in the antechamber of his office. Although Ginchy was a Quaker, from Pennsylvania, he was also a longtime college football coach and Boy Scout leader. His camp had a bugler who began the day with reveille and ended it with taps, a cook whose job title was quartermaster, and now, in Russ, an aide-de-camp. Ginchy liked everything about military life except the killing part.

One morning in the spring of 1945, the sun rose on a dusty black relic of a truck parked outside headquarters. Inside it, upright and silent, since sometime in the night, had been sitting four Navajo men in black felt hats. They were elders from Tuba City and had come to petition the camp director. George Ginchy welcomed them, widened his eyes at Russ, and asked him to bring coffee. Taking a pot into the office, Russ found three of the Navajo men standing against a wall with their arms crossed, the fourth studying a framed topo map in the corner, all of them silent.

Russ had never seen an Indian before, and he had so little worldly experience that he didn't recognize the sensation in his heart as love at first sight. He thought the Navajos' faces moved him because they were old. And yet, if he'd been asked to describe their leader, who wore a turquoise-clasped string tie beneath a fleece-collared coat, stiff with dirt, he might have used the word *beautiful*.

Ginchy uncomfortably said, "How can I help you gentlemen?"

One of them murmured in a strange tongue. The leader addressed Ginchy. "What are you doing here?"

"We, ah—this is a service camp for men with a conscientious objection to war."

"Yes. What are you doing?"

"Specifically? It's a bit of a hodgepodge. We're improving the national forest."

This seemed to amuse the Navajos. There were chuckles, an exchange of glances. The leader nodded at the pine trees outside and explained, "It's a forest."

"Land of many uses," Ginchy said. "I believe that is the Forest Service motto. You've got your logging, your hunting, your fishing, your watershed protection. We're improving the basis for all that. My guess is, somebody knew the right people in Washington."

A silence fell. Russ offered a mug of coffee to the leader, who wore a wide silver ring on his thumb, and asked if he wanted sugar.

"Yes. Five spoons."

When Russ returned from the antechamber, the leader was explaining to Ginchy what he wanted. The federal government, through its agents, had impoverished the Navajos by requiring severe reductions of their stock of cattle, sheep, and horses, and by unfairly siding with the Hopis in their land disputes. Now the country was fighting a war in which the Navajos sent their young men to fight, and conditions were bad on the reservation—fertile land eroding, the remaining stock fenced out of good pasture, too few able hands available for restoration work.

"War is bad for everyone," Ginchy agreed.

"You are the federal government. You have strong young men who won't fight. Why help a forest that doesn't need helping?"

"I'm sympathetic, but I'm not actually the federal government."

"Send us fifty men. You feed them, we'll shelter them."

"Yeah, that's . . . We have procedures here, roll calls and so forth. If I sent people to your reservation, they'd be off *my* reservation, if you take my meaning."

"Then you come, too. Move your camp. There isn't any work to do here."

"I don't have authority for that. If I asked for authority, the government would remember I'm here. I'd rather they not remember."

"They'll forget again," the leader said.

Already, in his first minutes of acquaintance, because he instinctively loved them, Russ grasped that the Navajos weren't lesser than white men but simply very different. In his later experience, they were unfailingly blunt about what they wanted. They didn't say please, didn't bow to convention or authority. Disqualifications self-evident to white men were meaningless to them. White men chalked up the frustrations of dealing with them to orneriness and stupidity, but Russ, that morning, saw nothing stupid in them. It hurt to think that they'd come all the way from Tuba City, a drive of several hours, and sat for further hours in a freezing truck, with an idea that made sense to them. It hurt to think of them returning empty-handed, in some unguessable state of mind—disappointment? Anger at the government? Embarrassment for having been naïve? Or just mute perplexity? Russ had been thirteen when his beloved farm dog, Skipper, fell sick with what his mother said was cancer. The dog's pain and infirmity soon reached the point where she made Russ ask a neighbor to shoot him and bury him. For Russ the hardest part of saying good-bye had been that Skipper couldn't understand what he was doing to him, or why. The Navajo elders were the opposite of dumb beasts, but this only made imagining their perplexity more painful.

When the sugared coffee had been drunk, Ginchy took down the elders' names and offered to send them a truckload of food and clothes.

The leader, whose name was Charlie Durochie, was unmoved and didn't thank him.

"That was a strange one," Ginchy said when they were gone.

"They're right, though," Russ said. "The work here seems like make-work."

"That's some other fellow's decision. I have to tread carefully, you know. Roosevelt wanted the army in charge of these camps."

"But we're supposed to be here serving, not building picnic tables."

"The service I perform is keeping men out of the war. If that means building picnic tables . . ."

Russ asked him for permission to deliver the supplies to Tuba City.

"They didn't seem much interested in charity," Ginchy said.

"They didn't say no."

"You have a tender heart."

"You do, too, sir."

The next morning, in a truck driven by the quartermaster's assistant and loaded with flour, rice, beans, and some work clothes left behind in the Depression, Russ rode north to Tuba City. In his innocence, he'd pictured tepees or log cabins in Indian country, tall trees with horses tied to them, clear streams running past mossy stones; he'd actually pictured mossy stones. The arid bleakness of the landscape he entered, after crossing Route 66, had not been imaginable. Dust hung in the air and coated every rock along the road. Lifeless buttes shimmered in the distance. Out on the parched plain were hogans more like piles of refuse than dwellings. In the settlements were houses of unpainted gray wood, roofless adobe ruins with holes in their walls, expanses of ash-darkened sand littered with rusted cans and broken roof tiles. Some of the smaller children, black-haired and round-faced, waved tentatively at the truck. Everyone else—old women wearing leggings beneath their skirts, old men with caved-in mouths, younger women who looked like they'd been born brokenhearted—averted their eyes.

Tuba City was a proper town, better shaded by cottonwoods, but scarcely less bleak. Russ now saw how comparatively much like Lesser Hebron the high forest was; how comparatively paradisal. The streams there were full, the forest double-carpeted with snow and pine needles, everything wet and white and fresh-smelling, and the men there, too— every last one of them—were white. To enter the reservation was to become aware of whiteness. Until he took a train to Arizona, Russ had never been more than sixty miles from Lesser Hebron, and although some of the non-Mennonite farmers had been ruined by the Depression, he'd never seen true privation. The Navajos had been stuck with barren land, seldom rained on. Witnessing their endurance of it, he had a curious sense of inferiority. The Navajos seemed closer to something he hadn't known he was so far from. He felt, from his white height, like a Pharisee.

"Jesus Christ, this place is depressing," the assistant quartermaster said.

The house to which they were directed seemed unfittingly tiny for a tribal leader, but a familiar black truck was parked in the dirt outside it, its front end elevated on stacks of earthen bricks. Charlie Durochie was watching a younger man hammer on a wrench connected to the truck's undercarriage. One of the tires lay next to an emaciated dog licking its penis. From the doorway of the house, which stood open to the cold, a little girl in a frilly, faded dress stared at the white men in their better truck. Russ hopped out and reintroduced himself to Durochie, who was dressed exactly as he'd been the day before.

"What do you have," Durochie said.

"What Mr. Ginchy promised. Some food, some clothes."

Durochie nodded as if the delivery were more burden than relief. From beneath the old truck came a thud, a strong oath, a wrench skittering out into the dirt. In Russ's grandfather's shop, it was a sin against a wrench to hammer on it. Always better, Clement said, to use leverage.

"Do you have a longer wrench?" Russ couldn't help asking.

"If I had a longer wrench," the younger man said coldly, "would I be using this one?"

He reached for the wrench, and Russ extended a hand to shake. "Russ Hildebrandt."

The man ignored the hand and picked up the wrench. His shoulders were broad in a chamois shirt, his hair tied in a ponytail that had no gray in it. He might have been fifteen years older than Russ, but it was hard to tell with Indian faces.

"Keith is my brother's son," Durochie remarked.

In a canvas bag in the cab of the camp truck, Russ found a longer wrench. Keith took it from him as if he expected no less. Russ asked Charlie where they should put the supplies.

"Here," Charlie said.

"Just on the ground?"

Apparently yes. By the time Russ and his partner had unloaded the sacks of food and two bales of clothing, Charlie had disappeared. The little girl now sat in the dirt watching Keith hammer on a steering arm. "What's your name?" Russ asked her.

She looked uncertainly at Keith, who stopped hammering. "Her name is Stella."

"Nice to meet you, Stella." To Keith, Russ added, "You can keep the wrench."

"Okay."

"I wish there were more we could do."

Keith sighted along the steering arm, checking its shape. Already then, he had a presence that later served him as a tribal politician, a charisma that invited touch and trust. Russ just wanted to keep looking at him. The assistant quartermaster was in the camp truck, tapping his fingers on the wheel. The thing about a Navajo silence was the sense that it could last indefinitely—all day.

"Say we sent a crew up here," Russ said. "What would we do?"

"I told my uncle not to bother with you. All he got was a broken truck."

"I'd like to help, though."

"My uncle thinks from a different time. I try to tell him the new lesson, but he won't learn."

"What is the lesson?"

"Your help is worse than no help."

"But if I came back with a crew? What would be entailed, exactly?"

"Go home, Long Wrench. We don't want your help."

When Russ returned to the reservation, two months later, Keith Durochie continued to call him Long Wrench, possibly a reference to his height, more probably to his thinking he knew better. Being given a nickname was traditional, but he didn't know this when he left that day. He felt disliked by someone he wished had liked him. In the weeks that followed, whenever he had hours of leave in Flagstaff, he went to the library and read what he could find about the Navajos. Despite being intransigent and thieving—to the point where they were rounded up and marched, en masse, to a prison camp in New Mexico—they'd been granted an immense piece of territory, which, according to various authors, and in contrast to the peace-loving, farm-tending Hopis, they'd proceeded to overgraze with herds of horses too numerous to be of practical use. To the U.S. government, the Navajos were a problem to be solved by force. To Russ, who was haunted by their faces, what needed solving was the mystery of them. He later had the same feeling about Marion.

In June, after Germany's unconditional surrender, when the mood in camp was festive, he again raised the question of the Navajos with Ginchy. "We should be there, not here," he said. "If I could show you the reservation, you'd see what I mean."

"You want to go back there," Ginchy said.

"Yes, sir. Very much."

"You're a strange one."

"How so?"

"A lot of men would kill for what you've got. People used to come here and vacation."

"It doesn't seem right to be on vacation when other men are dying."

"You don't feel fortunate. You're not happy to be my aide-de-camp."

"No, sir. I feel very fortunate. But I'd rather serve people in real need."

"That speaks well of you. I'm afraid you'll have to wait another twenty months, though."

Russ's disappointment must have been obvious. An hour later, when he was typing a report on camp hygiene, Ginchy came out to his desk with a roughly scrawled letter and asked him to do it up on letterhead. Reading the scrawl, Russ felt as though warm syrup were being poured over his head. It was love that worked miracles; no force on earth was more powerful.

To whom it may concern: I am the director of etc. etc. My assistant
R.H. wishes to inquire into work needing performance on the N
reservation. Please give him any assistance he may require. Yours etc. etc.

"Nobody cares what I do anymore," Ginchy said. "My only concern is your safety. You can take the old Willys if you can get it running, but you'll need to bring a partner."

Though Russ was friendly with the men in his cabin, Ginchy's favoritism hadn't endeared him to them, and neither had Russ's seriousness. The camp was like college that way.

"I'd rather go alone, sir."

"That's very Indian of you, but I'm the one in hot water if something happens to you."

"Things can happen to two people, too."

"Not as often."

"I don't need a partner. You can trust me."

"That also is Indian. I offer you an apple, and you want the whole basket. Speaking of which—'Thank you'?"

"Thank you, sir."

"I will, of course, expect a full formal report."

For his mission, after he'd repaired the Willys, Russ packed a bedroll, a change of clothes, his Bible, a notebook, twenty dollars of saved allowance, a canteen, toilet paper, and a box of food. He was still so dazzled by his luck that he was halfway down the forest road, on the morning of June 20, before it occurred to him to be afraid. He could be robbed or beaten up. The truck could wind up in a ditch. By the time he reached Tuba City, he ached from the work of keeping the Willys on the road. His shirt was soaked in the June heat.

Neither Charlie Durochie nor his truck was at the little house in town. When Russ found a woman down the street who spoke English, she said that Charlie was gone for the summer and Keith was with his wife's people, up on the mesa. She nodded in a direction where there was only glare and dusty vacancy, no mesa.

Russ was now additionally afraid that his mission would be a bust, because, in all the vast reservation, he knew only two men to speak to.

Inside the baking Willys, he shut his eyes and prayed for strength and guidance. Then he drove in the direction the woman had indicated.

The road up to the mesa was in places barely passable, the country relentlessly deserted but nevertheless dotted with bleached, shriveled cow patties. The Navajo men Russ encountered, one whittling a stick in the shade of an outcropping, two others watering horses at a tank beneath a rusted windmill, seemed to assume that a twenty-one-year-old white man looking for the Fallen Rocks people, as Keith Durochie's in-laws were evidently known, must have had some reason. The men stressed, in their crude English, that the distance wasn't short.

He had to stop every half hour to shake his cramped hands. When the air cooled and the shadows grew long, he pulled over by a decrepit stock pen and a tank into which water trickled from a crusty pipe. Small birds, ghostly in the twilight, were drinking from the seepage. The water was bitter, but his canteen was empty. On the mesa road, in six hours, he'd seen two women on a motorbike, one boy with a dog herding sheep, one old man driving a truck with coils of wire strapped to its bed, various free-roaming horses, and nothing resembling a town. He ate pork and beans from a can still warm from the day's heat. Then, fearing scorpions, he bedded down inside the Willys. He missed George Ginchy. Through the windshield, he could see a sky clotted with stars and nebulae, but he was too homesick for the camp to get out and admire it.

In the cool of early morning, he traveled through an upward-sloping basin forested with juniper and pinyon. Along the road, on flats too dry to be called meadow, sheep grazed among thorny shrubs. There was a magnificent desertion to the country, rutted tracks branching off with mysteries at the end of them, a sense of lives present but hidden. He drove fifteen miles before he saw another person, and then it wasn't one but a hundred.

Close to the road, beside a corral, were cook fires, horses, some trucks. Older men and women of all ages stood or sat around a structure of tree boughs festooned with scraps of red cloth. When Russ stopped and asked the nearest man, who was saddling a horse, where he might find the Fallen Rocks people, a scent of fried mutton entered the Willys. The man nodded up the road.

"At the chapter house. Follow the wash."

"What does the chapter house look like?"

The man cinched the saddle and didn't answer.

A long way farther up the road, Russ came to a neat, unmarked structure of mud and split logs beside a wash. The track next to it looked passable, and he followed it up into a shallow canyon, past fallen rocks the size of haystacks, an encouraging sign. In a side canyon still shaded from the sun, he found a proper small house, a stock pen, a yard with chickens in it. Beyond the pen was a hogan outside which women were cooking on an open fire. In front of the house, a little girl, Stella, was watching her father chop wood. At the sight of Keith Durochie, the tension of Russ's long drive drained out of him. He felt like he'd come home.

Keith approached the truck, trailed shyly by Stella. "What the hell?"

"I'm back," Russ said.

"What for?"

"Forgot my wrench."

There was a silence before Keith smiled. He led Russ into the house, which had two rooms, one with a bed in it, and gave him sweet coffee and a cold, unsweetened sort of doughnut. When Russ explained that he was on a fact-finding mission, Keith said it would have to wait—he was doing a sing. He left Russ alone, by no means for the last time. Life among the Navajos meant a lot of waiting and not much explanation.

What a sing was he learned later in the morning, when a dust cloud boiled up from the canyon. The people he'd passed on the road were now on horses adorned with brightly colored yarn, followed by trucks similarly adorned and tooting their horns. The entourage proceeded past the house to the hogan where the women had been cooking. Nervous but curious, Russ crossed the yard for a closer look.

The lead rider was a short-haired young man whose face was painted black and red; in his hand was a tasseled black stick. He waited in the saddle until others from his group could help him down. Moving with a bad limp, he took the black stick into the hogan. Children were piling from the trucks and running to a shed where the food was. Keith and his kinswomen quietly greeted the adults. No one paid any attention to Russ.

From inside the hogan, a male voice rose tremulously in off-key song. Russ didn't understand the words, but they went to his heart. The voice was like his grandfather's, singing hymns in Lesser Hebron; Clement, too, sang off-key. After the song had ended, the hogan erupted like a small volcano, boxes of Cracker Jack flying out through its smoke hole. While the children pounced on them, Keith's people distributed blankets to the older guests, who'd taken up a different song.

he-ye ye ye ya ŋa
'ëëla do kwii-yi – na
kị gó di yá – 'e – hya ŋa
he ye ye ye ya

Though the language was foreign, the voices of a congregation, raised in bright morning sun, deepened Russ's sense of having come home. As the singing continued, Keith invited him to join the group for mutton and corn bread.

Only the children, Stella in particular, looked at him, and for a long time Keith was busy hosting. Russ might have grown bored if he hadn't been so fascinated by the faces. When the party finally broke up, the entourage returning to their horses and trucks, Keith sat down and asked him where he was going next. Russ again mentioned his charge from George Ginchy.

"I told you not to bother," Keith said.

"You said you'd talk to me after the sing."

"It just started. We still have three days."

"Three days?"

"That's the new way. We don't do the long sings anymore."

"The thing is, the only people I know here are you and your uncle."

"You won't get to my uncle in your truck."

"Well, so."

Keith turned and, for the first time, looked at Russ directly. "What are you doing here?"

"Honestly, I want to know more about your people. The work is just an excuse."

Keith nodded and said, "That's better."

He went to help his kinspeople, and Russ fell asleep on the ground.

He was awakened by the smell of gasoline. Keith was filling the tank of a small truck through a funnel with a muslin filter. Already seated on the cargo bed were Stella and a slender young woman with a bundled baby. "You ride in front with me," Keith said.

Making the woman sit in back didn't seem right to Russ, but to Keith the matter was already settled. The little truck had a suspension well suited to the rutted canyon road. After a long while, as Keith drove, his silence became so trying that Russ asked him what a sing was.

"We're helping our friend," Keith said. "He came back from the Pacific out of harmony. He walks bad, from shrapnel, and he doesn't sleep—the enemy's burned flesh is in his nose. The enemy looked like us, not like the *bilagáana*, and their spirits got inside him. He brought home an enemy shirt that he can smell the war in. It will be part of the sing."

Though Russ didn't understand every detail, the communal healing of a man brutalized by war made thrilling sense to him. He had many more questions, but he made himself parcel them out slowly as the truck retraced his morning drive. He learned that the woman in back was Keith's wife, the baby his two-month-old son. Keith's father-in-law, riding ahead of them on horseback, carrying the ceremonial black stick, was a medicine man and a friend of Charlie Durochie from a boarding school in Farmington, New Mexico. Keith had attended the same school and worked for some years on oil rigs before he married into the Fallen Rocks clan. He now managed his in-laws' ranch on the mesa.

Each fact Keith offered seemed to Russ a precious stone. He felt hopelessly inferior to Keith, as lovers do, and was reluctant to take his eyes off him. What Keith thought about Russ was less clear. Russ had the sense of being more than just tolerated, of being at least amusing in his ignorance, but Keith showed little curiosity about him. The only question he asked on the drive was "You a Christian?"

"Yes," Russ said eagerly. "I'm from the Mennonite faith."

Keith nodded. "I knew their missionaries."

"Here? On the reservation?"

"In Tuba City. They were all right."

"So—are you—do you worship?"

Keith smiled at the road ahead of them. "Everyone drinks Arbuckle's

coffee. All over the world, Arbuckle's coffee. Your religion is like that—
I guess it must be pretty good coffee."

"I don't understand."

"We don't send our coffee around the world. You have to be born here
to drink it."

"But that's what I love about the Bible. Anyone, anywhere, can receive the Word—it's not exclusive."

"Now you sound like a missionary."

Russ was surprised to feel ashamed.

Many miles down the main mesa road, they reached an encampment
where fires were being built, blankets shaken open, slabs of raw mutton handled, a flaccid basketball kicked around a grassless pasture by
shouting boys. Several hundred people were at the camp. The sight of
them created a pressure in Russ's head, a sense of too much immersion
too quickly. To relieve it, he set off down the road by himself, into the
setting sun.

A raven was croaking, jackrabbits browsing in sagebrush shadows. A
snake, both startling and startled, went airborne in its haste to leave the
road. As soon as the sun dropped behind a ridge, a breeze came through
the valley, carrying smells of warmed juniper and wildflower. Turning
back, he saw smoke rising from a distant bonfire, the cliffs behind it pink
with alpenglow. He saw that he'd been wrong about the Navajos' land.
The beauty of the national forest was friendly and obvious. The beauty of
the mesa was harsher but cut deeper.

Feasting was in progress when he returned to the camp. He hadn't
known to bring anything but the clothes he was wearing, his pocket knife
and wallet, so Keith gave him blankets from the truck. Even if Keith's
wife hadn't been nursing, Russ would have been too shy to speak to her,
because she was Keith's wife. While he ate mutton and beans and bread,
competing songs wafted over from other cook fires. Someone was beating
on a drum.

The dancing started when the sky was fully black. Standing with
Keith, Russ watched a young woman circle the bonfire, stepping in
rhythm with the drum, while a crowd clapped and chanted. Other
young women joined her, and soon some of the older men were dancing,

too. The pressure in Russ's head had given way to exhilaration and gratitude. He was a white man alone among the Indians, hearing the women sing and chant. Resinous knots of juniper exploded in orange sparks, the stars dimming and brightening in swirling smoke, and he remembered to thank God.

One of the younger girls peeled off from the fire and came over to him. She touched his shirt sleeve. "Dance," she said.

Alarmed, he turned to Keith.

"She wants you to dance."

"Yes, I see that."

"Dance with me," the girl insisted.

She wore a bulky shawl and a skirt with a Mexican ruffle, but her calves were bare and slim. Her forwardness was so alien to Russ's experience, she was like a threatening animal, and he didn't know how to dance; it had been verboten in Lesser Hebron. He waited for her to go away, but she stood patiently, her eyes on the ground. She couldn't have been older than sixteen, and he was a tall, white, older stranger. He found himself touched by her courage.

"I'm not a dancer," he said, taking a step toward the fire, "but I can try."

The girl smiled at the ground.

"You need to give her a little money," Keith said.

This bewildered Russ. But the girl, too, seemed confused. Her smile, in the firelight, was edged with disappointment. Not wanting to offend her, he took a greenback from his wallet. She snatched it and hid it in her skirt.

He had no idea what to do, but he joined the circle and stepped as well as he could, following the girl, who did know what to do. The slimness of her legs and the shimmy of her hips brought out the queasiness in him. But now, in the flickering orange light, amid the beating of the drum and the chanting of female voices, he understood that the queasiness had nothing to do with pity or revulsion. It was heart-quickening excitement. Beneath the girl's shawl and skirt was a body that a man could want; that Russ himself could want. A suspense that had hitherto existed only in disturbing dreams, dreams that ballooned into apocalyptic heat and ruptured in the soiling of his pajamas, had invaded the world he was awake in. What made the dreams so disturbing was how painless it was, how ecstatically pleasurable, to be consumed in flame.

The girl's interest in him seemed to have expired when he gave her money. After a politely long interval, he stepped out of the circle and retreated into the dark. As soon as the girl noticed, she ran over to him. Her expression was now closer to angry.

"Keep dancing or give her money," someone, not Keith, called to him.

He couldn't imagine what money had to do with healing a soldier's psychic wounds, but he fumbled with his wallet and gave her another greenback. Satisfied, she left him alone.

He awoke in the morning, on the ground beside Keith's truck, still excited, still prickling with his new awareness, and daunted by the prospect of further immersion. Feeling the need for a walking cure, he told Keith he was going back to the ranch and would wait for him there.

"Take a horse," Keith said. "You could die in the sun."

"I'd rather walk."

The walk was brutal, seven hours under a sun ever hotter and whiter. Keith had given him a skin of water and some bread wrapped in a rag, and he'd exhausted both before he reached the turnoff at the chapter house. By then, in the white heat, the road had ceased to be a line leading rationally from an origin to a destination. It had become, in his mind, the defining engenderer of everything that wasn't road—stony slopes boiling with grasshoppers, stands of conifers made blacker by the blazing light, seemingly proximate rock formations whose respective positions his progress refused to alter. Either his ears or the air rang so loudly that he couldn't hear his footsteps. He mistook a hovering falcon for an angel, and then he saw that the falcon *was* an angel, unaffiliated with the God he'd always known; that Christ had no dominion on the mesa.

By the time he reached the ranch, he'd walked his way out of all certainty, and the cure hadn't worked. The very thing he'd been fleeing awaited him in Keith's little house. The spirit of the girl he'd danced with had preceded him, outrun him, to the bedroom. Parched and sunburned though he was, he lay down and opened his pants to see if the dreamed apocalypse could be achieved while he was awake. He discovered that, with a bit of chafing, it very quickly could. The pleasure that tore through him was the more glorious for being waking, and there wasn't any punishment; he wasn't struck blind. He wasn't even ashamed of the splatter. No one could see him, not even God. For the rest of his life, he associated the mesa with the discovery of secret pleasure and permission.

When Keith came back with his family, two days later, he put Russ to work on the ranch. To the farming skills Russ already had he added new ones. He learned how to lasso a calf, how to catch a horse on a range without fences, how to compel a cow to walk backward in a narrow gully. He experienced the misery of sheep dip for all concerned, both the sheep and anyone who touched the vile liquid. Keith's brother-in-law castrated a stallion and threw a bloody testicle at Russ, and Russ threw it back at him. He and Keith rode far up the canyon and camped beneath a milky host of stars, saw the silent silhouettes of gliding owls, heard spirits whistling in rock crevices, ate roasted pinyon nuts. When his worst fear was realized, in the form of a scorpion sting on his ankle, he learned that it merely hurt like the dickens.

The longer he stayed with the Diné, the more resemblance he saw with his own community in Indiana. The Diné, too, preferred to live apart and seek harmony, and their women were like his mother—sturdy and patient, permitted to own land. In the stories kept alive by medicine men, the original divine mother, Changing Woman, who was named for her seasons, had partnered with the Sun and given birth to twin sons. Like Russ's mother, Changing Woman was associated with the fruit of the land. She'd raised the sons and instilled them with practical wisdom, while the solar father, though necessary for creating life, remained aloof. And just as Mennonites recalled their martyrs, so the Diné sang of their Long Walk to the prison camp in the 1860s, the years of disease and hunger inflicted on them there. The Diné, too, defined themselves by persecution, and their country, close to nothing, welcoming to no one, a desert, was even godlier than Indiana. It was in the desert, after all, that the Israelites had received the Word of God, the one God of all mankind, and that Jesus, while summoning clarity for his ministry, had prayed for forty days and forty nights.

During Russ's forty days in Diné Bikéyah, Keith advised him not to point at shooting stars, not to whistle at night, not to look a stranger in the eye, and not to ask a man his name before it was offered. When a Diné man died in his hogan, his family had to burn it and destroy whatever had touched him. Out on the open mesa, Keith nodded at a sun-bleached horse skeleton, still saddled a decade after the horse's rider had been struck by lightning, and told Russ to stay away from it. Keith said the man's bad luck adhered to the spot, and Russ, in the shimmering heat, the rarefied air, found that this made sense to him. While man experienced time as a progression, from unknown past to unknowable future, to God the entire course of history was eternally present. To God, the site of the lightning strike wasn't just the spot where a man *had* died but the spot where he would *later* die and the spot where, in God's perfect knowledge, he was *forever* dying. Being in the desert made a mystery like this accessible.

Because he was working hard, for people who could use the help, he didn't feel guilty about his official mission, but George Ginchy had told him that if he wasn't back by August he would send a search party. Accordingly, at first light on the thirty-first of July, he packed and fueled the Willys and took his leave of Keith and Stella, who were the only others awake. Stella ran up to him and wrapped her arms around his leg. He picked her up and stroked her head.

"I'll come back," he said. "I don't know when, but I will."

"Careful what you promise, Long Wrench."

"I wasn't talking to you. Was I, Stella?"

She squirmed bashfully. He set her down, and she went to her father. Ever unsentimental, Keith was already walking away.

Russ still knew hardly anything about the Diné, but at least he knew how much he didn't know. The desert had only strengthened his belief in God, but he was no longer certain that his ancestral faith was the truest version of the one true faith. After he returned to the service camp, where Ginchy, not punitively, simply out of practicality, had found another worker to be his aide-de-camp, Russ began to investigate the many ways there were to skin a cat. He now worked for the quartermaster and could safely take an extra hour, on a Flagstaff supply run, to stop at the library and read books shelved in the Dewey decimal 290s, world religions. At the camp, on Sunday mornings, he tried worshiping with Ginchy and the Quakers. Their silences, though agreeable to him, seemed shallower than Navajo silences, less embedded in a comprehensive way of being. But he could never be a Navajo; their coffee wasn't for him to drink.

One Sunday morning in November, continuing his investigation, he drove the old Willys to the Catholic church in Flagstaff. He'd detected, in a book about Saint Francis, an appealingly uncompromising spirit. From a pew at the rear of the church, amid the fragrance of burning tapers and the feeble light from colored windows, he could see the mantillas and gray braids of old Mexican women, the more modern American dress of middle-aged couples, and the pale nape of a woman whose head was deeply bowed. The priest, who was elderly, with a serious tremor, spoke a language as unintelligible as Navajo, and the service wasn't short. Russ's eyes kept returning to the pale neck in front of him. It aroused a sensation he'd formerly misapprehended as queasiness and now associated with pleasure in secrecy. The woman was small and delicate, her hair cut in a bob.

In Lesser Hebron, Communion was a major semiannual event taken in full fellowship, using bread that the women had communally kneaded and baked. Catholic Communion seemed almost as alien to Russ as a Navajo sing. The priest invited sacrilegious comparison to a doctor with a tongue depressor, the congregants to children queuing up for lunch. Only the woman with the pretty neck received her wafer with visible feeling. She kneeled with a quaking vulnerability, reminiscent of his mother's intensity of faith. As she returned to her pew, he saw that she was full-mouthed and dark-eyed, possibly no older than he was.

After the service, he asked the priest if he could come again and receive Communion as a visitor. The priest explained why he couldn't, but he said that Russ was welcome to observe and worship. Russ duly revisited Nativity the following Sunday, but this time he was defeated by the Latin of it all. The church's thick walls, which a week earlier had felt sheltering, now struck him as a monument to a living faith gone dead, a once-molten spirit congealed into cold stone by the passing of centuries. The dark-eyed young woman was there again, alone again, but the fervor of her faith now seemed to exclude him.

Abandoning his experiment, he returned to worshiping with his fellow Mennonites in camp, but he felt no great fellowship with them. The truth was, he missed the mesa, the immanence of God in every rock, every bush, every insect. He took to hiking up the forest road, alone, on Sunday mornings. There he did sometimes sense God's presence, but it was feeble, like sun hidden by winter clouds.

One afternoon in March, while he was at the library in Flagstaff, abusing his camp privileges, leafing through a book of photographs of Plains Indians, a young woman sat down across the table from him and opened a math textbook. She was wearing a plaid cowboy shirt and had her hair in a bandanna, but he still recognized her. In the library's better light, she was easily the most handsome woman he'd seen since his eyes were opened by a Navajo dancer. Embarrassed to be looking at a picture book, as if he were illiterate, he stood up to fetch a different book.

"I know you," she said. "I saw you at Nativity."

He turned back. "Yes."

"I only saw you twice. Why?"

"Do you mean why only twice, or why was I there at all?"

"Both."

"I'm not Catholic. I was just—observing."

"That explains it. Young Catholic gentlemen are few and far between. I notice you never came back."

"I'm not Catholic."

"So you just said. If you say it a third time, I'll think you're warding off some hex."

Her sharpness surprised him, as did the directness with which she proceeded to question him. Having sensed a resemblance to his mother, he might have expected softness and modesty. While learning nothing more about her than her name, which was Marion, he told her where he came from, why he was in Flagstaff, and how the Navajos had led him to explore other faiths.

"So you just took a truck and disappeared for a month?"

"A month and a half. The camp director was very generous."

"And you weren't scared to go there by yourself?"

"I probably should have been more scared. Somehow it didn't occur to me."

"I would have been scared."

"Well, you're a woman."

The noun was innocuous and everyday, but he blushed to have spoken it. He'd never engaged in conversation with a woman he consciously found attractive—wouldn't have guessed how taxing it would be. That she seemed impressed with his story made it all the more taxing. He finally, awkwardly, said he ought to let her get on with her studying.

She regarded her textbook sadly. "The mind so drifts."

"I know. I struggle with math myself."

"It's not a struggle, it's just dry. I get hungry to be with God." Her tone was matter-of-fact, as if God were a sandwich.

"I do, too," Russ said. "That is—I know what you're saying. I miss being with the Navajos. They get to be with God all day, every day."

"You should come back to Nativity. You might find what you're looking for. I didn't even know I was looking till I went there."

Another man might have been put off by her religiosity, but to Russ it was no more than a version of what he'd grown up with. Less placid, but familiar. It no longer disturbed him that a girl called his mother to mind. It had dawned on him that his mother wasn't simply his mother, wasn't merely a figure of sacred devotion. She was a flesh-and-blood woman who herself had once been young.

When he returned to the Catholic church, the next Sunday, Marion sat beside him and whispered brief explanations of the liturgy. He tried to connect to Christus, as the priest called him, but he was thwarted by the proximity of her little self. She wore a coat dyed bright green and collared with darker green velveteen. Some of her nails were chewed, the torn cuticles edged with dry blood. She knit her fingers together so tightly in prayer that her knuckles whitened, her breath faintly rasping from her open mouth. Because her passion was directed at the Almighty, Russ felt safe to be excited by it.

After the service, he offered her a lift in the Willys.

"Thanks," she said, "but I have to walk."

"I like walking, too. It's my favorite thing."

"I have to count the steps, though. I did it once, a couple of years ago, and now I can't stop, because . . . Never mind."

Two old, slow women had emerged from the church speaking Spanish. Cherry Avenue was so quiet that pigeons were camped out in the middle of it.

"What were you going to say?"

"Nothing," she said. "It's embarrassing. I have to start at the door of the church and make sure it's the exact same number of steps every time, because that's how I know God is still with me. If I ever counted one step too many, or too few . . ." She shuddered, perhaps at the thought, perhaps with embarrassment.

"My number of steps wouldn't be the same," Russ offered, although she hadn't invited him to join her.

"That's right, you're tall. You'd have your own number—except you shouldn't have a number. *I* shouldn't have a number. I'm too superstitious already."

"The Navajos have all sorts of superstitions. I'm not sure they're wrong."

"It's an insult to God to think that counting steps has any bearing."

"I don't see the harm in it. The Bible is full of signs from God."

She raised her dark eyes to him. "You're a kind person."

"Oh—thank you."

"Maybe you can walk with me and distract me. I think, if I could walk even once without counting, I wouldn't have to count anymore. Unless"—she laughed—"I get struck dead because I wasn't counting."

She was a mysterious combination of sharp and odd. The delicacy of her neck, visible above her velveteen collar, continued to fascinate him. In Lesser Hebron, and at Goshen, too, female napes had been concealed by plaits or tresses. As he walked her home, he learned that she'd grown up in San Francisco and had dreamed, foolishly, of being a Hollywood actress. She'd worked in Los Angeles as a typist and stenographer before moving to Flagstaff to live with her uncle. For a short while, she'd considered entering a convent, but now she was studying to be an elementary-school teacher. Being small, she said, she'd found that children trusted her, as if she were one of them. She said she hadn't been raised Catholic—her father had been a nonobservant Jew, her mother a "Whiskeypalian."

Each disclosure widened the vista of what Russ didn't know about America. Although, by his calculation, she was only twenty-five, the place-names she dropped so casually, San Francisco, Los Angeles, were totemic of experiences more various than a woman from Lesser Hebron could expect in her entire life. As with Keith Durochie, he felt ignorant and inferior, and again the feeling was indistinguishable from attraction. It never crossed his mind that Marion might be attracted to him, too; that in her narrow Flagstaff ambit, with most of the country's young men overseas, his apparition at Nativity had been as singular to her as hers was to him. Even if she hadn't been significantly older, he had no concept of himself as an object of desire.

Her uncle's house, on the outskirts of town, was low and ramshackle, its yard overrun with prickly pear. In the driveway stood a Ford truck blasted paintless by Arizona sand. Marion ran up to the front door and stamped on the mat there, spread her arms, and raised her face to the blue, blue sky. "Here I am," she called to it. "Strike me dead."

She looked at Russ and laughed. Trying to keep up, he managed a smile, but now she was frowning. Part of her oddness was how suddenly her expressions changed.

"I'm terrible," she said. "This could turn out to be the moment when my fatal cancer started."

"I don't know that God minds a joke. Not if you sincerely love Him."

Still serious, she came back down the walk. "Thank you for that. I do believe you've cured me. Would you like to stay for lunch?"

When he demurred—he was already derelict, owing to the length of Catholic mass, and he still had to retrieve the Willys—Marion insisted on walking back to the church with him. The taxation of being with her grew heavier as they retraced their steps. She admired his pacifism, admired his impatience at the camp, admired his compassion for the Navajos. Every time he glanced down, her brown eyes were glowing up at him. He'd never felt a gaze so unconditionally approving, and he lacked the experience to recognize the willingness it signaled. By the time they reached the truck, the stress of it had given him an actual headache. He offered to run her back to her uncle's, but her face had clouded again.

"What you said earlier—that it doesn't matter what we do as long as we love God. Do you really think that's true?"

"I don't know," he said. "The Navajos don't accept Christ, and I don't know that they're eternally damned. It doesn't seem fair that they would be."

She lowered her eyes. "I don't believe in an afterlife."

"You—really?"

"I think the only thing that matters is the state of your soul while you're alive."

"Is that—Catholic teaching?"

"Definitely not. Father Fergus and I discuss it all the time. To me, there's nothing realer in the world than God, and Satan is no less real. Sin is real and God's forgiveness is real. That's the message of the Gospel. But there's not much in the Gospel about the afterlife—John is the only one who talks about it. And doesn't that seem strange? If the afterlife is so important? When the rich young man asks Jesus how he might have eternal life, Jesus doesn't give him a straight answer. He seems to say that heaven is loving God and obeying the commandments, and hell is being lost in sin—forsaking God. Father Fergus says I have to believe that Jesus is talking about a literal heaven and hell, because that's what the Church teaches. But I've read those verses a hundred times. The rich young man asks about eternity, and Jesus tells him to give away his money. He says what to do in the *present*—as if the *present* is where you find eternity— and I think that's right. Eternity is a mystery to us, just like God is a mystery. It doesn't have to mean rejoicing in heaven or burning in hell. It could be a timeless state of grace or bottomless despair. I think there's eternity in every second we're alive. So I'm in quite a bit of trouble with Father Fergus."

Russ stared at the little green-coated woman. He might have just fallen in love with her. It wasn't only the depth of her engagement with a question of urgency to him. It was hearing, in her words, a thought that had been latent in him without his being able to articulate it. His sense of inferiority became acute. Paradoxically, instead of making him shy of her, it made him want to bury himself in her.

"I should go inside and pray," she said. "It stinks to feel so close to God and not be a better Catholic. My progress has been stymied for quite some time."

"Can I come again next week?"

She smiled sadly. "If you don't mind my saying, you're not the most promising candidate, Mr. God Doesn't Mind a Joke."

"But you're struggling with the creed yourself."

"I have good reason to."

"What—reason?"

"I'd frankly rather—do you think you'll ever go back to the reservation?"

"Sometime, yes, absolutely."

"Maybe you can take me along with you. I'd like to see it for myself."

The thought of taking her to the mesa was like a reward in heaven, amazing but remote. For now, it felt more like a brush-off. "I'd be very happy to show it to you."

"Good," she said. "Something to look forward to." She turned away and added, "You know where to find me."

Did she mean that he could find her whenever he pleased, or only when he was returning to the reservation? As the words of Jesus were ambiguous, so were hers. He was still struggling to parse the ambiguity, two days later, when an envelope bearing only a Flagstaff postmark, no return address, arrived for him in camp. He took it to his cabin and sat down on his bunk.

Dear Russell,

I was remiss not to thank you again for curing me of my superstition. You were so lovely to put up with me—I felt as if the sun had come out after a month of clouds. I hope you find everything you're looking for and more.

Yours in God and friendship,
Marion

Here, too, in the farewell flavor of *I hope you find*, a doubting mind could see ambiguity. But his body knew better. The sensation that gripped it was familiar in its emanation from his nether parts, entirely novel in its suffusion with emotion—with hope and gratitude, the image of one particular person, her soulful eyes, her complicated mind. It was inconceivable that a person so fascinating might feel lesser, and yet there it was, in her own handwriting, unambiguously: *put up with me*. The words excited him so much, she might have been whispering them in his ear.

The next day, when he requested leave for the afternoon, the quarter-master didn't even ask what for. George Ginchy still enjoyed his roll calls and assemblies, but since the war ended the camp had only been go-ing through the motions; Ginchy's quest of the moment was to procure equipment for the football squad he'd organized. The old Willys was somehow still operable, and Russ drove it first to the public library and then, not finding Marion, to her uncle's house, which he identified by its prickly pears. He was curiously unafraid to knock on the front door. He knew that the marriage of men and women was in the natural course of things, ordained by God, but in his mind, already, the world wasn't full of women he might potentially someday meet, there was only one woman. In retrospect, their chance encounter at the library had had God's seal on it. To knock on her door was no more than what God had intended when He created man and woman; which was to say that Russ was now conscious of being a man.

She came to the door in dungarees and an oversize white shirt, knot-ted at her midriff. That she was wearing pants, like a man, was inordi-nately incredible to him.

"I knew it would be you," she said. "I woke up this morning with the strongest feeling I would see you."

Her lack of surprise reminded him again of his mother, her serenity. If Marion's presentiment could be credited, it suggested that Russ's com-ing to see her, which had felt to him like an act of personal agency, had merely been part of God's design. She led him through a parlor hung with landscape paintings, all similar in style, and into a kitchen with a view of a mountain. At the rear of the back yard, which was strewn with rusty metal forms, perhaps sculptures, stood a tin-roofed structure.

"That's Jimmy's studio," Marion said. "He won't come out till dinnertime. Antonio's at work, and I am—studying." She indicated an open textbook on the table. "We also have two cats, who seem to have disappeared. They were just here."

Jimmy was her uncle, but Russ wondered about the other man. An unpleasant new feeling, possessiveness, came over him. "Who is Antonio?"

"Jimmy's companion. They're—you know." Marion looked up. "Or maybe you don't."

How was he supposed to know anything?

"They're like husband and wife, except Antonio's a man. It's a terrible abomination." She snickered. "Are you hungry? I can make you a sandwich."

There were, at camp, two Quaker boys whom Russ's cabinmates referred to as *fairies*. Only now did he understand that the appellation might encompass more than just their manner. He felt a queasiness, not only at the abomination but at Marion's snicker.

"I'm sorry," she said, as if sensing his discomfort. "I forgot where you come from. I'm so used to Antonio, it seems ridiculous that anyone could disapprove."

"So, you, uh—what part of Catholic teaching do you actually accept?"

"Oh, lots of it. The Eucharist, Christ's absolution of our sins, Father Fergus's authority. Jimmy and Antonio would definitely have things to repent if they were Catholic, but I don't see that it's any of my business. Jesus says I shouldn't cast stones."

Russ's empathy for homosexuals began with Marion. Once he was in love with her, it became axiomatic that every conviction of hers deserved strong consideration for adoption. Alongside his craving to bury himself in her was a wish to be filled up with her—to feel his heart pumping her essence, as if he were a butterfly emerging from a chrysalis, into his unfurling, birth-damp wings. She'd spent three and a half more years on earth than he, had lived in San Francisco and Los Angeles, and was a deeper and more incisive thinker. Because she swore by Roosevelt, Russ registered to vote as a Democrat. Because she read secular literature—

Evelyn Waugh, Graham Greene, John Steinbeck—he read it, too. The same thing with jazz, the same thing with modern art, the same thing with clothes, and the same thing, especially, with sex.

They passed his first visit at her kitchen table, talking about the soul and teachers' college, about his grandfather and his doubts about his family's faith. On his second visit, five days later, they hiked so far up the mountain behind Jimmy's house they had to race the setting sun back down. Marion then sent him a letter in which there was little of substance, just a breezy account of her day, but he couldn't stop rereading it. Each detail—that one of the cats had coughed up a hair ball on her bed, that her uncle had asked her to cook lamb chops for his birthday, that she might stop at the butcher on her way back from the post office, that she thought it might snow again—was more magically interesting than the next. He remembered hungrily rereading his mother's early letters to him, which were likewise full of the quotidian. Now his mother's letters so bored him that he barely skimmed them once. He couldn't have cared less if she thought it might snow.

His mother had taken to mentioning that one girl or another in their community had "really grown up," a short phrase that encoded a longer message: he was to finish his service, choose a wife from one of a score of acceptable families, and settle down in Lesser Hebron. What he could write back to his mother without revealing his doubts had dwindled to the point of his repeating, essentially verbatim, not just sentences but whole paragraphs. Of his time with the Navajos, he'd written little more than that they were a proud and generous people who had great respect for the Mennonites. Of Marion, he wrote nothing at all. His sense that he and she had been ordained to meet was growing stronger by the day, and his family's community didn't forbid marriage to outsiders, merely discouraged it, but Marion was a pants-wearing, half-Jewish Catholic who lived with homosexuals. The safe course was to conceal her existence and hope for the best.

Every second Friday night, most of the camp workers piled into trucks and went down to the movie house in Flagstaff, chaperoned by George Ginchy himself. The first time Russ had joined them, after losing his religion on the mesa, he'd been transfixed by the window movies opened on the larger world, and he'd been going ever since. On a Friday night in April, when he and the others trooped into the Orpheum, a small, green-coated figure was waiting for him, by secret prearrangement, in the last row of seats.

Very soon, almost as soon as the lights went down, four soft fingers slipped into his callused hand. To hold a woman's hand was so absorbing and momentous that the shouts of the Three Stooges, in the first short subject, were unintelligible to him. While Marion, for her part, seemed perfectly at ease, laughing at the twisting of ears and the collapse of a stepladder, the spectacle of violence struck Russ as a profanement of his moment with her; it hurt his eyes.

When the feature started, a Sherlock Holmes picture, she lost interest in the screen and rested her head against his shoulder. She extended an arm across his chest, pulling herself closer. Basil Rathbone, meerschaum in hand, was speaking unintelligibly. Russ tried not to breathe, lest she let go of him, but she stirred again. Her hand was on his neck, turning his face toward hers. In the flickering light, a pair of lips surfaced. And, oh, their softness. The intimacy of kissing them was so intense it made him anxious, like a mortal in the presence of eternity. He turned his face away, but she immediately drew it back. By and by, he got the idea. He and she weren't there to watch the movie, not one bit. They were there to kiss and kiss and kiss.

When the credits rolled, she wordlessly stood and left the theater. The house lights came up on a world comprehensively transformed, made more vivid and expansive, by the joining of two mouths. Feeling wildly conspicuous, hoping he wasn't, he slipped into a group of workers exiting the theater. Marion wasn't in the lobby, but George Ginchy was.

"You never cease to surprise me," Ginchy said.

"Sir?"

"I took you for a God-fearing country boy. You almost squeaked with clean living."

"Am I in trouble?"

"Not with me."

Marion led him, in the weeks that followed, up a long and twisting stairway, scary to climb but delightful to linger on each step of—the first *I love you* in a letter, the first *I love you* spoken, the first kiss in public daylight, the hours shortened to minutes by kissing in her uncle's parlor, the more frenzied nighttime grappling on the seat of the Willys, the unbelievable opening of her blouse, the discovery that even infinite softness had gradations, *softer yet, softest of all*—which finally led, on a cloudy afternoon in May, to her locking her bedroom door, kicking off her shoes, and lying down on her little bed.

Through the sheer curtain on her window, Russ could see her uncle's art studio.

"Should we be in here?" he said. "It would be awkward if someone . . ."

"Antonio's in Phoenix, and Jimmy's not my keeper. It's not as if we have a better place."

"It could be awkward, though."

"Are you afraid of me, sweetie? You seem afraid of me."

"No. I'm not afraid of you. But—"

"I woke up knowing today would be the day. You just have to trust me. I'm scared, too, but—I really think God intended this to be the day."

It seemed to Russ that God was in the cloudy light outside but not inside her bedroom. Somewhere on the stairway to this moment, he'd lost hold of the importance of preserving his purity until they were married.

"Today's good for other reasons, too," she said. "It's a good safe day."

"Is Jimmy not home?"

"No, he's in his studio. I mean I can't get pregnant."

He didn't love feeling always slow, always behind, but he did love Marion. It wasn't accurate to say he thought about her night and day, because it was less a matter of thinking than of feeling filled with her, filled in the unceasing way that he imagined a more truly religious person, a Navajo on the mesa, might be filled with God. And she was right: if not today, in her room, then when and where? He never wanted to stop touching her, but merely touching was never enough. His body had been telling him, albeit mutely, and yet so insistently that he got the message, that the pressure of her presence in him could only be relieved by releasing it inside her.

Which he now did. In the gray light, on the quilted coverlet of her bed. The release came very quickly and was disappointing in its suddenness, surprisingly less satisfactory than his solitary chafings. An act no less crucial in his life than being baptized had lasted scarcely longer. Ashamed of how unmomentous the act had felt in the event, he became more generally ashamed. His proportions were as ungainly as hers were ideal, his boniness an affront to her softness, his skin a dismal gray against the creamy white of hers. He couldn't believe she was smiling up at him, couldn't believe the approval in her gaze.

"Just rest there for a second," she said, stroking his hair. "We're only starting."

He didn't know how she knew this, but again she was right. As soon as she said *starting*, his body told him she was right. The word in itself reelectrified it. That the crucial act could be repeated, after the shortest of breathers, would never have occurred to him. That it could be done *four times*, before the light faded and he had to rush away, was a dazzlement from which, he could already feel, as he urged the Willys up the steep road to camp, there would be no recovering. The Mosaic commandment against adultery, the plain dress of the women in Lesser Hebron, the proscription against dancing, the concealment of women's necks: it was as if he'd grown up inside an ancient fort whose parapets and cannons faced out on peaceful fields, toward an enemy he'd seen no trace of. Now he understood why the fortifications were so massive.

The next time they sinned, in her little room, on an unusually warm and muggy afternoon, with a cat thumping against her locked door, he fell from a height of carnality into an abyss of moral anxiety. He trusted Marion because of her unfeignable love of God, her self-blaming goodness. What she wanted was no more than what he wanted, and the spilling of seed wasn't shameful per se. An arousal and emission that occurred in dreams, without his volition, could only be a natural function of the body. But to release his seed inside a woman he wasn't married to, to lose himself in her flesh, to wallow in her private aromas, was manifestly different. He extricated himself and, despite the heat, pulled the coverlet over him.

"Aren't you worried," he said, "about committing a mortal sin?"

She scrambled to her knees. Her nakedness, blinding in its beauty, seemed of no consequence to her.

"I don't need to be a Catholic," she said. "I want to be whatever you are. If you want to be Navajo, I'll be a Navajo with you."

"That's not a possibility."

"Then whatever you like. I needed to be at Nativity because—it was something I needed to do. I needed to pray and be forgiven. I prayed and prayed, and then there you were—my reward. Am I allowed to say that? You're like my gift from God. That's how miraculous you are to me."

"But then . . . don't you think we should be married?"

"Yes! Good idea! We can do it next week. Or tomorrow—how about tomorrow?"

As if the blessing of matrimony had already descended, he pulled her onto him and kissed her. She threw aside the quilt and straddled him, handling him with an expertness he didn't question; she was naturally expert at everything. Only in her whimpers, which she emitted in rhythm to their coupling, was any sense of lesserness detectable. She whimpered and spoke his name, whimpered and spoke his name. In his mind, she was already his darling little wife. But after the culminating pleasure had coursed through him, he returned to being a sinner in a sweat beneath another sinner.

Her mood, too, had changed. She was crying, voicelessly, miserably.

"Is something wrong? Did I hurt you?"

She shook her head.

"Marion, I'm sorry, my God—did I hurt you?"

"No." She gasped through her tears. "You're wonderful. You're my—you're perfect."

"Then what? What is it?"

She rolled away and covered her face with her hands. "I *can't* be a Catholic."

"Why not?"

"Because it means I can't marry you. I was—oh, Russ." She sobbed. "I was already married!"

A sickening disclosure. Jealousy and uncleanliness, both bodily and moral, were compounded in the image of another man possessing her as he just had. A woman he'd believed to be pure and purehearted was previously used—befouled. He felt sick with disappointment. The depth of it revealed the height of the hope she'd given him.

"It happened in Los Angeles," she said. "I was married for six months and then divorced. I should have told you right away. It was terrible of me not to. You're so beautiful and I'm—oh—I'm so—I should have told you! Oh God, oh God, oh God."

She thrashed in her misery. A cruel part of him thought she deserved any amount of emotional punishment, but the loving part of him was moved. He wanted to kill the man who'd polluted her.

"Who was it? Did he hurt you?"

"It was just a mistake. I was still a kid—I didn't know anything. I thought I was supposed to—I didn't know anything."

The idea of an innocent girl's mistake, for which she was now piteously remorseful, further softened his heart. But his anger and disgust had a life of their own. He'd thrown away his virginity on a woman who'd given hers to someone else, and now her nakedness was repellent, her smell appalling. He wished to God he'd never left Lesser Hebron. He swung his legs off the bed and roughly dressed himself.

"Please don't be angry with me," she said in a calmer voice.

He was too angry to speak.

"I made a mistake. I made lots of mistakes, but I'm not wrong about us. Please try, if you can, to forgive me. I want to marry you, Russ. I want to be yours forever."

He'd wanted the very same thing. Disappointment welled up in him and erupted in a sob.

"Sweetie, please," she said. "Sit down with me, let me hold you. I'm so very, very sorry."

He stood shaking and crying, torn between disgust and need. The self-pity in his tears was new to him—it was as if he'd never appreciated, until this moment, that he, too, was a person, a person he was always with, a person he might love and pity the way he loved God or pitied other people. Feeling compassion for this person, who was suffering and needed his care, he unlocked the bedroom door and ran out through the house, jumped into the Willys and drove a few blocks. He stopped beneath a cypress tree and wept for himself.

She sent him two letters, on consecutive days, and he opened neither of them. The woman he loved was still there but occluded from him, separated by her own doing. It was as if his Marion were imprisoned in a Marion he didn't know at all. He could almost hear his dear one crying out to him from inside the prison. She needed him to come and rescue her, but he was afraid of the other Marion—afraid of finding that it was she who'd written the letters.

He'd done very little praying since he met her. Returning to it now, he laid his situation out to God and asked Him what His will was. The first insight to emerge was that God required him to forgive her. In trying to explain to God why he was angry, he saw that Marion's offense—she'd been too embarrassed to mention her marriage sooner—was paltry; that, indeed, the greater offense was his own hard-heartedness. This led him to a second insight: for all his doubting, for all his liberation, he was still a Mennonite. At some level, he'd assumed that he would one day bring Marion home with him and there, although they might not settle in Lesser Hebron, receive his family's blessing. Now the fact of her divorce had snuffed any chance of that. The extremity of his disappointment pertained not to her but to his parents, because he hadn't yet fully broken with them. He was angry because her divorce compelled him to make a hard choice.

Unready to make it, still afraid to open her letters, he wrote to the only person who might understand his quandary. His grandfather must have replied to Russ's letter immediately, because the reply arrived in camp just eight days later. The advice in it was unexpected.

You don't have to marry her—I'm here to tell you the sun will still rise in the morning. Why not enjoy the moment and see how you feel when your term of service ends? You'll have plenty of time for marrying if you still feel the same, but a young man doesn't always know his heart. Your gal already made her own mistake, and it sounds like she knows how to look after herself. That's pure gold—yours to enjoy if you're careful. So long as she's not in a family way, there's no reason to be hasty.

A year earlier, Russ might have been alarmed by how tumorously his grandfather's debauchery had consumed his moral principles. Now, instead, he felt a fraternity. It seemed to him that Clement was right in every respect but one—Russ already knew his heart, and it belonged to Marion. But there was more.

As to your parents, I don't guess they'll forgive you if you marry her. Your father doesn't look to our Savior but to what other men think of him. He preaches love but holds a grudge like no man's business. I know firsthand the vengeance in his heart. Your mother's a good woman, but she lost her mind to Jesus. She's so deep in her faith you can scream at the top of the lungs and she won't hear you. She thinks she loves you when she prays for you, but she only loves her Jesus.

Russ didn't need to reread Clement's letter, then or ever. One reading was enough to burn every line of it into his memory.

What the Bible meant by *joy*, and by the related words that recurred in it so frequently, *joyful*, *joyous*, *rejoicing*, he learned the following afternoon, when he went back to Marion's uncle's house. There was joy in his unconditional surrender to her—joy in his apology for the hardness of his heart, joy in her forgiveness, joy in his release from doubt and blame. How many times had he read the word *joy* without having experienced what it meant? There was joy in making love on a thunderstormy afternoon, and there was joy in not making love, joy in just lying and looking into her fathomless dark eyes. Joy in the first trip they made together to Diné Bikéyah, joy in the sight of Stella on Marion's lap, joy in the sweetness of Marion's way with children, joy in the thought of giving her a child of her own, joy in the desert sunset, joy in the star-choked sky, joy even in the mutton stew. And joy in George Ginchy's invitation to a private dinner with him, joy in seeing her through Ginchy's eyes. Joy when she first put her mouth on Russ's penis, joy in her wantonness, joy in the abjectness of his gratitude, joy in its sealing of the certainty that he would never leave her. Joy in the corroborating pain of being apart from her, joy in their reunions, joy in making plans, joy in the prospect of finishing his education and catching up with her, joy in the mystery of what might happen after that.

The joy lasted until they were married, on the day his term of service ended, with George and Jimmy as their witnesses, at the courthouse in Flagstaff. They'd abandoned their respective religions and were seeking a new faith to share, but their slate was still clean and they didn't have a church to marry in. Russ felt obliged to write to his parents the very same day, and he didn't sugarcoat what he'd done. He explained that Marion had been previously married and that he had no interest in rejoining the community, but that he would like to bring his wife to Lesser Hebron and introduce her to the family.

His father's reply was brief and bitter. It grieved him but didn't entirely surprise him, he said, that Russ had been infected by a pestilence stemming from elsewhere in the family, and neither he nor Russ's mother had any wish to meet Marion. Russ's mother's reply was longer and more anguished, more a descant on her own failures, but the point was the same: she'd lost her son. Not *rejected* him (as Marion, ever defensive of Russ, was quick to point out) but *lost* him.

The rejection confirmed the rightness of his choice—shame and blame on anyone who refused to meet the most wonderful woman in the world—and he adored being wedded to Marion, adored having her always at his side, on his side. And yet, in his innermost heart, a shadow fell when his parents disowned him. The shadow wasn't quite doubt and it wasn't quite guilt. It was more a sense of what he'd lost in gaining Marion. He no longer belonged in Lesser Hebron, but he was still haunted by it. He found himself missing his mother's little farm, his grandfather's shop, the eternity in the sameness of the days there, the rightness of a community radically organized around the Word. He understood that his father was a deeply flawed person, his stringency a compensation for an underlying weakness, and that his mother had indeed, in a way, lost her mind. But he couldn't help secretly admiring them. Their faith had an edge that his own never would.

When he accepted a rural ministry in Indiana, four years later, he hoped he might regain a bit of what he'd lost. He was certainly glad to see more of his grandfather, who, in spite of himself, had married Estelle and now lived in her hometown, two hours to the north of Russ. But the sense of loss was spiritual, not geographical. It was portable and its name was Marion. As his reliance on her became routine, her capabilities merely useful to him, their lovemaking duly procreative, his misgivings about her first marriage returned in the form of grievance. He began to wonder why he'd been so determined to ignore Clement's advice and marry the first woman he'd loved.

On his bad days, he saw a rube from Indiana who'd been pounced on by an older city girl—snared by the sexual cunning of a woman who'd developed it with a different man. On his worst days, he suspected that Marion had known very well that he could have done better. She must have known that as soon as he left the little world of Flagstaff he would encounter women younger than he was, taller than Marion, less odd, more awed by his own capabilities, and *not previously married*. She'd seduced him into a contract before he knew his value in the marketplace.

And still, even then, he might have made peace with having married her, if only she, too, had been a virgin when he met her. His grievance was no less gnawing for being trivial and godless. In the final, hard form it had taken, after his dream about Sally Perkins had opened his eyes to the multitude of desirable women, the grievance was that Marion had gotten to enjoy sex with a second person, he only with her. He could tolerate her superiority in every other regard, but not in this one.

Boarding the bus in New Prospect, he'd been unhappy to find Frances sitting with the other parent adviser, Ted Jernigan, in the seats behind the driver. Ted was a threat—every other man was a threat—but Russ had learned his lesson: it was better to withhold than to pester. Better to ensconce himself with the kids in back, bat around a Nerf ball, sing along with songs whose words he now mostly knew, take instruction in the playing of an E chord and a D chord, compete in an endless license-plate game, and let Frances feel left out. His acceptance by the cool kids, a result of his more laissez-faire approach to Crossroads, was such a gratifying contrast to his previous Arizona trip, he almost could have done without the complication of her.

Now they'd entered the Navajo Nation. Along the highway, in evening sunlight, were children hawking juniper-berry necklaces, billboards advertising HAND WOVEN BLANKETS and TURQUOISE JEWELRY, a souvenir shop overflowing with generic kitsch, behind it an AUTHENTIC NAVAJO HOGAN, a wooden Plains Indian in full headdress, and an enormous tepee. The last of the five guitars on the bus had gone quiet. Carolyn Polley, across the aisle from Russ, was reading Carlos Castaneda. Kim Perkins was teaching the cat's cradle to David Goya, other girls were playing Spades, other boys openly hooting over a pornographic comic book that Keith Stratton had bought at a truck stop in Tucumcari. Russ could have confiscated it, with some words about its demeaning of women, but he was tired and the kids in his group were all basically harmless. Roger Hangartner had smoked pot on a Crossroads retreat the year before, Darcie Mandell needed to be watched for her diabetes, Alice Raymond was grieving the recent death of her mother, and Gerri Kohl was an irritating trumpeter of hackneyed phrases ("Feeding time *at* the zoo" "Velly stlange"), but there weren't any real problem kids—Perry was on Kevin Anderson's bus. In Tucumcari, when Russ asked Kevin how Perry was doing, Kevin had said he was overexcited, had talked nonstop all night, and didn't feel like leaving the bus. Russ could have boarded it and spoken to Perry, but Perry was Kevin's problem now, not his.

When the Many Farms water tower appeared on the horizon, he ventured forward and made Ted Jernigan trade places with him. Taking the Ted-warmed seat, he asked Frances if she'd gotten any sleep.

She leaned away from him and gave him a cold look. "You mean, between hearing how Ted would have handled the Viet Cong and how much I overpaid for my house?"

Russ laughed. He couldn't have been happier. "I kept waiting for you to come and join us."

"One of us knows every single person on this bus. The other one doesn't know anyone."

He lost his smile. "Sorry."

"When you told me you could be a jerk, I didn't believe you."

"Very sorry."

She turned to her window and didn't look at him again.

The sun had dropped behind the Black Mesa, beginning the long dusk in Many Farms, the somber illumination of its overwide roads, its identical BIA-sponsored houses, its utilitarian school buildings and dusty warehouses. Russ directed the driver to the council office and hopped out while the other two buses pulled up behind him. The air had a wintry bite, a thinness that his heart immediately registered. As he approached the office door, a sturdy young woman in a red wool jacket came out. "You must be Russ."

"Yes. Wanda?"

"Russ, if I may say so, we were expecting you earlier." In person, too, her voice was plangent. "I would like to discuss your plan with you."

"The, ah—mandate?"

Wanda's emphatic nodding matched her voice. "We have the mandate and you can help us. However, because you prefer to stay in Many Farms, we are willing to accommodate a second group here. I have spoken to the director and he is okay with it."

"What is the mandate?"

"To conform with the mandate, we need handicapped access ramps at Kitsillie. A ramp for the front and a ramp for the fire exit. The toilet also must be handicapped-accessible. But may I be completely open and honest with you? I feel you would be more comfortable in Many Farms."

Over the idling of three buses came the crunch of boots on gravel, the growling voice of Ambrose, a murmur from Kevin Anderson. If Russ's group stayed in Many Farms, he would have to be with Perry, and Frances with Larry. Quickly, before Ambrose could interfere, he told Wanda that he'd rather stick to the original plan. Her emphatic nod said one thing, her troubled expression another.

"You may go to Kitsillie," she said, "but I would ask you, in all respect, to stay close to the school. No one should walk alone, and no one should be outside after dark."

"That's fine. We've had the same rule in the past."

She stepped away to greet Ambrose and Kevin. Not for the first time, Russ was impressed by Ambrose's way of forging a connection with a stranger, the compassionate scowl with which he conveyed that she was being seen as a person, taken seriously. Scowling as if nothing on earth mattered more to him, he asked Wanda how Keith Durochie was. It should have been Russ who'd asked the question.

"Keith is not good," Wanda said, "but he is resting comfortably at home."

"How bad is it?" Russ said.

"He is resting comfortably but I am told that he is very weak."

Into Russ's throat came the sadness of life's brevity, the sadness of the sunless hour, the sadness of Easter. God was telling him very clearly what to do. He had to stay in Many Farms, where Keith had lived since 1960, so he could visit Keith and keep an eye on Perry. In light of Keith's condition, his wish to enjoy sex with a person not Marion seemed even more trivial, and he'd been insane to imagine it happening in Arizona. He'd let himself forget how bleak the reservation was in late winter, how demanding it was to lead a work camp.

And yet, when he thought of doing God's will, at the cost of his week with Frances on the mesa, he felt unbearably sorry for himself. It was strange that self-pity wasn't on the list of deadly sins; none was deadlier.

The swing driver, a gaunt lung-cancer candidate named Ollie, had taken over the wheel of the Kitsillie bus. From the seat beside Frances, Russ directed him to Rough Rock and from there up the side of the mesa. The road was stony and narrow, and there was still enough light to see how close to the edge of it they were, how fatal a plunge would be. At a particularly harrowing bend, Frances gasped and said, "Oh Jesus, *Jesus*." She clutched Russ's hand, and, just like that, he was holding hers. She'd said it herself: jerks turned her on. Behind the bus, a horn began to honk.

"Yeah, where am I supposed to go?" Ollie said.

The honking persisted until they reached a straightaway. Ollie pulled over, inches from the edge of a chasm, and a pickup truck, still honking, gunned past them. One of its bumper stickers said CUSTER HAD IT COMING. Its driver stuck out his arm and gave the bus the middle finger.

"Charming," Frances said.

"Are you okay?"

She let go of Russ's hand. "I'm waiting to hear there's a better road back down."

As if from a different world, the gentler world of New Prospect, Biff Allard's bongo drums started up, joined by one guitar and then another, and then by Biff's reedy voice.

Bus driver Ollie, bus driver Ollie
Rollin' through the hills, movin' down the valley
Some folks like to drink, some folks like to cuss
Ollie gets high on a TWELVE-TON BUS

A cheer went up, and Ollie waved his thanks. He didn't know that Biff had written the song for the earlier driver, Bill.

Up on the mesa, as the sky darkened, the moon highlighted patches of snow on the north-facing slopes. Russ struggled to integrate his memories of the mesa and the sadness of Keith with the new possibility embodied in the woman next to him. He felt warmed not only by her shoulder but by the triumph of having brought her, after so many complications, to a place that had formed him. He wondered if she could love the place herself—love him—and if he might yet grow old with her. Though the road had leveled out, he put his hand on hers again. She gave it a squeeze and didn't let go until he stood up to address the group.

"Okay, listen up," he said. "We're going straight to the chapter house and see if we can get some dinner. I don't want to hear any complaining about the food. You hear me? We'll see a lot of mutton stew and frybread—if you don't like it, you'll eat it anyway. We need to remember, at all times, that we are guests of the Navajo Nation. Our attitude is gratitude. We come with our privilege, come with all our nice things, and we need to remember how we look to the Navajos. Do not *ever* leave your things unattended, except where we'll be sleeping. Do not *ever* leave the school area by yourself. Are we clear on that? I want to see groups of four people or more, and no one *ever* leaves the school after dark. Understood?"

There was no electricity or telephone at Kitsillie—except for the chapter house and the school building, still unfinished after five years of work, there wasn't much of anything—but, Wanda be praised, Daisy Benally and her sister were waiting for the bus. Daisy, an aunt of Keith's by marriage, hadn't been young when Russ met her in 1945; now she was stooped and shrunken. Her sister, Ruth, was nearly as fat as the average Hopi. The two of them had made a vat of stew in the chapter-house kitchen, which smelled of hot oil, and they now proceeded, by lantern light, while the Crossroads group settled into the common room, to cook the frybread. The room's chill pervaded the concrete floor, the dented metal folding chairs, the particle-board tables. Russ asked Frances what she was thinking.

"I'm thinking, yikes. You told me it was primitive, but."

"It's not too late to go to Many Farms. Ollie can take you back."

She bristled. "Is that how you think of me? The lady who can't hack it?"

"Not at all."

"I wouldn't mind finding a bathroom, though."

"Brace yourself."

As he weighed whether to sit with Alice Raymond—whether it would make her self-conscious about her mother's death, and whether his concern about making her self-conscious concealed a craven fear of her bereavement—he thought of Ambrose, whose instincts with teenagers were unerring. He was relieved when Carolyn Polley sat down with Alice. He didn't have to be good at everything, he only had to be good at getting Frances. He ate his dinner with her and Ted Jernigan.

"Not to complain," Ted said, "but there's something not right about the bread."

"The oil's a little rancid, maybe. It's only a taste—it won't hurt you."

"Where is the mutton?" Frances said, poking at her bowl. "All I have is turnips and potatoes."

"You can ask Daisy for some meat."

"I'm dreaming of the beer nuts in my suitcase."

Outside the chapter house, a truck banged by in a roar of downshift.

Russ didn't give it a thought until he'd finished his dinner and stepped outside. The temperature had plunged but Ollie was in shirtsleeves, smoking a cigarette and looking up the rough road to the school building. A hundred yards up, a pickup truck's headlights were aimed down at the bus. The sound of its engine was distinct in the still, cold air. Wanda had promised to come up and check on the group, but Russ didn't think the truck was Wanda's. Hoping there might be some other benign explanation, a lost calf, a relative fetching Daisy and Ruth, he rounded up the group and got everyone on the bus.

In its headlights, as Ollie steered it up the road, Russ recognized the pickup from their encounter with it earlier. Ollie slowed down and tapped the horn, but the truck didn't move. There was menace in its headlights. Frances again clutched Russ's hand.

"Stay here," he said.

As he got out and approached the truck, its doors opened and four figures jumped out. Four young men, three of them in hats. The fourth, in a jean jacket, his hair loose on his shoulders, stepped forward and looked directly, insolently, into Russ's eyes. "Hey, white man."

"Hello. Good evening."

"What are you doing up here?"

"We are a Christian youth fellowship. We're here to perform a week of service."

The man, seeming amused, looked back at his companions. Something in his manner reminded Russ of Laura Dobrinsky. *The younger Navajos don't like you, either.*

"Would you mind letting us through?"

"What are you doing here?"

"In Kitsillie? We will be working to finish the school building."

"We don't need you for that."

Anger rose in Russ. He had an angry white thought—that, year after year, the tribe itself did little to finish the school—but he didn't speak it. "We are here at the tribal council's invitation. They've given us a job, and I intend to do it."

The man laughed. "Fuck the council. They might as well be white."

"The council is an elected body. If you have a problem with our being here, you can take it up with them. I have a busload of very tired kids who, if you wouldn't mind, need to sleep."

"Where you from?"

"We're from Chicago."

"Go back to Chicago."

Russ's blood rose further. "For your information," he said, "I am not just another *bilagáana*. I've been a friend of the reservation for twenty-seven years. I've known Daisy Benally since 1945. Keith Durochie is an old friend of mine."

"Fuck Keith Durochie."

Russ took an anger-managing breath. "What exactly is your grievance?"

"Fuck Keith Durochie. That's my grievance. Get the fuck out of here—that's my grievance."

"Well, I'm sorry, but this is council land, and we have an invitation to be here. We will stay at the school and be gone in a week."

"You people are polluters. You can pollute Chicago, but this isn't Chicago. I don't want to see you here tomorrow."

"Then you'll just have to look the other way. We're not leaving."

The man spat on the ground, not directly at Russ, but close. "You had your warning."

"Is that a threat?"

The man turned away and walked toward his companions.

"Hey, *hey*," Russ shouted, "are you threatening me?"

Again, over the shoulder, the middle finger.

Russ hadn't been so angry since he fought with Marion at Christmas. He stalked past the bus, back down to the chapter house, and found Daisy stooped in the light of a lantern, her expression unreadable. As the truck screamed past them, he asked her who the young man was.

"Clyde," she said. "He has an angry spirit."

"Do you know what his problem with Keith is?"

"He's angry at Keith."

"I can see that. But why?"

Daisy smiled at the ground. "It's not our business."

"Do you think it's safe for us to be here?"

"Stay close to the school."

"But do you think we'll be safe?"

"Stay close to the school. We'll have breakfast for you in the morning."

The sensible thing to do was to concede defeat and retreat to Many Farms, but Russ's blood was raging with testosterone. He felt wronged and misunderstood, and the progress he'd made with Frances had elevated his hormone levels. When he returned to the bus and saw the worry and the admiration in her face, the hormones urged him to stand his ground.

The following day, Palm Sunday, passed without a sign of Clyde. Russ established a perimeter comprising the table of land on which the school was set, a lower yard with a netless basketball hoop, and the arroyo behind it. Sunday was a rest day, and it was hard on the kids to be surrounded by interesting country and not be allowed to explore it, but they had their relationships and their suntans to work on, their books and their playing cards, their guitars. Russ was grateful to see Carolyn Polley, who was going to be a fine Christian minister, introducing Frances to the various girls. He was struck, as he'd been when he first took Frances to Theo Crenshaw's church, by her hesitancy in an unfamiliar setting, and again it moved him.

Ted Jernigan had a problem with the mandate. While Russ and the other alumni adviser, Craig Dilkes, were inventorying the ramp-building supplies, which had been dumped in an otherwise empty classroom, Ted remarked that the money might better have been spent on central heating.

"Government money comes with mandates," Russ said.

"And I'm saying it's an idiotic mandate."

Testosterone stirred in Russ. "I'll remind you," he said, "that we're mainly here for ourselves. The point is personal growth, individually and as a group. If the Navajos want handicapped ramps, that's good enough for me."

"How does a kid in a wheelchair get up that road? How does he get across the ditch? Are they planning on landing him in a helicopter?"

"You can lead the bookcase-building crew. Would that meet your high standard of utility?"

The sarcasm drew a frown from Ted. "I don't get you."

"What don't you get?"

"That was quite the welcoming committee last night. We might as well be under siege—I don't get why you're so hell-bent on staying."

"I just explained the point of it."

"But a place where the kids can't even take a shower? When we're obviously not wanted?"

"If you don't like it here, I can find you a ride back to Many Farms."

"You're telling me you don't think this is dangerous."

"Kitsillie can be rough," Craig Dilkes interposed. He'd been a sophomore on the fellowship's first trip to Arizona. "It's the roughness that really pulls the group together—people taking care of each other."

"Maybe," Ted said. "Provided no one gets hurt. If someone gets hurt, in a place we should know better than to be, the buck stops with the leader."

He left the room, and Craig raised his eyebrows. They were blonder than his mop of red hair. "I'm not liking the vibe here."

With Craig, Russ could be honest. "I agree," he said. "Keith warned me about it."

"There's that, but I meant Ted."

In the evening, the group gathered around a single flame in their dark room. The "candle" began with the singing of two songs and the giving of what Ambrose called strokes—a stroke to someone for having a great sense of humor, a stroke for trading potatoes for nasty turnips, a stroke for taking a risk in a new relationship, a stroke for being smart, a stroke for letting go of being smart and speaking from the heart, a stroke for sharing a candy bar, a stroke for teaching someone how to tie a bandanna. Frances herself spoke up and stroked the group for welcoming a middle-aged housewife. Kim Perkins, whom Russ had so far left alone, owing to his troubles with her sister, surprised him with a stroke for his courage in handling the four angry Navajos. His heart swelled with the contrast to the last Arizona candle he'd led. Here, unpoisoned by Laura Dobrinsky and Sally Perkins, were forty good kids in thick socks and thermal underwear, with sleeping bags draped over their shoulders, and his beloved boy-haired woman on the far side of the circle, holding the hands of two girls she'd only just met. How much better his life was now! How nearly joyful again!

And then Ted Jernigan raised the issue of security. "I don't know about the rest of you," he said, "but I don't enjoy feeling threatened every time I step out for a meal. Do you mind if we have a show of hands? Does anyone else think we'd be better off closer to civilization?"

The memory of Russ's expulsion three years earlier, the traumatic call for a show of hands, triggered a fight-or-flight response in him.

"Ted," he said hormonally, "if you have an issue with my leadership, you should direct it to me personally."

"I already did that," Ted said. "What I'm looking for now is a sense of the group. Is anyone else thinking what I'm thinking?"

He raised his hand and looked around the circle. Russ glanced at Frances and found her smiling at him, perhaps conveying her opinion of Ted, her hand unraised. Among the kids, only Gerri Kohl, she of "velly stlange," raised a hand. Russ, sensing victory, was all over it.

"Gerri, thank you for your honesty," he said, sounding like Ambrose. "That is a brave thing to admit. That took real guts."

Gerri lowered her hand. "It's just one vote," she said. "I can go with the flow."

Though Russ felt bad for her, knowing she wasn't well liked, her unpopularity was an advantage to be pressed. "Ted is right," he said. "The energy up here is somewhat negative. I intend to find out why and see what we can do to repair it. But if anyone else feels the same way Gerri does, now is the time to say so. If you'd rather go back to Many Farms, we can still be together as a group there."

"Is there hot water in Many Farms?" a girl asked.

The discussion devolved into bitching and laughter at the bitching, followed by a final song and a closing prayer, which Russ handed off to Carolyn Polley. He blew out the candle, relit the Coleman lanterns, and checked the kerosene heater. There was a rush for the bathroom, which he'd plumbed three years earlier, and squeals of mock horror, the nightly Crossroads silliness, a sophomore boy prancing in his BVDs and singing "Let Me Entertain You," an ovation for Darcie Mandell when she took off her sweatshirt, a screaming discovery of a rubber scorpion, cries of dismay at a leak in an air mattress, a posse of ticklers bearing down on Kim Perkins, David Goya pissed off at them. Russ tried to have a private word with Gerri Kohl, but she was embarrassed by her vote and didn't want to talk about it.

He was an old-school camper, eschewing a sleeping bag, preferring blankets. In dim moonlight, after the flashlights had gone out and the room had quieted, and after the comedy of breaking the silence with a loud random remark had been exhausted, he got up in his long johns and went down the hallway to take a late leak. Among his hundred worries was the bathroom water supply. The tank on the hill above the school was filled by a windmill, and he had no way to gauge if it was full enough to last them for a week in which he had to mix concrete and clean equipment. He'd asked the kids to flush only solid waste, but they were kids and forgot.

Leaving the toilet unflushed, he opened the door and was startled by a figure standing outside it. In her own thermal underwear, her hunting jacket. She backed him into the bathroom and put her arms around him. He could feel her shivering, presumably with cold.

"I made it through the first day," she whispered.

He clasped her delicate head to his chest, and his testosterone manifested itself in his long johns. A possibility he'd been too obtuse to be aware of on his previous Arizona trip, before Sally Perkins had appeared to him in a dream, a possibility inherent in the nighttime mixing of sexes in close quarters, on the margins of civilization, was now being realized.

"I felt so lonely on the bus," Frances whispered. "I was wishing I hadn't come."

"I'm sorry."

"I don't even know what I'm doing here. It only makes sense with you."

In the intimacy of her *you*, he detected an invitation to kiss her. But she lowered her arms and turned away.

"Just please include me," she said. "I need to know you're there."

The next morning, after a breakfast heavy on grits, he began work

on the handicapped ramps. David Goya did the math on the ramp angles while Russ and Craig Dilkes sorted lumber for the pouring forms
and the rest of the crew moved earth. In previous years, when Keith
Durochie was involved, Russ had sent crews to nearby ranches. This
year, with forty kids penned up at the school, where the only other
work was building bookcases, he was at once overstaffed and worried
that the ramp-building job was too large to finish in five days. Stripped
down to a T-shirt, under a warming sun, he worked with the focus of
his mother and his grandfather, and the long morning seemed gone in
ten minutes. At lunchtime, he asked Daisy Benally again about Clyde's
grievance with Keith, but Daisy again declined to elaborate. He reproached himself for having been too scattered to get the story from
Wanda when he had the chance. Now there was nothing to be done but
wait for Wanda to come and explain.

In the evening, when the group was eating dinner and he heard a
vehicle on the school road, he briefly hoped it might be Wanda, but he
didn't stop to wonder where the vehicle was going. Not until it came
roaring back down the hill did he wonder. Stepping outside, he saw
Clyde's truck turning onto the main road.

Only he had seen it. The group's merriment level was high; a piece
of turnip had been flung. He had to pretend to be surprised when, after
dinner, he led the group back up the hill and found the school door,
which he'd been careful to padlock, standing open. The doorframe was
splintered, the hasp dangling from the lock.

David Goya, speaking for everyone, said, "Uh-oh."

Quietly, as a group, in wandering flashlight beams, they went inside
and surveyed the room where they slept. Suitcases and duffel bags had
been emptied on the floor, sleeping bags tossed around, a bottle of tal-
cum powder thrown against a wall, but Bobby Jett's expensive camera
was sitting where he'd left it. Frances took Russ by the arm. He could
feel her looking up at him, but he didn't want to look at anyone. The fault
was clearly his.

"Where's my guitar?" Darcie Mandell said.

"You're missing your guitar?" Russ said in a choked voice.

"Uh, yeah."

"They took mine, too," another girl called from across the room. "It's definitely not here. They freaking stole my Martin!"

Catching a note of hysteria, Russ removed himself from Frances and found his voice. "All right, ah—listen up. This is obviously not good, but we need to stay calm. Let's get the lanterns on and do a careful inventory. If anything's broken, anything's missing, I want to hear about it."

"My guitar is missing," Darcie Mandell reported dryly.

"So, yes, we seem to be missing two guitars, but let's see if there's anything else. We're in a place of underprivilege, and sometimes these things happen. The important thing is that we're together as a group. We're safe as long as we stay together."

"I'm not feeling especially safe," Darcie said, "despite our being together."

"Let's straighten up the room and see what we've got."

Still unable to look at Frances, he lit two lanterns and checked his own belongings. He wasn't angry; he was struggling not to cry. The sorrow pertained to everything—the hardness of reservation life, the fears and hurt feelings of forty good kids, the cultural and economic gulf between New Prospect and Kitsillie—but especially to his own vanity. He'd imagined himself a friend of the Navajos and a bridger of divides, imagined he knew better than the people who'd warned him not to come here. He hated to think what God thought of him.

It emerged that only the two guitars had been stolen. The greater damage was in the violation of their space, the chill that Clyde's aggression had put on their fellowship. When the group gathered again around the candle, the contrast to the previous night couldn't have been starker. Unhappiness or fear was in almost every face.

"So we've encountered our first adversity," Russ said. "Adversity can strengthen us as a group, but it's important that I hear from every one of you tonight. We'll go around the circle and hear what each of us is feeling. Speaking for myself, I'm very sad—sad for us and sad for whoever broke in. It could be that we'll decide not to stay here, but my own inclination is to stick it out and deal with the issue, not walk away from it. In practical terms, at least one adviser will now stay in the building at all times, and tomorrow morning I will deal with this. I will try to get Darcie and Katie's guitars back."

"How about just calling the police?" Ted Jernigan said unpleasantly.

"We can report this to the tribal police, but I'd like to understand better why it happened. Let's see what we can achieve with listening before we bring the law in."

It took more than an hour to go around the circle, and Russ wasn't Ambrose. He didn't have limitless patience with the self-drama of adolescents, the Crossroads-encouraged inflation of emotional scrapes into ambulance-worthy traumas. He himself was upset, but his fault gave him the right to be, and although he'd asked to hear from everyone, because this was the Crossroads way, it tried his patience to sit in a world of real social injustice, real suffering, and make such an opera of the theft of two guitars, easily replaceable by their owners' parents. The outpouring of support for Darcie and Katie was comparable to what Alice Raymond had received when her mother died. Of all the feelings voiced at the long candle, the only one Russ respected was the group's frustration with being quarantined from interaction with the Navajos. He shared that frustration.

In the end, they voted to stay at least one more day. All the advisers except Ted Jernigan favored staying. Afterward, while the group bedded down, its spirits subdued, Russ went outside to look at the sky. He hoped to reconnect with God, but the door behind him opened. Frances had followed him.

"I thought you handled that well," she said.

"I feel bad for the kids, especially the sophomores. This is their first experience here."

"They respect you—I could see it. I don't know why you thought you shouldn't be a youth minister."

His eyes filled with gratitude. "Now I'm the one who needs a hug."

She gave it to him. The blessing of her touch, the palpable reality of the woman in his arms, was making a believer of him. It was as if he'd yearned to know God without actually believing that He existed. Now he could feel that, far from overhoping, he might have underestimated his chances—that Frances's decision to come to Arizona had been, in fact, a decision about him.

"We're having the full experience," she said.

Behind them, the door creaked open again.

"Whoops," a girl said.

As if excited to be discovered with him, Frances squeezed him harder, and again he thought of kissing her. To let himself be seen as the man she'd chosen, to cement his status with a public kiss, was worth the cost of what Becky would learn from her friends, what Ambrose would say. But to do it on a night when his group was in crisis could send a bad message. He contented himself with breathing his thanks into her hair.

The next morning, very early, after sleeping essentially not at all, he stole out of the school and walked down the road. The sun hadn't cleared the ridge, but a flock of mountain bluebirds was awake, foraging among bitten tussocks, perching on fence posts glaucous with frost. Daisy Benally was chopping onions in the chapter-house kitchen, her sister still asleep. When Russ told Daisy what had happened, she just shook her head. He asked where he could find Clyde.

"Don't go there," she said.

"But where is he?"

"You know the place. Up the canyon where Keith lived."

"Are you saying Clyde is a Fallen Rocks?"

"No, he's a Jackson. You shouldn't go there."

Russ explained why he had little choice but to go. Daisy, who'd reached an age where she greeted anything the world did with resignation, allowed that he could borrow Ruth's truck. He would have liked to leave immediately, before he had time to be afraid, but he waited until the group came down for breakfast. Everyone's hair was flat and dirty, every eye red from a night on a hard floor. By way of mending fences, Russ asked Ted Jernigan, who'd sat down with Frances, to take charge of the group for the morning.

Frances, too, looked dirty and poorly slept. "You're not going alone," she said.

"It's fine. I can take care of myself."

"She has a point," Ted said. "Why don't you and I go together?"

"Because I need you to stay here with the kids."

"I'm going with you," Frances said.

"I don't think that's a good idea."

"I don't care what you think."

Her eyes were on the table, her expression sullen. Russ wondered what he'd done to make her angry.

"Are you sure you want to do that?"

"Yes I want to do that," she said crossly.

He guessed she was embarrassed. Embarrassed by her fear for his safety, embarrassed by her need to stay close to him.

Ruth Benally's truck was barely big enough for him to fit behind the wheel. If the fuel gauge could be trusted, there was half a tank of gas. As he followed the old road along the wash, he told Frances about the first time he'd driven it, the Enemy Way ceremony he'd blundered into. The road had since been widened, but the surface was no better. Negotiating the ruts and stones, he was slow to notice that Frances wasn't listening. Her eyes were fixed on the windshield, her mouth tight. He asked what she was thinking.

"I'm thinking," she said, "I'd rather just buy two guitars with my own money."

"Do you want to go back?"

Not getting an answer, he stopped the truck. "I mean it," he said. "I can easily take you back."

She shut her eyes. "I don't know if you've noticed, Russ, but I'm a fearful person."

"Someone else could have come with me. It didn't have to be you."

"Just drive."

He reached for her, but she jerked away from him. "Just drive."

He didn't understand her. He couldn't sort out the mixture of confidence and fear, self-love and self-reproach. In her own way, she was as odd as Marion. He wondered if all women were odd or only the ones he was attracted to.

The farther he drove up the valley, the less he recognized it. The land had always been dry, but he didn't remember it being so utterly denuded. Gone were the sheep and cattle, gone every conceivably edible leaf and shoot, gone even the fence wire. All that remained were rough-hewn fence posts and erosion-scored slopes. Except that the rocks were white, not red, the landscape could have been Martian. Even the sky had a strange yellowish-gray pall. The haze was too pale and diffuse to be from a fire, and it wasn't a dust storm—there wasn't any wind. It was more like the pall over Gary, Indiana, on a clear Chicago day.

The alienation deepened when he passed the last of the fallen rocks and saw, in the distance, Keith's old farmstead. He'd assumed he would find people here, maybe Clyde himself, but there was nothing. No grass, no garden, no animals, only gnarled junipers and dead cottonwoods, their broken limbs barkless and silvery. In his mind, the farmstead had remained unchanged, alive with Keith and his extended family, their chickens and goats. To see what time had done to it was to become aware of how old he was.

"Amazingly enough," he said, "this is where I spent a summer."

Frances wasn't listening. Or was listening but was too tense to speak.

The little house, where he'd had his sexual revelation, had been stripped of its doors and its windows and its roof, leaving only the walls. The sunlight on it was bright but not as bright as it should have been. As Russ proceeded along the road, across the canyon and up the ridge opposite the farmstead, the yellowish pall became more pronounced.

Reaching the top of the ridge, he saw where it was coming from. In the middle of the wide plain below, the earth had been torn open—was being torn open. Dust was billowing from a gash that might have been a mile wide. Industrial trestles and a raw new road extended from the gash to the northern horizon. Russ had a sense of betrayal, born of his loyalty to the primitive mesa of his memories. Keith had mentioned that the tribal council permitted coal mining on the reservation, but Russ hadn't had any reason to travel in this direction until now. He hadn't imagined that the mining was so close to the Fallen Rocks land—so close, indeed, to Kitsillie itself—or that the scale of the operation was so immense.

Half a mile down the road, he saw Clyde's pickup. In a clearing among sparse, stunted pine trees were two unhitched camper trailers, a structure of sticks and tarpaulin, a woodpile, and a larger, rusted truck with a water tank on its bed, everything filmed with road dust. Russ pulled over behind the pickup and cut the engine. A second sticker on its bumper said CRAZY HORSE WASN'T.

"So," he said to Frances. "Maybe you should stay here."

She was still staring at the windshield. "What did I ask you."

"I'm sorry?"

"What was the one thing I asked you to do."

It was interesting that her fear expressed itself as anger, as if it were his fault that she needed him to include her.

"Okay, then," he said, opening his door.

As they approached the trailers, the flimsy rear door of one of them banged open. Clyde came out in his bare feet, dressed only in brown jeans and a fleece-lined denim jacket, unbuttoned. His chest was bare and hairless. "Hey, white man."

"Hello, good morning."

"That your wife?"

Frances had stopped a step behind Russ.

"No," he said. "She's an adviser in our fellowship."

"Hey, pretty lady." Again the smiling insolence. "What brings you up here?"

"What do you think?" Russ said.

"I think you didn't get the message."

"I got the message, but I didn't understand it."

"Get the fuck out of here? Seems pretty clear to me."

"But why? We're not bothering you."

Clyde smiled at the sky, as if his amusement were cosmic. He was handsome in a strong-browed way, handsome and fit. "If I walked into your house in Chicago and you said, 'Hey, red man, get the fuck out, I don't like you people'—I'd get the message."

Russ could have objected that his group wasn't in Clyde's house. But the Navajos' home was in the land, not in structures, and white people had certainly given them reasons to hate them. It was only by chance that Russ, until now, had dealt with Navajos who didn't hate them. He glanced back at Frances. She seemed entirely occupied with managing her fear.

"You're right," he said. "If you don't want us here, we shouldn't be here."

"That's better."

"But first I want you to hear me as a person. Not as a white man—as a person. I want to hear you, too. I didn't come here to argue with you, I came to listen."

Clyde laughed. "Like hell you did. I know why you're here."

"If you're talking about the guitars, then, yes, we will need those back. We're not leaving the mesa without them."

"You people are all the same."

"No, we're not."

"Your possessions, your money. You think you're different, but you're all the same."

"You don't know me," Russ said angrily. "I don't give a damn about possessions. I do care about the two young girls you hurt by stealing from them."

"How many guitars do you need? I left you three of them."

"How many do *you* need?"

"I already gave them to my buddies. That's the difference between you and me."

"That's bullshit. The difference between you and me is you steal from teenaged girls."

Clyde's smile became pained. He looked around at the pine trees and then, shaking his head, walked over to the other trailer. From the dirtied sky came a faint sigh of industry, from the trees the chirring of a nutcracker. Frances's eyes were fastened on Clyde as if she expected him to get a gun.

"We're safe," Russ said gently.

Her eyes moved to him without seeming to see him. Clyde emerged from the other trailer with the two guitar cases and set them on the ground. "Now get out of here," he said.

"No."

"Seriously, white man. You got what you came for."

Clyde went inside his own trailer, and Frances gripped Russ's arm. "We should go."

"No."

"Please. For God's sake."

Russ's anger had turned to sorrow. There was beauty in a young man's righteous anger and no joy in overpowering it—no satisfaction in bringing a white man's legal rights to bear, asserting white ownership, reclaiming his possessions from a man who had nothing. The moral victory was Clyde's. Thinking of what it cost him, Russ felt sorry for him.

He went and rapped on the door of the trailer. Rapped again.

"Listen to me," he said to the door. "I want to invite you to come down to the school and talk to our group. Will you do that for me?"

"I'm not your performing Navajo," came the voice from inside.

"Goddamn it, I'm showing you respect. I'm asking you to do the same."

After a silence, the trailer shifted with movement inside it. The door opened a crack. "You're a friend of Keith Durochie."

"I am."

"Then I have no respect for you."

The door fell shut. Russ opened it again. Inside the trailer were the smells and disarray of solitary male living. "We came here to listen," he said.

"Your lady looks at me like I'm a rattlesnake."

"Can you blame her? You make threats, you break into the school."

"But you're not afraid of me."

"No. I'm not."

Clyde pursed his lips and nodded to himself. "All right. I'll show you who your friend is."

He stepped into a pair of boots, and Russ gave Frances a reassuring smile. She looked furious about what he was putting her through, but when Clyde came outside and led him down a sandy trail, through the pine trees, she followed them.

The trail was short and ended at an outcrop overlooking the devastated plain. Dust continued to billow from the strip mine, and the intervening slopes were treeless, lifeless—water-starved and grazed to death. Clyde stood so close to the cliff's edge that Russ's rectum tightened.

"Looking at this," Clyde said, "is like watching you rape my mother."

"It's bad," Russ agreed.

"It's sacred land, but it's full of coal. You see that smoke?" He gestured to the north. "That's electricity for your cities. It's not for us—there's no electricity on the mesa."

"Do you want electricity?"

Clyde looked over his shoulder at Russ. "I'm not a moron."

"I'm just trying to understand. Is the problem the coal mine, or the fact that you don't have electricity?"

"The problem is the tribal council. Your friend thinks this shithole is a good thing. Modern economy, man. Gotta deal with the *bilagáana*, fact of life, can't live without 'em. That's what your friend says."

"Keith cares about his people. I don't like what I'm seeing here any more than you do, and I don't guess Keith likes it, either. But the money has to come from somewhere."

"Keith doesn't have to see it. He's down in Many Farms."

"He's not well, you know. He had a stroke last week."

Clyde shrugged. "Somebody else can cry over that. He fucked my family, and we're not the only ones. The leases are shit and they last forever. We should be getting two or three times the money. And the jobs? My buddies are down there right now, eating coal dust. That's the new Navajo—Peabody Fucking Coal Company."

Frances was faintly shaking her head, her expression neither frightened nor angry, merely desolate, as if here were another door she was sorry to see opened.

"What did Keith do to your family?" Russ asked.

"This whole slope, he had the grazing permit for it. His wife had the permit on the back side, too. We knew the back side was no good—you probably saw it, coming in. But this side was still good. Keith cleared out and sold us the permit, and bang, a year later the council signed the deal with Peabody. He knew what was coming—we didn't. We had healthy herds, the maximum allowed, and now look. You see any stock down there?"

There wasn't an animal to be seen, not even a raven. From the direction of the mine came a muffled boom.

"The mine sucks water," Clyde said. "Peabody could shut it down tomorrow, the water wouldn't come back for twenty years. And you think Keith didn't know that? He read the leases, and the leases came with water rights. He knew exactly what he was doing."

Russ didn't want to believe it—there had to be another side of the story. And yet what did he really know about Keith Durochie? He remembered being smitten with him, remembered the delight of feeling accepted by him, the pride he'd taken in being friends with a full-blooded Navajo. What he couldn't remember, now that he thought about it, under the dust plume from the strip mine, was any particular warmth from Keith's side—any real curiosity or sentiment.

"That's your friend," Clyde said bitterly. "That's your tribal council."

"I feel for you," Russ said.

"Oh yeah? You know the Sierra Club? They're the crazy *bilagáana* that stopped the government from flooding the Grand Canyon. We went to them to try to stop the mine. We said we didn't want a power plant on sacred land, and they were exactly like you. They said, 'We feel for you.' And they didn't do shit for us. They only care about saving white places."

"So what are we supposed to do?" Frances said suddenly.

Clyde seemed startled that she had a voice.

"If we're the bad guys," she said, "if everything we do is automatically bad, if that's the way you feel about us, why should we try to do anything?"

"Just stay the fuck away," Clyde said. "That's what you can do."

"So you can go on hating us," she said. "So you can go on thinking you're superior to white people. If somebody like Russ comes along, somebody who actually cares, somebody who takes the time to hear you, somebody who's *good*, it messes up your whole story."

"Who's Russ?"

"I'm Russ," Russ said.

"I don't hate your guy," Clyde said to Frances. "At least he came up here—I respect that."

"But we're still supposed to get the fuck out," she said. "Is that the idea?"

Talking to a woman appeared to discomfit Clyde. He kicked some gravel over the edge of the cliff. "I don't care what you do. You can stay the week."

"No," Russ said. "That's not enough. I want you to come down and talk to our group. You can do it tonight—bring your friends."

"You're telling *me* what to do?"

"It won't change anything. You'll still have this nightmare on your mesa—nothing's going to change that. It makes me sick to see what's happened. But if you're angry enough to steal from us, we have a right to hear why you're angry. I promise you the kids will listen to you."

"Have their little Navajo experience."

"Yes. I won't deny it. But you'll experience who we are, too."

Clyde laughed. "The thing about your promises? There's always something you didn't tell us."

"That's bullshit," Russ said. "That's self-pitying bullshit. If you keep getting cheated, you need to be smarter. If you end up feeling like we've cheated you, you can go ahead and say so—we can take it. The question to me is whether you have the guts for an honest dialogue. From what I've seen, the only thing you're any good at is saying 'Fuck you' and walking away. I'd hate to find out you're nothing but a bully and a thief."

Did words give expression to emotion, or did they actively create it? The act of speaking had uncovered a love in Russ's heart, a love related to Clem, and he could tell, from the uncertainty in Clyde's sneer, that his words had had an effect. But the fact of the effect was problematic. The very act of caring was a kind of privilege, another weapon in the white arsenal. There was no escaping the imbalance of power.

"I'm sorry," he said. "You don't have to talk to us."

"You think I'm afraid of you?"

"No. I think you're angry and you have good reason to be. You're under no obligation to spare us the discomfort of your anger."

Now every word he said seemed to aggravate the imbalance. It was time to swallow his love and shut up.

"Thank you for giving us the guitars," he said.

He beckoned to Frances to go ahead of him on the trail through the pines. Following her and looking back, he saw a complicated smile.

"Fuck you," Clyde said.

Russ laughed and proceeded up the trail. Halfway up it, Frances stopped and threw her arms around him. "You're amazing," she said.

"I don't know about that."

"God, I admire you. Do you know that? Do you know how much I admire you?"

She held him tight, and there it was: the joy. After all the dark years, his joy was shining forth again.

Returning to the camp, they collected the two guitars and laid them on the bed of Ruth's truck. The sun was now white, the glare intense on the road down the back side of the ridge. (To Russ, when he'd stayed with Keith, it had been the "front" side.) Dangling from the rearview mirror was a small plastic Snoopy, not necessarily an indication that Ruth liked *Peanuts*. All sorts of random trinkets turned up on the reservation.

"I'm sorry about this morning," Frances said.

"Don't be. It was brave of you to be here at all."

"It's like the feeling comes over me and I can't control it. I wonder if it has to do with Bobby—the way he died. I don't remember always being so afraid."

"The important thing is that you did it. You were afraid, but you did it."

"Can I say something else?"

Russ nodded, hoping for a stroke in return.

"I desperately need to pee."

The canyon was devoid of shrubs to pee behind, but the old farmstead was close ahead. Russ increased his speed, Frances squirming at every bump. When he pulled into Keith's old yard, she had the door open before he stopped. She hobbled behind the shell of the little house, and he took his own leak behind a cottonwood. Watching the wood go dark with his urine, he thought of the bare ground going dark with hers, her pants around her ankles. In the sun and the thin air, he felt dizzy.

Returning to the truck, he saw her inside the roofless house and joined her there. The bedroom wall was still extant, but the door and its frame were gone, the floor covered with drifted sand. Nearly thirty years had passed since he'd lain in the bedroom and pictured the Navajo dancer. Even now, when he was enlightened enough to deplore a white man's lust for a Native American fifteen-year-old, the thought excited him.

"I don't know what to think," he said.

"About what?"

"About everything. About Keith. I hate to think he deliberately cheated Clyde's family. But that's the thing about other cultures—an outsider can never really understand what's going on."

"That's why you have your own culture," Frances said. "That's why you have me. I'm easy to understand."

"I'm not so sure about that."

"Want to bet?"

In two quick steps, she was pressing against him. Her hands were inside his sheepskin coat, her neck straining upward for a kiss. He gave it to her, tentatively.

She wasn't tentative. She gave a little hop and he lifted her off the ground. She was a very determined kisser, harder of mouth than Marion, more aggressive, and it was entirely up to him to keep her aloft. How sharp the discontinuity between fantasy and reality! How disorienting the step from the generality of desire into the specificity of her kissing style, the hundred-odd pounds of dead weight he was holding. When he set her down, she backed against the wall and drew him after her. Her hips were as aggressive as her mouth, denim grinding against denim, and he thought of the heart surgeon. He thought of the lakefront high-rise apartment in which, he could now be certain, she'd done with the surgeon exactly what she was doing with him. Far from dismaying him, the thought helped him make sense of her. She was a widow who wanted sex; was good at it; had recent practice at it.

She paused and looked up at him. "Is this all right?" She seemed genu-inely worried that it wasn't. He loved her all the more for that.

"Yes, yes, yes," he said.

"It's the nineteen seventies?"

"Yes, yes, yes."

With a sigh, she closed her eyes and put her hand between his legs. Her shoulders relaxed as if feeling his penis made her sleepy. "There we are."

It might have been the most extraordinary moment of his life.

"We should get back, though," she said. "Don't you think? They're probably wondering what happened to us."

She was right. But now, being felt by her, he lost his mind. He covered her mouth with his, unbuttoned her jacket, pulled out her shirt-tails, reached underneath. The smallness of her breasts, in contrast to Marion's, was extraordinary. Everything was extraordinary—he'd lost his mind, and she wasn't saying no. She wasn't saying they had to go back. The sun was warming his head and raising a smell of old smoke from the wall, but the place had lost its sound. Not a vehicle had passed on the road. No croak of a raven bore tidings of a reality larger than the two of them. In his madness, with the back of his hand scraping against her open zipper, he dared to part her private hair. She tensed and said, "Oh, Jesus."

His madness made him bold. "Just let me."

"No, it's fine. It's just—hoo. Shouldn't we go back?"

They definitely needed to go back, but he was touching Frances Cottrell's vagina, a few steps from the spot where he'd entered the world of conscious pleasure, and there was no withstanding it. He'd come too far and waited too long. He opened his own pants.

"Oh, wow, okay." She looked down at what was pressing against her belly, and then at the hole in the front wall where a window had been. "Maybe this isn't the best time?"

His voice wasn't his own; wasn't under his control. "I can't wait any more."

"It's true. I did make you wait."

"You tortured me and tortured me."

She nodded, as if conceding the point, and he tried to take her pants down. She looked around more nervously. "Really?"

"Yes, please."

"I had no idea you were like this."

"I am utterly in love with you. Didn't you know that?"

"No, I guess I did wonder."

When he tried again to get her pants down, she gently pushed him away. "Can we at least be less visible?"

In the time it took him to lead her into what had been the house's bedroom, remove his coat, and spread it on the floor, the character of his madness changed—became less of the body and more of the head. Now everything centered on the deed and its attendant practicalities. She sat down on the coat and pulled off her shoes and pants. "I'm on the Pill," she said, "in case you were wondering."

He wanted to ask if she truly wanted what he wanted, but there was a chance that her assent would lack enthusiasm, a chance that it would start a conversation. The air was still cold enough that she left her hunting jacket on. At the sight of her lying back in it, naked below the waist, he thought he might throw up with excitement. Before she could change her mind—before he could lose the mad determination to do the deed, before he could consider how far from ideal the time and the setting for it were—he tore off his own pants and kneeled between her legs.

"My goodness, Reverend Hildebrandt. You're rather large."

If *large* meant *comparatively large*, it was a comparison that no one had ever made. The stroke (oh, what a suggestive term Ambrose had coined) made him even larger. To his surprise, he found the largeness to be a difficulty.

"Sorry," she said. "You're big, and I'm—tense."

It couldn't have been clearer that he was making a mistake. Each passing minute would only add to her tension. But he simply couldn't wait any more. As if time were a thing he could grasp in his arms and bend to his will, he kissed her and touched her with soothing unhurry. Her responses were ambiguous, speaking possibly of arousal, possibly of tenseness. Gone, either way, was her aggressiveness.

"We can wait," he admitted.

"No, try it again. Just go slow. I don't know why I'm so tight."

How quickly, once clothes had been shed, the wildly unmention-
able became the casually discussable. It was like being whisked to a
different planet. He felt as if he'd learned more about Frances in an
hour than he'd learned in half a year. Thankfully, his heart still recognized her; his reservoir of compassion was still there to be tapped. He
loved that a woman so confident of her desirability should have trouble
relaxing for him. But alongside her specificity as a person, the sweetly
imperfect person in whom he'd invested so much hope and so much
longing, was the necessity to be, if only once, inside a woman who
wasn't Marion. How absurd the necessity, and how funny and human
the constriction that impeded it, the quarter-inch out for every half-
inch farther in, the lump in the sheepskin jacket that was murdering
his elbow. In the end, he didn't make it quite all the way in, and his
satisfaction was pinched. But, God help him, he was keeping score,
and this absolutely counted. Freed, at long last, from the weight of his
inferiority, his heart returned to Frances. He shuddered with gratitude
for the woman whose grace had saved him.

"So, number one," she said, "I need to pee again. Number two, we
should definitely go back."

She gave him a sloppy kiss, the pleasure of it heightened by their
union, their mouths like twins or proxies of other wet parts. He didn't
want to leave her. He didn't want to feel that he'd had, by far, the better
half of the experience. He wanted to satisfy her, too. But the desire he'd
turned on with his taming of Clyde now seemed to be turned off. She
scrambled to her feet and put her pants on. Two minutes later, they were
in the truck again.

"So," he said.

"Right, so."

"I love you. That's where I am."

"I appreciate that."

He started the truck and drove for a while in silence. There was no
point in repeating that he loved her—he'd already said it twice.

"It's strange," she finally said. "The thing that makes you so attractive
to me is the thing that makes it wrong of me to want you."

"I'm not so good. I think I told you that."

"But you are good. You're a beautiful man. It's all very confusing to me."

"You're regretting what we did."

"No. At least not yet. It's just confusing."

"I'm fantastically happy," he said. "I have no regrets at all."

The hour was nearly noon, and he was driving as fast as he dared, too focused on road hazards to sustain a conversation, even if Frances had been inclined to say more. And so it happened that when he approached the chapter house and saw a big Chevy truck and a red-jacketed figure, Wanda, standing with Ted Jernigan and another man, Rick Ambrose, the latter glowering at Russ and Frances and registering their guilty lateness, waiting with the only kind of news that could have brought him to the mesa—bad news—the last words Russ had spoken were that he had no regrets at all.

In the beginning, there was only a speck of dark matter in a universe of light, a floater in the eye of God. It was to floaters that Perry owed his discovery, as a boy, that his vision wasn't a direct revelation of the world but an artifact of two spherical organs in his head. He'd lain gazing at a bright blue sky and tried to focus on one, tried to determine the particulars of its shape and size, only to lose it and glimpse it again in a different location. To pin it down, he had to train his eyes in concert, but a floater in one eyeball was ipso facto invisible to the other; he was like a dog chasing its tail. And so with the speck of dark matter. The speck was elusive but persistent. He could glimpse it even in the night, because its darkness was of an order deeper than mere optical darkness. The speck was in his mind, and his mind was now lambent with rationality at all hours.

On the bunk mattress above him, Larry Cottrell cleared his throat. An advantage of Many Farms was that the group slept in dorm rooms, rather than in a common area, where any of forty people could have noticed Perry leaving. The disadvantage was his roommate. Larry was myopic with adulation, useful to Perry insofar as his company displaced that of people who might have given him shit about his effervescence, but very unsound as a sleeper. The night before, returning to their room at two a.m. and finding him awake, Perry had explained that the frybread at dinner had given him an attack of flatulence, and that he'd crept out to a sofa in the lounge to spare his friend the smell of his slow burners. A similar lie would be available tonight, but first he needed to escape undetected, and Larry, above him, in the dark, kept clearing his throat.

Among Perry's options were strangling Larry (an idea appealing in the moment but fraught with sequelae); boldly rising to announce that he was gassy again and going to the lounge (here the virtue was consistency of story, the drawback that Larry might insist on keeping him company); and simply waiting for Larry, whose bones a day of scraping paint had surely wearied, to fall asleep. Perry still had an hour to play with, but he resented the hijacking of his mind by trivialities. His rationality was blazing and tireless and all-seeing, and the problem of Larry made him sensible of the cost of ceaseless blazing, the body's need for a little boost. The emptier of his two aluminum film canisters was in his pants pocket. He could rub sustenance into his gums without a sound, but he was plagued by unknowns, such as whether his sleeping bag would sufficiently muffle the sound of a lid's unscrewing. Whether he could open the canister blindly without spilling. (Even a microgram of spillage was unacceptable.) Whether it was wise to partake at all from a canister already so depleted. Whether he shouldn't at least wait until he could give himself a superior boost nasally. Whether, on second thought, it wasn't such a bad idea to strangle the person whose interminable throat clearings were standing between him and that boost . . .

Unh! The whether whether whether was of the body and its arrangement, its side deal, with the powder. Wholly apart from his body, lambent in his mind even now, was a key to millennia of fruitless speculation. It happened that, very recently, less than a week ago, he'd solved the puzzle of the world's persistent talk of God. The solution was that he, Perry, was God. The realization had frightened him, but it was followed by a second realization: if a felonious and drug-addicted New Prospect Township High School sophomore was God, *then anyone at all could be God.* This was the amazing key. The amazement, indeed, was that he hadn't seen it sooner. It had stared him in the face the previous summer, when he'd inked out the *God*s in the Reverend's clerical magazine and replaced them with *Steve*s. How had he failed, that day, to grasp a key so exquisitely simple? The key was that Steve could be God. So could every other Tom, Dick, and Harry—all any of them had to do was open his eyes to his divinity. The instant a person experienced the mind's truly limitless capacities, God's existence became the opposite of preposterous. It became preposterously self-evident.

The revelation had occurred on Maple Avenue, minutes after he'd withdrawn $2,825.00 from his brother's passbook account at Cook County Savings Bank. The teller had counted the bills and then counted them again out loud, *twenty-seven, twenty-eight, twenty, and five*, and tucked them into a nifty brown envelope. The rush of success was so titanic, he imagined an ejaculation blotting out the heavens. Knowledge so perfect could only have been God's, and if he, Perry, possessed it, then what did this make him? In his earlier lunch-hour casings of the bank, he'd ascertained that the older, gray-haired teller, with whom he'd had dealings, was nowhere to be seen at 12:15. Behind the window, instead, was a frizzy-haired mademoiselle still sporting orthodontia, thus undoubtedly (beyond all question!) *too new at the bank to know Clem*. The scarlet-nailed hand that had taken his passbook was marvelously inexpert.

"That's a lot of cash. Are you sure you wouldn't rather have a cashier's check?"

"I'm buying a sailboat."

"Wow. That's exciting."

"It's a beauty. I've been saving for three years."

"Do you have some ID?"

She couldn't have asked a question more perfectly foreseen. Everything had been foreseen: withdrawing an innocently precise number of dollars; wearing a nerdy cardigan and the disguise of his new eyeglasses; not only replicating and laminating a University of Illinois student ID card but meticulously abrading and soiling it with an emery board and charcoal, labors performed within feet of his soundly sleeping little brother and underwritten by his powder, which was also a focuser of attention, an enhancer of manual precision. He'd invested rather a lot of little boosts in his project, but the investment would be dwarfed by the avalanche of dividends he perfectly foresaw. When the metal-mouthed teller returned the ID card, having scarcely glanced at it, the investment had already paid off handsomely. Counting time spent manufacturing the card and practicing Clem's signature, minus incidental drug expenses, he'd made $236.25 an hour. Not bad. But still far less than he stood to make—even factoring in the additional hours of labor in Arizona and the return of Clem's money—after his transactions had unfolded as foreseen.

There was no peyote, not one button, in Chicagoland.

Thousands of Chicagoland hippies were desperate to try it.

Only one person in the world had identified the demand and positioned himself to meet it.

He owed the development of this logic to an earlier realization: for three years, he'd been treating the wrong disorder. He'd believed his mind to be diseased, in want of chemical palliation, when in fact the problem was somatic. It was his body, its exhaustible muscles, its irritable nerves, not his mind, that needed support. As soon as his guy had introduced him to Dexedrine and he'd learned the proper function of a Quaalude, which was to let his body rest, he'd entered a phase unprecedented in its excellence and serenity. Each day, the world was like pinball played in slow motion. His timing with the flippers was precise to the millisecond; he could run up the score arbitrarily high. He also knew exactly when to stop, allow the ball to drain, and eat his 'ludes. Everything he did in early January had a rightness so complete that it controlled the world around him. Example: the very day he exhausted his Dexies, *the very day*, three thousand dollars appeared in his savings passbook, courtesy of his sister. Example: his bank did not require parental countersignatures. Example: his guy was not only at home and not only compos mentis, more or less, but willing to part with the entire remaining contents of his Planters Peanuts jar. The thought did cross Perry's mind that he was overpaying, but the agreed-upon price was a minor fraction of three thousand dollars, and the guy fell upon his twenty-dollar bills with poignant greediness, suggestive of an individual who'd seriously hit the skids. As Perry fled down Felix Street, chewing pills, the world seemed even righter. His money had brought great happiness to both him and the guy. Their transaction, in theory zero-sum, had somehow doubled the money's value.

For yet a while longer, all had been righter than right, but by the time Bear delivered his judgment of speed, Perry was ready to hear it. What had seemed in the moment of purchase an all but inexhaustible number of pills had dwindled unexpectedly fast, and although their function was somatic he was experiencing less than salubrious mental side effects. Jay in particular was intolerably impatient-making, their sharing of a room a misery. Likewise his mother's tender touchings. Likewise any Crossroads activity requiring physical contact. The world's slowness had become more infuriating than capacitating, and meanwhile his body kept saying, "More, please." His body had created a problem. He hated it for its inroads on his dwindling supplies, hated its drag on the flight of his mind. In a state of towering crankiness, when he ran out of pills, he returned to the guy's little house on Felix Street, and this time no dog was there to howl at him. The front stoop was littered with rain-eaten advertising folios. Pasted to the door was a bright-yellow sheriff's notice that he didn't dare step close enough to read.

"I'm not surprised," Bear said. "That shit is pure evil."

That Perry liked Bear was irrelevant. That Bear liked Perry, and allowed him to make house calls, was a blessing portending a new phase of rightness. Bear, who'd also sold to Ansel Roder, had zero personal attributes in common with the guy on Felix Street. He was burly and mellow, seemingly unafraid of the law, and reassuringly acquainted with several such Crossroads alumni as Laura Dobrinsky. His house, a trek of thirty minutes from the Crappier Parsonage, belonged to a grandmother who now dwelt in a nursing home. Perry had never had a grandmother, but he recognized the grandmaternal smell in the walls, the grandmaternal hand in the embroidered sheer curtains in the living room, where Bear, of an afternoon, drank Löwenbräu and read the many magazines he subscribed to. Clearly, the key to longevity as a dealer was to be like Bear. He dealt exclusively in naturally derived substances, mostly pot and hash but also, as Perry learned after explaining his energy requirements, the odd gram of cocaine, to oblige some of the musicians among his clientele.

On his first visit, Perry left with a forty-dollar sample. Did someone say love at first snort? He was back two days later. This time, Bear had company, a comely personage in a leather miniskirt, drinking her own Löwenbräu, and Perry feared that his arrival was unwelcome. But Bear was mellow, and his lady friend, on learning what Perry was about, brightened as though she'd remembered that today was a holiday. Already, after only two days, Perry wondered how a person even casually acquainted with cocaine could ever, for a moment, not be wondering if some of it might be close at hand; how the thought had managed to absent itself from her head. Further speeding his heart, as Bear convivially treated them, was the thrill of his singularity (if anyone else at New Prospect High had used the fabled drug of Casey Jones, Perry was unaware of it) and his inclusion by two sophisticated people in their twenties. Among their topics of lively discussion were the most interesting drug they'd ever taken, the drug they were keenest to try ("Peyote," Bear declared), the lucky star that Perry could thank for not having been robbed by a needle-using freak, the contrasting benignancy of a plant-based alkaloid that didn't turn its users into paranoid maniacs, the experiments of Dr. Sigmund Freud, the hypocritical distinction between prescription drugs and street drugs, and the rumors of the Beatles reuniting, the grating self-importance of Grand Funk Railroad. Perry was very merry, and his very merriness served the ends of his unsleeping rationality. His first-order need was that Bear like him and trust him. His second-order need was to deflect attention from a glaring difference between himself and Bear, namely, that Bear was mellow. One snort made Bear an even happier Bear and was enough. Perry, who was the nth degree of the opposite of mellow, struggled fiercely to control his eyeballs, which wanted only to follow the coke.

Bear's mellowness, it emerged, concealed a stubborn will. His coke sales were a sideline, subject to constraints of availability at the wholesale level, and his other buyers, though few and irregular, were loyal to him. Perry, as a newcomer, was eligible for only half a gram. When he offered to pay a premium for more, Bear pretended not to hear him. Bear was being irrational—it was tiresome and risky to make Perry come a-scoring so often—but Perry, guided by rationality, gave their relationship some weeks to grow before he made his proposition.

Bear whistled. "That's a shitload."

"I'm more than happy to prepay you for your trouble."

"Cost isn't the issue."

"As much as I enjoy our little chats, it might be better if we had them less frequently. Don't you think?"

"Honestly? I think you'll blow through whatever you get and be back here in a week."

"Not true!"

"I'm not cool with where this is going."

"But—you'll see—that is—it's cool. Just give me a chance."

It might have been the sight of twenty fifty-dollar bills, crisp from the presses, satisfying to riffle, that turned the tide in Perry's favor. Bear grumpily took the money and sent him away with his nearly weight-less allowance. In the ensuing fortnight, Perry visited him twice more without getting his thousand dollars' worth. Did there then come a night when he focused the full might of his mind on imagining into existence—*on willing into being*—a trace of the powder that had so lately and whitely existed but now, owing to a traitorous improvidence of the body, did not? There came more than one such night. And did there then come a day when Bear answered the doorbell and merely handed him a slip of paper?

"His name is Eddie. He's got what you paid for."

"May I come in?"

"No. Sorry. You're a sweet kid, but I can't see you anymore."

The door closed. For various reasons, sheer physical exhaustion per-haps primary among them, Perry burst into tears. Was it then that the speck of dark matter first appeared? He felt that he loved Bear, admit-tedly on short acquaintance, more than he'd ever loved any other per-son. His forfeiture of Bear's affection was a blow so devastating that it actually chased from his mind all thought of white powder. Only when he was home again, having blubbered himself out, did he recollect what the seven digits on the slip of paper represented. His mind exploded as if he'd inhaled the whole of it.

He did not love Eddie, and Eddie did not love him. Their first en-counter had a flavor of Felix Street, and their one subsequent transaction, which more than completed the exhaustion of the funds that Becky had transferred to him, left him seething with hatred of Eddie, who he was absolutely sure had cheated him. Again, it was only afterward that he recalled how fucking much drug, even after being cheated, he'd come to possess. Three tightly lidded film canisters: that was something. Never again, or at least not for an extremely long while, would he find himself dying of empty-handedness.

And yet, if three canisters was excellent, how much more excellent six would have been. Or twelve. Or twenty-four. Was there a multi-ple of three of whiteness large enough to permanently set his mind at rest? The dark speck, the mental floater, was there again. It no longer seemed that money spent brought double benefit. Money spent was simply money gone. In his savings passbook, perilously exposed to prying parental eyes, stood the sorry figure of $188.85, and even genius had its limits. He didn't see how one hundred and eighty-nine dollars could be compounded, quickly, into thirty-five hundred . . .

Larry was snoring. The sound accorded so closely with the platonic form of "snore sound" that Perry wondered if it might be fake. He lay still, and the snores grew louder. By and by, they terminated in a choking gasp, the rustle of Larry repositioning himself. There followed fainter snores, unquestionably authentic. Perry now dared—first things first; throw the nerves a bone—to open the canister and insert a moistened finger. He tapped the finger on the canister's rim, very carefully, and introduced it to his mouth. He dipped again and pushed the finger deep into a nostril, removed it and breathed deeply, sucked the finger clean and used his tongue as a gum swab. The localized numbing was metonymic of a more general cessation of his nervous system's hostilities against the mind. Although the rush had of late been feeble, he at least was no longer at odds with himself. He capped the canister and slowly sat upright. His boots were by the door, the money in the toe of one of them, everything perfectly foreseen. The now deafening beating of his heart served also to deafen Larry, because it had to; because the sound was God's own. As maternal heartbeats were said to soothe prenatal babies, His own cosmic heartbeats lulled every one of His children. Oh, how He loved them! He felt He could have killed them all or saved them all, just by willing it, so loud were His coked-up heartbeats as He proceeded to ease open the dorm-room door.

An exit sign glowed in the dark hallway. At the far end, fluorescent light spilled weakly from the lounge. It was difficult to return to human chronology and make sense of his watch, but he grasped that he still had thirty-five minutes. He pocketed the money, put on his boots, and crept past other rooms commandeered by Crossroads. From one of them, he could hear the muted squeak of girl voices, distressingly awake. What needed to be done about them must have been self-evident, because he found himself, a seeming instant later, sitting in a bathroom

stall and propelling into his sinuses, from the base of his thumb, a large
and sloppy pour. It was very curious. How did an all-seeing Entity end
up on a toilet seat without knowing how he'd gotten there? Casting his
mind's eye back over the preceding moments, he encountered an occlu-
sion. The speck of dark matter now seemed larger; could, indeed, no longer be referred to as a speck; was perhaps better described as an uneasy
semitransparency, a poorly demarcated blob. He couldn't pin it down
for examination, but he sensed its malignant saturation with knowledge
contradicting his own. It was unbelievable! Unbelievable that God Himself should have a floater in His eye! God was very, very wrathful. His
wrath, having nowhere else to vent itself, took the form of three further
massive boosts in quick succession. If wild excess killed the body, then
so be it.

He got his pants down just in time. The body, rather than dying, was
defecating like an upside-down volcano. Into the stench, amid a flashing
of alien lights, an apocalyptic pounding in his chest, came a blessedly
rational insight: this was what happened when a person overindulged.
To entertain this thought, however, was to perceive its irrelevance. Overindulgence had shattered his lambent rationality into myriad splinters,
each consisting of an insight unrelated to any other, each brightly reflect-
ing a star-hot whiteness now blazing in his stomach; he thought he might
vomit. Instead he shat again, and none of this had been foreseen. If fore-
knowledge of this supremely unpleasant lavatorial digression had resided
anywhere, it had been in the hazy blob of dark matter, not in his mind.

Wiping his ass in a cramped Navajo bathroom stall, shackled by
dropped trousers and distracted by the flashes of a thousand splinters,
by the choking engorgement of his carotid, he forgot to be mindful of
his canister's whereabouts. As soon as he remembered, he confidently
foresaw that he'd capped it and set it aside. But no. Oh, no no no no no.
He'd knocked it over on the floor. Its scattered contents were thirstily
absorbing a trickle from the toilet's leaking seal. They'd formed a watery
paste that he now had no choice but to urge, with the side of his finger,
back into the canister, even at the cost of dampening the powder still
inside it. Nothing made any sense. The embodied clairvoyance that
had crept down the hallway toward the execution of its masterstroke

was now wiping up, with bits of toilet paper, a whitish alkaloid smear contaminated with fecal and perhaps even tubercular bacteria, sullying itself with the question of whether the alkaloid had antiseptic properties, whether the toilet paper could later be applied to his gums without the swallowing of pathogens, and whether, although he still felt close to throwing up, it wouldn't be better to lick the floor than let any milligrams go to waste.

A gag reflex dissuaded him from licking. He tamped the saturated toilet paper into the canister and screwed on the lid. And just like that—in an n-dimensioned wave of ecstasy, a rolling pan-cellular orgasm—he recalled that the object of his masterstroke was to secure an abundance of drug better measured in kilograms than in milligrams. Just like that, he emerged from life-threatening turbulence into the smoothest of highest-altitude flying, and everything made sense again. How had he questioned the rightness of his actions? How had he imagined that he'd overindulged? God didn't err! He was superb! Superb! He'd pushed through the body's limits to the highest realm of being. The speck of dark matter had shrunk to the point of disappearing, was again so tiny that God could love it, was dear and unthreatening and did not, after all, know anything, or maybe one small thing . . .

now you've seen hadn't you better won't take but a minute

Getting the speck's message—that there might come, tonight, a moment when he felt a notch less superb, which couldn't be allowed to happen—he stole back down the hallway and slipped into his room. His other canister, the full and fully dry one, was at the center of a sock ball in his duffel bag. He'd brought it along with no intention of dipping into it. He'd been motivated by a last-minute paranoia, a seemingly irrational fear of leaving his entire reserve in the parsonage basement, well hidden behind the oil burner but unguarded. Now he saw that it hadn't been irrational at all. It had been perfect foresight.

"Perry?"

The voice, in the dark, sounded like Larry's, but this didn't mean that Larry was awake. Part of becoming God was hearing the voices of His children's thoughts. So far, the voices had been too low to be intelligible. More like the random murmur in Union Station. He unballed the sock and put the wonderfully weighted canister in the leg pocket of his painter pants. Sweet-caustic alkaloid juices continued to drain behind his septum.

"What are you doing?"

If Perry's vision had truly been perfect, unmarred by the dark speck, he might have succeeded in extinguishing Larry. The power to kill by thinking was divine. The flaw in his power was like a smudge on the lens of an infinitely powerful telescope.

"Perry?"

"Go to sleep."

"What are you doing?"

"I'm going to the lounge. Stick your nose in the bathroom if you don't believe me."

"I'm having the opposite problem. I'm totally constipated."

Perry stood up and moved toward the door. Already he felt a notch less superb.

"Can we talk for a minute?"

"No," Perry said.

"Why won't you talk to me?"

"All I do is talk to you. We're together all the time."

"I know, but . . ." Larry sat up on his bunk. "I don't really feel like I'm with you. It's like you're in some kind of . . . place. Do you know what I mean? You haven't even had a shower since we got here."

If Larry couldn't see the absurdity of showering, didn't have a deity's intense distaste for it, there was no point in explaining.

"I'm trying to be honest," Larry said. "I'm telling you how you seem to me. And one thing I think is you really need to take a shower."

"Understood. Sleep tight."

"It's not just me, though. People think you're being really weird."

Perry now sensed an alliance between Larry and the speck of dark matter, a kindred possession of contradictory knowledge.

"I just wish you'd tell me what's going on with you," Larry said. "I'm your friend, we're in Crossroads. You can tell me anything you want."

"I think you're evil," Perry said. The rightness of this verdict was thrilling. "I think the powers of darkness are gathered in you."

Larry produced an emotional sound. "That's—a joke, right?"

"Far from it. I think you want to fuck your mother."

"Jesus, Perry."

"My dad's the same way—I have it on good authority. You need to mind your own business. All you people, just stay the fuck out of my way. Can you do that for me?"

There was a silence made imperfect by a Navajo's distant hot rod. Larry's pale face, in the obscurity above, was like a death's-head. The thought came to Perry that infinite power was infinitely terrible. How could God endure all the smiting He had to do? With infinite power came infinite pity.

Larry swung his legs off the bunk. "I'm getting Kevin."

"Don't do that. I was—my joke was in poor taste. I apologize."

"You're really scaring me."

"Do not get Kevin. What we both need now is shut-eye. If I promise to take a shower, will you go back to sleep?"

"I can't. I'm worried about you."

However he might extinguish Larry, whether with blunt-object blows or strangling hands, there was bound to be an overhearable commotion.

"Just let me visit the facilities again. I'm having quite the roiling and boiling. Quite the industrial gas factory. Just stay here, okay? I'll be right back."

Without waiting for a response, he darted from the room and flew down the hallway on wings of powder. As if he'd sailed off a cliff, he achieved fabulous velocity before hard ground, in the form of coronary limits made stricter by low atmospheric oxygen levels, stopped him dead. He turned, gasping, to see if the evil one had left their room. Not a sound!

The dormitory doors were locked at night, but from the lounge's window to the pavement was a jump (or climb, as the case would later be) of only five feet. Outside, in freezing air, he paused to touch the money in his jacket, the canisters in his pants. One more quick boost: advisable? Though he was now perhaps two notches below the most sensational high he'd ever experienced, the cold was bitter. A metallic taste of blood was in his windpipe, and he still wasn't far from throwing up. Press on, sir. Press on.

The young Navajos he'd befriended the night before were meeting him at the off-brand gas station up the road from the dormitory. He'd found the two of them shooting baskets beneath a billboard for the Best Western Canyon de Chelly whose lights indirectly illuminated a hoop and a crude backboard bolted to one of its stanchions. The younger Navajo had a deep, irregular scar from the bridge of his nose to his jaw. The older fellow was groovier and longer-haired, dressed in bell-bottom corduroys with a large silver belt buckle. At their urging, Perry had displayed his pathetic lack of ball skills, and by submitting to their derision, giggling along with it, he'd secured their trust. When he then broached the crucial subject, their laughter reached new heights.

"But seriously," he said.

Their hilarity was ongoing. "You want to try *peyote*?"

"No," he said. "That is—no offense intended—it's not for my own use. I'm looking to obtain a large quantity. Perhaps a pound of it or more. I have the money."

Of everything he'd said, this was apparently the most pants-wettingly funny. His foresight had allowed for the necessity of casting many a line before he got a bite, and he judged that it was time to try a different pond. He sidled away.

"Hey, wait, man, where you going?"

"It was nice to meet you both."

"You said money. What's your money?"

"Do you mean, is it legal tender?"

"How much you got? Twenty?"

Offended, he turned back to them. "A pound of peyote for twenty dollars? I have a hundred fifty times that much."

This disclosure ended the hilarity. The groovier Navajo asked him, with a frown, what he knew about peyote.

"I know that it's a powerful hallucinogen employed in Navajo ceremonies."

"That's wrong. Peyote isn't Navajo."

No word in the world hurt more than *wrong*. All his life, it had made Perry want to cry.

"That's disappointing," he said.

"Peyote's not our thing," the groovier fellow said. "It's only for people in the church."

"They take it and they sweat," his friend said.

"It doesn't even grow here. It comes from Texas."

"I see," Perry said.

Out of the now revealed imperfection of his knowledge rose a weariness compounded over many weeks of sleepless nights, a weariness so immense that he suspected no amount of boosting could overcome it. He shut his eyes and saw the überdark speck against the blackness of his lowered eyelids. The two Navajos were exchanging words that he was tantalizingly close to understanding. The gap between knowing no words of Navajo and knowing all words of Navajo seemed no wider than a micron. Were it not for the dark speck, the weariness, he could have crossed it effortlessly.

"So there's a guy," the groovier fellow said to Perry. "Guy named Flint."

"Flint, *right*." The younger fellow seemed excited to remember him. "Flint Stone."

"He's in New Mexico, just over the state line."

"Just over the state line. I know the place."

"Who is Flint?" Perry said.

"He's the man. He's got what you need. He brings peyote up from Texas."

"He's a Navajo?"

"Didn't I just say that? He's in the church and everything." The groovier fellow turned to his scar-faced friend. "Remember that time we went out there?"

"Yeah! That time we went out there."

"He had a bag of buttons in his shed. It was like a five-pound bag of coffee, pure peyote."

"That wasn't coffee?"

"No, man. I saw it. He opened the bag, he showed me. It was all peyote. He gets it for the church."

Flint Stone was a name from a cartoon. Perry's doubts about the story, which were substantial, all emanated from the speck. The speck's essence was that everything was hopeless and he was deathly tired. For a moment, in the billboard's reflected light, he sank deeper into weariness. But then—O ye of little faith!—his rationality blazed forth. His weariness was itself the proof that he could go no farther; didn't have the strength to accost further Navajo strangers. *By definition*, if he could go no farther, he'd reached a logical terminus. In the light of perfect logic, the coffee sack overflowing with peyote became incontrovertibly real. The surety was the balance of $13.85 in his passbook account, the scarcely larger sum in Clem's. The only way to replenish these accounts, while realizing a profit sufficient for his ancillary drug needs, was to buy peyote in bulk and resell it at a fivefold markup in Chicago. Ergo, there had to be a man by the unlikely name of Flint Stone, the man had to sell peyote at a depressed reservation price, and the first individuals Perry had accosted had to know it. Had to! It couldn't have been otherwise, because God had only one plan.

Weightless with logic, ebullient, he'd arranged to return in twenty-four hours. In the small eternity of those hours, the sack of peyote had become even realer, so real that he could feel the heavy weight of it; he could smell its earthy fungal smell. The weight and the smell were a turn-on that persisted through a morning of scraping paint from the side of a tribal meetinghouse, an afternoon of holding forth to Larry on the atomic structure of matter, the creation of matter in a Big Bang that even now propelled the universe ever outward, the key role of Cepheid variable stars in the discovery of this expansion, the unbelievably providential circumstance (*it had to be*) that a Cepheid's period of variation was proportional to its absolute luminosity, thus enabling precise measurement of intergalactic distances, across which an all-seeing mind could zip at will, zoom in for closer looks at the quasars and nebulae of its Creation, survey the dark outer limits of material existence . . .

Along the deserted road to the gas station were mercury-vapor lights that seemed weaker than those in New Prospect, as if Navajo impoverishment extended even to amperage. The air had an acrid scent of burned heating oil, and the only glow of warmth was in his head. He considered the possibility that he'd erred in not wearing long johns and a second sweater before dismissing it as incompatible with perfect foresight. His nose and mouth were so numb that his snot ran onto his chin before he noticed it. He pushed it into his mouth and savored the ever-freshness of the naturally derived substance dissolved in it. Conceivably he'd snorted more than half a gram . . .

The gas station was closed. Standing outside its dark office were the scar-faced fellow and, smoking a cigarette, a shaggy figure Perry didn't recognize. *Mr. Stone, I presume?* The figure was much younger than he'd imagined Flint.

"This is my cousin," the scar-faced fellow said. "He's driving."

The cousin had a thick neck and radiated stupidity. Types of this sort haunted the high-school locker room.

"Where is our other friend?" Perry said.

"He's not coming."

"That's a pity."

The cousin threw his cigarette toward the gas pumps, as though daring them to ignite (stupid), and walked over to a dusty station wagon parked in shadow. When Perry saw that the car was of the same make and model as the Reverend's, and of similarly advanced decrepitude, he felt a pinprick on his scalp. Pure goodness and rightness coursed through him, washing away his last lingering speck-sponsored doubts. The cousin's vehicle *had* to be a Plymouth Fury. As it was in the beginning, is now, and ever shall be!

He wouldn't have guessed the speeds of which a Fury was capable. On the state highway, from the back seat, he saw the speedometer needle enter regions that recalled his overindulgence in the bathroom. But there had been no overindulgence, and the cousin wasn't stupid. To the contrary, his driverly intelligence was profound. Lone lights flashed by like the galaxies God glimpsed in his zooming. Supernaturally invisible, slouched behind two Indian heads silhouetted like rock formations in a desert lit by headlights, he stickied his finger inside the tainted canister and applied it to his gums and nostrils. He took a deep, sweetened breath and sniffed repeatedly.

"You can totally trust me," he said. "I couldn't be more perfectly indifferent to the particulars of our buttons' provenance. Whether every last link in the chain of possession was strictly legal is no concern of mine. Indeed, I might argue that larceny, being forbidden, entails a level of risk that could be considered hard labor, as deserving of reward as any other form of labor."

He chuckled, divinely pleased with himself.

"The counterargument would be that larceny deprives a second party of the fruits of his own hard labor, and it becomes an interesting economic question—how value is created, how lost. If we had time and you had basic algebra, we could look into the mathematics of larceny— whether it really is zero-sum or whether there's some x factor that we're failing to account for, some hidden deficit in the party who's been stolen from. Although, again, for the narrow purposes of our transaction, it's no concern of mine. By the same token, if there's one link in the chain that you don't have to—"

"Man, what are you saying?"

"I'm saying that however legitimate, or perhaps less than legitimate—"

"Why are you talking? Shut up."

His scar-faced best of buddies! Perry giggled at how colossally he loved him. That God had chosen specially to favor a disfigured Navajo whose education had probably ended in eighth grade: all the angels in heaven were laughing with Him.

"What's so funny? What are you laughing at?"

"Stop laughing," the cousin said. "Shut up."

He kept laughing, but at a wavelength deeper than hearing, a radio or telepathic wavelength that entered every heart, waking or sleeping, around the world, and brought a comfort that human understanding could not explain. Into his own hearing came a multitude of voices, a collective murmur of gratitude and gladness. One voice, rising above the murmur, distinctly said, "That's a crock."

The voice was insidiously close and stopped his silent laughter. The voice sounded like Rick Ambrose, and the sentiment was odd. Crock of what? Only shit and butter came in crocks.

"Not butter," the voice clarified. And added—one was tempted to say snarled—something in a language (Navajo?) that would have been intelligible if spoken more slowly. Hearing an alien language in one's head was nearly as frightening as recognizing one's divinity, but it was likewise followed by a reassuring realization: the mind that could speak all human languages without having studied them could only be God's. *Quod erat demonstrandum.*

Like overindulgence inverted, the Fury's smooth sailing gave way to spine-crunching turbulence. On a narrow dirt road whose craters were inky in the headlights, the cousin maintained a speed inviting reassessment of his intelligence. One needed both hands to steady oneself, three further hands to ensure that the two film canisters and the folded envelope of cash weren't falling from one's pockets. A chalky-tasting powder filled the passenger compartment, and the road went on and on. One could only hope that they were rushing to meet an impatient seller at some appointed hour; that the return drive could be taken at lower velocity. Beneath the physical pain of being battered by armrest and door and one's own flying limbs, a deeper kind of pain began to grow, but the accelerations and counteraccelerations were so unpredictable and violent that to open a canister was out of the question . . .

The Fury stopped.

No longer the best of buddies, the scar-faced fellow turned and put his elbow on the backrest. "Give me the money and wait here."

"If you don't mind, I'd rather go with you."

"Wait here. He doesn't know you."

This made enough sense to be construed as foreordained necessity. The fellow took the envelope of money, and his cousin cut the engine and the lights. The sky must have clouded over the moon. After the door had opened and closed, the only light was from the fellow's flashlight. Its beam, crisply defined by the dust the car had raised, caught barbed-wire fencing, a corroded cattle guard, pale weeds along a rocky driveway, before it receded into negligibility. The cousin lit a cigarette and inhaled like a gusting wind. There was much to say and nothing that could be said. The speck of dark matter was malignant, and yet its darkness was tempting. One became so very tired of the brightness of one's mind . . .

The flashlight beam bobbed back into view. The back door opened.

"He's got the peyote, but he wants to talk to you."

As cold as the air in Many Farms had been, it was twice as cold in the dark of nowhere. The flashlight beam kindly pointed out stones and holes to be avoided on the driveway. Ahead, in its incident light, a stone structure became visible, a fence of bleached wood, the rear end of a skeletal truck. The fellow kicked open a sagging gate in the fence. "Go on," he said.

It was difficult to speak with jaws clenched against the chattering of teeth. "Give me the money."

"Cliff's got it. He's counting it."

"Who's Cliff?"

"Flint. He wants to talk to you."

Deep pain and brutal cold, a shuddering of chest muscles. He'd still had his wits in the warmth of the car. The thing he'd always had was wits, but now they'd abandoned him. He was stone-cold stupid.

"Go on. Take the flashlight."

He took the flashlight and proceeded through the gate. Stupidity had reduced him to hoping for the best. Hope was the refuge of the stupid. A paddle-limbed cactus loomed up, a nest of rust-eaten oblong cans, ragged sheets of unidentifiable building material, a charred tree stump. The signs of abandonment were unmistakable, but he went around to the back of the stone structure.

There was no back of it. Only the edges of a wall that had collapsed into rubble.

He heard a sound as familiar as his father's voice, the whinny and rumble of a Fury wagon's engine starting up. He heard wheels spinning, an automatic transmission shifting gears.

He was too cold to be angry, too shaky-limbed to run.

The speck of dark matter had been tiny only in spatial dimension. It was the negative image of the point of light that had given birth to the universe. Now, in its explosive expansion and consumption of the light, the speck's hyperdensity became apparent: nothing was denser than death. And how tired he was of running from it. All he had to do was lie down on the ground and wait. He was so malnourished and exhausted, the cold would quickly do the rest—he knew this; could feel it. The dark negative that had replaced his rationality was equally rational, everything equally clear in its antithesis of light.

But the body wasn't rational. What the body's nervous system wanted, absurdly, at this moment, was more drug. His money had been stolen but not his canisters.

He jumped up and down to warm himself, he did deep knee bends until he couldn't breathe, and then, clumsily, with stiffened fingers, he got a canister open and conveyed the saturated wads of toilet paper to his gums.

Though malign and sickening, the boost was a boost. Though everything was inverted, his rationality now reduced to a floater against a black infinity of death, the light hadn't entirely left his mind. Stumbling, falling, dropping the flashlight, picking it up, he made his way back to the dirt road.

Where he'd formerly entertained a thousand thoughts while taking a single step, he now had to take a thousand steps to complete one thought.

His first thousand steps yielded the thought that he was walking only to warm up.

A thousand steps later, he thought that warming up would restore enough manual dexterity to take a proper whiff from his thumb.

Farther down the road, he thought he was in trouble.

Later yet, after reaching a fork and randomly bearing right, he understood that he couldn't report his money stolen without revealing that he'd taken it from Clem.

Still later, he realized that he was tasting only toilet paper, which he might as well spit out.

The moment he stopped to spit, his chest was gripped with chills. He was getting no warmer, and the flashlight's batteries had failed to the point where he could see no worse by turning it off.

This was a thought and his last one. His mind went dark with the flashlight, and then there was only a frigid blackness, its only features a slightly less black sky, a matchingly less black passage forward. The passage seemed eternal, but by and by it developed an incline. At the top of the incline, the sky lightened to reveal a boxy shape in the distance, darker than the road, higher than the horizon.

He was still trudging toward this shape after flames had engulfed it.

He still wasn't there when he'd been there for a while.

Even as he stood clear of the inferno and toasted himself, he was still on his way to it.

A thing that hadn't happened yet had happened. A large wooden building with a metal roof and wide doors had been broken into. The frozen metal of the tractors it contained, the deep chill of its concrete floor, had made the inside even colder than the outside, but the totality of the darkness had made even a dim flashlight useful, and there had been a box of matches. There had been a tower of wooden pallets. Gasoline. A splash of gasoline, just enough to kindle one pallet for some warmth. And then a blue flame snaking with terrible speed.

A bird blazing yellow, an oriole, was singing in a palm tree. In the background, around the pool at the apartment complex, she could hear the cheeping of smaller birds, the clacking of hedge clippers, the sighing of the megalopolis. Somewhere in the night, her third in Los Angeles, she'd regained an acuity of hearing that she hadn't noticed losing. A similar thing had happened toward the end of her confinement in Rancho Los Amigos. A return of ordinary presence.

Of the city she remembered, only the mild weather and the palm trees hadn't changed. East of Santa Monica, where the streetcar had run, there was now a freeway ten lanes wide, an elevated immensity of automotive glare. Driving from the airport, she'd been tailgated, veered in front of, honked at. Formerly orienting mountains had vanished in a claustrophobic smog. The buildings that loomed up in it, mile after mile, were like players in some cancerous game of trying to be the largest. The city no longer invited her mind to be sky-wide. She was just a frazzled tourist from Chicago, an ordinary mother who was lucky that her boy could read a road map.

It wasn't so bad, being ordinary. It was nice to be present with the birds again. Nice to be unembarrassed in a bathing suit, nearly at her target weight. How nice it would have been to spend the whole day in Pasadena, see Jimmy in the nursing home again, and let Antonio, who'd become quite a chef, make dinner. How unexpectedly unfortunate that she had to get into her rented car and navigate the freeways.

She'd misplaced the urgency of seeing Bradley. For three months, consumed by the urgency, focused on losing weight and getting to Los Angeles, she'd given little concrete thought to what would happen when she got there. It had been enough to imagine a wordless locking of gazes, a delirious reblossoming of passion. When Bradley, in his second letter to her, had offered to come to her in Pasadena, she hadn't foreseen the terrors of freeway driving. She'd insisted on going to his house, because Antonio's apartment in Pasadena, with Judson underfoot, was obviously not a place for passion.

"Mom, look at me."

Judson, on the neighboring recliner, in baggy new swim trunks, was aiming his camera at her. The camera briefly whirred.

"Sweetie, why aren't you in the water?"

"I'm busy."

"You have the whole pool to yourself."

"I don't feel like getting wet."

Something moved in her, a flutter of fear or guilt—a memory. The girl she'd been in Rancho Los Amigos had had a phobia of water on her skin.

"I want to see you dive in the water. Can you show me your dive?"

"No."

He hunched over the camera and adjusted a dial. The camera seemed too complicated for a nine-year-old, and she'd tried to discourage him from bringing it on the trip. On the flight from Chicago, instead of reading a book, he'd fiddled with the thing incessantly, clicking and turning every clickable or turnable part. He'd done the same thing at Disneyland. He had only three minutes of film, and he was anxious, visibly stressed, about misusing it—kept raising the camera and hesitating, fiddling with it, frowning. She was anxious herself, about the freeway, and needed more cigarettes than she felt she could smoke in front of him. It was only three thirty when he ran out of film. Money had been spent, Frontierland not yet visited, but he said he'd had enough. In the Disney parking lot, before returning to Pasadena, she'd smoked two Luckies.

"Put the camera down," she said. "You've played with it enough."

He set it aside with a theatrical sigh.

"Are you unhappy about something?"

He shook his head.

"Is it me? Is it my smoking? I apologize for smoking."

The oriole was singing again, so very yellow. He glanced at it, reached for the camera, and caught himself.

"Sweetie, what is it? You haven't seemed like yourself."

His expression became morose. With the return of ordinary hearing came a more general sharpening of her senses.

"Will you tell me what's bothering you?"

"Nothing. Just . . . nothing."

"What is it?"

"Perry hates me."

She had another flutter of guilt, more pronounced.

"That's not true at all. There's no one Perry loves more than you. You're his special favorite."

Judson's mouth curled inward as if he might cry. She moved over to his recliner and pressed his face to her chest. He was so skinny and unhormonal, she could have gobbled him up, but she could feel his resistance. Her old bathing suit now gaped at the top and gave her breasts a wanton latitude. She let him pull away.

"Perry's sixteen now," she said. "Teenagers say all sorts of things they don't really mean. It has nothing to do with how much your brother loves you. I'm sure of that."

Judson's expression didn't change.

"Did something happen? Did he say something that upset you?"

"He told me to leave him alone. He used a bad word."

"I'm sure he didn't mean it."

"He said he was sick of me. He used a really bad word."

"Oh, honey, I'm sorry."

She embraced him again, this time positioning his head on her shoulder. "I don't have to see my friend today. I can stay here with you and Antonio. Would you like that?"

He squirmed out of her grasp. "It's okay. I hate him, too."

"No, you don't. Never say that."

He picked up the camera and clicked something. Clicked it. Clicked it. She'd never had to worry about Judson, but his absorption in the camera recalled her own unhealthy absorptions. Out of nowhere, she was seized by an image so vivid that she quaked with it, an image of her soul mate on top of her, rampant in her utter openness to him. Her bathing suit was loose on her—she'd lost thirty pounds—for him—it was crazy. Oh, the relief of being obsessed, the blessed banishing of guilt. The switch in her was still there to be flipped.

"Judson," she said, her heart beating hard, "I'm sorry if I haven't been myself. I'm sorry Perry hurt you. Are you sure you don't want me to stay here with you?"

"Antonio said he'd play Monopoly with me."

"You don't want me to stay?"

He gave a shrug, a child's exaggerated shrug. The right thing was to stay with him, but an afternoon of Monopoly would pass quickly enough, and Antonio had promised to make crispy tacos. Nothing she could do today was so urgent that it couldn't be done tomorrow, except seeing Bradley.

"Let's go inside, then. Maybe Antonio will make you a smoothie."

"I'll be there in a minute."

"Did you not see the sign? No unaccompanied children under twelve."

Antonio had introduced Judson to the concept of a "smoothie," a sort of milkshake blended with banana. Antonio had retired from the job that had brought him and Jimmy to Los Angeles, but he was still vigorous, his hair splendidly white, his face handsomer than ever. He could easily have found a new lover, but instead, every morning and every evening, he visited the nursing home where Jimmy was bedridden. She saw that in her youthful prejudice, because Antonio was Mexican, she'd misread his relationship with her uncle. Antonio, not Jimmy, had always been the man of the house. Jimmy's art had never really found a market, and now he was just a sack of bones, his vertebrae so badly crumbled that even a wheelchair was uncomfortable. All he had left were his wits. When she'd inquired about his brother, Roy, he'd mentioned that Roy's first great-grandchild had been born on the day Nixon was elected. "I'll let you guess," he'd said, "which of those two events made him happier."

It wasn't easy to apply eyeliner with a shaking hand. The face in the guest-room mirror again had prominent cheekbones, but her skin was finely scored with wrinkles previously hidden by fat; poor light was required to see her as the girl she meant to be. At least her new dress fit this girl. She'd asked the dressmaker on Pirsig Avenue for something summery, something of the sort that Sophie Serafimides said *lifted a man's spirits*, and she'd delayed the final fitting as an incentive to keep shedding pounds. The dressmaker, declaring that she looked darling, had taken the money she'd earned by proofreading a reader's guide to Sophocles.

When she'd exhausted the money embezzled from her sister's estate, and had charged as much as she dared on the family BankAmericard, she'd asked around the church for leads on work suitable for a literate person with no employment history, and a parishioner had connected her to a woman on maternity leave from the Great Books Foundation. The proofreading work was tedious but doable with frequent cigarettes. It kept her mind off food and further limited her interactions with Russ and the kids. In four weeks, she'd made nearly four hundred dollars, enough to pay the credit-card bill, cover the cost of a rental car and Disneyland, and buy sundries like the rolls of film that Judson wanted for their trip. Bradley had once said it himself, in a sonnet: she was capable.

Before going to say good-bye to Judson, she stepped onto the guest-room patio with her purse. It took her a while, after she'd smoked, to notice that she was crossing the lawn toward the parking lot, rather than going back inside. Apparently it wasn't necessary to say good-bye?

She was too terrified to judge. Her brain felt like a banana in a blender. It was unclear if the source of the terror was the prospect of the freeway or simply the arrival of *the moment*—the moment when past and present would connect and thirty intervening years would disappear. Obsessed though she'd been with creating this moment, its arrival had caught her by surprise.

She wasn't capable. She'd memorized the directions that Bradley had sent her, she'd tested herself by reciting them verbatim, and now she couldn't remember a word of them. She had his last letter in her purse, but she couldn't read and drive at the same time.

She started the car, which was baking in the sun, and turned the air-conditioning on full blast. The fabric of her dress had sparse green paisleys on a background of ecru that would show her sweating, which was already considerable. She would have to talk to Mr. Shen, the dry cleaner in New Prospect. Mr. Shen was ever pessimistic when she showed him a bad stain, ever able to perform the miracle of removing it. The thought of Mr. Shen returned her to ordinariness. The worst case—that she'd be back in Pasadena in four hours, able to swim in the pool, unphobic, ordinary—wasn't such a bad case. Tiny treats, an air-conditioned car, a drink by the pool, an after-dinner cigarette, could get a person through her life. Looking forward to treats was a coping skill for which Sophie Serafimides had praised her. It was strange that she'd felt compelled to inflict such terrors on herself.

Another adage of the dumpling: *It's better to function than not function.* Once she was on the freeway, she found that she remembered the directions perfectly. The freeway experience was itself a helpful obsession, a state of mind so consuming that the world outside it barely registered. All she had to do was stick to the rightmost lane and attend to road signs. Of the millions of people who drove in Los Angeles every day, very few were killed. When she'd made it past the San Diego Freeway without dying, she had the thought that, if she ended up moving here, she might even come to enjoy driving.

It was a mistake to think this. Only by luck did she emerge from her fantasies in time to take the exit for Palos Verdes. Pushed relentlessly by cars behind her, she drove all the way to Crenshaw Boulevard before she could pull over and collect herself. She angled a cold-air louver at her face, which felt red, and patted her underarms with a tissue from her purse. The haze outside the car had a marine quality, cooler in color than smog, merely dimming, not effacing. A sign on a nearby awning said PERRY SUMMONS REALITY.

The words swam in her vision.

Their reemergence as PERRY SIMMONS REALTY didn't lessen her fear. Not wanting her dress to stink of smoke, she got out of the car. The air was ocean-cool and sharply scented with asphalt from a repaving job across the street. The words on the awning were too strange, too apt, to be anything but a sign from God. But what did it mean?

She hadn't had a real talk with Perry since the night of his sixteenth birthday, three weeks ago. She'd detained him in the kitchen, after dinner, and privately handed him two hundred dollars, the same amount she'd given Clem at Christmas. After Perry had thanked her, she'd noticed that someone's slice of cake had hardly been touched, and he'd admitted it was his. *Did he not like chocolate cake anymore?* "No, it's delicious." *Then why wasn't he eating it?* "My butt is fat." *His butt wasn't fat in the slightest!* "You're the one with the crazy weight-loss program." *She was just trying to get back to her proper weight.* "I'm doing the same thing. You don't have to worry about me." *Was he sleeping?* "Sleeping fine, thanks." *And he wasn't still . . .* "Selling weed? I told you I wouldn't." *Did he still smoke it?* "Nope." *And—did he remember what else he'd promised her?* "Trust me, Mother. If I notice anything amiss, you'll be the first to know." *But he seemed a little—agitated.* "Said the pot to the kettle." *What did that mean?* "Your own mental health doesn't strike me as the finest." *She was—it was only some trouble between her and his father. The point here was that a growing boy needed to eat.* "What sort of 'trouble'?" *Just—nothing. The sort of trouble that married couples sometimes had.* "Does it have a name? Is it Mrs. Cottrell?" *What made him—why did he ask that?* "Things I've heard. Things I've seen." *Well—yes. Since he was nosy enough to ask—yes. And, well, yes—it was very upsetting. If she hadn't seemed like herself lately, that was why. But the point—*"The point, Mother, is that you should worry about yourself, not me."

With the help of two Luckies, by the side of the road, she understood that the building with the awning was just an ordinary realtor's office. Looking around, she saw ordinary asphalt, ordinary streetlights, a hillside covered prettily with coastal heather. She unwrapped a stick of Trident and got back in the car.

Palos Verdes was one of countless neighborhoods she'd had no reason to visit in her youth. The streets were empty of pedestrians, and the houses were blander, more homogenous, than the ones in West Los Angeles. In the dimming marine mist, the place seemed abandoned and melancholy. Reaching the street called Via Rivera, she found that she was ten minutes early.

Bradley's house was less than grand, and it didn't have the ocean view that she'd imagined; a burgundy Cadillac was in the driveway. She stopped her own car well short of it and took the gum from her mouth. Would her smoking repel him? Or would the smell of her Luckies take him back, as it took her, to the Murphy bed in Westlake?

His first letter, which had arrived a week after she'd written to him, contained sentences of inexhaustible interest—*I can't tell you how often I've thought of you, how often I've wondered where you were, how worried I was that something terrible had happened to you*—and many smaller items of interest, such as the fact that he wasn't married. He'd been divorced from Isabelle after their younger boy finished high school, and divorced a second time, more recently, from *a woman I should have known better than to marry*. Also of interest were the excellence of his health and certain suggestions of wealth. He was now in the vitamin business, not as a salesman but as the owner of a company, based in Torrance, that employed more than forty people. Although his report on his sons was not of interest, she'd studied the details and filed them in a mental drawer that also held the name of every member of First Reformed. She was a pastor's wife, skilled at politely remembering, no longer scary, and she wanted Bradley to know it.

At one minute past twelve thirty, she rang his doorbell.

The man who answered was somewhat like Bradley but jowlier, sparser of hair, wider in the hips. He was wearing loose linen pants and an oversize sort of toreador blouse, pale blue and halfway unbuttoned. Also a frightful pair of sandals.

"My God," he said. "It really is you."

She had two related thoughts. One was that she'd somehow projected the height of her husband onto her memory of Bradley, who in fact had never been tall. The other was that Russ, besides being tall, was by far the better-looking man. The man in the doorway was blowsy and yellow-toenailed. If she'd daydreamed for a hundred years, she couldn't have imagined him in sandals. This led to a third and very unexpected thought: she was doing him a favor by seeing him, not the other way around.

"I was afraid you wouldn't be able to find me," he said, beckoning her inside. "How was the freeway? It's usually not bad at this time of day."

He shut the door and made a move to hug her. She stepped sideways.

The house was a split-level and smelled faintly of old person. The art and the furnishings were tamely Far Eastern.

"What a lovely house."

"Yeah, I have the vitamin craze to thank for that. Come in, come in, I'll show you around. I was thinking we could eat on the patio, but it's a little too cool, don't you think?"

"It was nice of you to make lunch."

"God, Marion. Marion! I can't believe you're here."

"I can't either."

"You look—you look like yourself. A little older, a little grayer, but—great."

"It's good to see you, too."

Broad in the beam, favoring an apparently sore hip, he led her down into the living room, from which a tall hedge and a flower garden were visible. The clamminess of her dress, a vestige of her terror, seemed sad to her now. On a wall lined with bookshelves, she noticed recent Mailer, recent Updike.

"I see you still read."

"God, yes. More than ever. I'm still working, but the company kind of runs itself. A fair number of days, I don't even go down to the office."

"I don't read the way I used to."

"With a house full of kids, that's not surprising."

Her fourth thought was terrible: she'd killed the baby he'd fathered. Not once in three months had it occurred to her that she might have to mention this to him. She wondered if she should do it right away. Their entire history was coiled up tightly in her head. If she let it out, it might obliterate the reality of how he looked to her, the sad smell in his house. But was this a favor she felt like doing? It was confounding to recognize how *much* she had, compared to him. Not only many more years to live but full knowledge of their history. The story resided in *her* head, not his, and she felt a curious reluctance to share it, because she was its sole author. He'd merely been the reader.

He was staring at her, his smile almost goofy. In her evident fascination to him, she felt a stirring of the role she'd once played, the role of dangerous-crazy, the role of bluntly saying whatever came to mind.

"Did you live here with your second wife?"

He didn't seem to hear her. "I cannot believe I'm seeing you. How many years has it been?"

"More than thirty."

"God!"

He came at her again, and she slipped away to the rear windows. He hastened to open a French door. "I'll show you the garden. I love the privacy of it."

In other words, he didn't have an ocean view.

"I've got the gardening bug," he said, following her outside. "It comes on like clockwork when you're sixty. I always hated yard work, and now I can't get enough of it."

There was a large bed of roses. The sky was gray-blue in the haze, the shadows of the patio furniture indistinct. A bird was buzzing in the hedge, perhaps a wren. She could hear it very clearly.

"Your second wife," she said. "Did she live here with you?"

He laughed. "I'd forgotten how direct you are."

"Really? You forgot?"

It was an unfair thing to say. She'd forgotten, too, for many years.

"I want to hear about everything," he said. "I want to hear about your kids, I want to hear about—your husband. Your life in Chicago. I want to hear about everything."

"I'm just curious about your second wife. What was she like?"

His face soured. "It was painful. A mistake."

"She left you?"

"Marion, it's been thirty years. Can't we just . . ." He gestured limply.

"All right. Show me your garden."

The wren buzzed again in the bushes, as uninterested as she in Bradley's gardening. While he held forth about aphids and pruning cycles, morning sun versus afternoon sun, the mysterious death of a lemon tree, her idealization of him entirely disintegrated. The stiffness of his joints, when he crouched to show her a virginal hydrangea blossom, foretokened a near future in which, unlike Jimmy, he wouldn't have a loyal mate devoted to his care—not unless he married a third time. And why should she, who already had a husband, even younger than herself, do a blowsy old man such a favor? Why, indeed, if she wasn't going to marry him, had she come to his house at all?

It was true that, in a different chamber of her mind, their reunion was unfolding as she'd imagined it, a trail of discarded clothes leading down a hallway, lunch forgotten in the frenzy of their coupling. From Bradley's little glances at her figure, his touchings of her shoulder as he steered her through his plants, she guessed that he'd imagined the same thing. But now she could see, as she never had before—as if God were telling her— that the obsessive chamber of her mind would always be there; that she would never stop wanting what she'd had and lost.

The wren in the bushes erupted in full song, liquid, melodious, achingly clear. It seemed to her that God, in His mercy, was speaking through His birds. Her eyes filled.

"Oh, Bradley," she said. "Do you have any idea how much you meant to me?"

She meant something definitively past. In the present, he was holding some weeds that he'd pulled, perhaps unconsciously.

"You were good to me," she said. "I'm sorry for what I put you through."

He looked at the weeds in his hand, let them fall to the gravel path, and took her in his arms. The two of them fit together as they once had. His chest, against her cheek, exposed by his half-open blouse, was still nearly hairless. Her eyes moist with pity for him, pity that he'd gotten older, she held him tight. When he tried to raise her chin, she averted her face. "Just hold me."

"You're every bit as beautiful to me."

"I haven't eaten in three months."

"Marion—Marion—"

He tried to kiss her.

"What I'm saying," she said, extricating herself, "is I'm extremely hungry."

"You want lunch."

"Yes, please."

The tacky Oriental screen in his dining room saddened her. The disclosure that he'd become a vegetarian and a teetotaler saddened her.

The vitamin pills he swallowed with his iced tea saddened her. The hemisphere of egg salad, on a bed of lettuce, saddened her so much she couldn't touch it. Her chest was obstructed with the wrongness of her being there at all. That she'd imagined *fucking*—because this was what it was, this was the truth, this was why she'd starved herself and invented a pretext for going to Los Angeles—seemed so senseless to her, she wished she'd never done it with Bradley. She wished she'd never done it with anyone. To be fifty years old in a convent, to rise every morning and hear the sweet birds, to devote herself to loving God, to have *that* have been her life, instead of this one . . .

"I thought you were hungry," Bradley said.

"I'm sorry. The salad looks delicious. I'm just—do you mind if I have a cigarette first?"

His expression told her that he minded. He'd really become quite the health nut.

"I can step out on the patio."

"No, it's fine. I have an ashtray somewhere."

"I know," she admitted. "I'm still the same mess. I was hoping I could fool you."

A suspicion appeared to dawn on him. "Do you—you do have a family?"

"Oh, God, yes. That's all real. I've got pictures I was going to show you. Here—"

She jumped up and went to the front hallway. There, uppermost in her purse, were her Lucky Strikes. It wasn't as if one cigarette would ruin his curtains. As she returned to the dining room, smoking it, she saw that there was no telling what else she might do. The intention to be *fucked*, her pesky little obsession with it, was, however senseless, persistent.

Dropping a stack of snapshots on the table returned her to her senses. Invisible among the smiling faces of her children was the fetus she'd aborted. Bradley, too, no longer seemed sure he wanted her in his house. He went so far as to wave her smoke away from his nose. The pictures lay on the table unexamined. She asked him if he believed in God.

"God?" He winced. "No. Why do you ask?"

"God saved my life."

"That's right. You married a minister. It's funny it didn't occur to me."

"That I have a relationship with God?"

"No, it makes sense. You were always . . ."

"Crazy?"

He stood up, with a sigh, and went to the kitchen. She had no reason to keep starving herself, but cigarettes had become part of her autonomy. Bradley returned with a yellow ceramic ashtray. On its side were the words LERNER MOTORS.

She smiled. "What ever happened to Lerner?"

"He sold out after the war. The dealerships were moving farther out, and nobody wanted custom bodywork. That was always where Harry's margin was."

She tapped the ashtray with her cigarette. "To Harry's memory I dedicate this ash."

Sadness made Bradley look even older. Talking about any subject but the two of them was all it took—all it had ever taken—to illuminate their unsuitability for each other. What was best and most essential in her had been wasted on him. The converse was probably also true. She'd been too disturbed in Los Angeles to even know what love was. The real love had come later, in Arizona, and she was pierced, now, by homesickness for New Prospect. For the dear, creaky parsonage. Daffodils in the yard, Becky steaming up the bathroom, Russ buffing his shoes for a funeral. It was worth it, after all, to have aged thirty years. It was worth it to have taken the arduous steps to arrive in Bradley's house, because the reward was clarity: God had given her a way of being. God had given her four children, a role she was skilled at playing, a husband who shared her faith. With Bradley, there had really only ever been fucking.

She put out the cigarette and took a bite of salad. Bradley picked up his own fork.

Only when she was leaving, an hour and a half later, might something have happened. She'd showed him her few photos, noting how he lingered on a recent school picture of Becky, and suffered through an interminable showing of his own. She would happily have spent another hour in his garden to spare herself a minute of his grandson pictures; her boredom was so aggressive, it verged on loathing. But she played the role of pastor's wife, fascinated by Bradley's offspring, and said nothing further to provoke him.

At the front door, as she was leaving, he tried to revive her interest. To her loose farewell hug, he responded by gripping her fanny and pulling her into him.

"Bradley."

"Please kiss me."

She gave him a brisk peck, and his hands were all over her. There was a blindness to his pawing, his nuzzling of her throat, his squeezing of her breasts, and this was how she knew for certain. She felt invisible, not excited. She patted his head and said she needed to get back to Judson.

"You can't stay another hour?"

"No."

This wasn't true. She'd told Antonio she might be out all evening. Bradley gripped her head and tried to make her look at him.

"I never got over you," he said. "Even when you were crazy, I didn't get over you."

"Well. Maybe now is a good time."

"Why did you write to me? Why did you come here?"

"I guess—" She laughed. Everything was light. The world was full of light. "I guess I wanted to finally get over it. I didn't even know what I was doing. It was God's plan, not mine."

At the naming of God, Bradley let go of her. He ran a hand through what was left of his hair.

"I'm sorry," she said.

"It's not—I have a perfectly nice lady friend from work. Better than I deserve."

"Oh."

"It's just—she isn't you."

"Well. I suppose no one is, except me."

"Her family's Japanese. She does our books."

"And I'm so grateful that you mentioned that." She picked up her purse and clicked it shut. "I'd hate to think of you alone."

To walk away from his house without having surrendered herself—to be bathed in God's approval; to know, for once, that she deserved it—was immeasurably better than to surrender. She felt so elated, she almost floated to her car. And she recognized this elation. A similar feeling had filled her thirty years ago, after Bradley, at a Carpenter's drive-in, had ended their affair. It was true that the earlier elation had only intensified her obsession, had unspooled into madness, the making and unmaking of a baby. But this time it was she who'd done the ending. This time, the elation was of God, and she was sure that He would keep her safe.

To survive the grandkids, she'd promised herself a cigarette, but now she saw that she didn't have to smoke. God took and took, but He also gave and gave. Freed of the ghost of Bradley, freed of the morbid urgency of dieting, she could be free of cigarettes, too. Her elation held until, north of downtown, the freeway traffic came to a dead halt. She wanted to get back to Pasadena in time to swim before dinner, to be enveloped by water, and the traffic jam infuriated her. It turned out that she needed to smoke after all. And there was something else, a nasty little itch. With a glance at the car to her left, she felt herself between her legs. It was shocking how Bradley's assault, which had left her unmoved in the moment, now aroused her. Would it really have been so bad to give him what he wanted? For the sake of her private parts, which three months of longing had tantalized and primed, she was sorry that she hadn't. Smoke was drifting from the driver's side of the car in front of her. She unrolled her own window and punched the lighter on the dashboard.

Antonio's apartment, when she finally got back, smelled of fried onions. The Monopoly box was on the living-room coffee table, evidence of an afternoon of fun. As soon as Antonio heard her, he came hurrying from the kitchen.

"Russ called. You need to call him back."

She wondered if Russ had somehow sensed, via God, the choice she'd made; if he missed her, too. But a foreboding told her otherwise. God gave and God took. There was no phone service in Kitsillie.

"Did he say what it was about?"

"Just to call him right away. He left three different numbers."

"Where's Judson?"

"He's grating cheese. I left the numbers by the bedroom phone."

And so began the remainder of her life. In the glass doors of the master bedroom was a lovely honey-toned light, in the garden the cheeping of birds, from the swimming pool the shouts of children, from the kitchen a smell of fried onions and beef, above Jimmy's bare dresser his painting of the old Flagstaff post office, atop the other dresser a sepia photograph of Antonio's mother in a filigreed silver frame: the first impressions were the ones that stayed with you forever.

Russ's voice was piteously pinched. He was at a hospital in Farmington, New Mexico, and Perry was—sleeping. They had him heavily sedated. The attempt—he'd tried to—dear God, he'd tried to harm himself. They'd brought him to the hospital, his head was bandaged, he was heavily sedated. Thank God, thank God, the juvenile hall hadn't wanted him—at least the police knew enough to take away his shoelaces. All he could do to himself—all he had was an ugly bump on his forehead. But the reason—what had happened was—he'd burned down a farm building on the reservation. And then felony drug possession. Felony—two felonies. The lawyer—it was a mess—the crimes were federal but Perry was not of sound mind. They were taking him to Albuquerque in the morning because nobody in Farmington wanted the responsibility. The cops didn't want him, the sheriff didn't want him, the hospital didn't want him, the juvenile hall absolutely didn't want him—there was a place for mentally ill minors in Albuquerque. If she could get a flight to Albuquerque, he could meet her at the airport.

Each fact that Russ conveyed fell into place as if it had been meant to be there all along. Without noticing how, she'd come to be holding a burning cigarette on the patio outside the bedroom. The base of the telephone was at her feet, its cord stretched to its limit. Although the sun was still golden in the west, its light seemed dark in a deeper dimension, but this didn't mean that God had left her. With the new darkness came a feeling of peace. To bask in His light, to experience the elation of that, was a privilege to be earned, a privilege to feel anxious about forfeiting. Now that her long-deferred punishment had commenced, she didn't have to struggle or be anxious. Secure in God's judgment, she could simply welcome Him into her heart.

"Marion? Are you there?"

"Yes, Russ. I'm here."

"This is terrible. It's the worst thing that's ever happened."

"I know. It's my fault."

"No, it's my fault. I'm the—"

"No," she said firmly. "It's not your fault. I want you to make sure Perry's being looked after. If you think he'll be all right, I want you to get some sleep. See if one of the nurses will give you a sleeping pill."

A wet, choking sound came through the long-distance hiss.

"Russ. Sweetie. Try to get some sleep. Will you do that for me?"

"Marion, I can't—"

"Hush now. I'll be there tomorrow."

Her calmness was like nothing she'd ever experienced. It seemed to reach to the very bottom of her soul. In everything she proceeded to do—carrying the phone back inside, finding her plane ticket and calling the airline, speaking to Russ again briefly, calling Becky and then explaining the change of plan to Judson, assuring him that Becky would be waiting at the airport in Chicago, and finally sitting down and eating, with leisurely relish, three crispy tacos dripping with warm beef fat—she could feel her feet securely grounded. She wasn't afraid of what was still to come, wasn't afraid of seeing Perry and dealing with the consequences, because her feet had found the bottom and beneath them was God. In coming to an end, her life had also started. *Within you a calm capability*—how funny that Bradley, in his sonnet, had been the one to notice. She wished the calmness had descended a day sooner, before she'd gone to his house. She could have said everything to him, instead of hardly anything, although maybe, not knowing God, he wouldn't have cared to hear it.

In the morning, at the airport, after meeting a gate agent and a stewardess, Judson asked why he couldn't have stayed on with Antonio through the week. He was pouchy-eyed and grumpy from a short night of sleep. She, for her part, had slept astonishingly well, not waking once. The worst had happened—she didn't have to fear it anymore.

"You'll have fun with Becky," she said. "I bet she'll take you out for pizza."

"Becky isn't interested in me."

"Of course she's interested in you. This is a chance to spend some time alone with her."

He looked down at his camera. "When is Perry coming home?"

"I don't know, sweetie. He had a kind of breakdown. It could be a while before you see him."

"I don't know what 'breakdown' means."

"It means something went very wrong in his head. It's frightening, but there is a bright side. Whatever bad things he said to you, he wasn't himself. Now that you know that he wasn't himself, you don't have to feel hurt."

"That's not a bright side."

"Maybe consolation is a better word."

"I don't want consolation. I want Perry to come back."

Outward the ripples of harm expanded: Judson would henceforth be a boy with a mentally ill brother. His own first impressions, the sound of her phone calls the night before, the morning smog on the freeway, the airplane he had to board by himself, would always stay with him. But God had made Judson healthy and strong. She could sense it in his love of Perry and in the contrast between them: Perry had never, in her hearing, expressed anxiety on his siblings' behalf. The harm her sins had caused was immense, but only with Perry was it potentially irreparable. Judson bristled when she offered to go on the plane with him and get him settled. He said he wasn't a baby.

Before she boarded her own flight, she bought a paperback, *The Prime of Miss Jean Brodie*. She didn't expect that she could focus on a novel—it was several years since she'd been calm enough to read one—but she was sucked right in. She read all the way to Phoenix and then, on a second plane, all the way to Albuquerque. She didn't quite finish the book, but it didn't matter. The dream of a novel was more resilient than other kinds of dreaming. It could be interrupted in mid-sentence and snapped back into later.

Her reading had turned morning in California into late afternoon in Albuquerque. Russ was waiting just inside the gate, in his sheepskin coat. He looked ashen and unslept. When she put her arms around him, she felt him shudder. As a kindness, she let go.

"So," he said. "They did transfer him."

"Have you seen him?"

"No. You and I can go together in the morning."

In her homesickness, she'd lost sight of the trouble in their marriage. To see Russ in the flesh, so tall, so youthful, was to recall her cruelty to him and his pursuit of the Cottrell woman. Although she gathered that Cottrell had opted out, plenty of other women were available to distract him from the awfulness of a mentally ill son. In the wake of the calamity, it seemed all the likelier that he would end up leaving her. And she deserved to be left; she felt as capable of accepting divorce as she was capable of everything else. But the prospect did remind her that she hadn't had a cigarette since leaving Pasadena.

When she lit up, in the baggage-claim area, he sighed with displeasure.

"I'm sorry."

"Do as you please."

"I'm going to quit. Just not . . . today."

"It's fine with me. I'm tempted to take it up myself."

She extended the pack to him. "Want one?"

He made a face. "No, I don't want one."

"You just said you were tempted."

"It was a figure of speech, for God's sake."

Even his sharpness was sweet to her. She and Bradley had never come close to being sharp with each other. It required long years of togetherness.

"We need to rent a car," he said. "Kevin Anderson drove me down here—he's on his way back to Many Farms. Do you have the credit card?"

"I do."

"You didn't wear it out in Los Angeles?"

"No, Russ. I did not wear it out."

In the rental car, which conveniently already stank of smoke, he acquainted her with the financial dimension of the calamity. A tribal council administrator, Wanda, had recommended a lawyer from Aztec, oddly named Clark Lawless, whom Russ had met the day before and been impressed with. Because Lawless was the best, he was expensive, and Perry had committed two felonies in the state of New Mexico. As a mentally incapacitated juvenile, he would be charged with the crime of "delinquency," for which the sentence would typically be confinement in a mental-health facility, followed by at least two years in a reformatory. But Perry was an Illinois resident. Provided that his parents agreed to have his mental illness treated, at their own expense, Lawless was optimistic that a judge would grant them custody. Lawless was well liked at the district courthouse.

"That's a blessing," she said.

"You haven't seen Perry. He hasn't said a coherent word since they picked him up. He just moans and covers his face. I give a lot of credit to the Farmington police. They put him in the cell that was closest to the desk. If they hadn't been on top of it, he might have broken his skull open. My guess is that he's—I mean, based on my counseling experience—I suspect he's manic-depressive."

She gasped, in spite of herself, at the evil hyphenated word. Outside the car, a blighted part of Albuquerque was passing by. Warped plywood on storefronts, broken bottles in the gutter. Her father in the evil state, playing ragtime at three in the morning, before the crash.

"Are we sure it wasn't the drugs? What drugs did he have?"

"Cocaine."

"*Cocaine*? I've never heard of such a thing."

"Neither have I. Neither has Ambrose. Where he got it, why he had so much of it—no idea."

"Well, could that be why he crashed? If he was withdrawing—"

"No," Russ said. "I'm sorry, but no. It's my fault, Marion—I knew he wasn't right. David Goya told me he wasn't right. He was obviously not right, and now—there was another thing, last night. Early this morning. When he came out of sedation, they had to restrain him again. He's psychotically depressed."

A pair of hands was moving randomly in front of her. She directed them toward the cigarettes in her purse. It was good to give them a task.

"Anyway," Russ said, "we're looking at a long recovery. I don't know if they'll bill us for his time in the facility here, but Lawless is going to cost at least five hundred dollars, probably a lot more. Then however many weeks or months in a private hospital, and further treatment after that. Are you sure you want to be hearing this now?"

She'd got a cigarette lit. It helped a little. "Yes. I want to know everything."

"We also need to pay for the barn he burned. It was on tribal land, and I'd be shocked if the owners had insurance. I gather there were tractors, other equipment, plus the building itself. I don't know how many thousands of dollars, but it's thousands. I called the church office while I was waiting for you, and Phyllis checked the liability policy—it won't help us. We do have the three thousand that Becky gave Perry. We can also borrow some of the money she gave Clem and Judson. But we're going to need a lot more."

"I'll get a full-time job."

"No. This is my responsibility. The question is whether I can get a big enough loan."

"I'll work until I'm eighty, if that's what it takes."

Russ veered over and braked to a hard stop, so he could look at her directly. "We need to get something straight. This is entirely my responsibility. Do you understand?"

She shook her head emphatically.

"I didn't listen to you," he said. "A year ago. You wanted to send him to a psychiatrist, and I didn't listen. Five days ago—again, I didn't listen. He was as good as telling me he'd lost his mind. And—God! I didn't listen."

She sucked on the cigarette. "It's not your fault."

"And I'm telling you it is. I don't want to hear another word about it."

Through the windshield, she watched an emaciated kid, not much older than Perry, shamble out of a liquor store. His shirt was untucked, his pants barely clinging to his hips. He had a bottle in a paper bag.

"Where are we going? I'm already sick of this car."

"It is entirely my fault, and that's the end of it."

"I don't care whose fault it is. Just get me out of this car. I'm having a panic attack."

"Maybe you shouldn't smoke."

"Where are we going? Why are we stopped here?"

With a heavy sigh, Russ put the car back into gear.

The next thing she knew, they were in the parking lot of a Ramada Inn, and her desperation to leave the car had passed. The car now seemed relatively secure to her. She closed her eyes while Russ went inside to register.

It was strange, considering God's everpresence in her, how rarely she felt moved to pray. In her guilt, in Arizona, she'd prayed incessantly, but she'd stopped when she married Russ, just as she'd stopped keeping a diary. Only after the births of her children, for which thanks were manifestly due, could she remember really praying. The weekly prayers she said in church were more lateral than vertical, more about belonging to a congregation. God already knew what she was thinking, so she didn't need to tell Him, and it seemed silly to trouble an infinite Being for minor favors. But the favor she needed now was large.

Dear God, I accept your will, and you've given me no more than what I deserve. But please let it be your will that Perry gets better, the same way you once let me get better. Please also let it be your will that I don't go crazy again. I want to be myself, I want to be fully present for Russ, and you know how I love you. If you would keep my mind clear enough to recognize your will, I would be so very grateful. Whatever your will requires of me, I will gladly do.

She opened her eyes and saw two sparrows, one more boldly patterned than the other, picking through detritus at the base of a concrete parking strip. She felt calmer for having asked. It was the asking that mattered, not the answer. She decided that, for the remainder of her life, she would pray every day. In a world suffused with God, prayer ought to be as regular as drawing breaths.

Cheered by this insight, she got out of the car with her purse. Russ was crossing the parking lot with the room key. She ran up to him and said, "Have you prayed?"

"Uh, no."

"Let's go do it. We can get the luggage later."

He seemed worried about her, but she didn't feel like stopping to explain. Their room was at the very end of the first floor. She hurried ahead while he followed with the key.

The room was stuffy, the late sun beating on the curtains. She immediately kneeled on the floor. "Here, anywhere. It doesn't matter. Will you kneel with me?"

"Um."

"We'll pray, and then we can talk."

He still seemed worried, but he kneeled by her and knit his fingers together.

Oh, God, she prayed. *Please be merciful to him. Please let him know you're there.*

This was all she had to say, but Russ apparently had more. It might have been five minutes before he stood up and turned on the air conditioner.

"I know it's private," she said, "but—did you find Him?"

"I don't know."

"If we're going to get through this, we need to stay connected."

"I'm not like you. You were always so—it was always easy with you and God. It's not so easy for me."

He made her access to God sound slutty, like her talent for quick orgasms. She joined him in the air conditioner's coolish outflow. It was a very long time since the two of them had been alone in a hotel room, almost as long as since Bradley had taken her to one. Had she ever been alone with a man in a hotel room without having sex? Possibly not.

"Usually it helps to be in a bad place," Russ said. "But the place I'm in now is so bad . . ."

His shoulders began to shake, and he covered his face. When she tried to comfort him, he shuddered.

"Russ. Honey. Listen to me. I ignored things, too. I could see Perry wasn't right, and I ignored it. This isn't your fault."

"You have no idea what you're talking about."

"I believe I do."

"You have no idea what I've done! No idea!" He looked around wildly. "I'm going to get the luggage."

She took her purse to the bathroom and unwrapped a drinking glass. The thinness of the woman in the mirror was a continuing surprise. Russ would now be stuck with this woman indefinitely, and she wondered if he might want her again. However deserving she was of God's punishment, she was surely still allowed some pleasure. She wondered, indeed, if priming herself for Bradley but returning to Russ, excited and unsatisfied, had been part of God's plan. She freshened her lipstick.

Russ was sitting on the edge of the bed, his face in his hands, as if replicating Perry's condition. She sat down by him and touched him. When he shuddered, yet again, a suspicion crept into her.

"So," she said. "What is it that you think you did?"

He rocked himself and didn't answer.

"You said I had no idea. Maybe you'll feel better if you tell me."

"It's all my fault."

"So you keep insisting."

"I—oh. What to say. God told me what to do, and I didn't listen. And then Ambrose . . ."

"Ambrose?"

"He was waiting for me. Kevin reported Perry missing, and the sheriff had already put out a bulletin, so Kevin went straight to Farmington, but Wanda and Ambrose had to wait for me in Kitsillie. They waited an hour. An *hour*." He shuddered. "I don't think I mentioned to you— I didn't mention that one of the parent advisers in Kitsillie was . . . So, Larry Cottrell was down in Many Farms, and his mother was on the mesa, and we'd had some trouble. The group, I mean. One of the Navajos broke into the school, and I had to . . . we had to . . . that is, I and, uh . . ."

"Larry's mother."

"Yes."

"Frances Cottrell was with you in Kitsillie."

"Yes."

Now, at last, she saw the totality of the punishment God intended. Since her fight with Russ at Christmas, he'd made any number of overtures to her, and she'd spurned every one of them. From the overtures, and from his generally low spirits, she'd inferred that the Cottrell woman had opted out of an affair; Marion had gone so far as to make fun of him. Now, in a flash, she saw why he'd returned to Crossroads. Once upon a time, he'd beguiled her with his talk of the Navajos, and it had worked, and so he'd tried it again with the Cottrell woman, and again it had worked. The Cottrell woman was a fool. She herself was a fool. She had no one but herself to blame.

"And now you're here with me," she said. "It must be very strange for you. That we have to deal with this together. That we still happen to be married."

He gave no sign of hearing her.

"I want you to leave me here alone," she said. "Let me take responsibility. I want you to go and be as happy as you can. This isn't your problem to deal with."

He was hitting himself in the head with the heels of his hands. He was lost in his misery, like a little boy, and she couldn't bring herself to hate him. He was her big little boy, entrusted to her care by God, and she'd driven him away. She grabbed one of his hands, but he kept hitting himself with the other.

"Honey, stop. I don't care what you did."

"I committed adultery."

"So I gather. Please stop hitting yourself."

"I was committing adultery while our son tried to kill himself!"

"Oh dear. I'm sorry."

"You're *sorry*? What is wrong with you?"

The ground beneath her was firm. She was secure in God's punishment.

"I'm just thinking how terrible that must feel. If the two things really did happen at the same time—that's terrible luck. No one deserves that."

"Terrible?" He staggered to his feet. "It's beyond terrible. It's beyond redemption. There's no use in praying—I'm a fraud."

"Russ, Russ. I'm the one who gave you permission. Don't you remember?"

"Stop looking at me! I can't stand you looking at me!"

She wasn't sure, but he seemed to be saying that he still cared what she thought of him, still in some way loved her. To spare him from her gaze, she went outside with her purse.

The sun was low, the distant mountains furrowed with deep shadows. At the edge of the parking lot, in the dry residue of a puddle, a sparrow was giving itself a dust bath. The air smelled like Flagstaff and was cooling off rapidly, as it had in the years when she'd walked home at this hour from the Church of the Nativity, counting her steps. She lit a cigarette and watched the sparrow. It was groveling on its belly, prostrating itself, raising its little face to the sky, flicking up dust with its wings, cleansing itself in dirt. She saw what she had to do.

She put out the cigarette and returned to the room. Russ was slumped on the edge of the bed.

"Are you in love with her? You can tell me the truth—it won't kill me."

"The truth," he said bitterly. "What is the truth? When a person is utterly fraudulent, what does love even mean? How can he judge?"

"I'll take that as a qualified yes. And what about her? Do you think she loves you?"

"I made a mistake."

"We all make mistakes. I'm just trying to think practically. If you love her and you think she might love you, I don't want to stand in your way. You can let Perry be my responsibility."

"I never want to lay eyes on her again."

"I'm saying I release you. This is your chance to walk away, and I'm warning you. Right this minute is the time to take it."

"Even if she loved me, which I doubt, the whole thing is too vile."

"That's only because you're feeling guilty. The minute you see her again, you'll remember that you love her."

"No. It's poisoned. Having to sit in that truck with Ambrose for three hours . . ."

"What does Rick have to do with it?"

Russ shuddered in his sheepskin coat. She'd bought it for him in Flagstaff.

"Do you know what I did to you?" he said. "Three years ago? Marion, do you know what I did? I told a seventeen-year-old girl that I'd lost interest in you sexually."

Suddenly cold, she went to her suitcase for a sweater. The summer dress was uppermost. She couldn't bring herself to handle it.

"And you know what else? I never told you the real reason the group kicked me out. It was because I was drooling all over that girl. I didn't even know I was doing it, but she could see it. And Rick—Rick was there, too. He knows who I am, and—God, *God*."

A low voice spoke, her own. "Did you touch her?"

"Sally? No! Absolutely—no. Never. I was just lost in my vanity."

She had her own vanity. She no longer felt like reciprocating his confession.

"It wasn't even true," he said. "When I saw you coming off the plane—what I said to that girl simply wasn't true. You are very, very attractive to me."

"Yeah, wait until I'm fat again."

"I don't expect you to forgive me. I don't deserve to be forgiven. I just want you to know—"

"That you've humiliated me?"

"That I need you. That I would be completely lost without you."

"Nice. Maybe you should fuck *me* while you're at it. It seems to be your thing."

This shut him up.

"Better do it while you can. I've started eating again." She moved into his field of vision and ran her hands down her flanks. "These hips aren't going to last."

"I know you're hurt. I know you're angry."

"What does that have to do with fucking?"

"I mean, yes, if you could forgive me—if we could find our way back—then, yes, I would very much like to . . . find our way back. But right now—"

"Right now," she pointed out, "we're alone in a hotel room."

"And our son is in a ward three blocks away."

"I'm not the one going on and on about what I've fucked. Or couldn't fuck but really, really wanted to."

He covered his ears. Her chest was heaving, but not only with anger. In taunting him with the dirtiest of words, in a hotel room, she'd accidentally turned herself on. There was an itch to be scratched, and it really did seem as if everything else could wait. She pushed his knees apart and dropped to her own.

"Marion—"

"Shut up," she said, unbuckling his belt. "You have no rights here."

She unzipped him, and there it was. The beautiful and hateful thing. Interested in seventeen-year-olds, interested in home-wrecking forty-year-olds, apparently even somewhat interested in his wife. She lowered her face to it, and—good Lord. He hadn't showered.

A noseful of Cottrell ought to have sobered her, but somehow everything was interchangeable. It was as if, instead of repulsing the assault she'd provoked from Bradley, she'd surrendered to it and were catching a whiff of the aftermath. Though the matter of the seventeen-year-old still had to be dealt with, the Cottrell matter seemed settled. Withholding her mouth would suffice as punishment. She pushed him onto his back and stretched out on top of him.

"With a kiss," she said, "I forgive thee."

"You don't seem right."

"I suggest taking the kiss while you can."

"Marion?"

She kissed him, and everything was interchangeable. Not just he and the other man, not just she and the other woman, but past and present. They hadn't made love in so long, it might as well have been twenty-five years. She in her younger body, he pulling off the coat she'd bought, the air as dry and thin as Arizona's, the fading light a mountain light. And how easy it had been in Arizona. Along with a faulty mind and a believing heart, God had given her an oversexedness so scratchable that she could relieve it in a public library without attracting notice. And how easy it was again. Seizing on some incidental contact and running with it, she promptly convulsed. She opened her eyes and saw gleaming, in Russ's eyes, a memory of that orgasmic girl. He'd liked that girl, oh, yes, he had. The gift she'd been given had made him feel powerful. Although she'd misplaced it in the swamp of motherhood, lost it altogether in the wasteland of anxious depression, her refinding of it made him powerful again. His thrusting abandon hurt around the edges, and she would pay for it later, but his excitement excited her. She urged him on, urged herself on. She heard an almost barking sound, an ongoing laugh of surprise, until further convulsing silenced her. He redoubled his efforts, but here, too, the past recurred. As in Arizona, once sated, she remembered her guilt.

When he'd finished, he rested his full weight on her, his scratchy cheek against her neck.

"Not so bad," she said. "Right?"

"I don't want to leave."

"Well. No rush."

The only light remaining was from the bedside alarm clock, the only sound the passing of cars in the distance. He kissed her neck.

"To be with you like this—I'd forgotten."

"I know," she said.

"It's such a simple gift."

"Shh."

The sound of a car passing was like a breaking wave of water. Guilt fluttered in her again.

"Turning and turning," he said. "'Till by turning and turning, we come round right.' That's how this feels. Like I've been turning and turning . . ."

The song was devotional, but she knew what he meant. *To bow and to bend, we will not be ashamed.* In the plain words of the song was a joy so deep that its roots were inextricable from sorrow's, and the release of sorrow was even sweeter than the other kind of release. Sorrow was of the heart, and she gave herself to it. As she wept, she felt him hardening inside her. It made her cry harder. She was his again.

He brushed at her tears with his fingertips. "I never want to leave you."

"That's nice," she said, sniffing. "But I should probably use the bathroom."

"I'm no good for this world. We never should have left Indiana. We should have spent our whole life there, just the two of us and the kids, a community of believers . . ."

She moved beneath him, hinting at the bathroom, but he wouldn't let her go.

"All I want is a family to provide for. A Lord to worship. And a wife who . . . Marion, I swear. If you'll forgive me, simple gifts will be enough."

"Shh."

"You always know the right thing to do. How you knew we should— this is the last thing I would have imagined happening, but you were right. You're always right. You were right about—"

"Shh. Just let me pee."

Careful not to stub a toe, she felt her way to the bathroom and sat down on the toilet. There was a magician's trick to be performed, a snap of the fingers that would make Russ's remorse disappear. His confessions had been piteously sincere, like a little boy's, and it was time to make her own confession. The sparrow had told her it was time.

And yet: what if she didn't? What exactly would be gained by dragging him through Bradley Grant, through Santa, through the abortion, through Rancho Los Amigos? She could clear her conscience by groveling in the dirt, but was it really a kindness to her husband? Now that Perry's calamity had brought Russ back to her, might it not be better to simply love him and serve him? He was like a boy, and a boy needed structure in his life, and wasn't remorse a kind of structure? She would never be simple, but she could give him the gift of thinking he'd wronged her more than she'd wronged him. Might this not be kinder than dumping her complexities on him?

It could have been Satan asking, but she didn't think it was, because the temptation didn't feel evil. It felt more like punishment. To not confess her sins to Russ—to renounce her chance to be chastised, maybe pitied, maybe even forgiven—would be to carry the burden for the remainder of her life. The unending burden of being alone with what she knew.

I need help here. Any kind of sign would be welcome.

She waited, shivering, on the toilet seat. If God was listening, He gave no indication of it, and while she waited something shifted in her. Although she could always ask Him again later, she'd made her decision.

Russ had peeled back the bedspread and pulled a sheet over himself. She joined him beneath it. "I have something to say to you, and I want you to listen."

He put a hand on her breast. She gently removed it.

"So you know," she said, "my father was manic-depressive—"

"I didn't know that."

"Well, you knew he was a suicide. But I never told you about my own troubles. I never told you how disturbed I was when I was Perry's age. I was afraid of scaring you away, and I couldn't bear the thought of losing you. Russ, honey, I couldn't bear it. I loved you so much, I couldn't bear it."

"I knew you were a little crazy."

"But it was more than a little. You had a right to know before you married me. I knew what the danger was, and I didn't tell you. So I don't want to hear about this being your fault."

"It is my fault. I was the—"

"Shh. Just listen. You're mixing up two different things. You feel bad about your . . . indiscretion. And even that, you shouldn't feel bad about. I gave you my permission."

"That doesn't mean I had to use it."

"You were hurt. I hurt you because you'd hurt me—these things happen in a marriage. My point is that you had bad luck. You're embarrassed by what happened in Kitsillie, you feel guilty about it, and I understand that. But it's enough. You don't have to feel guilty about Perry, too. His troubles all come from me."

"I knew very well what God wanted me to do."

"Sweetie, I didn't listen to Him, either. From now on, we'll have to try to do better. That's why I want us to pray together every day. I want us to change. I want us to be closer. I want us to experience the joy of God together."

He shuddered.

"A terrible thing happened, but there can still be joy. I was looking at the birds outside—can't we still take joy in Creation? Can't we take joy in each other?"

He gave a cry of pain.

"Shh, shh."

"I don't deserve you!"

"Shh. I'm here now. I'm not going anywhere."

"I don't deserve joy!"

"No one does. It's a gift from God."

And Becky had been so happy. Finally a spring-semester senior, walking among underclassmen but feeling a new commonality with the Class of '72, she'd made a point, every day, of being friendly to at least one classmate she'd never spoken to before, a boy taking metal shop, a girl from the Baptist church where she and Tanner had worshiped. It was a kind of daily Christian service, and then, on the weekend, if she and Tanner had time, they stopped by a party approved by Jeannie Cross and stayed for half an hour, not drinking, just putting a seal on the proceedings, before slipping away to a realm beyond high-school reckoning.

By late March, she had an acceptance letter from Lake Forest College and realistic hopes for Lawrence and Beloit. The anticipation of sweater weather in Wisconsin, a dorm room looking out on a quadrangle dappled with fallen leaves, new school spirit to be developed, new social heights to be scaled, was almost one blessing too many, because she already had a summer in Europe to look forward to. Earlier in the month, at a gig in Chicago not attended by her, Tanner had met a young couple from Denmark who'd loved his show and happened to be the organizers of a folk-music festival in Aarhus. American folk was huge in Europe, a whole circuit of summer festivals had slots to be filled by American performers, and a solo billing in Aarhus, *which the Danish couple had offered Tanner*, could open doors to all of them. Tanner had returned from the gig more excited than Becky had ever seen him. Wouldn't it be amazing, he said, to experience Europe together, be part of the scene, and meet the likes of Donovan, if not Richie Havens?

Becky hadn't been thinking of Europe at all. After Christmas, to abide by her promises to Jesus, she'd shared her inheritance with her brothers. She could no longer afford a big European trip with her mother, and given how her mother had been acting, smoking her cigarettes, paying little attention to anyone but herself, she'd quietly decided to stay home with Tanner. But to be in Europe *with* him? To whirl in his arms on the Champs-Élyseés? Cross the Alps together in a sleeper car? Toss coins into the Trevi Fountain and make wishes for each other? All she needed to do was save up money and disinvite her mother.

Owing to some marital strife about which Becky had learned only enough to be revolted by her father, her mother had moved into their house's third-floor storage room, fashioned a bed for herself in a low-ceilinged corner of it, and positioned an old escritoire beneath its window. When Becky ventured up to the third floor, after a school day rendered useless by visions of Europe, her mother was sitting at her desk in a haze of stale smoke. In lieu of smoking, she twisted a mechanical pencil while Becky laid out her plan.

"I don't need to go to Europe," her mother said. "But I'm not sure your going with Tanner is a good idea."

"You don't trust me."

"I'm not questioning your good sense. I was impressed by the decision you made about your money—it was a very loving thing to do. But my understanding was that you were saving your share of it for college."

"I hardly have to pay for anything but the plane ticket. If Tanner gets into other festivals, they'll cover our expenses."

"And if he doesn't?"

"I'll still have enough for two years of school. After that, I'll be working summers, and I can get financial aid."

Her mother continued to twist the pencil. She'd lost so much weight that a resemblance to Aunt Shirley had emerged. It couldn't have been healthy to lose that much weight so quickly.

"I haven't wanted to ask," she said, "because I know it's uncomfortable for you. But—have you and Tanner had sex?"

Becky felt her face burn.

"I'm not trying to embarrass you," her mother said. "A simple yes or no will do."

"It's complicated."

"Okay."

"That is—no. We haven't."

"That's fine, honey. It's more than fine—it's lovely. I'm proud of you. But if you want to go to Europe with your boyfriend, I'll need to know you have good protection."

Becky blushed again. Her friends all assumed that she and Tanner were having intercourse, and she'd done nothing to disabuse them. She'd enjoyed the secret that she and Tanner shared, the secret of her chastity, and the feeling of power and goodness it brought her. But to hear the same assumption from her mother was weirdly awful.

"Do you have protection?" her mother said.

"Do you *want* me to be having sex?"

"Dear God, no. Why would you think that?"

"I can take care of myself."

"Honey, I know you can. It's just—I also know how things can happen."

"What are you doing up here, anyway?"

Her mother sighed. "I am proofreading for the Great Books Foundation."

"I mean sleeping up here. Hiding up here."

"Your father and I are unhappy with each other."

"Yeah, who would have guessed."

"I know. I know it's been uncomfortable for you. I apologize for that."

"It's your life. I just don't feel like listening to your advice."

Her mother set down the pencil. "It's not advice. If you want to go to Europe with Tanner, it's a requirement. In fact, I think you should see a doctor right away. Will you let me make you an appointment?"

"I can make my own appointment."

"Whatever you prefer."

"I'll go do it right now. Do you want to listen on Dad's phone? Make sure I get my *appointment?*"

"Becky—"

There were three doors to slam on the way to her bedroom, and she slammed all three. The world seemed upside down to her. Premarital sex was supposed to be wrong, but Tanner had already had it with someone else, her friends expected her to have it, Clem expected her to have it, even her mother expected her to have it. Probably Judson, too, if anyone had asked him!

She wasn't a prude. She liked necking and petting and—coming. There had been moments when she was carried away into wanting Tanner inside her, moments when sex seemed like a blessing that God intended her to crave. What had saved her, each time, was Tanner's own hesitation. By firmly defining her limits from the outset, she'd made her virginity a thing for which the two of them shared responsibility, a jewel they participated equally in guarding, so that, when she forgot herself, Tanner was there to catch her. If this wasn't how real love worked, she didn't know what real love was.

Resentfully, as though forced to do chores while her friends were at the swimming pool, she went to her mother's gynecologist and submitted to being "fitted" for a diaphragm and tested on her ability to properly insert it. She was given a tube of jelly like the one that Laura Dobrinsky had once thrown at her face. The gear she brought home reduced love to something medical. It connected her, sordidly, to all the other girls in New Prospect with similar gear in their drawers.

And yet: wasn't it wrong to feel superior to those girls? Despite much prayer and reading of the Gospels, she had yet to recapture the spiritual ecstasy she'd experienced after smoking pot, the bodily yearning to be Christ's servant, but the essence of her revelation had stayed with her: she was sinfully proud and needed to repent. Ever since that revelation, and beginning with the sharing of her inheritance, she'd endeavored to be a good Christian, but the paradox of doing good was that she felt even prouder of herself. It was as if, although the terms had changed, she was still pursuing superiority. In the Gospels, Jesus paid more attention to the poor and the sick, to the iniquitous and the despised, than to the righteous and the privileged. Now that she'd taken the step of obtaining contraception, she wondered if withholding herself from the man she loved might constitute, in itself, a kind of vanity. Hadn't God revealed Himself to her precisely at her lowest moment? Might it not paradoxically be *more* Christian to humble herself, accept that she was one of those girls, and yield up her jewel?

As soon as she had the thought, she knew what she wanted. She wanted to fall, and by falling to deepen her relationship with Tanner and Jesus. And she knew exactly how it would happen.

Her fervor for Crossroads had cooled when her father returned to the group, and she'd been too busy with Tanner to earn the "hours" she needed to be eligible for Arizona. Kim Perkins and David Goya had pressured her to do some marathon last-minute hours-earning, so she could join them in Kitsillie, but when the trip roster for Kitsillie was posted she saw the name not only of her father but of *Frances Cottrell.* Kim and David still expected Becky to come along with them, but now she had a better plan for Easter vacation. She wouldn't give herself to Tanner in his van. She would do it with proper ceremony, in the privacy of her otherwise empty house.

Her only misgivings were related to her family. She was disgusted with her father, because she had reason to believe that he was trespassing against her mother, committing adultery with Mrs. Cottrell. Although Becky wouldn't trespass against anyone by giving herself to Tanner, she would still, in a sense, be sinking to her father's level. Worse yet, she'd be sinking to Clem's, and she was very sorry to give him that satisfaction.

She hadn't missed Clem at Christmas, not one bit. His insult of Tanner, his uttering of the word *passive,* continued to rankle in her heart, and she was sure he would ridicule her discovery of God as well. The mere sight of his empty bedroom, the reminder of the many late nights when she'd lain down on his bed and confided in him, was upsetting to her, vaguely sickening. Her aversion was so strong that it extended to Tanner's room at his parents' house. When Tanner showed it to her, during Christmas vacation, she gave it a once-over from the doorway without going in. The room reeked of Laura, who'd been a kind of foster sister to him, a sister he had sex with, and Becky wanted nothing to do with it.

When her parents, at Christmas dinner, in a rare moment of unity, lamented Clem's betrayal of the family's pacifism, she didn't say a word in his defense. When Tanner, to her surprise, declared that he was blown away by the courage of Clem's moral convictions, she insisted that Clem was just being an asshole. When Clem proceeded to send her a letter, apologizing for missing the holidays and laying out his rationale for quitting school, she crumpled it and tossed it in her wastebasket, because he hadn't apologized for insulting Tanner, and when he began to leave phone messages with her mother, asking Becky to call him at such-and-such time on such-and-such day, she ignored them.

The night before he caught up with her, in February, she'd accompanied the Bleu Notes to a cocktail lounge surprisingly more crowded than it had been in January. Parties of older women had claimed the tables nearest the band, and they were obviously there—drinking away, spending money—because of Tanner. Halfway through the second set, Gig Benedetti himself showed up and joined her at a table in the rear. Gig did the booking for a great many bands, and it pleased her to think that by letting him admire her looks and touch her elbow, by letting him believe they had a private understanding, she'd increased his attention to Tanner. "It hurts me to say it," Gig said, "but you were right. He's better off without what's-her-name. He's packing in the ladies, and that's dynamite." To be complimented on her intelligence, and to see the adoring expressions of Tanner's fans, to hear their tipsy hooting when he strapped on his twelve-string and played a solo number, and to know that she was the girl who got to be alone with him: she was almost too happy with her life to breathe.

She came home, well kissed and well petted, at two in the morning. Not many hours later, she was awakened by a ringing phone, her mother knocking on her door. The light in her window was still gray. "Leave me alone," she said. "I'm sleeping."

"Your brother wants to talk to you."

"Tell him I'll call back after church."

"Tell him yourself. I've had enough of taking messages."

The intensity of Becky's irritation cleared the sleep from her head. She threw on her Japanese robe and stamped past the doors of her sleeping father and younger brothers. In the kitchen, she fumbled with the phone, pressed its cold plastic to her ear, and heard her mother hang up on the third floor.

"Sorry to wake you," Clem said. "I didn't know what else to do."

"How about calling at a decent hour?"

"I already tried that. Like, eight times."

"Give me your number. I'll call you back after church."

"I have a job, Becky. I can't just talk when it's convenient for you. Which apparently is never."

"I've been really busy."

"Right. Although somehow you're free every night for your boyfriend."

"So what?"

"I just don't get why you're avoiding me."

He seemed to think he owned her. She seethed with silent irritation.

"Is it that thing I said about Tanner? I'm sorry I said that. Tanner's fine. He's a perfectly decent guy."

"Shut up!"

"I can't even apologize?"

"I'm sick of you poking around in my life."

"I'm not poking around in your life."

"Then why did you call me? What did you wake me up for?"

Over the phone lines, from some unpicturable room in New Orleans, came a heavy sigh. "I'm calling," Clem said, "because everything's gone to shit and I thought you might sympathize. I'm calling because I'm fucked. The draft board fucked me over."

"What does that mean?"

"It means they don't want me. Their quota was tiny, and they'd already filled it. I could still theoretically get called up, but not for Vietnam. Everybody there is coming home."

Far from sympathizing, she was wickedly pleased his plan had failed. "You're probably the only person in America who's sorry we're getting out of Vietnam."

"I'm not sorry, I'm just frustrated. I thought I'd be in basic training by now."

"Then maybe you should volunteer. If killing people is so important to you."

Another sigh in New Orleans, more patronizing. "Did you even read my letter? It's not about wanting to fight. It's a question of social justice."

"I'm saying, if that's so important to you, why not volunteer? Or do you just passively do whatever the draft board tells you?"

"I took an action, Becky."

"Yeah, you scored your point. Too bad it didn't count."

Stretching the phone cord, she filled a glass with water at the sink.

"I made a mistake," Clem said. "I should have quit school a year ago. Do you think I'm happy about it?"

The water was deliciously cold, February cold.

"No," she said, "I'm sure it's very frustrating. When do you ever make a mistake?"

"I called you because I was thinking of coming home for a while. You're not exactly making me want to."

"What did you expect at seven in the morning?"

"How else was I supposed to reach you?"

"I'm really busy. Okay? I don't care if you come home, but don't do it for my sake."

"Becky."

"What."

"I don't understand what's going on with you."

"Nothing's going on. I'm really happy. At least I was until you woke me up."

"I turn my back for one minute, and it's like you're a different person. I mean—the Baptist church? Seriously? You're going to the Baptist church? You're giving away your inheritance?"

Now she saw why he'd been trying to reach her: he had no other way to control her from a different city. She additionally resented her mother, for telling tales to him.

"I'm not your baby sister anymore," she said. "I can do my own thinking."

"You don't remember talking about this? You don't remember me fighting with Dad about it? You said you were keeping the money. You said you wanted to go to a great school."

"That's what *you* wanted for me."

"And you don't?"

"Not that it's any of your business, but I still have enough money for two years at Lawrence or Beloit. I can do the rest with financial aid."

"But I don't *want* your money."

"If you don't understand Christian charity, there's no explaining it."

"Oh, there we go. Is this something Tanner talked you into?"

"You mean, because I'm too stupid to think for myself?"

"I mean the Holy Roller thing. He was always kind of a Jesus freak."

She was flooded with pure hatred. Clem had managed, in a single breath, to insult her intelligence, her boyfriend, and her faith.

"For your information," she said coldly, "Tanner loves First Reformed. I'm the one who doesn't."

"And he goes along with it? 'That's cool, babe, whatever you say'?"

So much for his being sorry he'd called Tanner passive.

"Tanner accepts who I am," she said. "That's more than I can say for you."

"Accept what? That you believe in angels and devils and Holy Spirits? That I'm bound for hell because I don't believe in fairy tales? Forgive me for thinking you were smarter than that."

"Do you have any idea how sick I am of hearing that?"

"Hearing what?"

"'You're too smart for this, you're too smart for that.' You've been saying it all my life, and you know what? Maybe I'm sick of being made to feel stupid."

"Yeah, well. I guess you don't have to worry about that with Tanner."

She was too offended to speak.

"Maybe you should go ahead and marry him. Pop out a kid, forget about college, join the Baptist church. Nobody will expect you to be smart there. I'll be roasting in hell, so you won't have to worry about me."

"This is why you woke me up? You needed to insult me?"

Something rustled at Clem's end of the line. "I was pissed off," he said, "that you never call me back. But you're right—I get it. If I were you, I'd rather be out boning a rock star myself. He has such a cool van."

"Jesus. Are you drunk?"

"You think I give a shit who's boning who? You've got your rock star, Dad's got his little parishioner—"

"What are you *talking* about?"

"I'm talking about penis and vagina. Do I really have to explain it to you?"

She was appalled that she'd ever confided in him, appalled that she'd admired him.

"What parishioner?" she said.

"You didn't know about that? Him and Mrs. Cottrell? Why do you think Mom is on strike?"

Becky shuddered with disgust. "I don't know anything about that. But I would appreciate you not making false assumptions about *me*."

"Whoa. Really? False assumptions?"

"Yes, really."

"You're, what—too Baptist to go all the way? Or do you just like controlling him?"

"Fuck you!"

"I'm sorry, but it's kind of pathetic. If you're not even having sex, I honestly don't see the point. The least you could do is learn something about yourself."

Her hatred had entered a new dimension—Clem seemed outright evil to her. His antipathy to God, his contempt for every prohibition, had destroyed his soul. Her hand was shaking so badly, she could hardly hold the phone.

"You're the pathetic one," she said, shaking. "You think you're so superior and rational, but your soul is dead."

"My *soul*? That's another fairy tale."

"I don't know what happened to you, I don't know what your girl-friend did to you, but I don't even recognize you."

"I'm the same person I always was, Becky."

"Then maybe I'm the one who's changed. Maybe I'm finally old enough to see how totally different we are."

"We're not so different."

"How totally different! You make me sick!"

She slammed the receiver into its holster. Then she lifted it again and set it on the floor, to forestall his calling back, and wandered out of the kitchen, sick with hatred. She tried going back to bed, but her hatred wouldn't let her sleep. When Tanner picked her up for church, two hours later, she was reluctant to look at him, for fear of polluting him with Clem. At the Baptist church, she sang hymns and sat through the sermon with hatred in her heart.

Only at the end of the service, during the final prayer, did she reconnect with Jesus. Picturing the face of her Lord, the infinite wisdom and sadness of his gaze, she was seized with pity for her brother. She would never understand why he'd tried to go to Vietnam, but going to Vietnam was what he'd set his heart on, it was what he'd proclaimed to everyone that he was doing. Beyond his disappointment, he must have felt *embarrassed* when his plan fell through. Unhappy in New Orleans, presumably friendless, working the deep-fry station at Kentucky Fried Chicken, he'd repeatedly left messages for his sister, who in the past had always been there for him, and when he'd finally reached her on the phone she'd rejected him. In her sinful pride, her offended vanity, she'd lashed out at a person who'd loved and protected her all her life. If he'd lashed out at her, too, it was only because he was hurt and embarrassed.

She returned to the parsonage intending to call him and apologize, but when she went upstairs and saw his empty bedroom the sickness boiled up in her again. A visceral loathing, compounded by his contempt for everything that mattered to her, overwhelmed her sentimentality. Clem had actively attacked her, she'd merely defended herself. It seemed to her that he, not she, should be the first to apologize. For the rest of the day, and for several days afterward, she expected him to call her again. Even a small gesture of regret and respect, if he'd offered it sincerely, might have opened the door to her better self. But apparently he had his own pride.

In her abundance of happiness, as February turned to March, their fight receded in her mind. Tanner had sent letters to a dozen festivals in Europe, along with copies of a solo tape he'd recorded in his basement and clippings of a newspaper review of the Bleu Notes. Becky had helped him with the letter, rewording it more assertively, and the two of them now dwelt in states of parallel anticipation, he waiting to hear from Europe, she from Lawrence and Beloit. After a thorough, Crossroads-flavored discussion of her readiness to give herself to him, they also shared the anticipation of a week alone together in the parsonage.

Whatever Clem might think, she wasn't stupid. Though it had warmed her heart and deepened her faith to share her inheritance with her brothers, she'd kept enough money to attend an expensive private college, surrounded by people as ambitious as her aunt Shirley had encouraged her to be. She'd encouraged Tanner to be similarly ambitious, and if he happened to get a record contract, and started touring nationally, she could see herself taking time away from college to be part of that. But going along with him to gigs had made her aware of how many other musicians had the same ambitions, how much competition even a brilliant talent faced. She didn't like to think of Tanner languishing in New Prospect while she moved into new social spheres in Wisconsin; it didn't bode well for their future as a couple. But her own personal future held two equally luminous possibilities, either the glamour of the music world or the privileges of college, and she was very happy.

On the Friday before Palm Sunday, as she walked home from school, her heart began to race. Easter vacation had commenced; her moment of falling was suddenly at hand. She and Tanner had chosen Monday as *the night*. She'd wanted to make him something special and European for dinner, possibly a cheese soufflé, but after consulting with her mother, who actually knew how to cook, she'd settled on beef bourguignon. She'd already bought two long candles for the table and, boldly, at the liquor store, a bottle of Mouton Cadet red wine. For the night to be perfect, it had to be about more than just sex.

She came home to a house in the process of emptying for her and Tanner. Her father had left for First Reformed, and Perry's duffel bag was packed and waiting by the door. The only sign of her mother was a note asking Becky to drive Perry to the church. Upstairs, she found Judson neatly packing his own suitcase for his Disneyland trip. He didn't know where Perry was. Returning to the kitchen, she heard a dull clank from the basement. She opened the door and peered into its gloom. "Perry?"

No answer. She turned on a light and ventured down the stairs. From the far corner of the basement, where the oil burner was, came an odd huffing, another clank of metal.

"Hey, Perry, you ready?"

"Yes, I'm ready, can't a person be alone?"

"If you want a ride to church, now is when I'm offering it."

He came sauntering out from behind the oil burner. "Ready."

"What are you doing down here?"

"The question seems more apposite to you. You're supposed to be a creature of the light. Why aren't you shining in the world where you belong?"

He skipped past her and up the stairs. She didn't smell pot, but she wondered if he might be doing drugs again. For a short while, at Christmas, she'd enjoyed the novelty of hanging out with him, but their "friendship" hadn't taken off. Since she'd added a shift to her schedule at the Grove, to earn money for Europe, she'd barely spoken to him.

Emerging from the basement, she saw him lugging his duffel bag into the bathroom.

"What are you doing?"

"A moment of privacy, sister, if you would be so kind. Would do me that gentle favor."

He locked the bathroom door behind him.

"Hey, listen," she said, through the door. "You seem weird. Are you okay?"

She heard him huffing, heard the rasp of a heavy-duty zipper.

"If you're doing drugs again," she said, "you need to be open with me. Remember what we said about walking away? I'm not the enemy."

No confession was forthcoming. Behind her, in the kitchen, the telephone rang.

She expected the caller to be Jeannie Cross, but it was Gig Benedetti, asking for Becky. She hadn't known Gig even had her number.

"This is Becky speaking."

"Ha, didn't recognize your voice. How is our beautiful girl today?"

"She's fine, thank you."

"Do you have a second?"

"Actually, it's better if you call me back a little later."

"Reason I'm calling is—Tanner tells me he's going to Europe with you. Were you aware of this plan? Did you know about this plan and not tell me?"

Her heart clutched. Apparently she'd betrayed their special understanding.

"I talked to him this morning," Gig said. "I've been working my butt off, booking him into the Holiday Inn circuit, and what do I find out? He's ditching the band and taking you to Denmark!"

"Well—yes."

"Do you realize what a toilet Europe is, professionally? Do you know why his Danish pals are so happy he's coming to Aarfuck? It's because any act with half a brain can see it's a freaking waste of time! I thought you and I were on the same wavelength!"

He was yelling, and she wanted to tell him not to. She couldn't stand being yelled at.

"We are on the same wavelength," she said. "This is only for one summer."

"Only one summer—I like that. Only one summer. And Quincy and Mike? While the lovebirds are off on their honeymoon, Quincy and Mike are supposed to do what? Twiddle their thumbs and hope you send a postcard? It'll take Tanner four months, minimum, to put together new backup and break them in. Suddenly we're in 1973 and nobody remembers him. Does that sound like a plan to you? I thought you were *smart*."

"There's a huge folk scene in Europe," she said stiffly.

"Pfff. If we were talking about the UK, it sort of halfway might make sense—the labels still scout London. But the Continent? Are you kidding me? Can you name one Top Forty hit that *ever* came out of France or Germany?"

"It's not just about the labels, though, right? It's about developing an audience."

"Damn straight it is. And how do you do that? You play the Holiday Inn Rockford and then you move on to Rock Island. Hit enough big little cities, you start to get a name, and that's what the A&R guys are looking for. You've got to trust me on this, Becky. Your guy is literally better off playing Decatur, Illinois, than Paris, France. There's an act I booked into Decatur eight months ago that just signed a major-label deal. I'm not lying to you."

"But he can still do that—I mean, the Holiday Inns. He'll come back even better, with new contacts."

"Listen. Baby. Sweetheart, listen. Your guy's okay. I admit I kind of signed him as a favor, because I like your style, but I'm not keeping him on as a favor. He's a pro, he takes direction, he's a hit with the ladies, everybody's making money. But my honest opinion? I'm not in love with his original material, and neither are the audiences. Time will tell if he's got better songs in him, but there's a million and one acts at his level. The best thing he's got going is he's young and super easy on the eyes, and you know what they say about the record business—the vampire thirsts for youth and beauty. The last thing your guy needs is to sit on the shelf for a year."

"Okay," she said in a very small voice.

"I told him, if he wants me to represent him, he's got to flush this Europe thing where it belongs. He didn't want to hear me, but he'll hear it from you. You need to take him in hand and lay down the law. Will you promise to do that for me?"

"I don't know."

"You're the brains of the outfit. He'll do whatever you say."

When she hung up the phone, the sun was still strong in the windows, but the kitchen seemed dusky, as if what had brightened it weren't the sun but the dream of Europe. She felt punished and guilty and disappointed; sorry for Tanner, sorrier for herself. Tuning out Perry's weird patter, she mechanically drove him to the church and mechanically drove home again. Never had she felt less like working her Friday-night shift.

To ignore Gig's advice, at the cost of his firing Tanner, would obviously be the height of selfishness. But Shirley had died imagining her niece on a Grand Tour of Europe, Becky had already given away nine thousand dollars of her money, and the alternatives to Europe were dismal: either another summer with her parents, waitressing at the Grove, or a succession of cornfields and depressing small cities, the steambath of July in the Midwest. She understood that this was the reality of the music business, but the vision of going to Europe *and* advancing Tanner's career was too perfect to be defeated by reality. She didn't see how she could give it up.

Her problem was still there in the morning, when she took her mother and Judson to O'Hare. She'd expected to feel liberated by her family's absence, but Gig's judgment of Tanner, its echoing of Clem's, had deflated the romance of the coming week. As she watched Judson run ahead of their mother with his little suitcase, the two of them bound for a city of palm trees and movie stars, she felt desolated.

From the airport, she went straight to the Grove. Gig's first move as Tanner's agent had been to pull the plug on his Friday-night shows there, and Becky, having now seen better places in the city, understood why. The Grove's earth-tone decor and potted trees were tired, not trendy, its lounge acoustics lousy, its patrons tightfisted and Nixonite. By the time her shift ended, she felt so worn down that she called Tanner's house and left a message with his mother, excusing herself from his gig in Winnetka. Interestingly, Tanner didn't call her back.

The next morning, however, his van rolled into the parsonage driveway at the usual Sunday hour. For reasons she didn't immediately understand, she'd not only put on her best spring dress but applied a lot of makeup. The face in the bathroom mirror was not at all a girl's, and maybe that was it. Maybe she wanted to place herself in a future from which she could look back at herself.

Tanner had dressed up, too. In the misty morning light, wearing the suit he'd bought for his grandmother's funeral, his hair thick and glistening on his shoulders, his eyelashes batting at the sight of Becky in her finest, he was absurdly gorgeous. Whatever else might be the case, she could never get enough of looking at him, and she was the woman whose mouth he then kissed. The kiss, exciting her nerves in the usual places, made her problem seem less consequential.

"I was thinking," he said, "do you want to go to First Reformed?"

"Is that what you want?"

"I don't know—it's Palm Sunday. It might be nice to be someplace familiar."

"I would love that." She kissed him again. "It's a great idea. Thank you for suggesting it."

She was happy that he'd made a definite wish explicit. And happy, after all, to return to First Reformed, on a Sunday when her father wasn't there. Happy to see faces of surprise when she and Tanner made their entrance, happy to accept a palm twig from the greeters, Tom and Betsy Devereaux, happy to claim the pew she'd shared with Tanner at the first service she'd attended with him. It was strange to recall how she'd imagined, at that service, that they were there as a couple; strange how wishing for a future life and then actually inhabiting it made time feel unreal. As she sat with him now and received the word of God, muted but not defeated by Dwight Haefle's delivery of it, she wondered what the purpose of a person's life was. Almost everything in life was vanity—success a vanity, privilege a vanity, Europe a vanity, beauty a vanity. When you stripped away the vanity and stood alone before God, what was left? Only loving your neighbor as yourself. Only worshiping the Lord, Sunday after Sunday. Even if you lived for eighty years, the duration of a life was infinitesimal, your eighty years of Sundays were over in a blink. Life had no length; only in depth was there salvation.

And so it happened. Near the end of the service, when she stood with Tanner to sing the Doxology and heard his tenor voice ringing forth, heard her own voice quavering to stay in tune with him, the golden light entered her again. This time, not being veiled by marijuana, it was even brighter. This time, to see it, she didn't need to look down into herself. She could feel it rising up in her and brimming over—the goodness of God, the simplicity of the answer to her question—and she experienced a paroxysm so powerful it took her singing breath away. The answer was her Savior, Jesus Christ.

She hadn't found the answer in the other churches where she'd been looking. She'd found it where she'd started. This seemed to her a crucial fact.

The spring morning into which she and Tanner emerged, after being cooed over in the parlor, admired by dewy-eyed matrons, was the warmest of the year so far. In the wake of her paroxysm, her senses were alive to the caressing breeze, to the fragrance of flowers and spring earth, to the blazing of the dogwoods by the bank building, to the song of unseen birds, and to her body's own springtime urges. Because a visitation from God had stirred them up, they didn't seem the least bit wrong to her. They were simply part of being His creature.

"Let's take a walk," she said.

"Your feet are going to hurt in those shoes."

"It's so beautiful, I'll go barefoot."

The sidewalk on Maple Avenue still had winter beneath it, a thrilling contrast to the warmth of the sun. She couldn't remember the last time she'd gone walking barefoot. The eight-year-old girl she'd once been was now eighteen and someday might be eighty. Her sense-memories of spring were confirming her insight from the sanctuary: time was an illusion.

"It just happened again," she told Tanner. "What happened at Christmas—it happened again while we were singing the Doxology. I saw God."

"You—really? That's far-out."

"What's strange is that yesterday was the total opposite. Yesterday I felt so dead, and now I'm so alive. Yesterday I had no idea what to do, and today the answer is so clear to me."

"What do you mean?"

In a few words, she recounted her conversation with Gig. To spare Tanner's feelings, she omitted Gig's judgments, but Tanner was angry even so. Although she gathered that Laura had been quite the screaming bandmate, Becky had only once seen him really angry, when Quincy made the band late for a gig in the city.

"What the fuck? He called your house? Behind my back?"

"You didn't give him my number?"

"That guy? No way. If he has something to say to me, I'm the one to say it to. Did you tell him that? Tell him he should be talking to me, not you?"

"All I did was answer the phone."

"God, I am sick of this. He's a good booker but a total sleaze. He's been all over you since day one. I can't believe he called you behind my back!"

Tanner's outburst, its assertiveness, was extremely pleasing to her.

"I guess he thought," she said, "that I was making you go to Europe."

"I already *told* him why I'm going. I told him I'll find another agent if he can't deal with it."

"Yeah, but, here's the thing. Tanner, here's the thing. Maybe we shouldn't go."

He stopped dead on the sidewalk. "You don't want to go?"

"No, I do, but—that's just vanity. I couldn't see it yesterday, but now I do. I want what's best for you, not me. And Gig says it's better not to go."

"Of course he says that. He's all about the money—if I'm in Europe, he's not taking his cut."

"But what if he's right? What if it's a career mistake?"

"He knows zilch about the scene there. He said it himself—'I know zilch.'"

"He knows about the business here, though. If you want a record contract and you want to really break out, don't you think you should listen to him?"

Tanner stared at her. "What did he say to you?"

"Just what I told you."

"I thought Europe was a thing we were doing together. That it wasn't just about the music—I thought we wanted to have an experience together."

"That's what I want, too. But . . . maybe it doesn't have to be this summer."

"Becky. Do you not want to be with me?"

There were tears in his eyes. They made her want to be with him.

"Of course I do. I'm in love with you."

"Then fuck it. Let's go to Europe."

"But, sweetie—"

"Who cares if it's a 'career mistake'? The only things I care about are being with you and celebrating life with music. As long as I'm with you—Becky. As long as I'm with you, there's no such thing as a mistake."

Across the street, in a yard dotted with eruptions of shaggy green grass, a man started up a lawn mower. It coughed and backfired in a cloud of blue smoke. The day was getting warmer by the minute, and the parsonage was just around the corner. Seeing the tears in Tanner's eyes, and hearing him express, spontaneously, the exact same thought she'd had in the sanctuary—that only love and worship mattered—she felt as if her body might float into the sky. She took his hand and pressed it flat on her hip.

"Let's go to my house."

He knew right away what she was saying. "Now?"

"Yes, now. I'm so ready."

"I've got practice at one thirty."

"You're the front man," she said. "You can tell them it's canceled."

In Rome, in early September, in the apartment where they were crash-ing, they met a German couple in their twenties who were heading to a farmhouse in Tuscany that the woman's father owned, and Becky had jumped on their invitation to come along with them, although technically it was Tanner, not she, whom the Germans had invited, after hearing him play. Her own fishings for an invitation, her feigning of a lifelong desire to see the Tuscan countryside, her unfeigned rapture at the description of the farmhouse, had gone unnoticed, and this was ironic, because Tanner cared more about people than places and had no gripe with Rome. Becky was the one who couldn't wait to get away. The heat in Rome was suffo-cating, and the crash pad, though huge and well situated, within sight of the Campo de' Fiori, was essentially unfurnished—room after room with sun-damaged parquet floors and nary a table, nary a chair. She and Tanner were camped out in the corner of what might once have been a ballroom, beneath a window open to a smell of rotting vegetables. In the far corner was an unfriendly young couple, purportedly from behind the Iron Cur-tain, who traipsed around naked and coupled, unquietly, on the room's only piece of furniture, a gilded sofa twelve feet long. Half a dozen other long-haired travelers were accepting hospitality from a man named Edoardo, a spritelike Italian who wore tight white pants and thin-soled loafers, without socks, and lived in two properly furnished rooms behind the kitchen. Becky and Tanner had met Edoardo on a side street where Tanner was busking and Becky was sitting on the pavement, writing in her travel diary. When Edoardo had dropped a five-thousand-lire note in Tanner's guitar case and invited them to crash with him, they hadn't needed to be asked twice. The night before, under a pillow in their tiny hotel room, near the train station, they'd discovered a balled-up, crusty tissue that hadn't been there in the morning.

The folk festival in Rome took place in the last days of August, and the organizers, while rejecting Tanner's application, had allowed that performance slots sometimes opened up at the last minute. On the strength of that hope, and because Aunt Shirley had especially loved Rome, and because their Eurail passes were about to expire, they'd come down from Heidelberg four days early. In Heidelberg, where Tanner had played as an official invitee, albeit at eleven in the morning and to a disappointing crowd, they'd eaten free food, slept on cleanly sheeted German beds, and avoided cashing any of their remaining traveler's checks.

In Rome, they subsisted on *tavola calda* and agonized about buying a gelato. There were a thousand sights to see, but the only safe place Becky could be while Tanner busked was either right beside him or in the baking, furnitureless apartment; she couldn't walk alone without being hassled by Italian men. Although Edoardo had urged them to stay for as long as they liked, they were camping on a parquet floor with only sleeping bags for padding. The image of a Tuscan farmhouse, shared with a pair of privacy-respecting Germans, was like a dream of respite. The Roman heat had frayed her nerves, no performance slot had opened up for Tanner, and they had a week to kill before they hitchhiked to Paris for an outdoor concert, headlined by the Who and Country Joe McDonald, that people had been talking about all summer. There was also the matter of Becky's period being overdue. She was only a few days late, but she worried that the exhaustion of her tube of jelly, which she'd understood to be redundant and hadn't replaced yet, had been a bigger deal than she'd supposed.

The overnight flight from Chicago to Amsterdam, the cool rainstorms in Denmark, the warmth of Tanner's reception in Aarhus, were now memories so distant that they might have been a different person's. According to the little check marks in her travel diary, she and Tanner had made love three times in Aarhus and forty-six times since. Every day, whether she was seeing the sunflowers of van Gogh or just hanging out with American musicians, whether picnicking on the green flank of an Alp or being confounded by a shower that sprayed all over the bathroom floor, without a curtain or a sill, she'd felt delighted afresh to be in

Europe, but every night she'd returned to a bitterness from which being loved and possessed by Tanner was her only escape.

Tanner's kindness, to her and to everyone they met, was basically a miracle. Even when she was bleeding and bitchy, he didn't get cross with her. When they sprinted to catch a train, only to watch it pull out of the station, he just shrugged and said it wasn't meant to be. When she had the stomach flu in Utrecht and begged him to go alone to the mainstage event, he not only refused to leave her, he said that even the sound of her throwing up was dear to him. When she caught herself wishing he were more assertive, she had only to think of his openhearted curiosity, his readiness to be amazed, his honest praise of singers farther along in their careers, his head-shaking bemusement when someone insisted on being a jerk, and his beautiful way of slipping into a jam session—how he followed along unobtrusively, observing the other players, and then, when the moment was right, cut loose and really jammed, displaying his superior musicianship, and was always happy to explain, if someone asked, how he'd played some difficult lick. The back pages of her travel diary were filled with addresses of Europeans who hoped to see him again and had offered him and Becky lodging. The Continental music scene, with its ethic of sharing, could sustain them long after their traveler's checks ran out. Though Rome and its heat, all the assholes on their scooters, weren't to her taste, and though Tanner would eventually need to restart his career in the States, she was in no hurry at all to go home.

With the exception of Judson, who was too young to be relevant, her family had abandoned her. She hadn't heard from Clem since their fight in February, Perry had spent four months in residential psychiatric treatment, at ghastly expense, and her parents had done their best to ruin her life. Not only had her father dispossessed her, with scarcely an apology, but her mother, instead of siding with her or sympathizing, had deferred to him without a murmur of resistance. Never in her life had her parents been so united against her or so cloyingly into each other. They'd returned from Albuquerque, after Easter, like a pair of newlyweds— little pats on the fanny, wet smooches, treacly endearments, her father mooning at her mother, her mother breathy and submissive. Equally obnoxious was their new religiosity. Her father now began every meal with a lengthy prayer, applauded by her mother with tremulous amens. Although Becky had her own faith, she knew better than to inflict it on people waiting to eat. Although she herself had been guilty of public smooching, she had the very good excuse of not being a parent with grown children.

Again, as when she received her inheritance, there had been a summons to her father's home office. The third floor smelled of cigarettes—her mother had returned to her proper bed, but she hadn't quit smoking—when Becky climbed the stairs to it. Her father's desk was strewn with bills and legal documents. He kept glancing at them, repositioning them, while he explained his financial predicament and her mother gazed at him supportively. The upshot was that, to pay reparations to the Navajos whose barn Perry had burned, he wanted to "borrow" Becky's college money.

"It seems to me," she said, "that Perry should be the one to pay for that."

"Unfortunately, there's no money left in Perry's account."

"I'm talking about the money *I* gave him."

"It's gone, honey," her mother said. "He spent it all on drugs."

"It was three thousand dollars!"

"I know. It's a terrible thing, but it's gone."

The news was both sickening and vindicating. Becky had long suspected that Perry was soulless and amoral. At least she could stop pretending she wanted a relationship with him.

"What about Jay, though? What about Clem?"

"We are borrowing the money you gave Judson," her father said. "I've also obtained a loan from the church, which will help with the legal and medical expenses. But we still have a large shortfall."

"And Clem? It's not like he even wanted my money."

Her father sighed and looked at her mother.

"Your younger brother is very seriously mentally ill," her mother said. "At some point, in the course of his illness, he emptied Clem's account as well."

Becky stared at her. She was the victim, and her mother didn't even have the guts to look at her.

"Emptied," she said. "Don't you mean *stole*?"

"I know it's hard for you to understand," her mother said, her eyes on the floor, "but Perry was too disturbed to know what he was doing."

"How do you steal without knowing what you're doing?"

Her father gave her a look of warning. "Our family has a very pressing need for money. I know it's hard for you, but you're part of this family. If the situation were reversed—"

"You mean, if I were a thief and a drug addict?"

"If you had a serious illness—and, make no mistake, Perry has a very serious illness—then, yes, I think your brothers would make any sacrifice we asked of them."

"But it's not even for his treatment. It's just for the Navajos."

"The loss of the farm equipment was devastating. It's not the Navajos' fault that your brother destroyed it."

"Right. And it's not his fault either, because he's so seriously ill. Apparently it's *my* fault."

"Obviously," her father said, "it's not your fault, and I know how unfair it must seem to you. But we're only asking for a loan, not a gift. Your mother will be looking for work, and I will be looking for a better-paid position. By this time next year, we might be able to repay some of what we've borrowed. We'll also be more eligible for college financial aid."

"It's only for a little while, honey," her mother said. "We're only asking to borrow what Shirley gave you."

"In case you've forgotten, Shirley gave me *thirteen* thousand dollars."

"You'll still have your own savings. If you want to start college in the fall, you can go to U of I for a year or two. Then you can transfer anywhere you like."

Becky had received her acceptance letter from Beloit three days earlier. The idea of being a transfer student there, missing the freshman experience, entering a class whose social order had long since coalesced, seemed worse to her than not going at all. Of the thirteen thousand dollars she'd inherited, she'd given away nine with the assurance that the remaining four were hers alone to spend; that she still had special things coming to her. But her parents had disapproved of the inheritance from the start. They'd disapproved of Shirley, and now they'd gotten what they'd wanted all along, which was for Becky to have nothing. It was as if they were in league with God Himself, who, knowing everything, knew that beneath her Christian charity was a tough little core of selfishness. Her cheeks burned with hatred of her parents for exposing it.

"Fine," she said. "You can have all of it. It's fifty-two hundred dollars—take all of it."

"Honey," her mother said. "We don't want to take your own savings."

"Why not? It's not like they're enough to do me any good."

"That's not true. You can still go to U of I."

"As long as I don't go to Europe. Right?"

Her mother, knowing what Europe meant to her, might at least have expressed some sympathy. Instead, she deferred to her husband.

"Unfortunately, yes," he said. "If you go to U of I, you'll need money for room and board. I know you were looking forward to Europe, but we think it's better if you postpone that plan."

"The two of you. That's what the two of you together have decided."

"This is hard for all of us," her mother said. "We're all having to give up things we might have wanted."

There was nothing more to say. When Becky returned to her bedroom, she didn't even feel like crying. A bitterness had entered her soul, and there it stayed. She could forgive the injury of being dispossessed, because Jesus promised a reward to those who gave away everything and followed him, but the insult of it only grew deeper: her parents cared more about her amoral brother, more about each other, more even about the blessed Navajos, than they did about her. When, at dinner, on the day she'd transferred four thousand dollars, her father raised thanks to the Lord for the gift of family and the gift of his daughter, Rebecca, her bitterness was so intense she couldn't taste her food. Although her mother was courteous enough to thank her directly, she failed to say, as she'd said so often in the past, that she was proud of her. She knew very well what she'd taken from her daughter, the injustice she'd been party to; it would have been obscene to speak of pride. Only in Tanner was there relief from the bitterness. He was too kindhearted to join Becky in hating her family, but he understood her as no one else did, understood both the goodness and the selfishness in her. She'd surrendered the last of her inheritance, she'd lost Beloit and the future it stood for, she was looking at a year of full-time waitressing or a shitty high-rise dorm room in Champaign, and Tanner had understood why she had to go to Europe.

Like all of Edoardo's guests (it was evidently a requirement), the German couple, Renata and Volker, were notably good-looking. Volker, who resembled a blond Charles Manson, had lived in Morocco and traveled as far east as India, exploring non-Western ways of being. Renata had amazing blue eyes and a style that Becky envied. Nowhere in America were there pants and tops like Renata's, cut simply and practically without being masculine, their fabrics faded but durable, or leather sandals so elegant and obviously comfortable. Becky had grown very sick of her own sneakers and Dr. Scholl's.

The night before they left for Tuscany, Tanner stayed up late with Edoardo and the Germans while she retired to the stifling ballroom. Worse than the smell of rot were the voices coming through the window, young men yelling in Italian perhaps the very same vulgarities they yelled at her in English. Even the fainter sound of Tanner in the kitchen, singing "Cross Road Blues," was oppressive to her in her condition. Stopping her ears with her fingers, she lay sweating on her sleeping bag and focused her entire will on bleeding.

It was like trying to will a heat wave to break. She awoke to an even hotter day, a sensation of menstrual operations firmly shut down, which was to say an absence of encouraging sensations. Her body had always performed its duties without being asked, and the flip side of this, now, was its perfect indifference to her entreaties. After she and Tanner had helped themselves to stale cornetti from the kitchen, they gathered their luggage and found the Germans in a room darker than theirs, perceptibly less hot. They were rolling up air mattresses, another thing to envy.

Down on the steaming street, around the corner from Edoardo's building, Volker led them to a large, low-slung Mercedes, parked halfway up on the sidewalk, and opened the trunk.

"This is your car?" Becky said.

Volker extended a hand for her backpack. "What did you expect?"

"I don't know, a van or something. I thought you guys were more—I don't know. Poor."

"We love Edoardo," Renata said. "He brings together such interesting people—like you."

"You don't mind that there's no furniture?"

"We visit with him three times now," Volker said. "He is a really great guy."

"I wonder why he doesn't have any furniture."

"Because he's Edoardo!"

The back seat of the Mercedes was so roomy that she could stretch out her legs and Tanner could open his guitar case. He immediately began to play, because playing was what he did, day and night. Becky was so used to the sound of his Guild that she only paid attention when other people were listening, as Renata was doing now, from the front seat, her body angled toward him, her blue eyes more fervent than Becky cared to see. Where the harassment she'd endured in Rome was strictly about her as a sex object, Tanner's fascination to women seemed more romantic, and she'd come to resent that other women felt free to imagine romance with her boyfriend. It occurred to her that Renata had invited Tanner to Tuscany because she was very into him.

Hanging on a string from the car's rearview mirror, lurching and spinning with Volker's brakings for rude Italian drivers, was a painted plastic Buddha. Along the narrow streets were tiny trattorias, inviting but unaffordable, and bars with colorful bottles doubled by the mirrors behind them, and long, unpainted walls gouged by trucks and plastered with posters for a circus, for an automobile show, for *FOLKAROMA, 29–31 Agosto*. Wider avenues offered glimpses of churches and ruins and monuments, pastel in the haze, that Becky might have visited with Shirley, or with her mother, but hadn't with Tanner, because theirs was not that kind of trip.

There ensued an uglier Rome, more sprawling than the pretty Rome. They passed scooters in buzzing packs of twenty, apartment blocks bedecked with drying laundry, pyramids of car tires, gas station after gas station. Tanner was improvising and the Germans speaking German, Renata consulting a map, while Becky monitored her condition. For four and a half years, her period had arrived as reliably as the thunderstorms that ended a sweltering Midwestern day. Now she felt nothing in her belly, no change at all, an ominous stasis. Even before the last of ugly Rome fell away and they reached the autostrada, a dread had taken root in her.

Volker's acceleration pressed her back into her leather seat. He was driving so fast that the trucks they passed looked stationary. She saw the speedometer needle trembling at two hundred kilometers an hour, climbing higher. The sky was white hot and the windows were down, the roar of air so loud that she could hear only Tanner's high notes. He was still immersed in his music, Renata gazing at him again, Volker serene at the wheel. The Buddha's string tightened and tilted as he braked for a car going only recklessly fast, not insanely fast.

Stiff with dread, barely able to raise her arm, Becky touched Tanner's shoulder. He smiled and nodded in time with his strumming. She was too frightened to move again or speak. Beyond the dangling plastic Buddha, another nearly stationary car rushed up to meet them. Volker flashed his headlights, the Buddha smiled, and her dread branched out in all directions. What did she know about Volker, except that he looked like Charles Manson? Did he believe in Buddhist reincarnation? Was he trying to crash them to a higher plane, beyond the whiteness of the sky? And the weirdness of Edoardo, his thing for pretty houseguests, the vacancy of his apartment—was everyone perverted? Was this why Volker and Renata stayed there? Did they pay Edoardo to cruise the streets and find fresh meat? Was the farmhouse in Tuscany just a lure for unsuspecting Americans? She'd placed herself and Tanner in the hands of people *she knew absolutely nothing about*. She wanted to ask Volker to slow down, but her jaw was locked, her chest muscles petrified. The Mercedes was flying at airplane speed, meteor speed. It telescoped the passing trees and road signs, smashed them together in a blur of violence. Was this how she would die? She could see her death as clearly as if it had already happened. It filled her with sadness, but at least she'd had a chance to live in the world, at least she'd experienced real love and beheld the light of God. The unborn soul in her had never even seen the light.

Dear God, she prayed, *if this is the final test, I accept the test. If my time has come, I'll die rejoicing in you. But please let it be your will that I live. If it's your will that I live, I promise I will always serve you. If it's your will that I be pregnant, I promise I will never harm my baby. I will love her and cherish her and teach her to love you, I promise, I promise, I promise, if you would only let me live. Please, God. Let me live.*

Clem met Felipe Cuéllar at a construction site where the work consisted of shoveling sand, under a sand-colored Lima sky, and pushing it up narrow planks in a wheelbarrow. For a month, they shared a corrugated metal lean-to near the water treatment plant, shared food and beer, awakened to the smell of each other's farts. Like other young men from the highlands, Felipe had come to the city in the winter to earn some cash. When it was time for him to go home, in November, Clem offered to join him and work for his family in exchange for food and shelter. The nonweather of Lima, the identically beige-skied days, was oppressing him, and throughout his months in Peru he'd seen the Andes in the east, the sun reflected on their heights, without getting any closer. He knew so little of farming, it didn't occur to him that planting season coincided with the arrival of the rains.

He'd thought he knew what labor was. He'd carried tons of tar paper up six flights of stairs, a hundred-pound roll at a time, at a building site in Guayaquil, he'd stood in raw sewage outside Chiclayo and shoveled for ten hours, he'd raked hot asphalt under midday sun, but not until he was slipping and crawling in the mud of the Andes, in freezing fog and pelting hail, pulling out stones with cracked and swollen fingers, hacking at the earth with a dull-bladed implement, the altitude sharp-bladed in his brain, the blood from broken capillaries in his throat, did he put to rest the question of his strength.

When he'd left New Orleans, a year and a half earlier, his only plan had been *to have no plan*. With a few hundred dollars and the Spanish he'd taught himself while waiting for a passport, he'd crossed the Mexican border at Matamoros and headed farther south, intending to be gone for two years, the same term he would have served in the army. When he'd exhausted his money, on a boat passage to Guayaquil, he'd become an itinerant day laborer, motiveless in every respect except the need to work. If he saw a bus packed with other workers, he squeezed onto it without caring where it was going, not because he wished to understand the underprivileged but simply because, if he didn't work, he didn't eat.

Neither having nor seeking a larger motive, he'd been surprised to find one in the highlands. The fundamental equation of human existence—soil + water + plants + labor = food—was the most applied of sciences, nothing philosophical about it, but the Andean farmers' way with their seedlings and their tubers, their wresting of sustenance from the harshest margins of arability, was a fulfillment of the plant physiology and genetics, the physical and atmospheric chemistry, the nitrogen cycles, the molecular jujitsu of chlorophyll, that he'd studied in school without appreciating their existential crux; and it had given him a plan. He would stay on through the potato harvest, complete his two-year term, and return to Illinois to study the impure science of agronomy.

The Cuéllars lived in a hamlet an hour's walk from the town of Tres Fuentes. Once a week, after the crops had been planted, Clem descended on a boggy track through the puna, past pockets of hardwood forest whose recession upslope made the gathering of firewood arduous, to a post office conceivably colonial in age. Unlike the Cuéllars, whose first language was Quechua, the postal clerk spoke perfect Spanish. He was Clem's sole connection to the world beyond the highlands, his *fútbol*-themed calendar the only marker of that world's chronology. Every week, Clem returned to find another line of days x-ed out.

One afternoon, when x's had consumed half of February, the clerk had a small package for him. He took it outside and sat down on the rim of a dry, ruined fountain. The air was scented with the smoke of kitchen fires, the sun hidden by a ceiling of pale cloud through which he could feel its warmth. In the package were three pairs of wool socks and a letter from his mother.

There were two kinds of letters, the ones you eagerly tore open and the ones you had to force yourself to read, and his mother's were of the latter kind. Others she'd sent him, in Guayaquil and Lima, had made him angry, especially at Becky. If Becky hadn't been so bent on her religious do-goodery, Perry couldn't have pissed away six thousand dollars and she could have gone to college, instead of getting herself pregnant and married, at nineteen, to an affable lightweight. But there was nothing he could do from South America, and his anger had passed in the daily struggle for bread, the dysentery he was prone to, the repeated theft of his spare clothes, the bother of acquiring new ones without resorting, himself, to stealing. Experience had taught him to live with nothing of value except his passport, and so it was with the news of Perry's collapse and Becky's disastrous choices, his mother's sorrows: it was better to travel light.

January 26, 1974

Dear Clem,

Your father and I were blessed to receive your letter from Tres Fuentes and learn that you are safe and well there. Even if you're working hard, it must be a relief to be in the beautiful High Andes after all your time in cities, and I'm so glad to have an address where I know a letter is sure to reach you. (You didn't mention the second letter I sent to the post office in Lima—I assume you didn't get it?) It must be difficult to summarize so many interesting experiences in a short letter home, so many thoughts and impressions, and I understand you can't write every week, but please know that every word you write to us is precious.

We enjoyed your thoughts about agricultural science but of course I'm especially curious about the people you're with. It warms my heart to hear of the interest you've taken in Felipe's family and your willingness to share in their hardships, and I think your father is more than a little envious. If our lives had gone a different way, he would have liked to be a missionary—he has such deep empathy for people whose existence is a struggle. We miss you more and more with every day that passes, but it's a comfort to know that you're developing that empathy yourself. I can't imagine a better reward for your two years of "service."

The big news here is that your father has accepted a new position, and we're moving to—Indiana! The town is Hadleysburg, about an hour outside Indianapolis, and the U.C.C. there has a very engaged congregation. The interim pastor is leaving at the end of June, and we'll relocate as soon as Judson finishes the school year. Hadleysburg is attractive for many reasons. The cost of living is lower, your father will finally have his own church again, and his pastoral duties will be lighter, so he can do other work for pay. Perry's second stint at Cedar Hill was a terrible financial blow, and we haven't been able to repay the money we borrowed from your sister, let alone the money of yours that was lost. Your father had talked about going back to Lesser Hebron (!) and petitioning the brethren for reacceptance in their community, because he wants a simpler life, but financially that's no longer an option and Hadleysburg is plenty simple for me. Judson can go to a regular school and I can have a glass of wine without being excommunicated, but it's a small and close-knit community, with fewer temptations for Perry. He swears he doesn't have more drugs hidden away, but after his relapse I don't know that I can ever trust him, and I won't be sorry to leave this house—all I can see is places where he might have hidden drugs.

Perry is polite to us and seems to appreciate our help, but he has no energy and very little "affect." He says the electroshock harmed his powers of recall, and he hates the side effects of his new medication. Even if he could finish high school (he hasn't completed a course in almost two years), I don't yet see how he could go away to college. For the moment, I'm afraid there's nothing to be done but watch over him and pray that he gets better on his new medication. Dear Clem, I know your feelings about the efficacy of prayer, but if you could ever find it in your heart to say a little prayer for your brother, even if you don't think it will change anything, it would mean a lot to your mother, and to your father too.

Judson remains a joy. He's starring in the sixth-grade "musical" and reading at tenth-grade level. He feels for Perry and he understands how burdened your father and I are, but he never seems to brood about it. When Perry had his calamity, I worried it would take away Judson's childhood and he would lose that innocent capacity to enjoy things. I can't tell you what a blessing it is, when I'm having a bad day (I won't bore you with that), to see him playing outside with the Erickson girls or watching the news with your father (he's tape-recording all the Watergate news for a social-studies report) or just eating his dinner with so much gusto. Perry says the medication makes everything taste the same to him, and if there's something Judson is especially enjoying, Perry passes his plate and lets him take more of it. Since he came back from Cedar Hill, the only real glimmers I've seen of his old self are when he's with Judson. David Goya stopped by twice at Christmas (he's a sophomore at Rice now), and Larry Cottrell, God bless him, comes over every week (his mother left the church, but he's still in Crossroads), but Perry doesn't seem to care much either way. The fear that he'll try to harm himself again is with me night and day, and I'm afraid it always will be.

We continue to see your sister and Tanner in church. They sit at the back in case Gracie starts crying and Becky needs to step out. I make an effort to talk to her after the service, but it's like talking to a locked door—she will not take her eyes off Gracie. I think I told you they have their own apartment now, above the record store, and I offered to come by with some things, some old linens and baby blankets and toys, because I know money is tight. Becky didn't get her back up, she just smiled and said no thank you, they didn't need anything. Everything is done with a smile—declining my invitations to dinner, excusing herself from the holidays, refusing to let me hold her baby (and then I turn around and see a parishioner holding her). Lord knows, she has reason to be angry with me, but her coldness just breaks my heart. Tanner is as nice as ever but gets nervous when Becky sees us talking to him—she pretends to be immersed in Gracie, but she's obviously watching him. She says she's very happy, and maybe she is. I imagine she'll be even happier when we leave for Indiana.

There's a search committee for the new associate minister, and we hear that Ambrose is at the top of the list. I think, if he takes the job, it will help your father close the door on New Prospect. He's been so changed since the calamity, so chastened and humbled, I honestly think he could have wished Rick all the best, if only Rick hadn't officiated at Becky's wedding. (It was her choice, but, really, what was Rick thinking?) My hope is that having his own church, with no Rick in the picture, will give your father a fresh start, because he still has so much to give. I'm enclosing a sermon he wrote about coal mining on the Navajo reservation, after Keith Durochie died. It was so good, I sent it in to "The Other Side," and now your father is a published author. He wasn't happy I submitted it without telling him, but I don't think he'll mind me sending it to you.

Dear Clem, you mustn't think your father doesn't write to you because he isn't thinking of you. He thinks about you all the time, and you should see the way he talks about you—the way he shakes his head with admiration. I've begged him to write and let you know how proud he is, but he's convinced that he let you down as a father, and he's afraid a letter would be unwelcome. I don't want to burden you with a second request, but, if you're ever inclined, you might let him know that you'd be happy for a word from him.

It's cold and late here, and I want to put this in the mail in the morning. Your father just went upstairs to bed and asked me to send you his love. You needn't worry about us—God never asks for more than we can give. Just know that nothing in the world could bring us more joy than to see you again. Please take very, very good care in the mountains.

All my love,
Mom

P.S. Now that I have a good safe address for you, I'm sending a very belated little Christmas present and the last of the money from your savings account, which might help with your trip home. (Do you know when that will be?)

Maybe it was the twenty-dollar bills in the envelope, the impending return they represented, or maybe the image of his father broken and remorseful, his weakness merely pitiable, not embarrassing, but the letter didn't anger Clem. It made him very anxious. The feeling was like something from a dream, a dreamer's panicked sense of needing to be somewhere else, of being late for an important exam, of having forgotten he had a train to catch. How absurd that he'd thought he needed to prove himself stronger than his father. He'd been fighting a battle long since won, in an irrelevant sector of the dreamworld.

Whatever else Becky was, happy or unhappy, she'd always been straightforward—sincere to the point of naïveté. It was hard to imagine a person so clearhearted giving phony smiles to her mother, a person so naturally guileless calculating how to stab her parents without leaving prints on the knife. Ever since he'd learned of her marriage to the lightweight, Clem had done his best not to think about her; a baby was a baby, and there was nothing to be done. He'd been disappointed in her, but he'd lacked the empathy to imagine her own disappointment. How miserable she must have become, to be cruel to a person as harmless as their mother. And this, yes, was the source of his anxiety, this was the thing he was late for, this was the vital matter he'd forgotten: he loved Becky.

He went back to the postal clerk and parted with some coins. Standing at the end of the counter, with a pen borrowed from the clerk, he covered an aerogram with tiny handwriting. He apologized to Becky for having criticized her, he described his daily life in the hamlet, and then he paused. He was in the same position as his father, afraid that an avowal of love would be unwelcome. It might seem inflated to Becky after such a long silence, and so he went at it sideways. Using terms in which he hoped love would be implicit—she was a person of strength, clear of heart, a shining star—he asked her to consider the trouble their parents were in, consider her many advantages, and try to be a little kinder. Without rereading the letter, he wrote his parents' address and PLEASE FORWARD on the aerogram and gave it to the clerk. Then he put on a pair of new socks (much needed) and walked back up the valley.

It was generous of his mother to suppose he'd developed greater empathy in South America. Empathy was a luxury a day laborer couldn't afford. When a truck pulled up at dawn and fifty men fought for space on it, empathizing with the man trying to yank you off the tailgate could result in having nothing to eat that day. If Clem had developed anything in Tres Fuentes, it was simply admiration for the men who tilled the unforgiving puna, the women who rose at the night's coldest hour to boil their *mote* and their *mate*. He didn't have to empathize with Felipe Cuéllar. It was enough to know that he was durable and trustworthy.

Having taken action against the anxiety, Clem returned to his elemental existence. He woke and worked, drank chicha and slept in a shed with the Cuéllars' donkey. The month of March brought finer weather, dense nitrogen-fixing growth on the bean slopes, alpacas fattening themselves with ceaseless chewing. Lacking the finer skills of farming, he earned his keep by rebuilding a pen for the hamlet's livestock, repairing stone walls, and gathering firewood. The donkey was old and tolerant, and he did it the favor of leading it up to the forest, rather than riding it. He was amazed that hardwoods could survive at all at such an altitude, far higher than a temperate tree line, and he felt bad about hacking at them with a machete. They had small, silvery leaves, twigs encrusted with lichen, branches hairy with epiphytes and tortured in their angles, as though they'd been thwarted at every turn by the harshness of their environment. He suspected they grew too slowly to keep up with the demand for firewood, but the hamlet had no other source of fuel. He tried to cut judiciously, taking only dead limbs, but every branch seemed half dead and half alive. Even as the bark peeled away, exposing xylem to the weather, it managed to convey nutrients to an outpost or two of fresh leaves. Each tree, indeed, was like a miniature of the highlands. The branches resembled the ancient, gnarled pathways that led to the patches of arable land, leaf-green, that were scattered among stony fields and bogs of tannic standing water. The half-dead trees recalled the human settlements as well: for every dwelling in good repair were several in a state of ruin, some no more than heaps of rock, possibly dating from the Incas; the birds he flushed from the trees were like the ponchos of the women of the hamlet, gold and blue, black and crimson. When he'd cut as much wood as he and the donkey could carry on their backs, they made their way down a slope already cleared of trees. He noticed that its soil was badly eroded, less water-retentive, than the loam in the forest, but the nights here were frigid and the *almuerzo* waiting for him at the Cuéllars', a thick soup he never tired of, could not have been cooked without firewood.

In hindsight, he wished he'd come to the Andes a year earlier, instead of wasting his time in cities. And yet maybe it was for the best. Maybe he'd needed to serve a term of hard labor, to work off the shame of his mistake with the draft board, to punish himself for the pain he'd point-lessly inflicted on Sharon and his parents, in order to earn his reward in the highlands. The labor here was even harder, but he felt restored to a self he'd misplaced for so long that he'd forgotten it, restored to a world of earth and plants and animals, restored to his curiosity and his ambi-tion to do something with it. The excitement of returning to school and pursuing a career in science propelled him through his days and kept him awake at night. It was a very long time since he'd wanted something larger than his next meal.

The afternoon he got Becky's letter in Tres Fuentes, the page of the postal clerk's calendar was gravid with x's. It was the twenty-seventh of March. Clem went out to the dry fountain and tore open the envelope eagerly.

Dear Clem,

Thank you for your apology, thank you for bringing me "up to speed" on your travels (it all sounds very interesting), but please don't tell me what to do. You made a choice not to be here, and it's pretty late in the day to suddenly play the peacemaker. You were off on your adventure, you don't know what M & D did to me, you don't know how obsessed they are with Perry (I know he's sick but he's unbelievably selfish and deceitful and has cost them well over ten thousand dollars, no end in sight), you have no idea how unbearable they are, you haven't had your stomach turned. I've forgiven their financial debt to me, I don't want or expect <u>anything</u> from them, and whatever Mom tells you, I'm always friendly to them. I don't wish them ill, I just don't enjoy being around them. The Bible doesn't tell us to <u>like</u> our neighbor, because a person can't control who she likes. I do struggle with honoring one's parents, but in fairness they don't give me much to work with. Dad is more grotesquely insecure than ever, the whole church knows about his affair with a church member (did Mom happen to mention he nearly got fired for that?), he's grown a goatee that looks like pubic hair, and Mom acts like he's God's special gift to the world. Try honoring that. I'm perfectly cordial to them, but no, I don't invite them over and no, I don't go there for holidays, because A, I'm part of Tanner's family too, and B, I want Grace to grow up in a house of peace and harmony and I'm afraid of what would happen if I spent more than fifteen minutes with them. I'm married to a wonderful, talented, generous man and I have the most beautiful baby, I'm really overwhelmed with what God has given me, I wake up every morning with a song in my heart, and I would ask you not to blame me for trying to keep it that way. Some people are lucky enough to like their parents, but I'm not one of them.

I owe you an apology in turn for saying hateful things when you couldn't go to Vietnam. It was wrong, and I apologize, but there was something weird about the way we used to be together and maybe we needed to grow apart and become our own people with separate identities. I used to love talking to you about everything under the sun, and I do sometimes miss having a brother to look up to and tell things to. If you ever come home, maybe we can give it a try again. The second you meet Gracie, you'll understand why I'm so crazy about her, and I want you to get to know Tanner as he really is. You never gave him a chance, but if you care about me you should care about the person in my life who's best to me, best for me, best everything. I don't mean to make rules, but if you want to be in my life again I guess there are some rules. Number one is <u>respect my feelings about M & D</u>. That one is nonnegotiable. But also, when you see the situation with Perry and what the two of them are like these days, you might understand better why I feel the way I do. I'm sorry they're unhappy, but I can't make it better, even if I wanted to, because I don't matter to them enough. They made their choices, you made yours, I made mine. At least one of us is happy with her choices.

Love, Becky

The letter was like a match struck in the dark. In the light of it, he saw his old bedroom at the parsonage. It was there that Becky had come to him late at night, offered up stories, and, more than once, in her straight-forwardness, fallen asleep on his bed. Why hadn't he woken her up? Told her to sleep in her own room? It was because she'd meant too much to him. To know that she preferred his room, preferred him to anyone else in the family, was worth the discomfort of sleeping on the floor. And if she'd been embarrassed to wake up and see him on the rug, had apologized for appropriating his bed, or if it had happened only once, it wouldn't have been *weird*. But when she'd done it again, and again—let him sleep on the floor without embarrassment or apology—the terms of their arrange-ment had been clear: he would do anything for her, and she would let him. To anyone else, it might have looked like she was being selfish. Only he understood the love in her consenting to be so loved.

Then he'd gone to college and met Sharon, who'd wanted nothing more than to be so loved, and in his wretched honesty he'd admitted that he didn't love her to the degree he knew his heart was capable of. In the light of the match the letter had struck, he saw that his heart had still be-longed to Becky; that this was the real reason he hadn't stayed with Sha-ron. But while he'd been sleeping with Sharon the terms had changed, Becky no longer needed him, and in trying to hold on to her, trying to recall her to their arrangement, trying to interfere with her decisions, he'd lost her love entirely. She'd been so angry with him, her hatred so unbear-able, that he'd boarded a bus for Mexico without a plan. In the light of the match, he saw that he'd tried to displace one pain with another, the pain of losing her with the pain of hard labor, and this was the terrible thing about her letter: nothing had changed.

Striding along the track to the hamlet, the incendiary letter in his pocket, he overtook Felipe Cuéllar, who was carrying a stout-handled hoe on his shoulder. Felipe was slight of build and a head shorter than

Clem, but there was no physical task he couldn't perform with less effort. Following him up the track, keeping clear of the hoe, Clem asked him when the potatoes would be harvested.

When they're ready, Felipe said.

Yes, Clem said, but how soon?

Always in May. It's very hard work.

Not harder than planting in the rain.

Yes, harder. You'll see.

They walked in silence for a while. Clouds were building behind the mountain at the upper end of the valley, Amazonian moisture, but lately the rains hadn't come down as far west as the hamlet. The track through the puna was drying out.

I have a question, Clem said. If I had to leave now—soon—could I come here again? I meant to stay through the harvest, but I think I need to see my family.

Felipe stopped on the path and swung around with the hoe. He was frowning.

Did you get bad news? Is someone sick?

Yes. Well—yes.

Then go right away, Felipe said. Nothing is more important than family.

His last ride, from Bloomington to Aurora, early on the Saturday morning before Easter, was a twice-divorced fertilizer salesman, named Morton, who drove a sleek Buick Riviera and wanted to talk about God. Morton had pulled over on a ramp outside the truck stop where Clem had casually lifted and eaten the leavings from a table in the restaurant, taken a shower, and caught a few hours of sleep behind the parking lot. The money his mother had sent had got him by plane to Panama City and by bus to Mexico, but from there he'd had to hitchhike, mostly with long-haul truckers. When Morton learned that he hadn't had a proper meal in five days, he took an exit for a Stuckey's and bought him a stack of pancakes with fried eggs and bacon. Morton had the sunken face, the stained skin, the reassembled-looking body, of a man with hard drinking in his past. It seemed to give him pleasure to watch Clem eat.

"You know why I stopped for you?" he said. "When I saw you with your thumb out—the reason I stopped was I thought you might be an angel."

Clem had wondered about that. He was the antithesis of a hippie, but in his hooded Peruvian sweater, his beard and long hair, he looked like one. He'd been surprised when the Riviera pulled over.

"I know what you're thinking," Morton said, "but they exist. Angels. They look like ordinary people, but after they're gone you realize they were angels of the Lord."

Clem was still getting used to speaking English, the remarkable fact that he could do it. "I'm pretty sure I'm not an angel."

"But that's the way God works. That's how He takes care of us—by having us care for each other. When you refuse a stranger in need, you might be refusing an angel. You know the day I got the message? It was the twenty-seventh of June, four years ago. I was a mess, my second wife had just left me, I'd lost my job at the high school, and my car broke down in a thunderstorm. Not far from here, actually. It was a county road, rain coming down in sheets, and the alternator shorted out. I was as low as I ever was in my life. I sat there in the car feeling sorry for myself, soaking wet, and right behind me, in the mirror, I see this figure walking towards me. You'll think I'm making this up, but he's a young man about your age, dressed in white. I roll down the window, and he asks me what the problem is. He's as wet as I am, but he looks under the hood and tells me to try the ignition. And damned if the car doesn't start right up. I let it run for a second and then I get out to thank him, maybe give him some money, and he's gone. We're in the middle of the cornfields, flat as can be, and, poof—he's nowhere. Gone. And just like that, the rain stops, and you'll think I'm making this up, but there's writing all across the sky, and I can see that it's *numbers*. Numbers horizon to horizon. I realize there's a number for every day of my life—the angel is showing me my entire life, past and future. And then, for a split second, the numbers line up in perfect formation, and I see it. I see eternal life in Jesus Christ. I hadn't set foot in a church in years, but I got down on my knees, right there on the road, and poured out my heart to Jesus. That was the day my new life started."

There was no denying Morton's Christian kindness, no arguing with flapjacks and syrup and whipped butter, and he'd told his story with impressive conviction, but the story couldn't begin to withstand objective scrutiny. In Peru, Clem had worked alongside men with all manner of superstitions. There was a crucifix in the Cuéllars' hut, and he'd seen Felipe cross himself outside the church and the cemetery in Tres Fuentes. But those had been simple working folk. Morton was an educated American, by his own account the top seller in his territory, the owner of a Buick built on scientifically verified principles. Stranger yet, the other adults in Clem's own family, his mother and his father and now Becky, modern people of high intelligence, spoke of God as though the word referred to something real. Being the nonbeliever among believers was even lonelier than being the gringo in Tres Fuentes. A gringo was different only on the surface and could look for common ground. Science and delusion had no ground in common.

Morton would have taken him all the way to New Prospect if he hadn't been collecting his daughter in Aurora at ten o'clock. He dropped Clem at the train station and gave him a five-dollar bill. Leaning across to the glove compartment, he produced a card densely printed with devotional matter.

"You've been incredibly generous," Clem said, taking the card. On the front side was a halftone Jesus, on the obverse a halftone Paradise.

"I hope you have a blessed Easter with your family."

Alone on the train platform, Clem dropped the card in a trash can. While he was at it, he ditched his filthy knit shoulder bag and the filthy clothes in it, keeping only his passport. Today was the day his own new life was starting. An inbound train was waiting with open doors.

That he recognized New Prospect and had a claim to it, knew every building and street name, seemed as remarkable as his command of English. He could have called his parents from the road, to let them know he was coming, but the discomforts of hitchhiking were best survived by not looking ahead, and his parents weren't the reason he'd left Tres Fuentes anyway.

The air on Pirsig Avenue was heavy with spring, its smell unlike anything in Peru. In the window of Aeolian Records were sun-damaged jazz and symphonic albums, seemingly untouched since he'd last been in town. Inside the store, under the owner's untrusting eye, two long-haired boys were flipping through the Rock bins. Clem went around to the alley behind the store. At the bottom of the stairs to the second-floor apartment, he hesitated. He remembered similarly hesitating on the landing below Sharon's room in the hippie house.

Tacked to the apartment door, at the top of the stairs, was a file card on which someone, surely Becky, had written *Tanner and Becky Evans* ornately, in cursive, and drawn little flowers to either side. Eyes filling, Clem knocked on the door. He couldn't remember Becky ever playing house as a girl. In Indiana, where he'd had her all to himself, she'd fol-lowed him wherever he went. He'd taught her to throw a baseball, taught her to watch it into the glove (his glove, their only glove) when he threw it back. She'd chased him with a dried-out piece of dog crap, screaming, "Petrified poo! Petrified poo!" And the gleeful savagery of the tortures she'd devised for a toy rabbit that had fallen out of favor, the giggling wickedness with which she'd enumerated its transgressions: since when had that girl wanted to play house?

He knocked again. Nobody home.

Overcome, all at once, by the miles he'd traveled, he returned to the street. He'd wanted to see Becky before he saw his parents, to make clear that she was the reason he'd come home, but all he could think of now was his bed at the parsonage. The day was warm, the sun near the zenith. A nap on a real bed would be delicious. Already half asleep, he bent his steps homeward past the bookstore, the drugstore, the insur-ance broker.

He was jolted awake when he came to Treble Clef. Behind the front window, Tanner Evans was showing an electric guitar to a middle-aged customer, someone's mother. Clem stopped on the sidewalk uncertainly. Tanner glanced at him and returned his attention to the woman. Then he looked again, eyes widening, and came running out of the store. "What the hell?"

"I'm back," Clem said.

"I'm thinking, do I know this person?"

Tanner, for his part, seemed perfectly unchanged. Perhaps would always be unchanged. He spread his arms, as he'd done so readily in Crossroads, and Clem stepped in for the embrace.

"This is fantastic," Tanner said. "Becky will be so happy."

"Really?"

Tanner's face clouded to the extent his native sunniness allowed. "I mean—yeah. Definitely. She missed you."

"Congratulations on everything. Marriage, fatherhood. Congratulations."

"Thanks, it's been amazing."

"I want to hear about it, but—where is she?"

"Probably at Scofield, with Gracie. Jeannie Cross is in town."

After a second hug, from the man who was now his brother-in-law, Clem headed up toward Scofield Park. The trees of New Prospect were a hundred percent alive, gripped jealously by their unblemished bark, and every house looked like a palace. The wet, emerald grass that a man was removing from a lawn-mower bag, discarding as waste, would have been the sweetest meal for an alpaca. Clem stopped to take off his sweater and knot it above his hips, and the man looked up from his mower suspiciously. Maybe he sensed the comparisons Clem was making, the implicit critique, or maybe he just hated hippies.

Becky wasn't among the mothers at the Scofield playground, and she wasn't at the picnic tables. Farther back in the park was a ball field with a backstop. Fully grown young men, several of them shirtless, were playing softball. The guy at the plate, connecting with a pitch and sending it high over the head of the left fielder, was a detestable jock Clem recognized from high school, Kent Carducci. He pumped his fist and gave a brute roar as he rounded first base.

The girls—where there were boys like this, there had to be girls—were grouped along the first-base line, around a set of aluminum bleachers. Becky was seated on the lowest bleacher with Jeannie Cross. Taller than the others, her old aura intact, she might have been a queen holding court. Lesser girls sat cross-legged on the grass below her, one of them holding up the arms of a little child who'd achieved a standing position.

Jeannie Cross spotted Clem first. She grabbed Becky's shoulder, and now Becky saw him, too. For a moment, her expression was uncomprehending. Then she ran up behind the first-base line to meet him. He spread his arms, but she stopped short of hugging distance. She was wearing a corduroy jacket that had once been his. Her smile was perhaps more incredulous than joyful.

"What are you doing here?"

"Came to see you."

"Wow."

"Is it okay if I give you a hug?"

She didn't seem to remember the joke, but she stepped up and put one arm around him, briefly, and pulled back. "Everybody's home for Easter," she said. "I guess you are, too."

"I wasn't thinking about Easter. I only came to see you."

Kent Carducci shouted something abusive on the ball field.

"So come and meet Gracie," Becky said. She ran ahead of Clem and scooped up the little child. "Gracie, I want you to meet your uncle Clem."

The child hid her face in Becky's neck. Clem probably looked to her like a hairy monster. He realized that, until this moment, he hadn't quite believed that his sister had procreated. The child was perfectly formed, her hair fine and thin on top, thicker on the sides: a new little person, ex nihilo, with a mother scarcely past childhood herself. He could almost remember Becky as a one-year-old. His eyes filled again.

"Here, you can hold her," Becky said. "She won't break."

Watched by Becky's friends, he took Gracie in his arms. She was radiantly warm in her cotton sweater, squirming with vital energy, reaching back for her mother. He didn't think he'd held a baby since Judson had outgrown being portable. He gently bounced his niece, trying to postpone the inevitable crying, but Becky's gaze and smile were fixed on her, as if to remind her of where she'd rather be. She let out a wail, and Becky took her back.

The physics of their reunion were nothing like what he'd imagined: a ball field populated with guys whose muscles had been developed by athletics, not hard labor, eight flavors of pretty girl arrayed by the bleachers, some of them from Crossroads (Carol Pinella, Sally Perkins's younger sister), others from the cheerleading squad, most of them home from college, at least one of them still local, and none of them remotely capable of imagining the world in which he'd lived for two years. His shirt stank, his dungarees were stained with Andean mud, and his affinities were with the Cuéllars' hamlet. New Prospect was still New Prospect, and Becky was evidently still at the social center of it, while he, who'd always been far from the center, had moved radically much farther. He would have liked to talk to Jeannie Cross, who was more sensationally desirable than ever, but his alienation was so extreme that he could only stand behind the backstop, watching people he disliked play softball, and wait for Becky to find a moment for him.

Gracie had fallen asleep in the flimsy stroller that Becky wheeled over to the backstop. "Somebody needs her diaper changed," she said. "Do you want to walk home with us?"

"What do you think I want?"

"I don't know."

"You're the reason I'm here. I came back as soon as I got your letter."

"Yeah, okay."

She pushed the stroller toward the nearest pavement, and he followed her. "I'm glad to see you're still wearing that jacket."

"That's right," she said, "it was yours. I've had it so long, I forgot."

Reaching the pavement, she crouched and inspected her baby.

"She's beautiful," he offered.

"Thank you. I love her like you wouldn't believe."

She was right in front of him, the person he loved best, still matching his mental image of her, but his own sudden apparition was apparently unremarkable to her. As she proceeded out of the park with the stroller, peering down at her baby, he feared that he'd made another bad mistake; that he should have stayed in Tres Fuentes for the potato harvest.

"Becky," he said finally.

"Yeah?"

"I'm sorry I tried to tell you what to do."

"It's okay. I forgive you."

"I don't want to interfere in your life. I'm just asking for a chance to be a part of it again."

She didn't seem to hear him, didn't speak again until they were crossing Highland Street. He could see the taller of the parsonage oak trees in the distance. He didn't feel especially forgiven.

"Have you been home yet?" she said.

"No. I wanted to see you first."

She acknowledged this tribute with a nod. "Mom showed up at my door the other day. She didn't call, she just showed up. She wanted us to come to dinner tomorrow. She tried to lay a guilt trip on me, how it's Dad's last Easter in New Prospect."

"Well. She's right about that."

"I already invited Tanner's parents to our place. It's Gracie's first Easter. I bought a ham."

Clem could feel that he was being tested—being dared to point out that, unlike his parents, a one-year-old couldn't tell Easter Sunday from Guy Fawkes Day.

"So, uh. Why not invite Mom and Dad?"

"Because that means bringing Perry, which doesn't sound like a holiday to me. He uses up all the air in the room, even when he's just sitting there. If you start talking about something that isn't him, he'll make some remark about how shitty he feels, or something completely random, whatever it takes to get the attention back on him, and they fall for it every time."

"He's sick, Becky."

"Yeah, obviously. I get why they have to take care of him. But it isn't fair to Tanner's parents to have his sickness be their whole evening."

"Mom and Dad have to live with it every night of the week."

"I know. I'm sure it's really hard for them. But he's their son, not mine, and I already made my contribution as a sibling. I think I'm entitled to not deal with it on a holiday."

Clem suppressed an impulse to say more. Obeying her first rule, respecting her feelings about their parents, was going to be a struggle. At least there was no rule against being kind to them himself.

As if she'd sensed his thought, she stopped on the sidewalk and turned to him.

"So," she said. "Will you have dinner with us?"

"Tonight?"

"No, tomorrow. Easter. I'm inviting you."

His heart leaped at the invitation; it couldn't help itself. But it had leaped into a trap. He'd been away for so long, it would be cruel to leave his parents alone on Easter, and Becky knew it.

"I don't know," he said.

She looked away with an expression of not caring. All he'd asked for was a chance with her, and she was offering him that chance. Whether she genuinely wanted him in her life or was simply testing his loyalties, he couldn't yet tell. But it was clear that, in his absence, far from having diminished herself, as he'd supposed, she'd become a dominating force. She had the grandchild, she had the absolutely loyal husband, she had her charisma and her popularity, and she needed nothing from him or their parents. The terms were hers to set.

"Let me think about it," he said, although he already knew what he would do.